ISBN 978-1-334-14308-3
PIBN 10654741

English
Français
Deutsche
Italiano
Español
Português

www.forgottenbooks.com

Mythology Photography **Fiction**
Fishing Christianity **Art** Cooking
Essays Buddhism Freemasonry
Medicine **Biology** Music **Ancient
Egypt** Evolution Carpentry Physics
Dance Geology **Mathematics** Fitness
Shakespeare **Folklore** Yoga Marketing
Confidence Immortality Biographies
Poetry **Psychology** Witchcraft
Electronics Chemistry History **Law**
Accounting **Philosophy** Anthropology
Alchemy Drama Quantum Mechanics
Atheism Sexual Health **Ancient History**
Entrepreneurship Languages Sport
Paleontology Needlework Islam
Metaphysics Investment Archaeology
Parenting Statistics Criminology
Motivational

REMINISCENCES OF

(*née* PRINCESSE GALITZINE)

"Lived through but not forgotten"

WITH TWO PORTRAITS

LONDON

JOHN LONG, LIMITED

12, 13 & 14 NORRIS STREET, HAYMARKET
MCMXVII

REMINISCENCES OF

BARBARA DUCKHOVNY

(*née* PRINCESSE GALITZINE)

" Lived through but not forgotten "

WITH TWO PORTRAITS

LONDON

JOHN LONG, LIMITED

12, 13 & 14 NORRIS STREET, HAYMARKET
MCMXVII

Preface

THIS book was not intended to be published, and it is to accident that we owe its appearance.

The author, from her childhood, followed affectionate advices and good examples, and noted every day her impressions of everything she saw and heard about her. She puts in these pages all the freshness and sincerity of her woman's heart.

Circumstances placed the author in the centre of remarkable events. Remaining faithful to the principle of not interfering with her husband's business, she becomes, however, unwillingly, the spectatrix of particularly interesting facts: the outside of war, of different centres of Russian society, of exotic life in foreign colonies and on our remote frontiers, including the regions of the river Amour in Eastern Siberia.

Our author does not pretend to give a thorough and complete study of political events and society customs. But here we have vivid pictures of different impressions which, linked together, give us a living picture of places, events, and persons; real life in fact is delineated in this book, which has thus become a considerable work.

The author's innate talent, her education, her faculty of observation, and her deep study of the best Russian and foreign writers, are the cause of the vivid impression produced by her light and clear style. Some portions of these studies entitled " Fragments of the Diary of a Russian woman in Erzeroum," were printed in one of the most famous Russian periodicals. The welcome they received showed the author to what use she could turn her book for her works of charity, and it is her desire to assist the poor which gave to Barbara Doukhovskoy the idea of publishing her " Memories," though the great realism of them did not permit of their publication as a whole.

Profiting by the right of having been a friend and a playmate of the author's husband, I insisted on the necessity of publishing this work.

Not only by the truth and the spontaneity of her impressions, but by the profoundness of her observations and the artistic conception of the whole, the author of this book now embellishes our literature by a work of an exceptional and original character.

C. SLOUTCHEVSKY

Constantin Sloutchevsky, Russian poet, one of the most famous of the end of the nineteenth century.

Contents

Contents

Contents

Contents

The Diary of a Russian Lady

BOOK I

CHAPTER I

EARLY RECOLLECTIONS

MY father, Prince Theodore Galitzine, married my mother being a widower with five children, three of whom died before my birth. My earliest vivid recollections begin when I was two years old. I distinctly remember feeling a terrible pain in parting with my wet-nurse, to whom I was passionately attached. I got hold of her skirt and wouldn't let her go, weeping wildly. It was my first bitter affliction. I could not put up with the new nurse, whom I hated from the depths of my little heart, and I would not call her otherwise than *Wild Cat*, with baby petulance, having already at that early age pronounced likes and dislikes. We were in perpetual state of warfare. When I was about three years old that nurse was succeeded by a pretty Belgian girl named Melle Henriette. The tutor of my two step-brothers, Mr. Liziar, made love to her and finished by marrying her some time after. He seemed somewhat half-witted ; by night he went to chime the bells at the belfry of our village church in Dolgik, a fine estate belonging to my father, in the government of Kharkoff, and also amused himself by breaking, in the conservatory, the panes of glass with big stones. One day he frightened his sweetheart nearly to death by throwing a snake under her feet. After all these pranks it is no way astonishing that Mr. Liziar finished his days in a lunatic asylum. The tutor who succeeded him, asked my parents to bring his wife with him. He hastened to pocket the hundred roubles taken beforehand on account of his salary, and departed suddenly to Kharkoff to fetch her. Meanwhile my father received a letter from this tutor's legitimate wife dated from St. Petersburg, in which she entreated papa to send her the half of her husband's monthly salary, telling him he spent all his money on his mistress, whilst his wife and children had not a morsel of bread to put into their mouths. Of course, this too *Don Juanesque* tutor was instantly dismissed.

My parents at that time kept an open house. On great

occasions my smart nurse would appear in the dining-room carrying me in her arms, attired like a little fairy, all ribbons and lace, to be admired by our guests. She put me down on the table, and I promenaded quite at my ease between the flowers and fruits.

I was born under fortunate auspices, there could not be a happier little girl; good things were thrown down upon me: presents, petting, admiration. At an early age I chose as my motto: "*Fais ce que voudras.*" Whatever I wished for, I very certainly had, and I didn't see how anybody could want to refuse me in anything.

I was often sent down to the drawing-room to be admired by the afternoon callers, and mamma ordered me to let myself be kissed by unkissable grown-ups, who paid me those compliments shown to children, who are precious to their parents, and which made me intolerably conceited. I stood in great danger of being completely spoilt, and mamma, who was afraid that I received a good deal more flattery than she thought good for me, ordered me to answer what I was told: "*Comme Vava*[1] *est jolie!*"—"*Vava n'est pas jolie, elle est seulement gentille.*" But, nevertheless, I knew that I was pretty, my glass told me so.

At the age of four I could read and write fairly well, and chatted freely in French. I was immensely proud when my nurse ended putting me to bed in the daytime, and when I was old enough to sit at table, able to handle my knife and fork properly. My greatest delight was to ride on my brothers' backs and to be swung by them in a sheet, that they held by the four corners and lifted me as high as they could, whilst I crowed gleefully, my bare legs waving happily in the air. Mamma hastened with my nurse to my rescue, and carried me off, paying but little attention to the wild shrieks with which I requested to be tossed higher and higher. There was a speedy end to all this fun; destiny itself interfered to stop these aerial gymnastics: I had a bad fall one day, tumbling out of the sheet, and my infatuation for this sport disappeared completely.

It was a source of infinite delight to me to creep on the knees of Mr Vremeff, an intimate friend of my parents, a charming old gentleman with snowy white hair, and hear him relate entrancing fairy tales for which I had an insatiable appetite. As soon as he had finished one story, I asked for another and another.

At that time my father was marshal of nobility of the district of Kharkoff. One day he was suddenly called to St. Petersburg, and, during his absence, we received the news that he was appointed chamberlain to His Majesty the

---

[1] Vava: diminutive of Barbara.

Princess Vava Galitzine
Aged 4 years.

occasions my smart nurse would appear in the dining room, carrying me in her arms, attired like a little fairy, all silk and lace, to be admired by our guests. She put me down on the table, and I promenaded quite at my ease between the flowers and fruits.

I was born under fortunate auspices, there could not be a happier little girl; good things were thrown down upon me: presents, petting, admiration. At an early age I chose as my motto: "*Fais ce que voudras.*" Whatever I wished for, I very certainly had, and I didn't see how anybody could want to refuse me in anything.

I was often sent down to the drawing-room to be admired by the afternoon callers, and mamma ordered me to let myself be kissed by unkissable grown-ups, who paid me those compliments shown to children, who are precious to their parents, and which made me intolerably conceited. I stood in great danger of being completely spoilt, and mamma, who was afraid that I received a good deal more flattery than she thought good for me, ordered me to answer what I was told: "*Comme Vera est jolie!*"—"*Vera n'est pas jolie, elle est seulement gentille.*" I knew that I was pretty, my glass told me so.

At the age of four I could read and write fairly well, and chatted freely in French. I was immensely proud when my nurse ended putting me to bed in the daytime, and when I was old enough to sit at table, able to handle my knife and fork properly. My greatest delight was to ride on my brothers' backs and to be swung by them in a sheet, that they held by the four corners and lifted me as high as they could, whilst I crowed gleefully, my bare legs waving happily in the air. Mamma hastened with my nurse to my rescue, and carried me off, paying but little attention to the wild shrieks with which I requested to be tossed higher and higher. There was a speedy end to all this fun; destiny itself interfered to stop these aerial gymnastics: I had a bad fall one day, tumbling out of the sheet, and my infatuation for this sport disappeared completely.

It was a source of infinite delight to me to creep on the knees of Mr Vremeff, an intimate friend of my parents, a charming old gentleman with snowy white hair, and hear him relate entrancing fairy tales for which I had an insatiable appetite. As soon as he had finished one story, I asked for another and another.

At that time my father was marshal of nobility of the district of Kharkoff. O suddenly called to St. Petersburg, and, during his absence, we received the news that he was appointed to His Majesty the

Princess Vava Galitzine
Aged 4 years.

Emperor. I wept bitterly when I was told that papa must wear the chamberlain's key, persuaded that he would be obliged to adorn even his *robe de chambre* with that ugly ornament, which must completely transform my dear old dad.

My parents, going to St. Petersburg, generally paid flying visits to my aunt Galitzine, who lived in Moscow. I made my first journey with them at the mature age of four. If the faults of children develop as they grow older, I was to become a pick-pocket, for I had the bad habit of hiding in my pockets all sorts of broken toys belonging to the Karamzins, —two little pupils of my aunt! When I went to bed my nurse emptied my pockets, crying out at the enormity of my dreadful conduct.

My birthday was a great day for festivities. I received lots of lovely presents and sweets. On the eve of my birthday I went to bed with expectations of a pleasant awaking, and the first thing when I woke up in the morning was to put my hand under my pillow and pull out the presents, laid there by my parents during my sleep.

On my seventh birthday my grandmother presented me with a beautiful watch with diamond settings. From the very first moment I harboured a guilty determination to get the diamonds out, just as I broke my dolls' heads in order to see what there was in them, a resolve, alas! very soon put into practice. Mamma entering my nursery one day saw me perched on the top of my high stool, occupied in drawing out the diamonds with a long pin. Moral: "It is superfluous to give such rich presents to small persons of my age."

The object of my first love was a simple servant-girl who lived in the next house. Every day I watched for her, and rushing to the window I flattened my tiny nose against the glass, and devoured her with eager eyes.

We used to live in Kharkoff in winter and passed the summer months in Doljik, our beautiful estate which claims to be counted amongst the stately homes of Russia, situated forty miles distance from town. Our removal to Doljik was a regular treat for us children, our joy and the servants' nuisance, for when they began to pack up, we were only in their way, under pretence of help, poking about among the straw, scattered in the yard, throwing it over one another whilst playing hide-and-seek.

Doljik is a delightful place. The castle, a stately white mansion of commanding appearance, is very grand with its suite of lofty rooms ; portraits of ancestors, the former Galitzins, very good-looking all of them, adorn the walls. The park is beautiful, with long alleys of elm and oak and vast lawns with skilfully sorted flower-borders, I had a doll's house in the park, furnished with every convenience, with a garden of my own in which I spent happy hours gardening eagerly, weeding and watering, I also bestowed a great part of my affection on pet animals: dogs, cats, squirrels and tame rabbits. My brothers and I were fond of all kinds of fun; early in the morning we used to start for the meadows with baskets to gather mushrooms for our breakfast, and went for rambles in the woods. We also did a lot of fishing and bathing. My parents presented me with a prefect dream of a pony. How proud I felt when I was lifted on my " Scotchy's " back for my first ride!

Dolls took no leading part in my childhood, and I had often wished I had been a boy. I climbed trees and tore my frocks and engaged in all sorts of wild pranks.

There was much excitement on my father's birthday. The house was full of guests, and an orchestra came down from town. At dinner when papa's health was drunk, two large cannons, placed at the principal entrance, were fired, which made me crawl on my hands and knees, shamefully, under the table. We had in the evening grand illuminations in the park, with fireworks which did not enrapture me, for at every burst of rockets I had to put my hands over my ears.

On the day of our village festival there was a fair on the square opposite the church. I threw sugar-candy and handfuls of pennies to the peasant children.

I had now passed my eighth year and the time for lessons had come. I was given over to the care of a French governess, Melle. Rose, who was very badly named, for she was a horrid lemon-coloured old creature, wearing a hideous curled wig, and always looking as though she had just swallowed a spoonful of vinegar. I hated plain people about me and could not bare the sight of Melle. Rose, disliking her from the first. What a life I led her! Plaguing her was a charmingly pretty sport for me. My governess was always scolding and fault-finding; she forced me to make her every morning and evening a low curtsey, which made me long to kick her. Melle. Rose held up as an example to me a little friend of mine, the Princess Mimi Troubetzkoy, who was a well-behaved child, doing credit to her governess's bringing up, and never giving her any trouble. But I despised sheep-like docility and was weary of hearing of all the beautiful things Mimi did and said.

Being deprived of the bump of respect, I did exactly what my governess told me not to do, refusing to be put into harness. When the fighting-blood stirred in me and made me too horribly naughty, I was sent for punishment to bed, but I would rather be cut to pieces before I would deign to apologise to Melle. Rose. That disagreeable person was succeeded by Melle. Allamand, a French lady educated in England, the most delightful of old maids, whom I loved fondly, for she was never cross, and since she came to me, I began to understand that it was possible for a governess to be nice, and that the term is not necessarily synonimous to frighten and bore.

We got on very well for Melle. Allamand bore with my caprices, which were many, I must confess. But though she was always in a good temper we had little quarrels sometimes, which we soon made up. I studied my piano with Melle. Allamand and learned English, which soon became a second mother-tongue to me. When we went out walking, my governess's soft heart was full of pity for the poor starving homeless dogs which she picked up in the streets and brought home to be fed; the ugliest and shabbiest had her tenderest care. Melle. Allamand was called back to England and my parents had to get another governess. An English young lady was engaged, named Miss Emily Puddan. My brothers made her rage awfully in calling her Miss Pudding. She had no authority over me whatever, being in fact rather silly, but she was a very pleasant companion—so well up in all games. We were enthusiastic croquet-players and had sometimes desperate quarrels, being very near scratching each other's eyes out. "I tell you I hit your ball!"—"You didn't!"—"I did!" etc., our arguments becoming very hot and uncivil; soon we dropped our mallets and ran and complained to mamma, both governess and pupil.

When I was past my twelfth year I grew very fond of reading the books of the "Bibliothèque Rose." I pitied mamma because she read deadly uninteresting English Tauchnitz novels, when there existed such enrapturing books as *Les petites filles modéles, les malheurs de Sophie,* etc. But this childish literature did not hinder me from flirtation. I used to long for adventures; and here I was having one, notwithstanding that I had only just grown out of pinafores. My parents took me sometimes to the Italian opera and I conceived a romantic admiration for the tenor of the troop, who was, as I thought adorable beyond words. I raved about him. When out walking with my governess, I dragged her in the direction I knew the tenor would take, in the hope of meeting him. I began to knit a prosaic cache-nez for the object of my dreams, which mamma confiscated, happily, in time.

From my earliest years I had a great love for acting; we gave, from time to time, little theatrical entertainments; we dressed up and played fragments of Shakespeare's dramas, and I was the leading-lady in these rehearsals. When I took up the high tragic part of "Desdemona," Nicolas, the brother of my little friend Sophy Annenkoff, was the personator of "Othello," he sacrificed his appearance so far as to blacken his face. During the murder scene, when the situation grew particularly tragic, Nicolas displayed such a realism of the Shakespearian meaning, that I began to fear being choked in reality.

B

I was a half-grown girl now, arrived at the age of fourteen, envied awfully my friends, the countess Sievers and Mary Podgoritchany who were grown-ups and wore long frocks. Some day, I said, it will be my turn to be introduced to society. I looked forward to the day when I should reach the age of seventeen and appear at my first ball with a long train, and be able to flirt to my heart's content.

I felt now that I had enough of governesses. My last one, Melle. Annaguy, bored me awfully, being extremely particular about my manners ; it was preach, preach all day long. Melle. Anna gave me continually a string of instructions consisting chiefly of "don'ts," which I listened to impatiently. I couldn't go here, I couldn't go there, I couldn't eat this, I couldn't eat that ! My governess was indeed too exasperating, and I had a furious inclination to consign her to very warm quarters. Melle. Anna was besides intensely devout ; being very anxious about the welfare of my soul, she crammed me with pious lectures, but books of this sort were not in my line, and I read everything I could lay hand on. Papa's library was full of interesting books, and I spent whole nights greedily devouring in bed works written by Paul de Kock, a jolly author, but rather improper. In the morning I hid these books under my mattress. My childhood days had passed by Poor " Bibliothèque Rose," thy time was well and duly over !

CHAPTER II

MY FIRST TRIP ABROAD

WHEN I was fifteen, mamma decided to take me abroad to be " finished." Stuttgart was chosen for our winter residence ; we were to get there towards the end of October, after having visited Paris and made a water-cure at Spa.

I was intensely interested in all my surroundings ; it was all new to me. We spent a fortnight in Paris, visiting the curiosities of that splendid city from morning till night.

I delighted to walk on the boulevards. Though a minx of fifteen I had already an insatiable thirst for admiration, and loved to attract attention, I did not look a " bread and butter Miss " and men stared at me in the streets. One day a passer-by, giving me a glance of approval, said to his companion : " Look at this little girl, she promises much ! " I need not say that I was much flattered and laughed outright, but mamma didn't.

From Paris we went to Spa, a bright watering place, lying in a high valley of the Belgian Ardennes, three hours by rail from Brussels.

We took an apartment in the house of a coach-maker ; his daughter waited on us. Insignificant in her work-a-day clothes, she looked quite a lady on Sundays, dressed in her smartest frock ; but her work was badly done that day.

Our programme was as follows : we rose at six, swallowed hastily a glass of mineral water and went to take a walk on the broad avenue named *Allée de sept heures*. In the afternoon we listened to the band playing in the principal square bearing the name of *Pierre le Grand*. (Spa's iron waters had saved the life of our Tzar, Peter the Great, nearly two hundred years before).

Profiting by the occasion of being in the neighbourhood of Brussels, we went to visit the famous lace factory. I remarked that the poor work-women all had sore, inflamed eyes.

On our return to Spa, we took a wrong train and arriving at the humble little station of Pepinster, which stood in the open country, we were very much disconcerted on being told to get out, for our train took an opposite direction to Spa, and there was no other train that day. And thus we had the cheery prospect of spending the night in this solitary station with no dwelling in sight. It was too bad! We quitted the train rather out of sorts, and looked round about in helpless bewilderment. The station consisted of a bare hall only, giving one the impression of being all windows, with a telegraphic office at one end. As there was no lock on the outer door, the porter advised us to barricade it with a large table. But we were not left alone, however, someone put his long nose through the small ticket-window, which troubled us somewhat; nevertheless we laid ourselves down on the hard benches to sleep, which was easier said than done, for we had just begun to doze, when the table, which being weak on its legs performed very badly the function of safety-lock, gave way with a bang and six tipsy porters, arrayed in blue cotton blouses, precipitated themselves in the hall, disposed to pass the night in our company. What was to be done to turn them out of doors? The situation was becoming critical, but mamma did not lose her presence of mind, and spreading a shawl over me, she whispered into my ear not to give the slightest sign that I was awake, and approaching bravely these rascals, she ordered them out, telling them that the station-master had promised that no one should disturb us. After many debates five men went out, but the sixth declared that he had the settled resolution to sleep there. My poor mamma half dead with fright, sat down on the bench by my side, and holding up a warning finger, she entreated the man, in an anxious whisper, not to wake her poor invalid child. Feigning sleep, I had much ado to stifle the laughter which bubbled in my throat. Then our night-mate drew nearer to mamma and said: "I see, madam, that you are not a bit sleepy, nor am I either, so let us chat together." To cut him short mamma began to tell him all sorts of fibs; she announced that she was the wife of the Russian Ambassador in Brussels, and invited him to come and pay her a visit at Spa, giving him a false address. Flattered and stunned by all this magnificence, her interlocutor removed to the opposite end of the hall, and very soon we heard him snoring in Wagnerian volume; and in the morning how astonished he was to see the wonderful transformation of the poor invalid child into a tall, rosy-cheeked maiden, looking the very picture of health. As I was getting into the train I heard the porters saying, pointing me out: "*Tiens, la petite moribonde d'hier, est-elle tout plein gentille!*"

From Spa the doctor sent us to Boulogne-sur-mer. From the top of the belfry of the cathedral of "Notre Dame de Boulogne," one discerns the shores of England in fine weather. I burned with impatience to cross the channel, and one bright morning my desire was accomplished; we embarked on a ship going to Dover. It was the first experience I ever had of the sea, and nevertheless I proved a very good sailor, though the passage of the " Pas-de-Calais " was not at all pleasant ; there was a heavy swell and the sea-breeze was so sharp, that I had to hold my hat all the time. There was a curate on board with his son, an Eton boy, who fell in love with me on the spot, but I did not take much notice of him, for he looked such a baby that one would be positively ashamed to bother with him.

When we reached Dover we caught the special train waiting to take us to London. When it drew up at Charing-Cross station, a porter took possession of us and our luggage, and conveyed us across to the Charing-Cross Hotel. I was somewhat abashed when we were invited to enter a small cage, which shut upon us with a vicious snap and then tossed us up, and before I had time to do more than gasp, we were on the sixth storey. It was my first acquaintance with the lift, a means of conveyance which substitutes so advantageously the legs of fatigued travellers. A new surprise awaited us : when we rang for the maid, ordering her to bring us some sandwiches, she whispered something into a pipe-tube in the wall, and in a moment a shutter was set open and the sandwiches, appeared like magic, served automatically on a tray.

I was delighted with London. In this great city life is full and stirring ; but the English Sunday is rather a trying affair, for there are no theatres, no entertainments whatever. We wanted to explore the British Museum that day, and it was with great difficulty that we caught a drowsy porter who turned on his heel and went away after having declared, very rudely, that we were troubling him in vain, the Museum being closed, considering that the day of Sabbath was for rest and peace, and that all good Christians kept it holy. We turned sorrowfully away and went to our Russian church. When the service was over our priest, a charming old gentleman, invited us for a cup of tea. My patriotic sentiment was agreeably flattered when I saw the works of Tourgenieff, our great writer, translated into English, in his drawing-room.

From London we went straight to Stuttgart, where we settled down to a peaceful winter. We looked about for furnished apartments and took one in Köning-Strasse, the principal street.

Mamma devoted herself to give me the best finish in her power. Our Grand-Duchess, Olga Nikolaevna, queen of Würtenberg, was at that time educating her niece, the Grand-Duchess Vera, and I had the benefit of her masters. I worked terribly hard, remaining at my studies till dinner-time. Trying to stimulate my zeal, mamma resolved to give me two marks for my weekly reports if they were all fives, permitting me to spend my pocket-money on theatre tickets.

A singing mistress was sought for me, who rejoiced in the poetical name of " Fraulein Rosa." When I was presented to her I gave way to a fit of most indecent laughter, for this Rose looked such a guy—a veritable old caricature. Outraged she left the room and never after returned. I was very glad to be rid of that fright, and clapped my hands in naughty glee.

I took a great liking to a young compatriot of mine, Mary Vietinghoff, who lived abroad with her mother, by reason of her delicate health. She was one year younger that I, but for good senses she was ten years my senior. I used also to see a great deal of the Rydes. Mrs. Ryde was the widow of a Scotch curate and the mother of twelve children. I liked the Ryde family *tutti quanti*, especially Ettie, a girl of my own age, a most jolly lassie. Her brother, Willie, a youngster of fourteen, took a fancy to me. This shrewd young Scot glided one day on tiptoe behind me and stroked my cheek, exclaiming: " How smooth it is." He wanted to repeat this manipulation with his lips, but received a smart slap across the face in recompense ; a very rude demonstration, indeed, but I was an awfully quick-tempered young lady and hated to be touched. The Rydes were astonished at what they termed my " colossal good English," which I had got from my childhood. To complete my education, Willie offered to teach me some of his best slang.

Though I was still in short frocks, I was already a dreadful flirt and had all sorts of love affairs, but all the stock of my affection was exclusively bestowed upon Robert Jeffrey, a pupil of the English school in Cannstadt, a small town in the neighbourhood of Stuttgart. He was a Scotch lad of eighteen summers, blue-eyed, brown-haired and white-toothed. I was drawn to him from the beginning, for Bobbie was a real darling, and I considered him the sweetest boy in the world. I had other admirers, but Jeffrey was by far the handsomest and the dearest ; I was quite silly about him and had eyes and ears only for him alone. He was my " Prince Charming ;" my imagination adorned him with the attributes of all possible and impossible heroes. It was my first serious affair, the first love of my girlhood. The passion was reciprocal and Jeffrey said I was the first girl who had yet disturbed his peace. Mamma went to Paris for a few days, leaving me under the care of the Baroness Vietinghoff. She hoped that Mary, who considered herself a sort of guardian of mine, would prevent me doing anything rash while she was away. Part of her duty was to keep off boys, (other boys, not Jeffrey.) Mary promised mamma to play a mother's part to me ; she wouldn't let me commit any eccentricity. But I did an enormous one. Jeffrey was a somewhat green and inexperienced youth, too timid for my taste, and wanted a little go and rousing up. Wishing to sharpen his wits I sent him a wild letter, telling him that he was all the world to me. I did not expect that he would answer personally, that same day, my foolish *billet-doux*, and when Mary announced that my youthful sweetheart was waiting for me in the drawing-room, I sat down on my trunk, declaring that nothing in the world would force me to move from my place. I don't believe I am weak in the way of shyness, but I didn't find strength at the moment to think of facing Jeffrey. Mary went to fetch him and left the room, feeling herself an uncomfortable third. I continued to stick to my box, my chin upon my folded hands. At first we did not utter a single word, as silent as two stones. Some minutes later we were quite ourselves again, and Jeffrey from that day proved extremely teachable, and soon lost his shyness ; I had trained him thoroughly.

This foolish " boy and girl love " lasted during all our stay in Stuttgart. We arranged clandestine meetings at the Rydes. Ettie was a staunch friend, full of sympathy, and we poured into her willing ears the story of our love, having found a comfortable ally in her. We used to have great fun together. One evening we were in the wildest spirits, playing charades, and Jeffrey was just going to accomplish one of his forfeits : he had to kneel down beside the prettiest girl of all the company and kiss the one he loved best. He had chosen me for both manifestations. In the midst of the fun mamma appeared. *Tableau!* She didn't approve of kissing, mamma—and soon put a stop to the delightful game.

Mamma kept me very strictly, and did a good deal of weeding in the selection of my friends. She did not consider, alas! the Rydes the best of companions for a girl of my temperament, who was always on the look out for wickedness, fearing that they stuffed my head with all sorts of silly nonsense. On holidays she caught me flat-nosed, with my face glued to the window, looking out for the Rydes.

I went with Mary Vietinghoff to Dr. Roth's gymnastic class, and enjoyed meeting there girls of different social classes. Forgetting that our stations in life were widely apart, it amused me to shake hands with daughters of shop-keepers as well as ladies by birth, without distinction. Dr. Roth made us march up and down the hall with our hands clasped behind our backs. At each step we made he repeated like a pendulum, " *Kopf, Rücken, Kopf, Rücken!* " and I mimicked him in the anteroom where we put on our hats, throwing my audience into convulsions of giggling. My foolish tricks drove Dr. Roth to despair. When his back was turned I dashed on to the window, raised up a corner of the blind which was generally let down during our exercises, and stared at the passers-by.

As we lived within two minutes' walk of Dr. Roth's dwelling, I begged mamma to allow me to go unaccompanied to his class. Mamma objected at first, for she said she could not have me running alone in the streets, but I soon overcame her prejudice and profited by my liberty for paying flying visits to the Rydes on my way home from Dr. Roth's. Being such a romp I wanted a lot of looking after and gave much trouble to poor mamma, who never knew what I would do next. My apparent frivolity deeply wounded her, but remonstrance always led to scenes. One night, coming home from a dancing-party, where my conduct had been more disgraceful than usual, after a miserable scene that we had had together, mamma fell into hysterics. It drove me nearly mad to see her in such a state, and I dashed into the street and raced headlong, hatless, my hair loose, flying wildly about my shoulders and waving in the wind. Whilst I fled in terror across the street I heard two well-known voices calling: "Vava! Vava!" screamed mamma, "Fraulein Princess!" roared our cook, running after me in pursuit. This only increased my speed, and I ran as fast as my legs would carry me. A group of students, wearing coloured caps and followed by huge dogs, who were coming out of a restaurant before which I was galloping at that moment, were soon at my heels. I never stopped running till I found myself breathless at the door of the Vietinghoffs, having taken that way by instinct, and I flung myself panting into their appartment, where I felt safe at last.

On Sundays we went to the Russian chapel. It amused me enormously to watch the secretary of the queen, a gentleman looking excessively pleased with himself, who made the sign of the cross only when the priest pronounced the names of the queen or the Grand Duchess Vera.

My health began to alarm Mamma; I was growing thin and pale. Our doctor believed I was overstraining myself with lessons, and instead of prescribing me a lot of horrid drugs, he had the capital idea of sending us to sun ourselves for a week or two on the Riviera. We followed willingly his agreeable prescription and set off speedily to Nice.

Mere child as I was, I already indulged in a decided taste for adventures, and experienced one on the road. During the night, we were pushed into a railway carriage full of passengers; one of them, a very good-looking young man, made room for us and went to find for himself another place. The next morning, whilst we were breakfasting at the Station of Marseilles, a waiter brought me a beautiful bouquet, followed by our amiable fellow-passenger of the previous night, who proved to be a Mexican fresh from South America. He opened the conversation by telling us that his name was *Gallardo Alvarez*, and hinted that he was an unmarried millionaire, making his first pleasure tour in Europe. Studying him stealthily I decided that he would do.

We stopped at the same hotel with Señor Alvarez, who soon began to show me that he was deeply interested in me. In fact I won him entirely. He was a man of volcanic passions and inflammable as gun-cotton, his eyes said even more than his words. Unfortunately the liking was not mutual, he did not make my heart beat. Though I was a girl to change her passions in a hurry, I was so taken up with Jeffrey, that I had no thought for any one else, just then ; my Mexican conquest was rather amusing and kept me from yawning, that's all, but nevertheless I gave him a fair amount of encouragement. I suppose I am a flirt, but I cannot help being nice to men. My Transatlantic adorer followed me about like my shadow ; go where I would, he was ever at my heels and at last it became quite wearisome. I was awfully bored and did the utmost to show it to him by being uncivil and not nice, and he only received hard words from me. Oh ! I can easily snub anyone if I wish ! I told him one day, he needn't stick to me so, but no, in spite of my rebuffs, he wouldn't stir from my side ; he only exclaimed piteously : " Princess Vava, why are you so awfully hard on me ? " He was a persevering wooer that Don Alvarez, telling me that he had already fallen a victim to my blue eyes in the sleeping-car, and that he thought of me all day and dreamt of me all night since, then and a lot more idiotic bosh. He often bothered me with compliments that I affected not to hear. He likened me to Venus and told me that I was his goddess and the wonder of the world, a being created to be fallen in love with, and that I would remain as a gem set in his mind for evermore. But I only made fun of his high-flown sentiments. One night at the Opera, whilst Faust was " cooing " his romance to Margaret, Senor Alvarez asked me suddenly : " Tell me, who is the prettiest person in this house ! " I raised my opera glasses and looked about me at the audience, but he told me it was useless work, for there was no looking-glass near me.

I went out shopping with my Mexican friend one afternoon. In a shop-window, with a variety of nicknacks offered for sale, I saw a small box of powder in the form of an ivory apple, a perfect darling, which took particularly my fancy. I had a craving to possess it, but as I had only a few coppers left in my purse, I could not purchase it, and looked at the tempting apple with longing eyes ; but crushed by the scorn of the stylish person behind the counter, I left the shop dismissing it from my mind. On the same night, going to bed,

I noticed a parcel lying upon my toilet table, which contained the apple that I had resisted, bought by my Mexican Paris for his Russian Helena.

We left Stuttgart in winter, and there we were in full blooming-time of violets and roses. We made several excursions and went as far as the wicked little principality of Monaco. Mamma gained large sums of money at the roulette tables of Monte-Carlo. I was also longing to try my luck, but roulette was prohibited, alas for youngsters like me.

We were invited to a ball given on an American man-of-war, the "Franklin," which anchored in the harbour of Villefranche. The ball was too delightful; I highly enjoyed myself and nearly danced my shoes off. There never was anything to equal the amiability of the officers of the frigate; their commander, Captain Folger, was awfully charming to us and hoisted the Russian flag in our honour.

We had such a delightful fortnight in Nice. The days went like lightning and the hour of our departure approached. I detested the idea of going back to dull Stuttgart to pursue my studies, but I had a compensation in the person of my darling Bobbie.

Senor Alvarez pined with grief at being obliged to part with me. He accompanied us as far as Marseilles and delivered to me, whilst travelling with us, a Spanish poem, of his composition, dedicated to me, speaking of delirious passion, broken heart and other fiddlesticks. One of our fellow-passengers, a handsome Canadian girl begged him to dedicate at least three lines to her. Alvarez at once pulled a note-book out of his pocket and scribbled down three words only: *Adieu pour toujours.* Not very amiable on his part! Bidding me good-bye, Alvarez took hold of my hands, squeezing them as if they had been shut in a door, and looking at me with an expression of entreaty, he requested my permission to pay us a visit in Russia. By the manner I answered him, I would not in his place have undertaken such a long journey.

Here I was again in Stuttgart, carried back to lessons. In January, on the occasion of my sixteenth birthday, mamma gave me a coming-out dance. I considered myself fully grown now, having put up my golden mane and let down my frock for the first time that night. I was awfully unhappy to leave Stuttgart in April, for I left my heart behind. It was such a sore trial to part with Jeffrey. He was unwell on the day of our departure and could not see us off. I was in despair at not being able to bid him farewell and sobbed desperately at the thought that I should never see his darling face again. At that moment he was more indispensable to me than air and light. Being ashamed that mamma should see me cry, I swallowed my tears and tried to look cheerful, but when the train began to move, I crept into a corner of the railway-carriage and sobbed my heart out in childish grief, little fool that I was.

Before returning to Russia we made a trip to Italy and travelled as far as Naples in the company of the Italian Consul of Manchester, Signor Raphaello Giordano, middle-aged and perfectly gentleman-like. He promised to be our cicerone in Naples, where we arrived at night, rather disconcerted by the hubbub of the clamerous Neapolitans. When we found ourselves on the crowded platform, noisy *fachini* (porters) besieged us and snatched away our bags. Signor Giordano had to desert us on the quay, whilst we went to get our luggage through the Customs promising to be back soon. In his absence a young man began to hang about in front of us, staring at me all the time with frankest impertinence. He came close to me and managed to whisper in my ear : " What hotel are you going to ? Do stop at the hotel where I am staying." Impudent fellow ! I was greatly astonished at his audacity. Fortunately Signor Giordano strolled in at the right moment and rescued me. Both men were standing nervously facing each other and Giordano exclaimed in arrogant tones, his eyes blazing with wrath : " What right have you to speak to that young lady ? " " And you, how do you dare to speak to me ? " was the impertinent answer. A squabble sprang up between them ; it was so hateful to have a scandal ! Giordano went to seek a policeman and we remained alone, dreading to move in fear of losing sight of our protector, and our boxes were so long in coming. At last we decided to be bold and wait no longer. We hailed a carriage and rode off to Victoria Hotel, recommended by Giordano, and were very glad when he made his appearance an hour after.

Early next morning I opened the shutters and was fascinated by the splendid panorama of the bay of Naples and Vesuvius with its cone rising against the azure sky. How glorious it all was !

We spent three weeks in Naples making excursions and visiting all the curiosities in the neighbourhood. Pompeii produced a very painful impression on me by its atmosphere of death and disaster. We were present at the digging up of vases, bracelets and other curious relics of by-gone days.

Wishing to give a surprise to my father, mamma had my portrait made by a horrible little hunch-backed painter of modest pretensions. After my very first sitting we did not appreciate this Quasimodo's manner of painting. Mamma took great pains in pointing out to him his mistakes, but instead of repairing them, the little fright contemplated that abominable painting with his ugly head first on this side and then on that, as if lost in admiration, repeating all the time :

"*Bellissimo, grazioso!*" The portrait was, as we expected, a great failure, but we had to take, nevertheless, that spoilt canvas, unworthy of preservation, paying for it the sum of 200 francs.

One day, having to change some Russian coins, we entered an American bank, where I made, as it appears, a great impression upon one of the clerks, a very good-looking chap, with light hair and brilliant black eyes. He found a pretext to come and see us at the hotel next morning. After that, we saw him nearly every day; he spent all his spare time with me. This youth, named Alphonso Shildecker, was of cosmopolitan origin, born in America of a German father and an Italian mother. Though only a banker's clerk, Shildecker was nevertheless very well educated and spoke several languages fluently. He had an agreeable tenor voice and taught me some popular Neapolitan songs. This poor youth was getting seriously in love with me, which was perfectly ridiculous. I liked him pretty well in the beginning, and rather encouraged his hopes and accepted his advances in a friendly spirit, but if he thought I was serious, he was making a great mistake. It had all gone much deeper with him than with me. To me he was only a new toy; I was delighted with any one who could amuse me and was simply playing with him out of girlish perversity.

An American boy, Floyd Reynolds, a student of the University of Bonn, who lived in our hotel, was burning with impatience to be presented to me. One day he sent me up an enormous bouquet with his card pinned on it. Shildecker took it into his head to be detestably jealous of Floyd. Giordano was not dangerous to him being no longer young and not particularly good-looking, but he was wild at my flirting with Floyd, in who's company he did not show to advantage. He soon became very tedious, never leaving us alone and coming in our way when we wanted to be free and quiet; he seemed to take a perverse pleasure in interrupting our conversation. I considered two a better number than three, and as for Shildecker I would have liked to have kicked him round the room. He followed me everywhere, but I turned my back and devoted myself to Floyd, and left him out in the cold. He caught me in all the available corners, when we visited churches and museums, and made love to me, telling me that he adored me to madness, and that he was going to cut his throat, or hang himself, or I know not what, unless I gave him hope. That sounded very tragical indeed! It may be all stuff and nonsense, but, nevertheless, I undoubtedly played with fire and was in a constant fear that he might do something wild and desperate; I am sure it's enough to make any girl nervous! But I was not going to let him spoil our trip, and tried to keep away from him, thereby driving him into a more feverish condition than ever. He grew perfectly ill with jealousy. How black he looked that love-sick boy! He suffered and I enjoyed myself; that is the way of the world! The day we left Naples, Shildecker wanted to go with us to the train, but I determined he should not have the chance, and indicated to him a wrong train. I was awfully vexed when I saw him at the station, looking down the platform with anxiety. Despite all my precautions he had tracked me. When he asked permission to write to me, I looked at him as though suddenly remembering his presence, and answered with an air of royal condescension: " You may do as you like!"

We spent three days in Rome, roaming through the splendid museums and churches, and had the chance of seeing the Pope officiate in St. Peter's Cathedral, which was a very imposing spectacle.

On the eve of our departure I received a letter from Shildecker, who wrote to me that he had taken leave of absence for a fortnight and was coming to rejoin us in Rome; but it did not detain us, to be sure, and the next morning we started for Florence without leaving our address at the hotel. I had had such an awful dose of Shildecker at Naples that it was quite enough! But " La Donna é mobile," I found myself at intervals thinking about him, and strangely enough, I missed him now not a little that he was altogether lost and done with, and felt tenderly towards him. Such is the consistency of human nature! Being a girl of prompt action, I wrote to him, not foreboding the consequences, to come speedily to Florence. To days later a waiter came to tell me that a young gentleman was at the door and wished particularly to speak to me. It was Shildecker in person, who rushed forward, took my hands in his and kissed them passionately, looking happy and proud beyond words, but I did not let him make too much display of his flow of tenderness and, wrenching my hands from his grasp, I told him to follow me. We entered the drawing-room together, and I blushed up to the roots of my hair when I saw mamma's bewilderment at the unexpected appearance of Shildecker, who, without preamble, solicited my hand. Mamma with ideal composure told him that we were far too young, both of us, to talk of marriage, and that my father would certainly never give his consent. Shildecker's face lengthened visibly, but this check did not, however, abate his hope of taking possession of me one day.

I had again enough of Shildecker, but it was no such easy matter this time to get rid of him; having gone so far, he was not to be turned back, he meant to follow us to Venice. (He would have followed me to the end of the world if I had let him!)

For some time past I had noticed that my wooer **was** altered, not the same fellow at all, looking like a phantom of his former self, a wreck of the handsome Shildecker of former days. I knew it was all my doing, but asked him impishly what was the matter with him and if he could ever manage to stop looking as if he were in a dentist's chair. He told me that my coolness gave him innumerable sleepless nights, and that I ruined his life.

We arrived at Venice in the night. That aquatic town seemed very beautiful to me with its magnificent palaces reflected in the water, and poetic gondolas, but I found Venice less interesting when seen in disenchanting day ; the beautiful palaces appeared ancient and decayed, and the poetic gondolas, resembling coffins, gave rise to lugubrious thoughts. How insufferably dull it would be to dwell here ! To live a day, buried in that monotonous silence, is quite enough, I thought.

We parted with Shildecker in Venice. He accompanied us to the boat sailing for Trieste, and was sadly broken down, poor boy. When he bade me a dramatic farewell, his face was pale and his eyes had a world of grief in them, and he told me in a voice which trembled, that even if years were to pass, and continents and oceans divided us, I had only to say come, and he'd come. His last words were that he would ever be true to me, and always keep me in his heart, and though always is rather a tremendous word, still, to judge by his dejected aspect, he looked likely to fulfil it. When our boat swerved slowly from the shore, my poor worshipper stood forlorn, contemplating our ship with tortured eyes, and then I vanished out of his life for ever.

On my return home my father and brothers found that I looked quite grown-up with my long dress and new style of coiffure.

Though far away, I could not forget Jeffrey, and was very happy to receive a long passionate missive from him, enclosed in Mary Vietinghoff's letter. I devoured the pages with eager joy. Jeffrey wrote that he was broken-hearted since his darling Vava went away, and that he smothered her sweet face with thousands of passionate kisses. My poor, dear, bonny lad ! I too was hungering for the sight of him, but half Europe, alas, divided us !

For some time I kept up a correspondence with Ettie Ryde, and inspired her with the following poem, in well turned rhymes :—

> From this large, bustling city
> My friend has gone. Oh, what a pity !
> With her I laughed and sang and danced,
> Since she left me my love is much enhanced
> She was merry, she was very, very wild,
> My friend was a naughty, disobedient child.

She fell in love with handsome men and boys,
And broke their hearts, as children break their toys.
   She first loved a Greek, of colour dark and sallow,
" I always thought him like a candle made of tallow."
But she much admired that dark-eyed Greek ;
She used to sit by him and softly stroke his cheek.

(White lies.)

   At length of this Greek youth she grew quite tired,
And her heart with love to a young Scotchman was fired.
He was young, just turned nineteen,
Hair brown, eyes blue, by nature somewhat green.
   Oh, I can't tell of that long, long tale of love !
He thought her constant, sweet, gentle as a dove.
She believed him mild, kind-hearted, very true.
Can you tell the names of this young couple, can you?
   Well, she was no other than Vava, the young princess,
She ought to have had more sense, you must confess.
He was Jeffrey, the youth from Glasgow town.
If they read these verses how they both would frown !
   Oh, I should like to see dear Vava again !
She gave me pleasure, never a moment's pain.
Now, my sweet girl, this poetry I must end,
Don't, oh don't forget your fond Scotch friend !

HENRIETTA RYDE.

I was delighted with her poetry, which incited me to write the verses that I venture to give here, written in the slang style that I had picked from my Stuttgart English friends. The lines ran thus :—

   Dear Ettie, spare some minutes few,
To read this poetry, will you?
It's awful, stupid balderdash,
And nothing better than mere trash,
But be indulgent, damsel sweet,
And mind, you puggie, be discreet,
Don't show this rubbish to your beaus,
Nor to your friends, nor to your foes,
For I'm afraid to be laughed at,
And to be called a stupid brat.
   Do you remember, darling child,
How I was fast, and oh, so wild?
But I'm not changed as yet the least,
Now, am I not a horrid beast?
   Oh what a booby, dear, I was,
To care for so many fellows.
But the real object of my flame,
I truly should not know—to name.

(Ungrateful being.)

   I liked Jeffrey pretty well,
Because he was such a swell,
I liked Skinner very much too,
Somebody else did, don't you know who?
   Oh, Ettie, you were an awful flirt,
The idea of my being so pert !
But it's the truth, dear, isn't it, dove,

You must confess it as a love.
  Poor old girl, how you must feel forlorn,
Now that sweet Teddie Thomson's gone !
He was a darling little man,
But as dark as a frying pan.

(My revenge for the comparison of my Greek adorer to a candle made of tallow.)

Just remember, at Mary's party,
You nearly fainted, my hearty,
Then Teddie with a haggard face,
Bustled near you with a great deal of grace.
He ran for water, for Eau-de-Cologne,
And went right smartly through his *besogne*
  Now, old girlie, I must bid you good-bye,
Really, duckie, 'tis not without a sigh ! "

VAVA GALITZINE.

CHAPTER III

MY FIRST APPEARANCE IN SOCIETY

I WAS to be taken out in St. Petersburg for my first season, and presented at Court. How my heart palpitated at the idea of my first dance! I made my appearance in public in Kharkoff, at a ball given by the Count Sievers, the governor of the town. I am not afflicted with shyness, nevertheless I was seized with a sudden access of bashfulness on entering the ball-room, and feeling horribly uncomfortable with the big bouquet that my brother had given to me, I flung it on the floor in the ante-room. It was not long, however, before I was quite at my ease again, enjoying the ball enormously, and dancing to my heart's content all through the evening.

I came to St. Petersburg full of happy hopes and expectations, and an eager desire to spread my wings in the wide world. It would be a delightful existence—every hour filled with enjoyment.

I plunged at once into all the gaieties of St. Petersburg society. Everything was so new and delightful to me! My first social appearance was at a great Court ball. I was brought out by my aunt, the Princess Kourakine, a lady of honour to the Empress. I had such a ravishing ball dress with a very long train. One of mamma's friends had lent me a carved ivory fan of great value, which I dropped in the snow stepping out of the carriage. The fan lost some of its lustre, but what a dazzling lustre presented itself to my eyes when I entered the palace and mounted the splendid staircase lined with powdered footmen in gorgeous liveries. Everything was magnificent and I enjoyed the ball madly. I was not acquainted with a single soul in the place, nevertheless I became instantly surrounded by a circle of partners. I never amused myself so much before. The first dance over, my cavalier, a brilliant officer of the guards, piloted me through the ranks of dancers to the refreshment-room to get an ice. As we passed by the Emperor, who was engaged in a conversation with my Aunt Kourakine, His Majesty gazed at me fixedly and asked who I was. My aunt came over and led me to the Emperor and formally introduced me. His Majesty began by questioning me about myself, my home and my parents. I forgot to be frightened and answered without the slightest flutter of embarrassment, and we soon fell into a comfortable talk. The Emperor asked me if it was my first grown-up dance. " Oh, no, Sir, it's my second one," I announced proudly. The Emperor smiled and expressed his desire to see me henceforth at the Court balls. Perceiving my partner, who was trying to conceal himself behind a column, the Emperor asked me if it was my cavalier. " Oh, yes, Sir, and I am keeping him waiting such a long, long time," I blurted out in one breath. It was indeed a dreadful breach of court etiquette, but I was so inexperienced in the ways of society that a transgression against Court laws appeared of little importance to me. The Emperor seemed much amused by my outspoken manner and said : " Well, go on dancing, I will not deprive you any longer of that pleasure."

I returned home enchanted, and went to bed in a delirium, but I had had too exciting a night to find it easy to fall asleep.

Some days later, at a musical party, given by my uncle, the Prince Prosorowski-Galitzine, the master of the house said to me significantly, " Well, Vava, I congratulate you ! " But he did not conclude his phrase, for mamma, who tried to preserve me from the intoxication of overpraise, made haste to change the subject of conversation. I was tortured with curiosity and got the whole story out of my cousins, the Prosorowskis', who told me that the Emperor at the fox-hunt had asked their father all about me and said a lot of flattering things, congratulating him on having such a niece.

The gaiety and the bustle of St. Petersburg life bewildered me. I went out a great deal, fluttering from amusement to amusement : balls, dinners, theatres, concerts, etc., etc. Unfortunately I couldn't be in two places at the same time.

Papa took me to another Court ball, where I distinguished myself, making such a stupid blunder. Overheated by dancing, I was dying of thirst, and rushing up to a smart-looking individual, clad in bright red, I told him to bring me some iced lemonade, taking him for a Court official. He returned in about five minutes, closely followed by another personage arrayed likewise in red, who carried a tray, and making me a most refined bow, he named himself " Senator K——." In an instant I had guessed the whole odious situation. I had made an awful mistake, having confounded a red-livered laquey with a senator. How could I have been so clumsy ? It was a horribly awkward moment, and I thought I should die of shame. It was really very difficult to find something to say. Covered with confusion I blushed all over my face and muttered hastily some excuses, wanting the floor to open and swallow me up.

There was to be a grand fancy-dress ball at Court, in which I was invited to participate. It was to be one of the best things of the season, one of the eight marvels of the world. The Grand Duke Waldemar, representing the sun, was to open the cortège sitting in a triumphal car drawn by pages and surrounded by twelve sunbeams. I was designed to represent one of them. We were to follow the car in a semi-circle, the tall ones (I being one of the number) in the middle. I had the most bewitching costume that heart of girl could desire. It consisted of a Greek tunic in rose satin, draped on the shoulders with golden gauze; a small sun-dial on the top of my coiffure, powdered with golden powder, was to indicate the hour (mine pointed out six o'clock.) My costume was quite ready, and I gazed at myself in the looking-glass with rapture, arrayed in it. I was a good deal excited about this ball, and could think of nothing else, when suddenly came the tidings of the death of a prince belonging to the Prussian Imperial family, and the ball was put off. I was awfully disappointed and nearly cried my eyes out. I had looked forward to it so!

A love affair sprang up between me and the Prince of Montenegro, brother of the reigning prince of that country. We met for the first time at a ball at the French Embassy. The prince was astonishingly handsome, quite a show creature, looking very picturesque in his native costume, consisting of a white woollen skirt and a jacket with golden embroidery. There was an air of *Veni, vidi, vici,* about him. The prince was made much of in society; never was a man so run after. I was surrounded by a flood of partners when the prince came up, claiming a dance, but I had to refuse him, being already engaged. He was by no means discouraged, and established himself on the other side of my chair, and thus I found myself sitting between two devoted cavaliers. The prince danced divinely, and I waltzed with him pretty nearly all the evening. As the ball went on mamma, who found that my partners were becoming alarmingly enterprising, wanted to carry me off home at once, but a chorus of protestations arose from them, and I, too, began to implore mamma not to be obliged to leave the ball just when the fun was at its height. The prince added his entreaties to mine and gained the victory, taking me to supper. I never had a more entertaining neighbour. The prince had lived a great many years in Paris and spoke French perfectly. He was so clever, full of spirits and daring; in short he was a number of charming things, and I lost my heart a bit. The temptation to play with fire had seized me and I desired to prove my power to charm him. The prince lost no time in letting me see the impression I had made on him, and though he had the reputation of preferring the society of married women to that of young girls, I saw that he was inclined to enter into a flirtation with me.

The champagne had warmed him up and he became very audacious. He slipped his hand under the table-cloth and our fingers touched and communicated fire. Meanwhile, a not very attractive damsel, deeply impressed by the prince's good looks, was gazing at him with eyes of passionate adoration across the table. I noticed it to the prince, but he replied that as for himself, he had no eyes for anyone but me. And he had indeed very expressive eyes, the prince, and knew how to use them! I tried to keep a cool head during the siege of my admirer, but though I had been an iceberg, it was impossible for me not to thaw in his presence. My pulses quickened and I felt an odd little thrill of emotion, while my tell-tale eyes betrayed the truth and looked pleased. After the cotillon mamma took me reluctantly away. Whilst we were putting on our cloaks in the ante-room the prince appeared and came out in the cold to help us into our carriage, and pressing my hand to his lips, he begged permission to call on us the next day.

I was playing the piano frantically, absorbed in my performance of one of Chopin's nocturnes, when the prince was announced, but mamma being out, I gave orders to tell him that there was nobody at home. The prince was a good deal nettled, and when I met him at a ball a few days afterwards, he greeted me somewhat chillingly, but I soon smoothed him down and we were good friends again.

The prince's marked attention to me soon became the topic of much gossip. He was hit, I knew he was, and I, too, was not very far from being in love with him. At the end of the season the prince's white skirt began to be slightly grizzly, and as I had remarkably sharp eyes and a tongue to match, I looked him over critically and declared that I would not dance with him until he had changed his skirt for a new one. Brazen girl that I was to say such shameless things!

We left St. Petersburg in February and came to Moscow for a few days to my grandmother Galatzine. I caught a bad cold on the way, and a doctor was hastily summoned: a fat little old man with a face like a wrinkled apple. He was so funny that I had an attack of laughter at the sight of him which he took for delirium. I had been allowed on that day to have my friend Mary Grekoff with me for an hour or two. She sat on the edge of my bed and we were both soon engaged in eating pounds of chocolate, which did not improve the state of my health, to be sure. Small wonder then that I got worse with every minute; my temperature rose alarmingly and I began to be delirious. My illness declared itself plainly, typhoid fever was the verdict pronounced by the doctor. The case was going to be an anxious one, and the chances were two to one against my recovery. The doctor said it would be well that mamma, who was almost distracted with anxiety and grief, should be prepared for the worst. I passed many sleepless nights tossing in my bed in a restless manner ; at daybreak, when the windows were beginning to whiten, I listened with envy to the joyous "coquerico" of neighbouring cocks, who woke up gay and brisk after a good sleep, whilst I, poor thing, had not closed my eyes for many nights.

I sat up in bed, propped with pillows, and sobbed bitterly, moved to pity for myself. I was so unused to illness. Mamma, who slept in my room, came and sat by me and we had our cry together.

Feeling my end drawing nigh, I sent for a priest and received the Holy Sacrament. Soon after came the crisis. I suffered tortures that day, one could hear my shrieks two streets off. Gasping for breath I tried to bounce out of bed and had to be kept there by main force. Happily complications did not arise, my constitution triumphed, and by the mercy of heaven, life conquered death, and I was pronounced out of danger,

My convalescence was slow ; I was laid up for six long weeks, coming round from my illness day by day, and nursed with much tenderness. As soon as all danger was over, the doctor permitted me to be transferred to Dolgik, though I was still weaker than a new-born babe—a mere shadow of my former self.

The wholesome country air put me quite on my legs again, my health was entirely restored, and I recovered my good looks and my spirits, but I had such a shock when I found all my hair had to come off; I was obliged to have it shaved after my illness. It did not hinder me, however from having three or four admirers here, waiting on my very words. One of my chief victims was Aksenoff, a chum of my brother's, who was completing his studies at the University of Kharkoff that year. Aksenoff was not a bit the hero of my girlish dreams and had no chance whatever of attracting me ; he was a clumsy, athletic-looking lad, with feet like fiddle-cases. Rough on the outside, but the best fellow in the world, he improved on close acquaintance. One could easily see that he was falling seriously in love with me in spite of my shaven head, covered, it is true, with a coquettish cap which suited me wonderfully. I seemed to him a pearl beyond price, and he spent all his time in gazing up at me as a unattainable star. He was my devoted slave in everything, following me about with a sort of dog-like fidelity. I could twist that giant round my little finger ; he was as wax in my hands and would go through fire and water for my sake, but I was a very cruel girl, I delighted to torment my admirers and I only made a laughing-stock of Aksenoff, and began to order him about mercilessly.   Enjoying to impress my sweet will upon the poor boy, I teased and tormented him atrociously. Had I not had plenty of victims already?   Why should I want that poor boy to be tortured?   But my desire for conquest was insatiable, I couldn't leave a man alone.

We had a continual succession of guests in our house.   In the middle of May there was a large party staying at Dolgik-castle, and Aksenoff was kept by me as usual in the background ; he accompanied us in our excursions, carrying cloaks and umbrellas.   I used him barbarously and abused my power over him.   I was pitiless, making the most use possible of my willing slave, and invented many nasty tricks to annoy him.   When we arranged dances in the evenings I sent him to gather roses in the garden, promising him, with my most winning smile, a waltz in recompense, whilst another partner carried me off in his arms from under his nose, leaving him standing there in great dismay.   My simple-hearted lover had no suspicion that I was only fooling him, he went and picked the roses, and when he returned with an armful of flowers, I started him out again on the same errand, and the much-enduring Aksenoff went off crestfallen, with a face a yard long.   One must allow, poor boy, that just then he happened to be supremely unattractive.   When he came back this time, I flung off his roses and said with my most princess-like air, dropping into an armchair, that I was too tired to dance with him now.   Seeing the look of suffering in his face, I thought that I had teased him enough for that evening, and coaxed him with some sweet words.   Poor Aksenoff only heaved a sigh like a March-gale and looked at me with kind, forgiving eyes.   He told me one day that the lines of his hand predicted him a short life, and his prediction was realised ; soon after we heard of his death in Kharkoff, of smallpox.

CHAPTER IV

MY SECOND TRIP ABROAD

IN order to recover entirely from the effects of my illness, the physicians sent me to Biarritz. I was taken abroad by mamma. Towards the latter end of July, travelling from Berlin there was a nice German lady with her niece in our compartment, and I was delighted with my new acquaintance, a girl of about my own age, ever ready for frolic and fun. As soon as the whistle of our train announced an approaching station, we hung our heads out of the window and exchanged glances with groups of German students, in red caps who promenaded on the platform, shouting to them : " *Rothkapchen* ! " But as soon as they approached, our heads were hurriedly withdrawn.

We established ourselves in Biarritz at the delightful Hôtel d'Angleterre, full of English tourists. The outlook from our windows was splendid ; in the distance came the incessant wash of the ocean, and at night, the murmur of the waves was a sweet lullaby soothing me to sleep.

On the first day of our arrival, at table-d'hôte, my eyes travelled round the table and noticed an attractive-looking English trio sitting opposite to us : Mr Delbruck, his son Alfred and his nephew Walter Heape, a fine, fresh-looking boy, with whom I made a nice little bit of flirtation during our stay in Biarritz. He was very much drawn towards me ; I also entertained tender feelings towards him. (And what of the prince of Montenegro ?) But, never mind the prince, he was far enough away, just then, anyhow !

In Biarritz you are next door to Spain and I longed to snatch a glimpse of that poetic country of fans, mantillas and serenades. The Delbrucks agreed to go with us to San-Sebastiano, a Spanish town near the frontier. We could easily go there and be back by dinner-time. We started at an early hour, half asleep all of us, but were soon cheered up as we came out into the freshness and crispness of the early morning.

As we passed the frontier, I was very much disappointed to see that the Spanish officials, walking on the platform, looked just the same as the French ones,—not a bit like opera *Toreadors* or *Tradiavolos* !

After a speedy breakfast at the London Hotel we loitered about the town of San-Sebastiano in a labyrinth of narrow streets, and mounted to the top of the citadel. The climb proved to be a long, hot and fatiguing one. Half way up we saw the monument of a German merchant who, after having become bankrupt, had thrown himself into the ocean from that spot. When we reached the citadel we went groping along silent passage-ways; the semi-darkness within began to provoke a disagreeable impression on me, especially when I perceived a ghastly face peep in at us through the bars of a dungeon window. The prisoner was beckoning to us, trying to explain by an expressive pantomime, that he was going to have his head cut off. I regarded him with eyes of terror and alarm and remarking my fright, the prisoner amused himself to increase it by shouting to me : " Senorita, *escucha Vd !* " (Listen to me Miss !) which I certainly declined to do, and hid myself behind the backs of my cavaliers.

We returned to the hotel thoroughly done up. After dinner, as we took our seats in the train carrying us back to Biarritz, an elderly Spaniard came in, cigar in mouth. He sat down and sent a dense cloud of horrid smoke right into our faces, making mamma feel faint. Noticing that, Mr. Delbrück requested our unpleasant fellow-traveller to stop smoking, but he only sneered, puffing away at his cigar.

The next day the Delbrucks proposed another expedition to the convent of the " Bernardines," where the nuns took vows of perpetual silence. When we came within the enclosure of that monastery, situated near Bayonne, there was an ominous deep stillness around us. In passing through the garden we saw a group of nuns sitting in pairs under the trees, with their backs turned to each other reading their *bréviaires*. These poor cloistered women were draped in long white robes with a black cross embroidered on the back ; an enormous hood covered their faces entirely.

Mamma, having enough of hotel life, began to look for a private villa, and I triumphed inwardly each time she did not come to a right understanding with the proprietors, for it did not suit me a bit to be separated from Walter Heape. But mamma made her choice at last, and before long we were installed in a pretty cottage called " Maison Monheau." Happily the day of our removal coincided with the day of the departure of my English friends. Mr. Delbruck gave us a pressing invitation to come and have a grape-cure on his property, situated in the neighbourhood of Bordeaux. This suggestion was seized upon by the boys with enthusiasm ; they promised me a warm reception and said they would do anything they could to make my visit a pleasant one, and painted me entrancing pictures of the good times they would give me ; they could offer me fishing, a pony for me to ride, and other enticing things. For my part I thought it would be splendid fun, and the invitation was so tempting that I was ready to embrace Mr. Delbruck, but mamma declined it to my intense disappointment.

Towards the end of September we started on our homeward journey.

CHAPTER V

MY SECOND SEASON IN ST. PETERSBURG

I HAD again my heart's desire. I was invited by my aunt, Swetchine, mamma's sister, to spend the winter with her in St. Petersburg; I was in the seventh heaven of delight, nothing çould please me better.

How pleasant it was to be in St. Petersburg again; I felt so self-dependent in it! It was my first taste of liberty; I was my own mistress at last, and I should have plenty of opportunity to spread my wings and see the world, of which I knew nothing, but expected everything. I had a chamber of my own and felt that I had never lived till now, it was simply a foretaste of Paradise.

I got on admirably with my cousin, Kate Swetchine, the most good-natured girl in the world; her sister, Sophy was much too serious for me. I had all my days free to do what I desired. Music became an actual passion to me; I practised the piano a good deal; Liszt being one of my favourite composers, I played his rhapsodies stormingly. I began also to study singing, and in spare moments wrote stupid verses, which all my admirers thought beautiful. That winter I raved about officers belonging to the horse-guard regiment, and dedicated to them an atrocious poem that I sang on the motive of *L'Amour*, the fashionable chansonette of the season.

A young engineer occupied an appartment in the house where we lived; our rooms communicated. My neighbour possessed a loud baritone voice and sang very improper songs for a young lady to hear. Though unacquainted, we chorused sometimes to each other, and when I sang my horse-guard chansonette, from my neighbour's room came the most sonorous second.

A gentleman of quite different style, who was acutely sensitive to noise, lived side by side with our drawing-room; a stern, frozen-up human being, grey and wrinkled. When we were not behaving too quietly, he sent the maid to request us to moderate our gambols, but we were not in the habit of being silenced.

My singing mistress procured us tickets for the distribution of prizes in the St. Petersburg conservatory, where I attracted the attention of one of the professors, Mme. Everardi, who gave me an appreciative glance and said, pointing me out, "Look at this young lady, she is destined for the stage."

I was enjoying the many pleasures St. Petersburg could offer, and was bombarded with invitations of every kind; people were asking me to dinners, dances and all sorts of delicious things. We came home at most eccentric hours, turning night into day. I liked the admiration I excited. As soon as I entered a ball-room, I became surrounded by a circle of partners, quarrelling with each other for the privilege of a dance with me. My ball-programme was soon scrawled all over; I mixed up my dancers and began to wonder how I could possibly manage six youths at once. They drew lots for the right of dancing with me, and as neither seemed inclined to give way, they would end by half tearing me to pieces between them. I danced nearly every dance with two partners, and how I danced, with all my soul in it, for I never did things by halves. Hot but indefatigable, I flew round the room, dancing as though I would never tire. My partners wanted to flirt with me in the intervals but I never gave them the time, keeping them whirling me round till they had not much breath left for talking. Towards the end of the evening my hair became untidy and my train torn to pieces, every scrap of trimming on it destroyed.

My admirers were of all ages, from mere boys to wrinkled greybeards. I received their attentions as a matter of course, and though I flirted with many men, I never really lost my heart to any of them.

A young officer appeared at last on my horizon, with whom I almost convinced myself that I was in love. He carried my photograph in a locket on his watch-chain, and brought me flowers and bonbons, and spoilt my appetite, making me eat lots of sweets before dinner. One day I scratched my finger with a pin; it was nothing but a simple scratch, but a drop of blood appeared and my chivalrous admirer tore his handkerchief instantly to pieces and bound up my wound. He preserved that rag, stained with my precious blood, as a sweet remembrance. Very touching indeed !

A general with lumbago, full of years and honours, who was looking about him for a wife, began to lay siege on me. I saw a great deal more of him than I wished to, and as I didn't like to have that tiresome old man bothering after me, I often pretended to have a bad headache and went to my room. His company was too odious for words, he was dull as ditch water. This general got me alone one day, and proposed to me, saying that his hand, his heart and his purse were freely at my command. The idea of that old scarecrow indulging in matrimonial schemes ! A husband of that sort would never do for me, and I gave him a brilliant rebuke.

Distressed by my unreachableness, he disappeared from our horizon.   I was so happy to be rid of him!

I took a walk between two and three every afternoon up the " Nevski Prospect," a place of *rendezvous* with a number of my admirers.   I came back one day from my walk with a terrible headache and throwing myself on my bed, I burst into a loud fit of hysterical laughter and weeping which terrified my cousins who stood beside me wringing their hands, and wanted to send the maid after the doctor, but my aunt, who came home at that moment, did something more practical : she stamped her foot and ordered me to stop instantly all that nonsense, otherwise she would countermand the dancing-party that was to take place that evening.   My hysterical fit passed as if by magic ; I recovered my self-control, and bounding to my feet in the liveliest manner, I began to prepare the dessert for our *soirée.*

The young men about me were very incendiary, a tiny spark thrown among them set them on fire.   Stenger, one of my most ardent partners, a youth of about nineteen years of age, took a desperate fancy to me ; when we danced together he held me in his arms so tightly I could hardly breathe, and as we swung round he murmured soft things into my willing ears.   That boy managed to make his way into our house and found means to see me almost daily.

One beautiful frosty night we went out sledging to the Islands in the outskirts of St. Petersburg ; we drove in troikas, wide sleighs drawn by three horses.   It was very cold ; I was quite frozen and rubbed my fingers, and Stenger, who sat opposite to me, slipped his hand into my muff, and under pretence of warming my hands, pressed them, almost crushing them in his grasp, but my aunt soon put a stop to this massage, saying that my muff would do the business much better.   Stenger's adoration was too bothering, and as I did not happen to be consumed with passion myself, I grew weary of it and lavished my attention upon Ofrossimoff, a very good-looking boy, a scholar of the Lyceum.   Naturally, Stenger was full of bitter envy towards his successor, and strongly disapproved of him.   I tried to pacify his jealousy, but it was not to be subdued and I made his eyes look angry very often.   Stenger grew altogether impossible, and his fits of jealousy became disagreeably frequent of late.   I scarcely had a moment alone with Ofrossimoff, Stenger resolutely determined not to let us sit together, and was always in our way and came and spoilt our talk.   Wherever we went he turned up unexpectedly and looked upon us with suspicious eyes.   I have never felt so watched, and mentally sent him to the antipodes, for I was always the same, with no idea of constancy ; I simply tossed aside my admirers as an old glove,

as soon as anybody more attractive turned up. For me that tiresome Stenger was already a broken toy; I did not wish to spend my time looking at him when I could spend it looking at Ofrossimoff.

Wanting to be rid of him at last, I made him understand, very clearly, that he was a bore, telling him, naughtily, there was no room for him here, and making him feel that three is an awkward number and that he was one too many; then Stenger fell upon me with reproaches, saying that I take all and give nothing, winning all hearts just because I myself had none, and that I was a monster in a woman's shape to torture him so, a sort of vampire who sucked every drop of happiness out of him. He concluded by telling me that he had given away his heart to one who was utterly unworthy of it. I did not suspect that I was treading on such dangerous ground, but my aunt felt that we were going to have trouble with this too ardent youth; she was sure there was going to be a row. Had I pushed my game too far after all? I had never taken Stenger very seriously and began to feel uncomfortable.

One day when I was shamelessly flirting with Ofrossimoff, absorbed in each other we had forgotten the presence of Stenger, who came to us in a storming rage, his face a thunder cloud, and told Ofrossimoff he wouldn't play second fiddle, nor submit any longer to a cat-and-mouse game, and also would not permit any other man to usurp his place, especially to such a baby not yet out of the school-room. (Ofrossimoff at that time was a moustachless youth and Stenger had already a slight shadow on his upper lip, of which he was immensely proud.) My aunt was right: there was a frantic personal affair between these two boys, and Ofrossimoff flaming angrily at Stenger's insult, challenged him to a duel. That was a nice piece of work indeed! The two rivals were going to fight and all through me; they had already invited seconds. Happily the duel did not come off, Stenger was forced to appolgise, but nevertheless I was now feeling myself to be a heroine, as for Ofrossimoff, he seemed to me to be as bold as a young lion, and went up twenty-five per cent in my estimation. I had a good scolding, nevertheless, from my aunt, who said I was a fearful little flirt, playing merry games with the affections of men. She accused me also of having given Stenger every encouragement, and said that I must do everything now to cure him of his infatuation and stop all this nonsense. Following her advice, I tried to be as frigid as a whole iceberg to poor Stenger, and told him he was a fool to break his heart for me, and that he must try and find another object for his affections. I hope now I had been unfriendly enough and had brought him to his senses; but it came to nothing, and his parents decided that the best thing was to get him out of my way and send him away from St. Petersburg ; so they accompanied their " Benjamine " to the train, and after having installed him in the railway carriage, they returned home peacefully, far from the thought that in spite of his appearance of filial obedience, Stenger had conceived, beforehand, the audacious project of running away, and great was the amazement of the old couple, when their son reappeared that same day, declaring that decidedly he would not be separated from me.

Time went on with the most extraordinary rapidity ; winter was over and my happy time at St. Petersburg came to an end all but too soon.   I adored the place and a great many people in it, and having seen a little of the world and tasted of its pleasures and temptations, I was awfully sorry to leave this delightful life behind me, and to lose my independance.   I wrote home entreating permission to prolong my stay ; I would have given ten years of my life for a month more of St. Petersburg, but the answer had just come, and mamma said, " No."   I was delivered soon after to the care of my aunt Leon Galitine, who volunteered to see me safe to Moscow ; mamma would come and fetch me from there in a few days.

Before my departure I had a long conversation with Ofrossimoff ; that silly boy actually proposed to me.   In an amazingly sudden way he blurted out, with a voice which was eloquent of many things, how madly he loved me, and asked me if I'd marry him.   I tried to turn all he said into a joke, and told him to put that ridiculous idea out of his head, for I couldn't quite take him seriously, like a regular grown-up man.   He was so disastrously young in fact, just turned nineteen.   " Ah, that will remedy itself soon enough!" exclaimed my suitor, adding that he would wait for ten years if he were sure of getting me at last ; and when I told him that love did not grow with waiting, he said that, as far as he was concerned, he promised me the devotion of a lifetime and a lot of other nonsense.   Upon this we decided that we should wait for three or four years, and concluded a compact of eternal friendship.   We parted with a lingering hand-shake and tender glances.   There was a tear in the corner of my eye, for I did care for him in a way.   But " out of sight, out of mind ! "   His face haunted me for some days, and in a week's time I had forgotten the poor boy's existence.

Mr. Swinine, a friend of my aunt Galitzine's, greeted us cordially in Moscow, and offered us the hospitality of his splendid home, where everything spoke of wealth.   The house was a veritable museum ; all the rooms, of great height and good proportion, were furnished with every luxury, and filled with pictures of old masters and bronzes and antiquities of immense value.   There was a painting of the

utmost impropriety but it was covered with a veil during
our stay.

Mr. Swinine was a very charming and courteous old gentleman, a real *Grand Seigneur* of the past generation, and a
wonderful man for his age, light of step and young of spirit ;
there was nothing decrepit or infirm about him. The old
beau, in spite of his eighty years, was a delightful host, and
treated me with an old-world gallantry. His heart was not
altogether withered, and in extraordinary circumstances he
could even be moved. He felt a new sense of renewed youth
in my presence, which heated his old blood ; he told me that
I seemed to have a talisman about me, and that he had never
met a woman who could quicken his pulse like me. His face
had the expression of a satyr and his little eyes twinkled
merrily when he related to me a number of his feats and love-
affairs of "auld lang syne." He preserved, among other
remote remembrances of by-gone days, a beautiful Indian
shawl with which I was not a little surprised to see my bed
covered; in his opinion I only was worthy of such an honour.

At the end of the week mamma rejoined us and carried me
off.

CHAPTER VI

DOLGIK

DURING the summer manœuvres a squadron was quartered in our village. The chief, a provincial "lady killer," with a face upon which high-thinking had never been expressed, was the possessor of a very inflammable heart; he fell a victim to my blue eyes, and it wouldn't have been me if I hadn't tried to get up a flirtation with him, though he was ridiculous to the highest degree, and saluted me so funnily, bringing his heels together with a snap. He used every means in his power to conquer me and made the most wonderful eyes at me; (when mamma was not looking of course). He began to be immensely sentimental and sang to me to a guitar accompaniment, old love songs, something very pleading and lamentable, with a burden of " I love thee so!" turning up his eyes a good deal as if he was in pain. He was not gifted with much perception of time and tune, my Troubadour, and I could hardly keep serious when he looked so doleful, with his hand pressed to his breast and his eyes devouring me with a passionate gaze.

I used to ride on horseback a great deal, accompanied by my sentimental officer. One day, whilst my white mare was galloping wildly across the open moors, my saddle unbuckled and I felt it turning with me; I slipt out of it and found myself sitting on the grass, unhurt, and was on my legs all right in a moment, having luckily disengaged my foot from the stirrup.

A few days afterwards I escaped from another danger. We were to take a drive in the woods that evening; Mr. K., a friend of my brothers, asked me to take him with me in my dog-cart. As I didn't care particularly for his company, I contrived to put off our drive for some time and suggested a game of croquet. In the middle of our game Mr. K. uttered a piercing scream and fell down in a violent fit of epilepsy. I was dreadfully frightened and scrambled, without ceremony, over the fence of the croquet-ground. None of us had before suspected Mr. K. to be epileptic, and if I hadn't delayed our drive, this attack would have happened in my dog-cart and the consequences might have been terribly disastrous. It makes me shudder when I think of it!

I went out driving one day with a dashing young officer,

Count Podgoritchany, his sister Mary and my dolorous Troubadour. I was in a mood just then to do something foolish, and it struck me that it would be charming fun to take a ride astride on the horse which drove us, and thus, becoming deaf to Mary's frantic remonstrance and casting dignity to the winds, I perched myself on our steed, who broke into a gallop, whilst my cavaliers ran by my side holding me steadily. That was certainly very unladylike and shocking of me!

We were near neighbours with the Podgoritchany's, their estate is within a few miles from Dolgik. The young count was always devoted to me ; he believed that we were destined for one another, and it was the hope of his life to make me his wife, but my heart was still entirely at my own disposal and I never gave him more than a passing thought, being hard to catch as a sunbeam. It wasn't very fair, however, to keep him dangling after me like that if I didn't mean that it should come to anything. One day, as I was practising one my favourite Chopin's Études, the count came in and leant on the piano, his eyes dwelling upon me with a passionate expression ; suddenly he seized my right hand and kissed it, whilst I played accords with my left one. I knew quite well what he was going to say. He implored me to marry him, but I had not yet made up my mind to part with my liberty and said "No" point blank, telling him he would have to get on as best he could without me. His face fell and he looked very miserable, my rejected lover, his matrimonial hopes being rudely shattered.

A wealthy country squire, the possessor of a fine adjoining estate, who had the reputation of being a very good catch, came to pay us a visit. I made no attempt whatever to show off my best points and made up my mind, on the contrary, to make a guy of myself, putting on my most unbecoming gown and dressing my hair unfashionably, so that he might see me at my worst. Our guest was all sentiment and poetry, his language was "music spoken," and I responded by the most crude prose. He asked me at luncheon : "*Mademoiselle aime les fleurs.*" "*Oh, non, monsieur, je préfère le jambon !*" I answered, helping myself to a second portion of ham. Mamma looked very annoyed indeed at this unromantic turn of conversation.

I surely had not the vocation of a domestic paragon ; when I poured out tea it was done the reverse of neatly, and the spotless teacloth was spotless no longer, for I poured more water on to it than into the cups, and mamma regretfully decided that I hadn't got the right turn for housekeeping. My culinary efforts were also not to meet approval, and the cakes that I amused myself in baking, one day, were recognised, I am aggrieved to say, as not being fit to eat.

D

CHAPTER VII

IN ST. PETERSBURG AGAIN

My thoughts flew back constantly to St. Petersburg. Being a girl who had already tasted city life, it did not please me in the least to bury myself in the country, and I longed to mix with the gay world again. One day, an invitation came from my aunt Léon Galitzine, asking me to spend two or three months with them. That was indeed a piece of good fortune! What could be more exciting, more delicious! Visions of balls floated before my eyes and I simply danced with joy, meaning to amuse myself tremendously.

Mamma brought me to St. Petersburgh and left me in charge of my aunt, who did all she could to make my stay pleasant. The vanities of the world took complete hold of me; I had a very gay season, being out nearly every night and dancing to my heart's content with my band of last year's admirers. Stenger continued to care for me as he did at first, and was more than ever my slave. Everywhere I went he would find out and go too, for he had a true heart, poor boy. I had such a thirst for pleasure that my evenings at home appeared awfully long; I found it dreadfully dreary and yawned in the most distressing fashion, sitting half-dozing in an armchair beside the fire, and constantly asking what time it was, having a most natural desire to go to bed.

I met many nice fellows of the *corps des pages* in the house of a great friend of mine, the countess Aline Hendrikoff, all chums of her brother's. The boys were charming fellows and I flirted shamelessly with them. My more sedate admirers began to tease me about the way I caught mere babes into my net, they said that a chap of twenty was too old already to attract my attention. We really did have great fun at the Hendrikoffs and gave way to wild mirth, such a noise, such laughter! We played hide-and-seek and climbed on the top of cupboards, and when we girls were found, before tumbling down into the arms of the pages, we commanded them to turn their heads the other way and to shut their eyes tight, very tight. One evening we got up some *tableaux-vivants* in which I exhibited myself as Cleopatra the Egyptian queen, stretched at full length on a tiger skin and holding in my hand the fatal asp, artfully composed of green paper. I had to be just stung by it, but instead of simulating the agonies of death, I burst out laughing, to the scandal of the spectators. In the next *tableau* we represented a flock of woolly lambs, spread on all fours on the carpet, and wrapped up in our pelisses turned inside out.

By the end of April mamma came to take me home. I reluctantly left St. Petersburg and took a long farewell of my freedom.

CHAPTER VIII

THE CRIMEA

A totally unexpected stroke of luck was in store for me. My aunt, Zoe Zaroudni, who was going to spend a month in the Crimea with her two little daughters, offered to take me with her, promising mamma that I should be well looked after.

We travelled from Sebastopol to Jalta in a mail-coach. It was such a beautiful drive, but seemed all too short. I am not given to sentimental rhapsodies over the beauties of nature, nevertheless, I was very much impressed by the divinely lovely scenery. I had no end of a good time at Jalta and danced a great deal at the military club, making conquests by the dozen. Time flew rapidly and the date fixed for our departure drew near ; it was a great misfortune for me that our stay was so short.

On the eve of our departure, I amused myself more than ever at the military club. At supper my cavaliers entreated me to arrange somehow or other not to leave Jalta next day. Mrs. S., a jolly middle-aged lady whose acquaintance I had just made that evening, offered to take charge of me and proposed to go instantly and persuade my aunt to let me stay with her a few weeks longer. I said "yes" on the impulse of the moment to Mrs. S., not stopping to think that I ought first to ask permission of my parents by telegraph. We set forth at once to our hotel under the escort of my partners. Daylight was beginning to break, and the ship which was to carry me away in a few hours had been brought up alongside of the pier, and our trunks were already buckled and sent off to the steamer.

Mrs. S. came up to my aunt's bed, my cavaliers waiting at a respectful distance behind the door, and expressed her desire. My heart was beating wildly, I wondered what my aunt would say, would she let me stay, and I uttered a prayer inwardly for the happy issue of our request ; poor aunt Zoe, who was sleeping soundly, awoke with a start and gazed perplexedly at Mrs. S., who pledged herself to mind me as her own bairn during my stay in Jalta, and promised to bring me back to Kharkoff in the autumn. Mrs. S. came out victorious and remained slumbering in an armchair till daylight, lest my aunt should alter her mind when wide awake, as for me I was too excited to go to bed at all. As soon as Mrs. S. went away, my aunt who seemed to have little faith in my power to look after myself, decided that she could not trust me out of her sight and leave me under the guardianship of an unknown chaperon, and went to ask another aunt of mine, a Princess Galitzine, who possessed a beautiful villa in Jalta, to look after me ; but the Princess refused downright, unwilling to be responsible for my extravagances ; she strongly disapproved of me, I believe, and said that I was just the sort of girl to make trouble. I did not want anyone to worry about me, I could take care of myself and get along all right, I should think, and wanted to be treated like a rational human being ; I was eighteen after all, and a person of eighteen isn't a child and doesn't need a nurse. My aunt and cousins did all in their power to persuade me to return home with them, but I and reason had never marched together, and I remained firm in my intention to stay in Jalta.

I accompanied my aunt to the ship. After the first whistle she called to mind the old proverb saying : "Better late than never," and unheeding the protests of the captain, she jumped into a boat wishing to carry me off, willing or unwilling ; but the piercing shrill of the second whistle forced her to turn back speedily. My fate trembled in the balance as long as I was within my aunt's reach, and I felt myself in utter security only when I lost sight of the ship completely.

It was done. I got my liberty and Mrs. S. was left sole guardian over me. I was so happy to go about alone, free as the mountain air. I might flirt with what men I pleased, and meant to make the most of my independence and to enjoy my free life thoroughly.

Mrs. S. was the most convenient of chaperons, very comply inig ndeed. I danced and rode and picnicked to my heart's content. It was all rather dangerous for a girl of my age and temperament, and with all that, I was absolutely without knowledge or experience of the world, exposed to all the temptations of a modern sea-bathing place. One began to gossip on my account and to say nasty things of me, but it did not affect me in the least. I was doing no harm and was happy—why couldn't people leave me alone ?

I had a great number of admirers, an old admiral over seventy years old among them. My charms had captivated his elderly fancy, and his old heart caught fire. This "Methuselah" was an old silly about me and spent his time in making love to me as any "Romeo" of twenty. My company had for him the fascination of the forbidden fruit, but I was not at all ready to play "May" to his "January," and was afraid even to shake hands with that ancient Marionette, for fear he'd fall to pieces.

The Princess Troubetzkoy invited me one day to come and dine with her in her beautiful villa, situated a few miles from Jalta.   My old admiral offered to take me in his brougham, but being a trifle afraid of him I would not consent at first, remembering his atrocious behaviour, when he arranged to see me home and drove me one night from the military club.   I suddenly felt an arm steal about my waist in the dark, and that old wretch lent close over me and wanted to embrace me.   "May I give you a kiss, just only one?" said that disgusting old man, looking at me as if he would like to eat me, and licking his lips in the anticipation of that pleasure.   "Certainly not!" I shrieked emphatically, wrenching myself free and ordering him to keep his hands off.   But he reiterated his demand saying that it could not matter, for he was so old and his kiss wouldn't leave any trace on me, as for him, it would transport him into "Paradise."   Horrible old man!   And, notwithstanding all that I accepted the admiral's offer, hoping that he would conduct himself better in daylight; nevertheless I stepped into his carriage with a vague feeling of uneasiness.   It was the most horrid ride I had ever had.   At first we conversed by fits and starts, for my cavalier was as deaf as a door-post, and I had to scream very loud into his ear; it had its good points, for I could make my reflections aloud and call him a lot of bad names.   Unfortunately that day the admiral was in an alarmingly amiable frame of mind and more inflammable than ever.   I found his manner anything but reassuring, and began to be vaguely uneasy at the sight of the nasty face he turned towards me, looking at me with eyes that made me wish myself well out of his carriage.   He sat inconveniently close beside me, and I got as far from him as the carriage allowed.

As soon as we were out of town, his quick small eyes roved in all directions, and having satisfied himself that there was no one to see us, he became enterprising, and grew every minute more and more amorous.   His sentiments were rather thinly veiled, and I knew what he was driving at.   All at once, before I had time to do so much as think of resistance, he pushed back my sleeve and ran up my arm with his horrid old lips as far as he could reach, whispering in a hissing voice that I was a tempting morsel, and that he adored me.   I was absolutely disgusted, but what could I do then but turn upon him with flashing eyes, trying to make him ashamed before his coachman, but the fact was that he too was as deaf as his master.   It was a most unfair advantage, and I told him so, adding that he was a brute and that I hated him, and that if he didn't leave me alone at once, I should jump out of his carriage. I was a fiery girl, and had at that moment a ferocious desire to box his ears, but happily by that time the brougham was stopping before the Villa Troubetzkoy. I gave a great sigh of relief. Thank heaven we had arrived! It had the effect of chilling my "Methusalah's" emotions, and making him recover himself quickly. In parting with my old cavalier I treated him with the contempt he deserved, dropping his outstretched hand like a hot coal, and declaring to him, with my chin in the air, that I was not going to have anything more to do with him, and that henceforth I would not permit him even to kiss the tips of my fingers. After that I ran away, feeling like a nymph flying from a satyr. I certainly didn't want to trust myself alone with that admiral again; he never forgave me for it, and I looked the other way when I used to meet him.

We continued to lead a very gay life. Dances, picnics, rides, were in full swing. In the midst of most delightful people and amusement I was quite happy, and far from imagining that my horizon was not clear, and that my happy time at Jalta was coming to an end all but too soon. One fine morning we were all assembled on the pier to watch the mail boat coming in, chatting away gaily, when suddenly I heard a sharp voice calling me by my name. I turned round, and was amazed to behold amongst the passengers my mother's sour-faced maid, Mary—a terrible creature who had lived with us ever since I was a baby. She announced that my parents would not have me staying in Jalta by myself any longer, and had sent her to fetch me, insisting on my immediate return. I was never so overwhelmed in my life, and quite furious at being packed back home in disgrace. My wings were clipped, my freedom lost! When I got into my room I locked myself in and spent an hour weeping passionately.

Of course, I had to obey my duenna, and the following day started homewards with her.

Well, it was a pretty home-coming! I had expected a scolding under the paternal roof, and got a sound one.

CHAPTER IX

WINTER IN ST. PETERSBURG

To my great delight mamma decided to pass the winter in St. Petersburg. I was enchanted to meet my pages again. We contrived to encounter everywhere. One evening I went to the circus accompanied by my aunt, the Princess Koudasheff, as chaperon. Entering the circus I looked round for my young cavaliers who waited for me at the appointed place of meeting. On our right was an empty box; I signalled to them, and they stepped into it, appropriating it in spite of the energetic protestations of the circus grooms. I enjoyed my pages neighbourhood immensely; we were all of us in buoyant spirits and became wildly gay. I declared suddenly that I should like something to drink, and my worthy aunt, who was propriety incarnate, looked horribly shocked when the pages began to uncork a bottle of lemonade, apprehending that the spectators would take my innocent beverage for champagne.

Princess Mimi Troubetykoy, a jolly playmate of my childhood, came to pass Christmas in St. Petersburg. We were both glad to be together again, having known one another from infancy, we had many interests and tastes in common. Mimi was such a dear, delightful girl, and we had an uncommonly good time together. In our daily walks we used to meet a handsome, blustering officer, who managed to give us a good stare each time we passed him in the street. We decided one day, Mimi and I, to fling a pelot-balloon in order to know which of us attracted his attention, and crossed to the other side of the street. Mimi went on the left and I on the right side, and oh, triumph!—our follower came after me. I was very flattered, and rejoiced at my victory over Mimi. Her companion, a charming old lady who had once been governess to her, seeing that the affair was taking a serious turn, hurried us off home. That officer had been extremely useful to me one frosty day; he picked me up when I stretched myself at full length on the slippery pavement, and profiting by the opportunity, he murmured *sotto voce* compliments into my willing ear.

A young official, Mr. Ladigenski, occupied an apartment adjoining our drawing-room. One evening, recalling with

Mimi the old school-room days, we played hide and seek, and profiting by the absence of our neighbour, I hid myself in his bedchamber; Mimi having found me, we began to examine with much curiosity the frivolous pictures that adorned the walls of his bachelor apartment, which was indeed very improper in us. What would Ladigenski have thought of us if he had caught us in his room? He paid us a visit a few days afterwards, and I decided at the first sight that our neighbour was not nice at all; I could even by no stretch of imagination find him passable. He looked moth-eaten, and was quite too old for my taste—thirty at least. He came nearly every day to see us, entering our drawing-room, a bouquet in one hand and a box of bon-bons in the other. It was evident that he took more than an ordinary interest in me, but I took none in him, however. Nevertheless, in a very short time he became a nearly acknowledged suitor, forgetting that in questions of marriage there are two people to be considered. Ladigenski was looked upon as an exceedingly promising young man, and was spoken of by indefatigable matchmakers as a suitable marriage for me; they said I would be an idiot if I refused him. Horrid, meddling old cats! As a simple acquaintance he was well enough, but could I accept the love of such a one? I didn't want to marry him, l didn't want to marry anyone! The time for that sort of thing had not come, and the right man hadn't yet arrived. I should surely have to marry one day, but the later the better, for I hadn't got the solid domestic virtues which one wants in a wife, besides I was in no hurry to give up my freedom.

Most people think that marriage is the sole aim of a girl's life, but I chose to differ from them, for I despised a girl who sold herself for gold, and as for me, I was not to be appropriated against my will, certainly. I began to hate Ladigenski with some intensity, and had made up my mind I shouldn't marry him even if we two happened to be shipwrecked on a desert island.

I was always alarmed when my love affairs seemed to be approaching matrimonial engagements, and hated all the men who were in the mood for marriage. I knew just when to draw the line when they wanted to propose to me, and managed to keep my suitors sufficiently at a distance to prevent any of them from making an offer. It was now the case with poor Ladigenski; his chances were very small indeed, the warmer his manner became, the more I froze. If he had eyes in his head he ought to have seen how I detested him, but he was not a man to take a hint, and the deprecating glances I threw in his direction met with no visible acknowledgment, and he could hardly be made to understand that his company was an intrusion. I grew deadly sick of my unwelcome suitor, who was becoming the nightmare of my life. The sight of his face acted on me as an ice-cold shower bath, but he continued to force his hateful attentions upon me, and was not easy to break with.

The moment for decisive action had arrived; I felt that I must put an end to all this business once for all and take measures to suppress him. As my rebuffs had not the slightest effect upon him I planned an experiment to cure him of his passion swiftly. I knew that he could hear every word pronounced in our drawing-room, and I addressed myself to an imaginary interlocutor, making disastrous revelation of my sentiments towards our neighbour. " I find Ladigenski perfectly horrid," I said in a very loud voice, with a very strong accent on horrid, and put on the crowning touch in saying that his whole aspect was disgusting, a positive eye-torture. It was candid at any rate. This little manœuvre proved perfectly successful, and my purpose was attained. For several days after that we saw nothing of Ladigenski, and I rejoiced in his absence. But soon things took another turn. Money had become scarce of late, and my parents found their pecuniary difficulties increasing. I had to make up my mind to a quieter life, so I decided to marry the first decently marriageable man who should come my way, and after mature reflections I came to the conclusion that Ladigenski was to be called back again, and that I must make it right with him. I had been too hot-headed for a dowerless girl like me, and was determined to mend matters roughly.

The important thing just then was that I should recover ground with Ladigenski, which I had evidently lost. I would have given worlds to have undone what I had done. Ladigenski had not actually said anything that I could take as an offer of marriage, but he had gone very near it, and being on the point of proposing to me, if he was to speak now it would be something definite, and so I decided to give him hope and encouragement. I sat down and wrote a letter in which I expressed regret in being deprived of his society and told him that he was to forget the stupid proceedings of my monologue, invented to tease him, and made him understand that I was ready now to accept his offer. I enclosed my note in a book that Ladigenski had lent me and sent it with our maid Olga. I waited in a fever of impatience for his answer, desperately afraid lest my letter had not safely reached its destination. Suppose mamma should catch Olga in the corridor and discover my letter! At last Olga came back with the answer. With fingers trembling I broke open the envelope and read the following phrase : " It does not suit me to be trifled with any longer, so please forget all about me." Oh, the shame, the humiliation experienced by me! And just at that moment, to my horror, I heard mamma asking Ladigenski, through the wall of our room, to come and dine with us at the restaurant.

How on earth could I face him? My only hope was that he would refuse, but he answered that he would be delighted to come. What was I to do? I could not plead a sudden indisposition, mamma wouldn't believe it, for I was so distressingly healthy in appearance. Small wonder then that my heart sank within me when Ladigenski came walking into the restaurant, clean-shaven, a white gardenia in his buttonhole. I was in the most awfully awkward position, and felt upon thorns all through dinner. Ladigenski settled himself beside me, perfectly at his ease; his voice was as usual cool and quiet, but I could not pluck up courage to look at him, and steadily refused to meet his eyes, assuming a wooden expression, and remained tongue-tied, giving my whole attention to the contents of my plate, with a longing to crawl under the table.

After dinner Ladigenski invited himself to come and take tea with us, but I received him very ungraciously, being in a very beastly humour, and did not attempt to conceal my vexation in having to endure his presence. I made myself as disagreeable as possible, and answered him in mono-syllables, glancing nervously from time to time at the clock on the mantelpiece, but he showed no inclination to rise, and would not leave my side. I sent him mentally to Lucifer, that little abomination! Mamma, rather surprised at my want of courtesy, was engaged all through the evening in the serious business of keeping our guest in a good temper. Losing my patience at last I went to bed demonstratively, leaving Ladigenski alone with mamma. I was sure that I had shown him clearly enough that I did not want to have anything more to do with him. It was the last time I saw his face. He went away the next day, bag and baggage, without even saying good-bye. So much the better; I did not miss my departed admirer, he might have gone to Jericho for all I cared.

We came back to Dolgik at Easter but for a short while, for my Aunt Staritzki, mamma's sister, who lived in Tiflis, the capital of the Caucasus, invited us to come and spend some time with her.

CHAPTER X

THE CAUCASUS

WE went to Tiflis towards the middle of May. On the way I made the acquaintance of two cadets of the *corps des pages*, grandsons of the Shah of Persia. The youngest prince, Rouknadine-Mirza, a charming chap with exquisite oriental eyes, took particularly my fancy. He had already fallen a little under my spell, and I looked upon him as a kind of blessed invention for my entertainment on this trip. As for his eldest brother, he seemed to be of rather a quiet disposition, and I did not care a rap for him.

It was almost dark when we reached Tiflis. The Staritzkis received us in the friendliest way. We were also kindly greeted by my aunt, Nathalie Roerberg, the wife of the Chief of the Military Engineers of the Caucasus. She wanted me to come and see her just as often as I could. I can't say how good and kind she was, we got on admirably.

It became my favourite pastime to watch through the iron-barred gate of the Roerberg's garden, opening on the summer-theatre, the endless string of people promenading between the acts. My guilty curiosity was noticed by an elegant swell, whom I saw staring and making eyes at me. I met him a few days afterwards at a dancing party in the casino. He was quick to seize the chance of talking to me and exclaimed, "How happy I am to meet you! I have desired it so tremendously!" Impudent fellow! As I was not a bit disposed to be gracious to him I stopped his effusions, turning my back pointedly. When I met that brazen-faced individual after that in the streets, he raised his hat in vain to me; I pretended not to perceive him.

I found a jolly companion in the person of my cousin Nathaly Staritzki. One evening we went to see *La Traviata* sung in Armenian, which rather disagreed with Italian music. Nathaly was, like me, easily moved to laughter. As the opera proceeded we became more and more hilarious, and our behaviour was such that caused many disapproving glances to be cast in our direction. At the most pathetic moment, when the prima-donna breathed her last breath, we ran out of our box, putting our handkerchiefs to our mouths and overturning the chairs on our passage.

I used to see a great deal of the Persian princes; Rouknadine-Mirza was rapidly losing his heart to me. One day we went out riding together, and whilst our horses were galloping at full speed, the idea came to me to make my page gather a wild flower growing in the grass. He managed to do it, but during that acrobatic exercise his *casque* rolled off, and instead of treating him commiseratingly I only snubbed him for his pains.

Horsemanship was my ruling passion. I easily found partners to accompany me in my rides, and careered through the streets of Tiflis, followed by my cavaliers, enjoying to overtake them like a cyclone. I cantered home in high spirits, with a heated face and my hair coming down, most of it outside my cap, not in it. I frequently brought my cavaliers home to tea, and if they didn't happen to be particularly interesting, I proceeded straight to bed, and the Staritzkis had to sit with my guests and entertain them as best they could, whilst I slept the sleep of the just.

One day, in turning over an album, I came upon a photograph the sight of which made me exclaim: "Oh, who is that good-looking officer?" "That is Serge Michailovitch Doukhovskoy, a young general attached to the person of the Grand-Duke Michael, commander-in-chief of the army of the Caucasus," said my aunt Roerberg. She told me that he was the youngest general in the Russian army, being only six-and-thirty years old, that he had a splendid career before him, and was in short everything desirable; she added that now I had a capital opportunity of making a brilliant match, and that I must spread my net to catch that big fish and set immediately to work to captivate him. That was enough to set me against the general; there was something very distasteful in the idea of such a marriage, and I was not at all willing to sacrifice my youth to the advantage of rank and money.

When first General Doukhovskoy was introduced to me I was slightly disappointed; he was so reserved in manner and did not condescend to take much notice of me, a method of treatment to which I was not accustomed, being brought up with the idea that I was to be petted and bowed down to by men; I had been adored all my young life and this indifference stung my vanity. I was far from the idea of falling in love with General Doukhovskoy, nevertheless I was annoyed by the coolness with which he regarded me; admiration was my daily bread, he failed to offer it to me and that instantly aroused in me an intention of making him display some interest in me. Serge Michailovitch was quite unlike all the men I had ever met before, he was immovable as a stone, and didn't look like the sort of man whose head could be easily turned, and would surely never become a girl's plaything.

Nevertheless there was something which drew me towards him, and day by day he got hold of me and I meant to win his heart if it only could be done. All my passing fancies only kindled the spark that was to burn for another man's benefit. But why, oh why, was this ice-berg of a human being incapable of understanding? He was so queer; I did not know how to manage him; it was impossible to draw him into the mildest flirtation, we were on the polite conversation footing, nothing else.

In mid-June I was left all of a sudden on my aunt Roerberg's hands. Mamma started off for Russia for a few weeks, and the Staritzkis went to Beloy-Klouth, their summer residence, and as I did not like to leave Serge Michailovitch behind, I preferred to remain in Tiflis. Day by day the general's visits grew more frequent, One evening he got up a picnic in his garden to which he invited us. Whilst we had tea laid under the trees, I remarked that a change was coming over our host; he seemed in a boyish mood, and altogether forgetful of his usual careful correctness, and put aside all his reserve; he lay at my feet and tickled my cheek with a blade of grass. This was the hour of my triumph! I caught his eyes and they said quite plainly " I like you." Could he be catching fire at last? I saw now that I was not wholly indifferent to him; he was looking at me with new eyes, the eyes of an awakened sleeper. Was it the awakening germ of some deeper feeling, perhaps? In parting he squeezed my hand and held it in his for a few seconds longer than the conventions allowed. Every day drew me closer to Serge Michailovitch; the more I saw him, the more my affection deepened, and I soon found that he was for me the dearest of created beings.

The heat in Tiflis was very trying, there was scarcely air enough to breathe, and my aunt decided to go to Borjom, the summer residence of the Grand-Duke Michael, a delightful watering-place buried in verdure and surrounded by mountains covered with thick forests. Serge Michailovitch came round occasionally to see how we got on. I looked forward eagerly to his visits; his society became very dear to me for he succeeded in winning my love; my heart had spoken at last and I was sensible of the tremendous power he exercised over me. I was beginning to know that I too, had a little power over him. Serge Michailovitch appeared so pleased when he saw me; his hand trembled when it touched mine. His affection seemed to rise with extraordinary rapidity from zero to boiling point, and it was whispered that General Doukhovskoy had serious views towards me; my aunt with her all-seeing eyes had perceived for some time already the turn events had taken.

In July the general had to go to Russia for a short time; On the eve of his departure he came to Borjom. That evening altered the course of my life. He managed to get me away from the others on the terrace; we were so happy to be left alone and drew closer to each other, watching the glow-worms' fairy lamps amidst the shrubs below. For some time there was no conversation between us, but there was no need for words, we looked into each other's eyes and found that one can kiss even with looks. Suddenly Serge Michailovitch bent over me, his face drawn with emotion, and asked me if I cared for him a little bit? The moment was decisive; my head dropped on my arms on the table and tears were my only answer. I felt assured of one thing now, that he loved me; yet, what had he said to me? Nothing and yet everything!

On the next day, when Serge Michailovitch came to bid us good-bye, he seemed quite altered; he was changed altogether, exceedingly cool and formal in his manner to me, his greeting was gravely courteous, that was all. What was this sudden change in him, in voice and eyes? His entirely incomprehensible attitude made me horribly unhappy; had he changed his mind at the last moment? All through his visit he maintained his air of frigid reserve; he was so cold that he froze me. An icy feeling crept over me and I suddenly had the sensation of being a great way off from him. I could not help feeling hurt and wounded and struggled hard to keep the tears from my eyes; not for worlds would I have appeared disappointed. Serge Michailovitch went away saying good-bye frigidly, and we parted upon very cold terms. When he had gone, I missed him more than I could have imagined possible; his face haunted my dreams and my waking, and I thought of him the first thing in the morning, the last thing at night. I see now that I didn't know what love meant until I met Serge Michailovitch. How I longed for his first letter, but the days slipped away without a word or sign from him. I was so horribly disappointed and tortured with doubt. Had he forgotten then all about me? I began to feel extremely uncomfortable, seeing him slipping away from me and wished I had not let him go.

I could bear it no longer and wrote a volume to him, telling him I wanted him to cheer me up, and that I was looking forward impatiently to seeing him soon. Day by day I waited for his answer; at last the post brought me a letter from him. I tore the envelope open, with trembling hands and scarlet cheeks, but there was nothing in it to gladden my longing eyes or to fill my empty heart. His letter was short and scrapy, with no words of endearment; it might have been written to a sister. He told me so little about himself, and hardly anything at all about myself, and addressed me in such a formal way, ending his letter with sincere regards to me. (I hated sincere regards)!

I continued to be quite in the dark as to his plans for the future and didn't like at all to be fed upon chance scraps, I wanted a whole bone. I don't know when in all my life I had been more vexed and had shed such hot passionate tears; but pride arose, forbidding my heart to ache for the loss of his love. What was the use of crying my eyes out? I was determined to forget Serge Michailovitch, putting him as much as possible out of my thoughts and passing a sponge over our love affair. To keep my spirits up, I rushed into all sorts of adventures, exposing myself to ill-natured comments. People began to say nasty things of me, and my aunt Roerberg implored me to put a stop to my disgraceful flirtations, warning me that the talk would reach the ears of Serge Michailovitch. She tried to excuse his conduct in my eyes and said that, as his experiences were much wider than mine, he was more cool-headed, and knew what he was about, therefore he could not act inconsiderately in such a serious matter as marriage. Yes, but as for me, being prompt and vivacious I hated delays, and could not possibly just take time and think things over like him, I can't. I can't stop and wait!

I continued to wear a steel armour over my heart, and I now spent much of my time out of doors, riding. Serge Michailovitch had permitted me, during his absence, to mount his lovely arab, a young and spirited horse who proved sufficiently troublesome the first time I mounted him I had to spring hastily into my saddle, the horse gave a bound when the groom left his head, and set off galloping like the wind. My hand was nearly dislocated with the strain of holding him; I succeeded in managing my fiery steed and brought him to a stand-still before a villa inhabited by Mrs. Blicks, a charming lady whom I knew only by sight. She happened to be on her balcony just then, and invited me to dismount, in order to recover myself from my fright. My wrist was aching a good deal and had begun to swell. After Mrs. Blicks had bound it up, I remounted my arab who behaved perfectly well on our way home. After my first break-neck ride I succeeded to be mistress of my horse; he went like a lamb now, and I felt as much at home on his back as in a rocking-chair.

I liked Mrs. Blicks and her two daughters very much, and often dropped in for a chat. I met in their house two schoolboys, a prince and a simple mortal. I kept the prince in the background and displayed a marked preference for the simple mortal, welcoming him as a relief to threatened monotony. There was nothing particularly entrancing in him, but he was still better than no lover at all, and I began to flirt with him until he was half mad. We wandered away from the others on every available occasion, and sauntered together into the park; he drew my arm within his and pressed it tenderly to his heart, whilst our eyes met, speaking volumes. In that moment we seemed very much in love with one another, and wanted to put off as long as possible getting back home. I took a fancy, one day, on visiting Mrs. Blicks, to stimulate a fainting-fit. I lay at full length on a low sofa, wrapped up in a loose white dressing-gown belonging to Mrs. Blicks, whilst my affrighted school-boys made a great fuss over me; they bathed my temples with eau-de-cologne and put a bottle of sal-volatile under my nose. I took delight in prolonging that mistification as long as I could, surveying them out of the corners of my half-closed eyes.

Though it was only September, the weather suddenly turned cold and wet; the sky was low and grey, a gusty wind was driving the fallen leaves across the park. We decided to return to Tiflis; mamma was back already from Russia, and soon after I heard that Serge Michailovitch had come also.

We met at a dinner-party a few days after his arrival. At the sight of him my heart began to beat very quickly. Do what I would to banish him from my thoughts, I never ceased to love him; but he looked so frigid when he came up to me that I was cut to the quick. Surely he might look a little more pleased at seeing me! Was he doing it to provoke me? I felt that something had broken between us and that we should never be the same to each other after that night. My anger rose against him and I tried to look stolidly indifferent, and if possible, to be more frigid than he was. I ignored Serge Michailovitch the whole evening and behaved shockingly, talking a lot of stupid nonsense; I did not know myself what I was saying and mamma looked disapprovingly at me across the table. I own that my behaviour was shameful and that I deserved to have lost the best husband that ever a woman desired. When I got home the evil spirit went out of me and I felt awfully remorseful. I would not lose Serge Michailovitch for anyone or anything in this world. I was not going to run away from my happiness, and at any price I had to see him again and make it up with him; whatever happened, I must not let him go. I resolved therefore upon the desperate step of writing to him, and it had to be done at once or my courage would fail me. I sat down and scribbled a few lines telling him that I wanted to apologise for my extremely silly conduct. His answer contained an appointment for the following afternoon at four o'clock; he asked me to come out for a ride with him. I passed a restless night glowing with impatience at the next day's rendezvous. I wanted to see him so much, yet I dreaded the ordeal. How could I meet him? How could I look into his face again?

I got up nervous and excited. The whole morning I had been in a fever; my hands were as cold as ice and my cheeks burned like fire. How slowly the hours did pass! When Serge Michailovitch was announced I went hot all over, and my emotion was so uncontrollable that I fled into my room, in which I felt more safe. My cousin Nathaly dragged me out by force and the next minute we came face to face, Serge Michailovitch and I. The first step was made, we mounted our horses and set off at a trot; soon after we walked them slowly, riding side by side. For some time we did not exchange a word, then suddenly Serge Michailovitch put his arm round me and drew me towards him till our lips met; he told me then that he loved me and asked me if I cared enough for him to become his wife. I only answered with my eyes, which spoke the plainest "yes," and thus, under the open sky, we pledged our troth, for a minute forgetting everything but our two selves. I gave him with happiness the gift of myself. Nothing could shake my faith in him now. For me that day marked the red-letter day of my calendar. I rode back to Tiflis an engaged girl, and announced our betrothal to mamma; I longed to inform the world at large of it. Our betrothal was made known the next day, and hearty were the congratulations addressed to us. I wrote to my father to ask for his consent and blessing, which he gave with pleasure.

Our wedding was to take place at Dolgik in the beginning of April. Serge Michailovitch, Sergy as I called him now, spent a good deal of his time with me; we used to pass all our evenings together in the library, where we contrived a sort of recess, furnished with a sofa, in which we could talk in peace. Nothing will ever make me forget the hours we passed together, hours which were all but too brief for us; we forgot that clocks existed. Dear days! so long ago, yet so vivid to me! We sat on the sofa with our heads very close together, pretending to read out of a book that lay on my lap face downwards. One evening as I sat thus, side by side with Sergy, my hand imprisoned in his, developing our plans for our future happiness, the footsteps of my uncle Staritzki recalled us to reality. Seeing that I held my book upside down, uncle went to fetch a venerable calf-bound volume containing the code of laws, and gave it to me saying laughingly that, perhaps we should be more interested with that sort of literature.

I was the happiest girl on earth; it was so good to feel that Sergy cared for me! He became my world, my all. I was no longer the same girl I had been, my time of playing with the sentiments of men was over; surely there were two *Vava Galitzines:* one that had been blessed with the happy faculty of dismissing one love from her mind the moment that she began to occupy herself with another, and one who, in spite of her frivolous outside, loved only one man in the world—her Sergy!

Now and then I had little fits of ill-temper, days when I was out of sorts with myself and everyone else. My griefs did not last long, but while they lasted they were very strong. Sometimes, after short quarrels between us, I would lock myself up in my room and flinging myself across my bed, burst into stormy tears, my hair all dishevelled and hanging loose like a repentant " Magdalena." These sudden outbursts of passion cleared off quickly, and I soon made it up with Sergy.

Nearly a month had passed since our engagement, and our visit was near drawing to a close ; it was time to start on our homeward journey. I left Tiflis with heart-breaking regret ; I hated to leave Sergy behind, he had grown into my heart and I could not bear the idea of being separated from him. I didn't know how I was going to get along till April without a sight of him ;. deprived of his company my life would be lonely beyond words. Five months were such an awfully long time to wait ! We promised to write to each other every day, but that was a poor consolation.

We travelled to Russia *via* Poti. Early the following morning our boat was to leave that town and we had to pass the night at a hotel. I was tired and depressed ; directly after dinner I got into bed and cried myself to sleep. When I woke up in the morning the wind moaned outside and the rain poured down in torrents. I went to the window and looked at the unquiet sea ; great waves were tumbling over the pier ; it was a very unpleasant day indeed for a sail, there-fore, we decided to travel back to Tiflis, and afterwards take the carriage road that leads to Vladicaucasus.

We reached Tiflis in the evening and gave Sergy a pleasant surprise. Oh ! there was no mistake about his being glad to see me !

Much to my egotistical delight, the roads were encumbered by falls of great masses of snow, and we were to have a whole week of each other's company until they were cleared away. In my secret heart I was cherishing a wild hope that new avalanches would fall and that we should be the longer together, but, alas, the roads were getting all right and the dreaded day of our second separation rapidly approached. I grumbled a good deal at having to leave Tiflis again ; I had never been so sorry to quit any place before.

The high road from Tiflis to Vladicaucasus is called the " Military Georgian Road." The scenery is magnificent but dreadfully wild, and I was awfully frightened to see that we were within a yard of the brinks of horrible precipices. As we got higher up in the mountains the air became so rarified that it was difficult to breathe.   Our sledge, drawn by two horses, one in front of the other, dragged on slowly, rising. The blocks of snow that bordered our way formed a prison wall between the road and the world outside.   Everything was a sort of wild, white sleepy stillness; no sound arose but the clink of the harness.   A large wooden cross rose on the highest point of the road ; a flock of black crows flew across the leaden sky, and wheeled about it, croaking piercingly. Everything looked so grey and cold ; we found ourselves as in a bewitched icy kingdom in a fairy tale.   There was something very awe-inspiring about it all.

It was night when we arrived at Vladicaucasus, where we took the train to Kharkoff.

CHAPTER XI

MARRIAGE

I LONGED for the winter to be over ; the days passed slowly, very slowly. I was in very low spirits and wanted Sergy most awfully, my one desire was to see him ; I thought of him morning, noon, and night. He had grown so dear to me that I could not do without him. We corresponded regularly and I only lived from letter to letter. Every morning my father entered my room, sat down on the edge of my bed and dropped a letter into my lap. Sergy wrote such delightful epistles which I devoured greedily.

In order to cheer me up my parents proposed to take me to Kharkoff, where the governor of the town was to give a couple of grand balls, but I refused outright ; what pleasure could I derive from them without Sergy ! I no longer knew myself, I was a new creature ; Sergy certainly had worked wonders ; my craze for pleasure, for excitement, my vanity and coquetry, well, all this was over and done with.

For a whole week I had no news from Sergy and was beginning to get very anxious. One rainy afternoon, as I was sitting in the drawing-room, hemming towels for our future household, I heard the sound of wheels on the gravel. Oh ! there is the door bell ! It is some intrusive country-neighbour that had burst upon us for sure. This irony of fate exasperated me beyond measure ; suppose that instead of that boring visitor it was my welcome bridegroom who had come ! But no, that was not possible, I was stupid to think about it, it was just as well to desire the moon. As I could not possibly see any strangers now, I gathered up my needlework and fled into my room, Soon after I was called by mamma, and directed my steps *adagio* towards the drawing-room. But lo ! what was that ? the clinking of spurs ? I opened the door, my heart beating wildly, and stood dazed and unable to believe my own eyes. There, on the threshold, was Sergy, my beloved Sergy ! It was no dream and the next instant his arms were thrown eagerly round me. Sergy had contrived to obtain a few days leave, on the most urgent private affairs, and run over to Dolgik, crossing the Black Sea, so stormy at this time of year, in order to spend a week with me. It was so very sweet of him to come all that long way, that horrid November month, to see me! So that was the reason of his long silence.

I was beside myself with joy, it was simply glorious to have Sergy here, but his flying visit only sharpened my desire to have him always near me. The days that followed his departure were long and dismal; I was literally pining for him and counted the weeks and days like a school-girl.

So time went on. As the day of our marriage approached, my spirits rose. Sergy announced by wire his definite arrival for the first day of Easter. I was in a terrible state of nervous excitement on that happy day, and felt so impatient to see him that I could hardly sit still! Hark! There's a carriage rumbling round the porch. Oh rapture, oh joy! It is he, my bridegroom, whom I have wanted so greedily! I have him now for good and all; except death there is no power on earth which can divide us!

April 11th, 1876, our wedding day, was a red-letter day for me. Our house was full of guests and relations assembled to see me married. The marriage ceremony was to take place at ten o'clock in the evening in our village church. Before starting for church my father and mother gave me their blessing and cried a good deal. My bridegroom came forward to meet me on the threshold of the church and led me to the altar. We stood before the old priest who was to unite us, a little pale but quite self-possessed. He pronounced the words of the Sacrament that had been said over to so many millions of human beings: "Until death us do part!" and we became man and wife. The priest had concluded his marriage benediction, and after the usual congratulations, Sergy offered me his arm and we passed out of church, going together into a new life. We proceeded to our chateau, where my parents gave us and our numerous guests a sumptuous supper, enlivened by a military band that they sent for from Kharkoff. Whilst my health was drunk Sergy pressed a kiss on my lips, then followed a clinking of glasses and wild cheers of felicitations and blessings without end. Amidst this hurly-burly I saw a spider that crept up my nuptial gown. That was a cheerful omen for our wedding. A French proverb says: *Araignée du soir grand espoir.* God grant it to be so!

When the meal was over I went speedily to put on my travelling dress, for it was nearly daylight and we had to drive a long way to Mertchik, a fine estate belonging to Sergy's elder brother, situated at about fifty miles from Dolgik, where we were to spend our honeymoon.

Before leaving the home that had sheltered my happy girlhood for ever, I went to bid my last farewell to the room of my girlish days. I knelt down at the side of my forlorn bed, and with my head on my folded arms I prayed.

Then I parted from my parents, shedding copious tears. Good-bye Dolgik, good-bye my dear old life!

I stepped with my husband into the handsome victoria, given to me by my brother for a wedding present, and we rode away, driven by four spirited horses. On crossing a bridge one of our steeds slipped and went down ; the carriage passed over him, throwing the coachman and the footman off their box-seat. The frightened animals, feeling themselves at liberty, tore away down the road at a frightful pace. We were sitting terror-struck, seeing ourselves shut up in the carriage. Sergy made an attempt to squeeze himself through the pane of glass on the box, in order to catch hold of the reins and stop the horses. I divined his crazy purpose and cluched at him with all my force. Luckily at that moment the reins entangled themselves between the wheels, bringing the maddened animals to a stand-still within two steps of the river.

We had all miraculously escaped from death, and weren't hurt at all, only scared. When we sprang down, I shook with nervousness, and began to sob convulsively. It is easy to conceive the fright of Sergy's brothers who were following us behind. They made us mount into their brougham and soon after we arrived safely at Mertchik. My favourite dog, a beautiful St. Bernard, who had been sent to Mertchik the day before, stood wagging his tail to welcome us on the doorstep.

My parents with some friends came to visit us the next day. I put on for that occasion a dressing-gown with a long train and felt very proud to be called Madame and said " my husband " on every available opportunity.

I had won the great draw in the matrimonial lottery, for Sergy was the best of husbands. I had found true happiness and felt that I had just begun to live. We were all in all to each other ; how I had existed so long without Sergy, passes my comprehension. I couldn't believe that any man could have such a power over me ; my whole heart belonged to him. There seemed no disparity in our ages, for Sergy was so full of the joy of life. He fondled me and fulfilled all my wishes, giving me everything I could wish for before even I asked ; he literally read my thoughts. Sergy was, in short, a darling, and I have only the old story to tell :

> I love you and you love me,
> And oh! how happy we shall be !

But our honeymoon was short, alas ; the clouds came on all but too soon. We had been married about twenty days, and my cup of happiness was full, when matters took a turn for the bad. There came a telegram calling my husband back to Tiflis on account of the preparations for war with

Turkey.   This unexpected turn of events fairly stunned me.
What awaited us, I wondered?

I was heart-broken at parting with my parents, who
accompanied us to the railway station with a great number
of friends.   Parting is so horrid; I always hated good-byes.
I gave kisses and shake-hands to right and left, and cried a
good deal, crushing unmercifully my pocket handkerchief, a
dainty thing not made for woe.   It was time to enter our
compartment; I stood at the window to say a last farewell.
The engine whistled and the long train groaned and moved
away, carrying me away speedily to my new home.

At one of the big stations a young officer came up to me,
a tall, good-looking fellow, in whom I recognised one of the
victims of my St. Petersburg doings, a former page who had
been enamoured with me once upon a time.   He was greatly
altered, having attained the age of adolescence; a slight
trace of a moustache was visible.   His face was aglow with
the pleasure at seeing me.   He took my hands in his and
said in a low aside to me that he continued to adore
me, and a lot more things that were enough to move a stone.
But all this seemed exceedingly foolish to me, and I was a
little uncertain whether I ought to be flattered or affronted,
but he looked so doleful that I had not the heart to snub
him and treated him with a soft graciousness which raised
him to the seventh heaven and induced him to devour my
hands with kisses.   One more good-bye and then farewell;
we had gone away!   My ex-page stood staring ruefully after
the departing train, which-stole me away, whilst I lent on the
window squeezing tightly Sergy's hand and nodding him
adieu.   How ridiculous seemed to me all the passing fancies
of by-gone days.   I see now that I never loved anyone
until I met Sergy; he was absolutely and indisputably sole
master of my heart.   All the others served only as a pastime

CHAPTER XII

TIFLIS

THE carriage road that leads from Vladicaucasus to Tiflis is equally dangerous in winter as in summer, for instead of snow avalanches there are falls of stones. I shuddered when I passed under these treacherous rocks, dreading every time we passed them to be smashed to pieces. I was startingly impressed by the scenery; it was a wild, primeval landscape, great old mountains all around. Sharp turns were to be made and we had often to stop the carriage to let omnibuses and camels pass, a process for which there was scarcely enough room.

We reached Tiflis in the evening and established ourselves very comfortable in Sergy's spacious appartments. It was the prettiest home that could be imagined; my pink boudoir was lovely, a real bonbon box. I had all the world before me and everything to make me happy. Wearing rose-coloured glasses through which one looks at the outside world, I felt in particular good-humour with life in general and with my husband above all. But all joys have an end. These two delicious months passed over only too swiftly; storm-clouds rose quite unexpectedly upon our horizon and a shadow of trouble hung over us. A few years before, an insurrection broke out in Herzegovine; later on the Bulgarians made an attempt to throw off the Turkish yoke, but the Osmanlies made short and terrible work of the unfortunate Bulgarians, and Serbia and Montenegro maddened by the spectacle of horror, declared war. We were expecting with dread lest Russia should meddle in that sad affair, when all of a sudden rumours of war spread abroad. Whatever I thought will now become of me, should I have to part with Sergy, who had crept into my life as a necessity? It did not seem possible; sooner might I lie down and die!

About this time general Loris Melikoff was appointed commander of the army of the Caucasus, and my husband chief of his staff. Towards the middle of June Sergy was ordered to "Manglis" to inspect our artillery, a part of which quartered there. He offered to take me with him and I accepted gladly, for the heat in Tiflis was excessive and everybody was out of town at this season.

It was very late at night before we were able to reach the

village of " Bely-Kloutch," for though we had a beautiful moon to help us on our way, we advanced very slowly, thanks to the bad state of the roads.

I was very much frightened to hear that "Manglis" was dangerous on account of the brigands, and scarcely closed my eyes the whole night, as the windows of the room that we occupied at the small hotel were nearly level with the garden walls, and it seemed to me all the time that someone was climbing up through the window

The next morning at six o'clock we started on horseback to "Manglis." The road was steep and very fatiguing, but my brave little Cossack horse went an excellent pace ; he seldom stumbled and was thoroughly intelligent in dangerous places. We plodded on steadily till midday, when we reached a big wood, and feeling horribly hungry, we dismounted, sat on the grass in the shade of a big tree, and had luncheon.

It was about six o'clock when we arrived at " Manglis." We stopped at the house of Colonel Gourtchine, a friend of my husband's. I was so dead-tired that I went to bed immediately and slept soundly.

On the following day the regiment of Erivan, who held his quarters in " Manglis," was on the march to Alexandropol, a small town situated on the frontier of Russia and Asiatic Turkey. The troops stood in lines for a review in the Public Square, where a Te-Deum was sung. The spectacle was most imposing and my whole heart rose up in pity for our poor soldiers, who prayed so fervently, at the thought that in case of war a great number of them would never see their native land again.

We travelled back to Tiflis on that same day. A week later, in order to escape the intolerable heat, we set off to Borjom.

A few days after our arrival, I had to be presented to the Grand Duchess Olga Fedorovna. Whilst waiting to be received by Her Imperial Highness I was shown into a big library; I sat down and began to turn over some illustrated magazines when the Grand Duke came in and shook hands with me with his usual graciousness. His Highness drew my arm through his, telling me that he wanted to present me himself to his spouse. Whilst we proceeded to the ·Grand Duchess's private appartments, the Grand Duke asked me, all of a sudden, if I hadn't had enough of my husband yet. I wonder what put such a poor idea of my constancy into his head ! At all events it was a little too soon to ask that question.

The Grand Duchess got up to receive me in a most cordial manner, at once setting me at my ease. I didn't feel shy at all in her presence, and returned home enchanted with my visit.

Towards the end of September we came back to Tiflis ; a week later general Loris-Melikoff was called away for a few days to Alexandropol to inspect our troops and Sergy had to accompany him. I accepted philosophically that short separation, for just then I had the joy to see mamma arrive. Soon after my busband returned, and mamma went back to Russia.

It was sweet to have Sergy home again, but he soon announced to me that it was necessary for him to return to Alexandropol for the whole winter, perhaps, on account of the hostile attitude of the Turks. That was a source of great affliction to me. Less than ever I was able to spare him, and told him that nothing could induce me to remain alone in Tiflis and that I was determined to follow him to the Turkish frontier. For his sake I would gladly travel to the end of the world ! After many discussions Sergy yielded.

CHAPTER XIII

ALEXANDROPOL

WE drove the hundred miles to Alexandropol in a post-chaise, bringing over with us my old maid Helena, who was both a faithful friend and servant.

We installed ourselves at Alexandropol in the house of a rich Armenian merchant. It was a dreary home, my new one, with its cross-barred windows, and suggested to my mind being in prison. I suffered a great deal from the cold, for our apartments were very badly heated, and we were obliged to put up an iron stove in the drawing-room.

Alexandropol is surrounded by high mountains; one of the summits named "Alagöse" is always covered with snow. The town with its low houses and flat roofs, uniformaly built of grey stone, reminds one of Pompeii. The costume of the native women is as gloomy as everything else in this town. Enveloped in a yashmak, a piece of white muslin leaving only the eyes exposed, they looked exactly like ghosts.

We lived in a very unpretending style. General Loris-Melikoff, who tried his best to cheer our Russian colony, pursued me with invitations, which I generally managed to evade.

One of our favourite diversions was to visit the citadel, a miniature fortified town, situated at about a mile's distance from Alexandropol. General Kobsieff, the commander of the citadel, was awfully nice to me; he lent me books and sent me flowers.

One of our most frequent guests, General S—— was so old that I was afraid all the time he'd go to pieces. He showed a distinct preference for my society and looked at me as if I were something good to eat. This old general gave me to understand that I had captured his venerable heart and that he was deeply enamoured with me, which sounded somewhat ridiculous from that aged warrior, and though he was far too ancient for my taste, I let him make love to me, for what harm could come of it? My old admirer was dying to show me the renewal of his vigour, lost in the night of time; an occasion soon presented itself. One rainy day I went out for a walk accompanied by two cavaliers, my out-of-date adorer and a sprightly young officer. Whilst I held my nose up in the air looking at the state of the sky, a gust of wind tore away my umbrella and the old warrior, trying to get it before the young one, ran as fast as his old legs could carry him towards the rolling parasol, and brought it back triumphantly to me, like a perfect knight. Gallant old creature!

A score of " djigites " belonging to General Loris-Melikoff's escort, consisting of different Asiatic tribes, gave circus performances on the square, where a military band played every afternoon on the roof-platform of the house opposite our abode. Below, a band of Armenian street urchins went through all sorts of military evolutions, under the command of a little chief, decorated with Russian paper-stars and crosses.

I had a great desire to cross the Arpatchai, a small frontier river between Alexandropol and Asia Minor, in order to be able to say that I had actually stepped upon Asiatic ground. The Arpatchai was frozen at this time of year. As soon as I found myself with Mrs. Zezemann, one of our military ladies, on the other side of the river, a group of Cossacks who guarded our frontier cried out to us to go back, apprehending, surely, that we had the intention of running away to Kars, where the Turkish army was concentrated. The Turkish sentinels, in their turn, regarded us with suspicion. Finding ourselves thus between two fires we had to retreat speedily, to my great disappointment, for we had nearly reached a small cottage inhabited by a Turkish major, with a dozen of soldiers. But " well begun is half done," I made a fresh attempt at my exciting expedition, accompanied this time by Sergy and his interpreter. My heart beat quickly as we went under the roof of our future enemies, encircled by a group of red-fezzed soldiers who stared very hard at us. When the usual greetings had been exchanged, our courteous host, who seemed quite willing to be friendly, offered us black coffee, served in tiny cups. Fearing that the beverage was poisoned, I entreated Sergy not to taste it, but, notwithstanding, he drank a whole cupful and I hastened to follow his example, for if the coffee had been poisoned, we should undergo the same fate, both of us. In bidding good-bye to our host I expressed my intense desire to possess a white Persian cat with silky long wool, and the Turkish major promised to send me a beautiful specimen of that feline race. It was very charming of him, but though we had been treated first rate, I must say I was glad when we were safely home again.

Meanwhile the political horizon grew very dark, and the shadow of evil hung over us. A great number of the heroes of the last Russo-Turkish war are buried in Alexandropol in the " Dale of Honour," and when I thought that a new war was very near to bursting out, I had a ferocious desire to fling myself into the Arpatchai. I tried to keep up my spirits as best I could, deluding myself with vain hopes that in a short time we should return safe and sound to Tiflis; but the menace of coming war became more evident every day, it was no use deceiving myself.   "Is war inevitable then?"   I asked Sergy a hundred times a day, and he could give me but little comfort.   How could I live then with this sword of Damocles hanging over me?

CHAPTER XIV

THE TURCO-RUSSIAN WAR

THERE were new complications and things began to look more and more serious. Every day when I awoke a fear came over me that the news would be brought: "we are to march."

From time to time disguised Turkish officers, spies for certain, began to appear in Alexandropol. There were some skirmishes in the town, unfriendly demonstrations between the Christians and the Mussulmans. A great activity was noticeable in Alexandropol, and I listened to the sounds of drums and the rumble of the big guns through the streets with increasing uneasiness.

On Easter night we went to the citadel church for divine service; a score of Cossacks lighted our way with torches. The next day we had a great number of congratulators who came in to embrace us, according to our Orthodox practice, in commemoration of Christ's Resurrection. It was curious to see amongst them "devil-worshippers," belonging to Loris-Melikoff's escort.

Events were advancing faster than I anticipated; the storm-cloud which had been gathering had burst at last, and the time of trial had come. A telegram informed Loris Melikoff that the Ambassador of Russia had received the order to quit Constantinople; a second despatch followed saying: "if Turkey did not consent to sign the conditions that Russia exacted, war would be declared in the lapse of two days." And Turkey did not consent.

On the 11th of April, the first anniversary of our wedded life, we invited some friends to dine with us. Just when our health was going to be drunk, my husband was hastily summoned by Loris-Melikoff whom he found reading a cyphered telegram which announced the declaration of war against Turkey.

Having agreed not to divulge these alarming tidings, Sergy tried to look cheery when he returned home, but I saw at a glance that he was very pale and nervous, and guessed at once that he had brought bad news; when I heard him give orders to have his horse ready at any time of the night, I understood all. He had to go! Oh, to think of it! Oh, to think of it!

For some minutes I could not collect my faculties, everything swam before my eyes, it was altogether such a terrible blow! The first shock of horrible surprise over, I resolved to show myself as self-possessed as I could. Time enough for tears and grief when Sergy would be gone!

The order was given to our cavalry to attack the twenty Turkish posts who guarded the frontier at nightfall; only three of them defended themselves, all the others were taken unawares; being plunged into deep sleep, they were taken captives. It was the first act of open hostility.

Oh, the terrible night! Of sleep there was no question whatever! Before the stepping out of our troops, in the cold grey light of a rainy dawn, a Te-Deum was performed in the square in front of the cathedral. The soldiers, after having concluded their fervent prayers, took a pinch of earth, kissed the dear ground and laid it in their knapsacks. Many eyes filled with tears at this touching spectacle.

Until this moment no one in town had suspected that war had been declared. All Alexandropol was in a great state of excitement; the Armenians, especially, were awfully frightened and depressed.

At seven in the morning our troops left Alexandropol. The heart-breaking hour had come, the sad word "farewell" was to be said. I cried out, "Good-bye my all, good-bye!" and pressed my wet cheek to Sergy's tear-stained one, like my own. After a short prayer, we held each other in a close embrace; I couldn't believe that he was really going. At last I mastered myself with an effort, and disengaged my clinging arms with a last kiss. It was the worst moment I had ever had in my life. There was an instant of unconsciousness, and when I recovered myself he was gone! I hadn't the strength to accompany Sergy to the front door, and flinging myself upon my bed, face downwards, I sobbed as I had never sobbed before. Oh! now I was alone, alone, alone! Suddenly I sprang up and stretched out my hands to the blank distance, cried aloud: "Come back, Sergy, come back, my sweetheart, I cannot let you go!" But he was already gone past recall. I shall certainly never forget that day. It seemed as if my life had ended. Oh, my God, if I could only die!

I sent Housnadine, our Tartar servant, to the Russian frontier with the orders to return only after my husband had crossed to the other side of the Arpatchai. After two hours of agony, Housnadine brought me a few hasty words, scribbled by Sergy, while the pontoons were laying a bridge across the river for our artillery to pass over. Sergy entreated me to be brave, and promised to send me news as often as he could. Whilst he was writing that note, a notice came from head-quarters that the enemy had appeared. It was only a false alarm; a detachment of Turkish irregulars belonging to a tribe named "Karapapaki," who had promised to serve the Russian cause if war would be declared, came now to join our army, with a banner and in full battle array.

A long, miserable night followed. Oh, what I was suffering! What agonies, what tortures! Worn out with tears, I fell asleep, but was suddenly awakened by a loud voice pronouncing my husband's name. A moment later I was out of bed and rushed to the window, seized with a sudden dread that some misfortune had happened to Sergy. It was an express messenger covered with dust, who had brought a letter from my husband. He wrote from the first halting place of our army, a Turkish village situated about ten miles distance from Alexandropol. I read that epistle till the pages were blotted with tears. Short as it was, there was enough love in it to make the letter doubly dear. I kissed the paper over and over again; then I kissed the "My own darling" with which the letter began, kissed the "Your loving husband" with which it ended.

Early next morning I rose from my bed to look out upon a world suddenly become empty. It was like an awful nightmare from which I couldn't wake up.

The succeeding days were the most trying I had ever known; I was so miserable, so wretched, and needed comfort so badly, and here I was left alone to wither away! It was altogether too cruel! I was so young, and my trouble was so great! For twenty years I had lived and had never been acquainted with adverse circumstances, and the troubles which had been averted were now beginning to come thickly upon me, and I could not possibly endure it patiently, my heart overflowed with self-pity. I will not deny that I displayed a pitiful lack of moral courage, but I was neither a philosopher nor a stoic, alas! It is a fact that I had always lived on the sunny side of life, and was born to be petted and made much of. Fairies had brought their offerings at my birth, and I took the rose-leaf pathway as my due; and now my eyes began to open to the realities of life!

Oh, how I did pine for Sergy! I wanted him now as I had never wanted him before; I wanted the sound of his voice, the touch of his hand. Oh that he may soon come back to me! He was in my mind and in my heart day and night; in every dream I saw him: I stretched my arms out to him, but I awoke with sobs and in torment, for he was not there!

One can easily imagine what an anxious time I passed through, living in a constant state of alarm. Sergy's telegrams brought me the assurance that he was still alive and unwounded, but what might be in an hour—to-morrow? The minute just past might have made me a widow!

I lived a mechanical existence ; at ten o'clock I got out of bed, at twelve I went back to it again.   One day was the same to me as another ; I would not take interest in anything, and was only thirsting for news from the seat of war. Our military ladies, who were not depressed like me, though their husbands were also at the war, visited me frequently, being prompted by kindly wishes to raise me from my apathy. They succeeded somewhat to break the monotony of my life, bringing in the freshness of the outer world.

Mrs. Zezemann, dropping in one day to cheer me up, succeeded in forcing me to come out of my shell.   She took me to the citadel to see a detachment of Turkish prisoners ;   I perceived among them the major who had promised me a cat.   He gave me a broad grin of recognition, and when I recalled his promise to his mind, he assured me that he would fulfil it without fail as soon as he was set at liberty by the Russians.

The list of killed had already brought the names of several officers I had known personally.   Naturally I became very anxious concerning my husband's safety.   The thought that he might meet the same fate drove me to madness.   What the newspapers had to tell about the war was not of a nature to set my mind at ease.   I began to dread the arrival of the post, lest it should bring me the news of Sergy's death ; I fancied ten millions of accidents.   My old Helena, who served me with loving fidelity, tried her best to comfort me, and said it was no good imagining horrors, but I would not be comforted, and continued to be in an agony of terror.

I preferred to remain in complete seclusion, and shut my door to all callers, but one evening Helena acted against my orders, and let Mrs. R., one of our military ladies in, a person with whom I had never succeeded in making friends.   She came and sat by my bed in spite of my desire for solitude. As I presented an unresponsive cheek to her lips, she inquired suavely if I had read the papers that day, and though she saw that this talk was most distasteful to me, she gave herself great trouble to make it quite clear to me that the day before, in a great clash, Sergy had been exposed to sharp artillery fire.   Being on the brink of an outburst of hysterical sobbing, I exclaimed : "Don't, it hurts me ! " But that vixen of a woman, who, if she could say bitter things never lost an opportunity of doing so, continued her horrible descriptions.   The aims of my tormentor were attained ; I flew into a passion, and turning upon her war-like eyes blazing through a flood of tears, I told her that it was cruel and shameless to come and frighten me like that. Mrs. R. sailed away very much offended, and thus ended that pleasant visit.   In fact, what right had that disagreeable lady to disturb me like that ?   I had never known anything but love, and expected it from everything and everybody, but my eyes commenced to open now to the reality and bitterness of life, and I began to experience things which astonished and disgusted me. I had found out at last that the world was hard.

Meanwhile good tidings came from the seat of war; a conference, which assembled in Paris, occasioned a suspension of hostilities. It must surely be the presage of peace, and I clung with all my might to my hope that war would soon be over, and that all my anxieties, my worries, would be at an end. Cheered and strengthened, I so far recovered my spirits as to be able to receive Colonel K., but that gentleman proved to be very unsympathetic and disappointing, for instead of confirming my happy expectations, he prophecied dreadful things, and when I said I hoped better days were in store for me, he replied that it was easy to hope, that hope's cheap, but nevertheless any possibility of peace was held to be out of the question, and that war would go on for a long time yet. But I refused to face that picture. "It won't, it won't," I screamed out, but it was only to make myself believe it wasn't true. At that moment my anger had risen so high that I struggled against an impulse to fling him out of the room. At last, no longer able to contain myself, I lost all self-control. "I hate you!" I cried out vehemently, and darted past him into Helena's room and locked myself in. It was certainly very rude of me to give way to such an undignified outburst of passion, but I was so furious with my visitor that I could not be polite to him at that moment, to save my life.

One of my St. Petersburg ex-pages, B——, a newly promoted officer, was passing through Alexandropol to the seat of war, and paid me an unexpected visit, but I was in a mood which makes one long to mope in solitude, and could not endure callers, so he was turned from my door greatly disappointed. That officer, as well as all the rest of the unfair sex, (I beg your pardon, gentlemen!) was naught to me; my husband being the one man in the world for me, my heart being true as steel to him, I wanted him alone and no one else.

By this time there were little reconnoitrings of cavalry. Musket shots were exchanged, with great damage on both sides. The news of more fighting, more bloodshed, had just reached me; a great battle was being fought near Alexandropol; we could plainly see the fire and hear the roar of the cannons from the citadel. The Turks were threatening Alexandropol now, and we were in immediate danger of seeing our homes invaded by the hostile army. Fantastical reports circulated that Mussa-Pasha, the commander-in-chief of the Turkish army, had informed Loris-Melikoff that he would dine on the following day at Alexandropol. The *mouchir's* visit hung over our town as a nightmare, and a panic arose which drove our military ladies to distraction. They all persuaded me in vain to flee with them, and Helena, who easily lost her head, implored me in her turn to start immediately for Tiflis ; but I was not afraid of anything, I felt I did not care what became of me, and declared that I should certainly not stir from Alexandropol. On that same evening our soldiers turned the Turks back, and our ladies grew calm again.

The idea came to me to become Sister of Mercy in order to have the possibility of following our troops. Here again I was destined to meet with disappointment. General Tolstoi, a member of the society of the Red Cross, had refused to take me seriously, saying that I was far too young and inexperienced for such hard work. How perfectly horrid of him !

Oh, what agonies I endured during the hours of fighting ! I fancied the raging battle going on in which Sergy might at any moment be killed. One whole night I sat at the window-seat waiting nervously for news ; the stillness was broken only by the measured tramp of the sentinel who paced to and fro under my window, and also by the mewing of marauding cats on the terrace roofs. At dawn I received a reassuring telegram from Sergy.

At the end of April my husband came home to spend a whole day with me. Oh, the joy of being together after those two horrid weeks of separation and suspense ! Those few hours of calm, of quiet, put life into me again, and roused me from my lethargy. Everything changed when Sergy was while he was with here ; me I felt no fear whatever, but I knew that very soon Sergy would have to go back to that dreadful war, and I should be left all alone, lonelier than ever. That short visit only increased the bitter pain of renewed parting. " How shall I ever let you go away again," I murmured, embracing Sergy tearfully. But I had to do it, and my sorrows came back, and the house seemed blank again.

Meanwhile the Russian army continued to advance boldly. The telegraphic despatches gave the description of a fiery battle between our Cossacks and the Turkish pickets. In May the siege of Ardagan took place ; Sergy entered the town at the head of a big detachment of soldiers, and notwithstanding the ·energetic resistance of the Turks, the citadel of Ardagan was obliged to capitulate. The battle was hot, and the Turks who had fought desperately for eighteen hours, sustained great losses. The streets were literally filled with dead and wounded ; the corpses were crowded in heaps, one upon the other, and it took three whole days to clear them away. It was frosty weather fortunately, otherwise one couldn't have breathed for the dreadful smell.

On the 13th of May (evil day) a great battle was fought near Zevine. On the same day the Turks blockaded our fortress of Baiazette. A small number of soldiers shut up in that citadel showed great steadiness under fire, and rained shells upon the enemy, defending themselves desperately. Their situation was very critical indeed. They were short of water, and had to leave their shelter to draw water from a source running under the rocks, whilst the Turks opened a terrible fire upon them. It was certainly a very perilous undertaking. The Russians held the town ten days until a reinforcement arrived which put the Turks to flight and delivered the Russian garrison.

The Grand Duke Michael had proceeded to the seat of war whilst the Grand Duchess, his spouse, established herself for an indefinite period in the citadel of Alexandropol. Miss Ozeroff, one of her maids-in-waiting, came to see me, and hinted to me that the Grand Duchess expected a visit from me. My first impulse was to decline this honour and say, "No," but Miss Ozeroff, catching me like a fish in her net, invited me one afternoon for a cup of tea. As it was one of my good days, for I had just received a telegram from Sergy, I accepted her invitation, and picking myself up, I put on my plainest walking-dress and a broad-brimmed garden hat and set off for the citadel. I gave my card to a tall lackey in glittering livery, and ordered him to conduct me upstairs to Miss Ozeroff's private apartments. My cunning hostess, in spite of my protestations, insisted on carrying me off to the Grand Duchess. I was quite unprepared for that and very much upset. The Grand Duchess, however, most kindly rose to embrace me and placed me on the sofa by her side. She began directly to talk of the war operations and related to me that during the siege of Ardagan, for which Sergy had received the Cross of St. George, he had been in great danger, his horse having been shot from under him. When I heard this I turned very pale and burst into a storm of tears. The Grand Duchess tried vainly to sooth me, telling me that perhaps it might not be true that Sergy had been in such mortal danger, but I continued to sob hysterically, for I was not altogether a Spartan, I must confess.

I continued to display an obstinate preference for seclusion, and refused myself to callers. I might as well be shut away in prison. I had, moreover, imposed on myself the vow never to set foot out of my room until Sergy's definite return. This life was telling upon my nerves and I fell into a condition of dreadful mental apathy. I had no wish for anything and fretted myself into a kind of low fever. I had lost my sleep and hated the sight of food, and became thinner and more wretched every day, until at last I was a shadow of myself. I nearly drove my poor Helena mad with my pale face and tear-sodden eyes. At length she became so uneasy about me that she wrote the most alarming reports of my health to my mother, who started immediately for Alexandropol with my cousin, Kate Swetchine, to help me bear my grief and soothe my sorrows. They were certainly a dear comfort, both of them, but I wanted Sergy, and continued to send him daily laconic despatches with one word only, "Come."

My condition was so alarming that my husband decided to beg for a leave of absence as soon as he could, in order to take me abroad for a short time. Meanwhile a suspension of arms had been agreed upon, and our troops remained in inaction before the fortress of Kars. Profiting by that short calm, Sergy had obtained a leave of absence on the plea of urgent private affairs. It was a very great surprise to me, almost too good to be true. Happy days were yet in store for me!

It was decided that we should spend a week in Paris; the project was a delightful one. With what impatience I awaited Sergy's arrival! Though for a short while, I said still I'll have him all to myself now!

On the day of my husband's proposed arrival I sat at the open window in joyous excitement and expectation, listening l intensely, with every nerve tingling, to the sounds in the street outside. What a day it had been—a hundred hours in it! The clock-hands seemed to crawl on purpose. Seeing my agitation, Helena mounted on our roof, but as Sister Anne on her watch-tower, she didn't perceive my knight. Suddenly I heard a rolling of wheels under my window and a carriage drove up to the door. Mamma flew out to greet Sergy, but instead of him, rushed into the arms of a total stranger. She had got hold of the wrong man and found herself confronted by an officer who brought a letter from Sergy, explaining his unexpected delay. And I had been just withering up with impatience to see him!

Two days later a telegram announced my husband's definite arrival. On the eve of that happy day I went to bed very early and awakened the next morning with the pleasant sense of anticipation of the coming journey.

Hurrah! My husband had arrived at last! I should have gone mad if he hadn't come that time. With what joy I ran forward and hugged him! He was given back to me, thank God! I put my arms round his neck and cried over him for happiness.

So it was decided at last, and we were to start for Paris in a few days. I was now all impatience to be off. The first

thing we did after Sergy's arrival was to order a *Te Deum*
of thanksgiving. What a joy I felt when I went out of doors
for the first time after my voluntary days of jail. I was very
tired after my long imprisonment, and found myself coming
to life again. The next day we were on our way to Tiflis.
My nerves being tiresomely on edge just then, I was in a
horrible fright all the way, and before approaching a steep
hill that we had to ascend, I jumped out of the carriage and
sat down in the middle of the road, and folding my arms I
declared that I would not proceed further. My cousin Kate
followed my example and established herself on the *chaussée*
beside me, saying that she wouldn't move either. As we
could not take up our quarters on the highway for ever, I
gathered up my somewhat scattered courage and remounted
the carriage.

From Tiflis we went straight on to Paris, and mamma
returned to Russia with my cousin.

Our stay abroad was not altogether a very agreeable one,
for Sergy was all the time very nervous and careworn, dreading to arrive too late for the siege of Kars. As to me, this
trip brought the roses back to my cheeks, but as the time for
my husband's return to the war drew near, my face grew
sadder. I dreaded going back, having the painful knowledge
that we must return to all the horrors of war again.

We came back to Alexandropol before my husband's
holidays expired. To his great disappointment, and to my
immense delight, General Komaroff had already taken
possession of Kars, which was thought to be impregnable.

After my installation in the house of an Armenian, an old
dismissed officer, I had the horrible pain of seeing my
husband depart to the campaign. We had again to endure
separation which might end in death.

The room which I was to occupy was low-ceilinged and
bare-looking, with a bit of looking-glass nailed to the wall;
a table, three chairs and a sofa, which had evidently attained
the dignity of old age, composed all the furniture. I had to
sleep on that hard sofa, from which nearly all the horse-hair
and springs had gone.

Things had returned to their usual state; I was again in
terror and suspicion through an eternity of days. My hosts
showed me the greatest hospitality. The master of the house
had served about twenty years before in the escort of our
Emperor in St. Petersburg, where he had been renowned for
his martial air and ferocious black moustache, which was now
painted blue-black and was still startling. My host was a
good old chap; under his strong outside, he had a heart as
soft as a pincushion. He was always very desirous to please
me and did all my commissions with the greatest pleasure.
I was thirsting for information from the seat of war and sent

him on exploring expeditions every morning. His wife was a fat, double-chinned matron who looked good-natured enough but possessed the very slowest of brains; I had no patience with a person of such indolent temperament, for I had more life in my little finger than she had in her whole voluminous body. She conceived a prompt affection for me, but it was dull work sitting all day with that gossiping, childish woman, who was not an exhilarating companion, to be sure; her attempts to cheer me up were not brilliant and failed to bring the faintest smile to my lips. All day long my hostess did nothing, and ate everything; anyone would be fat leading such a life. Her sole occupation was to string pearls for her head attire; lazy, unoccupied, she shuffled about in her slippers, or sat twiddling her thumbs. Her favourite pastime was bathing; she went to the bath-establishment with female friends, supplied with provisions; these daughters of the East remained there nearly all day long, babbling and chatting like magpies. It took a long time for me to get used to my hostess, but I ended by liking her quite well. I was so miserable and felt so utterly alone, that any friendly, seeming companionship was welcome, and it was a balm to feel the good woman's sympathy.

I was living like an anchorite and had no one to talk to but my hosts, a very poor resource indeed. When the weather was fine I sat on an old bench near our gate and watched the native women who came to draw water from a fountain just opposite; they carried it on their shoulders in large clay jugs just as in the times of Rebecca. In November the weather was bitterly cold. Sometimes, in moments of supreme depression, I would go out and stand at the gate hoping to catch a bad cold. My poor Helena, terror-stricken, raised her hands up in horror and drew me indoors by force. Often, after our meagre dinner, when it grew dark, I sat on the hearth-rug, drawing my shawl close about me, and shivering looked with dreary eyes into the dying fire, big tears rolling down my cheeks.

A message suddenly arrived from Sergy, an astounding piece of good news; he was coming to spend Christmas with me. I was delirious with joy at the thought of seeing him, and eagerly awaited his arrival; it filled my days with hope and excitement. I was sick and weary and hungry for the sight of his face and the sound of his voice. I counted the days and planned how we should spend Christmas together.

On Christmas Eve I went to bed immediately after dinner, in order to shorten the hours, and dreamt all night of bliss and joyous meeting. Early in the morning Helena came to announce that an officer had arrived from the seat of war and wished to see me. He brought awful news; Sergy wrote to me that he had just been ordered with a detachment of soldiers to Kniss-Kala, a place very far away at the very bottom of the Kurdistan, where a strong epidemic of typhus-fever was raging. It was a terrible disappointment and grief. What a sad Christmas it would be for me now! The shock was almost more than I could bear; I speedily sent a telegram to Sergy beseeching him not to accept that mission. Very unsoldier like it was of me and not sufficiently heroic; my husband certainly paid no heed to my entreaty and started off for Kniss-Kala.

Ten months were already passed since war had been declared, and I was still at Alexandropol, when one happy morning my host brought me news that peace had been signed. I was beside myself with joy, and feeling the necessity to share my happiness with some one, I ran off to Mrs. Odnossoumoff, one of the few military ladies whom I could tolerate; but she clouded my perfect happiness in telling me that it was an armistice only, which had been signed, and that war would soon break out again. I went home awfully sad at heart, and back to my room, flinging myself on my bed, I wept passionately; worn out I sobbed myself to sleep. With what bliss I would have slept for ever!

The armistice was announced at Kniss-Kala on the same day that the Turks were to attack the detachment commanded by my husband. What a terrible misfortune there might have been for me, had the announcement not come in time, and what a narrow escape Sergy had. I shudder when I think of it.

CHAPTER XV

KARS

A NEW post was offered to my husband. He had recently been nominated President of the Commission of Demarcation, and was obliged to start for Erzeroum, the capital of Anatolia. I felt a burning desire to see Sergy before his departure, and acting upon the impulse of the moment, for I am a person of prompt action, I rushed off to Kars at once, without stopping to think of the state of the roads or anything else ; determined to brave all dangers, I felt adventurous enough to undertake this voyage through Asia.

It was five o'clock in the morning when I started on my journey in a hired carriage, accompanied by my faithful Helena. All the way was strewed with corpses of horses and camels. We encountered on our road bands of wandering Asiatic tribes very fierce-looking and armed from head to foot.

We reached Kars without any adventure whatever towards night. A crowd of red-fezzed Turks surrounded our carriage as soon as we arrived at the market-place, and stared at us in a rather hostile manner. We tried in vain to make ourselves understood and looked helplessly about us, when I suddenly perceived in the crowd Mr. Danilevski, a Russian officer whom I had known at Alexandropol. I greeted him with a radiant smile, for if he was not the rose, he had been near the rose. My heart was inclined to fail me when I asked for Sergy, and my discouragement was profound when Mr. Danilevski told me that my husband had already started for Erzeroum. Fate treated me with exasperating asperity, and his departure left me inconsolable ; I wondered what on earth I should do with myself in Kars ; fortunately Sergy had kept his lodging, and Mr. Danilevski proposed to escort us thither.

Our carriage stopped before a shabby little house, and we made our way up a dark and tortuous stairs to a room which had a dreary deserted appearance. A rickety table and two lame chairs formed almost all the furniture. The proprietor, an old Turk wearing an enormous white turban on his head, came in and welcomed me graciously, putting his hand to his heart and to his forehead. He offered me a little refreshment, which one of his wives brought in to me on a tray laden with all sorts of sweets; but what I wished for most at that moment was that my host would go away, for I was very weary and exhausted after the journey. When the old Turk had paid me all his oriental civilities and I had got rid of him, I lay down upon a mattress which had been spread on the floor, for there was no bed in the room, but nevertheless I was asleep almost before my head touched the pillow.

I woke up the next morning feeling very miserable, very desolate. Here I was alone in a land I knew not, among people whose language I could not speak.

How dark those days were! I wanted my husband so badly! oh, so very badly, and he was so desperately far away! In every letter Sergy announced his speedy return, and I was looking forward to the happy time that would unite us again. But he failed to arrive, and I felt myself the most forsaken and miserable of women. I was here within four walls, leading such a weary, grey life. I had nothing to fill up my time with and didn't know what to do with myself all day, and was in such a state of melancholy that I wished myself dead a thousand times. And in these moments of wretchedness, except Helena, I had not a human being to speak to; I was all alone in my misery! The few Russian ladies staying at Kars saw everything through black spectacles, which irritated me, and I preferred to shut myself up in my room in order to escape from the great trial of their sympathy and condolences; I felt myself far better alone. The ticking of the clock and the wind in the chimney were the only sounds that broke the silence around me. I hadn't talked for so long that I felt myself growing dumb. My life was made of nothing but privations; I reduced my own personal requirements to the strictest minimum: a plate of soup and gruel, that was our usual fare. Luckily a sort of torpor came over me which made me indifferent to my surroundings.

A long, heavy winter was drawing near. I felt the cold terribly; my broken window was stuffed up with paper instead of panes, of glass and the stove smoked atrociously, it was impossible to heat it on windy days.

Thus went day after day. At length a telegram came from Sergy. I was sure it was announcing his arrival and burst it open with a smile of triumph, but this smile very soon disappeared, for the telegram was an awful surprise, and shocked me dreadfully, saying that my husband was appointed governor-general of Erzeroum. For three weeks I had already lived this loathsome life and I had still many more weary weeks to pass before Sergy could return to me! What would I not give only to be able to go to him! Once the idea entered my mind, I communicated my wish to join him to Sergy, who treated the subject as an insane one, apprehending the state of the roads, quite impracticable in that season.

The epidemic of typhus that seemed softened down, broke out again, sweeping away whole villages. The death-list of my husband's companions of arms swelled. I was present at the funeral service officiated over by General Goubski, a good friend of ours, and was very painfully impressed by it; all who stood by were dry-eyed, his servant only seemed somewhat afflicted. I returned home in a most depressed state of mind. As I entered my room I perceived on the flat roof of the house opposite my lodgings an unusual animation; there was a table in the middle surrounded by officers and soldiers; I was told that it was a public sale of all the articles that had belonged to an inhabitant of that house, a Cossack colonel who had just been carried away by the typhus. On the other side of the roof the clothes of the deceased officer were burnt on a wood-pile. At the sight of that my nerves utterly gave way, and I was seized more than ever with a strong desire to rejoin my husband. I was so awfully anxious knowing him to be in Erzeroum, where the disease was at its height, that I could endure the separation, the uncertainty, the suspense no longer. My pillow that night was all moistened with tears. I lay in the dark, save for the ghastly light of the smouldering fire on the opposite roof, with my pessimistic thoughts to keep me company; I turned my face to the wall and sobbed hot, miserable sobs until I fell into an uneasy slumber.

The next morning my mind was made up and I despatched a telegram to my husband, telling him that, come what might, I would start for Erzeroum. It was all to no purpose again; Sergy showed himself the most inexhorable of husbands and wrote to me that I must listen to reason and wait patiently until his return after the ratification of the armistice. But I was not in a humour to listen to reason. "Wait patiently," I cried out with unusual heat in myself, "Patience be hanged! I'll go crazy if I don't go to Sergy; I cannot possibly sit still and wait!"

An officer who had just arrived from Erzeroum came on purpose to try to dissuade me from undertaking such a long and dangerous journey. He told me that even for him it had been awfully fatiguing; the roads were so horrible that the committee of the Red-Cross could not find it possible to send even one Sister of Mercy to Erzeroum. These descriptions of the state of the roads were certainly not encouraging, but nothing could shake my determination, I felt heroic and was prepared to brave all dangers and risk anything for Sergy's sake, and no human powers should prevent me from starting at the first opportunity.

Oh, joy! Oh, rapture! A telegram had just been brought

to me in which my husband announced that the preliminary
discussions were settled, and that peace was definitely signed.
It seemed almost too good to be true. I was happier than
words can tell. This piece of good news spread through the
town like wild fire. The cannons began to thunder, and the
church-bells pealed merrily all day.

Soon after, a messenger from Erzeroum brought me an
urgent letter from Sergy, telling me that he must remain in
Erzeroum until the evacuation of our troops. He advised
me to return to Tiflis until then, but instead of that I was
determined to start for Erzeroum and rejoin my husband. I
implored Mr. Danilevski to send me there with the first
military conveyance, but better fortune awaited me: Mr.
Danilevski was sent himself as a courier to Erzeroum, and
having taken compassion on me, he proposed to take me
with him in his post-cart, warning me that I must be ready
to start at any moment. As there was but small chance that
I would find a better occasion, I accepted gladly and began
hastily to prepare for our journey. There was only one
drawback, I couldn't take Helena with me, there was no
room for her in the post-cart. But I could not let such a
chance slip, and was willing even to sacrifice Helena. The
poor old woman entreated me with tears not to undertake this
mad journey, but it was no time to show weakness, my courage
seemed to have developed itself rapidly, for adversity is a
great teacher; distance was nothing to me. I trusted my star and
laughed at the most gigantic obstacles, and Helena had to submit to the painful necessity of letting me go. I did not allow
myself to sleep that night lest I should not be awake when
the hour came for starting. The next morning I received a
note from General Kousminski; that gentleman, whom I
had never known before, the chief of the military communications, extended a helping hand to me and proposed
to take me with Helena in his comfortable travelling-coach.
This was awfully generous of him and I hastened to accept
his offer thanking him profusely. I was so happy I would
have kissed everybody, but there was only Helena, so I
kissed her. Dreading that long voyage for Helena I told
her that I could very well do without her and proposed she
should return to Tiflis, but the dear old woman protested
hotly and said she was quite decided to fellow me anywhere.
It was all settled, we were to start next day at dawn. I
went to bed radiously happy at the thought that on the morrow
I should be far away from Kars, and closing my eyes, I
departed to sweet dreamland, seeing myself already in my
husband's loving arms.

CHAPTER XVI

ON MY WAY TO ERZEROUM

At seven o'clock in the morning General Kousminski was at my door, and I started bravely for Erzeroum, full of happy hopes and expectations. A crowd of Turks gathered round our carriage, wishing us Godspeed.

For the first mile or two all went well, but soon there was an accident ; the road was heavy and one of our horses slipped and fell down. It was not a good beginning, but we still had the worst before us, and a long way to go. We only made a hundred miles that day, the roads being shockingly bad, all covered with big stones over which we rumbled down, our carriage bouncing like a roasted chestnut. I tried to console myself with the thought that the way which led to "Paradise" was also covered with stones and strewed with pebbles. We stopped for the night in a small Turkish hamlet and continued our journey at dawn ; the worst bit of it now began. The road which led to the next station was a terribly bad one ; we had to abandon our comfortable coach and take a sledge. The road grew steeper with every mile ; it was a succession of hills, one after the other. Up and down we went all the time, but I felt a wonderful access of courage at the thought that each mile drew me nearer to Sergy. I could already feel myself flying into his arms. In descending a terribly steep hill our sledge was upset and bang—there we were in a deep ditch! Happily we had come to no harm, and after having assured ourselves that we had no broken limbs, we remounted into our sledge and travelled on till sunset. Dreading to be overtaken by darkness in the mountains, we made a halt in a village under the hospitable roof of Mr. Iliashenko, a Russian officer who took up his quarters there with some dozen soldiers. I was pretty well fagged out and hurried off to my room. It was so nice to sleep again like respectable people, between sheets, on our second night's resting-place.

A most dreadful surprise awaited me in the morning. I was roused by Helena coming to tell me that General Kousminski was summonded back to Kars at once. The prospects of so long a journey without my protector was the most distressing thing that could befall me. The worst of all was that we were in danger of dying of starvation, for we were not supplied with provisions. The next stage was known to be a very risky one, and I had to make all the way on horseback. Helena had set out before in a peasant's cart with an old military doctor who was also proceeding to Erzeroum, and to whose care General Kousminski had entrusted me. It was not nice at all to be left behind! Our horses were led up, but I couldn't manage to climb into the saddle which one of the soldiers had lent me; the clumsily tied arch would not hold and I slipped down continually. I was growing quite desperate, when it occurred to Mr. Iliashenko to propose for me his transport-van, an enormous vehicle with a team of six horses. I climbed into it tremblingly, and off we went.

After crossing a bridge thrown over the " Arax," we began to mount the slopes of the opposite bank, creeping along the high shelf roughly bedecked with fallen stones. Here we met a long caravan of camels; our horses took fright at them and drew back till we were almost on the very brink of a precipice, perhaps three hundred feet deep. Though Mr. Iliashenko made an attempt to hold me in I jumped out of the van and scrambled up the steep hill dabbling in the greasy mud flushed and breathless. Suddenly a happy idea struck Mr. Iliashenko, he proposed to me to mount his horse, saddled with a wide Cossack saddle. I settled myself down comfortably in it and went valiantly onwards. My anxious Helena awaited me at the next station. I was already beginning to feel General Kousminski's absence, and now learned what it was to be desperately hungry. I was as a ravenous wolf, seeking what I might devour, but we had only a meagre luncheon of bread and cheese. Here I had to bid good-bye to Mr. Iliashenko, who proposed for me to keep his horse as far as Erzeroum, thinking he might be useful to me in dangerous places, too bad for carriages; he gave me, besides, a Cossack.

After many difficulties, we succeeded in reaching the next station. We were obliged to advance very slowly; it took nearly seven hours to get there, although the distance was only sixteen miles, for there was no road as the Europeans generally understand it. Our horses plunged in the snow up to their necks. We met on the road groups of soldiers returning to Kars, who seemed greatly astonished to meet a woman in these dull parts. It was almost dark when we reached a tiny village, where we stopped for the night in a dirty dairy-hut, and slept in the company of my brave little horse who shared all my mishaps. I had to lie down on a mat stretched upon the floor, and being tired out, I slept the sleep of the just, when at dawn an enormous tongue, trying to find my face, woke me. I soon realised that the tongue was my horse's, who had freed himself from his bridle and came to bid me good-morning. When I got up I saw the snow falling heavily. We weren't able to start before the following day until the snow-storm had passed away. A young officer on his way to Kars took shelter under the same roof with us, which helped me to while away the weary hours of waiting-time.

We started at cock-crow, and soon discovered that we were in no path at all. There was no road, not even a track; our driver was compelled to clear a way for himself *à la grace de Dieu*, as best he could over heaps of snow. We came near falling into a hut through a big hole in the roof, which, instead of a chimney, gave passage to smoke. In comparison with the enormous heaps of snow on our untrodden road this hut presented but a mere mound. We were now in the most dangerous parts and followed a track winding round precipitous ravines. On the narrowest part of the cliff, just over a deep precipice scarcely three inches between the wheels and the brink, we met a field-battery and there was hardly room for our sledge to pass.

We intended to reach the village of Yus-Veran that day, which we succeeded in doing, though not without considerable difficulties, pinched with cold and very miserable. For the night we stopped at a wayside farm-house, a dingy, uninviting place. I was immediately surrounded by a group of native women, whose noses were adorned with metal rings. After they had lavished on me their *selamaleks*, Helena made me up an impromptu bed upon the bare boards covered with straw. To my disgust the room was invaded by sheep, pigs and goats, nevertheless I slept soundly.

After freeing my hair and clothing of the straw and chaff, we set off at sunrise. When we passed the village of Kepri-Kay, a pestilence-stricken Russian camp, I had to put my handkerchief up to my nose for the horrible smell which hung in the air.

From Kepri-Kay I made all the way on horseback, the roads being too rough for carriages. I felt tired, so very tired, and oh, so cold! The wind began to blow harder every minute, and made me nearly lose my equilibrium. On the top of a steep mountain we encountered General Avinoff, who was returning to Kars. Seeing me so lightly clad he made me put on his big fur boots, which had to be held up by bits of rope tied on by my Cossack attendants.

In the middle of the passage of Deve-Boynou we perceived, all of a sudden, a cloud of dust and saw a group of ferocious-looking horsemen, armed from head to foot, who came galloping up, shouting and gesticulating vehemently. I was horribly frightened, taking these individuals for highwaymen. The seeming brigands proved to be peaceful Turks sent by my husband with shawls and furs to bid me welcome. And I had expected my arrival would be such a surprise to Sergy! It was the young officer with whom I had passed the night under the same roof during the snow-storm who had betrayed my secret and announced my arrival to Sergy by wire.

It was nearly night when we perceived the tops of numerous minarets. My long journey had come to an end ; Erzeroum was reached at last.

As soon as we stopped before the house inhabited by my husband, I jumped out and bounded upstairs three steps at a time, and rushed into Sergy's study, my heart beating wildly. The next instant I was in my husband's strong arms, listening with rapture to his voice. "My wife, my love," he repeated constantly and smothered my face with kisses. It was no dream, I was resting on Sergy's breast and felt plainly that one can become mad with joy. What ages we had been apart, and now my darling husband was wholly given back to me. I nestled against him and the world seemed to me a pleasant place again and I forgot that I had ever been wet and cold and lonely. I have him now for good and all and always. The day of suffering was over !

CHAPTER XVII

ERZEROUM

IT is all cheery, homelike and delightful out here after my lonely life in Alexandropol and Kars. I began to take an interest in all my surroundings once more. When I waked up next morning my first thought was, "Can it be true, or is it only a dream that I have my husband to myself?" and I almost cried for joy when I was quite sure it was true.

March 16th.—Life in Erzeroum is an Elysium after my lonely life in Alexandropol and Kars. I am in such a radiant mood that I think everything I see is perfect. I have nothing left to wish for and am able to allow myself the luxury of a piano, a lovely saddle-horse, and all sorts of nice things. Our house is one of the biggest in Erzeroum; it looks palatial after my lodgings in Alexandropol and Kars. From the top of our terrace-roof one can see the whole town from a bird's eye view, with its sixty-six minarets rising to the sky, its imposing citadels and floating flags over different Consulates. In the far distance there is the encircling chain of the Palantek mountains, with glittering snow-peaks. The houses are low, with balustrades round them like those in Biblical pictures. There are about 15,000 inhabitants in Erzeroum; the majority are Turks, then come Greeks and Armenians. After sunset the town looks gloomy, only soldiers can be seen in the streets. As for the population, it is represented only by a multitude of errant dogs, the usual street-sweepers of Turkish towns. I hear every evening the voices of the muezzins (Turkish priests) calling to prayer: "*Alla huac bar, Alla huac bar!*" (God is great.)

I had a nightmare last night, and with a loud scream I woke up. I dreamt that Sergy was ordered to the war and clung to him, fearing to be parted again. Sergy held me close to him and kissed away my tears, assuring me that nothing and nobody could part us now, and that I shall be with him always, night and day. He succeeded at length in calming my fears. I felt safe again under his wing and fell peacefully asleep.

March 17th.—My arrival caused the greatest excitement among the Christian inhabitants of Erzeroum. They are all singing my praises for having come out here by those shocking roads, and they say that I certainly deserve a medal as a reward for my bravery.

Was it curiosity to see a European woman, or was it a desire to show devotedness to the Russians? Perhaps both reasons together made visitors overflow our drawing-room. All the big wigs of the town came to pay their respects to me. To-day, for instance, I received the family of George Effendi, one of the richest Greek merchants of Erzeroum. His wife wore a splendid silk dress interwoven with gold and silver, and a small velvet cap adorned with gold spangles and tassels. Her daughter-in-law, a woman of fourteen, of childish stature and appearance, was obliged to keep the most absolute silence in her presence, whilst her own daughter chatted in very bad French all the while. After them came the family of Antoine-Effendi Schabaniane, the most noted Armenian inhabitant of the town, who had come to present his respects to me the day before.

The native Christian women, being under the dominion of Turkish rule, find themselves here in such a state of degradation, that their husbands consider it unsuitable to appear with them anywhere. Antoine Effendi speaks very good English for a foreigner; he has been a correspondent of the *Times* during the Russo-Turkish war. Other guests came in quick succession, amongst them the French Consul, M. Gilbert, with his wife, a charming young woman, so bright and winsome. Mme. Gilbert seems very friendly; she has put her books and music at my disposal. We propose to see each other often, and to take long walks together. During the Gilbert's visit an old Pasha came in. That ancient fanatic, more than eighty years of age, didn't venture to look into my face, but kept his eyes fixed chastely on the carpet, murmuring *sotto voce* something I didn't understand. Mme. Gilbert, who speaks Turkish, explained that the aged mussulman was making oriental compliments to me. Just before dinner an Australian doctor came in, holding a stick and a Scotch cap in his hand. That young physician is summoned away to Constantinople and has come to ask Sergy for a passport. He is the son of a rich cattle-breeder residing in Melbourne. I saw on his arm a white band with a red crescent and the letters S.H.S. on it, indicating that he belonged to the "Stafford House Society." There is a great number of European doctors attending the Turks in Erzeroum; nearly all the nations have sent their contingents of medical men. These Christians in the Turkish service produce rather a painful impression on me.

A telegraphic office is just opened. No telegram can be sent without my husband's permission as censor. Heaps of telegraphic despatches are brought to him every day. The first telegram was sent by Sergy to Ismail-Pasha, the former

governor of Erzeroum, in which he congratulated the Turkish
warrior on the inauguration of the telegraph.

March 18th.—To-day my husband gave a grand dinner in
honour of a dozen officers belonging to the Turkish army
who happen to be staying here at present. A military band
announced the arrival of our Turkish guests by a loud march.
The dinner was a very gay and long one, consisting of twelve
courses. Our guests, not being fanatics, did ample honour
to the champagne. I sat opposite Sergy, between Houssein-
Pasha and Daniel-Bek, a smart young officer of the Turkish
staff, *aide-de-camp* to the celebrated Moukhtar-Pasha. This
young Turk wore his fez jauntily on one side, and looked
quite European, having been educated in Paris. He has
been military attaché at the Turkish Embassy at St.
Petersburg for three years and speaks perfect French and
Russian. Daniel-Bek surveyed me with appraising eyes and
set himself to be charming to me all through the meal. I
found him most amusing, and was soon chatting away to
him as if I had known him for years. Houssein-Pasha teased
me all through dinner by insinuating that his subordinate
was paying court to me too openly.

March 19th.—It is Sunday to-day. We have attended
mass at the Greek Cathedral. Though it is situated far
away from the centre of the town, we proceeded thither on
foot, escorted by Hamid-Bey, an officer attached to the
person of my husband, a dragoman, a Turkish zaptieh, and
about a dozen Cossacks. The attitude of the Armenian
inhabitants that we met on our way was most cordial and
sympathetic towards us, but the Mussulmans showed open
hostility by the glances full of hatred that they cast upon us.
By these glances it was easy to distinguish the Turks from
the Armenians, notwithstanding the similitude of their
garments.

The Greek Cathedral was erected in honour of St. George
the Conqueror. There is a throne in the middle for the
Archbishop who said mass, arrayed in his sacerdotal vestments; he wore on his head an immense mitre adorned with
the Byzantine Eagle. The prayers were sung in Greek with
a very nasal sound. Our Russian officers have made a
present to this church of the image of St. George with the
following dedication: " In commemoration of the sojourn of
the Russian army in Erzeroum in the year 1878."

We didn't remain till the end of the service, for on that
same morning a requiem was sung in the Armenian Cathedral
for the repose of the soul of General Shelkovnikoff, my
husband's predecessor. I aroused much curiosity and
attention at church, where an enormous congregation had
gathered. The Cathedral appeared very imposing with all
the wax lights and chandeliers ablaze, and the Metropolitan

looked magnificent, clad in a robe that was stiff with gold embroideries. About a hundred chanters, in black and red surplices, sang melodious hymns ; from time to time choristers shook big silver disks with much noise. The loud voice of the Metropolitan was suddenly drowned by a deafening uproar above in the choirs. A loud squabble arose among the Armenian women, who protested loudly at seeing me down in the nave of the church where they were not allowed to penetrate. As soon as the service was over the Metropolitan delivered a long sermon of which we couldn't make out a word. It proved to be an ovation in favour of the Russians, as well as a demonstration against the Turks. I fear that he will have to pay dearly for his eloquence as soon as we leave Erzeroum. After service the Metropolitan invited us to have a cup of tea. During our visit Sergy asked him the reason of the women's screams in the choirs, and he explained to us that it was quite natural that the liberty given to European women had created an animosity between these recluses, who protested against it in that noisy way.

We have spent the afternoon in paying calls in a victoria belonging to General Heimann, the only carriage in all Erzeroum. After our visit to Mme. Gilbert, we went to George Effendi, where we were received with effusive cordiality. As soon as we were seated on a low divan, Turkish coffee without sugar, and different sorts of preserves were served to us. Oriental politeness required us to take a very small quantity of jam and to drink a whole glass of water after it. When we got up to say good-bye, George Effendi threw upon my shoulder a shawl of great price that I had just admired, and his daughter undid her beautiful necklace of heavy coins and clasped it round my neck. Of course I refused both presents outright, but I was told afterwards that it was an Oriental custom to offer as a present the object just praised. I will certainly abstain from admiring anything in the future, because the natives say directly : " It is yours, take it ! " and that is very embarrassing.

When we got home we found an old Turk at our door who held a paper in his hand. He was robbed the previous night and came to complain to my husband. I had hardly time to take off my hat when three French sisters of mercy were announced. After that came the Persian Consul, accompanied by his interpreter. The Consul is a honeytongued personage, who made graceful speeches to me ; flattering phrases came so readily to his lips, and I did not particularly like him..

March 20th.—My riding habit of dark-blue cloth and a jacket made after the style of a Turkish uniform, have just been brought to me. When I appeared for the first time in that costume, Hamid-Bey saluted me in military fashion because the sleeves of my habit were made with gold embroideries like those of a pasha.

I spend much of my time in the saddle, accompanied by my husband and a large suite. Such freedom given to the young "giaour," is incomprehensible to the inhabitants of Erzeroum, who find it very improper. I have stirred up a stormy discussion in many Christian families ; newly married women begin to protest against the ancient order of things, and the old ones, on the contrary, faithful to the ancient traditions, show themselves indignant against European liberal customs.

The Persian Consul has sent me this morning a large basket of fresh oranges and lemons, which came from Trebizonde, and Erzeroum is still buried in snow. I had another present to-day, a splendid roasted turkey-cock sent to me by the wife of the President of the Turkish Municipal Council, who warned me of her visit, so as to be quite certain of meeting no man in our house.

This evening about twenty doctors of Russian, English and Turkish nationalities came to debate upon the indifferent sanitary conditions of the town. During this winter about 1500 Russian soldiers have been buried here ; their graves were of such small depth that when the melting of the snows had begun, many tombs were exposed to view and it was necessary to fill them up once more. Doctor Remmert, the chief physician of the army of the Caucasus, sent up to Erzeroum in order to inspect the military hospitals, was agreeably surprised to see the town so clean and so well arranged. The innumerable canals have been cleaned out and the slaughter-houses banished from the town. The heaps of snow, of more than three metres in height, that encumbered the streets, are completely cleared away, The inhabitants, seeing the Russian workmen occupied with the improvements of the general state of health of their own town say : "How funny these Russians are to spend so much money for an affair that a month later nature would do for nothing ! "

In returning from our ride this morning we saw a group of mollahs assembled before our house. They had come to complain against the Russian police that had arrived to take an inventory of all their goods, and had begun to make an account of their wives and cattle, it proved to be the Sanitary Commission who were obtaining necessary information. My husband took immediate measures to calm the population.

The Armenian-Catholic Archbishop, Melchisedec, called before dinner. Though he is suavity itself, there is something about him which gives me a feeling of distrust. He pretends to be very happy that the Russians still occupy Erzeroum,

and dreads our departure, fearing cruel treatment from the
Turks towards the Christian population.

March 21st.—My husband introduced an American clergy-
man to me this morning, who is working as a missionary in
Erzeroum. He has come to ask Sergy to give him a large
supply of bread and money, but Sergy said that he could
give him but a small sum. The Russian government has, in
fact, assigned a monthly subsidy for the poor population of
Erzeroum, not only for the Protestants, but for all the
indigent, independent of their religion or nationality.

Later on came Ibrahim Bey, one of the dignitaries of the
town of Khnyss, who had to proceed further on to Ernzindjane,
the head-quarters of Ismail Pasha. This Turk kissed the
lappets of my husband's coat slavishly, and drew backwards
towards the door, putting his hand to his forehead and heart.
As an example of Turkish barbarism I shall note an exploit
that he related to Sergy and of which he boasted, a truly
disgusting story. At Khnyss some Kurdes dug up the
corpse of a Russian soldier and stripped him of his clothes
and boots. As a punishment for their sacrilegious misdeed,
Ibrahim Pasha obliged the Kurdes to eat these boots, chopped
up into small bits.

March 25th.—On account of ill-health, General Loris-
Melikoff, by his own request, was released from the command
of the main army, which was given over to General Heimann.

The contents of the political telegrams received to-day are
rather alarming ; England decidedly plots a war afresh, and
a rumour of the approaching breaking of peace has spread in
the town. We must be prepared that the Turks will assail
us at any moment.

This morning a soldier of the light infantry, belonging to
the Malakani sect, desiring to embrace the Orthodox religion,
came to beg me to stand God-mother to him. This soldier
made a vow to be baptised if he escaped war safely ; he has
been in all the fights without having received the slightest
wound, and thinks it proper now to fulfil his promise, I of
course consented willingly.

March 26th.—The baptism of the Malakan soldier took
place to-day in the Armenian cathedral, which was so crowded
that the "cavasses" had to clear a way for us to pass. The
Metropolitan officiated in Greek and addressed himself
continually to me in that language. As I couldn't understand
a word, I didn't know how to answer and what to do, and was
very comic, I am sure, in repeating aloud the Greek phrases
that he dictated to me. Mr. Popoff, an officer of the light-
infantry, acted as God-father. Our God-son had to be completely undressed, which took place behind a screen, and
then brought in to us covered only with a white sheet.
I didn't know where to cast my eyes whilst he was being

dipped in the font, which was no other than the big soup-boiler of the brigade to which our God-son belonged. I did not dare to glance at Sergy and pressed my lips together, trying not to shake with laughter, and drew a breath of profound relief, when I realised that the ceremony of baptism was over.

From church we went to visit the bride of Egueshi, our Armenian interpreter. The walls of her sitting-room were all hung up with her drawings, amongst which we saw the portrait of our Emperor painted by our hostess in the space of two days, during the time when the Christian inhabitants of Erzeroum expected their town to be invaded by the Russians. Dreading to see our soldiers enter their homes by force, in order to plunder them, they put out big wooden crosses before their houses in the hope of mollifying the hearts of our soldiers, trusting to escape thus from the general fate. Our hostess told us candidly that she concealed that picture when the Turkish officials visited her house, but during our visit the portrait of His Majesty occupied the place of honour.

To-day my husband has ordered Shefket Bey, one of the oldest members of the Ottoman officers left in Erzeroum, to fire a cannon from the citadel at twelve o'clock precisely, employing for that purpose a Turkish gun and Turkish powder. Ten of our soldiers have been appointed for that special service by Sergy. Shefket Bey was obliged to submit, swallowing his wrath. He took it with outward meekness, whilst his eyes gave a flash, and answered humbly, " *Pek-ei.*" (I'll obey you.)

Amongst the Turkish telegrams that my husband received this morning there was one to Ismail Pasha with a complaint against Sergy for having forbidden the Ottoman flag to be hoisted over the tower of the principal citadel of Erzeroum. In answer to this telegram Ismail Pasha gave orders that every command given by the Russian authorities should be strictly executed.

Among the representatives of the different churches here it is only the Mussulman "moufti" who has not presented himself to my husband. Yesterday evening a group of Turkish inhabitants came to ask permission to hoist their flag on Fridays, but Sergy told them that they interfered with things that didn't concern them, and that it was their "moufti" who had to solicit this permission. The "moufti" arrived to-day accompanied by a great number of white-bearded and white-turbaned "imams" (Mahometan priests) dressed in long furred robes. This time my husband has given them the permission to hoist their standard on Fridays, and has been warmly thanked for it.

We had two interesting guests at dinner to-day, a young

Persian prince, nephew of the Shah, who serves as dragoon officer in the Russian army, and is attached to the police-master of Erzeroum for the present, and Daniel Effendi, a Turkish bureaucrat, who was sent to Constantinople last year as member of the new Turkish Parliament. After dinner, as we sipped our coffee on the roof-terrace, Egueshi, with a rather scattered expression, came up to Sergy and led him away, whispering something into his ear. Later on I was informed that there had just been an earthquake, and as the second shock is generally stronger than the first one, Egueshi came to advise my husband to make us all come out into the street. Some years before there had been such a terrible earthquake in Erzeroum that the inhabitants were forced to camp out in the open air for a whole month. After to-day's earthquake one of the walls in the citadel has partly fallen down, and a great number of houses have cracked. It's very strange that I haven't felt anything at all, not the slightest shock. In order to prevent accidents in Erzeroum, where earthquakes are frequent, big beams are put into the masonries of nearly all the buildings. Two great shocks and some slight ones have succeeded each other during the night, and this time I felt them. It's my first experience of an earthquake, and my last one, I hope.

March 28th.—The weather being comparatively fine, we have taken a long walk this afternoon in the direction of the Tap-Dagh, a beautiful valley situated at the foot of a high mountain from whence one discovers the source of the Euphrates, the famous Biblical river. Behind the Tap-Dagh, according to Armenian traditions, Adam's Paradise was situated, with the two rivers mentioned in the descriptions of Elysium. This is where fate has brought me. The scenery is said to be exquisite, the vegetation luxurious.

The future is already brightened. The terms of the treaty of peace have finally been signed at San-Sebastiano on the 1st of February. This glorious piece of news has reached us only to-day in this out-of-the-world place.

April 1st.—Mr. Kamsarakan, our Prefect of the Police, is a very jolly fellow, fond of playing jokes on his friends. To-day, for instance, he has invited to dinner all his acquaintances belonging to the Russian colony whom he met in the street, promising them a splendid Russian cabbage-pie. His guests rejoiced beforehand at the thought of partaking of that famous national dish, but as they began to arrive, there was no sign whatever of any preparations for dinner, and Kamsarakan's servant announced that his master was out and would probably not dine at home to-day. The guests' countenances expressed the blankest dismay ; being far from their father-land no one had remembered that the first of April was the day of traditional mystifications. As for

Kamsarakan, he went at the same time to Mr. Eritzeff's, one of his invited guests, and asked the servant to give him something to eat. He devoured all the supper, and when poor Eritzeff returned home dismissed from Kamsarakan's house, he found himself deprived both of his dinner and his supper.

April 22nd.—The Catholics celebrate to-day their Palm-Sunday. We went to their cathedral where Capuchin monks, in brown garments, wearing a cord instead of a girdle, officiated. After mass we visited the school directed by the French Sisters of Mercy. The Turks had shown themselves very uncivil to these Sisters when they arrived at Erzeroum, but they got accustomed to them afterwards, and begin now to esteem the good sisters for their attendance on the sick and wounded.

April 4th.—Our Tartar servant Housnadine has arrived from Kars. He has made that journey in sixteen days, being upset several times. Housnadine has brought me different indispensable articles. Until now my wardrobe was in a shocking condition; a small portmanteau contained all my belongings.

We walked down to the ramparts this afternoon with the Gilberts, and rambled over the old fort, surrounded by high massive walls through the embrasures of which cannons are to be seen During all these eight years of their sojourn in Ezeroum the Gilberts are entering this citadel for the first time, it had been *terra prohibita* to all strangers up till now. Pushing forward we climbed up a high tower by a narrow winding staircase; my long habit was dreadfully in the way and I stumbled over it continually. The citadel is now occupied by the Russian regiment of Bakou and three or four scores of Turkish soldiers entrusted to watch over the warehouse, who presented arms to my husband. There is a great bond of sympathy between these Osmanlies and our soldiers; though not one of them can speak a word of Turkish, they explained themselves quite easily in a highly fantastic language of their own. Maksoud Effendi, the chief of this small Turkish detachment bewitched us by his aimiability and led us to admire the edifice of *Chifket-Minaret*, a beautiful Arabian building of the ninth century, with two formidable pillars of the Byzantine style at the entrance. According to what the Armenians say a saint of their nationality reposes in that minaret, but the Musselmans pretend that it is the burial place of one of their most celebrated " imams." For the moment this mausoleum, as well as the innermost recesses of that edifice, are encumbered with guns, bombs, shells and other objects of but little religious character.

April 6th.—The officers of the rifle battalion invited us to come and take tea in their camp. At our approach a military band struck up a march. The musicians were surrounded by a red-fezzed mob, and the natives, generally lank and thin, looked contemptible little pieces of humanity beside our tall portly soldiers. We were invited to dismount and entered a great tent where we sat down at a long table. Our hosts who were awfully nice to us, proposed a little refreshment and drank our health.

April 7th—Our landlord, an Italian chemist named Ricci, has transformed himself into a famous physician here, his daughters go to the French school and wear " tchartchaffs," when they start out of doors. Eleonora the eldest Signorina Ricci, came in this afternoon to announce to me the visit of the wife of the President of the Town Council ; I ran to the window and saw an *araba* (a Turkish chariot,) covered inside with red cloth approaching our house. The araba was drawn by a pair of beautiful white bullocks, a red-fezzed boy of about twelve was following behind mounted on a tiny pony, and two male servants were running on each side of the vehicle. When the carriage stopped at our door, three women, wrapped up in black veils, stepped out of the chariot and entered our drawing-room. The President's wife, an outrageously painted young woman, was followed by her little son and two female slaves, a white one and a negress ; Turkish ladies of fashion never go out without their attendants. The negress in her scarlet vestment with large printed black flowers reminded me of "*Asucena*" the *Troubadour's* mother. She has been brought over from Stamboul where her mother still resides in the Sultan's harem. This black Venus was bought by the President's wife for the sum of a thousand francs. Through Eleonora as interpreter, I was able to carry on a conversation with my Turkish guests, in which harem life was the only topic. The Mussulman women are incapable of seeing anything beyond it, their souls are asleep, they are dull and unimaginative, without any keen interests, and deplorably ignorant ; most of them never turn the leaves of a book or trace a word upon paper. The President's wife told me that she was surnamed " Blue Hanum " on account of her blue eyes. She paid me a lot of compliments and appeared very astonished that my husband allowed me to associate with men and that he permitted me to appear before them unveiled. She plagued me with childish questions about my sentiments towards my husband, and in her turn she related to me the sensations that she experienced at the time when her husband had two wives ; both consorts cried bitterly each night when their Pasha gave his preference to the rival spouse. She told me with a smile of satisfaction that her rival died a few years ago, leaving her an undivided sovereignty over her husband. Harem slavery begins at the age of twelve, till then Turkish girls are as free as European children, but on her twelfth birthday the girl becomes a woman, she adopts the "tchartchaff" and is condemned to see the world darkly through a veil. Henceforth she is a prisoner in the harem.

The negress slave proposed a nigger-boy to me, when suddenly tbe idea struck her that I should wish to appropriate her little son, and she hastened to warn me that he was a mulatto and not a thoroughbred nigger ; she told me that I could order one from Diarbekir, and that he wouldn't cost more than five hundred francs, and added that I could also procure for myself from that same place a splendid young negress who could speak several languages, but she warned me charitably that these learned negresses were often unprincipled, and dangerous to keep, on account of their propensity to seduce the master of the house! I replied laughingly that in that case I should certainly prefer to buy a nigger boy. When coffee was brought in, the negress and the slave sat down on their heels upon the floor to sip it, they daren't do it otherwise in the presence of their mistress. After a while the negress asked permission to go and smoke in the corridor ; it was only a pretext to have a peep at Sergy and his aide-de-camp, who were just then in the next room. In leaving our house the President's wife, who had severely, remonstrated with the negress for her improper curiosity revealed to her by her little son, could not resist the temptation of stealing a glance at the imprisoned gentlemen through the chink of the door. She invited me to come and see her soon, promising to show me the best dancing girls (bayadères) in Erzeroum.

Now, to turn to the other side of the medal, I must say that during our stay at Erzeroum our roses weren't entirely without thorns. The typhus-fever continued to rage, and mowed down whole ranks of our soldiers. Every day there were new victims. The Russian cemetery is quite full now, and we are obliged to bury our soldiers in a common grave. Nearly every morning I see sinister waggons carrying away the unfortunate victims of this dreadful epidemic to their last dwelling-place. I shudder when I think of it!

We are warned that a fanatic society under the name of "Avengers" (Christian haters) is newly organised, and that we run great risks during our rides through the bazaars and Turkish quarters.

April 8th.—To-day we revisited the camp of the light-infantry, desiring to see my godson, the newly converted *Melakani* soldier, who by the way, is several years older than his godmother. I was horrified to hear that he had just been sent to the hospital. Presently, amongst our soldiers, the comparitively healthy ones are only those who have recovered already from the typhus-fever ; it is pitiful to see their pale and meagre faces. Mr. Popoff told me that the sight of a

Russian woman would help them to forget, for a moment at least, that they find themselves in a strange and hostile land, so far away from their native country.

April 12th.—To-day is Maundy-Thursday. The Catholic Archbishop has invited us to assist at the ceremony of the washing of the feet of twelve little boys belonging to the best Armenian families of Erzeroum. These children dressed in long white garments and wearing crowns of flowers on their heads, had taken their seats on a long bench, covered with red cloth. After having each one bared the right foot, one of the priests poured some water into a golden dish and the Archbishop, in rich sacerdotal vestments, knelt before each of them on one knee, took the bared foot, washed it and dried it with a towel. After this he offered each child a lighted wax-taper and a box of bonbons tied with a green ribbon.

In the evening a service was held in the dwelling of General Heimann, who was in Kars at the present moment, danger-ously ill. The reading aloud of the twelve Evangelists by our Russian priest, in this foreign land, to a mass of Russian officers each holding a wax-light, produced a great impression upon me. After the second Evangilist an officer came into the room, a telegram in his hand, and gave it over to my husband who perused the despatch with an air of consternation, and whilst it passed from hand to hand, I noticed the troubled expression of the faces about me. This telegram announced the decease of General Heimann, carried off in five days by the typhus. Is then the prediction of one of our friends going to be realised ? He said that we should all die here, and that none of us should see his native land again ; the turn of each one is the only thing unknown to us. After the reading of the twelve Evangelists, a requiem was sung for the peace of the soul of General Heimann.

April 13th.—The Russian colony at Erzeroum decided to celebrate the Easter-night ceremony with great pomp ; a rather difficult thing to do in this Mussulman country. An attempt was made to illuminate the streets leading to the Greek cathedral, but the inhabitants hadn't the slightest idea how to do it, and it was our house only which was lighted with lanterns taken from "mosques." When my husband had put on his uniform and red ribbon, we proceeded to church on horseback, in complete obscurity, with a dozen Cossacks and zaptiehs to protect us. It is very sad to feel oneself in a Mussulman country on this great Christian feast. Nothing recalls to mind the customary animation of that holy night ; the streets are so dark and silent ! On approaching the cathedral we saw a detachment of Russian soldiers standing under arms. The church was illuminated *a giorno* and filled with officers, soldiers and Christian inhabitants, the latter take off their fezzes now in church, which they didn't dare to do before the entry of the Russians into Erzeroum. In a corner of the cathedral lay heaps of painted eggs and Easter-cakes brought by our soldiers to be blessed. Cannons were fired; the first shot was at midnight precisely. After mass, my husband invited all the Russian colony to supper. Our guests left us only at five o'clock in the morning.

April 14th.—On waking this morning I heard men's voices singing in chorus "Christ is risen!" It was a group of Cossacks who had come to congratulate us with Easter-Sunday. Later on, from ten o'clock, visitors of different nationalities continued to arrive until dinner-time.

It is reported that the Turks circulate exaggerated rumours about the pitiful state of our troops and say that the moment for revenge against the Christians has come. What trouble-some times we are living through, good God!

The Mussulmans had the custom of firing guns through the whole night during the eclipses of the moon, but my husband has forbidden this now, in order not to frighten the Christians.

April 17th.—It is the birthday of our Emperor to-day. After a Te Deum in the Greek cathedral, there was a great review of our troops on the square; four military bands executed our national hymn, whilst our soldiers acclaimed their sovereign enthusiastically. The square was crowded with lookers-on. Egueshi caught the drift of a dialogue between an Armenian and a Turk; the Turk announced, pointing to the citadel from whence discharges were heard: "The Russians are unable," said he, "To frighten us with their cannon-shots, one sees directly that these cannons are not Turkish ones for they make too little noise."

"You are much mistaken," broke in the Armenian, "They are precisely Turkish cannons, and it is Maksoud Effendi who has procured the gunpowder."

"Ah! now I see the reason why we are able to hear these cannon-shots, for if they were Russian guns, they would not be heard at all from the citadel," concluded the Osmanle, not a bit disconcerted.

In the afternoon the members of the Town Council came in to congratulate my husband on the occasion of to-day's solemnity; their President, Mehamet-Ali-Bey was accompanied by a group of white-turbaned "mollahs." Sergy made a long speech to them, translated by Egueshi. He thanked them for their activity, for the order that they maintained in the town, and promised them to express to Ismail-Pasha his gratitude for having chosen such worthy members for the municipal council; he ended his speech by telling them that the Russians occupied Erzeroum by the will of God, and that it was the duty of all the inhabitants to submit to their destiny and to strictly obey our authorities. My husband made a rich present to Ali-Effendi in the name of the Russian government; he gave him a beautiful gold snuff-box, adorned with diamonds which cost 4000 francs.

I didn't go out to-day, having to superintend the preparations for the official dinner that Sergy gave to the Russian and Turkish authorities. The table was richly decorated with flowers and fruits brought from Tartoum, where they are admirably preserved; last year's pears are still quite fresh. At about six o'clock the musicians mounted on to the roof of the opposite house by a ladder against the wall one after the other; street-lads climbed up after them in such numbers that one was obliged to turn them out for fear of the roof falling in. Another band was placed in the street just under our balcony. From my window I saw the Persian Consul approaching on his beautiful white Arab; in a few moments our drawing-room was full of guests. My husband placed himself at the centre of the table, having on one side the Metropolitan and on the other the Armenian Archbishop; I was sitting opposite. The dinner was very animated, much champagne was drunk. Maksoud-Effendi consumed this stimulating beverage more than anyone; he embraced his neighbour, Prince Tchavtchavadze, and exclaimed in a transport of tenderness: "If war had continued, I would have killed you, perhaps, but now I kiss you with all my heart!" My husband gave the first toast and drank to the health of our Emperor; everybody stood up crying out "Hurra!" After that Sergy exclaimed: "I drink to the duration of peace between Russia and the friendly powers, France, Turkey and Persia, as well as to the health of their representatives here present!"

The Metropolitan pronounced a long discourse in Armenian that Egueshi translated to us; he said that the Emperor of Russia had always been regarded with deep love and respect by the whole Christian population of Asia, and that he, consequently, proposed a toast to the health of our Monarch in the name of all the Armenians. Ali-Effendi, taking offence, proposed to drink the health of our Emperor in the name of all the Asiatic nationalities, without distinction of religion, as he could not admit any difference between them. The Metropolitan, wishing to expiate his awkwardness, held up his glass to Ali-Effendi, but the offended Osmanlie feigned not to notice it, and removed his glass. Never will the Koran and the Gospel, evidently, live in peace in Asia! Mons. Gilbert, in his turn, after having spoken of the sympathy that existed between France and Russia, exclaimed, "Long live Russia!" and my husband replied immediately, "Long live France!" The Catholic Archbishop said something very eloquent but rather incomprehensible. The last toast was drunk by Sergy to the prosperity of Erzeroum, whatever fate should befall it. After dinner we went out on the balcony and listened to the different *potpourris* on Russian national airs executed by our military bands. At our appearance hundreds of voices exclaimed, "Long live the Emperor of Russia!" It was night when the musicians returned to their camp, playing marches all the time. They were followed by a throng of street boys who carried their cymbals and their rolls of music.

April 18th.—On waking this morning I saw the street covered with snow, which continued to fall in big flakes, and it is spring in Russia now! Country, people, climate, everything is so gloomy out here!

In the afternoon I went on horseback to return my visit to the wife of the President of the Town Council. Mme. Gilbert followed with Helena in a cart procured by our ambulance people. Eleonora had entreated her father to allow her to accompany us, but he refused outright, saying that if the question was of visiting an Armenian or Greek family, he would have willingly given his consent, but he would certainly never allow his daughter to enter a Turkish harem.

The President's wife met us at the entrance door and led us into her private apartments, furnished in Turkish style with low sofas all round the walls, on which sat, cross-legged, five Bayadères dressed in green and pink robes; their faces were painted white and red, and their nails dyed with henna juice. After a slight collation, which consisted of coffee and different sorts of preserves served in silver vases, the Bayadères began to dance, clinking castanettes. Four music-girls sat on the floor and played the daira, a sort of cithern. Brandy and champagne was offered to the Bayadères to put them into still more depraved spirits, and they began to dance unlike anything I had ever seen. The master of the house who sat in the next room with a score of male friends left his door ajar, and the sight of these men inflamed the dancing-girls still more, and they took such liberties that I didn't dare to raise my eyes from the carpet. When the Bayadères approached Helena, making indecent gestures, my poor old nurse pushed them back, her eyes flashing indignantly. Her speechless horror amused me enormously, and it was a mercy that from the place where I sat I hadn't Mme. Gilbert to exchange glances with, or I couldn't have remained serious. Our hostess seemed astonished at Helena's repulse and asked why she did it, and if it was contrary to her religion? Anyone who reads this will suppose that I am describing a house of ill fame, but, on the contrary, it is one of the most respectable houses in Erzeroum, and all these enormities are of the exigencies of harem life. The little son of our hostess, aged twelve, an awfully vicious brat, was incapable of concealing the ardour with which he was gazing upon the contortions of the Bayadères ; he hardly heard when he was spoken to.

Dinner was served *à la franca*, but there were knives and forks for us only, our hosts did very well without them, helping themselves with their fingers. The meal consisted of a score of meat and sweet dishes intermingled. I did not know what I was eating, but was compelled to taste everything, to refuse would be a great offence to our hostess, and I resigned myself to swallow all sorts of nasty things. Our hostess, according to the custom of the country, tasted every dish before it was served to her guests, in order to prove that it wasn't poisoned. During the meal the son of our hostess behaved abominably. He tyrannised over the poor little mulatto, the son of the negress slave, and was awfully rude to his mother, daring to call her in our presence *kiopek*, which means dog in Turkish. After dinner a large copper basin was brought in to wash our hands, after which the dances were renewed. The face of one of the Bayadères was completely veiled. I was told that this woman had formerly been a prostitute. She is married now, but all the same she is obliged to cover her face in remembrance of her bad life. When the time came to bid good-bye to our hostess, I wanted to give a *bakshish* (a tip) to the dancing-girls, but she objected to this and told me that I had far better invite them to come and dance in our house. I promised to do it one of these days. I could not possibly imagine that our hostess's son, the perverse little despot, could show himself such a gallant cavalier towards me. In 'parting he wanted absolutely to kiss me, and declared that at first he had detested the Russians, but now he had seen me, he liked me so much that his most ardent wish was that the Russians would remain for ever in Erzeroum.

April 23rd.—To-day is the feast of the sapper battalion. Their chief, Prince Toumanoff, begged me to assist at the Te Deum performed on their camp, telling me that my presence would be a great treat to his officers and soldiers. I couldn't refuse his friendly invitation, and proceeded on horseback to the camp. When prayers were over, the officers invited me to partake of their repast served in a big tent. After Prince Toumanoff had drunk my health, I took my courage in both hands and gave a toast to the hospitality of our amiable hosts. An awful uproar arose, the officers called for three cheers for me and the soldiers cried " Hurra," throwing their caps in the air. A small bazaar was just opposite the tent, with nuts, plums, apples and different sweetmeats ; Sergy bought the whole contents and dealt them out to the soldiers.

At seven o'clock the sappers gave a banquet in the apartments of the deceased General Heimann. I begged for Mme. Gilbert to be invited to that dinner, so as not to be the only woman at that festival. Again numerous toasts were given. Doctor Reitlinger, a thorough Dorpat student, stood on a chair and gave a long discourse in praise of Erzeroum. When he had ended, Prince Toumanoff exclaimed that he had forgotten to mention in his panegyrics the most important point of all, namely, that Paradise happened to be only a few miles off from here. Everybody laughed, for the neighbourhood of Paradise was not perceptible in Erzeroum as we dabbled in mud and snow close by this Paradise, whilst it was already spring-time in Russia.

When we got home I went directly to bed, and was just falling asleep when the sounds of a march playing under our windows awakened me. It proved to be a group of sapper officers who had come to serenade me for having taken part at their festival.

April 30th.—I have been unwell all these days and was obliged to remain in bed. Yesterday I felt well enough to leave my room, and Mme. Gilbert hastened to call on me. She threw her arms round my neck and nearly strangled me with kisses, having been awfully anxious about me, for when one falls ill in this blessed country, one is sent beforehand *ad patres*.

April 31st.—I called to-day on Signora Lavini, a curious specimen of a Turkified European woman. She is the wife of an Italian druggist, who has lived here for many years. Their daughter was born and educated in Erzeroum, of which one is easily aware by her moral development. Nevertheless her parents seem very proud of their offspring ; they called her up to exhibit her musical accomplishments before us. The young *virtuose* betook herself to the piano, and first played some scales on the elderly instrument shockingly out of tune, toiling up and down the piano, and giving her wrist and arm a tremendous jerk every time it was her thumbs turn to go under. She ended her musical performance by the traditional *Cloches du Monastère*.

Profiting by the improvement of the roads, a great number of Turkish officers hasten to Erzeroum to see their families.

As soon as the pasture grounds were covered with grass, bands of brigands, belonging to the Kurdish tribe, began to appear. The Ottoman administration has tolerated the exploits of these highwaymen till now, especially the deeds of a well known bandit named Mirza-Bek, who carried in his expeditions his favourite wife, a young Circassian dressed in masculine clothes ; but we cannot maintain the same indifference to be sure! Last night there was a robbery connected with murder in a village near Erzeroum ; the villains were immediately found and arrested. I saw them this morning brought up to my husband, under a great escort. Oh, how awful-looking they were! All in rags, with dark vicious faces and rapacious glances resembling those of the hyenna who dreads daylight and human beings. We have been warned that a band of Kurds are going to assault the cloister of " Kermirvank "; my husband has sent a dozen Cossacks there and the would-be brave highwaymen hastened to run away. It seems that the Kurds venture upon robbery-expeditions only when they are sure of their grounds.

May 1st.—Our policemaster Kamsarakane organises all sorts of amusements for me; to-day, for instance, in honour of the 1st of May, he arranged a picnic out on the side of the Tap-Dagh. The Cossacks made a great fire and we roasted potatoes and boiled water for our tea, after which we sat down on carpets and did full justice to the contents of our luncheon baskets. Crowds of people from the surrounding villages had gathered around, and a mob of Armenian peasants organised a village-dance. We followed their example, trying our feet in a waltz on the uneven ground, the train of my long habit being very much in my way. A functionary of the intendance, an enormous giant, looked so comic waltzing with a tiny officer, who was scarcely up to his shoulder; it seemed all the time as if he wanted to swallow up his undersized partner, or to jump over his head. A group of Armenian urchins, armed with sticks instead of guns, appeared under the command of a little chief, wearing a Russian cap on his head and paper epaulettes; they looked like small lead-warriors taken out of a toy box. These boys executed all sorts of military evolutions, mimicking the training of our soldiers.

On our way home we visited a Turkish Coffee house. We entered a paved courtyard with a fountain basin in the middle, surrounded by big yellow flowers. The customers were sitting around the basin on low cushions; some of them were sipping their coffee and others smoked their narghile, passing it by turns from neighbour to neighbour. Thus occupied, the Turkish smokers pondered meditatively, whilst the Greeks and the Armenians argued about their commercial affairs. This coffee-house consists of several lofty rooms. In one of them the proprietor was sitting proudly behind his bar; a quantity of narghilez of all dimensions, richly adorned with gold and silver ornaments, lay in rows on the shelves fixed all around the wall. In the next room a barber worked, shaving a greater number of skulls than beards.

May 5th.—A Russian employer has been insulted this morning by an individual serving in the Persian Consulate, who called him a lot of bad names. The man came to complain to my husband just when the Persian Cousul was announced.

The culpable Persian was speedily sent for and brought in under the escort of a Russian gendarme and a Turkish kavass. The interview was not pleasant. Sergy told the Persian that it was only out of regard to his Consul that a severe punishment was not imposed upon him by the Russian authorities; he was handed over entirely to the discretion of his Consul.

May 8th.—Yesterday we went to a ball given at the Casino, the building of the ancient "seraglio," where all the festivities were organised before, being now transformed into a hospital for the Turkish wounded soldiers. This ball was to be a grand affair, the arrangements were splendid; the ball-room was fitted up as a big Turkish tent, decorated with plants and flowers. I had to sign a large packet of invitations for that ball, printed on gilt-edged paper, which indicated a long sojourn in the shop by its yellowish colour. This ball sowed discord in many Armenian families; the fair sex wanted to assist at it but the unfair protested energetically. Bulerian, one of the richest Armenians of Erzeroum, had proclaimed publicly that his compatriots who dared to conduct their families to that ball would have to pay dearly for it when Erzeroum was given back to the Turks. Bulerian was responsible for his reckless speech; after having been smartly lectured for it, he has undergone the most infamous Asiatic punishment, which was, being forbidden to mount his horse for a whole month.

The ball was a great success, and the whole entertainment went off admirably. Many Christian inhabitants brought their families to this ball; elderly Armenians and Greek matrons, gorgeously dressed, sat against the wall, and watched our dancing. Supper was served for two hundred persons, and continued till very late. We returned home at dawn, escorted by a military band. We had two Turks at dinner to-day, Ismael-Bey and Maksoud-Effendi. I could hardly keep from laughing in looking at the desperate efforts that they made in serving themselves with their knives and forks; how gladly they would have thrown away these instruments of torture to be able to tear their meat with their fingers!

May 30th.—This afternoon we made an excursion to the banks of the Euphrates. After having made about five miles on horseback, we arrived at a sort of paved dike, which seemed to have been built by giants; the stones are so enormous that it is quite incomprehensible how human beings could handle them. For many centuries whole generations have gone over this ancient dike without its being necessary to mend it. The Euphrates is very broad in this part, and in full rise just now. Frogs were croaking around us, and whole flocks of wild geese dived about ten steps from us; their tranquillity, as it seems, is rarely troubled by musket-shots. On the middle of the river a boatman was rowing his yawl, cut out of the trunk of an enormous tree, with a long perch.

On our way home we stopped at " Kian," a small village where we created a great sensation, and were stared at as if we were beings from another world. The women crowded around; one of them determined to examine me closely grasped my arm exclaiming, " I have touched her, she is alive!" (Did she suppose that I was a wax-doll?)

May 11th.—This morning a Turkish woman, holding a small boy dressed in the uniform of a pasha by the hand, has come with a petition to my husband. She began to relate different exploits of her ancestors, and concluded her long narrative by requesting Sergy to procure her means to return to Constantinople, her native town. Sergy tried to explain to her that the services rendered by her forefathers had nothing to do with the Russian government, but she continued to beg, and having received the sum that she requested, she whispered something to her little son, who came up to our interpreter and announced to him that he too, wanted a *bakshish.*

We went to visit the Christian schools in the afternoon. In the Catholic school one directly sees the active intervention of the clergy. The Archbishop Melchisedec takes a great part in the education of the children; the director and the tutors are all priests. The best scholars are sent to Rome and Venice to finish their studies. The pupils repeated compliments of welcome to us in French, and expressed their gratitude to our Emperor for the protection that His Majesty accorded to the Christian inhabitants of Erzeroum. The Greek school is also considered as a part of the church, but the priests do not assist in the teaching. The director of this school showed us his establishment in detail. It contains two hundred scholars of both sexes. Till the age of twelve boys and girls study together; they are taught both Greek and Turkish. This school being of the Orthodox creed, received a monthly subsidy of fifteen francs before the beginning of the war, now my husband has offered the sum of four thousand francs yearly as a support to the school. In the evening the Greek deputy came to thank Sergy for this rich offering; they told him that the remembrance of his generosity would remain for ever in their hearts as also in the hearts of their children.

May 14th.—My husband has received an important despatch from Constantinople, a circular of orders from the "Grand Vizir" to the high Turkish functionaries. Sergy thus acts the part of an Ottoman Pasha, which amuses me greatly.

After dinner we rode over to Abdurakman-Kazi, an antique mosque containing the mausoleum of a renowned Turkish saint and also a score of rooms for pilgrims. This monastery, on the mountain side looks splendid.

May 15th.—Yesterday on our way home from the cloister of Abdurakman-Kazi, we saw on our way some bomb shells. This morning, a little shepherd turned over one of these shells, which exploded and tore the poor lad to pieces.

May 17th.—Striving to invent all sorts of distractions in order to raise the drooping spirits of our Russian colony, horribly depressed by the epidemic of typhus-fever, we have organised races on a track of three miles. To-day a large crowd of inhabitants surrounded the racing-place. There were seven concurrent events—five Cossack and two native. When they started I followed them attentively, fearing to see our Cossacks outridden by the Turks. To my great joy a young Cossack gained the first prize, the sum of four hundred francs. He mounted a tiny insignificant-looking horse that he had bought at Khiva for forty francs. The Cossack was accompanied up to town in triumph by a big crowd, and two military bands.

May 21st.—The benediction of the common tomb of the soldiers of the regiment of Bakou, killed during the assault of the fort Azizie, took place this morning. A year has glided away, the fate of Erzeroum has changed, and this same regiment of Bakou holds garrison now in this fort.

Egueshi related to us the cruelties committed by the Mussulmans during that siege. He pointed out a Turkish woman who had cut the throats of many wounded Russian soldiers, thus avenging herself for the death of her husband on the battle field. The enormous tomb has been done up with stones, and a big wooden cross is fixed in the middle.

During the Requiem, at which I assisted on horseback, all the soldiers knelt down and prayed fervently for their comrades, the brave warriors who are sleeping their eternal sleep in this Mussulman ground.

After dinner we arranged an expedition to the monastery of Loussavoritch-Vank, situated about six miles outside the town. This monastery, built on the top of a high mountain and surrounded by a stone-wall, resembles a castle of the middle-ages. Three sides of this cloister are perpendicular and the fourth one, by which one mounts, is planted with a row of fine trees, an agreeable contrast to the rocky scenery all around. Two monks composed the whole establishment ; one of them, at our approach, began to toll a bell, whilst his companion came out to meet us, holding a big silver cross in his hand. He led us into the church, where he performed a Te Deum and made us descend afterwards into a dark dungeon where, according to a legend, Saint-Gregory, the propagator of Christianity, had taken refuge during the persecution of the Christians. We also visited an antique underground church, making our way to it by narrow dark passages. I drew a long breath when I found myself in the open air once more. On our way home we were overtaken by a terrible thunderstorm, which didn't last long, but was followed by a dreadful shower of rain. We put on mackintoshes with caps, which made us look like highwaymen, but we all got a thorough drenching, nevertheless.

May 27th.—The snow in the mountains transforms itself when thawing into big clouds, and it pours with rain nearly every day. The top of the " Palantek " is a capital weatherprophet ; when there are no clouds on the summit, even if the sky is heavy all around, it will not rain that day, and vice versa. From our sitting-room one can watch the mountains, and this barometer is of great use to us during our rides.

There was an awful storm last night ; the wind shook our house to its very foundation, it seemed as though it must be caught up and hurled headlong. I've never seen such dazzling flashes of lightning before, nor heard such formidable thunderbolts reverberating loudly with an echo in the mountains. I was in a terrible fright all the time lest the flag-staff, put on the top of our roof, would be struck by lightning. The rain came in through the ceilings ; I can well imagine what was taking place in the other houses in Erzeroum which had no clay roofs like ours.

May 28th.—A very disagreeable incident occurred last night, a musket-ball whizzed close past the sentry on duty near the guard-house. Investigations were made and the inhabitants handed over a Turkish solider this morning, who said that in jumping over a wall he had awkwardly let fall his gun, which fired itself. The culprit is arrested.

During our evening ride along the line of the fortifications, a bullet flew past me and made my horse start. The misunderstanding explained itself. The Cossacks of our escort were ready to retaliate, when it proved to be simply a Russian officer who, shooting at a target, did not perceive that his bullets passed over the ramparts. All the same it is evident that I stood in imminent danger of being shot through the body, and feel myself trained up in war now, having experienced the baptism of fire, which is a very peculiar feeling, indeed !

May 29th.—Troubles have arisen again. There has been a fresh underhand musket-shot which took place in town this morning. This time the ball lodged itself in the wall of a house inhabited by one of our functionaries. A group of " imams " from different parts of Erzeroum were gathered, and the order was given to them to find out the culprit, under the threat of making the whole Mussulman quarter responsible for his misdeed, and to deliver him immediately into the hands of the Russian authorities, as also all the firearms that the Turkish government had dealt out to the inhabitants during the blockade of Erzeroum. The " imams " listened woefully to the proclamation of that severe decree, and presented, a few hours later as culprit, the single Christian inhabitant of their quarter; it is quite evident that they accuse him wrongfully.

There came a telegram to-day which announced that a ratification of peace was going to be opened in Berlin on the 12th of June. That's a new gleam of hope that we shall soon leave Erzeroum.

I have often heard military bands playing in the streets of Erzeroum, but they generally executed funeral marches, whilst platoons of soldiers accompanied their chiefs, victims of the terrible epidemic, to their last dwelling-place, and one can easily conceive my joy when I perceived from my window the first detachment destined to reinforce our army, entering Erzeroum this morning, preceeded by a military band. The Mussulmans must be very much annoyed to see our troops increasing, as up till now the number of our soldiers diminished every day.

May 30th.—The Persian Consul presented Sergy with the portrait of the Shah and a piece of poetry which states that this portrait is given to the Russian governor of Erzeroum in token of gratitude for his kindness to the Persian inhabitants.

Though the sky was perfectly clear this evening, Egueshi warned us, pointing to the "Palantek," that there would be a shower before long, but we, all the same, started on our habitual ride, but had not gone half a mile when there came the rumble of thunder from afar; a flash of lightning shot across the sky and the rain came down in torrents. We galloped at full speed towards the village of Shakk, not far off, and took refuge under the roof of an old Armenian priest. On the walls of his parlour hung a whole gallery of pictures cut from French illustrated papers, representing chiefly heroes of the Russo-Turkish war, a present left for our host by a Russian officer who had put up at his house for a time. I wonder if the originals of these portraits will ever know that their visages adorn the walls of a humble cottage situated in one of the remotest parts of Asia Minor. On our way home we admired the beautiful growth of the wheat; the plain of Erzeroum being abundantly irrigated, the harvests are usually splendid, everything looks so green and fresh.

May 31st.—Storm clouds gathered again on the heights of the "Palantek" this evening. We had scarcely reached the camp when large drops began to fall and the storm came down in rolling thunder and lashing rain. Sergy hurried me into a great coat but nevertheless I got wet through. In an instant the whole camp, situated on a declivity, was furrowed by the impetuous torrents, and the water rushed in streams over the ground. When we reached the riflemen's camp, we dismounted and ran into Mr. Popoff's tent for shelter until the storm should clear away. In returning we had to go over gutters, which was difficult on account of their being full of foaming water. We saw a drove of cattle returning from the pasture grounds which found itself in great trouble before a usually dry ditch transformed for the moment into a torrent. The shepherds, mounted on donkeys, tried by gestures and voice to force the cattle to enter the water, in order to reach the other bank, but it was no easy matter; the cows ended by obeying, but the donkeys resisted energetically and nothing could be done with them.

The proprietor of the house inhabited by Eritzeff, a Persian who was noted for his vanity, stinginess, and cowardice, was determined to obtain a Russian decoration. He was a fearful bore to his tenant, repeating to him at every favourable moment his desire to be useful to the Russian government. Eritzeff lost his patience at last and determined to play him a trick; he announced confidently to him that he was sent on a serious mission to Bagdad and offered him to be his interpreter; Eritzeff also warned him that he was to fit himself suitably for that long journey. The Persian was delighted and replied that the expenses of equipment would not be a drawback, and in fact he delivered himself, in spite of his stinginess, to mad prodigalities; he bought a horse, a new saddle, a white mackintosh and a pair of yellow jackboots. His family could not understand whither he was starting, but submitted to Providence, and when the day of departure arrived, they all kissed and cried over him.

A dinner for the sham-parting was given to Eritzeff in the Musselman monastery of Abdurakman-Kazi, after which our would-be travellers were to start. During the meal a Cossack was to appear and hand over to Eritzeff a counter-order of departure. Unluckily someone had the awkwardness of revealing that plot before the repast began, nevertheless the guests were immensely amused. In fact, the poor Persian was such a picture to look at, equipped in his great mantle, his seven-leagued boots, furnished with gigantic spurs that reached well up to his calves, and armed up to the tip-top, sword and pistols in his sash; he was literally the personification of "Don Quixote." The poor creature looked as if he wasn't quite sure at first whether he was standing on his head or on his heels, but he soon controlled himself and bore his disappointment with serene resignation. Trying to put a good face on the matter, he regaled everyone with the big oranges that he had crammed into his pockets to quench his thirst during his long journey, and calling to mind a Persian song named, "I went in three days to Bagdad," he said good-humouredly. As to me I have made the trip much quicker!

This Persian was the hero of a new pleasant adventure. Last night, returning home, he perceived at the corner of his house someone smoking behind the fountain ; only the tip of a lighted cigarette could be seen. " Hello ! who goes there ? " he challenged the mysterious smoker loudly, but got no answer. " What are you doing there behind that fountain ? " Complete silence again. " Brigands for sure ! " vociferated the valiant Persian, and dashing into his house he returned reinforced by his servant, provided with a pistol which he pointed at the would-be malefactor, who continued to smoke peacefully. The fact is that there was no brigand whatever ; it proved to be simply the tip of a lighted cigarette laid down ont he border of the fountain by some nocturnal passer-by.

June 1st.—General Lazareff has come to Erzeroum to replace General Heimann. The Armenian inhabitants awaited him with impatience, very proud that he was the second commander of the main army of their own nationality. From early morning the whole town was put into a fluster ; the native women established themselves upon their roofs at daybreak, wishing to see the new Russian mouchir enter Erzeroum. As I also wished to be present, I accepted readily the Gilberts' invitation to come on their balcony which looked out into the square where the Guards of Honour, and a great number of officers in grand uniform, had assembled. Towards ten o'clock we heard the clamour of hurras and soon perceived a crowd of inhabitants coming up, followed by two hundred Cossacks with big banners ; behind them rode General Lazareff, accompanied by a numerous suite.

June 5th.—Kirkor-Effendi Schabanian gave an evening-party to-day. We remained in his fantastic garden, illuminated with many coloured lanterns, till late, admiring the gorgeous costumes of his Asiatic guests who promenaded round a marble fountain full of goldfish. It was all like a scene from the Arabian nights.

June 9th.—This morning we have visited the mill of Kireh-Bulak, the prettiest spot in the neighbourhood, situated in a narrow pass about eight miles from town. We brought our luncheon with us, hard boiled eggs, biscuits and salt in an envelope, and ate it with great appetite in this nice, cool resting-place. Large trees grow all around and a rapid torrent falls from high cliffs in a roaring cascade white with foam ; the noise of the mill at work sounded close by.

June 10th.—To-day a gala banquet was given at the Casino by Ali-Effendi. The most cordial union seemed to reign between the Russians and Mussulmans, but was it all very sincere ? At the end of the repast, when the champagne had loosened the tongues and quickened the spirits, Maksoud-Effendi came up to the Persian Consul, glass in hand, and proposed to drink to his health, but the Persian, a water-drinker, like every good Mussulman, refused the toast, at which Maksoud-Effendi took offence, and flying into a passion, dashed the contents of his glass into the face of the astounded Persian and vociferated with furious eyes and face aflame : " Ah, you wouldn't drink to my health by mere politeness, well, do it now by mere force ! " The Consul started up wiping his face and his clothes, muttering a prayer to be purified from the stains of wine.

June 12th.—To-day passing before the Casino, M. Gilbert witnessed a completely unusual event. He saw a mounted Cossack officer climbing up the steep wooden staircase leading into the Casino ; after having made a tour through all the apartments that officer returned the same way, without having run against anyone or anything. This equestrian prank made a strong impression upon a group of Turks who were standing in the street, they said that only a Cossack officer was capable of such a wild deed, because in their opinion all the Cossacks were possessed by the *schaitan* (the devil).

A fancy took me to drive with Mme. Gilbert to the monastery of Abdurakman-Kazi in an *araba*, a cart drawn by a pair of oxen, for thousands of years the unchanged mode of conveyance in Turkey, a mode of locomotion more comfortable than dignified, to be sure. The *araba* was furnished with carpets and cushions, and the oxen adorned with flowers and ribbons. I undertook to perform the part of driver, and succeeded to put my phlegmatic bullocks into a sharp trot.

June 20th.—Last night we visited the village of Laouk, inhabited by Christians and Mussulmans. My husband asked a white-bearded " imam " if the Armenians and the Turks lived on good terms with each other, and that old Osmanlie for answer, in order to prove his affection, tenderly embraced an Armenian priest who stood by. I wonder if these individuals will kiss each other when the Turks have re-entered Erzeroum !

June 22nd.—About a hundred fierce-looking men, who had formerly belonged to the brigand band of the famous Mechrali, assembled before our house after dinner with their chief, Temir-Aga, who is seventy years old but still as brisk and nimble as a young man. He had previously been chief of a band of highwaymen who had spread terror through all Anatolia about twenty years before. The Turkish Government could find no other means to subdue him than to appoint him chief of one of the districts in the province of Erzeroum. Temir-Aga profited by every available occasion to assure my husband of his entire devotedness. Sergy sent for these men to ascertain that they had received their soldiers' pay regularly. They were not pleasant men to meet in a dark lane, and are to be watched closely all the time, in order to prevent them from troubling the peace of the citizens.

July 4th.—There has been a conflict between a band of Kurds and Turks about twenty miles from Erzeroum; about a dozen Kurds were wounded and the rest of them made prisoners. Temir-Aga, who captured these highwaymen, brought them over to my husband this morning. I saw them advancing slowly towards our house, between a body-guard of Turkish soldiers, with their hands fastened behind their backs, having awfully ferocious expressions.

July 6th.—This morning we heard the welcome tidings that a private agreement had been decided upon between Russia, England and Prussia. God grant war won't begin anew!

To-day, in spite of the peaceful issue of the Congress in Berlin, a violent fighting broke out in Erzeroum between the Christian and Mussulman street-boys. The Armenians fought energetically and knocked down their adversaries, shouting, " Long live the Emperor of Russia ! "

Time is going on and we are still in Erzeroum, and though the certitude that war won't begin anew tranquillises me, still the ignorance in which we find ourselves about the time of our departure is very hard to bear.

The Catholic Archbishop invited us to assist at the distribution of prizes at his school. After we were seated at the head of a long table, the Sisters of Mercy presented to us the pupils deserving prizes, and I had to adorn them with crowns of flowers. After that the pupils played on the piano to us and recited French and Armenian poetry ; then the Archbishop led us into his library which contains rare and curious books, amidst which we saw a manuscript of the Lord's prayer written in fifty different languages.

July 10th.—The influence which the Russians exercise on the outward life of the Christian population is so great that the Armenian inhabitants have decided to organise a theatre in Erzeroum, an ignored luxury at the time of the sovereignty of the Turks. A stage with a score of boxes has been built in a spacious cart-house ; the curtain represents an allegory of Armenia amidst a heap of ruins. In these amateur performances all the womens' parts are played by men.

August 1st.—According to a Turkish legend, the eclipse of the moon proceeds from a " Flying Dragon " attempting to swallow up that planet. In order to prevent the monster from realising his sinister project, the native women climb on to their roofs and make a dreadful noise with different brass instruments to frighten the " Dragon " away, whilst the men discharge a number of musket-shots. Yesterday, for instance, there was an eclipse, but this time the inhabitants were strictly forbidden to shoot.

To-day an organ-grinder arrived from "San Stefano" and played the whole evening under our windows; he was surrounded by a throng of street-boys, who examined his instrument, completely unknown to them, with much curiosity.

August 9th.—This afternoon we took a trip along the right shore of the Euphrates. We came to an ancient grotto close to a basin of mineral water, about half a mile from the best quarries of the country. The stones drawn out of them are of various colours and serve for the construction of houses. The echo in these crypts, which served in former times as shelter to hermits, is remarkably sonorous. At present the natives who go on a pilgrimage to the Mussulman monastery of Hatcha-Vank, usually make a halt here. We sat down on a carpet spread under an immense tree and rested in dreamy quiet within its shade, near a big trench for irrigation filled with foaming water. The Cossacks of our escort made a fire and roasted potatoes in that sheltered nook, and the inhabitants of the neighbouring village brought jugs of excellent milk, new-laid eggs and salmon-trout that they had just caught close by. We returned home only at nightfall.

August 15th.—A Turkish kavass came this morning to complain that an Armenian zaptieh had insulted him and torn off his galoons. The Armenians, dazed by their momentary success after the arrival of General Lazareff, are very rude towards the Turkish inhabitants. As to the sly Greeks, they assume an entirely different behaviour, making themselves agreeable both to the Christians and Mussulmans.

A telegram has just arrived announcing that the Russians are to leave Erzeroum directly after the surrender of Batoum. Parleys with Turkish authorities are going to be immediately entered upon. Oh, what joy, joy, joy! It is almost too good to be true!

August 24th.—From to-day the Mussulmans are beginning to feast their "Ramazan," when they are obliged to fast till night-time. At nine o'clock precisely, as soon as a cannon-shot has announced the termination of fasting, which lasts again from dawn till the new sunset, the Turks revel frantically, eating, drinking and smoking to their heart's content. Hamid-Bek, who is possessed with a ravenous appetite, spends his afternoons in contemplating the citadel, and as soon as he perceives a little smoke arise, fortelling the cannon-shot, he rushes into his house to devour his supper, in the company of his wives who are as famishing as himself.

The Gilberts have left Erzeroum for good this morning. I got up very early to bid them good-bye, and saw two enormous vans standing before their house-porch. One of these vans was to serve as a carriage, for there are no post-chaises to be had in Erzeroum, and the other vehicle was assigned for the luggage. When everything was ready for starting, the Gilberts clambered into their waggon which began to move, jolting heavily on the rough pavement, and soon disappeared out of sight round the corner of the street. I was awfully sad to lose the Gilberts, but the thought that we should soon follow their example, consoled me.

August 28th.—A telegraphic message has just arrived announcing the surrender of Batoum. The official orders of the giving up of that town to the Turks will come to-morrow. Now we shall be able to get away soon ; I am wildly, madly happy !

I have been awakened this morning by the sounds of a loud conversation under our windows. An Armenian merchant came to complain that a score of Turks had forced themselves into his house last night, and after having bound him up with strong cords, they wanted to carry away his wife, a mere child of fifteen. This incident gave rise to a great commotion among the Armenians ; our approaching departure terrifies them. We have not left Erzeroum yet and the Turks have already begun to fulfil their threats. The whole town is in excitement, all the shops are closed. I hear the toll of the alarm-bell chiming for the assembling of the Christian inhabitants. Just before lunch my husband was told that several thousands of Armenians who had gathered before the dwelling of their Metropolitan, were now advancing towards our house and we already heard the ominous sound of treading feet and clamerous voices in the distance. In a second I was on the balcony and the first thing I saw was the figure of the Metropolitan making his way through a tumultuous throng of people, closely followed by all the members of the Town Council, in about two minutes there was a crowd of several hundred people about our house. I heard the roaring voices of an excited mob from below ; wherever I looked I saw a sea of anxious faces and gesticnlating arms and hands. The confusion became greater with every moment. Notwithstanding my entreaties, Sergy came out on the balcony with the Metropolitan and policemaster, who explained to me that this noisy crowd had come to entreat my husband to permit them to emigrate to Russia. The Armenians, who completely lost their heads and thought that their end was drawing nigh, wanted to follow us to Russia and declared they would not stir from the spot until they got a favourable answer from my husband. I was terrified beyond words when I saw an individual drawing a pistol out of his pocket and pointing it at us exclaiming : " In mercy kill me, I prefer to perish from your hands rather than be left to the mercy of the Turks ! " The policemaster, escorted by his agents, went down into the street in order to exhort the mob to disperse, but the infuriated Armenians continued to roar under our balcony; then Sergy addressed the crowd, persuading them to be quiet and promising that he would not leave Erzeroum before the Turkish army arrived, and that order would be maintained in the town till then. These words were greeted with a wild yell of exultation from the crowding masses, and the noise of the multitude gradually decreased. .Oh! it was a scene and an experience I shall certainly never forget! My husband ordered the number of patrols in the streets to be increased, and after dinner we rode through the Turkish bazaars in order to tranquillise the affrighted Christian inhabitants.

August 29th.—Order in town is reinstated. The merchants are beginning to open their shops, but before luncheon a new mob has gathered outside our house. This time the inhabitants of the neighbouring villages have assembled to beg for permission to emigrate to Russia, prefering rather to risk the uncertain future than to suffer the yoke of the Turks; but Sergy had to tell them that there was no convenient ground in our country to give them.

A rumour has spread that "Mechrali," the famous brigand whose daring was boundless, hearing of the Turkish occupation of Erzeroum, hastened to come here, and is now promenading in the streets without fear.

September 1st.—During our ride this evening I was very happy to see our camp diminishing; the regiment of Elizabethpol has left Erzeroum to-day, and the rest of our troops will depart in a few days. The Greek and Armenians that we met in the streets appeared to me greatly discouraged and very much depressed, but I remarked that they changed their countenances instantly and looked quite cheerful the moment they perceived a Turkish officer.

September 5th.—Hadji-Houssein-Pasha, my husband's successor, has arrived this morning with his policemaster and a squadron of "souvaris" (dragoons;) he has got orders to assist at the surrender of the town. Ismail-Pasha has sent an express command to the "mollahs" and other Mussulman representatives to maintain strict order in town. Houssein-Pasha paid us an official visit in the afternoon. He is an old man with a long white beard and rather an inexpressive face. Out of my window I saw him approach our house mounted on a beautiful Arab steed whose saddle sparkled with gildings and glittered blindingly in the sun.

September 6th.—A great many Christian and Mussulman inhabitants, who held different posts in the Russian administration of Erzeroum, have been gratified with presents and decorated with medals, therefore various deputations have come to take leave of us, assuring my husband of their deep gratitude and sympathy.

September 7th.—Great animation in town to-day on account

of the arrival of Moussa-Pasha, the chief of the Turkish army in Asia-Minor. The Russian commander of the citadel with a squadron of dragoons and a military band has gone out to meet him as far as the Postern of Kars. At about ten o'clock in the morning a Guard of Honour was placed before the house of the Mouchir. We mounted on the roof of the Turkish military school, from whence we could see the road leading to Trebizond. We waited a long time; at last sounds of music were heard from afar, a cloud of dust arose, and we discerned long files of cavalry. Our dragoons rode ahead, bringing in the Turkish commander mounted on a splendid horse and surrounded by a numerous suite. The Turkish troops brought up the rear. As soon as Moussa-Pasha perceived my husband he waved his hand to him exclaiming in perfect Russian: "Your Excellency, how happy I am to see you!" Moussa-Pasha is an aborigine of the Caucasus; he has been educated in St. Petersburg in the *Corps des Pages*, and has served a long time in the Russian army. It is only since he rose to the rank of general, that he turned traitor and went back to the Turkish government.

Moussa-Pasha dismounted and came up on to our roof to give my husband a warm greeting, holding out both hands. Then, in sight of the whole crowd of bewildered Turks, he kissed my hand gallantly. After having seated himself between us, the Mouchir ordered his troops to continue their march through the town, meanwhile being awfully nice to me; he expressed his satisfaction that I hadn't left Erzeroum before his arrival and told me that the rumours of my stay in Erzeroum had reached Constantinople, and that my bravery was held up as an example to the Turkish officers and soldiers. He also related to me that prude, Ismail-Pasha, was highly displeased that I rode through the streets of Erzeroum in the company of men and with my face uncovered, pretending that it thoroughly offended the notion of propriety in the Turkish and Armenian families. When the infantry had passed, Moussa-Pasha took leave of us and rode off whilst his troops continued to defile. Each battalion was preceded by sappers, each carrying a hatchet. The Turkish soldiers had a fine deportment and marched in good order, but their officers looked oldish and round-shouldered. The batteries began to defile now, followed by a regiment of "souvaris" (dragoons) in brilliant uniforms, laid all over with red and yellow galoons. Closed arabas, occupied by the families of the Turkish army, filed off now amidst luggage-vans. The occupants of these harem conveyances were invisible; one of the women having the curiosity to peep out was brutally pushed back by a soldier. A band of dervishes, bearing the standard of the Prophet, came galloping up, brandishing glittering swords; behind them advanced files of

Osmanlies striking up a clamorous flourish of trumpets, beating the war-drums and blowing the war-horns. The Mussulman schools brought up the rear carrying banners with inscriptions out of the "Koran." The scholars chanted verses and sung in chorus "Lah illah, illah lah!" in high-pitched voices. They were surrounded by a crowd of street-boys shouting them words of welcome. These urchins who had been very much annoyed in hearing their Armenian little comrades vociferate at every available occasion the Russian "hurra" had their revenge now.

It was decided that our sentinels should immediately be replaced by Turkish soldiers. I looked at that ceremony from the balcony of General Lazareff's dwelling, commanding a view of the guard-house and the public square where crowds were gathering. A Turkish patrol soon appeared, about a dozen soldiers with an under-officer swinging a long branch that he had just broken from a tree; but the chief of our patrol declared that he would certainly not give up the guardhouse to such singular substitutes. The new commander of the citadel with a detachment of soldiers arrived shortly afterwards, and this time our soldiers presented arms to their former enemies and resigned the place to the Turks. From henceforth Erzeroum has become again a Turkish town!

Our last dinner in Erzeroum was interrupted by the arrival of Houssein-Pasha, who came in full uniform to bid us good-bye, accompanied by his policemaster. After their departure we speedily finished our meal and started on horseback for the camp. Now, at last, all was over with Erzeroum! We had tea in our tent, which was pitched on the slope of a hill, and at seven o'-clock we remounted our horses and returned to Erzeroum, as guests this time; Ali-Effendi invited us to a grand dinner that he gave in our honour. When we approached his house, it was illuminated, and a Turkish band began to play. Ali-Effendi came out to meet us, and offering me his arm, he led me to the dining-room where all the Russian and Turkish authorities were already assembled. I sat on the right of Houssein-Pasha, who lavished compliments on me the whole time. Our host was also most charmingly courteous and proposed to drink my health with enthusiasm. The dinner consisted of fifteen courses and lasted it seemed a whole eternity. We returned to our camp late in the night, accompanied by an escort of Turkish dragoons who carried lighted torches.

September 8th.—A tent is a poor place to spend the night in, nevertheless I slept soundly in my narrow camp-bed. At day-break I was roused by the sound of trumpets and the beating of drums; the soldiers began to stir, in great excitement, and less than a quarter of an hour later the whole camp was broken up. Our soldiers having burned all their useless rags by the fire, hundreds of the indigent inhabitants of Erzeroum hurried down like birds of prey upon the place recently occupied by our camp and searched for the remains in the dense smoke. Meanwhile our troops drew up in a line while their commanders took a survey of their ranks and congratulated the men on the occasion of their return to their homes. After that public prayers were sung ; during the Te Deum the sounds of the trumpet resounded to signal our departure.

We mounted on horseback and left Erzeroum with our troops, with music playing and banners waving in the air. To-day is the birthday of the Grand-Duchess Olga Fedorovna, therefore twenty-one cannon-shots have been fired. We were already approaching the Postern of Kars when, in the middle of a cloud of dust, a cavalcade came into view. It was Mouchtar-Pasha who had come with a numerous suite to see us off. Suddenly we heard the sounds of a march, and saw a Turkish military band preceding a battalion of Turkish soldiers, marching also in the direction of the Postern of Kars in order to escort the departing Russian troops ; they drew up in a line on each side of the road. I was greatly impressed to see the enemy troops, who a short time ago fought ferociously with us, now presenting arms to the Russian commanders. There was a great crowd of Turks round about, but the Armenian inhabitants restrained from appearing. The Postern is left behind, the Russian and Turkish commanders have made their adieus, and we are marching off to Kars. Our cavalcade was very gay ; we were trotting fast and soon overtook our troops. In the afternoon we arrived at the spot where we were to lunch in a tent pitched on the banks of a river. After sunset, we came to Hassan-kala where we passed the night under the roof of the chief of the district. An impromptu bed was made up for me far too short, alas, for my long legs.

September 9th.—We continued our journey at day-break. The chief of the district of Kharoussan came to meet my husband on horseback, accompanied by an escort of Kurdes. The chief of their tribe, wishing to be agreeable to Sergy, told him how glad he was when the new frontier was made, that his land became joined to the Russian territory, when the land of his brothers was joined to that of Turkey.

September 10th.—After having made a long halt at Zevine, we overtook a large detachment of emigrants going to Kars on their way to America. On the passage of the Saganlough we rejoined the rifle battalion. The officers invited us to dismount and sit down to lunch on the grass with them. When we came to Karagalis, a tiny hamlet composed of a few cottages, the hut in which we were to pass the night appeared so dirty and miserable to us that we prefered to sleep in the open air, stretched on mats on the grass outside.

September 11th.—Rising early we remounted our horses. Amongst the crowd of villagers who surrounded us we saw a great many Armenians wearing fezzes on their heads. When one of our fellow-travellers asked an old Armenian the reason why he wore this Turkish head-gear instead of a cap, he replied candidly that he wasn't quite sure yet to what territory he was to belong, and said that if he belonged to the Turks he would have to pay dearly for the change of his head-covering.

We reached Kars in safety some little time before sunset, after having been in the saddle three days, riding at the rate of 50 miles a day, and intended to put up at the London-Hotel for rest, but General Franchini, the governor of Kars, took us off to his house. I was tired out and unable to do anything but rest and wanted a good sleep after our long journey. I hurried up to my room and stretched my tired limbs in the comfort of my bed.

Kars has changed considerably since my departure to Erzeroum ; sign-boards written in Russian are to be seen everywhere, and our language chiefly is heard in the streets.

September 18th.—From Kars to Alexandropol we travelled in a post-chaise. General Franchini and his colleagues expressed a desire to accompany us to the first station on horseback. On approaching it, we were very much surprised to hear the sounds of a military band and to see a large tent in which a farewell banquet was served. A greater surprise still awaited us ; Sergy found an address under his table-napkin a printed order proceeding from General Lazareff, in which he referred to my husband's first-rate administration of the country which had just been restored to the Turks. During the repast we all remembered the painful moments that we had passed during these two years of war. Thank God its happily over now ; all this nightmare of war done with and gone !

The first thing we did on our arrival at Alexandropol was to hire a carriage and go and pray on the tombs of our departed friends, victims of that terrible war. Quick ! let us get out of this land of mourning, grief and sorrow ! Let us come out of the darkness and gloom into the light again !

September 20th.—After a journey of two days we are comfortably reinstalled in Tiflis. How delighted I am to live again in our cosy nest, with all the luxury of civilisation round us. I do hope that the wandering existence that we have lived since our marriage has come to an end. My gaiety has come back to me and the world is beautiful again, and I am just going to live and forget the privations and dangers of the past months. All the horrors of war have vanished like a bad dream.

November 30th.—Our stay in Tiflis, alas, did not last long. The Grand Duke Michael, setting out to St. Petersburg, has charged Sergy to work out projects in case of a new war with Turkey, (Oh! horror!) and has ordered him to bring them personally to St. Petersburg. We are leaving Tiflis in the beginning of December.

CHAPTER XVIII

ST. PETERSBURG

WE have put up at the Grand Hôtel where we feel very comfortable. This winter I mean to lead a quiet, homely life, being wonderfully changed after my marriage. Out of a frivolous society girl, I have developed, thanks to Sergy, into a very domestic sort of person. I have seen enough of the world to understand how flippant it is, how empty—a vanity of vanities! Marriage has given me a new view of the world altogether, I have taken off my rose-coloured spectacles to look at life as it is, and have learned many things which I did not know.

Russia continues to outlive troublesome times ; after the war it is the anarchist conspirators who organise inquisitions, condemn to death, and hold themselves the office of executioners. A rumour has spread in town that on Easter Eve there will be a repetition of St. Bartholomew's night, and that all the wealthy inhabitants of the city will be massacred.

The life of our Emperor is in constant danger. An attempt to murder him was made whilst he was taking his usual afternoon walk. Luckily the malefactor's bullet missed the Tzar. Petersburg is all in a flutter through that attempt. Te Deums are sung in all the churches and the town is decorated all over with flags. The day of the attempt, during the performance of the opera "Life for the Tzar," a large audience packed the house from floor to ceiling. When the Emperor appeared in his box, the hymn "God save the Tzar," resounded through the hall ; the whole audience rose to their feet, and deafening cheers were heard. Our monarch bowed graciously in response.

Though the Neva thawed very late this year, larks were singing, and the sky was blue, and the whole air was full of the spring promise. It gave me a wild desire to go abroad and fly over hill and dale. Sergy wanted to take a two months' leave of absence, but the doctor that he had summoned to certify the absolute necessity of a cure, after having given his diagnosis, said that Sergy was blessed with excellent health. As it was absolutely necessary to find an ailment of some kind, I had recourse to artfulness. Before the doctor took leave, I put my head through the door and made faces behind his back, grimacing so wildly that Sergy had to struggle with suppressed laughter ; the muscles of his face moved and his lips twitched. "Oh, I don't like that at all!" cried out the mystified Æsculapius. "I see now what is the matter with you! your overstrained nervous system calls for energetic treatment, and a month's holidays, at least, is the sort of physic you want. Your ailment is overwork, pure and simple!" When the doctor left I burst into wild laughter, and thought him the nicest physician in the world. My scheme was thus successful, and Sergy, being ordered abroad by the doctor to take a long rest, had obtained a six weeks' leave of absence.

I was tremendously pleased to visit foreign countries, and looked forward to it with great anticipation. Quantities of pleasant things were planned. But, alas! it had only been a sweet dream! I soon awoke to grim reality. Quite unexpectedly Sergy was appointed chief of the staff of the circuit of Moscow. I was greatly disappointed that we had to give up our cherished trip abroad. It was all so sudden, so totally unexpected, and I cried that night when I went to bed. But it means a very brilliant future for my husband, and it would be madness to refuse it. We have to start without delay.

CHAPTER XIX

MOSCOW

WE arrived at Moscow in the beginning of May, and settled down for the summer months in a wing of the Petrovski Palace, situated in a beautiful park two miles out, to wait for our apartments to be got ready in town. This palace is a majestic building flanked with four red-brick turrets, looking like a mediæval castle.

The summer passed quickly. It was autumn now, and yellow leaves were falling thickly on the paths outside. The last week of September we took up our winter quarters in town. It was great pleasure to settle in our new home. We have bought a pair of carriage-horses, beautiful steppers, and a pair of lovely ponies to drive myself, sweet little pets they are.

We are leading a very happy life. Sergy keeps from me all knowledge of the world's misery and wrongs. I have really drawn the great prize in life's lottery, and am one of fortune's favourites. There never was a tenderer husband in the world. His one idea is to keep every cloud out of my life. He smooths my path and clears away all the thorns and briars. He is my protector, my guardian and my guide. If there were more men like Sergy there would be fewer miserable women. Sergy surrounded me with comforts and gave me everything my heart could desire, guessing my wishes before I knew them myself. There was nothing under the sun which he wouldn't do for me; I had only to reach my hand out for anything I wanted. I was really born with the traditional silver spoon in my mouth, and I think myself the most fortunate of human beings to have such a husband.

For social distraction I have now but little taste, and delight in staying at home with Sergy. My time is well filled up and my hours are regulated as clock-work. My daily life begins early in the morning. I usually rise at seven o'clock and am never for a moment idle, working, reading, playing the piano and trying to keep the house in order. I am rather new to housekeeping, it is true, but am determined to begin it in a thorough fashion. It is not a small affair to make myself respected by our servants. The management of that un-manageable creature, the cook, is especially difficult; I have had many struggles with him, and often see a sneer on his lips, but nevertheless I have never allowed him to fleece us too much. Sometimes I had a terrible turn for cleaning, and visitors often caught me perched upon a chair with my sleeves rolled well above my elbows, and my dress shielded by an apron, with a sponge in my hand, busy washing the plants in our drawing-room.

We had to mix a little in society, and Sergy took me out occasionally to pay formal calls, a task I particularly disliked. There seemed to be no end of card-leaving and card-receiving. It is such a bore going out visiting or holding a drawing-room— and this was my only crumpled rose-leaf. I had got thoroughly tired of the vapid folly and hypocrisy of social life, which is a daily lie, and mentally consigned all dinner-parties and deadly " At-Homes " to perdition. Nothing is more horrible than these " At-Home " days ; it is such a nuisance to have to be nice to people whom in the bottom of your heart you despise, and who devote their ample leisure to passing criticisms of no tender character on their friends behind their backs. All these *Grandes Dames* of the so-called Best World are more like mechanical dolls moving on wires, than living, feeling women. Their lives are framed uniformly on a fixed set of rules, and their gossip is perfectly intolerable to me. They talk either platitudes about chiffons, or make remarks about the weather ; they murmer mechanically hospitable phrases, and then tear their guests to pieces and mock the weak points of the very people whose hands they had just pressed.

I have the courage to order my life independently of the conventions which govern the existence of most women of my position, and I want to keep myself apart from the Great World. I am no longer fond of the pleasures and the admiration of society, finding no interest whatever in balls, which are insipid without a little bit of flirtation, for I can't enjoy the actual exercise of dancing quite irrespective of whom I dance with ; and now that I am married, I certainly will not admit any more courting. People wonder how I manage to kill my time, hiding myself from the world in a monastic seclusion. I am being talked about. " Mrs. This " and " Mrs. That " disapprove of my manner of life which gives rise to comment, but I am hopeless, and they have quite given up trying to reform me. They boycott me now when they meet me and cut me dead, giving me only the tips of their fingers. I pay them back in the same coin, even more, by giving them the ends of my nails. I do not care at all about what people say or think. Why should others busy themselves with my affairs ? I am perfectly well able to act for myself and intend to do so now, and to always brave public opinion. It is difficult to imagine my ranging myself among the slaves, and certainly I am not going to permit my life to be interfered with. If my husband is satisfied with me, it's all right then; only we two—the rest of the world does not count.

Sergy is occupied all day with his business, but in the evenings I have him to myself. He is the only man for me, the rest of the people are mere furniture. We understand each other perfectly; Sergy never plays the domestic tyrant over me, and is ready to do anything to please me, yielding in many respects for the sake of peace, but he knows how to manage me, nevertheless, and is a rock of resolution when serious things are concerned, and keeps his ultimatum for the great occasions. He has completely changed me from what I had been, and made me what I was to be. However, as I have a very inflammable temper, I often make shipwrecks in a tea-cup tempest, during which Sergy always acts like a tonic on my temperament.

Prince Dolgorouki, the Governor General of Moscow, gave great receptions on Sundays after mass held in his private chapel, where the fashionable world met to stare at each other and criticise each other. After service, the Prince invited everybody to take tea and chocolate in his apartments adjoining the chapel. During the reception I noticed that the over-ripe damsels, fearing to be classed as old maids, kept apart from the married matrons. It was very comical to see them planted stiffly on the edge of a sofa in their virginal nook, trying to look young and waiting for future husbands who did not come.

A new and desperate plot was hatched to assassinate the whole Imperial Family. The winter palace has nearly been blown up by dynamite which was to explode at a quarter past seven, during dinner, but luckily the Court was awaiting that day the arrival of a foreign prince, whose train was half-an-hour late, and this delay saved the Tzar and his family.

Sergy began to be anxious for my health; finding that I was looking rather pale, he wisely decided that I must have more exercise and made me go out for a walk every day. Hating to do things by halves, and wanting to prove to Sergy that I was a first-rate walker, the idea came to me one day, whilst taking my afternoon walk, to pay a visit to my aunt Galitzine, who lived about three miles away. I returned home dead tired and awoke next morning with a bad cold. I had to lie in bed with bronchitis for at least a week to be restored to health. For company's sake I always took Tiger, my big Danish dog, with me in my walks, whereat he rejoiced exceedingly, wagging his tail with violence. I had no need to elbow the passers-by with such a companion, every one cleared the way for us. There was much fuss with Tiger, he had to be led by a chain at which he tore with all his might, nearly choking himself with his collar in his desperate struggle to get free ; I had to do my best to keep his spirits within decent bounds. Sometimes he would stretch himself full length on the pavement, and it was hard work to make him get up without threatening him with his whip, at which he would stumble close against my skirt, doing the penitent, with the peculiar aspect of conscious wrong.

One day Tiger was more than ever demonstrative and nearly upset me with his rough gambols, jumping to my face in fierce joy and putting a cool nose against my cheek. Just at that moment we met an old woman carrying a full pitcher of milk, much to my quadruped's pleasure, and Tiger, his big mouth wide open and his pink tongue hungrily out, bounded towards her with loud barks of delight. The poor woman, frightened to death by Tiger's formidable aspect, gave a violent start and dropped her jug, spilling her milk all over the pavement ; Tiger licked it up with grunts of satisfaction. After having quenched his thirst, my agreeably animated dog bounced around the terrified granny, frolicking round her with an uncouth dance and yapping at her in ecstasy ; he put his huge paws over her breast and insisted upon licking her face, wagging his tail conciliatingly. When visitors entered our saloon and we were not there, Tiger usually stretched himself full length across the threshold so that our visitors could not leave the room without striding over him ; Tiger did not deign to budge and allow them to pass, but set up a most ominous growl like distant thunder, and when he was approached, he just opened his eyes and continued to growl until we came in and liberated the affrightened prisoners.

In the spring the unveiling of the newly built monument of Poushkine, our great poet, took place ; it was an event of considerable importance. A requiem in honour of the dead poet was sung on the square before the monument, covered all over with a white wrapper. It was a curious sight ; a great crowd was assembled there. Amongst many deputations a group of young maidens arrayed in Russian national costumes, holding garlands of roses, especially attracted my attention. After the service ended, the military band struck up and the statue was unveiled amongst enthusiastic cheers. The mayor of the town invited me that same day to a grand banquet given in honour of the son of Poushkine, who had just been promoted to the grade of general, telling me that as an authoress I had to take part at the festival, but I refused, giving a plausible reason. Next day I went to a meeting of a literary committee treating on the works of Poushkine, held in the hall of the Assembly. On the big estrade well-known writers, and professors of the different universities gave speeches. When Tourgeneff, our famous old writer appeared, great cheers rose from the audience.

In May we moved to Petrovski Palace, and on the last days of June Sergy went to review the troops at Yaroslaw. During his absence, I was invited by my aunt, Princess Leon Galitzine, to spend a week with her at Doubrovo, her splendid estate situated in the government of Kalouga. I welcomed the opportunity that was offered to me and accepted my aunt's invitation with pleasure. Another aunt of mine, Princess Safira Galitzine, was also going to Doubrovo and proposed to chaperon me. On our way there, great was my surprise to meet at one of the railway stations, Stenger, one of my old admirers of whom I had not heard for years. We both gave a violent start, and I uttered an exclamation of surprise: " Where on earth did you fall from ? " I asked.

My appearance nearly deprived Stenger of speech, then he took my hand and devoured it with kisses, much to the indignation of my aunt who was of the opinion that a married woman shares the dignity of her husband and, like Cæsar's wife, should be above suspicion of even the slightest flirtation. Whilst we paced up and down the platform, a pretty flood of eloquence rose to Stenger's lips, and I was aware that the constancy of his heart was as great as ever, and that he was still my devoted servant. He said with a quiver in his voice, looking me full in the face and nervously tormenting his very slight moustache, that after my marriage he had been moved to the desperate resolution to marry also ; but it did not help him to forget me, and that all these years he did his best to tear the thought of me out of his heart and could not. But I didn't love him, all the difference was there. I only shrugged indifferent shoulders and responded to his passionate eloquence with six degrees of frost. " Fiddle-de-dee ! old times are better left alone," I replied, looking upon his dismayed countenance with a cheerfulness which rather hurt his feelings.

" Why do you treat me like this ? " asked poor Stenger, looking very miserable and crestfallen. Really I am afraid I've been rather rude, to hurt anybody was quite contrary to my nature ; I called myself a monster of ingratitude and tried to be more friendly towards him. I ought to be grateful indeed for he was a faithful being ! Wishing, nevertheless, to get away from my impetuous lover, I hastened into my car. In bidding good-bye, Stenger captured my hands and squeezed them so horribly that he left the print of my rings on my fingers. He stood in a drooping attitude under my window, staring at me with eyes objectionably mournful and looking the very picture of despair. The train moved on and Stenger's pale face was lost to sight ; life had separated us for the second time! He was completely brushed away from my memory, and the whole episode fell away from my mind like breath from a mirror.

The journey to Doubrovo proved to be a tedious business. We had to leave the railway behind ; a coach drive of some fifty miles awaited us. We drove along a flat and somewhat desolate country road. The sun grew hot and so did I. Clouds of dust pursued us, and swarms of big flies attacked us ; we chased them away with branches cut from the trees. A drive of four hours under such conditions is a prostrating experience!

I spent a splendid time in Doubrovo with my cousin, Nelly Galitzine, and was sorry to leave her.

When I got back home, Sergy suggested a trip on the Volga, which I accepted with enthusiasm. We went by train to Nijni-Novgorod, where we had to take the steamer. We arrived at Nijny at about seven o'clock in the morning. I hid myself in my coupé from the military authorities who had come to greet my husband on the platform, but was dragged from my retreat by an officer, who insisted upon my following him into the state apartments of the station opened for us. I was half inclined to crawl under the seat, but there was no escape possible, and, conquering my impulse to flee, with tangled hair and unwashed face, horribly ashamed of myself, I had to walk with such dignity as my disordered condition would permit between two rows of brilliant sons of Mars. General Korevo, the chief of the division stationed at Nijni and its outskirts, offered me his arm and led me to his carriage to drive to the pier.

We took passage on a small steamer belonging to the company of "Caucasus and Mercury," and steamed down the Volga from Nijni to Kazan. In the beginning of our voyage, where the Oka flows into the Volga, the river is in many places half a mile broad. We glided between sandy and sterile banks. Towards evening we arrived at Simbrisk, where we were to pass the night. A rickety old cab drove us to the hotel creeping up the ill-paved hill of an old and dirty street. A shabby waiter showed us into a small room with one bed and a greasy sofa. There was a tournament of self-denial between Sergy and me about the bed, and as neither would give in we decided that we should toss a coin : heads, the bed—tails, the sofa. It came tails, and the sofa fell to my lot! It was not at all a bed of roses, and when I lay down I soon discovered that the repulsive sofa was the property of certain highly disreputable and painfully disagreeable insects. I tossed on my couch of torture until morning.

At eight o'clock we took the "Colorado," an immense three-storied vessel, replete with every luxury and convenience.

The first-class cabins opened on a spacious dining-room. There were many passengers on board, a doleful trio amongst them, a young sad-faced woman in the last degree of consumption travelling with her husband and baby. The poor invalid looked wretchedly ill and extremely nervous, her eyes were constantly filling with tears. Her husband was full of little cares and attentions about her. Another passenger, a lady of unpleasing appearance, more than fifty, but dressed like a young girl, with an artificial complexion and dyed hair, strummed all day long on the piano, which was much out of tune. She fell upon the defenceless instrument, dashing out marches and abominable polkas, making two false notes in every five. At last it was decided that an appeal *ad misericordiam* would be made to the noisy virtuose, and it was the captain who saved the whole company from the much dreaded musical entertainment and undertook to keep that peace-disturber away from the tempting instrument. He made her understand that her performance was not approved of by his passengers and that she had better give the piano a little rest.

After sight-seeing in the town of Kazan, we were back at Nijni the next day. In the morning Sergy went out to the camp, after which we had dinner on board with champagne and speeches, and were back at Moscow on the following day.

In September my husband was appointed military representative at the celebration of the twelve hundreth anniversary of the famous battle on the " Koulikovo Field." We had to be separated for more than a week. I profited by the occasion to visit my parents at Dolgik, my dear old home. It had been arranged between us that as soon as the festivals at Koulikovo were over, Sergy would come and join me at Dolgik. We travelled together as far as Toula, where we separated to go each our different ways. I found myself for the first time in my life travelling alone, but managed, however, to get to Dolgik without any adventure. I established myself in the train with pleasant books and papers to amuse me on the way, and never emerged from my compartment till the last station, which stands a few miles only from Dolgik, where I was met on the platform by my brother, who had come to fetch me in his carriage.

I spent such a happy week in my old country home ! What a lot of sweet reminiscences ! I was in my dear little room again, in which I recalled the old days. I saw myself as a child, a half grown-up girl and a happy bride. The old village people hadn't forgotten me and seemed glad to see me ; as to my parents, one can easily imagine how happy they were to have me with them again.

Fedia, the youngest of my nephews, is such a darling, with

a smile which says, " Please love me ! " One morning as he was just emerging from a battle-royal with his nurse whilst she was coaxing him into his clothes, she began to threaten him that if he continued to be naughty he would be devoured by all the animals mentioned in his favourite story-book, by the lions, tigers and wolves. Fedia, totally unabashed, his mischievous little face peeping from under the coverlet, burst out suddenly : " And the hippopotamus, you forget him ! "

Sergy came to meet me as it had been arranged and brought me back to Moscow.

The director of the " Foundling Hospital " invited us to. visit this interesting establishment, one of the largest in the world, founded by the Empress Catherine II. That huge asylum takes charge yearly of fourteen thousand babes. Many rows of cradles fill up the vast halls. About fifty little ones are brought here every day. The wet-nurses, chosen with the greatest care, carry them away to their villages afterwards, and continue to take care of them until they are grown up. These women receive three roubles per month for each child, who, on attaining the age of twenty, remains as workman in the family that has given him shelter. We saw a respectable matron who had been serving in the " Foundling Hospital " for forty years, and whose sole duty is to give the newly-arrived babes their first bath. The poor little things will never see their mothers again, for as soon as they are washed they are carried away to be mixed with thousands of other babies.

A terrible crime has just been committed at St. Petersburg. On the first of March our beloved Emperor, Alexander II., was murdered by the anarchists. This noblest of men has been killed by a bomb in the streets whilst returning from a visit to the Duchess of Oldenbourg. That day we went to a concert given by Marcella Zembrich, the celebrated opera singer. In the middle of the performance an officer came up to say that the Governor-General of Moscow, Prince Dolgorouki, wished to see my husband at once. Something serious must have happened, otherwise the Prince would not have disturbed Sergy who promised to be back soon. But I returned home immediately and would not go to bed before Sergy's return. I became very anxious at his prolonged absence and couldn't imagine what was keeping him so long. Eleven o'clock arrived and he had not yet returned. I could not help being very much alarmed, and as the minutes passed, I listened more and more anxiously for the sound of hoofs on the pavement, but still there was no sign of my husband. It was long past midnight when he came home in a great state of excitement, bringing the awful news of the murder of our Tzar. A bomb had been flung at his carriage, the back of which was torn away. His Majesty, luckily, was not hurt, but two Cossacks of his escort, and a boy who was passing in the street at that moment, were severely injured. The Tzar insisted upon seeing the wounded and approached the victims, when a second bomb was flung at him which tore off one of his legs and shattered the other. General Grösser, the Prefect of the Police, who always accompanied the Emperor wherever he went, had him lifted up into his sledge and transported His Majesty in that desperate state to the Winter Palace, where he passed away some minutes after.

The tragic death of Alexander II. filled the world with horror. The inhabitants of Moscow were thrilled by the news of that terrible event ; the streets are black with people in mourning, the bells in all the churches are tolling all day long.

The murderers of our Tzar were caught and brought to trial ; they were all sentenced to death. The sole executioner existing in Russia had been sent for from Moscow to execute them. Sophia Perovski, the daughter of a high Russian functionary, who had participated in the conspiracy plot, fled to Switzerland and for some time eluded her pursuer, a political spy who had been sent to trace her. The detective craftfully succeeded in making her fall in love with him and follow him to the frontier, where she was arrested and brought for trial to St. Petersburg. Not a very handsome proceeding on his part I must say ! When Sophia Perovski appeared before the tribunal, she was told that she would be hanged if she did not denounce all her accomplices ; but she absolutely refused to divulge their names, and exclaimed with splendid indifference, " I do not dread your gibbet, I only dread the misfortunes which befall my beloved brethren ! " However, when the choice was given to her to be hanged or delivered over to the mercy of her beloved brethren, she threw herself at the Attorney's feet, imploring him to condemn her to the cruelest punishment, but only not to give her up to the mob.

We are living through very troublesome times. Our new Emperor, Alexander III., receives anonymous letters with threats that he too, will be murdered and his son, the heir to the throne, stolen and taken away !

A secret notice was given to the police that the anarchists were preparing to blow up the Winter Palace, which is looking now like a fortress encircled with a rope ; even generals are not permitted to enter its enclosure.

It is an awful time altogether ! Alarming rumours continue to circulate. There is said to be a great deal of agitation in the country, especially in the south, where there is a special hatred against the Jews ; their houess are ransacked and plundered. The peasants begin to rebel and refuse to take oath to their new Tzar, stating that his father's murderers had been bribed by the Russian nobility, which was now avenging itself for the emancipation of the peasants, effected by Alexander II. Troops were obliged to be sent there to settle order amongst the rebels.

Kobzeff, one of the most important anarchists, a very stylish young man who hadn't at all the dynamite-look on his face, gained admittance under a false name into the most fashionable drawing-rooms of St. Petersburg. He went afterwards to Moscow and even forced his way into Prince Dolgorouki's palace on pretext that he was an engineer who had found out a new system of gas-light for the town.

The police had been informed that a quantity of dynamite has just been transported to one of Moscow's railway stations. But, when they wanted to confiscate it, the cunning anarchists disguised as policemen, took possession in full daylight of the murderous baggage under the very nose of the real police agents who arrived at the station a few minutes later and found all the dynamite gone.

The irritation against the anarchists is growing from day to day ; there are often scuffles in the streets. A masculine-looking girl, with short hair and glasses, was taken for a socialist by the wild mob, which stamped upon her reducing her nearly to the condition of a pancake. She had to be sent to the hospital with a bloody nose and black eyes. About the same time a French manicurist bought a paper from a news boy, in which the Emperor's funeral was described. Finding that the vendor had charged too high a price for his paper, the Frenchman asked him, in very bad Russian, why " he took so dear for such stuff," meaning the sheet of paper, but unfortunately he was understood in quite a different manner, and knocked down and beaten so severely that he died the next day.

In the middle of June the Tzar came to Moscow to review the troops on the " Khodinka Field." A warning had come from abroad telling the police to take great care of bomb-throwers during that review, and especially to mistrust the men wearing top-hats, which could hold engines ofe dstruction in them. Though great precautions had been taken, I felt awfully nervous whilst the review was going on. Count Brevern opened the parade on horseback, surrounded by my husband and a brilliant staff of splendidly uniformed officers who took up their position behind the Emperor. My fear of the anarchists did not hinder me from admiring the beautiful appearance of our soldiers. The artillery and infantry in compact rows, and the cavalry galloping very fast, produced an imposing spectacle. The regiments were splendid, they all came up and passed : cavalry, infantry, artillery, ambulance, doctors and all, with much music.

After the review the Emperor invited the chief-commanders to a lunch at Petrovski Palace. Some of the officers of the Emperor's suite came to pay us a visit in the afternoon, General Skobeleff, a brillant celebrity, amongst them. Though he was supposed to be a woman-hater, he gallantly kissed my hand, at which an enthusiastic lady-visitor, who happened to be present, began to examine my hand to see if a star had not incrusted itself on it after the kiss of such a man, every inch a hero.

A week afterwards the Grand Duke Michael arrived to be present at the grand manœuvres. I was on the Kodinka Field driving my pair of ponies when the order was given to the cavalry to attack the Petrovski Palace. Fearing to be trampled down by the charge of the cavalry, I jumped out of the pony-chase, leaving the ponies to the care of the groom, and started running home by the shortest cut, jumping over pits and ditches. The next day I drove to the spot where the mock-battle was to take place. The sound of the trumpets resounded from everywhere and the cannons kept up such a continual firing that the ground actually shook under us. The cavalry was prancing round. I soon perceived the Grand Duke and would have turned tail and fled, but I was not permitted to make my escape. I alighted and tried to hide myself behind my ponies, but for the first time I was dissatisfied with the diminutive stature of these little fellows; there was no concealment even for a rabbit. My position was awfully critical; I have never felt such a longing to sink into the earth and disappear from human sight. The Grand Duke, who had discovered me, laughed a great deal— I didn't!

We often spent our evenings at the Hermitage, a large music-hall, the entrance of which was strictly forbidden to collegians and cadets. One of them got in nevertheless, dressed in woman's clothes, a fair, effeminate youth. With his smooth girlish face he easily passed for what he pretended to be and played his part to perfection. He was soon surrounded by a crowd of admirers. But the poor boy got severely punished for his trick, and had to endure three days of arrest.

By the end of September we returned to town. Our new home was ready to welcome us: our house is said to be haunted, and the first thing we did was to order a Te Deum to be sung in our apartments. Now I hope we won't come across visitants from the other world!

We have been very busy settling into our new quarters. When all was arranged, we began to lead a gay life, and went to the best concerts and theatricals of the season. Sarah Bernhardt, an actress of world-wide renown, the greatest tragedian of the age, having conquered New York, achieved her next success in Moscow, which she took by storm. I was deeply interested to see her in *La Dame aux Camelias*, where she is at her best. Sarah, who is already well up in years, is a delicate-looking woman with a waist of painful slenderness. Her acting is simply wonderful. She was a glorious incarnation of *Violetta*, in the death scene, though I am not readily moved to the tears, I wiped from my eyes " *Una furtiva lagrime* " as Donizetti's song has it. The audience, which packed the house from floor to ceiling, was enthusiastic and applauded her much.

Sarah's name was on everybody's lips. The best milliners and dressmakers of Moscow went to her performances to copy her costumes, and the confectioners promised her portrait for every pound of bonbons. On our "At-home days," when I found myself searching for a suitable topic of conversation, the name of the great artist came to my aid, and I had every reason to be grateful to her without her being aware of it, for having helped me to entertain my guests. In comparison with Sarah the rest of her troop was very insignificant. The actor performing the leading part of lover, a gentleman by birth, had fallen under the spell of the enchantress and lost his heart to her. For her sake he became an actor and always accompanied her on her tours, following her wherever she went like the traditional lamb. The love-sick *Jeune Premier* looked extremely foolish when making love to Sarah on the stage, casting sheep's eyes at her. My goodness, what ridiculous creatures men are !

Anthony Rubinstein, the king of the piano, was giving his last public concert in Moscow. The whole town came in to be present at the leave-taking. When the great pianist appeared on the estrade, he was met by a roar of applause ; the wild enthusiasm of the house was indescribable. Rubinstein was a real treat, and bewildered me by his marvellous execution. This incomparable artist gave an interpretation of Chopin which sent a trill through me. His *touché* and his *technique* were wonderful and perfect, he made the instrument positively sob and sing. I was in an ecstasy of delight and listened entranced, having never heard anything so beautiful before. Rubinstein looks something like Beethoven, clean-shaven, with a powerful face ; his long locks, shaggy and picturesque, waved in sympathy with his excitement. When he had ceased, there was a moment of entire silence, that finest homage due to beautiful playing.

During Rubinstein's stay in Moscow he was bothered by a crowd of artists "in embryo," who all wanted to sing for "opera" without having the remotest idea how to sing, coming to ask him if he would try their voices and tell them if they had talent enough to follow the artistic career. A friend of ours happened to come on a visit to Rubinstein just at the moment when a fat, neckless lady of about fifty summers was making her rehearsal. She sang like an old cat; her one idea was to be heard and she howled all her top notes so hard as to make all the dogs bark in the street. Dumfounded and horrified, our friend stopped his ears and took to his heels, running away as fast as his legs could carry him.

One day we went to see a bird Exhibition at the Manège and were present at a horrible cock-fight—a most disgusting sight! White and red cocks were taken out of their narrow cages and settled on a small estrade covered with sand and surrounded by a railing. The combat began, the winged champions struck against one another, with bristled feathers which flew about on all sides, croaking piercingly all the time. By refinement of cruelty they had steel spurs fastened on their legs. The enraged birds picked off each others' skins by morsels, and long streams of blood spread on the sand. The white cock soon became purple-coloured; his red antagonist after having plucked out both his eyes, won the battle. I was boiling all over with indignation, but the cruel audience exhausted itself in frantic applause, admiring this miserable sport. The ganders' fight was not a less sickening spectacle. The males with wings outspread, prepared to battle, but only in the presence of their betterhalves, who ran after their "pachas" gabbling loudly.

I regretted still more to have accepted an invitation to be present at a wolve hunting on the race ground. The poor animals were brought on the arena in big wooden boxes. Exposed to the light of day and scared by the crowds of noisy spectators, the unfortunate wolves had scarcely the time to make two or three limping steps, both their hind legs being tied fast together, when a pack of starving hounds rushed upon them and tore them to pieces. It was a shame, a crying shame! Oh, how barbarous mankind is, I thought.

The Terrorists are continuing their work. It's getting positively dreadful, everyone's nerves are set on edge. Many rumours are circulating in St. Petersburg. The story goes now that the late Tzar Alexander II., proceeds slowly every night from the Winter Palace to the Kazan Cathedral, where he appears to the people. One of the chief rioters profited by this report, and one evening, during vespers, the Emperor's ghost made its usual appearance, pronouncing in a loud voice the following words: "Warn my son that I am waiting for him." But hardly had the admirably disguised sham-Emperor finished his public address, when the police laid hands upon him.

Moscow is now the rallying place of the anarchists. A band of malefactors had just been caught setting themselves upon undermining one of the theatres which was being built in the enclosure of the future French Exhibition on the

" Khodinka Field," a few paces from the Imperial pavilion which will be inaugurated in the month of May. By a lucky chance a factory where imitation oranges stuffed with dynamite were being made, was also discovered. The terrorists disguised as errand boys were to throw this murderous fruit into the midst of assemblages in order to produce a panic. I am greatly alarmed by all this !

Towards the beginning of May, in consequence of a sudden burst of hot weather, we left the town and betook ourselves to Petrovski Palace, the French Exhibition was just opposite the Palace. It was a grand affair ; lots of people were flocking in to see the splendid show. Punctually at ten o'clock in the morning we heard the whistle announcing the opening of the Exhibition. Everytime I visited it I felt myself as if transported by magic from Moscow to Paris. All the sections are very interesting and instructive. My cousin, Prince Leon Galitzine, one of the richest wine makers in the Crimea, had a splendid stand where he regaled everybody gratis with his wines. I dreaded to pass close by, because my cousin always forced me to taste the different sorts of wines, which made my cheeks, already burning like fire because of the great heat, pass gradually from red to crimson, and it was most unbecoming.

I had some accidental meetings with old friends at the Exhibition. One day, in the whirl of the crowd, I found myself suddenly face to face with Mr. O., my old love, for whom I had had a strong liking in my girlhood days. It was an age since I had heard anything of him and he was the last person I ever expected to see there. I had quite rubbed him out of my mind and there he was now. I could scarcely believe my eyes. My heart gave a little jump and I don't mind confessing, I was rather pleased to see him, although I thought I had long since given him up for ever. The sight of Mr. O. gave me an odd mixture of sensation, I was startled, I was disturbed, I was pleased. Time had made but few changes in his appearance, he had grown a trifle stouter, that was all, and I recognised him immediately. For the first moment agitation deprived us both of speech. On overcoming his constraint, Mr. O. began to talk of different things, he chaffed and laughed and told funny stories as of yore. Presently we discovered a comfortable seat and sat down near where the band was playing. Suddenly Mr. O. became serious and began assuring me of his love, of his fidelity. Oh, the things he said to me ! I wanted to put a stop to his passionate outburst, and felt very angry with my paralysed tongue. All the same I could not remain entirely unmoved, and to my extreme disgust I felt myself turning very red, and for the sake of doing something, I began drawing circles with my umbrella on the sand, looking anywhere but into his face. When recovering my composure I felt it my duty to lead the conversation into other channels and though my colour was beyond my control, my voice was steady, and with eyes which still declined to meet his, I told him he should leave off talking such nonsense, doing my best to make light of the matter. But he gazed at my downcast countenance and said, "I love you Vava!" to my very face, as if he had the right to call me by my Christian name. When we got up and passed through the section of toys, he asked abruptly if I had any children, and without waiting for my reply, he disappeared and returned soon after, holding a small india-rubber monkey by a long string. He thrust this little horror into my hand whispering, "That's for your baby." As it appeared Mr. O., who had married soon after me, had neither any babies of his own, and thus this nasty little monkey was of no good to either of us.

In September the Grand Duke Nicholas came to witness the grand manœuvres and stopped at Petrovski Palace. We lived in one of the wings of the palace, and wanting to see the Grand Duke's arrival, I had to mount a narrow corkscrew staircase, with shattered steps leading up one of the turrets. The walls were mouldy and hung with cobwebs which tumbled down upon my head. The view of Moscow and its surroundings, on reaching the top of the turret, was a thorough compensation for my disagreeable climb.

The next day I was invited to a dancing-party given in honour of the Grand Duke at the military summer club on the Khodinka Field. The Grand Duke was very affable towards me and contrived to put me at my ease at once. His Highness asked me to take tea with him. He seemed in capital spirits and talked in the most friendly way. He told me that he remembered me when I was quite a little thing and wore socks and pinafore, and said that passing through the town of Kharkoff he came to visit my parents and made me jump upon his knee. We sat round the tea-table for a long time. In bidding good-bye the Grand Duke proposed to me to come on the manœuvre-ground the following morning.

Getting up at break of day I hurried to our rendezvous and saw the Grand Duke in the distance standing upon a hillock amongst a group of generals and officers surveying the sham-fight with a field glass at his eye. On perceiving me the Grand Duke nodded and waved his hand, and when I approached His Highness, he inquired after the state of my health, fearing I had taken a cold in remaining out in the club-garden so long the night before.

A few days later a sham-alarm was raised in the camp. I was out before five o'clock in the morning and directed my steps towards the camp half asleep and yawning widely. There was still moonlight outside, and the breeze that ran before day-break was making me shiver a little. Suddenly cannon-shots were heard and in less than two minutes the the whole camp was astir. The soldiers rushed out of their tents and arranged themselves in battle-columns, whilst trumpet signals rent the air

No sooner had the Grand Duke Nicholas departed than his brother the Grand Duke Michael arrived to inspect the artillery. During his stay the artillery officers gave a lunch at the military club. I was invited to it, but was about to refuse, being very unwilling to go there alone, as Sergy was not quite well. But there was no escaping from it, and I had to accept the invitation. Countess Brevern, the wife of the commander-in-chief, who was also going with her two daughters to that lunch, offered to take me under her wing. When I was being presented to the Grand Duke he did not recognise me at first, and taking me for one of the young countesses he asked their mother which number I was. "Your Highness does not recognise me!" I exclaimed indignantly. When the countess named me, the Grand Duke pressed my hand warmly and said that I looked so absurdly young, that there was nothing surprising at all that he did not recognise in me such a respectable person as the wife of the chief of the staff.

Lunch passed off gaily, and I was glad after all that I went to it. The Grand Duke was charming to me and not at all ceremonious ; I soon felt quite at my ease with him, and entirely free from shyness. Altogether I enjoyed myself thoroughly, although I had been dragged there by force and considered myself a victim, feeling like a lamb about to be led to slaughter, and compared that lunch to a disagreeable pill which had to be swallowed.

In November Sergy had to go to St. Petersburg and took me with him. Whilst there, I had the chance to be present at a banquet given in the Hall of the Assembly on the day of the jubilee of the Academy of the General Staff. With difficulty I got a place in the gallery, from where I could see very well. As I was ascending the stairs, someone called me by my name, I looked round and saw the Grand Duke Michael hastening up to me. Putting out a welcoming hand His Highness exclaimed,

"You can't say now that I did not recognise you and it will atone for my former mistake, I hope!" to which I answered that the Grand Duke would only be completely forgiven when I receive his photograph from him. The very next day he sent me his portrait with his autograph.

· Spring came with galloping speed. The date of the Coronation was fixed for the 15th May. I went to see the Court

Regalias exposed to view in the Kremlin Palace. The crown and the sceptre, studded with precious stones as big as nuts, amazed me by their incredible richness. On the walls hung Gobelin tapestries and pictures taken from the Bible. Just opposite the Metropolitan's seat I saw a painting illustrating the story of Potipher's wife dragging Joseph by his legendary mantle. These heroes of the Ancient Testament being very lightly clad, the police censor had found it necessary to dress them in a more decent manner for the Coronation, leaving at the same time, just next to that picture, a large canvas representing a group of the " Happy Just " enjoying Paradise in a completely nude state. I also went to see a fine assortment of State carriages and the beautiful horses which were to drag them, pure white Hanovrians all of them.

In Moscow wonderful preparations have been made in the way of decorations. Our capital is in a state of extraordinary excitement. Triumphal arches and large tribunes are built on the principal squares. A great number of houses have their fronts decorated with carpets and flowers.

Our old capital is crowded to its utmost. People come from all parts of the world to see the ceremony of crowning. Every place in the trains was booked weeks in advance. The troops of the Guard Regiments continue to arrive from St. Petersburg. Along the streets move cavalry and guns. At our entrance door a placard says, "Staff of all the troops quartered in Moscow during the Coronation festivals."

My husband's eldest brother has arrived to be present at the Coronation. He had to take part in the equestrian procession of the Russian nobility. I went to see the rehearsal of it, and nearly choked with laughter at the sight of the timorous expression painted on the faces of some of these brave knights, who sat on their horses all of a huddle, and were wrapped up in observation of their own movements. The nobility certainly did not shine in the saddle. My brother-in-law's neighbour, a stout and rosy country gentleman, clutched at his horse's mane and asked him anxiously if his horse would not bite his heels, and confessed that he did not at all feel safe, being quite out of practice now, not having been for some twenty years on horseback.

The Emperor arrived at Moscow on the 8th May and drove straight to Petrovski Palace. There is much to be dreaded during the Coronation festivities, for the anarchists are not slumbering, and agents of the secret police had to be placed on the whole way. The triumphal entry of the Tzar into the town of Moscow took place two days afterwards. A great crowd had assembled in the streets through which the procession was to proceed to see the Emperor's entry. I and my sister-in-law had the privilege of being given good places on one of the tribunes built on the square just opposite the Kremlin. It was at the risk of our limbs and lives that we got there, being nearly crushed to death. We found ourselves in a dense crowd and marched boldly through the throng, our dresses leaving a good deal of themselves behind. We ventured within the rope drawn to keep back the crowd, and nearly reached our places when a new encumbrance arose, a row of soldiers refused to let us pass, but their chief took pity on us and cut our way through his men. At last we got inside the Kremlin with a deep sigh of relief.

We had to wait for the procession from early morning till two o'clock in the afternoon. The day was grey, the sky looked threatening, it was undoubtedly going to pour soon, and we risked being drenched as our tribune was uncovered and our umbrellas had been taken away from us at the entrance. But I was not made of sugar or salt, and preferred to have my dress ruined and to be drenched to the bone rather than be deprived of the beautiful sight which awaited us. To crown all, I was awfully hungry, not having had time to breakfast before starting, and it had been strictly forbidden to bring anything in one's pockets for fear of concealed explosions blowing everyone up. A lady sitting next to me had a squabble with a policeman through an inoffensive orange which she had taken out of her pocket. She was not allowed to eat it even in his presence.

Outside the rope there was an indescribable squeeze. The crowd swayed with a wavelike motion and made a rush besieging the barrier. The human waves were kept back by several lines of soldiers and a double row of policemen. Such a crowd was almost beyond imagination.

At two o'clock precisely the guns began to fire and the bells to ring a full peal, announcing that the Tzar had left Petrovski Palace and was on his way to the Kremlin. Soon the procession appeared in sight and the crowd began to acclaim their Sovereign by loud cheers; all the heads were bare. As I am a creature of strong emotions I, too, screamed to make myself hoarse. The procession advanced in the following order: First came a golden coach drawn by a teem of splendid white horses in which sat the Empress and the Grand Duchesses. The Emperor rode behind with the Tzarevitch at his side, on a lovely pony. The Grand Dukes and the officers of the guard regiments brought up the rear. The spectacle was most imposing.

For three days the Heralds in heraldic costumes rode about the town announcing by sound of trumpet that the ceremony of the Coronation would take place on the 15th May.

The great day arrived. Long before six o'clock in the morning the streets were black with excited crowds. I rose when it was only beginning to be daylight and at seven o'clock we were already driving to the Kremlin; it was printed on our tickets that after eight o'clock nobody would be allowed to enter its enclosure, and that was the reason we had to start so early. The large square was covered all over with red cloth. Ministers of the State and officers in full uniform began to assemble. The tribune on the opposite side was occupied by foreign Royalties and representatives of the different Oriental countries in gala costumes studded all over with precious stones. The Khan of Khiva was glittering like the sun. The Grand Duke Waldemar, accompanied by a numerous suite, came out of the palace and proceeded to the Cathedral of Assumption where the Tzars are crowned, followed by all the members of the Imperial Family, the ladies of the Court wearing the national dress of the richest style, the Court officials resplendent in their gorgeous uniforms, the Ambassadors of foreign countries with their spouses, the personages of the first two classes and all the authorities of the town with my husband amongst them. The bewildering variety of the many different uniforms, both military and diplomatic, was striking. Our troops standing in long rows, with the standard of every regiment, were an imposing sight. The Metropolitan, with a mitre on his head, in magnificent vestments thick with gold embroideries, followed by his Archbishops, came out of the Cathedral to meet Their Majesties who were slowly descending the steps of the wide marble staircase of the palace, coming out of the private apartments to proceed to the Cathedral. The Tzar gave his arm to the Tzarin, whose train was carried by four pages, behind came a long file of ladies-in-waiting and maids-of-honour. A company of the regiment of the Chevalier Guards walked ahead, behind them came forty-eight pages, and a second platoon of Chevalier Guards brought up the rear. The day was grey and wet, it soon began to rain, but it was indeed remarkable that at the moment Their Majesties appeared, the heavy clouds broke away and out burst sunshine, whilst a flock of white doves circled around them. At the foot of the staircase sixteen generals aide-de-camps to the Emperor supported a magnificent baldachin under which Their Majesties passed on to the Cathedral to be crowned, whilst guns were repeatedly firing. At the end of the ceremony there was a clamour of joy bells and the military bands began to play our National Anthem. It was a thrilling moment and my excitement was intense.

That evening Moscow was beautifully illuminated; the belfries of the numerous cathedrals and the towers of the Kremlin glittered with different-coloured lights. From all parts gushed out fountains illuminated by Bengal-lights. I felt myself transported into dreamland.

The following days were a whirl of festivities. There were

many entertainments given to which I was bidden, but it was difficult to get me to go anywhere. At the risk of being treated as a Vandal, I had arranged my existence nicely without going outside to look for amusement. I hate balls now, finding that dancing without a bit of flirtation is only a ridiculous jumping about, and loving my husband as I do, I am not the woman to be flirted with. I was told that the Grand Duke Michael repeatedly alluded to my absence at the Court balls. He hinted to Sergy that he was a Blue-Beard and kept me under lock and key inside a tower, like a tyrant knight of the middle-ages. Mrs. Grundy is ever on the war-path and people won't let me alone for having cut myself from the world. I wonder why they take so much interest in me when I do not take the faintest interest in them. I do not care a fig for any one, having the courage of my own acts and opinions, and care only to please my husband.

It is difficult to understand me at times. I am not quite like other people, being a thing of nerves and moods. One ball, I felt myself somewhat like Cinderella, and as I couldn't evening when my sister-in-law had driven away to a Court stand being left altogether out in the cold, I seized the opportunity for a few frantic tears in private. I daresay it was silly of me, but I couldn't help it. Only fancy, my sister-in-law is going to enjoy herself whilst I must pine away at home! But the odd thing was that even if I had been persuaded ever so much to go to that ball, I should not have gone.

A great festivity was given on the Khodinka Field for the people. On both sides of the Imperial pavilion large tribunes were built for the higher dignitaries of our town and the guests, and just opposite an immense stage was set up for the mob. I sat surrounded by all the great ones of the earth. As soon as Their Majesties appeared, surrounded by a glittering court, the performances in the different shows broke off and hurrahs were heard from all sides, whilst hats and bonnets flew up in the air. After the patriotic enthusiasm got appeased, an allegorical cavalcade in fancy dress defiled before us, after which baskets full of fruit and sweets were dealt out to the populace. We had to dine in a restaurant in the park, all our servants having a holiday that day.

The town-council organised a banquet for three thousand soldiers belonging to the Preobrajenski guard regiment within a few miles of Moscow, in a village bearing the name of that regiment. Our Emperor was present at the festival; he walked round the refreshment tables set up near the Imperial pavilion, and lifting up his glass, His Majesty drank to the health of his soldiers who threw up their caps in the air and shouted with all their might.

Many crowned heads had come to Moscow to see the

Coronation, Prince Amédée d'Aoste amongst them.   He is said to have the Evil-Eye, and as I am somewhat superstitious, I provided myself with a " Getattore," a tiny coral hand with two extended fingers.   This Prince has really brought many misfortunes during his life with him ; one day the part of the tribune on which he stood smashed and fell, another time a part of the ship on which he was sailing was blown up.

By that time much of the excitement had calmed down and Moscow relapsed into its former quiet.   At the end of May our troops began to leave Moscow.   The regiment of the Chevalier Guards, with their band marching in front of them, defiled before our windows on their way to the railway station.   At this sight, without knowing why, I burst into tears like a silly that I was.   I suppose it was due to the state of my nerves, irritated by the unusual mode of life I was leading during the Coronation.

A great number of rewards have been distributed on account of the Coronation.   My husband having already got all the rewards due to the rank of major-general, received as a present from the Tzar a rich gold snuff-box set all over with big diamonds—a custom dating from the times of the Empress Catherine II.

September came, bringing in premature cold weather, the rain fell continually.   These showers had their good side in laying the phenomenal dust in the streets of our venerable old city.

CHAPTER XX

OUR JOURNEY ABROAD

AN event occurred which overwhelmed me with joy. My husband was quite unexpectedly sent to Italy to be present at the Grandes Manœuvres at Milan. What a splendid surprise it was! We packed up and started on our journey in the first days of June. As the manœuvres begin only in July, we shall have plenty of time to wander about sight-seeing. First we are going to the seaside, and have decided upon proceeding straight on to Boulogne-sur-mer. That will be a treat indeed!

The country between St. Petersburg and the Prussian frontier is very uninteresting, nothing but flat cornfields, woods and wide expanses of pasture-land stretching on both sides of the railway.

When we arrived at the frontier some Prussian officials rushed into our compartment, and having taken possession of our passports, they declared, to our profound stupefaction, that we had to go out and began to fling our hand-bags out of the window. We had scarcely time to jump out when the train began to move, carrying away our heavy baggage which had been more lucky than we were, and we were left to our own devices. It appeared that our passports had not been signed by the German Consul in Moscow, and although it was stated in my husband's passport that he was going to Italy on a special mission, these horrid Germans tumbled us out of the train, finding sufficient ground for detaining us until permission be received by wire from their Consul in Moscow to let us proceed further. We stood for some time on the platform a picture of forlorn discomfort, looking at each other helplessly, and trying to collect our scattered wits. How perfectly dreadful it was! Our position can be better imagined than described. We had positively no notion where to go and what to do with ourselves. The day was closing rapidly, it would soon be night. What were we to do? Sleep in the open air perhaps, for except the station, there was not a house within sight, and to return to our frontier was impossible, there being no other train that night. Clutching our bags we mournfully entered a vast "Warte-Saal" where a party of bearded Teutons were loading themselves with beer out of huge pint-mugs, and were all talking at once amid clouds of tobacco smoke. The atmosphere making me feel faint and dizzy, we hastened back to the platform in search of the station-master to beg him to give us somewhere to lay our heads. He came up to us, a fiercely moustached man, awfully stiff and puffed up, and asked us what we wanted. We begged him, expressing ourselves somewhat lamely in German, to give us shelter for the night. He led us to his quarters and ushered us into a little slip of a room, low-roofed and white-washed, furnished with two huge feather-beds with eider-down quilts, where we felt ourselves as prisoners put under arrest. A bad night is soon passed after all! The first thing I did was to remove, with all haste, the obnoxious coverlet and lie down, but I could not sleep for the stifling air in the room; I tossed and turned in bed till morning.

We started back to Alexandrovo with the first train without taking any breakfast, not wishing to have anything to do with these detestable Prussians. On arriving at the station, whilst taking coffee, we received the longed-for telegram, and as we had to wait till evening for the North Express, we decided to drive to Tzekhotzinsk, a small Polish watering place, which is only a few miles distant from Alexandrovo. The journey was extremely trying on account of the excessive heat, and the flies which were pertinacious. We proceeded along a sandy road under a broiling sun. At last we arrived. The Casino, a red-brick house hidden among the trees, suggested repose and comfort. After having appeased our hunger and quenched our thirst in the restaurant, we took a room and locked ourselves up to have a good rest. After a refreshing nap, Sergy went to explore the place. He returned after his stroll rather dissatisfied with Tzekhotzinsk, and we decided to return to Alexandrovo at once. We were surely taken here for a pair of unlawful conjugators of the verb " to love," for we merely came to perch like a bird for a couple of hours, then to fly away.

When the North Express drew up at Alexandrovo we went to have a try for a carriage to ourselves and had to give a good tip to the conductor who ushered us into an empty compartment, assuring us that we should have it to ourselves as far as Berlin; but at the first stopping another guard came to announce that we had been placed here by mistake, this car being bound for another direction. He proposed for us a compartment in the neighbouring carriage; but if he imagined that he was going to be as liberally recompensed as his cheat of a companion, he was very much mistaken, for he did not receive even one kreutzer. We got thoroughly punished for it, however, for when the train was going to start and we had just composed ourselves for deep slumber, a lady and gentleman were ushered into our compartment, an elderly Englishman on the wrong side of fifty, particularly nasty-looking, and his spouse, a young person of about nineteen, very nice to look at. Her husband called her "Baby," and bestowed caresses upon her all the way; but she didn't seem to care a cent about him and responded very phlegmatically to his advances. Well, to have married such an individual she must have had great courage, with not so much as a pair of tongs would I have touched him, and couldn't have married him if he was the only man in the whole world.

CHAPTER XXI

BOULOGNE-SUR-MER

HERE we are at Boulogne, comfortably settled at the Hôtel du Pavillon Impérial. From the window I can see the broad Atlantic and the sea-shore which is so extensive that in 1855 Napoleon III. made the review of an army of 40,000 men on it. The tides are very strong at Boulogne, the sea is very high in the afternoon, the water rising rapidly with a great splashing of waves, and towards evening it is quite low again. Bathing is allowed only after the arrival of the life-boats at their station. In bad weather, when the signals of stormy weather are hung out, bathing is forbidden. We spent most of our time out of doors, taking long walks by the sea-shore or wandering up and down the winding, sleepy, streets of old " Haute-Ville," and climbing up the ramparts with their pleasant outlook on fields and ocean.

One day we visited the fish-market. The fisherwomen with their short skirts and large white flapping caps, holding their arms akimbo, reminded me of the traditional " Madame Angot." We crossed over in a canoe to a small beach where the fishermen anchor their boats at spring-tide. We returned to Boulogne with a grey-haired boatman wearing a silver ear-ring in one ear. He was a desperate Royalist, as it appears, and fumed all the time during our crossing against the French Republic, thanks to which, to his belief, morals had visibly decayed at Boulogne. He said that we had no idea of the extent of corruption in this unhappy country, and how disloyal the population was to their household traditions which they had cherished for centuries. Wanting to prove to us that he had remained a good Christain, he began to search in the pockets of his jersey for a small silver cross, forgetting to row in the meanwhile; and just at that moment whilst I was going hot and cold all over, a steamer came towards us full speed and we narrowly escaped being upset.

On clear days the coasts of England are discernable; it gave us the desire to cross the Channel. We never remained long in one place, possessed with an insatiable appetite for novelty, and always wanted to be somewhere where we were not; and now also we thought of remaining here three weeks, but at the end of three days we decided to turn our backs on Boulogne. I suggested that we should leave for London without delay, with the mail-boat which started for Folkestone in the morning. All the boats leave Boulogne when the tide is at its highest and not at set hours. We packed up our things at once and asked for our hotel bill, which proved to be a very long-tailed comet, quite three feet in length. It took us some time to settle it, as we were short of change, having only Russian money which was not accepted at the hotel, and as it was Sunday all the exchange offices were shut. Our situation was very embarrassing. At length the hotel manager took pity on us and accepted our Russian coins.

We were just in time for the Channel-boat, but our first impression when we stepped on board was not very favourable, thanks to a battery of basins placed under the sofas of the saloon ; I began to feel sick on the spot and hurried up on deck where the air felt cool and delicious after the close atmosphere of the saloon. Leaning on the rail, I looked out at the fast disappearing French coast. There was no wind and the ocean was as smooth as a lake. We had a first-rate passage and it only took us three-quarters of an hour to get to Folkestone. We soon perceived the white cliffs of England.

At Folkestone we took the express to London ; the train rushed across the pleasant English landscape. All around lay pasture of green velvet with flocks of sheep grazing on the meadows. Soon tall chimneys rose against the sky. Here was London ! its suburbs look like one immense building with an endless line of similar houses with boxes of red geraniums on the window-sills, surmounted by numerous chimney-pots smoking in the misty air.

CHAPTER XXII

LONDON

When the train drew up at Charing Cross platform, we hastened to collect our belongings for there was nobody to help us down with our luggage, and we had to find our way alone to Charing Cross Hotel loaded with our hand-bags. We were accosted on our way by a little hunchbacked man who pushed up to us on the crowded platform, a real ant's nest, and offered in very good Russian his services as guide, proposing to show us the principal sights of London. He must know foreigners by heart to have guessed our nationality at first sight. We turned deaf ears to his importunities, fearing that miserable Æsop to be a pickpocket, but he continued to trot steadily behind us and repeated: "Can I be of any assistance."

"Thank you," we replied, "None is needed," and we entered the hotel. The porter handed over the number of our room to us which proved to be No. 575, then we found ourselves in the lift en route for the fifth floor. As soon as we had repaired somehow, the ravages of sea and train, we went out to saunter through London. When we emerged from the gates of the hotel we again met Mr. Punch, our humpbacked pursuer, and this time we yielded to his assertions that without his aid we should be lost in the immense Metropolis, which he had at his finger ends, and arranged a meeting for the next day at the "Café Gatti" for ten o'clock in the morning. It appears that our guide is a Pole by birth, who had to leave Russia for political reasons after the rising in Poland, and has been settled in London for the last thirty years. This exile must be very trying in his old age. An intense compassion sprang up in my heart for the lonely old Pole, dismissed abroad to end his days, a friendless stranger in a foreign land.

Next morning our guide awaited us at our rendezvous at the appointed hour. We explored London thoroughly, crossing it from beginning to end with the underground railway and other conveyances. It was mid-summer, the season for London ; in the streets it is all haste and crowding, thousands and thousands of people all hurrying to some place or other. Especially the crossing of the London

Bridge, ploughed in all directions by omnibuses, cabs and private carriages, all tearing this way and that, made my head swim. We both drove and walked a good deal. The streets are very dangerous to cross; our old guide went before us, bent in two, one hand behind his back holding a stick. He was not very reassuring and said that in London, according to statistics, about a dozen persons were run over in the streets by carriages every day. In the City, the business part of the town, the heavy market waggons drawn by great powerful cart-horses especially attracted my attention.

We did a great deal of sight-seeing that day. We began with the Kensington Museum where we saw, amongst the many treasures which the museum contains, the first engine constructed by Stephenson, named by him "The Rocket." On leaving the museum we were privileged to see one of the most interesting sights of London, the Houses of Parliament, on the roof of which a lamp, the symbol of watchfulness and vigilance, is burning continually. On our way from there to Madame Tussaud's wax-figure show, we passed the noseless statue of Queen Anne. This damage was done by a hooligan who, profiting by the fog, climbed up the statue with the intention of mutilating it, but he had only time to cut off the nose when the fog cleared away suddenly and the miscreant was laid hold of.

In the main hall of Madame Tussaud's Museum an orchestra was playing. Amongst the many wax-figures we saw groups of Royalties in the robes and jewels of other times. We were in the company of all the remarkable old Kings and Queens of England and France. We stopped before William the Conqueror, asking Matilda of Flanders to sit down, and Richard Cœur de Lion in domestic argument with sweet Berengaria, whom Madame Tussaud describes in the catalogue as a "Fair flower of Navarre." Feeling thirsty we entered a bar-room, where we took a sherbet. The waitresses who served there were negligently dressed, with their fringes kept in curling-pins. Their reign only begins at night, when they put on their best attire and try to make themselves irresistible to their customers.

Still indefatigable, we went to visit Westminster Abbey, and saw the hall in the Temple where Shakespeare played before Queen Elizabeth. After that we had a stand up sixpenny lunch in a small and rather shabby establishment, which consisted of one room only, where a white-aproned cook fried mutton-chops served to us on a marble table on which table-cloth and serviettes were conspicuous by their absence.

After lunch we went again strolling about and left ourselves just time for a turn in Hyde Park before dinner. I begged for a four-wheeler instead of taking a hansom to drive there, dreading that sort of conveyence.

We were desperately hungry by this time and certainly we earned our dinner that day, which we took at "Monico's," a famous restaurant not only for the quality of the menu, but also for that of the guests. We ended our evening in a music-hall, and came back to the hotel after midnight to enjoy a well earned rest.

The following morning we ran down by train to the Crystal Palace where a great festival was given by the Temperance Society. This palace is used now for popular meetings, concerts, theatres, flower-shows, bazaars, etc. We entered a hall of enormous proportions where we found a monster musical gathering of some five thousand singers. A room was shown to us especially assigned for strayed children who had lost themselves in the crowd. In our presence a policeman brought there a small boy who was shouting desperately, "I want mother!" There was great animation in the extensive grounds all round. A dinner *gratis* was offered to the visitors, who belonged for the most part to the middle classes. They ate their meal under the trees, and the grass was all strewn with egg-shells and scraps of paper. As drink only beer was allowed. Two military schools, with their bands at the head, defiled before us.

The pleasure-train which brought us back to London was taken by assault. We ran from end to end of the long train in search of seats nowhere to be found, until at last we were literally hurled into a crowded compartment in which I squeezed myself between two fat ladies, taking up as little room as I could. Though we were returning from a temperance festival, there was a tipsy woman drunk with beer in the next car, who was leaning out of the window shouting bacchanal songs in a voice thick with drink.

We left London on the following morning. Our old Pole exhorted us to prolong our stay for another day, but we had no more time, and he saw us off at Victoria station. The mail train that was taking us back to France conveyed us swiftly to Newhaven from where we crossed by the ordinary steamer to Dieppe.

The train stopped close to the landing-place. The sea looked horrible from the pier, the wind was blowing strongly and black clouds hung over the sea. The prospect of crossing the channel in such weather was not enticing, and we were inclined to turn back to London, but it would be a shame to be so chicken-hearted, and braving sea-sickness we decided to go on.

We had hardly left the harbour when the steamer began to bounce and to pick its way from one wave to another, giving us the impression of a swing. I proved to be a miserable sailor and went below at once and put myself into the hands of the stewardess, who quickly placed a basin under my very nose. I lay prostrate on a sofa in the ladies' saloon ; my head was very bad and everything went round. What miserable creatures all my cabin companions were ! woefully sick all of them. Sergy, much less liable to sea-sickness, remained on deck all the time. He came to see how I was and said I had better come up on deck, but I was too deadly ill even to answer him.

It took us six hours to get to Dieppe. We looked ghostly when we landed on the pier, where a large crowd had assembled to see the passengers fresh from a rough channel passage. I was so happy to be on dry land. I would rather die than endure another half hour of sickness. We saw on the pier Mme. Kethoudoff, one of our Moscow friends, a French lady married to an Armenian. That couple was compelled to strictly fulfil the French proverb, *La parole est d'argent et le silence est d'or*, (speech is silver and silence is gold) as Mr. Kethoudoff does not speak a word of French, and his spouse completely ignores the Armenian language. Mme. Kethoudoff had settled at Dieppe for good. She received us with open arms when we stepped on shore, and carried us away to her own house, situated on the " Quai des Écluses."

I had not yet recovered from our rough passage and felt all the time as if the ground tottered under me. I tried not to think about the treacherous sea but couldn't, for the ocean was there, just in front of our windows, in all its vastness.

Mme. Kethoudoff had at dinner that day the *Vicaire du Pollet*, a rosy and plump curate. This gossip-loving priest was a great favourite among his lady parishioners, to whom he was very fond of confiding little bits of scandal.

We took our after-dinner coffee on the balcony and saw the swing bridge giving passage to a Spanish vessel which was leaving the harbour. At nine o'clock in the evening a retreat was sounded from the neighbouring barracks. At the first beat of the drum the soldiers hastened up to their quarters from all parts of the town.

In spite of Mme. Kethoudoff's hospitality, we moved that same night to the Hôtel des Étrangers, where we shall feel ourselves more at home and independent.

I lay in bed late next morning. After breakfast we went for a walk on the beach ; the weather was rainy and the sea uniformly grey, nothing but furious waves around us. The monotony of this sea-shore unnerved me. We shall probably not make a long stay here. Neither is the bathing very agreeable at Dieppe ; it only takes place at the hours of low water, and the bottom of the sea is so rough and stony that the bathers are obliged to put on sandals with very thick soles.

The rain having stopped in the afternoon, we drove to "Puits," a small place consisting of lovely villas. Our driver, who was very talkative, gave us the pedigree of all of them. The prettiest villa belongs to Alexandre Dumas Fils, who is residing here at the present moment.

The next day was the eve of the National Festival of the French Republic. There was a "Retraite aux Flambeaux" (a torch retreat) in the evening. The soldiers began to beat the tattoo and marched through the crowded streets holding lighted torches in their hands. They were preceded by a military band and a body of fire-men. The whole town had a holiday air about it. The carriages being stopped that day, the middle of the streets was occupied by groups of women wearing their best clothes, who promenaded to and fro, coquetting with their young men arrayed in blue blouses.

Very early next morning the maid came to knock at our door begging us not to shut our windows as the cannon was going to be fired. It appears that the proprietor of the hotel was afraid our windows would fly to pieces, although the cannon had been placed at a great distance and there could be no danger whatever that such a thing should happen. Guns must surely be very rarely fired at Dieppe to procure such a panic.

The greater part of the inhabitants of Dieppe are anti-republicans, and the Mayor of the Town had to go himself to the "Vicaire du Pollet" to beg him to hoist the Republican flag over his house.

At nine o'clock there was a review of all the troops quartered at Dieppe, consisting mainly of a battery of infantry, on the large square before the hotel. I threw on my morning-wrapper, and in slippers, my hair hanging loose, I made my way to the next room which was free at that moment, and the windows of which looked out into the square. I was busy critically observing the military evolutions when suddenly there was a sound of footsteps, the door opened behind me and an elegant couple was ushered into the room by the manager, who was going to let it to them. The pair surveyed me quizzically whilst I fled hastily, ashamed to be caught thus.

After lunch we went to see the games and all sorts of public amusements on the square: rocking-horses, targets, foot-runs and what not! A slight railing divided the fashionable world from the world that works, only the local aristocracy, ultra-provincial I must say, was admitted within the enclosure. The prizes for the most part consisted of different foods. The crowd gathered around the chief attraction, a climbing post with a gigantic leg of mutton at the top of it.   The native lads could not succeed in reaching it ; taking toss after toss they slipped from the pole to the ecstatic joy of the onlookers.   At last a young fellow had nearly attained the tempting prize, but he could not keep up on the pole and fell to the ground weakened by the strain of his position, without his leg of mutton.   We stopped before a stall with brass medals bearing the inscription *Vive la France!*   When I asked if there were any medals with *Vive la Republique* the woman who sold them answered in a voice full of indignation that she did not keep such horrors.

For some days the bad weather kept us indoors, it came on to rain as if it never meant to stop.   Warmly wrapped up in a shawl I passed many dull hours lolling rather disconsolately in an easy chair, listening to the monotonous song of the wind in the chimney—a lively way to pass the time ! We were growing very weary of Dieppe ; I am absolutely sick of the place, and the best thing we can do is to pack up and go.   As there was nothing to keep us here we decided, one wet, gloomy afternoon, to fling Dieppe to the winds and start for Paris, thence to travel right out to Switzerland.

CHAPTER XXIII

PARIS

WHEN our train stopped at the Gare St. Lazarre, we got a fiacre and drove to the Hôtel de la Paix, a large, ponderous edifice, one of the most stylish hotels in Paris. I waited in the cab whilst my husband went with inquiries for an apartment, hoping all the time that Sergy would not find one to his taste, for I hate these stiff and grand hotels. It turned out as I wanted, there was no room to our disposal, and so we betook ourselves to the Hôtel de Calais, an unpretending house situated in one of the most elegant quarters.

We spent a whole fortnight in Paris, which is a lively and beautiful city, the jolliest place in the universe. I was quite in raptures with the French Metropolis and the numberless attractions it offers. I woke the next morning in high spirits, pleased with the idea of being in Paris. The street-vendors and news-boys awoke me early, shouting each their wares. Here goes a woman wearing a hat with the inscription "I shave dogs," who is leading a beautifully shaven poodle by the chain. The poor animal seems quite worn out, and lies down on the pavement at every two steps. I was overcome with pity for that unfortunate living advertisment and felt still more sorry for a young woman turning a barrel-organ with one hand, and rocking her baby, laid down in a sort of cradle, with the other one.

Though we are of a roving disposition and seldom remain long in one place, being always between two trains, in Paris we never thought of being dull, rushing about to theatres, concerts, etc. The weather was faultless; after the London fogs and damps the sky appeared to be especially blue. In the afternoons I was out on shopping expeditions. The "Grands Magasins du Louvre," so well described by Zola in his novel *Au Bonheur des Dames*, especially attracted me. Before their huge stalls one might idle away many pleasant hours. There are such wonderful "Occasions" to be got, such lovely costumes, which fitted me like a glove, but cost a tremendous lot; I devoured them with greedy eyes. Sergy is awfully generous in money matters, there is nothing in the way of dress, jewels, luxury that I couldn't have if I wanted them; the instant I admired a dress, or a hat, he would say, "You shall have it." Sergy is such a delightful husband! he is so good that I look on his shoulders every day for wings. One afternoon between two fittings in one of the numerous dressing-rooms in the "Louvre," not much larger than a cupboard, I felt dreadfully fagged and entered the "Salon de Lecture" to rest a little. Turning over some French papers I came upon a paragraph entitled "Asia," and was awfully indignant to see that it contained recent news from St. Petersburg. Shall we ever be considered as Europeans, I wonder?

Walking one day on the Boulevards our eyes fell upon an inscription in large gilded letters "Korestchenko Magasin Russe." In one of its windows we saw a manifesto of the recent Coronation of our Tzar, and were told that a Russian traveller had left that paper to be sold for 40fr. The address of a Russian restaurant was given to us in that shop, to which we immediately proceeded, wanting to enjoy the different dishes of our national cookery, the foretaste of which was delicious to me. But a great deception awaited us. We didn't perceive any Russian element round about; the proprietor and the waiters were all French. Noticing our disappointment we were told that the cook was a Russian, and that was some comfort. We sat down at a table with a cloth that was not too clean, took up the menu-card and studied it through. It appeared very copious and made my mouth water. But alas! all the dishes that were served to us, beginning by the famous *stchi*, our national cabbage-soup, with scanty bits of over mature mutton, were horrid, and so was all the rest. We only lunched on a herring and a glass of milk. Hungry and cross we directed our steps to a neighbouring French restaurant, where this time the tasty menu did not deceive us.

We then went to the "Jardin des Plantes," visiting in the first place the part of the gardens where the useful plants of the whole world are exposed; amongst them we saw our native sunflowers, at the sight of which a sudden pang of home-sickness came over me. I was beginning to pine already for my dear old country, for my motto is and always will be: "There's no place like home." Life is so much more open and free in our Alma Mater! It is true that every piece of ground is cultivated abroad, but one feels restraint in everything here, everywhere one meets with peremptory orders to keep off the grass, and with placards saying, "Do not walk here, do not touch that." This restraint is especially felt by myself who am so fond of freedom and space. We just ran through the mineralogical museum, close to which grows a gum-tree planted in 1636, and then entered the Monkey Pavilion where the Fathers and Mothers of mankind (according to Darwin) performed all sorts of tricks and gambols, obtaining a great amount of laughter. Amongst other curiosities of the "Jardin des Plantes" we saw a white sheep with two black heads and a calf with five legs. In a separate Pavilion is shown the skeleton of an enormous whale caught in the waters of the Seine in 1847. I had a ride on the elephant and felt rather frightened to be perched so high up on the back of the great beast. I had also a ride in a car drawn by an ostrich; before starting I asked the conductor laughingly if his bird would not fly away up in the air with me. It was tremendous great fun!

We returned to our hotel for dinner and then went out for a drive in the "Bois," full of carriages, horsemen and pedestrians. In one of the remotest parts of the park a merry band of collegians were playing football whilst their tutors, black-robed curés, rested under the trees. On our way we passed the "Ecole de Médecine," on the front of which there is an inscription saying, "Liberté, Fraternité, Egalité," and just below some passer-by had written with a bit of coal, "Vive Henri V.," (the Duke of Chambord), meaning quite the reverse of these three words, and propagating Monarchy.

The next day being Sunday, we went to hear mass at the Russian church. The singing was beautiful, but our priest, with his hair cut short, did not at all harmonise with the rest of the Orthodox surroundings. After lunch, we had a nice trip by boat to St. Cloud. We had lunch there at a small inn over the entrance door of which we read with eager eyes, "Lait Frais," (Fresh Milk). A simpering red-armed and rosy-cheeked servant girl in a pink print dress, appeared wiping her hands with her blue apron; she spread a brown cloth upon a table standing in a green harbour under a big walnut tree, and served us a frugal repast, consisting of milk and eggs. A few steps from us stood a pair of scales with a placard saying, "Come and see how much you weigh before and after dinner," serving, surely, as a catchword to this inn, as over the door there was a painted hand pointing to the scales. After our cosy meal, we walked gaily through the grounds of St. Cloud, enjoying our walk as two big school children out for a holiday.

On our return to Paris we were not yet too tired to go to the "Musée Grévin," where we made a long halt before a group of wax figures representing the Coronation of our Emperor. All the personages were unrecognisable, the cadets of the "Corps de Pages" were arrayed in costumes dating from the time of Louis XV. Another group also represented a Russian scene, the capture of a band of anarchists at work in a secret printing office, in which it was the police agents who looked like villains, and the anarchists like innocent victims. It interested me greatly to listen to the opinions of the passers-by upon this group, they made such funny comments! Not wanting to disclose my nationality, the idea came to me to give myself out for an Englishwoman, and I asked Sergy, who didn't speak English fluently, to answer only in the negative or the affirmative to all I should say, and catching his eye I passed the signal, making him understand when he was to say "yes" or "no." He acted his part fairly well, and two French ladies were taken in. They endeavoured to make me understand the meaning of the criminal printing office, and one of them said to me in the very worst English, "This scene takes place in Russia, here is the Russian God," (pointing out to an Ikon of St. Nicholas hung in one corner of the printing office). Then, this well-informed person, wanting to flatter my national pride, added, that this Museum could not be compared to Madame Tussaud's wax-work-figures in London.

Our stay in Paris was drawing to a close. It was with much regret that we had to bring our delightful visit to an end. As we had plenty of time to spare before the beginning of the Italian manœuvres, it was settled we were to go first to Switzerland. The number of our trunks having considerably increased during our stay in Paris, we decided to cut down our luggage to the minimum, and left our big boxes to go straight on to Moscow through a transport-office. The chief of this office, a fat little jew, put himself quite at my disposal and proposed to forward to me in the future, all the *Nouveautés* appearing in the Paris shops for all the seasons, through his office.

CHAPTER XXIV

ON OUR WAY TO LUCERNE

WE started on our tour through Switzerland and went full speed in an express train to Lucerne. The scenery around us was lovely. Passing through the province " La Champagne," so rich in vineyards, we perceived small white cottages with the vines in front. On the mountain slopes bunches of newly-mown herbs were scattered; men and women were helping tò heap the grass into heavily laden carts. I was in ecstasies over the marvellous landscape that met our eyes immediately after leaving Liége. The delightful panorama reminded me of the Caucasus, only it was more pacific and thickly populated. Our train ran through countless tunnels and went twining in and out through patches of pasturage, so green, smooth and rich; big fat cows grazed lazily thereon. The road zigzags all the time, the sun appearing alternatively on our right or our left. The steep hills are covered with dense forests through which cascades are pouring down. We were winding higher and higher with every mile. The cars are very comfortable, with a long corridor along the side, where one can walk up and down. Feeling cramped with sitting, I went out there to stretch my legs, and saw a young man undeniably good-looking, whose appearance spoke the last word of fashion and who resembled a tailor's model from a Paris shop-window. He twisted his moustache and stared so hard at me that I hurried back to my place, but this hunter of petticoats followed me and sat down on the vacant seat opposite to me. I settled myself far back into my corner and tried to hide myself behind my book, but every time I raised my eyes I met his stare. A draught of air blew in from the corridor "Shall I shut the door?" suddenly ejaculated the passenger by way of opening conversation. I said "no," the "no" of a woman who was not to be drawn into a talk. Disregarding my cold tone, he insisted on lending me his rug, tucking it round my knees and under my feet, but I disencumbered myself hastily from his coverlet, which was very efficacious in lowering his enterprising spirits, and put that brazen-faced swell quickly into his place. It was a good blow to his self-conceit, he evidently took offence and left me alone.

CHAPTER XXV

LUCERNE

HERE are the Alps towering in all their glory, their immense contours sharp and clear. A few minutes more and our train stops at Lucerne. We were warned that the principal hotels at Lucerne were always full during the season, and that we had better order rooms beforehand by telegram, so we wired for an apartment at the " Hôtel Schweizerhof," but it led to nothing, and when the omnibus pulled up at this hotel we learned, to our disgust, it was quite full. A superior-looking gentleman at the desk announced that he had no single room disengaged at present. We were told to come next morning and there might then be an apartment free in the meanwhile. Thanks to our telegram a room had been provided for us in a private house just opposite. We followed a waiter who showed us the way there, and mounted to our room in anything but a sweet temper. It proved to be small but bright and perfectly neat and had nice beds disappearing completely under huge eider-downs, with linen smelling of lavender. The furniture was simple, the walls hung all over with framed portrait groups of antiquated photography ; amateur pictures of our landlady's parents stared down at us over the mantlepiece ; on one side of them hung a flaming heart made of red paper and on the other a small crooked mirror in which we could see only half of our faces reflected in it ; I have seen nature insulted but never to such an extent. On the mantlepiece enclosed in a glass case stood a clock which didn't mark the hour. Our landlady, a stout, comely-looking woman, proposed coffee and was altogether nice to us.

The next day we went for the promised room.at the " Schweizerhof," but the manager, with his hands in both his pockets, announced curtly that there was no room free until evening. There remained nothing else to do but to walk away in quest of another apartment. After a pretty hot chase we succeeded in finding a comfortable room at the " Hôtel National," on the second floor, with a good view on the lake, looking big as a sea, and the majestic Mount Pilatus, from where Pontius Pilatus is said to have thrown himself into the lake after the crucifixion. The legend goes that he fled from Jerusalem and wandered about the earth with a troubled conscience, and put an end to his misery on the heights of Mount Pilatus by drowning himself. From our windows we could also see the port where the steamers, black with people, were coming and going all the time, carrying away crowds of passengers in different directions of the beautiful lake.

We are going to be here a week and make trips round about. I am prepared to be delighted with everybody and everything.

Next morning we took our luncheon on our little railed balcony in cool comfort. The weather was clear and we had a very good view of the distant ranges of mountains and the snow-hooded Alpine peaks.

There are charming drives round about. After breakfast we took a carriage and drove out of town along a well kept road. We were out in the lovely undulating countryland amid vineyards and orchards. I feasted my eyes on the beautiful country-scene, and inhaled with delight the sweet smell of the perfumed meadows and fields, where the grain was tall and golden. We saw a tourist camping in the fields under an improvised tent made by means of his cloak suspended on his stick, making water-colour sketches of the lovely landscape. Our driver wanting to give a rest to his horse, stopped before the " Jardin des Glaciers," where an old guardian was explaining the museum belonging to this garden, to a little group of anxious sight-seers, in monotonous tones. An immense plan worked in relief of all the Swiss cantons especially attracted our attention. Close by the " Jardin des Glaciers," the " Lion de Lucerne," is carved out of the rock of the cliff. His size is colossal ; the great beast's protecting paw rests upon the " Lilies of France." This gigantic thing serves as a monument to the memory of the Monarchists killed in France during the horrors of the Terror. (A singular mausoleum for a Republican country !)

On our way back to the hotel, we crossed a long covered wooden bridge which contains about three hundred pictures by old Swiss masters. We got back to the hotel just in time for lunch. I generally avoid being on show at tables-d'hôtes and was very displeased with Sergy for insisting on my going down. My eyes wandered rapidly about the table and it did not improve my appetite, for everybody was so unattractive ! Just opposite me sat a fat bejewelled matron, who had made her appearance on this planet some seventy years ago at least, and who at a prehistorical period could have been rather nice ; but she did look such a guy now, dressed ridiculously for her age and outrageously painted, with black circles about her eyes which made them look like goggles, and a permanent blush palpably not due to nature. Her old face and youthful clothes presented an alarming contrast, but she considered herself still irresistible and affected little moues and attitudes that sat incongruously upon her elderly looks. She rolled her eyes like a love-smitten cat, showing off her rings and bracelets, and coquetted with her neighbours showing her false teeth in a hideous grimace. This old crony was a laughing-stock to everybody; she saw these mocking glances, but being completely satisfied with herself, she evidently attributed them to envy. She stared about her with a long-handled lorgnette and turned it rudely on me, eyeing me disagreeably. I returned her stare with a look of defiance. Already put into a nervous state by the cross-fire of masculine and feminine glances, I could not eat my lunch, and as soon as the horrid table-d'hôte was at an end, I hurried up into my room and indulged in a good cry. By dinner-time I was still in the same mood and would not go down, declaring that I had no appetite. I was much too disfigured by weeping to dine even at a separate table.

Next morning when Sergy went to take his bath in the Réus river, his bather, an old retired Swiss soldier, asked him if it was true that our Russian soldiers served under arms the whole year. In Switzerland, as it appears, the soldiers are only assembled during eight weeks; every two years they assemble again for the grand manœuvres, and this is all the service the Swiss warriors go through. It is true that they have not at all a martial air, arrayed in long coats that touch the ground and tangle about their legs. After lunch we went for a sail on the "Lac des Quatre Cantons," and had a delightful trip to Fluelen; with a gentle breeze we steamed off on the smooth waters. All the passengers, English for the most part, wearing leather gaiters and green Tyrolese felt hats with a feather in them, were laden with Alpenstocks with a bunch of Edelweiss on the top, and with cameras and knapsacks strapped upon their backs. We had dinner on board, whilst a troop of Tyrolese singers danced on the deck. On the blue and limpid lake fishermen were spreading their nets and preparing their tackle for the day's labour. Here is a steamer coming towards us; the waiters on it are waving their napkins, instead of handkerchiefs, saluting their comrades on our boat. We are passing now the tiny chalet of "Wilhelm Tell," situated on the shore of the lake. A little futher on we saw a large monument errected on the rock to the memory of Schiller. We glided for some time side by side with a railway train which made off in the direction of St. Gothard, appearing and disappearing in numerous tunnels. Roaring water-falls and picturesque cascades leap from the heights of high and steep hills. We are now approaching the village of Fluelen, the nearest spot to the snow mountains, whose white peaks were dazzling on the blue sky.

On approaching the small town of Viznau, from where one mounts by a funicular line on the summit of the Rigi-Kulm, a vast hill mounting to the sky, we saw an engine inclined almost perpendicularly, pushing one car up the steep mountain. From the peak, tumultuous torrents formed by the melting of the snow fell down. The road up the Rigi is an extraordinary piece of engineering, and how the funicular manages to climb it, is a matter of surprise. The weather was so clear that we could actually see the people walking about on the top of the mountain, and it gave us the desire to follow their example the next day.

We were back at Lucerne towards evening, and after taking tea, we sat for a short time in wicker-chairs under the chestnuts on the quay and went to end our evening to the theatre to see a new play. I felt thoroughly fatigued and dozed off during the performance. The play appeared awfully dull and I thought the acting was atrocious, so did everyone, for the curtain dropped and nobody applauded.

The next morning we started from Lucerne to make the ascent of the Rigi-Kulm. We went down the lake on a steamboat and got ashore at Viznau. I was eyeing the ascent above me with great awe. It was not an easy affair. We had to climb a road leading skyward, like an interminable staircase, by the funicular railway. It was incredible that the locomotive, standing on his hind legs so to speak, should creep up the mountain; I thought no one but a goat could surmount it. The funicular contains two cars, roofed but open from the sides, the seats are tilted back, which enables the passengers to sit level while going up the steep incline. Whether going up or down, the engine is always at the lower end of the train. The passengers sit backwards going up, and face forward going down. Our engine began to climb laboriously the steep mountain which is 6,000 feet high, grappling slowly step by step to the toothed rails, having on each side gigantic precipices clothed with pines. Loud cataracts roared below unseen. The road lay between high granite walls. Through a gap in the rocks unfathomable depths disclosed themselvs below us, chilling my blood and making me dizzy. I gripped Sergy's arm pinching him very hard, but Sergy, whose nerves were stronger than mine and who didn't see any danger at all, said laughingly to me that it was quite unnecessary to give him the blues, but I only grabbed his arm the tighter. The view grew fairer and fairer as we mounted. From here one could see the four lakes in the shape of a cross, on which the water appeared a smooth sapphire floor sparkling with sails no bigger than pin-heads, and the far stretching large and fertile valley. Now we began to climb up a narrow bridge thrown over a precipice at the bottom of which a rapid torrent rolled. I will not pretend I was not frightened, I was very. Footpaths are traced for pedestrians here and there. We saw a tourist resting against a huge stone in the crevice of a rock. We crawled higher and higher till we met the clouds that rested on the mountain sides. We are in the clouds now. The sun is shining above us and underneath the whole space is covered with thick clouds forming a milky ocean, and screening our way completely.

When the clouds dispersed, we discovered wonders in the immense Alpine landscape, and made out in the distance a group of cows with huge bells on their necks, lying phlegmatically amongst the clouds. All at once there was a full stop, it happened to be a drowsy black cow, immovable and contemplative, lying placidly on the rails, which we had nearly run over. The air grew quite chilly; though warmly wrapped up I was shivering with cold and Sergy drew his cloak close round me. Our fellow travellers had their collars turned up to their ears, I could only see the tops of their glowing noses; my neighbour, a thin, poorly looking individual wearing a chauffeur's cap, had tied his handkerchief over it. The wind was very strong and I was nearly thrown off my seat and clung terror-struck to the sides of the car, wishing that I had never consented to this aerial drive. We had left below us every vestige of vegetation. A flight of rooks are screaming overhead. At every stoppage our ears begin to tingle. At last we have reached the final bit of ascent to the summit of the " Rigi," and have to quit our car. We can hardly see two steps before us. Suddenly out of the fog came the sound of a bell: it was a sign given from the " Rigi Hotel " in order to aid us to find our way to it in the thick mist which enclosed us. We walked slowly one behind the other, following the direction the sound came from, and shivering with cold.

On reaching the Hotel, perched on the top of the mountain, we entered a large dining-room filled with a cosmopolitan crowd of tourists, sitting at a long table-d'hôte, who have assembled here to survey the sunset from the mountain top. It was delightful to get into the hall with the thick fragrant warmth of a fire of monster logs burning in a huge chimney-piece, reaching half way to the ceiling, which could easily contain a whole tree. We sat down at table and were soon thoroughly warmed by the steaming soup. There was a loud animated talk, in a curious mixture of languages; you might hear every tongue of Europe : there were Americans, Germans, Englishmen and a large number of countrymen of ours. Directly after dinner, the whole company climbed up the last bit of rough land which led to the top of the summit of the " Rigi-Kulm." I found it tiresome work ploughing our way slowly towards it, but the view from there was more than a compensation; we seemed to look into fairy-land, and though I was by no means a sentimental person, I uttered a cry of delight in looking forth on the wide expanse of hill, forest and plain that lay beneath us. Suddenly a cloud rolled by beneath our feet, completely obliterating the landscape. Sometimes the mists would part and disclose glorious views, then again they would form an impenetrable curtain. The keen mountain air was very fresh on the windy summit, and everyone was shivering and jumping about to keep warm. After having admired this spectacle, we returned back to the station in order to make the ascent of another peak of the " Rigi," the " Schneideck." We plunged again into an ocean of clouds, nearly at hand's reach.

When the clouds cleared away, we mistook forests for patches of green grass, and mighty trees for thorn shrubs. It was as if we gazed down from a balloon. An odd sensation, I had never experienced it before! When we reached the *Kaltbad* station, a group of yellow-haired children brought us bunches of Edelweiss, a small white flower which grows on the top of high mountains. *Kaltbad* is famous by its splendid and spacious hotel, full of bustle and movement. The vestibule was filled with English and American tourists, walking about and talking. They all seemed to know one another. The hotel has a splendid situation about two thousand feet above the sea-level, and offers every possible comfort to its guests. Notwithstanding its great altitude, it has every modern improvement, even gas-works. We were far above the clouds, whilst we took our coffee on the verandah. A storm broke out beneath us suddenly, peals of thunder resounded and the rain began to fall in torrents, whilst above us the sky was perfectly blue and the sun shone brightly.

On our way back to Lucerne, at the sight of the descent we had to make, terror seized me. It looked the most breakneck thing in the world, and it made me quite giddy to look down into the valley which is about nine hundred feet below. The hill was so steep that you felt as if you were going to pitch head first down it when you began to descend.

We got back to our hotel just in time for our well-earned dinner. The next day, having put our heavy luggage in deposit at the warehouse, we proceeded on our journey, and went to rove about Switzerland. In the first place we are going to Interlaken. We have reached Alpnacht by steamboat, and had great difficulties in getting seats in the brakes that run to Interlaken, the passengers had to take them by assault. We waited for our turn with a surprisingly long delay; the huge conveyances, with six powerful horses put to them, were filling fast, and there were still no places assigned to us. At last we were provided with a supplement in the shape of a landau. There was room for four in our carriage, two seats were already occupied by a very cross German lady and her daughter, who looked at us as if they wished to order our instant execution. They were most peevish companions and grumbled all the way that *der Papa* had been placed into another supplementary conveyance. We made sustained efforts at conversation, but only received rebuffs. Really, I quite expected them to bite us.

We proceeded at a brisk pace, changing horses only once. At twelve o'clock we stopped half-way in a little hamlet where luncheon had been prepared for us in an inn named *Au Lion d'Or*, whilst our horses were being changed. The table-d'hôte was served by pretty apple-cheeked waitresses dressed in the quaint costume of the Swiss peasant. They wore red skirts and black velvet bodices edged with little buttons of sparkling steel, with a flowered silk kerchief crossed over their breasts, and a golden cross on their necks.

It was time for us to move on. When we returned to our carriage we found it had another occupant, the cross lady's husband, *der Papa*, a little man with a big red moustache, who declared in a very rough tone that the seat belonged to him. It appears that it really was his place, and that his wife had exchanged seats of her own free will with two other German travellers. One of them immediately on starting, leisurely took off his coat, putting himself at his ease, and sat all the rest of the journey in his shirt-sleeves. The carriage went slowly winding up a long ascent. The road crept on between mountain slopes; close at hand the great form of the Jungfrau rose white to the sky. The ascent was difficult enough and when a specially steep bit was coming, the coachmen descended from their boxes to ease the horses up the rough track, walking by them and pulling vigorously at their long clay pipes.

CHAPTER XXVI

INTERLAKEN

CLOSE to Interlaken we took the train for about ten minutes. Interlaken is situated in a narrow pass encircled by a range of sparkling white mountains, behind which rises the majestic *Jungfrau*. This coquettish little town seems to be specially built for tourists, there are almost nothing but hotels in the place. The room which we occupied at the *Hôtel des Alpes* was furnished Swiss style, with a cuckoo-clock and cupboards in the walls; there were antimacassers everywhere, and two blue vases on the mantel-piece with everlasting flowers; on a small table lay a bible and a hymn-book.

Next morning when I looked out of our windows I saw a wonderful sight, the snow-capped *Jungfrau* emerged from a mantle of clouds, a glittering dazzling mass with a background of shimmering snow-clad mountains. It is most fortunate that the summit unveiled to-day, as it is only seen on rare occasions.

Our excursion to the Glaciers was arranged for eight o'clock, and the conveyance that we had ordered the day before stood at the door of our hotel, a mountain chariot with horses jingling with bells. We set off in the gayest of spirits. Our driver cracked his whip, and away rolled the carriage. Soon we were hurrying along the valley road, and passed meadows strewn with wild flowers. We took three hours to mount to the Hotel Eiger. On our way we met peasant girls with loaded baskets on their heads. On the slopes villagers in large straw hats were cutting down the grass, and women in bright-coloured skirts were working in the potato-fields. Here comes a procession of carts laden with blocks of ice procured from the Glaciers, dragged by patient sad-eyed oxen. In the distance the echo of an alpine horn and the cries of some peasants resounded. We overtook a peasant woman jolted like a basket on the back of her mule. After a mile or two the road began to mount, and our tender-hearted driver climbed down from the seat and walked at the horses heads, driving off the troublesome flies which stuck to his steeds. We crossed a tidy little village consisting of but one straggling street. The roofs of the houses are covered with lathings, with big stones laid over them, in order that the wind should not scatter them about. Behind the rusty gates flaxen-haired children stared at us. On the front of a tavern we saw the picture of a bear with the pleasant inscription, "*Lait Frais*," written underneath. Close by, on the front of an hostelry, we read, "*Les voyageurs qui descendent chez nous seront contents*"—(The tourists who put up at our house will be contented.) A year ago there was fearful damage done in the valley we were driving through, a huge block of rock fell down from the cliffs and hurled itself into the valley, destroying a house which was taken clear away. We had to pass that square stone that looked like a monument in the middle of the road. We wanted to stop before a wicket with a finger-post pointing to it with the inscription "*La Chute Noire, 25 centimes par personne*," but our driver said it was not worth while as we could see this same Chine at free cost a few paces off.

The road was interrupted here and there by gates which were opened by the village children, who received coppers for it. Before a wooden bridge in the form of a Swiss Chalet, we were met by a party of barefooted, yellow-haired brats, provided with long branches to chase off the flies, and square stones to put under the wheels on steep ascents. They followed us during a whole hour, waving their branches and singing Tyrolese songs. We plodded on steadily for three hours. Having reached the Hôtel Eiger we ordered saddle-horses, and went to the glaciers by a narrow way, with the rock-wall at one elbow and perpendicular precipices at the other. The rough path was so narrow that we had to ride one below the other, treading a road where a man would have scarcely room enough to pass.

The cleverness of our horses bewildered me, one false step would have thrown us headlong into the gap. We could ride no further and had to dismount at the foot of the glacier where we took a special glacier guide to take us up, and sent our horses to wait for us on the highway. Here the snow mountains rose close on us. Green pasturages had disappeared and all appearance of summer gradually faded into a perfect winter ; the snow began to fall in masses, all presented a Lapland scene, nothing but snow and ice. The guide after having provided us with alpenstocks and blue spectacles, made us pass through a damp cavern the soil of which was mouldy with dew and drippings from the roof.

Two shrivelled old women, wrapped up in shawls, with lilac cheeks and noses, were singing Tyrolese songs, with tremulous voices, in that grotto, accompanying themselves on the cithern, blowing their purple fingers in the intervals. When we came out of the cavern we saw a group of working-men occupied in sawing enormous blocks of ice which they dropped down the mountain on rails. Now we began to climb to the Glacier which was no childish play. The guide after pinning up my skirt led the way. We advanced very slowly, climbing higher and higher, pricking the sharp ends of our alpenstocks into the ice, running the risk of tumbling down into the deep ravines and leaving no trace behind. We had masses of snow to climb over and large abysses to leap over; soon greater difficulties awaited us. We had to climb a staircase simply propped up by a snow block; there was no path at all now, only crevices and precipices—it was chaos in short. The guide who had a sure foot, chopped steps with his ice-axe in the ice, and we were hoisted by him from a foothold to a foothold. He exclaimed at the courage I showed and said I was a capital hill-climber and called me "Sehr Brav." In the distance we heard the crash of a downfall of snow. Halfway up we sat down and took a brief rest, our backs against a rock and our heels dangling over a bottomless abyss. The guide insisted upon my swallowing a drop of brandy from a tumbler slung by a strap over his shoulder.

It was worth while to overcome all these difficulties to attain the "Mer de Glace" a fairy-like icy-kingdom. I was amazed by the vast and lonely beauty of these interminable uplands of ice; we were well repaid for our climb by this scenery of wildest beauty. On our way back we left the road and descended by the rough track to the lower route leading to the Hotel Eiger by a short cut, where we expected to find our saddle-horses, but when we had gained the road they were nowhere to be seen and we had to walk the entire remaining distance to the Hotel Eiger with the sun right over our heads. We got to the hotel red-faced, breathless and foot-sore. Our tempers suffered as well as our legs and we were so displeased with the manager for having given us such careless guides, that we wouldn't take any refreshment at the hotel and hastened back to Interlaken. On arriving there we had dinner brought into our room and then went straight to bed. It was an unspeakable comfort to stretch my weary limbs between the cool sheets.'

CHAPTER XXVII

MONTREUX

ON the next afternoon we started for Montreux intending to remain there about three days. We put up at the Hôtel du Cygne. Our windows opened on Lake Leman bordered by high snow-clad mountains, which lay like a mirror before us. Far away, the jagged summit of La Dent du Midi revealed itself in a dazzling and lovely garb; on the opposite side of the wide lake appeared the shores of France.

The next morning we rode to Chillon where we visited the mediæval castle, historically old and famous. The Château de Chillon stands on a small island which is reached by a bridge. An old guardian produced a large bunch of keys and took us all over the castle, down a labyrinth of mysterious echoing passages with many hidden nooks. It is a place full of thrilling historical associations; to hear the guide talk of the massacres that took place here, made my blood run cold. Down steep, winding steps we followed our guide into the secret chambers where the victims were kept. He brought us into a dungeon where Bonnivard, the famous "Prisoner of Chillon," endured his weary captivity, chained up to a post three hundred years ago. It has tall columns carved apparently from the rock, inscribed all over with a thousand names beginning with Byron and Victor Hugo. The torture-chamber was also shown to us, where the prisoners, after hideous martyrdom on the bed of tortures, were sentenced to death. We saw the huge stone upon which the victims condemned to death spent their last night. After long tortures to some of them it was announced that they were free, and believing that they were going into liberty, they joyfully descended the three steps which led into a deep pit and fell down upon sharp-pointed daggers. A shiver ran through me when I passed the open square where the gibbet stood, and saw the windows from which the corpses of the executed were thrown right down into the lake. Now we were entering the apartments of the duchesses which opened on the lake, whereat those of their husbands looked into the court-yard. As it appears in olden times also the first place was given to the ladies. Then pushing open a heavy oak door we entered a great vaulted hall paved with stone quarries and adorned with figures of knights in armour, with a monumental granite fire-place at one end. We went out of the gloomy castle as fast as we could, and were glad to be back at peaceful and modern Montreux.

The next day we went out on donkeys for an excursion up in the mountains. We were up very early, drank our tea in a gulp, and were ready to start by seven o'clock. Our long-eared steeds were already at the gates of the hotel, waiting for us; we mounted them and rode towards the mountain called Les Avants. My donkey's name was La Grise and Sergy's bore the valiant name of Garibaldi. Though the guide boasted of his donkeys being *bien gentils*, nevertheless, they had to be harpooned with a pointed stick all the way to make them advance. We were warned that Garibaldi, being a stallion, must not be allowed to walk behind La Grise, who pressed herself amorously to her companion, and stopped at every moment to clip the grass, stooping so low that many a time I nearly came to tumbling over her head. Still my donkey could be stirred up to a gallop, urged by our guide's stick; but Garibaldi was not true to his name, being very lazy, and every few steps he would stop short, and the guide had to walk at his side so as to keep him on his legs. Sergy, fearing to remain behind, was tugging at the recalcitrant quadruped, but this stubborn little ass was in one of his sulky moods and absolutely would not gallop. As we strolled along, gigantic flies pricked the poor animals, and La Grise strove to kick them off with her hind leg. One can easily imagine how comfortable I felt in my seat. We took three hours to mount to the summit of the mountain; the road was heavy and the heat overwhelming. We made a halt half-way and sat on the grass under the shelter of a great oak and ate the excellent lunch we had brought with us. A brook ran clear and shallow at our feet. The view from here spread on the whole valley of the Rhone, girt out with snow-capped mountains, Lake Leman, Vevey and Clarence. From where we sat we saw the lake on our left through a frame of foliage, and green mountains on our right where sheep were quietly brousing. During our *siesta* our donkeys were placidly cropping tufts of grass, whilst Garibaldi, being at war with the flies, slapped my umbrella with his tail all the time. We descended to Montreux by a cross-road, following a steep path in the hollow of the rocks.

Next day we started to Chamonix. On reaching Martigny we had to quit the train which was going to Simplon. The journey from here has to be accomplished in a wretched carriage, over precipitous roads and rough ground. A peasant, wearing a blue blouse, offered his *patache* to us, a battered, shabby-looking vehicle with a prodigious rattling framework, drawn by two sorry-horses. We jolted in our shaky, springless car, bounding over big uneven stones; the sky was laden with black clouds running before the wind, and soon rain began to fall. Whilst we were crossing a village where a group of women were washing their linen in a pond, one of the women, an acquaintance of our charioteer, offered him her blue cotton umbrella, big enough to protect a whole family from the downpour. The road narrowed and became rougher and rougher, the foot passengers even had to scramble on the rocks to give us passage. We began to climb a path lined with precipices winding and twisting through the mountain-passes, and here we met an old grey-haired curate mounted on a donkey, who called out to us saying that there was not much room for us to pass each other, and, in fact, the road was the worst to be met with in a civilized country. When we arrived at the summit of the ascent, we saw a big wooden crucifix standing against the sky and near it stood a pole with a placard stuck to it saying, that one-horse conveyance only could pass in this place; and so one of our horses had to be taken out and attached behind to the carriage.

Towards evening we arrived at Brientz, an Alpine village buried among the hills, at a few minutes' distance from the very summit of a huge mountain clad with perpetual snow. As it was getting dark and we had still a long way before getting to Chamonix, our charioteer pulled up his horses at the door of a cosy hostelry where we put up for the night. The inn proved to be old-fashioned and clean. We were shown by the inn-keeper into a clean, white-washed room, where supper was offered to us, consisting of cold chicken and eggs. A robust maiden with blooming country cheeks and rather staring eyes, came in and laid the cloth. Directly after supper, I returned to my room and was already in bed when Sergy brought me a glass of fresh foaming milk. The rain had ceased by this time and we breathed the good scent on the pasture grounds coming through the open window. A stream, tumbling its way busily over the rocks, made a never ceasing music of its own, and a jingle of bells came down from the village church ringing for vespers. The nights are chilly at the height of five thousand feet, and this time we were glad to have eider-downs to keep us warm. There was a great storm in the night; it is well our charioter advised us to stop here. We were out of bed at break of day to resume our journey. The weather promised to be fine, the sun shone brightly. We saw on the verge of a forest a withered old granny bending under the weight of a bundle of twigs and fallen branches that she was bringing home for fuel. As we drove along, whilst our horses were climbing slowly up a steep hill, we encountered a band of children with knapsacks on their backs, climbing up the hill on their way to school. The girls had quill-pens sticking from under their hoods. Sergy spoke to the children and made them a little examination in geography. Their answers were satisfactory, they pointed out on their maps the place where Russia stands and received some coins in recompense. Soon before our eyes, amongst the glittering peaks of the Alps, rose the majestic " Mont Blanc." Not long after, Chamonix was reached.

We put up at the Hôtel de la Croix-Blanche, facing the chain of the Alps, with " Mont Blanc " showing its snowy cone. On the public square, just opposite the hotel, stands an immense telescope. We took a look through it and saw the top of " Mont Blanc," brilliant with sunshine. With the naked eye we could dimly make out a house standing by the side of the great glacier and with the telescope we could see a caravan of eleven persons making the great ascent, surrounded by the eternal snows. I had a great wish to follow their example and go up the " Mont Blanc " to enjoy one of the most famous views in the Alps. The weather is most favourable for the ascent just now, and we decided to start on our " Mont Blanc " expedition on the following day. We got up early and equipped ourselves for the expedition, putting on proper mountaineering large nailed boots with heavy soles. Before starting we went through a hurried breakfast in the dining-room, in the company of a French traveller and an individual wearing a blue blouse, very dirty-looking and with a flavour of the stable about him. He appeared to be the charioteer who had brought that traveller from Martigny, and who had his driver at the same table with him. It was horrible to see how that creature half swallowed his knife when he ate. He was very familiar with his passenger and conversed with him as with an equal. Oh, republic! It was time to start on our thrilling mountain expedition. Our mules were led up. As our guide swung me awkwardly into the saddle, my mule " Nini " made a sudden start and I went sprawling full length on the ground. It was an excellent beginning! We followed a narrow track leading to the mountain " Montauvert." The road now threatened to dwindle into a goat-path. There were only a few inches to spare on each side of the road-shelf. We were surrounded by hideous desolation ; a more wild spot it would have been difficult to discover. Everywhere towered the great cliffs, destitute of tree and herbage. The cold increased the higher we got. By and by we seemed to have passed beyond the inhabited zone. The beautiful snows of the Alps towered in all their glory in front of us. An eagle was flying low overhead. Presently we came to the path in the hills which must be ascended on foot. We retained here a special guide with an alpenstock in his hand, an ice-axe in his belt

and a coil of rope over one shoulder, and proceeded to the
" Mer de Glace." We passed before a group of huge dogs
lying beside a cannon which was fired as usual when the
passage of the " Mont Blanc " is about to be undertaken. The
sound of the gun resounded a long time like a echo in the
mountains. The climb was excessively fatiguing. We were
roped to our guide and moved in single file ; the guide,
nimble as a goat, went in front, I next and Sergy behind.
We drove our alpenstocks in the snow, in order to support
ourselves ; the guide cut steps with his ice-axe with one
hand and held me with the other, and as fast as he
took his foot out of one of these holes, our feet occupied it.
After a quarter-of-an-hour's climb in the snow desert, we
arrived at the " Mer de Glace " and were filled with speechless
admiration at the splendid panorama which spread before our
eyes. We found ourselves in snow fairy-land. Oh, how
high in the air I felt ! The large continent of gleaming
snow was a spectacle of silent majesty and infinite grandeur.
Around us lay vast plains of untouched snow, a wonderful
white world ! The desert of ice that stretched far and wide
about was like a sea whose deep waves had frozen solid. I
have never before seen anything so impressive. Though very
weary I climbed conscientiously, dragged up by the guide.
The waves of ice were slippery and difficult to climb. We
took our way across yawning and terrific crevices, up to our
waist in snow, running the risk of being precipitated into the
abyss. This mode of ascent must surely cool the ardour of
the most enthusiastic Alpine climbers. All of a sudden we
heard, not far off, the cracking of the ice, and suddenly an
avalanche fell a few steps from us with a noise of rolling
thunder. We had a near escape, thank God ! Rapid torrents
produced by the melting of the snows tossed all around us
in cascades. I suffered from the so-called mountain sickness,
and becoming exhausted with thirst, I stopped kneeling to
drink greedily at a crevice from an icy stream ; the water
was deliciously cold and refreshing, but it was enough to
make me catch my death of cold. Overcoming almost un-
surmountable difficulties we arrived at the " Mauvais Pas,"
the most dangerous part of the ascent, a break-neck path
around the face of a precipice of fifty feet. We here had to
plant our feet on a piece of rock as large as a cricket ball,
on the very edge of a deep precipice and to creep insect-like.
This infernal passage well deserves its name, it is really a
veritable *Dante's Hell.* The road is a mere shelf projecting
along bottomless precipices. How to proceed became a
puzzle. There was hardly room to stand upon our feet and
nothing to hang on by but a thin iron rod to keep one's
equilibrium. I felt a nervous shudder come over me and the
guide did not soothe my fears by the cool observation that a

false step would send us headlong. I recommend that passage to persons searching for strong emotions. We reached the end of the dangerous passage safely; one last effort and the "Mauvais Pas" was got over. It took more than five hours to overcome all these difficulties. One minute more and I shouldn't have been able to make another step. At last we reached the "Chapeau," a sort of inn with a bar, serving as a shelter to Alpine climbers in case of bad weather. We found there a company of old fogies, wearing hideous hats with green veils and blue goggles. They appeared to be awful screws; finding that the milk offered to them was too expensive for their purses, they went themselves to draw water from a spring near-by. Now we began our descent and reached the high road by a short cut, where our guides were waiting for us with our mules. We descended by the valley and had another two hours' ride before arriving at Chamonix. I was so done up that I could hardly sit in my saddle, and envied our guides, who walked briskly alongside. They invited us to repeat the great ascent on "Mont Blanc" next year, and said that the mountain-sickness which I had felt was just the same as sea-sickness, one gets accustomed to it by repeated practice. Just now there are about 300 guides at Chamonix. They obtain their rank as Alpine guides when they reach the age of twenty-three, and only after having escorted a caravan of tourists, right to the top of "Mont Blanc;" before that they have to undergo a medical inspection, just like recruits.

We had left Chamonix at ten o'clock this morning and it was close upon eight when we were back to the hotel, simply expiring with fatigue and tanned red with the sun. When I looked into the glass I scarcely knew myself. I had no want, no desire except to stretch myself full length in a horizontal line. I stumbled into my bed and was asleep almost-before my weary head touched the pillow.

After a night's rest, we rose refreshed and invigorated; all the hardships of the ascent of the day before were forgotten, and I felt ready to recommence our Alpine exploits and go again mountaineering, but time pressing, we had to go on to Geneva. Our sojourn in the mountains is at an end.

After luncheon we packed ourselves into the huge two-storied diligence named *La berline du Mont Blanc*, which was to convey us to Geneva. Intrepidly I began the ascent of the steep ladder, of twelve steps, placed against the side of the omnibus. This giant coach, driven by three pairs of horses, contains twenty-five places. The postillon sounded his horn, the driver flourished his long whip, and we started off full speed surrounded by a cloud of dust. We sat higher than the passengers on the top of London 'buses, and I had the feeling as if we were looking out of a window from a house three stories high. We drove for some time along the picturesque sides of the river "Arve," which twisted like a silver ribbon through the smooth green pastures. The road led up and down a continual succession of hills. The coach soon turned into a woodland. My neighbour, an old lady who indulged in a sweet dose, her drooping head giving abrupt nods back and forward, gave little gasps and woke abruptly when we passed high trees, having to take care of the treacherous topmost branches which scratched our faces. The jolting of the omnibus made me also feel drowsy, but I was soon wakened up by the shouts of little peasant boys and girls who ran behind the diligence barefoot and bareheaded, and importuned us to buy the bouquets of wild flowers which they offered for sale, and fruit laid in baskets fixed to long poles. They continued to run and insisted until they lost breath. At the last station fiery, fretful horses were put to our carriage ; before starting they pawed the ground impatiently, tossed their heads and were disposed, in general, to give a great deal of trouble. When we started off at a rattling rate, I heard our coach-driver say to his neighbour that his horses weren't to be trusted ; of course it did not help me to feel safe, especially when we had to drive alongside the railway line, where a passing engine scared our steeds, who bolted and plunged wildly, nearly upsetting our coach. We made a smart entry into Geneva, at full gallop, with a loud jingle of harness-bells.

CHAPTER XXVIII

GENEVA

WE put up at the "Hôtel des Bergues." From the great bay windows of our sitting-room we could see far out over Lake Leman and the distant chain of mountains cut sharply against the deep blue sky. After having taken off the dust of the road, we went for a drive through the town, though I was awfully tired and felt the jolting of the omnibus still. Our driver having guessed our nationality, drove us straight to the Russian church. A party of English tourists were doing it with red Baedeckers in their hands. A guide, who was giving explanations to them, found it necessary to explain to us, pointing out the image of Alexander Nevski, one of our most venerated saints, that he had been "Un grand personnage de la Russie" (a notable Russian personage).

In passing the Public Gardens, we saw a coloured placard glued to the wall, announcing that a tribe of " Samoyedes," brought out from Russia, from the goverment of Archangel, were exhibited in the gardens-enclosure. As it was a little corner of our Fatherland we went in and were greatly disgusted to see these Samoydes devouring huge chops of raw meat, dipped in warm blood. Ugh! . . . the horror! . . . The Esquimos, after having ended their nasty meal, rode all around the gardens in small cars, driven by reindeers. There are only four of these animals left now, the rest have been devoured by the savages!

It is time for us to leave the land of William Tell, and to push on to the Italian lakes and to Milan. I am glad to leave this country, for the rarified mountain air does not suit me at all.

From Lucerne to Goeshenen the road is very wild and hilly. Our train plunged in and out through numerous tunnels and rushed round curves in deep cuttings. After having crossed a bridge thrown over a bottomless abyss, we arrived at Goeshenen, where we stopped to pass the night in a homely little inn, pompously called Hotel, with green shutters to the windows and a bit of flower garden in front. The inn looked very cosy and inviting. After having lunched upon a cup of tea, we took a carriage with a pair of horses, with brass harness and bells, to make the ascent of the famous St. Gothard road. The driver cracked his whip and off we went. The road mounted up and up, all over rocks and precipices and the wheels were perilously near the edge all the time. We wound through a narrow gorge, the river Reuss roared in the depths. Long lines of mountains were sharply defined against the profound blue sky, their summits veiled in clouds. Snow lay in dark hollows which the sun could never reach, and waterfalls poured down the hills. The higher the carriage rose, the more thrilling was the savage landscape. We approached now the famous *Pont du Diable* (Devil's Bridge) and saw on the polished surface of a rock an enormous coloured reproduction of Beelzebub, with a long tail and a red tongue hanging out of his huge mouth, holding in one hand a trident and a flaming torch in the other. Nothing remains now of the ancient "Devil's Bridge," which our field-marshal Prince Souvoroff had crossed with his army, going to fight against Napoleon Bonaparte. We passed over a modern bridge leading to the other side of the gorge. The spray from the Reuss ; which here drops a full hundred feet into the abyss, lashed our faces as whips. The foam of the river was splashing over it. We dashed now through a vaulted gallery where we found ourselves out of the reach of falling stones. It was very damp inside, the ceiling and walls are always dripping ; stalactites dangled heavy diamond fringes low over the roof. We drove against the wind and great clouds of dust swept across the road. We ran now into a zone of ice-cold air, there is no vegetation at all in these high altitudes, only the sides of the mountains are covered with thickets and bushes, where flocks of sheep and goats were grazing, under the guardianship of wild-looking shepherd boys. The great silence is only interrupted by a far-off ringing of bells from an Alpine village belfry, far below us. As we got higher up, the road was deep in snow, which continued to fall heavily. We ascended further and further and finally emerged upon a plain with a mountain lake formed by the melting of the snows, and came to the top of the ascent, having reached the height of over 23,000 feet. Suddenly after a steep ascent, we saw before us a tall lonely mass of grey stones, built upon a rock. It was the "Hospice" a sort of hotel, which used to be a monastery. Two big dogs of the St. Bernard breed welcomed us with joyous barkings. We ordered a dish of macaroni and a flask of *chianti*, and started back to Goeshenen. The atmosphere was chilly and the harsh, bleak wind made me shiver. Our driver taking pity on me, put his rug around my shoulders, but, alas, it appeared that it had many holes.

Our train left early in the morning, and we had to be up before six. We hastened to the railway station and took seats in the last car, in order to see the entrance of the great

St. Gothard tunnel. The guide cried out "*Partensa!*" the train moved, and we went with a rush into the black unknown for more than twenty minutes. A wavering light glowed here and there at long intervals. When the train flashed out of the tunnel, we entered the Canton of Tessino. Our train slid down zigzags through narrow passes, from valley to valley. After Chiosso—the Italian frontier—the railway line ran through comparatively flat country. At about nine in the evening we arrived at Milan.

CHAPTER XXIX

MILAN

WE have a vast and splendid apartment at the Hôtel de la Ville with a lovely ceiling, mostly angels and smiling cherubs floating about in the clouds, and a floor paved with marble. We passed a restless night; it was so hot, and the mosquitoes were such a nuisance! The roar of the street came to us, and till sunrise belated passers-by sang jolly songs at the top of their voices. The next day we took another room which looked into a quieter street. Even during the night the heat is intolerable, and I have to fan myself vehemently instead of falling asleep. We remained indoors the whole afternoon. From within came the sound of a piano. In this artistic city the air seems full of music, which is here as common as speech. There is nothing but singing from morning till night. We went down to dinner at table d' hôte. A queer company was dining at the next table: two extra-smart Brazilians and a young person of small virtue, with a thick paint on her face and a very loud voice. She seemed on easy terms with her cavaliers, who were on close attendance on her. They all looked as pleased as possible with each other and exchanged loving glances quite openly. The Brazilians made known to their lady-love, who was a Frenchwoman, in broken French, that they had been hunting all over the town for her, and as her address was unknown to them, they had to apply even to the police!

Immediately after dinner we went out for a drive. Milan is a very fine city. Our guide pointed out all the places of interest. The cathedral attracted our especial attention; it is a perfect lace-work of carving, all in white marble, marked, alas, by merciless age. We saw the *Castelli*, an immense open circus, which can hold thirty thousand spectators. Reviews of troops and public entertainments take place in it. In about half-an-hour the *Castelli* can be filled with water; it serves in winter as a skating rink, and in summer nautical fetes are organised there. We walked through the *Galleria Vittorio Emmanuele*, the largest arcade in the world, which has the form of a Latin cross, and contains a great number of shops, restaurants and cafés, with little tables all over it, and people sitting at them eating, drinking. The arcade is roofed over with glass, and illuminated by two thousand gas-jets, which can be lighted in one moment by the aid of small automatic engines. At nightfall the streets of Milan are filled with flirting couples, sitting in dark corners, the women's heads on their gallants' shoulders ; what they say to each other was not hard to guess. The masculine population is not to be pitied here, for the women, for the greater part, are very pretty creatures, wearing on their heads black lace mantillas like Spanish ladies. They don't look as if they felt the awful heat at all, the lucky creatures, whilst I am painfully hot and red. At every crossing we saw policemen dressed in long black coats and top-hats, holding great sticks and looking like funeral attendants. On our way back to the hotel we heard a funeral chant, and next moment appeared a processsion of monks, their faces covered and only their eyes seen, and their hands hidden in their full sleeves, walking two and two.

The following day at dinner we saw again the French *cocotte* and her bronzed cavaliers, who this time appeared insensible to her charms, their temperature having fallen to below zero. Her fickle lovers had only monosyllables at her disposal. They took no notice of her and ate their dinner.

The principal theatres of Milan are closed in summer, except the "Dal Verme," where we went to see a new play. The theatre is awfully dirty, the curtain all in holes and the chair-backs wear the trace of the spectators' feet. The performers were all second-rate and the play rather boring.

This night again we were roasted alive. It is impossible to remain longer in this furnace, and we decided to go on to the Italian Lakes to look out for a comfortable boarding-house where I could put up during the manœuvres. The morning, as if on purpose, was comparatively fresh, the sky overclouded and the rain coming on ; still we did not put off our journey and took the first train to Como. This town, with its Gothic cathedral, is very pretty. It is situated on Lake Como and surrounded by verdant mountains. Immediately on arriving, we took a carriage to Cernobbio, a little place where you take the boat to Bellaggio. The trip only occupies twenty minutes. Our driver pulled up at the entrance door of "Villa D' Este," a beautiful old palace transformed into a large palatial hotel, standing in a garden of orange and lemon trees. The house had once been the residence of Napoleon Bonaparte. The dining-room is decorated with rich tapestries incrusted with the letter "N" in gold, surmounted by the Imperial crown. In the library we saw a large veiled figure, the statue of "Love and Psychè," covered with gauze in order not to shock the prude spinster ladies of blameless morals dwelling in the hotel. After a hasty luncheon, we came out upon the beach, and I sat down to wait for the boat. I was that day in one of my nasty moods, in the humour to pick a quarrel with any-one, and Sergy's imperturbable good-temper was a source of greater irritation to me. Poking an inoffensive pebble viciously with my umbrella, I said some detestable things to Sergy and was altogether horrid. Fearing lest I should say too much, I made myself the solemn vow not to pronounce one single word until I went to bed that night. And there we sat, side by side, with faces apart, in gloomy silence, when suddenly the idea struck Sergy to establish me at Cernobbio, whilst he would attend the manœuvres. He sat thinking for a while, then rose and strolled down by himself, investigating the neighbourhood to try and find some hotel where he wanted me to spend about three weeks. He soon came back to tell me that he had found out a nice boarding-house kept by a German lady, Frau Weidemann, just opposite the landing place. Being tongue-tied I could only nod approval, meaning "Yes, it suits me exactly." In the meanwhile our boat ap-proached and took us to Bellaggio, where we had dinner at the Hôtel Grande Bretagne. It was a depressing meal, during which I maintained an absolute silence. After a stroll in the splendid park, which surrounded the hotel, the boat took us to Lecco, where we arrived too late to catch the evening train for Milan, and had to put up for the night at the modest little hotel bearing the name of " Zwei Thore." The hostess ushered us into a room with a pointed ceiling and an enormously high bedstead. How pleasant it was to get rid of my vow of silence, which was becoming unbearable ; for a whole day I had kept my lips sealed, although my anger had sensibly evaporated. When the hostess left us we became reconciled upon the spot, and all was right again.

Next morning we were back at Milan, and went to visit the "Campo Santo." This vast cemetery is a veritable museum. We wandered about, looking at the tombstones, reading names and epitaphs. I noticed a great many beautiful monuments, including those of some fearless people who gave themselves monuments and erected shrines during their lifetime. We admired the mausoleum of Mario, the celebrated tenor, which is surmounted by his bust, with his favourite "cavatina" incrusted on a metal plate. The poor folk are buried in a remote corner of the cemetery ; their tombs are all level, with black crosses and the number of the tomb painted on white labels. After the lapse of ten years all the bones are gathered together in heaps, in large boxes, and placed in the charnel-house. When we ap-proached the Crematory Temple, we saw smoke coming out from the chimneys, and were told that the corpse of an Austrian engineer was being consumed at that moment. This dismal procedure generally takes about an hour-and-a-half, and costs fifty francs. When we entered the Crematory

I felt somewhat frightened, and the odour was so sickening that I thought I must faint, and felt sorely in want of smelling-salts, but the guardian's pretty daughter seemed to feel quite at her ease in that ghastly kitchen, and ate her luncheon with great appetite. I hadn't the courage to peep into the Crematory furnace, but Sergy perceived the corner of the huge frying-pan upon which broiled the corpse of the Austrian engineer. His wife and children, who were present at this awful ceremony, didn't appear much impressed by it, and chattered on gaily all the time. It had been too much for my nerves, and when we were back at the hotel I went straight to bed and had a good cry.

CHAPTER XXX

VILLA D'ESTE

On the following day we started for Cernobbio to spend a week at the Villa d'Este. Our apartment was large and airy; the marble floor and white-washed walls looked agreeably cool, with windows and balcony looking out on the lake, and the hotel terrace with flights of white marble steps descending to the water's edge. A boat belonging to the hotel was anchored near it.

I went early to bed that night, and just as I was going to fall asleep, I heard a chorus of men's voices singing to a guitar accompaniment. I jumped out of bed and saw a boat moored to the terrace, in which a dozen men, gifted with fresh, strong voices, were giving us a serenade. The moon came up at that moment, silvering the lake and lighting up the scene. I leant out of the window to throw some coins in the direction of the singers, who were making the round of the group of visitors who had gathered on the terrace. I was very much disenchanted when I was told that these minstrels were, all of them, citizens of Como, who, having their day's work done, floated on the lake and sang ballads.

Time passed slowly, one day like another. The heat obliged us to stay indoors all the afternoon, and I was glad to rest in our cool room. After dinner, we took long walks in the park surrounding the hotel, with mediæval castles, turrets, fountains and water-falls. On the top of a hillock stands a pavilion named Il Bello Sguardo, from which you have a full view of the lake. One morning we went for a row on the lake. I was at the wheel, and Sergy, taking off his coat, rowed on for an hour or more. Our light skiff flew like a bird on the beautiful lake, which is fifty miles long. The shores are lovely, surrounded by hills covered with fig-trees, olive-trees, pine-trees, like big open umbrellas, and rich vineyards. The edges of the lake are strewn with pretty villas of the nobility of Milan, with splendid gardens stretching down to the water. The wonderful southern vegetation amazed us; orange and lemon trees, laden with fruit, grow in groves in the open air. As there is no road, there is no approach but by water to the villas; nearly all of them have a small separate embankment. One of the prettiest villas belongs to Taglioni, the renowned ballet dancer, who in long past days delighted our grandfathers. A little further on we saw the villa belonging to Mme. Pasta, the celebrated French actress. On its frescoed fronts different musical instruments are painted. Bellini once upon a time had been on a visit to Mme. Pasta, and the piano on which the great composer had improvised his music, is kept there as a relic.

We went another day by steamer to Menaggio. The hills that encircled these shores are covered by poor vegetation, only dull olive trees here and there. We were startled by the formidable report of the dynamite blowing up the rocks which are to serve for the building of houses ; the hills all around caught up the sound and echoed it from one to the other.

From Menaggio to Porlezza we continued our trip in a carriage, and took the boat again to Lugano. The Swiss frontier begins on the middle of the lake, and thus, for a short time, we found ourselves on Helvetic waters. Towards night we returned to Como by the railway.

Baron Rosen, the Russian military attaché at Rome, came to spend two or three days at the Villa d'Este. We saw a great deal of him ; he devoted his whole attention to me, and offered me his escort for moonlight promenades, but I preferred to regain prosaically my bed rather than stroll with him about the moonlit park. He called me obstinate and matter-of-fact, and said that I had warm water instead of blood, and that, like the " Sleeping Beauty in the Woods," I was asleep to the whole of life's pleasures, leading the existence of a nun ; but his agreeable task to wake me up did not succeed.

The heat continued to be overpowering, then one morning, after many days of waiting, the rain fell, but in the afternoon, the sun was ablaze, and again there was no breath of air in the over-heated atmosphere.

During dinner that same day, I saw by the expression of Sergy's face that he was preparing a surprise for me. And, in fact, he made me awfully happy by announcing that instead of establishing me at Frau Weidemann's boarding-house, he would take me with him to Piacenza, a small town in the neighbourhood of which the manœuvres would take place. And thus it was settled that we should start on the following day for the Baromees Islands on Lake Maggiore, and go straight from there to Piacenza.

We left the train at Verona and took the boat, coasting along Lake Maggiore. We passed Isola Madre and moored at Isola Bella, the residence of the Counts Barromée, who dwell here only in autumn, but the beautiful feudal castle and gardens are open to the public. A smart footman showed us all over the place, after which we took a row-boat and crossed over to Isola Peschia, a fishing village with only nets all along the shore hanging out to dry, and a fishy smell over it all. On the water edge small boats were moored and a group of fishermen were sitting on the shore, mending their nets and counting their day's catch. Suddenly I heard someone calling " Romeo ! " I turned round and beheld a fisherlad, bare-legged, with clothes in tatters, and a dirty fishbasket over his arm, looking most unromantic, and bearing very little resemblance to the Shakesperian hero.

On our return to Isola Bella, we took the train to Milan, where we arrived at sunset. Before we went to bed, it was settled that we should go next morning to Piacenza. When I awoke, Sergy made me understand that it would be far more convenient for him to go first by himself to Piacenza, in order to look out for a lodging for me. I was foolish enough to feel horribly hurt, and to take it into my head that my husband wanted to get rid of me. " Oh ! very well, be it so ! " I said to myself, and made the vow to await the end of the manœuvres at Cernobbio at Frau Weidemann's boardinghouse ; and, acting on blind impulse, with quick tears rising to my eyes, I told Sergy I did not want him to be bothered with me and intended to start with the first train to Como. Having said my say I began instantly to throw my things into my trunk in petulant haste, drying my tears with quick, impatient dashes. Sergy tried to talk some common sense into me, but to reason with me at that moment was impossible ; what I once made up my mind to do, I would do, no matter how hard it was. Sergy insisted upon accompanying me to Cernobbio. We had to be at the station by eight o'clock, but with all these parleys we missed the train, and Sergy, knowing my tempers to be of short duration, was very glad of it, thinking that it was just as well that I should be allowed a little time to recover my good-humour. But I made out that there was another train about nine. When we had secured a compartment to ourselves, I drew myself far into my corner and pulled down my veil to hide my tears, feeling as if I was going off to prison. We rolled on towards Como in gloomy spirits ; the journey was a very silent one. How stupid of me to have made that vow, but it was too late to alter matters now, and pride, holding me back, I had to stand firm. Nevertheless I blamed myself bitterly. All the pleasure of our trip was at an end.

CHAPTER XXXI

CERNOBBIO

FRAU WEIDEMANN, a comely, grey-haired woman, in a frilled cap and white apron, came out to receive us and wish us welcome. She had taken us for a honeymoon couple, and thought that we started forth on our wedding trip. Her boarding-house is a quiet family sort of establishment, but the whole effect of my apartment was rather cheerless, and the boarding-house surroundings were distasteful to me. The furniture was old and shabby, with faded curtains and threadbare carpet in the middle of the room. Frau Weidemann's prices are very moderate, I pay eight francs per day for board with a room. I have arranged to have breakfast and lunch in my own room, but must go down to dinner at table-d'hôte, which I do not like at all.

My windows look out on the lake and bit of garden belonging to our boarding-house. Just before dinner I looked out of the window and discovered our hostess sitting in the garden, holding a bit of crotchet in her fingers. I found that she had altered in a most surprising way, and was utterly metamorphosed and unrecognisable, transformed into a portly lady, wearing a black silk dress, with hair beautifully dressed.

When we entered the dining-room we saw Frau Weidemann presiding at the dinner table, looking very prim and dignified. All her boarders were present: A Russian lady—Mme. N—— and her daughter, Melle. Nadine, future opera-singer, studying singing with Professor Lamperti, the first singing master of the day. Then came Fräulein Weltmann, a maiden lady of ripe years, an ex-prima donna still dreaming of her successes, which she alone remembers, and who must have been once upon a time very good-looking, but it was a thing of the past, alas. All through dinner we had to listen to the endless stories of the brilliant days of her conquests in her vanished youth. I remarked that in speaking of herself she generally dropped dates. Last came an American lady, Mrs. G——, with her two children, a boy and girl aged eight and ten, called Hermann and Danys. Mrs. G—— is what one might call miscellaneous, she has an American father, a Spanish mother and a German husband. Little Danys is a Roman Catholic, and her brother is a Lutheran. Mrs. G—— crossed the ocean, coming all the way from New Orleans to Cernobbio, to prepare herself for professional work with Professor Lamperti, who inhabits Milan in winter and comes to Cernobbio in summer. The old meæstro has the custom to nick-name his pupils, thus Mrs. G—— is called "Norma" because of her two children, though they are not twins. Danys is a very clever little girl, and unusually sharp for her years. This small damsel, who sat next to Sergy at table, made shrewd observations and questions, not unfrequently astonishing her elders. Finding it her duty to entertain her neighbour, like a grown up person, she at once entered into conversation: "My name's Danys, what's yours? Have you got any children and how many? You are old enough to have a lot, though your wife looks so young!" cried out the ingenuous child in a breath, and when she was told by Frau Weidemann that little girls must not pass remarks, the bold little maid, turning scarlet, exclaimed: "One always asks how many children have you got when one meets for the first time!"

Sergy returned to Milan with the evening boat, and left me a grass widow in charge of Frau Weidemann. I suddenly felt utterly alone and so miserable, so desolate, with no one to care about my comings and goings! Our ladies took pity on me and said that they would try to make me feel at home with them. As soon as Sergy left the house, I shut myself in my room, and then my nerves failed me altogether. I sat down on my lonely bed and cried. Then I lay down and fell asleep and woke unhappy. Marie, the Swiss maid-of-all-work, in very creaking boots, brought in a telegram from Sergy with my breakfast. The day began well!

When I went down to luncheon I was taken by storm by Danys, who had felt one of these sudden fancies to me, which children sometimes do form for their elders. She rushed up to me, and flinging her arms tempestuously around my neck kissed me so rapturously that I was afraid of being smothered.

"Melle. Vava, you're a darling! I'm so glad you came down. I love you so much I should like to eat you up!" cried out Danys. I am called here by everyone Madame Vava, but Danys insisted in calling me Melle. Vava, saying that it didn't suit me to be called Madame because I didn't look at all like a married lady. Both children wanted to sit next me at table, "Oh! sit by me!" pleaded Danys, rubbing her cheek against my hand, "No, by me, please!" said Hermann, and I good-naturedly placed myself between them both.

For the first few days I got on pretty well with Frau Weidemann's boarders, who were all showing themselves very amiable and kind to me. One night they asked me to go to the theatre, where a travelling troop was giving a performance. And such a theatre! We found ourselves in a long room with a small stage at one end, lighted by three petroleum lamps suspended from the ceiling, which smoked horribly and were very dim; in fact they gave more smell than light. The grey holland curtain came up by the aid of two cords drawn through an iron ring. The band was supplied by local talent, all the musicians being labourers and workmen from Cernobbio, our gardener in the number, who received 20 centimes per evening. As to the performers they were all more or less bad. It was the benefit night of the leading actress, who was to be a mother in three months, and you could see it at a glance. Our seats in the first row cost only one franc. The audience consisted chiefly of Lamperti's pupils. Lamperti has produced many divas, Marcella Sembrich in the number. The mæstro was present at the play. He carries very lightly his eighty years, and has just taken, for second wife, one of his favourite pupils, a very pretty young creature.

I am having a very dull time, and my spirits are down to zero. I do want Sergy so badly, so very badly! Oh! if I had only not come to that horrid Cernobbio! I am spending my days stretched in an easy-chair, yawning over a book. Melle. Nadine's room is next to mine, and I can hear her singing or chatting with her intimate friend, Baroness B—— a tall, rather ungainly girl, with red hands and very bad manners. Her mother is a very troublesome, bad-tempered old lady, embellished by a horrid black wig. She is vulgarity itself, and resembles a cook trying to play the lady. That detestable woman generally makes her appearance with a horrid pug-dog tucked under one arm, which snarls at you, and flies out of her arms trying to bite your toes.

Melle. Nadine and her friend carried on a flirtation with a young Italian tenor, and ran after him in a most barefaced fashion, contriving both to catch him. Melle. Nadine, who was determined to keep him for herself, took him in hand and totally eclipsed the young Baroness, which led to a succession of stormy scenes. I perceived that the atmosphere was highly charged with electricity, and that there will be a row presently. One day they had a fearful dispute about the hero of their romance, after which the young Baroness did not appear for a week. Her mother, wishing to reconcile the rivals, brought over her daughter to make up her quarrel with Melle. Nadine, but the interview was not pleasant, Melle. Nadine. refused to see her friend's outstretched hand, at which the old Baroness flew into a rage and fell on Melle Nadine with fiery reproaches. "What!" screamed the old lady at the top of her voice and rolling infuriated eyes, "My daughter wants to make up with you and this is the

way you treat her. You base, ungrateful girl! I will
never allow her after that to set foot in your house!"
Having said her say, the old Baroness sank into an armchair, holding strong smelling-salts to her nose, and throwing
back her head, she waited for a fit of hysterics which would
not come, and two minutes after she made her exit, banging
the door after her. If I were in the place of Melle. Nadine I
should have nothing more to do with the Baroness and her
daughter, but half-an-hour afterwards I saw both young
ladies seated close together on a bank in the garden, hand in
hand, mingling their tears together, after having made each
other the vow of eternal friendship.

Melle. Nadine had another admirer in the person of Doctor
Bianchi, a forty-year old cherub, who worshipped the very
ground that she trod on, and cooed his romance into her
ears like a real troubadour. But he is far from being the
ideal Lohengrin, with his bald head and prominent abdomen.
He wouldn't have been my hero even with more hair on his
head, being rather a fool and very ignorant, especially of
geography. To him Russia represented only snow, bears,
and tallow candles. "May I ask you if you are English?"
he inquired when being presented to me.—"Russian?" he
exclaimed in blank astonishment. "Oh! I can't believe it,
you look quite European." Stupid fellow! I detested him
after that, for I am exceedingly tenacious in questions of
patriotic pride. Doctor Bianchi had made several times the
offer of his hand and heart to Melle. Nadine, but she
refused him flatly over and over again. She treats him very
harshly and hates the very sight of him. When Doctor
Blianchi enters one door she goes out by the other. But the
long-suffering physician makes an ass of himself and continues
to persecute his lady-love with his tenacious wooing and poor
Melle. Nadine dosen't know how to get rid of him. As for me
I would have known how to knock the calf-love out of him
soon enough. What awful idiots men make themselves
when they are in love.

Our landlord, Signor Bonsignore, is a magnificent old beau,
awfully stuck up and prim, belonging to the ancient school,
and suited rather to the eighteenth century than to our modern
era. He affected an antiquated style of dress, his chin
resting within the points of a high collar, which reached to
his ears. One day he came to keep me company whilst I
had my lunch in my room, and remained quite a long time
paying me old-fashioned compliments. He said that he
regretted that he had not met my second-self in his young
days, and that it was the reason why he is still single.
Signor Bonsignore is an awful old screw, one could see it by
the motto carved over the door of our dining-room saying:
"One never repents of having eaten too little." Frau

Weidemann follows the motto to the letter in respect of her boarders, practising rigorous economy, rarely varying her scanty menus and making mental photographs of the joints before they are removed. My frugal breakfast, day after day, has been coffee, one egg and insufficient bread and butter. My lunch is brought in to me on a tray; the limited menu is unvariably composed of cold meat, green beans and a dessert of two biscuits and half an apple. Marie, the household treasure, whilst clearing away my scanty repasts, always asks as if in derision : *" Madame a bien mangé ? "* which made me groan inwardly.

Mrs. G—— and Melle. Nadine came in hopelessly late to table, and sometimes didn't appear until after eight, keeping dinner waiting. One day when I descended to the dining-room, a smart young man, in the barber's block style, wearing very yellow gloves and yellow boots, walked in. He had a white gardenia in his buttonhole and an eyeglass, which made him squint. Frau Weidemann introduced him to me as Signor Gorgolli, the son of her close friend. He shook hands with me raising his elbow to his ear, and bowed his head as politely as the exigencies of his high collar would allow. Mrs G——, who lighted up when men were present, but languished if there were only ladies in the room, had taken extraordinary pains with her toilette for Signor Gorgolli, and came down to dinner having put on her most becoming gown. She was displaying her best graces to him, and laid herself out to be irresistible, and encouraged the young snob, which I regretted, because you could see at once that he wasn't the kind who needs encouragement, being thoroughly pleased with himself and seeming to think that every woman must fall in love with him. Edging his chair closer to where Mrs. G—— was sitting, he picked out a rose from a bowl of flowers that stood on the dinner-table, and pinned it into her low bodice. That coxcomb talked of himself all through the course of the meal, and didn't want to hear what you say, only to tell you about himself. The letter " I " was the back-bone of his conversation. He said " I this " and " I that " every time he opened his mouth ; a more conceited ass I never set eyes upon. His manner struck me as peculiarly odious. He was trying all the time to impress the company with the idea that he belongs to a circle in society in which he certainly never set foot, and confessed barefacedly that his finances, being at low ebb, he was on the look-out for a rich heiress to pay off his debts, but that in the meanwhile he was disposed to get all the fun he could out of life, feeling far too young to settle into a sober family man.

Signor Gorgolli came back the next day and the day after. He tried to get up a flirtation with me and was always hanging about me, twisting up the ends of his moustache and prepared for conquest. He paid me compliments upon my looks and said that he came to Cernobbio only on my account, at which I assumed an expression of extreme innocence, and pretended not to understand what he was driving at. He was certainly a very compromising young man, and I tried to avoid every occasion of meeting him, but he was such a fool, and would imagine anything except that he is not wanted. Presuming young idiot!

One afternoon I sat with a book on the veranda whilst our ladies were out shopping, and Signor Gorgolli, who was quick to take advantage of it, came to keep me company. I grasped the fact that he intended to stay with me, and began to wish the ladies would come back. In the street a hand-organ was reeling out a waltz, and I was reekless enough to give Signor Gorgolli a dance. He put his arm round me and held me very tight. I had done wrong in allowing my hand to stay in his a second or two longer than necessary. Dating from that afternoon he became bolder than ever, and ventured even to press my hand under the table-cloth during dinner. I never heard of such impudence! The matter was going a bit too far, and I began to crush him with my scorn, and soon put him back to his proper place in throwing his photograph, which he had just given me, into the waste-paper basket, whilst he pulled his moustache and looked silly. He left the room feeling terribly snubbed. A week went by and I saw nothing of him. I was awfully glad to be free from his detestable society. He might go to Jericho for what I cared.

The evenings were getting longer, and dragged like an eternity. To shorten them somehow we played society games and puzzles, which bored me to death and made me yawn.

One night after I had gone to bed, a terrible storm arose; ceaseless lightning harrowed the sky, and the rain came pouring down. Suddenly one of my windows was blown open. I jumped out of bed and went to shut it, and was nearly carried away by a gust of wind. After having wedged the frames with matches I crept back to bed, when bang! bang!! went the windows, and I had to get up again, and the match work had to be done all over once more. When I awoke next morning I opened the window and breathed the fresh pure air with delight. The mist was hanging like a grey curtain across the lake and the swallows were flying low over the water. From afar I heard the church bells ringing the *Ave Maria*. As a contrast to this peaceful scene, I saw under my window our cook chasing the hens, innocently awaiting their hasty doom in the patch of garden which was the resort of Frau Weidemann's fowls. The *pacha* of these poor victims, a little crested cock, didn't seem to remark the diminution of his harem, and continued to fling out his shrill *Koukarikou* joyously.

The little Americans are quite their own masters. They are running about all day without no one to look after them, and spend most of their time in quarrelling, flying at each other's faces, pulling each other by the hair, and pinching, and scratching. I hear Danys's shrill little voice coming from the garden, shouting orders to her brother, " Hermann, go in the shade ! " but he would not obey and paid no heed to her repeated calls to be quiet.

Hermann's sole idea of pleasure was making others miserable. He was full of mischief, and took delight in provoking his sister, and teased her constantly. One day he glued the hair of Danys's favourite doll, and she broke, in revenge, the legs of all the animals in his Noah's ark.

Another day Danys entered into a loud detail of grievances of which her brother was the cause. She had to keep strict watch on him ; but he did everything what he was told not to do, and gave her a world of trouble. When he got ideas into his head, there was never peace till he had what he wanted. He was mamma's own pet, and could get almost anything he liked out of her, and led her by the nose. Whatever Hermann did, whatever Hermann said, was always right, and Danys was always in the wrong, and had undeserved punishment even when she was behaving in the most exemplary manner. She was Hermann's scapegoat and accustomed to hear herself roughly spoken to by her mother, and always roared at. " I wish I were as small as a needle and Hermann as big as an elephant, perhaps I wouldn't have always to bear the blame then ! " said poor Danys, her eyes filling with tears.

" It is perfectly true," shouted Hermann, giving Danys a vicious little pinch, " I can thump her as much as I like, and she doesn't dare to touch me even with her little finger ! "

But Danys, who was in a rebellious mood just then, turned upon him in a rage, and a resounding slap came before we could interfere, thereupon Hermann belaboured her with his little fists, straining to get his teeth into her hands.

Hermann was a very wicked little boy, and took delight in torturing animals and insects. What pleased him more than anything was to help the cook to wring the chickens' and hens' necks and then to boast of it afterwards, showing us his blood-stained hands. Horrid little creature ! There never was such a child for mischief; he enjoyed playing all sorts of tricks on Frau Weidemann. That imp of a boy stole behind her chair when she was knitting in the garden, and took a malicious pleasure in tangling her skeins of wool. At dinner Hermann loved annoying Danys ; the little pig dropped hair into her soup and gave her furtive little kicks under the table. Frau Weidemann did all she could to train him a little.

One day, just as we were sitting down to table, Hermann brought me a radish, fresh from its bed of mould, and the hand that held it out was evidently the spade that had dug it therefrom, and in sore need of soap. Frau Weidemann told him that he must always be washed and brushed before he went down to the dining-room, and ordered him to go and wash his hands immediately, but Hermann, who had no acquaintance with the word *must*, set his mouth in a hard curve and didn't move; he looked so obstinate that I was strongly tempted to shake him. A more wilful boy I never saw: he'd try the temper of a saint. But this time Frau Weidemann had her own way, and ordered him out of the room. Hermann reluctantly obeyed, with rage in his little heart, and dashed from the room, banging the door with a shock that made the room rattle. Hermann ran straight to his mother, who didn't come down to dinner that day, to complain of Frau Weidemann, and instead of giving him a good scolding, Mrs. G. rewarded him with chocolates and kisses.

That night when I went to bed, passing through the dark corridor, I suddenly felt a tight grip on my wrist, it was Hermann, who giving an emphatic tug at my skirts, said in a husky whisper, "That's you who must have clean hands, because you are a young lady, and as to me, I may have them dirty as much as I like. I cannot be always washing myself and always thinking of my nails, like grown ups!"

Both children had got bad manners at table; they fidgeted on their chairs, kicked their legs right and left, and were eating noisily, rattling vigorously their knives and forks. They spilt their soup all over their napkin and spattered jam all over themselves. They also made a point of overeating themselves, transferring the largest and best pieces to their plates; they had several helps of pudding and wanted to have all the cake.

One morning Frau Weidemann caught Hermann throwing stones at passers-by over the hedge of our garden. "What are you doing, horrid little boy?" cried out our hostess.

"I am chasing these people away, I don't want them to stare at me!" declared Hermann vehemently.

"You are a bad, undutiful child!" exclaimed Frau Wiedemann, "go away, go away at once!"

But Hermann, who meant to go on being obstinate, jerking his shoulders, retorted rudely, "Mamma told me that I am not bound to obey Frau Weidemann, and I'll do as I please, do you understand, as I please, as I please!" shouted that delightful boy stamping viciously his little foot.

Frau Weidemann losing patience, said she would have him

punished for daring to be so rude, and wouldn't take him with his sister for their habitual walk next morning.

Danys, with tears coursing down her cheeks, implored Hermann to ask forgiveness, but tears and prayers were of no avail; he stuck firmly to his chair, his nose in his picture book, dangling his feet backwards and forwards, and would not apologise.

"I don't propose to ask Frau Weidemann's pardon anyhow, that's flat. When I am in a rage, I remain in a rage one week, two months, a whole year!" declared Hermann, doggedly, and remained sternly unapproachable.

When I came down to dinner that day I saw poor Danys, her eyes all swollen, her nose red, huddled up in a chair—a picture of misery. "We don't go for our walk to-morrow!" she said sobbing loudly.

The next day I was writing in my room upstairs, with the windows wide open, when suddenly I heard in the garden below my name called in a ringing voice, "Hullo! Madame Vava, look out of the window." It was Hermann, success written in his sunny little countenance, accompanied by Danys and Frau Weidemann, who having fallen into a melting mood, was taking out the children for their usual walk, and Hermann, radiant with triumph, wanted to prove to me that he had it all his own way. It was Hermann who had forced Danys to ask his forgiveness, and she had coaxed Frau Weidemann, with kisses and pleading words, to go out for a walk with them. She is a weak person, Frau Weidemann; I should have kept my word in her place.

Danys also was not quite easy to manage, and was liable sometimes to storms of temper. One afternoon all the company, except myself, went out for a sail on the lake. Frau Weidemann, who had forgotten to prepare a sauce for the trout we were to have at dinner, returned home before the others with Danys, in a small row-boat. Danys was in a fury to come back so early, and made an awful scene with Frau Weidemann, rocking herself to and fro in a paroxysm of grief; she fretted, foamed and turned nasty, shouting out all her bad words, for when she loses her temper she does not measure her lauguage. She called down curses on Frau Weidemann and sent her to Mephistopheles, and wished her at the bottom of the lake, and eaten up by the mermaids. As soon as they reached home the door of my room was dashed open and Danys flew in looking like a fury. "That's Frau Weidemann who insisted on coming back so early for that horrid old sauce. I hate it and shall never eat it as long as I live! I wish there were no sauces at all in the world, that I do!" cried out Danys. That same day at dinner Danys was tiresome with awkward questions: "why this," and "why that," and Frau Weidemann found it necessary to stop her. "Eat your soup," she said, "and remember that polite little girls never interrupt people's speeches." "But I say," exclaimed Danys, turning to her with blazing eyes and face aflame, "polite little girls can want to know what they do not know, can't they?" At which her mother administered a good scolding to her and told her that if she said one word more, she would give her a damned slap. "It isn't me that mamma curses, it is the slap!" said the bold little girl unabashed.

I hadn't got any news from Sergy for several days, and wrote to him six pages full of reproaches. I was expecting the postman's knock every moment, but nothing came. One morning I was sitting at my solitary breakfast, when at last a long letter from Sergy was brought to me. I devoured its contents. He wrote in high spirits and gave me all the details of his life at Piacenza, and glowing accounts of the manœuvres and all he was seeing. Two big rooms were reserved to him at the Hotel San Marco. After lunch, on the day of his arrival, he put on his uniform and went to present himself to the Commandant of Piacenza, in whose drawing-room a group of foreign officers, in the most varied uniforms, were gathered. Such a lot of strangers was quite an event for the little town of Piacenza, which was dressed all over with flags; a band played in the Square. When Sergy returned to the hotel he found on his table an envelope containing different instructions concerning the manœuvres, with maps and programmes for every day. The military representatives received a compliment in verse with the following inscription : *Dedica agli eccellentissimi signori, rappresentarano le nazioni, in occasione della lora venuta a Piacenza.* The representatives were entertained with much festivity; rich banquets were given in their honour. Twenty officers of different armies sat down to table every day : four Austrians, one Bavarian, three Germans, two Belgians, two Swedes, two Englishmen and three Russians. Sergy's neighbour was a Swedish general, an old trooper belonging to the school of "Gustav Vasa," who probably would never have stirred the world with any striking discovery, being rather narrow-minded. He said to Sergy that whilst travelling in Italy he was very much astonished that all the railway stations were named "Uscita" (which means exit), and was quite bewildered that in this country even children were able to surmount the difficulties of the language, and chatted Italian quite as a matter of course to each other! The manœuvres of one division against the other began on the 18th August. My husband with his brother-officers got up at daybreak and started by a special train to "Castello Giovanni," where a hillock, surrounded by vineyards, was chosen as point of observation. The Marchese Cambroso gave them a lunch in his splendid mansion that day, with champagne in abundance ; a military band played during the repast.   On the following morning the valiant sons of Mars went to Voghera, where they put up in private houses, as there was no hotel in that small place.   Their proprietors hoisted up the flags of the different nationalities who sheltered under their roofs.   Over the house where Sergy stopped, with two members of the Russian mission, a flag with a double eagle floated, and in their sitting-room stood a *samovar* (a Russian tea-kettle) deprived of its tap.   It was Count Bellisione who regaled the missions that day in his superb feudal castle.

My husband seemed to be quite happy while I am pining away at Cernobbio, and I positively could not admit that he was enjoying himself apparently while I was gloomily brooding here alone and miserable.   How I long to go away from that hateful Cernobbio!   I am quite out of place with my surroundings and feel like a fish out of water, thoroughly out of my element and out of tune with the whole atmosphere, which is a very different one from that to which I was accustomed.   The relations between Frau Weidemann's lady boarders were not so warm as they had promised to be at first.   I wanted to be very good friends here with everybody, but our way of life is so different and our natures are diametrically opposite ; we seemed to be as far apart as the poles.   The only topic of conversation of our lady-boarders was vocal matters, solfeggias and exercises.   I tried to keep out of their way and remained in my room as long as I could. Frau Weidemann was far more sympathetic than her boarders ; I liked her kind, motherly ways.   She tried to cheer me up and took the greatest pains to amuse me, but I refused all propositions of amusement and didn't care to join their out-of-door parties.   For two weeks I had been controlling myself, but it gets worse every day.   Our lady-boarders turn up their noses at me and cut me dead.   We scarcely notice each other and only meet at table.   What dismal meals we had!   It is Mrs. G— who has especially taken a dislike to me.   If wishes could have killed, I should have been dead long ago.   She detested me, I could read it in her eyes.   We were at daggers drawn.   I, too, was in entire readiness to show fight, for I like people who like me and hate those who don't like me ; it is unchristian, but I can't help it!   I am not a quiet, woolly lamb, and if Mrs. G— wanted to bite, I knew how to show my teeth too, and could take revenge on her, for to be silent and let others have all their say is not my nature.

Without the least intention of playing the eavesdropper I chanced to overhear a word or two spoken plainly on my account by Mrs. G—, which hadn't been intended to reach my ears.   I had not the temperament to turn "the other heek" at any insult ; I could take revenge, too.   I tried toc hold my tongue when I sat next to Mrs. G— at table, and had to close my lips tight—tight, or else a bad word would jump out, but the day would surely come when we should have a regular fight.   We were both in a mood when the merest spark would cause explosion, and the spark came ! At dinner one day Mrs. G—, in the presence of her children, boasted shamelessly that she could do very well without her husband, who, luckily for her, was retained by business in America, whilst she was enjoying herself across the ocean. Her vicious morality was so different from my own that I found it necessary to give her to understand that she was a heartless and undutiful woman, and losing all control over myself at such cynicism, I gave her a bit of my mind, and was obliged to tell her some truths which did not please her, after which Mrs. G—, who has a cutting tongue, made spiteful allusions concerning Signor Gorgolli, and asked if I ever practised what I preached, and added that I had better be careful of myself.   But I was not a bit baffled by the sharp prick of her poisonous arrow, and not a bit afraid of her back-handed little stabs.   I knew how to answer her and hold my ground, and got the better of her after all, having taught her not to interfere with me.

Our hen-coop is in commotion by the advent of a cock of very nasty plumage, it is true.   The new-comer is an American chanter, who has come from Chicago to study singing with Professor Lamperti.   At dinner I gazed with some curiosity at the Yankee, and found him helplessly shy and utterly unattractive, with sandy-coloured hair and features all wildly wrong ; his kindest friend could not have called him anything but ugly.   His clothes had the air of having been bought ready-made at a cheap shop and wanted brushing badly ; he wore a turned-over collar which showed his neck far down, and a white tie, tied a good deal on one side.   Our new lodger was painfully conscious of his physical shortcomings, and if ever a man wanted taming he did. At dinner he made all sorts of blunders, kept his eyes on his plate all the time and hardly spoke at all.   The advent of a man of that kind was not dangerous and far better for the peace of mind of our lady-boarders, for the new arrival was assuredly not of the type who seek adventure ; having nothing of the hero about him he would not play the Don Juan like Signor Gorgolli.

The Regattas had attracted a great number of spectators on the shore of Cernobbio.   Eighteen row-boats, adorned with wreaths of flowers, bearing each its number and denomination, were lining the coast like race-horses ready to start.   At a signal given by a cannon shot the boats spun along rapidly in the direction of Como. I didn't take any interest at all in these Regattas, my thoughts being miles away, for the manœuvres being over, I was leaving Cernobbio on the following day. To think that to-morrow at this time I shall be with Sergy again! I was getting so excited I didn't know how to wait till next morning, and went to bed as early as possible in order to reduce the evening to its very shortest proportions. It was my last night in that nasty place, and to-morrow I would shake the dust off my feet!

When I awoke in the morning I felt a great happiness. I dressed quickly and went to the window to look out for the carriage that was to take me to the railway station. To my great pleasure all our ladies, except Frau Weidemann, were asleep. I shall probably never set eyes on them again. If I ever see them, it will be only in my nightmares. I wanted to get away from here without the delay of a minute, and was leaving the house at a quarter to seven. I set out of Cernobbio deliciously light of heart, and hope I shall never return to this inhospitable place again. I had a first-class compartment to myself and felt like a schoolgirl off on her holiday. At every turn of the wheels my heart gave a glad throb at the thought that soon I would meet my husband, who was to arrive at Milan a few hours after me. I have left all my sorrows at Cernobbio : all the little bothers that were my lot were left behind. All that was done with now, and I'll make up for lost time, that I will !

On arriving at Milan I went straight to the Hôtel de la Ville. The manager came up to me and made me welcome, and told me that my husband was expected in the afternoon. I was shown into the same apartments we had before, which made me feel quite at home. I grew awfully impatient waiting ; I could not keep still and began to walk restlessly up and down the room, counting the minutes when Sergy would arrive, and every little while looking at the clock. At last I heard hurried steps in the corridor, and in an instant Sergy held me in his arms.

After luncheon, I drove with my husband in a smart landau with a pair of fine bays, put at our disposal by the Government, to the Hôtel Continental where all the members of the foreign missions had put up. Sergy wore his full uniform, on which shone many decorations, and created a great sensation ; people stopped and turned their heads when we passed through the street. In the long gallery of the hotel we saw groups of foreign representatives walking about. Sergy proceeded to introduce all the officers to me. Captain Sawyer, the aide-de-camp of General Freemantle, the English representative, was the best looking of them all. A Spanish colonel, Señor Achcaragua, came up by himself and begged for an introduction. His ardent eyes fixed on mine rather frightened me. One of his brother officers told Sergy that the colonel's brains were slightly touched, thanks to his somewhat stormy youth, during which he had spent himself too much physically, being not insensible to the Southern temperament of the Spanish ladies. During this edifying colloquy, General Fabre, the French representative, came up to Sergy and told him that he had just been appointed by King Humbert " Cavaliere " of the Order of the Corona d'Italia.

"It is the arrival of my wife at Milan, which has brought me that luck!" Sergy put in gallantly. We have invited the members of the Russian mission to dine with us at the National that night. Just as we were sitting down at table, an Italian officer brought the Order and ribbon granted to Sergy by the King, and I received in the same time a printed invitation from the Syndic of the town to assist at the grand review of troops which was to take place on the following day.

After dinner we removed to the Hôtel de la Ville, where an apartment was appointed to my husband. His name was on the door " Maggiore General de Doukhovskoy," in big white letters. I had scarcely time to take off my hat, when General Freemantle asked for permission to present himself to me. He was accompanied by Captain Sawyer, a very fair specimen of the English officer ; he was considerably over six feet and looked very smart and upright in his red uniform. That charming son of Albion paid me much attention and was extremely entertaining, he was astonished at my English, a language with which, from my childhood, I had been familiar. We didn't have five minutes' talk before Captain Sawyer defined my character. He called me whirl-wind, and nicknamed me " Quicksilver." I must confess I liked Captain Sawyer, he was quite my type of man.

When the members of the English mission left us, three officers of the German army came in, bowing with great clinking and much ceremony. They were martial-looking individuals, with fiercely twisted moustaches. The Teuton trio solemnly kissed my hand, sat down for two minutes, and stiffly bowed themselves off.

Italian orderlies, speaking the language of the members of the foreign missions, have been put to their service. The soldier alloted to my husband, Giovanni Varallo by name, a very handsome chap, spoke Russian very well, being born in Moscow where his parents have a little shop. Varallo is a funny sort of type. From the very beginning he made all sorts of blunders ; he disengaged himself of his knapsack in the drawing-room, and put his cap on the middle of the table!

At eight o'clock the following morning we were awakened by Varallo, who rapped sharply at our door and said that it was time to get up. I dressed quickly, and on entering our sitting-room I saw that Varallo had arranged it according to his idea of a lady's requirements. To complete all he he was holding my hat at the moment and insisted on brushing it with the blacking brush!

Mme. Favre, the wife of the French General, asked me to drive with her to the parade ground, our husbands having started together some minutes before us. We went first to the railway station to see the arrival of the King and Queen from Monzo, the Royal summer residence. On stepping out of the train King Humbert, mounted on horseback, and Queen Margareta took her place in a victoria, bowing graciously on right and left. The Italians do not cheer their sovereigns as we do in Russia, they applaud and shout "bravo," which seemed rather strange to me.

At the review we had seats in the Queen's stand. Queen Margareta sat a few paces from us, looking splendid in a beautiful gown embroidered with golden flowers. The King soon appeared, followed by his suit, my husband in the number. The throng was so great that the policemen had to use main force to procure free passage to the King. A crowd of lookers-on stood behind the double range of soldiers shouting bravo and clapping their hands to the King. In an open space of ground both infantry and cavalry were assembled. After all the regiments had defiled before the King, we went to the Continental where the representatives of the different nations were invited to a banquet given to them by the government. They came out afterwards into the courtyard to have their group taken. The photographer grouped the party according to his idea. Sergy and General Freemantle in the centre, while the others clustered round them. Many failures issued, as all these warriors, feeling themselves returned to boyhood, wouldn't sit still and laughed when they had to keep serious. The patience of the photographer was something wonderful. I looked at that comic scene out of the gallery facing the courtyard. Captain Sawyer came up to me and said that he had fixed me all the time whilst they were being photographed in order to have a pleasant expression and to look nice.

On that same day the missions were invited to dinner at Monzo. I remained alone at the hotel and sat in the deep window-seat to witness their departure. Varallo found it his duty to entertain me during my husband's absence and brought up an album with coloured views of Milan, which he began to explain to me.

Sergy returned enchanted with the warm reception of the Royal family. At dinner he sat next to the beautiful Countess

Barromée. All the ladies wore a daisy pinned on their bodices, in honour of Queen Margaret. When the guests were leaving Monzo, the King, speaking in Russian, bade Sergy adieu, saying *Do svidania*, which means "good-bye," and asked Sergy to transmit his est regards to our Emperor.

CHAPTER XXXII

VENICE

On the following day we took the Venice express at nine o'clock in the morning. Two Belgian members of the foreign missions travelled to Venice with us. Colonel Theuniss and Major Havard proved very entertaining companions, only their knowledge of Russia was sadly deficient. They believed that wolves prowled in the streets of St. Petersburg in broad daylight.

At eight o'clock in the evening we reached Venice and rolled slowly along a narrow pier. At the railway-station a group of gondoliers rushed up to us, offering their gondolas, just like cabmen. We stepped down into a gondola lighted up by lanterns on bow and poop. The gondolier pushed off from the steps and we silently glided along the Great Canal, surrounded by side canals crossed by small private bridges. Venice is built on piles, and stands upon many islands linked by bridges. At each crossing of the aquatic streets our strong-lunged gondolier shouted *Gia-e!* to escape collision. He brought us to the Hotel Danielli where we passed a sleepless night, not having followed the wise advice of the chambermaid, who told us not to raise the mosquito-nets. We were thoroughly punished for it, having been devoured by mosquitoes.

Lunch over, we went out for a walk along narrow little pathways leading to the Piazza San Marco. After a stroll in the arcades of the Square, we took a gondola for a sail on the Canale Grande. We glided smoothly on the silent waves of the Adriatic, passing before grim old buildings. The palaces in which Byron, Schiller and Lucrezia Borgia have dwelt are now transformed into hotels. Venice, the town of legends and dreams, has very unpleasant odours, and nearly all the windows are hung with a flutter of drying sheets and towels, flapping in the air like old tattered flags.

On the following day we took the boat to Lido, a fashionable sea-bathing-place, and returned to Venice just in time for the table d'hote. There was a great festival at night on the Canale Grande ; all the gondolas of Venice were on the water, lighted with coloured lanterns. On the broadest part of the Canal they were tied on to the other thus forming a large floating bridge, on the middle of which a group of street-singers were giving a serenade. Our gondolier, at our request, shouted out in a stentorian voice: *Funiculi, funicula*, and the singers performed with great emphasis that popular song, after which they crossed over from one gondola to the other, holding out their hats which were soon amply filled. We gave all the change we had in our pockets.

We only remained two days at Venice, having had quite enough of that aquatic town which does not suit my vivacious temperament.

CHAPTER XXXIII

FLORENCE

LEAVING Venice at ten o'clock in the morning, we arrived towards night at Florence, and took an apartment at the Hôtel de Russie, with a ceiling ornamented with flying nymphs in a blue sky all over, and an enormous bedstead on the top of which was placed a gigantic wreath of laurel. In my opinion, to sleep under it is an honour which few people deserve on earth.

The next day we went to the Pitti Galleries, to see the Exhibition of old Masters. This museum was formerly maintained by the monks, and the pictures were taken in preference from Scripture subjects, but at present the nude mythological element predominates. In the sculpture section we met a group of curates who were all in a state of sanctimonious adoration before the marble Venus. I could hardly keep from laughing at the sight of these tonsured admirers of art, whose expression of the face, for the moment, could easily serve for a picture representing the temptation of St. Antony. At the entrance of the Medici Chapel, an old curate impeded the passage of the turnstile, searching for his hat, which was hanging by the elastic on his back. Surely the venerable pater had also contemplated rather too much of the marble goddess.

After the Pitti Galleries, we were shown the Palace, maintained by the town, in which King Humbert is received in great ceremony, as a guest, when he comes to Florence. A carriage road leads to each floor separately replacing the elevator. The King was expected in a few days, and a legion of servants were cleaning the hangings and polishing the furniture whilst we went through the Palace.

On our way back we were driven in the "cascine," landaus, victorias, and open cabs of every variety, all filled with animated people, streamed along the wide road. We met in the park the famous American millionaire perched high upon the seat of his phaeton, who drives every afternoon in the "Cascine" a team of twelve horses, one pair in front of the other.

My old friends the Levdics have taken their abode in Italy having been expatriated by the doctors on account of their health. They spend the winter months in Florence and the summer at Viareggio, a little sea-side resort beyond Florence. We went to see them at Viareggio, and as we knew nothing of their address, we had to go to the post-office for information. Their home is a very pretty one, and the out-look from their terrace on the Mediterranean and the neighbouring mountains is wonderful.

Next day we visited the "Certosa," a convent situated on a high mountain in the outskirts of Florence. The cloister opens hospitable doors to strangers. We were gallantly received by the monks, who live here a luxurious life. Each monk occupies an apartment of several rooms, with a patch of garden. A tall, stout monk, in flowing white robes, served as guide to us. He conducted us, clacking his sandals on the stone flags, along white bare corridors paved with marble, which echoed to our footsteps. We were taken into a large refectory resembling much more an elegant Parisian restaurant. Then we went to the dormitory where the monks sleep. When our guide ushered us into his bedroom, I stealthily touched his bed and found it far too soft for a recluse. Before leaving the cloister we bought a few bottles of the "certosa liqueur" fabricated by the monks, for which we had to pay a considerable tax before entering Florence. Feeling awfully hungry, we stopped half way at an "Osteria" when passing through the little town of Galuppi. It was very cool and pleasant here after the dusty road, but our dinner had been uneatable : we had a dish of macaroni swimming in oil, and a fish fried also in oil. Ugh—the horror! Night was approaching and icy cold rain began to fall. We returned to Florence famished and chilled to the very bone. And our room at the hotel was so cold! You feel the cold much more abroad than in Russia, where the houses are much better heated. How I long for our warm Russian stoves!

Profiting by our stay in Florence, Sergy wanted me to be immortalised by brushes and chisels, on canvas and on marble. He ordered my portrait to be taken by Parrini, a well-known painter, and my bust by Romanelli, the famous sculptor, who took us to his "studio," full of nymphs and cupids and limbs ; a moving platform for the model occupied the middle of the room. I had to sit from nine o'clock in the morning until six in the evening, which was rather fatiguing. Whilst Parrini painted my portrait, his wife, Signora Adelgunda, a buxom, pleasant-faced lady, stood behind and generally approved, nodded her head and murmured, caressing her husband's cheek, "*Bene, bene, caro, Beppé.*" Signora Adelgunda was also a painter, and had exhibited several times. She has watched for eight years the right to obtain the first place to copy Rafaele's Madonna at the Pitti Galleries. Her picture had found its way into the Museum and was sold for the sum of two thousand francs. Parrini, during the sittings, told me little humorous things he could think of, trying to keep me amused. I laughed very much when he related to me that he had just received from America the photographs of a gentleman and his wife who wanted to have their portraits painted conformably to these photos, only the gentleman wished to be reproduced with less hair on his head and ten years more on his shoulders, whilst his spouse, on the contrary, wanted him to drop ten years of her age. Parrini related to me that when Mme. Lebrun, the celebrated lady-painter, in her old age, visited the Pitti Galleries and saw an oil painting of her, reproducing her young and beautiful, the poor woman had a fit of hysterics and nearly fainted away. Yes, certainly, it must not be pleasant to grow old, especially when one has been gifted by good looks. I felt very flattered when Parrini told me in his artistic language, that like Mme. Lebrun my face had warm and cold touches. Shall I ever fall into a swoon, if I ever reach old age, when looking at my portrait painted by Parrini, I wonder? The Parrinis have got a little son named Mario, a premature painter, who puts paint on the doors, walls and statues which adorn his father's "studio." He is a very lively and noisy little boy, who gives trouble and puts things out of place. His last exploit was to daub with red paint the statue of the daughter of Niobe, and to adorn her beautiful face with long black moustaches. Romanelli is over seventy years old but carries them lightly on his shoulders. He wears a red scarf round his throat, carpet slippers, and a black velvet "calotte" pushed off on the back of his bald head. At my first sitting I felt rather shy when the sculptor placed me in a seat standing on the turning pedestal, but at the second sitting it went off all right, I mounted bravely on my elevated throne. The bust of a young woman, made in clay, stood on my right hand and Romanelli modelled it here and there, according to my features, diminishing or adding small bits of clay. Sitting for my bust made me sleepy, and I waited impatiently when Romanelli, who was careful not to overtire me, would tell me to have a rest. Then I rose and went out into the garden, stiff with long sitting. I yawned and stretched my arms wearily and five minutes after I resumed my place on the "dais." When the turn came for my neck to be modelled, Romanelli told me to unbutton the upper part of my bodice, which made me burn with shame. The old sculptor laughed and said that he had lost the number of all the necks, a great deal more low-bodied than mine, which had served for models to him during his long artistic life. My bust advanced rapidly and the likeness was perfect, but Sergy, who had only too flattering an opinion of me in every way, and was very hard to please according to what concerned my precious person, found that the head was not well put on, and the back not sufficiently straight, and when Romanelli agreeably to his demands, began to take off layers of clay from my bust's back, Sergy turned away shuddering: it seemed to him as if I was being carved alive. Romanelli declared finally that the head had to be separated from the bust in order to place it more backwards; my husband would not consent to be present at this bloodless operation and carried me away promptly, when we returned an hour later, we found the head in its proper place again. My bust in clay was now completed and Romanelli promised to send to Moscow for Christmas my bust made in marble. The lump of clay representing the bust of a young woman, which Ramanelli manipulated according to my features, is transformed now, for another sitting, into a bust of a wrinkled old man. My portrait will be ready for Christmas also.

CHAPTER XXXIV

ROME

WE spent a week in visiting the city of the Cæsars, running through churches, art-galleries and other regulation sights, according to Baedecker, from morning till night. We followed our guide with uncomplaining stoicism from one Museum to another. I was not feeling altogether at my ease when visiting the catacombs, and wished myself anywhere else all the time. We had to come down slowly through dark stone passages with our folding lantern in which a reluctant wax-taper went out at regular intervals. We saw caverns containing skeletons which fell to dust when you touched them, and pertified corpses in coffins under a glass cover. Truly it was a ghastly sight! There are often crumbling stones too in the Catacombs, and you can easily find your death under them.

In the church of "Santa Croce" we saw the staircase (Scala Pia) brought forward from Jerusalem, reputed to have belonged to Pilate's Palace, where they were trodden by Christ at the time of his trial. Pilgrims are permitted to ascend the steps on their knees only. Two smart ladies were toiling slowly up the long ladder, stopping at every step to arrange the folds of their skirts. Some peasant women, who had begun their ascent much later, soon overtook them. I am sure that they have more chance of getting to the Kingdom of Heaven.

The Pantheon, where the remains of King Vittorio Emmanuele repose, is the only ancient edifice in Rome, which is conserved perfectly intact. It has no ceiling, and the Roman sun and the Roman moon shine through the open roof. The sepulchre in which the body of Vittorio Emmanuele is laid is covered all over with garlands of flowers and is guarded by three veterans of the Italian army, who watch over a big book in which all those who wish to honour the memory of the "King Galantuomo" sign their names.

We had to cross the Tiber to arrive at the Vatican, where we found ourselves on Papal territory, which has a particular clerical aspect. The population is very poor here, a great part of their existence is spent in the open. There was a crowd of women, ragged and unkempt creatures, sitting in front of their houses in a bath of sunshine, bearing the pure classical Roman type. They were surrounded by a swarm of children with unwiped noses, who stared at us with their fingers in their mouths. I can't make out how these matrons had the time to bring such a lot of children into the world. We met a number of prelates in the streets, and ladies in black dresses and long black veils, prescribed by etiquette for ladies going to an audience with the Pope, and wearing mourning in the memory of the abolished clerical potency. The Pope, deploring his decay, has shut himself up in the Vatican, vowing never to leave it until the King abdicates the throne. The doors of the Vatican are closed to all persons belonging to the Court of Italy, Baron Rosen, the Russian attaché, in the number.

There was much to see in the Vatican Palace. We went from room to room admiring the immortal master-pieces. In the "Sixtine Chapel" we saw the famous picture of the "Last Judgment" painted by Michael Angelo. We could hardly get away from the place. Then we stepped into a long gallery all lined with pictures on Scripture subjects, arranged like a museum and leading to the private apartments of the Pope. Groups of Papal guards, the last remains of the Papal power, in their picturesque uniforms, with striped yellow and black legs, were walking to and fro with a rifle on their shoulder. After leaving the Palace we strayed down the wide stairs into the beautifully kept gardens which surrounded it, and saw wild deer and pheasants walking about freely. The Pope feeds them himself every morning during the voluntary prisoner's drive in the alleys of the Park. On leaving the Vatican Gardens the head-gardener presented me with a splendid bouquet.

On the great Square before the bronze gates of the Vatican, in front of St. Peter's Cathedral, we saw the black statue of St. Peter, sitting in his stone chair under a golden baldaquin, holding in his hand the "Keys of Paradise." Through the continual contact of worshippers lips, one of the Saint's toes was almost completely worn out. After having admired the rich monuments of all the interred Popes, and the shrine containing St. Peter's relics, we drove along the ancient "Latin Road" to Monte Palanchino, one of the most interesting reminiscences of past ages. A whole army of workmen, under the superintendence of a group of engineers and archeologists, continue to excavate making splendid discoveries. A whole street intact has recently been dug out. The pavements and houses with their mosaic floors are marvellously preserved. We stood on the roof of one of the newly excavated houses watching the workmen who were destroying—on the mountain side over us—a splendid villa which had belonged to Napoleon the Third, in order to continue to dig out the street under its foundation.

On the eve of our departure from Rome we went to see the Coliseum, a ruin of former glory where gladiators have fought, the largest amphitheatre in the world, which could hold about ten thousand spectators. Before turning to the hotel we took a drive in Monte Pincio, the Hyde Park of Rome. The large alleys are filled with riders, drivers and pedestrians. On both sides of the drive stand white marble statues of gods and godesses. In the very beginning is erected the statue of Vittorio Emmanuele, in the memory of the taking of Rome by his armies. In front of the round tower of the summer-house, sheltered by magnificent magnolia and orange trees, there is a high terrace. We mounted on it, and Rome lay below us like a city from a baloon. It was very still and peaceful, the noise of the street did not penetrate to this place. Suddenly the evening bells began to ring all over Rome. On our way back, when passing before the " Trevi Fountains," we called to mind the popular saying that if you want to return to Rome once more, you must drink some water out of this fountain, and we swallowed two glasses of the miraculous water which we purchased at a little shop near by.

After having seen all the sights of the Eternal City we started for Naples. We had quite enough of all these churches and museums, and were tired out by too much admiration. The tenants of our railway carriage were but three, but they had managed things so nicely that not a square inch of spare room was visible, engrossed by a fabulous number of bags, baskets, etc., etc. " Partenza l" shouted the railway officials, bang-bang went the doors, and our train left the station and began to wind round the low hills of the " Campagna."

CHAPTER XXXV

NAPLES

WHEN we arrived at Naples a whole legion of porters assailed us. We took an apartment at the Grand Hôtel, situated on the New Quay. We had a disagreeable surprise when we awoke next morning; a grey mist veiled Mount Vesuvius, the sky and sea were of leaden hue, and rain began to fall, which is very rare in this place. We braved the elements, and went in the afternoon to try and find out what has become of Schildecker, one of my most devoted lovers in the blessed days of my girlhood. We had exhausted every means in our power to discover his whereabouts and have been all over Naples to find him, but nobody could tell us anything about him. We called at the Transatlantic Bank where Schildecker had been employed, but there also nothing had been heard of him for nearly ten years. We got, however, the address of one of Schildecker's friends, who perhaps could say where he was. But Sergy felt tired, and said that we could make far better use of our time than spending it in search of Schildecker. I despaired of finding him again, but did not insist, fearing to displease my husband.

After dinner, we drove to the Circus in a cab drawn by a queer-tempered horse, who at first would not move, and stood planted with rigid forelegs, tucked-in tail and ears laid back. Our driver made a great fuss with the reins and the whip, but his horse would not advance an inch. Suddenly the stubborn animal changed his mind, swerved aside, and commenced to rear, plunging rather wildly, and seemed to be in a fair way to kick himself free of everything. Perceiving the danger, I jumped out of the carriage, to Sergy's great horror, and went straight to the horse's head and snatched at the bridle, after which the nasty vicious brute became more manageable and consented to carry us to our destination.

Next morning, while still in bed, I could see the sunrise over Vesuvius, lighting the smoke which rose from the crater. After a hasty breakfast, we went for a drive in the outskirts of Naples passing through the " Pausilippe Grotto," which is about a mile long; it is supported by columns and lighted at long intervals by lanterns. The road leading to Virgil's tomb passes over the Grotto. We visited also the " Sulfre Grotto " with sulphur smoke coming out of the

Vesuvius and evaporating through crevices in the Grotto. The " Dog's Grotto " is full of sulphuric acid. A dog, serving for experiments, looses consciousness when kept inside one second, and breathes his last in the lapse of one minute. One of the ugly little mongrels, upon whom experiments are made, ran before us wagging his tail, but when the guide wanted to take him in his arms, the poor little brute began to whine pitifully. We would not have him tortured on our account, and the guide finding it necessary to show us another experiment, filled an earthen pot with gas, into which he dipped a burning torch which was immediately extinguished. We were back at Naples just in time for dinner. Before going to sleep we had an agreeable surprise. A troup of wandering singers gave us a serenade beneath our windows, and sung Russian folk-songs. I was so pleased I could have kissed them all. Next morning Sergy went out by himself to make inquiries about Schildecker, and started off to the address of his friend given in the Bank, and was told that Schildecker had died of consumption ten years ago. Poor fellow ! His death affected me, and I dropped a tear for him.

We devoted the whole of the next day to Pompeii, the long-buried city at the foot of the great destroyer. Nothing but desolation and silence around ! Walking amid the wrecks, the mystery of the past took possession of us and the busy lives which animated formerly the deserted town, rose before us. The cinder-choked streets have preserved their ancient denominations. The buildings remind me of those of Erzeroum, with a fountain in the middle of the inner court. The frescoed walls have kept their original colour, and the sign-boards over the houses and the indecent bas-reliefs (reminiscences of not over pure-minded antiquity) are perfectly intact. Here is the grand *Basilique* the symbol of an ancient disappeared civilisation and the pagan temples of Venus, Mercury and Jupiter. A little further, in the quarter of the Gladiators, is the *Forum* with the immense tribune in which the people assembled for all sorts of meetings. In a separate museum curious remains of past ages are gathered : artistically worked jewels, mosaics and petrified corpses in almost as fine condition as 1800 years ago in 79 A.D. There is a young woman lying prostrate on the marble floor ; the position of the hands indicate that she had instinctively tried to protect her face from the hot ashes when the death-storm broke and Vesuvius blotted out Pompeii. We saw objects just dug up : coins, vases and pottery. We passed before bars which looked as if they had just been freshly painted, where wine had been sold. Here are loaves of bread lying on the counter of a baker's shop, transformed into stone and looking as if they had just come out of the oven. Before the shop, a petrified dog, curled up, seems to be sleeping.

Our old cicerone, who had lived all his life at the foot of the great mountain, had worked as guide to Pompeii for fifty-five years. He told us that there were presently forty guides at Pompeii. When we asked if it wasn't dangerous for him to live so near to the volcano, the old guide replied, with pride, that they were all of them sons of Vesuvius, and had no need, therefore, to dread it.

We had to pass through the vestibule of the modern Hôtel Diomède to enter the domains of the past, and on our way back we had dinner there. I was glad to be out of the circle of the dead centuries and back into the world of living men. I had just read a French novel written by Georges de Peyrebrune in which the author described the wonderful beauty of Signorina Sofia Prospezi, the daughter of the proprietor of Hôtel Diomède, and wanted to see if the reputation of her beauty was not exaggerated. It appeared to be quite true. Signorina Prospezi was beyond question endowed with great beauty : she was tall, slender, with a pure oval face, finely chiselled features and luminous velvety, brown eyes, shaded by curling black lashes. I asked her to give me her photograph, and she begged for mine in return. Her father was wonderfully amiable and attentive towards us. Instead of regaling us with diluted wine, which was usually served to his customers, he ordered the oldest and best wine in his cellars to be brought to us. Our host evidently meant to be complimentary, and said that he thought me very much like his wife—who appeared to be a compatriot of ours—when she was young and beautiful.

On the following day we drove to Castellamare ; a succession of villages lined the way. The tramway took up half the breath of the road, encumbered with huge waggons drawn by great powerful horses ; I felt rather frightened. On approaching Sorrento we ran against a car drawn by a horse, a cow and a donkey as well ! There was a local feast of Saint-somebody, I didn't know who, at Sorrento, and flags were suspended from house to house across the narrow streets. We passed before the house which had been inhabited by Torquato Tasso transformed now into an hotel. Just in front of it stands the statue of the great poet. The distant sound of low chanting attracted our attention ; it grew louder, and presently, far up the street, we saw a religious procession come in sight. At the head came a pilgrim holding a high crucifix. Behind followed a group of curates in white surplices, bearing a large grotto in which stood the statue of a saint dressed as a Franciscan monk, surrounded by a number of statuettes representing worshippers kneeling to him. A number of little girls, arrayed in white, with crowns of roses on their heads, carried an altar decorated with vases full of paper-flowers, in the middle of which stood the statue of the Virgin, clad in a rich brocade dress and a long blue mantle embroidered with silver stars; the Madonna's long hair fell in ringlets on her shoulders. A large crowd of pilgrims came behind. We begged a constable to clear a passage for us through the throng and gained the high road by a back street. From afar we saw the lava running down Vesuvius. Our *vetturino*, turning round, said, "That's my home," pointing with his whip to a little village sheltered beneath the treacherous mountain.

On arriving at Castellamare we were just in time to catch the train with which we were to return to Naples. We got into the first railway carriage occupied by an ill-assorted Italian pair, a fat middle-aged lady and a good-looking young man resembling an opera tenor, and at least a quarter of a century younger than his companion, who made beside him, the sharpest contrast, looking very thick and clumsy. She gazed at her interesting cavalier with an admiration and tenderness in her old eyes, which was quite ridiculous. The evening being fresh, I closed the window, to the great displeasure of my voluminous neighbour, who began to grumble and said to her companion that she was on the point of being suffocated. "She must certainly feel hot, the fatty!" I exclaimed in Russian very imprudently, for after I had just made this flattering statement, the young Italian said to Sergy, in a most natural tone, that his wife, as it appears, is a compatriot of ours. I felt pretty bad at that moment, I confess, having got into a terrible scrape. I could have bitten off my tongue! Unfortunately I always speak first and think afterwards! But apparently the fat lady didn't hear my complimentary adverb, as she amiably entered into conversation, and in a few minutes we felt as if we had known her for ages. She became very confidential, and by the time the train reached Naples we were in possession of the entire history of her life. She told us, with a coquettish glance at her husband, which would have been very effective thirty years ago, that she had been married five years, and was feeling perfectly happy, only rather home-sick for Moscow, her native town. How in the world did she manage to catch that handsome fellow— who, for his part, certainly didn't seem to adore his caricature spouse.

Our great desire was to make the ascent by the Funicular Railway of Mount Vesuvius, whilst it was in eruption. Our wish was fulfilled on the following day. It took us three hours to drive in a carriage to the aerial railway-station. We passed a great number of macaroni factories, and saw rows of macaroni hanging on strings to dry. The road was most picturesque, having the blue Mediterranean strewn with white sails on one side and Vesuvius on the other. At length we reached the foot of the mountain. its head wrapped in a gloomy wreath of smoke and cloud. The volcano was in full activity at that moment, and a large torrent of lava was running down the right slope of the Vesuvius. We saw the Funicular Railway crawling up the steepest part of the cone. We began to climb a very steep ascent leading to the aerial station, paved with different-coloured tiles of petrified lava. On each side of our way rose mountains of black lava. A group of street-singers followed our carriage singing Neapolitan folk-songs. When we arrived at the railway-station, standing near the observatory and the carbiniers' lodge, the carriage-road ended. After having secured our tickets at the booking-office, we had lunch in the restaurant, and saw from the open window a funicular car crawling down the mountain. The Funicular Railway has only two cars, attached to an endless cable, named "Vesuvius" and "Etna," one at the top and one at the bottom of the mountain; the one that comes down pulls the other one up.

After lunch, when we made our way to the Funciular, we were accosted by a crowd of tattered boys, who proposed to clean our boots, and begged plaintively for some coins "*Per mangiare macaroni.*" We descended into a sort of dark cave and entered an open railway-carriage in sloping position, holding only ten passengers sitting in pairs opposite each other, the back seats on a level with their heads. Two carbiniers escorted our car. I shuddered when we began the ascent, for it was not at all comforting to be aware that lava only served as foundation to the Funicular Railway and might be falling to pieces at any moment. The mount which only takes a few minutes, seemed a whole century to me. Vesuvius was throwing great balls of fire all the time, and the smoke coming out of the volcano spread around us. We had arrived at the highest point that the waggon could reach and had to leave the Funicular and climb to the summit of Vesuvius on foot. We walked on very rough ground, steaming with sulphurous springs. A score of ragged fellows proposed to serve as guides to us, and said that we must absolutely take two men, each of us, to push and pull us up, but I announced proudly that I could perfectly do with one guide only. I hadn't made the ascent of Mont Blanc for nothing, I suppose! We walked on a moving soil, consisting of ashes and pumice-stone, sulphur smoke passed off in vapour from crevices beneath us; the soil burnt our feet and our shoes filled with lava. The smell of sulphur nearly choked me. I could not breathe without coughing or gasping. Our mount became more and more difficult: there was no longer any path, it was merely like going up a very steep cinder heap; with each step we sank in it to knee-depth. It was very fatiguing and I had to seek the aid of three guides; one guide took me by the right arm, another took me by the left one, and the third pushed vigorously behind.

By the time we arrived at the top my dress was in rags.
At last, after an hour's toil, we succeeded in reaching the
summit of the cone and were approaching the lip of the
crater. At the same time we heard a long low rumbling,
like the sound of the sea when the tide is breaking on a
distant beach. Right below us yawned an enormous pit,
whose sides were gnarled and twisted by the action of
terrible heat ; we saw the burning liquid issue from the
crater. I managed to get so near that the ashes fell on my
dress. It was a wonderful sight and needs the pen of
Dante to describe the awful impression received when I
stood on the brink of the crater and gazed into the depths
of an inferno. The head-guide requested me not to approach
too near its fiery mouth, but I felt it draw me like a magnet.
We could hear the roar of the fire beneath us. We stood
there fascinated when a loud report shook the ground and a
shower of hot cinders fell around us. We felt like being
under a war-fire. I never was in such a fright in all my
life and thought our last moment had come. "We are lost,"
I said to myself trembling all over.

Following the command of our guides we fell flat on our
faces, at once. All this happened in the space of a second.
A smell of burning wool spread around us. It was my dress
which had caught fire. Next moment we got up hurriedly
and fled in terror to the other end of the cone, as the
direction these rivulets of liquid fire take, depends entirely on
the wind. By some miracle nobody was hurt. We have
had evidently a very narrow escape of our lives. We were now
on our way back to the Funicular Railway. Oh! that
descent! We slid down as on skates and reached the
Funicular Station in shoes almost entirely without soles.

The next day we went to visit the "Certosa," an ancient
grey abbey perched on a high rock, a veritable eagle's nest.
Only six monks are left now in the monastery, to make the
famous "Certosa liqueur." They gather the herbs in the
mountains and keep the recipe of their liqueur as a great
secret. The convent is now converted into a Museum.
Among other curiosities we were shown a shallop in which
Charles the Tenth had landed in Spain. Looking out from the
terrace the whole city of Naples lay revealed ; only the
distant splashing of the sea below was heard.

A terrible calamity has befallen the Island of Ischia. The
little town of Casamicciola, destroyed by a recent tremendous earthquake, is nothing but a heap of deplorable
ruins. Through the awful cataclysm the inhabitants are
deprived of home and bread. In pursuit of strong
sensations we wanted to visit these ruins and embarked on a
small steamer which plied from the Bay of Naples to
Ischia. It takes only two hours to cross. There was not

a breath of air and the sea looked like a polished mirror. Whilst we gazed at the frolics of the dolphins from deck, we passed a man-of-war that had cast anchor in the Bay, and did not remark that it was a Russian cruiser. A young chap who sold photographs on board, offered to show us the ruins of Casamicciola. He could murder enough French to be our interpreter and we accepted his offer. He told us that he had lost both his parents and all his belongings in the recent earthquake ; the only object he had found amongst the ruins was his watch. The poor boy had remained several hours unconscious under the ruins and was just out of hospital. On approaching Ischia, we stopped before what had formerly been Casamicciola, a desolate black desert now. The earthquake had in a few moments changed the prosperous little town into a ruin. Hundreds and hundreds of homes had entirely gone. Many people were buried beneath the fallen houses. About two hundred corpses remained under the ruins and a terrible smell came forth. In fear of infection the inhabitants are forbidden to dig out the corpses. Another slight earthquake took place the other day : a rock tumbled down, destroying the remaining houses, and large crevices have been formed in the mountains all around. The whole population is in terrible distress. The only inhabitants who escaped death are those who were working out in the fields at the moment of the catastrophe, and had fled panic-stricken to the mountains for refuge. We were told that a Russian couple, living at the Hôtel des Etrangers, had been saved through their children who were having a fight in the park belonging to the hotel. Their parents had just come down to set them apart, when the earth shook, and the whole hotel came down, falling to pieces. Looking at this bright place and its luxurious vegetation, it seems to be a perfect paradise on earth, but this beautiful soil opens treacherously under your feet, transforming everything into a "vale of tears." Oh! the irony of the things of this world! And still men will build up new dwellings again and will not think of the danger of a repetition of the past catastrophe! An old cab, with a skeleton of a horse between the shafts, drove us through the demolished streets heaped up with stones, trunks of trees and plaster, but soon there was no road at all, and we had to walk amidst a mass of broken stones and woodwork. We saw women seeking forgotten objects on the threshold of their crumbled houses, a wreck of broken stones and fallen walls. A young girl sat with her head buried in her hands, rocking her body to and fro, and kept wailing " Why, oh, why was I saved! " It was a sorrowful spectacle and my heart bled for her. Workmen had been sent in haste to build barracks for the victims of the catastrophe, and huts have been erected in the vicinity of the ill-fated town.

We visited that sordid encampment where the poor wretches slept on the hard ground, pêle-mêle, like Bohemians. A troup of carbiniers have just arrived to keep order. We were surrounded by hundreds of poor starving creatures. Sad-faced women, with tragic eyes, stood in groups with children of all ages holding to their skirts. They spread out their hands in a gesture of despair and burst into lamentations, begging for bread. Sergy gave away nearly all the contents of his purse. The poor wretches murmured their thanks, pressing kisses on my hands, against my inclination. In token of gratitude, an old, toothless granny, wrinkled like a crumpled apple, her hooked nose nearly in contact with her chin, patted me on the back ; being very much afraid that she meant to kiss my reluctant cheek, I went prudently behind my husband. My one desire was to get back to Naples, and I breathed freely when our boat left the shores of Ischia. A group of Neapolitan women, with red handker-chiefs on their heads, had come out from third class on our deck to dance the *Tarantella*, to the accompaniment of a band of strolling musicians. One of the women had been hurt by the earthquake, and this was her first day out of the hospital.

On approaching Naples, I was delighted to see on the quay a group of Russian sailors belonging to the man-of-war which had cast anchor in the bay. I hastened to land, in order to boast of my country-men before our fellow pas-sengers. But, O horror! it appeared that the sailors were all desperately drunk, and looked awful. With bleeding faces, their clothes all in tatters, they made a disgusting spectacle of themselves. We were told that they had just had a fight with some Italian sailors who had cheated them in a tavern where they had been drinking together. Our compromising compatriots were shouting in Russian, " Give back our money or we'll throw you into the water ! " It was not a very edify-ing scene and made me blush for my country. On our way to the hotel we met another group of Russian sailors walking in a friendly way—arm-in-arm—with their Italian comrades, also tolerably drunk and zig-zagging somewhat, their two feet being hopelessly at variance. There will be a figh' between them ere long, I am sure. Passing by a co shop, we entered to purchase a necklace, and made out the owner of the shop was a fellow-countryman o living in Naples for the last thirty years. He sexton at the Russian church, and having r daughter of an Italian merchant, he had sett*bella* good in this country. His eldest son can j words in Russian, but the younger one word of our mother-tongue.

The next day we started back to P
Napoli with regret.

CHAPTER XXXVI

PEISSENBERG

ONCE back in Moscow, we resumed our usual mode of life. My husband is working very hard, and I see him only during our meals. Our doctor finds repose and change of air necessary for us both, and sends us to make a cure in the sanatorium of the famous Wunderfrau Ottilie Hohenmeister, at Peissenberg, in the Bavarian mountains. Our journey occupied three days. I grew rather excited as we neared our destination, and when the train steamed into the station of Peissenberg, I felt downcast and nervous at the thought that we should have to undergo a serious cure here. We drove in a carriage sent by Frau Hohenmeister to her sanatorium—beautifully situated on the slope of a hill—and followed her head-manager into a parlour where a fire was burning brightly. After having put our names down in the register-book, we climbed to the top-floor by a creaking staircase of seventy steep steps which led to our apartment, consisting of two rooms high up in the attic. Our turret bed-room was close under the roof, and our eyes were above the tree-tops. It had a window in its sloping ceiling through which stars might be studied at night. And we are first-class boarders at the sanatorium! How are the second-class tenants lodged, I wonder? In return we have a beautiful view from our sitting-room window, looking on to the vast forest and on snowy hill-tops in the background.

After having ordered a fire to be lit in our room, we went to present ourselves to the Wunderfrau, who lives in a private house close to the sanatorium. A number of people, coming from all parts of the world, sat about waiting in the drawing-room. Frau Hohenmeister has wide-world fame and works wonders. The doctoress welcomed us affably and gave me a friendly pat, calling me all the time, "*Mein Kind, mein Schatz.*" She is a short and fat woman, with a round face and round black eyes—in short, she is round everywhere. My German being very elementary, I called to my help all the German words I knew to answer the Wunderfrau's questions. That night, before going to bed, we devoured a whole box of caviare which we had brought from Moscow, as we were to be put on diet the following day.

Our cure began at six o'clock in the morning. First came a little wizen old woman, badly named "Greti" (diminutive of Margaret), who brought us a nasty drug which we swallowed with a grimace. At half-past six we had to undergo a massage performed by Fraulein Zenzi, Frau Hohenmeister's pretty niece ; at seven came the knock of the bathman (Herr Bademeister) announcing that our baths were ready. The water in the bath was dark, and smelt just like Grete's mixture. We had to lie down in bed for twenty minutes after our bath, and at eight o'clock Fraulein Zenzi reappeared bringing a bottle bearing the inscription " Medicine," and we had to swallow a table-spoonful of that horrid physic every two hours. It was only at ten o'clock that I got a cup of beef-tea, whilst Sergy (lucky man) was allowed a cup of coffee. At eleven o'clock repetition of the same broth with an egg, and a small roll in addition. At seven we went down to dinner after the table-d'hôte, and returned to our attic feeling very hungry, for the soup had been uneatable and the following dishes quite tasteless, as our doctoress strictly forbids seasoning of any kind. At nine o'clock we were obliged to go to bed, and at ten the gas was turned out all over the house.

Sergy was not a very docile patient, and felt rebellious to the authority of a person of the feeble sex, but I did all that the Wunderfrau ordered me to do without protest.

The village of Peissenberg—set upon a hill—is very picturesque. It is inhabited mostly by mine-workers. In the daytime the male population lives underground. When we went out for our every-day walk, the women on their doorsteps dropped us a curtsey with a muttered " *Grüss Gott.*" Sergy goes out on excursions sometimes. One afternoon he went to Steinberg, where he took the boat plying on the Lake Wurm. He met on board a very pretty and stylish woman, the Countess Dürkheim née Princess Bobrinsky, a compatriot of ours, who had married an aide-de-camp of the King of Bavaria. The Countess expressed her desire to make my acquaintance and wrote a note to me asking us to dine on the following day at Rothenbuch, the Dürkheim's beautiful estate at two hours' drive from Peissenberg. I scribbled off a line to say that I regretted I was unable to accept her amiable invitation, not being very well, but if she would come to see me, I should be very pleased. And the Countess came the next day. At the end of the week, we drove down to Rothenbuch to return her call. On approaching their estate, there came a sound of music from the forest surrounding the fine old mansion. The Countess and her husband came to meet us on the verge of the forest, and led us over a velvet lawn to a nook under a group of old trees where there was tea and cakes and all sorts of things laid on a long table, at which sat numerous guests, including the priest of the parish and the schoolmaster. The whole company went afterwards to shoot at targets near the brewery, where we saw a huge barrel filled with beer. The pencil drawings on the walls of the brew-house, of life-sized faces, depict every drunken emotion that the human face is capable of expressing, and represent red-nosed drunkards belonging to all classes of society, with a constable and a monk in the number. The young Count in shooting get-up, with his gun on the shoulder, looked very sportsmanlike. He is the best shot in the country, and now he carried off the first prize—a good fat goose. Then our hosts led us to inspect their magnificent property. The "Schloss" is a formidable square building with rounded towers at the four corners, full of mediæval reminiscences. The grounds around are beautifully kept.

As we were driven back to Peissenberg, we were overtaken by a terrible storm ; the thunder rolled, preceded by dazzling lightning, and rain began to fall heavily. We came home drenched to the skin ; my dress had the heavy soapy look that bathing-suits have, and my hat looked a sad object with its plume hanging lamentably, and rivulets of water falling from its brim.

Every year on her birthday the Wunderfrau gives a village entertainment followed by a rural ball. She invited us to a grand dinner during which a military band, imported from Munich, played marches and lively airs. After the repast we went to see the country-dance on the common. The merry-go-round was in all activity. The Wunderfrau, surrounded by her guests, was sitting on the grass, dowdily dressed and loaded with false jewellery ; her black silk dress was fastened at the throat by a brooch the size of a saucer, which contained the effigy of her late husband. There was a long file of tables laid out with dishes and bottles. Village youths and maidens had come from all around, dressed in their Sunday best. The lads, their vests hanging on one shoulder and their large-brimmed hats cocked on one ear, sat before large bocks, filling themselves steadily with beer and flirting with their sweethearts, talking and laughing uproariously. When it began to get dark there were dances in the big barn. Our cook and laundress opened the ball, swinging round the three-step waltz to the music of *Ach mein lieber Augustin* played by rural musicians. After them the whole company began whirling and twirling with shrill shrieks of merriment. We were very much amused by the gambols of these rustics. The lads in their thick boots and country clothes, carrying their partners clasped to their bosom like packets, were careering round, stamping the floor loudly with their nailed heels. We were much surprised to see among the dancers our doctoress, red and panting, turning round like a weather-cock, embraced by a ruddy-faced youth. All of a sudden the boys, brisked up by some glasses of wine, separated from the girls and began to turn somersaults, tapping themselves noisily on the thighs, at which Countess Platen, a Swedish lady who lived in our Sanatorium and gave tone to everything, gathered up her skirts majestically and swept out queen-like, bearing her head high and stepping as though she was mistress of the whole fair earth, followed by her satellites.

The days passed with despairing monotony. With admirable patience we were persevering in our cure, and took our medicine, our bath, our massage with great resignation. We shall finish our treatment in about a fortnight and have decided to go and take sea-baths at the Isle of Wight.

The day of our departure arrived at last. When taking leave of us the doctoress presented me with an enormous bouquet. Our train was crammed, and we were closely packed in our compartment, when the door was flung open and a breathless, panting lady of colossal dimensions, pushing parcels before her, clambered in, walking on everybody's toes. That fat creature had undergone a cure in our Sanatorium, and was also provided with a bouquet, only of much smaller dimensions than mine, because she had been a second-class boarder.

We made a short halt at Munich, just in time to make a round of the museums and to climb a dark staircase, lighted by a few oil-lamps, up to the gigantic statue of Bavaria, in the head of which two big iron sofas find place, and whose eyes serve as windows. We had a splendid bird's-eye view of the whole town out of them.

CHAPTER XXXVII

ON THE RHINE

WE arrived at Manheim at three o'clock in the morning and drove to the "Deutscher Hof." The entrance door was locked, and our driver had to ring vigorously several times before a dishevelled, drowsy waiter let us in. On the following day we travelled up the Rhine on our way to Holland on the "Elizabeth," a small merchant steamer, the only one starting that day for Coblentz. As there was no private cabin on the boat, we had to remain on deck all day. The "Elizabeth" was a shabby little vessel, very unclean, the uncovered deck was piled with boxes and barrels. Towards evening we approached Eltville, a small place where our boat moored for the night. We slept at a small hotel and had to be up at dawn, as the "Elizabeth" continued her way early in the morning. We got up long before light, and at four o'clock were already on board. The banks of the Rhine became more and more picturesque. The Rheinland seemed to be saturated with the life of the past. We saw ruined old castles perched high on the cliffs; one feels that they must have been the stage where many dramas of human life have been enacted. Here is the legend "Lorelei Felsen," so romantic and so mysterious. At every stoppage our boat took a cargo, which made us miss the Coblentz boat and we had to proceed further on by rail. Our road ran side by side with the river. The train was rapidly gaining headway, and at the second station we had overtaken the "Elizabeth" which had left Coblentz half-an-hour before us. We made a short halt at Bonn in order to pay a visit to Bonnegasse, the street in which Beethoven was born. The house No. 515 is commemorated by a tablet with his name and date of birth. At the last German station I saw, to my great fright, that we were descending straight to the Rhine, with no vestige of a bridge over it. When we arrived at the very edge of the river our train divided in two parts. Three cars, ours in the number, were placed on a large ferry and worked across the water by a wheel and a rope, to be hooked after to a Dutch train. It was a curious experience floating on a wide river without oars or any visible means of transport.

As soon as we entered Holland, the landscape changed at once. We rolled across flat expanses: all was level land. Vast fields of red and white tulips spread before us. Black and white cows, with huge bells on their necks, dozed in the high grass. The verdant prairies are variegated with bad-smelling canals filled with water, on a level with the ground. Quaint little houses with green and white shutters, that have sat themselves close to the water edge, border the road. In the distance windmills were turning slowly in the evening breeze, pointing their wings in all directions and filling the air with a ceaseless whir.

CHAPTER XXXVIII

ROTTERDAM

WE arrived towards night at Rotterdam, one of the most considerable sea-ports in Holland. How helpless we felt in this strange country! We had the greatest difficulty to make ourselves understood by the porters; our knowledge of Dutch being nil, we addressed them in German and English, and they answered in Dutch, which did not help us. We hailed a cab and tried to explain to the driver that we wanted to be driven to New Bath Hotel, and doubted somewhat whether we were understood, but our driver replied reassuringly, making our luggage a resting-place for his boots, and clambered into his seat. We arrived, in fact, at the designated hotel, situated on the quay of the river Maas.

Next morning Sergy went to secure tickets for the first boat leaving for London; there was one starting on the following day. When Sergy returned we drove to the Zoological Gardens, the best in Europe. Rotterdam does not inspire me; the houses are built on piles and look as if they were all on one side, and the canals, like those of Venice, are dirty and stinking. After the Zoological Gardens we visited an exhibition of Dutch painters, and saw posthumous pictures said to be painted by Rembrandt. Before returning to the hotel we drove through the park by a broad avenue bordered with elegant villas belonging, for the most part, to rich merchants. Dying of thirst, we drew up at a café and ordered tea. A waiter brought a teapot with boiling water and two cups and nothing else, and told us that the visitors had to supply their own tea and sugar in this singular restaurant!

When we were back at the hotel I sat a long time by the window looking at what was going on in the street, where the tram-cars, the carriages and heavy carts intermingled unceasingly. Muzzled dogs drew large waggonettes led by buxom peasant-women in stiffly starched gowns, who were faithful to their ancient costume and wore red bodices, brown skirts and a strange form of head-gear with heavy gold ornaments over flowing white caps. I was very much interested with the life and traffic in the port, on to a corner of which our windows looked. Large cargo-boats, exporting fruit and vegetables to England, were moored in the port, and numerous barges toiled steadily by, on their way to market, loaded to the water edge. A big American steamer was leaving for New York on the next day, carrying two thousand emigrants.

We spent our evening in a music-hall. The performance was very bad indeed. First came a French "chanteuse" in a short skirt and still shorter bodice, who rattled away indecent songs, then came the so-called tenor, who cooed a sentimental romance both out of tune and time, then a "basso profundo," who bellowed Mephistopheles' Serenade, made his appearance. The whole performance was accompanied by dead silence. The Dutch, in general, are a reserved people. All the faces are grave. I never saw a Dutchman smile. We were obliged to return on foot to the hotel and would have given anything for a carriage, but none was to be had and all the trams were overcrowded. So we walked, trying to find our way, which was not an easy thing to do, stopping at every corner to read the name of the street under a lamp-post.

On the following morning we embarked for London on a Dutch steamer named *Fjenoord*. The lower deck was closely packed with calves and sheep for sale. As soon as we were out in the open sea, we began to feel a slight rocking. It was too windy to remain on deck, and in our cabin the air was so close and stifling! We asked the stewardess to wake us before entering the Thames. I was up before six, dressed quickly and mounted on deck. It had been raining in the night and the wet wool of the sheep smelt very badly, whilst passing the English lighthouse, the syren on our ship whistled loudly, calling out the pilot, who came alongside on a small skiff; a rope-ladder was dropped, and the pilot clambered on board. At half-past six we landed at Blackwall. After having passed through the customs on a floating raft, we then took the train to London. We regretted that we couldn't enter London by the docks, but it was Sunday, and the boats going that way had a holiday.

CHAPTER XXXIX

LONDON

WE put up at Charing-Cross Hotel. After a good wash and brush-up, we went to find out the Rydes, my old Stuttgart friends who had settled in London for some years. I did not hear from Ettie Ryde, with whom I used to have great fun, since our school-days. What a chance to meet again! It was some little time before we found out the Rydes. We were received by Ettie's sisters, who had just returned from church. I was very much disappointed when I was told that Ettie was out of town at the present moment, but the Rydes are going to spend most of the summer at Blackgang, in the Isle of Wight, and I hope to see a great deal of Ettie.

It was Sunday that day, which reduced us to inactivity, and we had nothing else to do than to return to our hotel. There was a great demonstration in the streets, and we met on our way a procession of the "Westminster Democratic Society," composed of a deputy of cabmen and wine-merchants and other corporations, who were shouting and waving flags. They marched with their bands at the head, without disturbing the order in the streets. Three ragamuffins opened the march, mounted on decrepit old hacks, holding large banners. The police gazed upon this demonstration with the phlegm of an elephant whom a fly would like to sting.

The next day we visited the Health Exhibition in Kensington Palace. The trains left every five minutes and stopped with great jerks ; we were thrown out of our places so violently that I found myself sitting on the knees of my neighbour opposite. There were many interesting things to see at the Exhibition, but the Russian section was rather poorly represented—furs and stuffed animals predominated. We had a good laugh when we stopped before a manikin representing a Russian soldier, a frightful guy, more like a bear than a human being, with a beard right up to the eyes. The "quarter of old London," attracted us the most. Whilst walking the narrow dark streets lined with houses and shops, and crowded with people dressed in the costumes belonging to the fifteenth century, we had a vivid sensation of the past ages.

We returned to Charing-Cross Hotel longing to have a good rest, but on entering our apartment we found our beds upset, the sheets and blankets lying on the floor in a heap. It was the sour-faced chamber-maid who thought that we were leaving that same day, and was making ready the beds for new visitors. When we told her that we were going to remain another night in London, she picked up the sheets, flung them on the beds and carried away the clean linen. I could have smacked her!

We left London at ten the next morning, having taken our tickets straight to Ryde, the principal port of the Isle of Wight. On arriving at Portsmouth we embarked on a small steamer which corresponded with the train leaving for Shanklin, a sea-bathing place where we intended to spend about three weeks. The crossing, though short, was rather rough. It took ten minutes by train from Ryde to Shanklin station, where we got into an omnibus and drove to Hollier's Hotel.

Shanklin is a clean and pleasant village built on a cliff with trees planted along its streets, detached houses standing back amid gardens and a grey church reminiscent of rural England, with a spire rising from among the trees. We have taken an apartment of two rooms for two guineas a week. Hollier's Hotel is a white house overgrown with honeysuckle and sheltered by two enormous linden trees. Boxes of red geraniums hang out of the windows. There was a most charming air of home-like comfort about the whole house. Our sitting-room was prettily furnished, full of nick-nacks, with chintz covers, muslin curtains and vases of fresh flowers on the mantle-piece, and landscapes on the walls. Three bay-windows look on the front at the entrance and at the back into a railed-in garden with a broad, well-kept lawn like a green velvet carpet, shaded by cedars a century old. Before the entrance door stands the hotel omnibus, which is in ceaseless demand the whole day, bringing passengers from and taking them to the station. The driver, perched on his high seat, is dozing in the shade, with his nose on his paper.

On the following day of our arrival we were awakened by the sound of the rain beating against the window-panes. It did not hinder Sergy to go and take his first bath. It was low tide and the bathers were taken out into the sea in a small cabin drawn by a horse.

We have arranged to have our meals served in our apartment. At five o'clock a waiter brought in a neatly arrayed tray with nice tea, delicious cream and fresh-baked rolls.

In the afternoon the sun came out, and we went for a stroll to the Chine, a picturesque narrow pass which descends to the sea-edge. The Chine is, for its own sake, well worth a visit to Shanklin; the admittance is only twopence each. We sat down to rest on a crooked arm of a fallen tree, and listened to the music of a small water-fall down below.

After dinner Sergy went to Mew's post-office to hire a dog-cart for a drive to Sandown, a neighbouring watering-place. We have run the risk of breaking our necks during the promenade. I drove a restless horse who pranced and kicked all the time, taking fright at a passing train he jerked to one side, bolted and sprang into a furious gallop nearly dragging my hands off. I frantically tugged at the reins and managed to pull up the frightened animal some way down the road, driving him into a heap of stones. The season had not yet begun at Sandown, and the houses with their locked doors and closed shutters looked as if in sleep. Everywhere placards were to be seen bearing the inscription; "Apartments to Let," and announcements that pieces of ground were to be let. There was land to be sold for 999 years.

Having learned that the Rydes were living already at Blackgang, not far away from Shanklin, I hurried to let them know of our arrival, looking forward to seeing a great deal of Ettie. Although years had separated us, I was not one to forget old friends and had been simple enough to believe that Ettie, also, was burning with impatience to meet me. But one always believes what one desires, it is the weak point of human nature! Several days went by and it was queer that Ettie did not send any word of her coming. This meeting so hotly desired by me came at last, but in a fashion altogether different from that which I had pictured. One morning a knock came at the door, and the parlour-maid ushered in Ettie in person. I must say she was sadly altered, and I scarcely recognised her; time passing over her had modified her as it does everything in this world, nothing was left of the pretty Scotch lassie of bygone days. She was altered morally too; she looked so stiff, so unlike her old self. Ettie reminded me, nevertheless, of my youthful days, and memories which had slumbered for years awoke now in me. Stirring the cinders of our reminiscences we spoke of the dear old days gone by when we were both sixteen. We kept Ettie for dinner; when she went back in the evening her farewell seemed stiff and formal to me, she gave me a cold kiss on my cheek, and we were parting for no one knows how many years, for good and all, perhaps, for the Rydes were leaving Blackgang in a few days. I am a terrible creature for taking things to heart, and felt at the moment as if I had been drenched with cold water. She is a cold-hearted creature, Ettie, and I do not want to be friends with her any more. I should like to be cold-hearted too, and not to care for any one. When Ettie had gone, I remained for some time wrapped in thoughts the reverse of agreeable, and was not able to put Ettie out of my mind. Sergy, who has a wonderful soothing influence over me, set to work to comfort me, but he did not succeed, and this time I was not to be comforted.

There are delightful walks and drives in all directions of the Isle of Wight. We undertook to make excursions through the neighbouring country in a huge pleasant-tour coach named "Old Times." This coach can hold twenty people inside and is driven by four powerful horses gaily decorated with ribbons. We began our tour by Bembridge, and scrambled into the back seat of the immense car by a ladder of ten steps. The postilion frantically blew his horn, the coachman cracked his whip over the head of his horses, and the coach rattled full speed along beautifully kept roads. The drive proved long and interesting. We made three halts without changing horses. Our fellow-passengers were not very elegant-looking. I took Sergy's neighbour, a tall, bearded man, who was chewing a stinking cigar, for a German colonist, and he proved to be a German Royal Prince. Towards noon we drew up before the veranda of Bembridge Hotel standing on the beach, and had lunch on the spacious terrace, enjoying the sea-breeze. At the same time a pleasure-boat had brought a crowd of tourists to the hotel. We were back to Shanklin for dinner, having taken another road through the woods and corn-fields. Before us there was a lovely stretch of country with the gold of ripening grain and the scarlet glint of poppies smelling like honey; full blown blossoms of clover white and pink, scented the air. The Isle of Wight, so green and fresh, is well named "The Garden of England," really it is quite the nicest bit of England. Trees and grass are of a wonderful vivid green peculiar to this island. The climate is so mild that figs, laurel, and myrtle trees grow in the open air. Intense heat is quite unknown here.

The next day we had gone coaching again. This time I had the front seat of the coach. My neighbour was an elegant young man who had the manner and the bearing of a Prince of the blood Royal. Having taken the day before a Royal Prince for a colonist, Sergy this time promoted my neighbour to the post of State Minister at least, and I felt sure he was no less a person than a Royalty travelling incognito. At a stoppage one of the horses had cast a shoe, and one can easily imagine how we felt when my aristocratic neighbour began to shoe the horse—he was a blacksmith! Our driver put into good spirits by frequent sips taken at the stoppages, seemed to have completely forgotten his business. He drove recklessly, taking the corners in a way that made me gasp; I had to hold fast to the seat not to be thrown out of the omnibus at every turn. I couldn't bear it any longer and begged our driver to go slower, but it only made him rush down the inclines at the speed of an express train, turning in the same time his back to the horses and chatting with the passengers. He boasted of how well he could manage his long whip, and waving it right and left, he caught the rake of a villager who was passing on the road. Luckily the idea didn't come to our driver to lift the man like a spilikin in the air. Half-way on we stopped at Ventnor, a resort for consumptive patients, to give a rest to the horses. We saw numerous invalids drawn through the streets in their bath-chairs. We continued our way by an avenue of trees bending over and forming a roof, and towards four o'clock we rattled into the quiet village of Carisbrooke, and tore like a hurricane through the narrow streets, scattering the crowd of dogs and hens before us. The village with its white cottages and grass growing liberally out of the broken pavement, looked very cosy. We saw a group of women all down on their knees cheerfully doing their washing in the stream, laughing and chatting together, and village children who were playing at soldiers near a puddle where the ducks were quacking. The foaming horses came to a stop before the Red Lion Inn, and everyone descended. We had dinner at the inn, consisting of soup tasting like dish-water, and slices of mutton not thicker than a sheet of paper, and they charged us five shillings for the meagre repast! A two hours' halt gave us time to visit the picturesque ruins of old Carisbrooke Castle, after which we flung ourselves with satisfaction upon the grass under a stack of hay, and had for company an ancient white carthorse who chewed his bunch of hay under an old ash tree. We felt quite bucolic, it was so cool and nice here, and the new-mown hay smelt so sweetly. Meanwhile our coachman had put out his horses and gone to lie down. When we returned to the inn we found him stretched full length on the grass under the shade of a big tree, his face covered with his hat, sleeping the sleep of the just. The postilion put him on his legs with some difficulty, for the brave man had fortified himself still more with plentiful libations at the bar of the inn. The horses were put to with the aid of the postilion, and we drove back to Shanklin at the rate of twenty miles an hour. The photographer who had taken a photograph of our group in the morning, just before we had started for our tour, was waiting on the high-road and handed to each passenger a copy of it.

The next day we went to Cowes, the summer residence of Queen Victoria. We were speeding along level roads bordered by green woods—all soft grass and splendid trees— and rolled through fields golden with buttercups. The road now wound through bright green pastures where big fat cows dozed, lying in the shade of apple-trees. We passed neat little white cottages embowered in green, and a big farm-house belonging to the Prince of Wales. We drew now through an avenue sheltered by stately elm-trees and descended a steep hill leading to the river Medina, which we crossed on a ferry, and arrived at Cowes. Our coach drew up before a big hotel where we were to have dinner. The view from the terrace was one of exquisite beauty, the surroundings of Cowes being amongst the most splendid in England. We went and sat down on a bench beside the pier, waiting for the bell to call us to table-d'hôte. Two big yachts belonging to the Queen, the "Neptune" and "Man-of-War," were moored in front of us. Side by side with us on the bench sat an old man, with a face framed in a grey fringe of beard, wearing a cotton bonnet drawn over his ears, who held a short pipe in his toothless mouth. We fell into conversation with him and were very much surprised when he told us that in all his long life he had only been once to London.

Another day we went by rail to Ryde, the most frequented beach of the Isle of Wight. The esplanade with its elm-groves, different-coloured flower-beds, and well raked lawns, is magnificent.

The day after we went and spent the whole afternoon in the neighbouring town of Newport, to visit the Exhibition of Agriculture. There was only one passenger in our compartment, a stiff, solemn-looking lady, who plunged her nose in her book all the way without uttering one word. On arriving at Newport our silent companion dropped on my lap a small bunch of flowers and a leaflet describing the way to get to Heaven. It flashed upon me that, perhaps, that lady was some kind of missionary who wanted to snatch me from the grip of the Evil One, and rescue my soul from destruction.

The Exhibition, decorated with flags and banners, occupied a large space. In the first place we were taken to see the section of work-horses, cows, sheep and pigs in their stalls. All these animals, enormous in size, were well worth looking at, especially the pigs, long and low, with no legs to speak of, interested me much. The prize-animals had placards hanging round their necks, bearing the inscription: *First Prize, Highly Commended*, and simply *Commended*. On a big square we watched the show of the carriage, saddle and cart-horses, their manes plaited and interwoven with wild flowers and ears of corn, and their tails jauntily braided with red cords. Then came the jumping competition in which the first riders were to prove what they and their horses could do in clearing hedges, hurdles, water-jumps and other obstacles. Special experts were observing the print of the horses-hoofs on the sand, in order to see which one had made the longest leap. One of the horses bolted before a water-ditch and all the brave experts took to their heels, carrying off their chairs with them. There was suddenly a stir on the ring and stifled shrieks. It was a swarm of bees, which, leaving their hive, had settled on the head of a poor lady. Luckily a doctor who was present, rushed to her aid and began to scrape off with his pen-knife the bees from their victim's face, which had become all at once one blistered mass. We had dinner in a big refreshment tent, during which a red-coated military band played the best pieces from their repertoire. Towards evening it began to rain, and we hurried back to Shanklin.

One afternoon we saw a carriage stop at our entrance door, it held King Oscar of Sweden and his suite, who had come to take lunch at our hotel. After their meal the whole company withdrew to the lawn in front of our window. The Swedes threw themselves down on the grass, and the eldest member of the party, who was lying on his back in idle contentment, began to sing at the top of his voice a Swedish song with the burden of *O Matilde*, coming over and over again. Another Swede, forgetting his dignity, pirouetted and executed somersaults like a veritable clown, his legs making frequent excursions towards the sky, to the great indignation of one of the hotel tenants, a prudish maiden-lady of some fifty years, who was knitting in the garden. She rose suddenly, gathered up her work in dignified displeasure, and walked back to the hotel with an air of offended maidenhood, like a startled virgin whose virtue was being put to the test. King Oscar was travelling in strictly incognito under the name of *Count Haga*. When my husband asked our waiter, who had just brought in our tea, if the gentleman who sang *O Matilde*, was the King, he responded stoutly that it was not at all the King, but his first minister. Some time afterwards, during our stay in Paris, we saw the portrait of the Swedish King exposed in the window of a picture shop, and the fact appeared undeniable—that the singer was precisely King Oscar.

In Shanklin, like everywhere else in England, Sunday is a dull day ; the village is asleep, the shopkeepers put up their shutters and retire to the bosom of their families. Over the door of a thatched-roofed cottage just opposite Hollier's Hotel, the sign-board Library in big white letters, is taken off and the mistress of the shop does not sweep the steps on her threshold, as she does every week-day. The baths, even, are open only until eight o'clock in the morning. There are very few people in the streets, only at eleven o'clock a.m., and at eight p.m. you can see the inhabitants with their prayer-books, going off to Chapel.

We had quite enough of the Isle of Wight. Shanklin is such a dull and sleepy place ! It has only one advantage, you can't spend money there. The worst of the place is that there is nothing to do in the evenings; at nine o'clock all the houses close their shutters, and one can only go to bed. My pleasure-loving temperament revolted against this life, and I was very pleased when the day of our departure arrived. We went by train to Cowes, where we took the boat to Southampton. Before leaving British soil, we entered a druggist's shop and bought some homeopathic medicine against sea-sickness, for each crossing makes me horribly ill.

We arrived at Havre the next morning at sunrise. The fog was so thick that we could not see two paces ahead of us, and had to signal our approach by shrill sounds of the fog-horn. We took the express train at Havre and arrived the same evening at Paris, where we made a three days' halt, and then started back to Russia.

CHAPTER XL

WE are home at last! No more horrid hotels, no more travelling! We remained a few days in town and removed to the camp on the Khodinka Field, where a large barrack, consisting of a score of rooms, was assigned to us. I fully enjoyed our camp life. The trumpet exercises and the singing in chorus of the soldiers resounded from early morning until night.

One day we made an expedition to New Jerusalem, a large monastery standing in the neighbourhood of Moscow. It is a vast stone building surrounded by a high wall, one mile in circumference. There are forty-two altars in the church, which can hold up about ten thousand people. Every Sunday the Bishop, surrounded by a group of priests dressed in white sacerdotal vestments, performs the Easter mass before the Holy Sepulchre, the exact copy of the Sepulchre in Jerusalem. There is an hospice near the church where pilgrims find shelter and board for three days at the expense of the monastery.

Another day we drove to the Cloister of Simeon, where men and women possessed by the devil assemble for the expulsion of the Evil Spirit. When we entered the church we saw about a dozen women stretched flat on the floor before the Altar, in a fit of epilepsy. All at once they jumped up and began to shout: "There he is, there he is, he is entering into me, go away, go away, Demon!" But as soon as the priest called up the women by their names, they grew calm at once and began to drink a spoonful of oil taken from an image-lamp.

The rainy season coming on earlier than usual, we returned to town in the beginning of September. Moscow was very gay this winter; many celebrated artists visited our city. The appearance of Maria Van-Zandt, a lovely American Opera singer, was the great attraction of the season. I went to see her in "Lakme," Delibe's latest opera, and she gave me exquisite pleasure, being delightful to look upon and to be listened to. She was bewitchingly pretty, just like a dainty bit of Dresden china; her voice was clear as silver and she trilled like a bird.

Prince Dolgorouki, the governor-general of Moscow, arranged theatricals in his palace, in the presence of the Emperor and Empress, who visited in January our old capital. After a French one act comedy, came a tableau representing a banquet of Russian boyards in the ninth century ; the Prince invited me to take part in the tableau. My costume, pink and gold, was very pretty ; Sylvain the coiffeur of the Imperial Theatres, came to arrange my hair and make me up. At nine o'clock I set off to the Prince's Palace. The performers in the tableau had to wait till midnight in a close dressing-room before appearing. The temperature in our little dungeon became unbearable ; my headgear was awfully heavy and I was beside myself from heat and fatigue. Our tableau was a great success, and the curtain fell amidst a thunder of applause. When the performance was over, we came into the reception rooms, where we were presented to the Empress. We had supper afterwards, served on small separate tables.

In the first fine days of May we removed to the camp, where we remained until September, when my husband was to go to Brest, to take part in the grand manœuvres. It was settled that I was to join him in a few days, in order to proceed further on together to Biarritz, to take sea-baths. During Sergy's absence a telegram was received addressed to " General Lieutenant Doukhovskoi," and I hastened to be the first to congratulate my husband, by wire, on his new promotion.

CHAPTER XLI

BIARRITZ

I LEFT Moscow on the 10th of September and arrived at Brest on the following day. It was the first time in my life that I travelled alone, and it frightened me somewhat. I never left my compartment until Brest, and allayed my hunger by cramming myself with bon-bons. My husband was waiting for me at the station and we continued our journey together.

We took a day's rest at Verona. It was the anniversary of the occupation of Rome by the Italian troops, and the town was dressed all over with flags. On our way to the hotel we passed the house which had belonged to the Capulet family, and saw the balcony on which Juliet appeared to Romeo and listened to his serenades. After dinner we visited the splendid " Giusti Gardens," where we were shown a marble statue worth a fortune, resounding like bronze when you touched it, and for which an American collector of works of art had offered the sum of forty thousand francs.

Next afternoon we beheld Genoa, at the foot of the Appenines and the Mediterranean spreading far and wide, where we stopped a whole day. An old guide, aged seventy-five, took us through the town. That old man had been a brave soldier in his day, one of the 1,200 warriors who had fought and landed with Garibaldi in Sicily. He took us to his private dwelling to show us his Garibaldian costume, a piece of Garibaldi's famous red shirt, and the tip of a cigar which had been smoked by Garibaldi, which he kept as relics. On our way back to the hotel we passed before the monuments of Christopher Columbus, Garibaldi and Verdi. On the front of Garibaldi's house the Free Masons have carved a garland of flowers surrounded by hieroglyphics. After dinner we drove to the Villa Pallavicini. At the entrance into the park stand white marble statues of Leda, Pomona, Hebe, and Flora. We walked through alleys of lemon, laurel, cypress and myrtle trees in full bloom. We passed a lake in which salmon-trout swam, and mounted on the top of a castle of the Middle-Ages. We entered then a stalactite grotto, with an artificial lake in the middle, where a mysterious Carcarollo invited us to take a row in his boat, carrying the arms of the Dukes of Pallavicini. Further on we saw a pavilion bearing the tempting inscription *tête-à-tête amoureux*, and wanted to enter it, but our guide said that we had better keep outside, for as soon as you open the door a tub of water pours over your head, cooling instantly your amorous ardour.

On the following morning we started for Nice by the Corniche Railway. The road runs all the time by the sea-shore ; here and there it is barricaded with stones, in order to prevent the railway line from being washed away by the waves which broke against our carriage wheels.

We put up at Nice at the Hôtel des Etrangers. On entering the apartment that we were to occupy, we saw a placard stuck to the wall begging the visitors to turn the key in the lock when going to bed. This warning made me spend a restless night. I could not sleep, fearing that some-one would come and strangle me ; it seemed to me all the time as if a hand fumbled at the door. The mosquitoes were also awfully troublesome ; I began to chase these little vampires and execute them on the spot, I who could never hurt a fly ! Next morning directly after breakfast, we went to the Villa Bermont in which the Grand Duke Nicholas, our heir to the throne, had expired. A chapel has been built on the place where his bedroom stood. This villa is surrounded by a plantation of 10,000 orange trees. On our way back we visited the Russian Church ; the altar is constructed of oak brought from Russia, and a big silver cross is made of different objects taken away by our Cossacks from the French in 1812.

We continued our journey on the following day and arrived at sunset at Toulon, where we had to wait patiently for the train, which left for Biarritz at four o'clock in the morning, in a bare room at the station, where we had the privilege of dozing on hard horse-hair chairs given us. Our travelling companions lay curled up in uncomfortable arm-chairs, nevertheless their noses very soon emitted trumpet-sounds. I drowsed also, all in a lump on my chair and was chilled to the bone.

When we arrived at Lourdes on the following afternoon, we saw the platform crowded with pilgrims, crippled and impotent, who come here from all parts of the world in the hope of a miraculous cure.

The road from Lourdes to Bayonne has a desolate look, without any vegetation whatever, only groups of trees here and there. We saw labourers in the fields tilling the ground with oxen harnessed to ploughs, just as we do in Russia. During the twenty minutes' run from Bayonne to Biarritz two very prim, stately old ladies entered our compartment. They looked extremely haughty and unapproachable, and gave no outward signs of wishing to enter into conversation.

But their manner changed instantly, when they found out that we were Russians; they became amiability itself, and expressed their great sympathy for our country.

We put up at Biarritz at the Hôtel d'Angleterre, and had to be satisfied with a small room at the very top. Our windows looked seawards and showed the wide expanse of the Atlantic and the agglomeration of rocks of the most fantastic forms named The Chaos. From below we heard the thunder of mighty waves dashing on the cliffs with a sound like the booming of many guns.

In the night the noise of the ocean hindered our sleep, and we decided to move to the Villa Gaston, a comfortable boarding-house, where we paid five francs a day for an apartment of two rooms.

Above our heads two pupils of the Conservatory of Moscow played and sang all day long, practising their scales and vocal exercises not less than fifty times in succession. It was enough to make you hate music.

Biarritz is built on a rock. Over trenches excavated by the ocean picturesque bridges are thrown. The top part of the town consists of splendid hotels and lovely villas which stretch towards Bayonne and the road to Spain. It is from Biarritz that Christopher Columbus sailed to discover America. This queen of southern strands is very gay and fashionable. There are three beaches: La Grande Plage has a splendid casino; Port-Vieux, incased between rocks and is well sheltered against the assault of the big billows, where children and invalids bathe in preference. Above Port-Vieux a tunnel is cut through the rock for pedestrians, and on the summit of the rock rises the statue of the Virgin, held in great veneration by the seamen; near it stands a big cross and a pole with an alarm-bell to signal shipwrecks. A bridge is thrown over the dyke under which the ocean roars furiously producing sounds like continual cannon-shots. It is on the third beach, La côte des Basques, that the waves are the strongest. On Sundays the villagers from round about assemble here, dressed in their half Spanish costumes, to dance sprightly mouchachas and the fandangos, with the accompaniment of castanets and tambourines. Having danced to their hearts' content, they undress completely, and enter the water in a long file, holding each other by the hand, men and women pêle-mêle; after the waves have drenched them thoroughly, they come out and bake themselves on the sand for a while.

We took our bath every morning on the "Grande Plage," where the waves reached only to the knees, but they were so monstrously long that they splashed us from head to foot, and pushed us far away from the shore. One morning whilst my husband was taking his bath and I was merely present in the character of looker-on, someone called him in Russian by his name. Sergy turned round and saw Colonel Scalon, an aide-de-camp of the Grand Duke Michael. "What an unexpected surprise! How do you do, Colonel?" he exclaimed. "Thank you, I——" but at that same moment a gigantic billow had flung them apart without giving time to the Colonel to end his phrase.

Bathing hours are very gay on the beach. A crowd of people from all parts of the world are to be met there. Amongst the lady-bathers an American actress, wearing a white tight-fitting bathing costume, is the main attraction for the moment. I ordered myself a similar costume, which led to a very unpleasant incident. One morning after my bath, I was returning to my cabin with my soaked bathing-costume, clinging to my body. The bathing establishment was especially crowded that day, and the woman on service, who happened to be on my way, handed me the key of my cabin and led me through the throng, whilst two young ladies, seeing this favouritism, swelled with resentment at having to wait their turn longer than I. "Well," said one of them to her companion in Russian, throwing a murderous glance at me, " It is known that such creatures as this eccentric girl are always served the first; courtesans certainly know how to take care of themselves!" I had great trouble in controlling myself not to give her a good shaking. It appeared that these unpleasant compatriots of mine, who had so badly guessed my social position, were the noisy musical tenants of the Villa Gaston, who exasperated me daily with their scales and exercises. I shall have my revenge the first time I meet them. This occurred on the following day. The young ladies recognised me when I was going out to take my bath, and desirous to repair their silly mistake, they saluted me obsequiously, colouring to their hair, but I pretended not to see them and didn't recognise their bow.

One afternoon we went by train to Bayonne. There is nothing of much note in that town. The streets are narrow and encumbered with heavy carts and chariots. There was a crowd gathered before a small travelling-circus, where a self-named Hercules, in very dirty tights, lifted up weights of a hundred kilos, to the loud applause of his enthusiastic audience.

Another day we arranged to visit the "Couvent des Bernardines." This cold grey building is situated some miles off from Biarritz and seems to be shut away from all sounds of the world. From afar the dull sound of a bell was heard, denoting every half-hour the change of the nun on duty. Over the entrance door we saw a plate with the inscription to speak in a low voice when entering the cloister. We saw the nuns walking about two and two, shadowy white-robed women with black hoods that hid their downcast faces. There are many young girls belonging to the best French and Spanish families amongst them. Poor recluses who have taken their vows for eternal silence which would separate them from earthly love for ever. A defiance to natural laws I call it! The "Bernardines" are permitted to converse with their parents for half-an-hour once a year only. I wonder how they could preserve the gift of speech being deprived of it such a long time! A sad-faced lay sister ushered us into a large parlour with long windows and a polished floor. On the walls hung framed texts and coloured prints of the Virgin and Saints. We were shown all over the monastery and saw over the doors of the cells placards bearing the inscription, "God alone!" It was a very hard life in that Order, and silence was everywhere in this house of silence. In church even the nuns are hidden behind a curtain.

A pine wood separates the cloister from the convent of the "Servantes de Marie," where the nuns lead quite a different sort of life, working with their tongues just as well as with their hands. They are very industrious, do carpentry and photography and cultivate their flower gardens.

The rainy season was coming on. It was time to leave Biarritz and proceed to the country of "Carmen." From Biarritz the distance to the Spanish frontier is short. At Irun, the first Spanish station, we saw policemen wearing short black mantles and triangular hats, walking up and down the platform. After San Sebastiano, a picturesque town surrounded by fortifications, our train rolled along a curving road winding at the foot of the Pyrenees, vividly outlined on the deep blue sky. Just as we were preparing to arrange ourselves comfortably for our night's rest, travellers charged with parcels entered our compartment. A miserable child, who was cutting his first tooth, made us pass a bad night. Luckily I was not a bit sleepy, and leaning on the window I enjoyed the beautiful night, the moon and stars shining out gloriously.

CHAPTER XLII

MADRID

WE took seats in the omnibus belonging to the Hôtel de Paris, drawn by three richly harnessed grey mules with half-shaven tails like poodles. After lunch we went out for a stroll round the town, which does not differ greatly from other European cities. There is a continual thoroughfare in the streets of Madrid. We made our way with difficulty through a crowd of lookers-on surrounding a mountebank who was selling an elixir against toothache of his own concoction. He was standing on a chariot, dressed up in a swallow-tail and silk hat, and uttered in a loud voice the panegyric of his remedy. When passing the Royal Palace we saw a squadron of Blue Hussars, a company of infantry and two cannon drawn by mules, who came to relieve the guard. This cere-mony takes place every day, and always gathers a great crowd, kept back by a line of soldiers. Before returning to the hotel we went through the Museum where we admired the marvels of art painted by Murillo, Velasquez, Michael Angelo and other celebrities. Murillo's "Madonna Anun-ziata" and Tintoretto's "Paradise," an immense picture in which appears, between the chorus of angels, the lovely face of the painter's wife, attracted particularly our attention. A party of negroes, very up-to-date, were walking about the Museum and seemed very interested with all they saw.

After dinner we went to see the " Arenas " where barbarous bull-fights, the favourite spectacle of the Spaniards, take place. The bull-ring is a large round building which can hold up to 16,000 spectators. We entered a chapel where Toreadors, Matadors as they are called here, say prayers before starting for the bull-fight. In the next room we saw six beds prepared for the wounded Matadors. We were also shown the stalls where stood thirty horses doomed for the next courses. The poor animals didn't get any food or drink, "It wasn't worth while," said one of the grooms, as they would all be embowelled on the following day! The bulls travel by train to Madrid in a box put on wheels hardly big enough to hold them. On arriving at Madrid mules are harnessed to these boxes, and the bulls are brought behind the bull-ring where they are being kept in some dark place, and just before the beginning of the "Corrida" they are pushed into the arena, with long sharp iron rods, through a door which is opened from the top galleries by a cord on a pulley.

We drove back to the hotel through two beautiful parks, "Del Retiro" and "Reservado." After dinner we went to the Appolo to see a modern play "La Grande Via," about which the town was raving. The theatre was packed to the very ceiling. I perceived in one of the boxes a very ugly Matador who did not at all resemble Carmen's Toreador. After the second act I began to yawn, for the play was rather a bore, and the actors' appearance very unattractive. Sergy proposed to go and spend the rest of the evening in a Music Hall where painted women were sitting in a circle, singing and shrieking in oriental fashion, accompanied on guitars by suspicious-looking individuals. The audience consisted of rather ferocious-looking Spaniards with hair which seemed to have never been touched by the comb and eyes blazing under their wide black sombreros, who had the air of demanding "Your money or your life!"

The next morning we were again present at the ceremony of the change of watch, and saw General Pavia, the commandant of the town, enter the Palace, directing his steps to Queen Maria Christina's private apartments, with his report in his hand. To-day it was the Red Hussars, mounted on white horses, and a detachment of infantry, who relieved the guard. When the big Palace clock struck half-past eleven, a piercing horn gave the signal for the beginning of the ceremony which lasted about an hour, whilst a military band played selections from "Faust" on the Square before the Palace. Fair women are in favour on the other side of the Pyrenees, as it appears; I was the only blonde person in the place and most of the officers were paying attention to me, especially one of them, a very good-looking chap who was throwing fiery glances at me all the time, but I pretended not to notice him and he got nothing for his pains. After luncheon, we left Madrid for Saragossa, where we arrived in the middle of the night.

CHAPTER XLIII

SARAGOSSA

THERE happened to be a local feast of the "Madonna del Pilar," the patroness of the town, just now, and every hotel was crammed to the roof. The trains were bringing constantly new guests and the hotel proprietors profited by it in fleecing their tenants abominably. We had great difficulty in finding a shelter and were dragged in a crammed omnibus from one hotel to the other. We succeeded at last in installing ourselves at the "Hotel Universo." The entrance door was locked when we drove to it and our coachman had to give a vigorous pull at the bell; at length it brought a sleepy porter who told us that there was only the drawing-room, which had just been furnished with four beds, available for the moment. We hastened to occupy it, whilst the three Spanish travellers, burdened with their hand-bags, who had alighted from the omnibus together with us, went to seek a shelter elsewhere, muttering angrily " *Que diablo!* " We found ourselves in a spacious bare room which in the way of conveniences left much to be desired. Long cherished visions of cheering meals and soft couches vanished, and I felt so woefully tired that I was ready to weep.

The "Corridas" generally take place during Saint's days feasts, all the profit out of them is assigned to charity. The Spanish benevolence is of a very blood-thirsty nature as it appears, a queer pretence of religious feeling with barbarous cruelty. The excitement of the forthcoming bull-fight had invaded the town. The Matadors have just arrived from Madrid, accompanied by there " Quadrillas," and have put up at our hotel. They are travelling all the year round from one town to another. After Saragossa they are going to take part 'in the bull-fights of Sevilla. One of the waiters of the hotel procured tickets for us for the "Corrida," which was to take place on the following day, on the "shady side," which costs twice as much as those on the "sunny side." After lunch we sallied forth to the arenas, and had to walk all the way as there was no vehicle to be had. On the day of a "Corrida" the streets are alive with streaming crowds of people, in their gayest dress and mood, on their way to the " Plaza de Toros." The houses are adorned with flowers and

R

banners ; pretty women hung over the gaily-dressed balconies. When we approached the arenas a compact throng stood round the entrance door, and my heart gave a quick throb. Twelve thousand people could be accommodated in the great bull-ring, which resembles an enormous circus. Above was the clear blue sky. In the centre is a sanded place for the bull-fight, encircled by a wooden barrier, six feet high, over which the "Toreros" jump to escape the bull in wild pursuit. The bull-fight was to commence at two o'clock and we had more than an hour to wait yet. The tribunes were lined already with rows of gaily clad spectators. Some of them had brought baskets filled with empty bottles which they intended to throw at the head of the Matadors who happened to be clumsy in killing the bull. Soldiers were stationed everywhere; not unfrequently their services are called into requisition, for nothing excites a Spaniard more than his national bloody game, and disturbances often occur. We sat amid a haze of cigar smoke which made me quite giddy. Amongst a group of ragamuffins a quarrel arose which nearly ended in a fight. An army of grooms dressed in scarlet blouses and wearing yellow caps (the national colours) began to water the arena. The entrance of the President of the Bull-Fight was the signal for the band to strike up, and it continued to play at intervals during the horrible performance.

The door opposite the President opened wide and the procession began. First of all the "Alguazil" (herald) entered the ring, mounted on a beautiful bay horse adorned with a red velvet saddle. He himself was clad as if he had just stepped out of a "Velasquez" painting. He wore a black velvet suit and a large black hat ornamented with scarlet plumes. After having pranced round the ring he stopped beneath the President's box, and, taking off his plumed hat, begged to know if the performance might begin. Assent being given, the huge golden key of the door, behind which the six bulls who were to be killed that day were shut up, was thrown down and gracefully caught by the "Algua- zil" in his hat, after which he pranced to fetch his "Quadrilla." The gates on the opposite side of the arena were flung open, and a team of six superb grey mules, who were intended to drag out the dead bulls and horses, rushed in, decorated with yellow and scarlet ribbons, with pyramids of plumes and bells upon their heads, harnessed into shafts at the end of which a long iron hook was dragging. After having pranced noisily round the arena, the mules disappeared by the same door. Then the "Quadrilla" appeared on the ring and a roar of applause went up. First came Legartijo and Frascuello, the two most celebrated Matadors of Spain, who were to act that day, clad in spangled, coloured jackets, tight-fitting knee breeches, white stockings and leather slippers, wearing like "Figaro" a black wig with a short pig-tail and a three-cornered hat. Behind came the "Picadores" mounted on their poor decrepit horses. They were dressed in leather suits, their legs covered with armour to save them from the horns of the bull, and wore broad black sombreros. The Picadores blindfold their miserable steeds, tying a cloth round their right eye, and take them into the ring to be gored by an infuriated bull. The horses are slashed and spurred forward to a certain death on the pointed horns of the maddened formidable animal. At each "Corrida" there are about a dozen horses killed. Sometimes, when all the horses are exterminated, the insatiable audience claims new victims, shouting "*Mas caballos!*" (Bring on other horses!) The Picadores were followed by the "Capadores," the men who wave their scarlet cloaks in front of the bull to excite him, or to distract his attention as he rushes wildly after some one. They were dressed in beautiful costumes of varied colours with gold embroideries. Last came the Banderillos, holding a dart a couple of feet long and gaily decorated with ribbons in each hand. After waiting for the bull to charge, they rush right up to him and plant the dart into his shoulder, deftly jumping aside. The butcher, with his merciful knife, completed the "Quadrilla."

The signal for the beginning of the Bull-Fight was given. A man dressed in black, as if he had already donned mourning for the death of the bulls, went to the door exactly opposite to us and unlocked it carefully, concealing himself behind the door, and out rushed bull No. I., a magnificent black animal, with a rosette fixed on his shoulder representing the "hacienda" (torril) from which he came. The huge wild beast galloped into the middle of the ring and then stood still, as though bewildered by the noise and sudden transition from darkness to brilliant sunlight. A "Capador," running swiftly and waving a red shawl, darted before the bull and retreated rapidly backward, leaping over the barrier. The animal dashed at the shawl with a resounding bellow, and lunged with his sharp horns at the cloth. A Banderillo approached him now, holding in his hand his long darts, the ends of which were shod with little barbs that once firmly planted in the flesh, hold on tightly. He awaited the bull, like the spider watches for the fly, in order to plant his banderillas into him. If the bull is not sensitive enough, to complete the cruelty, the banderillas are charged with crackers (fuegos) which burst in his flesh. A slight stream of blood appeared trickling down the bull's shoulder ; he made a mad rush and stood now facing the Banderillero, strictly on the defensive, legs apart, head down, back humped, and tail lashing the air—a picture of power. The ferocious-looking animal with blood-shot eyes, his red nostrils quivering, pawed great lumps of sand and dug furiously with his mighty horns at the banks of the arena, giving thus the time for the Banderillero to jump over the barrier. We were told that at one of the preceding " Corridas " an infuriated bull, following the example of the fleeing Banderillero, jumped after him and found himself in the stalls amidst the audience. That did not sound very promising ! Soon the whole body of the bull became one bloody mass. The people shouted in the stalls. Both men and women became unconscious monsters excited by the horrible spectacle. It was too hideously cruel ! I burned with indignation and applied bad epithets to the Spaniards, calling them as many bad names as I could in Russian. The Picadores now pushed their horses on the bull, trying to prick him with their lances. The poor animal, with a loud snort, lowered his head, and with tail arched wickedly, he charged furiously upon one of the Picadores and plunged his horns into the horse's side, rolling him over. I covered my eyes with my hands to keep off the dreadful sight. Looking up accidentally, I nearly had a nervous attack, and started back with a cry of horror. A horse was there before me, his four hoofs up in the air, disembowelled, with two streams of blood pouring down its gored sides, rolling in convulsions in mortal agony. I shall never forget the sight of this quivering, dying creature ! The executioner, dressed in a red blouse, ran up to the horse and, with a butcher's knife, he deftly cut the poor animal's throat, giving him the touch of mercy. After fifty minutes of this horrid sport the bugle sounded for the final act, the putting to death of the bull. It was Legartijo's turn to kill the first bull. Wrapped up in his " capa " he strode out into the ring with a firm step and approached the President's box, whom he saluted with a theatrical flourish of his hat, after which he extended his " mulata " (sword) and made his announcement to present the bull to the President. Then he threw his hat to the audience, to be kept until his return, and advanced slowly, with an almost devilish expression of cruelty on his face, his sword hidden in the folds of his " capa," to his victim, and began his " passadas " (passes), whilst the bull, who was by now one bleeding lump, stood motionless and trembled all over, his eyes out of their sockets and tongue hanging out. For the space of half-a-minute both man and beast stood as if turned to stone, then with a quick move-ment Legartijo stuck his sword up to the hilt into the neck of the bull, nothing but the handle remaining visible. The tortured animal tottered to his knees, bowed his head in the dust, rolled over and died. It was a master-stroke, and the air resounded with deafening applause ; flowers and cigars (the highest token of Spanish approval) were thrown into the arena at the Torero's feet. More bugles, and at the same moment a door was flung open and in galloped the team of mules ; the bleeding corpses of the martyred animals were hooked to their yoke by the hind legs, and off they went full speed round the arena, dragging the corpses on the sand. It was unworthy of mankind ; my nerves could not staud it any longer, and I had but one desire—to flee from the spot. We struggled with all our might but couldn't pass, being encompassed on all sides by a dense crowd, and we had to return to our seats.

Hardly was the ring cleared before the second bull rushed in and the programme was repeated. The new bull looked quite peaceful, and, instead of rushing into battle, he walked from right to left, looking for a loophole to escape, but nevertheless he was made to go through all the traditional tortures. It was Frascuello's turn to march on the bull. The Matador didn't show any pluck. With the first passes of the "mulata" he had missed his bull and only injured the animal without killing him, at which shouts of encouragement to the bull were raised on all sides, " Viva el toro ! " they cried. The arena resounded with whistles and invectives to the Matador, and the populace fiercely threw orange-peels and empty bottles at him. Frascuello paled with suppressed rage, and had to strike several times before putting his victim to death. The Matador ventures to face the bull when the last spirit had been beaten out of him, and I find there is much less danger for them than for the Russian peasant going to hunt bears, armed only with a spear, whereas the Matadors charge on an unfortunate animal driven into a circle whence he could not escape.

After the second bull we pushed resolutely through the crowd, we had to fight our way as best we could by a series of manœuvres, and managed this time to decamp. I had my first, and I am sure of it, my last experience of a bull-fight, the one thing that makes Spain hateful to me. Outside the bull-ring we saw the carcasses of the martyred bulls, whose meat was sold at low prices to the lower classes.

We returned to the hotel in a cab. When we asked our driver if his horse was also doomed for the bull-fight, he answered that for some years yet his animal would escape the bull's horns.

My blood being still hot from the remembrance of what I had seen, I locked myself up in my room heart-sick, whilst Sergy went to make a tour in Saragossa. He crossed a bridge and found himself on the other side of the river Ebro. It happened to be a market day and there was a horse-fair on a large square, where more than ten thousand horses and mules were brought for sale.

I heard a carriage stop before our hotel, and thinking that it was my husband who was returning home, I went out on the balcony and saw Lagartijo, the hero of the day, stepping out of a smart phaeton. A rich marquis had begged, as an honour, to drive him up to his hotel in his four-in-hand. Behind the phaeton came the Picadores on their poor nags, who had been spared to-day, to be disembowelled to-morrow perhaps. There was great animation in the street, carriages drove by containing gaily dressed ladies, wrapped in soft lace mantillas, returning from the bull-fight. Newspaper boys were shouting the triumph of Lagartijo, and announced the issue of the bull-fight. It appears that after our departure two Banderillos had been severely wounded.

Sergy took me after dinner to see the dances of the "Gitanas" in a more than dubious-looking tavern, where the male audience consisted of individuals belonging to the "Fra Diavolo type," whom one would not care to meet at night turning the corner of a street. Four Andalusian gitanas and two guitarists, with red kerchiefs wrapped round their heads, and the *navaja* (knife) stuck in their belt, composed the troop. The gitanas, arrayed in scarlet frocks and different coloured shawls, with the traditional red flower stuck just over the ear, and huge gold ear-rings, bounced about to the sound of the guitars and the clinking of castanets, occasionally indulging in a sudden shrill shout, whilst the audience clapped their hands in tune. After that the gitanas went round for collections and came and sat at the guest's tables to be regaled with molluscs and snails, which they swallowed uncooked. A fat and rather unattractive terpsichore seated herself at the table next to ours, and cast alluring glances on the male audience, but lost her time in vain, for nobody paid attention to her. My neighbour, who with his savage-looking beard resembled a highwayman, offered me a cigarette and wanted me to taste some of those horrid molluscs, and was extremely astonished at my refusal.

CHAPTER XLIV

BARCELONA

THE following morning we took the train back to France, and shared our compartment with a pretty young woman from Seville and her two children, a fat-cheeked baby, who filled our car with its wailings, and a little girl holding a big doll in her arms, whom her mother stuffed with cakes to make her keep quiet. Both delightful children responded to her coaxings with piercing shrieks. Such a journey was not one to put you into good spirits !

We arrived towards evening at Barcelona and put up for the night at the " Hôtel des quatre Nations," situated on the "Rambla," the finest and gayest street of Barcelona. This town can easily rival Madrid. The streets are broad and beautifully lighted with electricity and the shops are splendid.

Feeling too tired to appear at table-d'hôte, I went immediately to bed, whilst Sergy made gastronomic purchases at the nearest grocery-shop. He came home laden with parcels, having converted himself into a temporary hanging-stand ; from every part of him suspended a loose parcel containing butter, cheese, sausages, etc., and under his arm he brought bravely a bottle of Malaga wine, which he added to his stock in order not to be taken by the shop-man for a famished wretch.

Early in the morning we continued our journey to Nice. The country is not picturesque, and the roads are very rough and badly kept. Towards sunset we approached the French frontier *Portou-Cerbère* and soon perceived a corner of the Mediterranean, lighted by a silver moon. It was very cold in our compartment, and the foot-warmers had to be changed several times during the night. We did not stop at Marseilles and went straight on to Nice, having decided to spend a few days on the Riviera. There were two French-men in our compartment going to gamble at Monte Carlo, who studied systems on a little roulette board. One of them descended at a station to buy a newspaper, whilst his friend slept on peacefully, nodding his head, in a corner of the carriage, and didn't come back when the train had started. I was watching wickedly the awakening of our fellow-passenger, to see the expression of his face when he would find out that his friend was not there. Suddenly waking out of his nap he opened his eyes very wide and fixed them upon us suspiciously. Did he think perhaps that we had pitched his companion out of the window? At the next stoppage both friends were reunited. The belated passenger, as it appears, had just time to jump in the next carriage when the train was moving.

CHAPTER XLV

SAN REMO

WE only remained ten days at Nice, for we were at the end of October, the season of gusty winds and showers. The weather was abominable, and we had to remain indoors all day. So we started for San Remo, where my husband's brother had settled with his family for the whole winter. The "Villa Maria," which they were to inhabit, was not ready yet to receive them, and they had to put up in the meanwhile at the "Quisisana," a boarding-house kept by an old German lady. The society offered by the few tenants of the "Quisisana" was not of a specially enlivening description. There was an English spinster lady on whom wooers had turned their backs long ago, dried up in celibacy, who never was kissed, I am sure, for with such a thin body you might get a bruise in coming in contact with her. She was a blue-stocking in the bargain, and read Homer in Greek ; a crushingly superior person who made other people feel ignorant. I was becoming intolerably tired of her superior culture and stopped her every time she began any long sentences. There was another British lady, who was a very different sort of person, her tongue being the only sharp thing in her whole stout person. What she lacked in height was amply made up in width : whichever way you put her down she'd roll. After dinner she regaled us with songs which she cooed raising her eyes to the ceiling, at which I had to make the greatest effort to keep serious. She was awfully sentimental, and when she turned her eyes upon me with so melting an expression that I thought she was going to kiss me, I precipitately fled. The third boarder was a consumptive German student, frightfully pale and thin, who, notwithstanding his malady, manifested an immoderate love for the flute, and practised it assiduously to the great annoyance of his neighbours.

San Remo is not very gay. The only distraction you get is to walk around a music-kiosque in the public garden, in the company of nursery maids wheeling perambulators in front of them. At nine o'clock of the evening the music stops, the shops are closed, and everybody goes to bed.

One morning we took a carriage and went over to Monte Carlo, situated at some hours' distance from San Remo. We followed all the time the beautiful *Corniche* road, cut out in the rock. Our driver, who made the journey for the first time, did not know that he had to take a pass, and was not allowed to go further. It is lucky that we found a carriage on the Italian side of the frontier, at Ventimiglia, which brought us to Mentone, where we took the train to Monaco. Here a new disappointment awaited us! We were too late for the train and had to wait hours for the next one. To shorten the time, we went for a stroll through Mentone, and entered the first hotel to have lunch, but it was not meal-time at the hotel, and we returned fagged out and ravenous to the railway station.

All Monte Carlo seemed composed of gardens, with the big, white building of the Casino in the midst, the whole ringed in by high grey mountains. We went straight to the Casino and looked in at the gambling-rooms. The tables were surrounded by anxious players with a preponderance of courtesans of high and low degree, with painted faces and rings down to their nails, who followed the game with breathless interest. An old woman, dressed in dyed silks and a home-made hat, was losing heavily, and staked her last francs with despair written on her face. Many players come to Monaco with their pockets full, and have nothing to pay their return journey. Suicides often take place here. I tried my luck, and lost something like ten francs.

The Principality of Monaco is quite a small one. It would take half an hour to walk over the island, from one end to the other. The reigning Prince has a diminutive army of sixty regular soldiers, two officers and three constables, and that's all! Sergy asked one of the constables who was on duty at the railway station, how their army could manage without any cavalry, and he answered that they wouldn't have known what to do with it, for it would take more time to saddle a horse than to walk around their whole territory!

Another day we went for an excursion to the monastery of *Notre Dame de la Garde*, where the church is decorated with little cardboard boats that the sailors' wives offer, with their prayers, to the Madonna, when their husbands are at sea.

We removed at last to the Villa Maria, where we felt the cold very much. The rooms were badly heated, and the draughts in the corridor were strong enough to work a windmill, and they gave me a horrid cold. In the night the noise of the passing trains and the roar of the sea hindered our sleep. We hastened our departure and started for Paris, where we intended to spend a few days before returning to Russia. Towards night three young Corsicans entered our compartment, and we were doomed to pass a sleepless night, for we couldn't stretch our legs, and felt very uncomfortable. Our fellow-travellers were the very image of Napoleon Bonaparte, and resembled each other like three peas.

CHAPTER XLVI

PARIS

MARY VIETINGHOFF, my old Stuttgart friend, who had married a Frenchman, Count Soligoux de Fougères, was in Paris for the moment. She used to be a dear girl, and so fond of me! We had not met for nearly ten years, but the friendship which had subsisted between us in the days of our girlhood had suffered no diminution through absence. How good it was to see her again. Mary smothered me with kisses and made me feel how her heart throbbed with joy at out meeting. She invited us to dine on the following day. There was a French minister among the guests, who began a political discussion with Sergy, which lasted during the whole repast. I must confess that political affairs rather bore me, and was very glad when Mary took me up to her room, leaving the gentlemen to sip their coffee. We sat and chatted happily together. We had not forgotten the old days, and had a thousand confidences to exchange. Mary told me that she had quitted the fold of our Church, and had turned Roman Catholic. She was afraid that my religious views would be hurt, and that her renouncement of our faith would stand as a barrier to our former friendship, but I assured her of my everlasting love. Mary's husband does not like our country, as it appears, and when his little daughter, called Baby, is capricious, he threatens her saying that if she continued to be naughty he would send her to Russia. How nasty of him!

Last winter a French Colonel, Baron Rothvillers, passing through Moscow, paid us a visit, and invited us to come and and see him in Paris and make the acquaintance of his wife, which we now did with pleasure. Baroness Rothvillers is a fine horsewoman and her stables are renowned in Paris. She invited me to drive with her in the *Bois de Boulogne*. I sat on the high driving-seat and trotted her handsome pair of browns round the Park. The horses were pulling and became somewhat restive, but I kept them well in hand, surveyed by the groom, immovable as a wooden image, with rigidly folded arms, seated on the back seat.

Though sorry to leave Paris, I was glad when the North Express carried us back to Russia.

CHAPTER XLVII

MOSCOW

ON returning to Moscow we found among our numerous correspondence a number of the Parisian paper *L'Evenement,* sent to us by the Rothvillers, with my biography and expressions of regret that the sojourn of the blonde young lady who had made a brief appearance in the " Bois," handling so surely a pair of restive horses, was of so short duration. It appears that when I entered a café to drink a cup of chocolate, during my drive in the Park with the Baroness Rothvillers, a reporter of the *Evenement* had asked our groom the address of the hotel where I had put up, and learnt from our hotel-keeper, who had known me a good many years, all sorts of things concerning my life. It is thus that my biography appeared in the French paper.

A Japanese Imperial Prince, who was returning from a long tour in Europe to his country through Russia, with his spouse and a numerous suite, stopped for a few days in Moscow. I went to see these Japs at the *Manège,* where a great festival was given in their honour. The Prince and Princess wore European costumes which did not suit them at all ; they would have been much better-looking in their own national costume. The Princess, into the bargain, had golden teeth (the sign of Imperial blood), which did not really embellish her.

In November my father came to pass the winter with my aunt Galitzine in Moscow. He had been ailing for some years, and I was painfully struck to see the change that had come over him. His illness took a dangerous turn, and soon after his arrival he departed this life. Father's death gave me a great shock. It was weeks before I got over it. I wouldn't see anyone, or take interest in anything. My health broke down completely and the doctors ordered me away from Moscow for some time. We decided to make a tour in Sweden and Denmark. So, at the end of June we started off to Stockholm, taking from St. Petersburg the Finnish boat " Döbbeln." The captain, a consummate patriot, had with extreme suddeness forgotten every word of Russian, and we had to talk German to him, though we knew, of course, that he spoke and understood Russian perfectly well. That detestable man made disparaging remarks about Russia to our fellow-passengers, foreigners for the most part, and prided himself that his steamer was named "Döbbeln" after a famous Finnish hero, who had distinguished himself in the war of Sweden against Russia. When we approached Kronstadt, I heard him say that this fortress had only two strong forts, and that the rest of them were good-for-nothing, and could be easily blown to pieces by one bomb. My patriotic pride was awfully wounded, and I did all in my power to resist the temptation to give the captain a bit of my mind.

On the right side of the bay of Kronstadt our cruisers stood in a long line, and huge German men-of-war were anchored on the left one. Numerous steam-launches were plying all the time from one fleet to another. On one of our vessels a band was playing on the deck ; it was our marine officers who were feasting their German comrades.

The weather was very fine and the sea had scarcely a ripple. Towards six o' clock dinner was spread on deck in Swedish fashion on a long table covered with appetising dishes, and you were asked to help yourself. That is a good way, because you have the opportunity of selecting what you prefer and of taking as much as you like.

At five o' clock in the morning we landed at Helsingfors and had only one hour to survey this pretty town. When we returned to our boat a fresh breeze arose and our ship began to pitch and rock. This disagreeable tossing of the waves made me feel sick and giddy. I hastened to my cabin and lay down. Early in the morning I was up and hastened on deck. The shores of Sweden had appeared at last, and soon we entered the port of Stockholm, the Venice of the North. The town, built upon islands, is very picturesque. As a rule, the Swedes are exceedingly courteous to strangers, nevertheless at the Custom House the officials burrowed into our trunks and opened all our bags, making a mess of everything. One of the men picked out a little folding looking-glass and turned it about in his clumsy fingers trying to find out what it was, till Sergy, at the end of his patience, opened the looking-glass and thrust it under the man's ugly face, after which he left us in peace.

We put up at the Grand Hôtel, just opposite the Royal Palace. After having taken a little rest we went for a stroll in the town and crossed in a small steamer to Djurgarden, a beautiful park on the other side of the bay, where we had dinner at a small restaurant. A waiter, napkin upon arm, came up to us, but as we couldn't speak a word of Swedish, we found it difficult to make him understand what we wanted, and had to converse by gestures to illustrate our meaning. But our attempts to describe a chicken being useless, the idea came to me to cry out cou-ca-ri-cou, and I came out of the difficulty. We ended our evening at " Tivoli," a fashionable music-hall, where we met several fellow-passengers of our boat. The performance took place in the open. The actresses who sang and danced were more or less bad, very short-petti-coated and very generously décolleté.

The next day we visited Drottningholm Palace, situated out of town, the summer residence of the King, who was for the moment in Norway, where he is obliged to live a part of the year. After dinner we started for Malmö, where we arrived early in the morning on the following day, and then took the train to Copenhagen.

CHAPTER XLVIII

COPENHAGEN

THANKS to the Exhibition in Copenhagen, all the hotels and boarding-houses were full, and it was with great difficulty that we succeeded in finding a shelter in a private house. By a winding staircase we were ushered into a dark, low room, looking into a grim back-yard, and scantily furnished with two beds, a few cane, inhospitable-looking chairs and a sofa losing its horse-hair through wide gaping wounds. Feeling very tired and sleepy, I lay down to rest a bit, but sprang up hastily, for the bed was abominable, the mattress as hard as stone and the pillows so thin that they could easily be folded in two. To crown all, behind the wall our landlady's children were shrieking with all their might. It was impossible to go to sleep, and we decided to go and take the train to Tivoli and explore the Exhibition, with its chief attraction, an enormous elevator representing a huge bottle of beer with a magnificent bird's-eye view of Copenhagen. We had dinner in a restaurant on board a ship of the middle-ages, and were brought in a barge with a three-storied poop to this curious establishment. The waiters were dressed in the costume of sailors belonging to that long past epoch, wearing broad-brimmed Rembrandt hats.

On the next morning an old friend of ours, Mr. Stcherbatcheff, the first Secretary of the Russian Embassy, came to see us. He was begged to wait for me in a small tobacco-shop belonging to our hostess, in the next house, while I finished dressing. Mr. Stcherbatcheff was horrified when he saw our lodging, and said that he had an apartment ready for us in the house where he dwelt, and we resolved to remove immediately to our new apartment, looking out into the most fashionable and animated quarter of the town, and furnished in showy fashion. It seemed palatial in comparison with our miserable room.

During our stay in Copenhagen the anniversary of the ninth century of the institution of Christianity in Russia was celebrated. Sergy went to the Russian church to be present at the official Te Deum, and was invited afterwards by our priest to take a cup of tea. On that same afternoon we visited the Museum where we saw prodigious sculptures, the work of Thorwaldsen, the famous Danish sculptor. After dinner we went by train, in an open car, to Klampenbrgə, about an hour's drive. A peasant woman, returning from market sat opposite to us with a basket on her knees, which contents appeared to be stinking fish. Our road ran along the sea-coast and was sheltered by roses and creepers. A strong odour of seaweed came over to us. When we arrived at Klampenberg we took a carriage to drive within the precincts of the beautiful park, and chose a coachman who could speak German. His comrades jeered at him and called his horse *Eine alte Katze*, out of spite, of course.

We hadn't time to have dinner that day, and we went to bed famished. I roamed about the room looking for something to eat, opening drawers and exploring them, but there was nothing, not even the skin of a sausage.

On the following morning we went out shopping and saw my picture painted in the Greenaway style on a cardboard plate exposed in a bookseller's shop window. When we entered the shop one of the clerks, who had noticed the resemblance at once, asked me if I had sat for that picture. It really bore a striking likeness to me and we bought it as a souvenir.

On the 16th of July we saw the arrival of Kaiser Wilhelm II. It was his first visit to Denmark after the taking of Schleswig by the Prussians. Our Ambassador, Count Toll, offered a window to us at the Russian Embassy, but we preferred to stand near the Royal Pavilion, erected on the landing-place for the reception of the Kaiser, so as to have the best view of the proceedings. Towards ten o'clock in the morning Mr. Stcherbatcheff, arrayed in full diplomatic uniform, covered all over with golden embroideries, came to fetch us in his carriage. Driving through the streets took a long time, the crowd was so great. When we approached the Royal Palace, we heard cannon reports. A stir among the throng heralded the coming of the King of Denmark, followed by his brothers and the Heir to the throne of Greece. Soon after appeared in a coach driven by a team of white horses the old Queen, aged seventy-two, but still very alert, accompanied by the Duchess of Orleans. Then a murmur arose among the crowd, and we saw a steam-launch, with the German flag flying at the prow, moored to the Danish shore, and Kaiser Wilhelm, his blond moustache curled upwards, stepped out upon the elegantly decorated pier, followed by a numerous suite. The King came up to him and embraced him. After a long exchange of amiabilities the Kaiser approached the Queen and kissed her hand, whilst the soldiers, standing in lines, presented arms to him. Only a few hurrahs were heard here and there. We were told that strong measures had been taken by the police to avoid demonstrations in the streets against the Kaiser. A squadron of hussars was given to him as an escort, and all the way to the Palace infantry regiments formed long lines. The Danish soldiers did not look very imposing, being mostly of small stature. The circulation of carriages and trams was stopped during the passing of the troops, and we had to walk home, running the risk of being crushed by the crowd.

Having passed a fortnight at Copenhagen we returned to St. Petersburg by the same way, taking at Stockholm the " Constantin," another Finnish boat. There were many passengers on board. During dinner I sat next to a young Mexican, Señor Lopez, who was very sarcastic, and found plenty to criticise. (The task is so easy!) He actually tore all our fellow-passengers to pieces. That snob thought himself very sharp-witted and was rather put out that I did not think him so. Opposite me sat an old Frenchman, M. Prévost-Rousseau and his pretty daughter Melle. Camille, who had been touring in Norway and were now on their way back to Paris, passing through St. Petersburg. Melle. Camille was an accomplished linguist, speaking English, German and Italian equally well. I discovered that we had a great deal in common, and an instinctive comradeship sprang up between us. I am not much given to making new friends, but I had a liking to Melle. Camille the moment I saw her, for I generally like or dislike a person at once.

We had a bad crossing; the sea was rough and the ship rolled very unpleasantly. Towards morning the wind having changed, calm came on, and I hurried on deck to rejoin Melle. Camille, my new-found friend. We established ourselves comfortably in a secluded spot on the prow of the vessel; scrambling over a pile of boxes we found a seat on a barrel of oil, and had a nice chat. Señor Lopez, who was in the mood of making the most open court to me, and followed me everywhere like a shadow, discovered our hiding place, but we packed him off very soon, and he had to withdraw, ruffled, and out of sorts.

We anchored at Helsingfors in the evening and went on shore to stretch our legs. I wanted to boast of the first Russian town before our fellow-passengers, who were visiting our country for the first time, but failed, alas, for the boulevards were full of half-drunken Russian sailors, loafing about, elbowing us and using bad language. Fearing a skirmish, we hurried back on board. At St. Petersburg we parted, with regret with our French friends, who invited us to pay them a visit, some day in Paris.

CHAPTER XLIX

MOSCOW

THIS winter we had to give tiresome "At Homes" every Sunday from four to six. I was so pleased when those tedious two hours were over.

Every morning I went out for a ride with Sergy and had a gallop round the Park on my beautiful horse named "Sailor," black as jet, with a coat shining like satin, which Sergy had just presented to me. In bad weather I went to a riding-school. I met there one day a stout lady perched on a pacific-looking horse, who was rolling like a barrel on her saddle. She wanted to try "Sailor," and I seated myself good-naturedly on her old hack. We had scarcely made two or three tours, when the "fatty" tumbled off my horse and lay sprawling on the sand, whilst "Sailor," feeling himself free from his heavy burden, went gambolling round the track, rearing and prancing after me with sheer joy of life, and trying to catch my habit with his long teeth. Loosing my head, I cried out shrilly, "Help! help!" and a gentleman who had come to the manége as a looker-on, sprang forward and was just in time to catch me in his arms as I fell from the saddle. He profited by the opportunity in coming to our "At Homes" the very next Sunday, and the Sunday after, and many other Sundays besides.

We frequented regularly the concerts of the "Philharmonic Society," where the audience, for the most part, was far more interested in themselves than in the music to which they were supposed to listen. I often met at these concerts an elegant young man, whose gaze followed me persistently; turning my head I always found his eyes upon me. One night he came up with a friend of ours and asked to be presented to me. When the concert was over, he followed us to the cloak-room, and helped me on with my pelisse, drawing it over my shoulders with lingering tenderness of touch, and squeezed my hand in a manner that spoke volumes. According to my permission, he came to call next afternoon, which happened to be a Sunday, and took advantage of every possible occasion to visit us. Wherever I was going he would find out and go too. I do not deny that I flirted a little with him, for I love to be loved, but it was really a shame of me to put ideas into his head   He flamed up one day, and looking admiringly into my eyes, burst into the most fiery declaration, telling me he had loved me since the first time he had met me, that the fever of love consumed him night and day, and all sort of other sentimental rubbish.   But my temperature, as far as he was concerned, was unvariably under zero, his great love left me unmoved, and his eloquence was all in vain.   He was extremely jealous into the bargain ; he was even angry with my parrot when the bird had too much of my attention.   I soon became thoroughly tired of him ; he exasperated me with his suppressed sighs and melancholy and I wished I hadn't made him so fond of me. I did all in my power to discourage him and heartlessly asked him to put himself out of my way, but he would not obey me, and regardless of the weather, it might rain, snow, or storm, he was always to be seen standing before my windows on the opposite side of the street, looking up through opera glasses trying to see what I was doing inside, and looking profoundly miserable, just like a stock figure weeping on a tombstone. To arrive nearer my heart my suitor loaded me with flowers and bonbons, and bored me with passionate letters in prose and in verse, but I tossed his epistles half-read into the waste-paper basket.   Everything wears out with time ; his broken heart began to mend ; he was seen no more and disappeared completely from my horizon.

CHAPTER L

PARIS

TOWARDS the end of June we went to Paris to see the World's Fair. We put up as usual at the Hôtel de Calais, a pleasant, quiet house. After having washed off the dust of our journey we started to visit the Exhibition. The passage of carriages was forbidden on the Pont d'Terra, and only foot-passengers provided with entrance tickets could cross that bridge. On entering the enclosure of the "Grand Fair," we took the Decauville, a toy-train, which carried us round the whole place. Every now and then our eyes were arrested by vivid printed notices on the walls, advertisements about cocoa and soap, and placards put everywhere, warning the passengers not to thrust out their hands or heads out of the window, written in all the European languages except in German. The Parisians, as it seems, have nothing to say against the Teutonic visitors of the Exhibition being deprived of heads or hands! In all directions small two-wheeled waggonettes called "puss-puss," circulated, pushed by yellow-faced Tonqinoise aborigines.

There was much to see at the Exhibition ; it just made my head swim. We unweariedly enjoyed all the sights of the Champ de Mars, the gayest part of the Exhibition, crowded with visitors from all the parts of the earth and moved with the throng, being pushed to-and-fro. The Eiffel Tower was the chief attraction of the Exhibition. It is by far the highest structure in the world, being 984 feet high, and took two years to build. There were five big restaurants on the first platform, where the charges were perfectly monstrous. We had lunch at the Restaurant de Russe, and paid ten francs for a roasted chicken. We waited more than half-an-hour our turn to enter the lift, which raised us to the third platform. Whilst we were mounting gently to the very sky, we saw through the barred windows the landscape gradually diminishing ; the whole horizon was disclosed and the people down below, walking about the Exhibition, appeared not bigger than flies. On each platform commemorative medals made of brass, bronze and silver were sold. The Tower had its own printing office where a newspaper, named "Le Figaro de la Tour," was printed every day.

Night festivals were given three times a week at the Trocadero, when the Eiffel Tower was illuminated with thousands of electric lights of all the brightest colours of the rainbow, as well as the beautiful "Fontaines Lumineuses," lighted up in a wonderful way.

We went almost every day to the Exhibition and sacrificed a whole afternoon to the French colonies: Tunis, Algiers, Dahomey and other transmarine countries, all clustered together near the Trocadero. In front of them were the cafés belonging to them. Here you could listen to the different national airs, see the different national types and costumes, and eat the different national foods.

The section named "Habillement des deux Sexes" is marvellous, with Paquin's and Worth's most divine combinations. I did not know how our purses were going to hold out. There was a dress I had been dying for, and Sergy, dear man, made me a present of it immediately.

The "Palais des Machines," a monstrous gallery full of machines, with glass walls and roof, was very fatiguing to go through. Sergy took great interest in all sorts of engines, and our guide bothered me with his technical explanations of which I understood nothing. On the top galleries a moving electric bridge, full of people, advanced towards us from the opposite side of the gallery, moving very slowly in order to permit the visitors to see all the machines at work. We were dying of thirst, and entered the English Dairy to drink a glass of milk, after which we visited the Cow-House, exhibiting superb animals, who stood in comfortable stalls with new clean straw under their feet. Whilst I petted a beautiful fat cow named "Every Inch a Queen," a milkmaid appeared with a stool and a pail and began to extract what the cow chose to give her.

Directly opposite the "Palais des Machines" is the "Vieux Paris." To visit it is to step back into the past. In the street La Huchette, the houses, the shops, the citizens, everything, transports you to the seventeenth century; the anachronism was ourselves in our modern clothes, which did not harmonise with the picture. Soldiers with their bands at the head, wearing white wigs, marched in the streets. On a raised platform the Mandolinists of the Duc de Guise played pretty gavottes and minuets. A few steps further the so-called "Sans-Chagrins" (street singers), standing on a table, sang popular airs. Through an open window we saw a dainty "Marquise" singing old-time love-ditties, to the accompaniment of a smart "Marquis" wearing a white wig and buckled shoes, who played a harpsichord. The illusion was complete, we had gone back a hundred years to Louis XVI. time. In the Rue Sainte Antoine we saw the exact copy of the church Sainte Marie, with a museum inside, where you could see the atrocities of the French Revolution, represented with horrid realism, and calculated to give even a strong man the creeps. Soldiers wearing pig-tailed wigs bellowed: "Come and see the execution of the Royal Family!" In dark alcoves different scenes of the French Revolution were represented. We saw the wax figure of Robespierre presiding at the Jacobin Club; of Charlotte Corday in the act of murdering Marat, etc., etc.

A fortune-teller, standing at the door of her dwelling, invited the passers-by to come in to hear their fortunes told. On the threshold of a house just opposite, a quarrelsome female, arms akimbo, was shouting and shaking her fist at her bourgeois; the discussion waxed hot, and a constable, dressed in the costume of the period, came running to separate them; the scene was only a sham. We entered a theatre on the Place du Guesclin, where we saw the escape of a prisoner from the dungeon of La Bastille. There was a great push at the entrance, and we got to our places with difficulty. The curtain rose showing the prisoner preparing to clamber out of the window, and falling down whilst he was dropping a cord exclaiming: "How dark the night is!" And, indeed, night came on when the spectators emerged into the square where stood the reproduction of the Bastille with its towers and raised bridges, to see the man, who appeared to be a skilful acrobat, making his escape from the prison. His flight was noticed by a group of soldiers, dressed in red uniforms, and wearing white wigs, who fired at him and began to climb over the walls in hurried pursuit, and seized the escaping prisoner, who was hissed by the crowd on the square. After that the taking of the Bastille, was reproduced. We could imagine all this taking place. A throng of 500 men, wearing Jacobin caps with tri-coloured cockades and armed with muskets and swords, began to climb up the Bastille by the aid of ropes and ladders, making a terrible noise. Suddenly a detachment of soldiers, dressed in the costume of the period, appeared, and a white-wigged colonel began to read instructions to the men, under a smoking lamp-post, urging them to serve their King faithfully and defeat the Sans-Culottes. Then began the charge of cannons and muskets, which soon made the huge building flame on all sides.

After the taking of La Bastille, we went to seek for something to eat and drink at the hostelry of the Lion d'Or, and ended our evening at the Palais des Enfants, a rather badly named theatre at the Exhibition, where we saw the La Belle Fatima, the renowned Eastern beauty, encircled by unattractive *houris* who set her off still more. La Belle Fatima looked amongst them, like some vivid brilliant flower surrounded by faded leaves.

We assisted one day at the representation of the Fakirs, a Hindustan religious sect given over to the mortification of the flesh. It was an impressive spectacle. The Fakirs, arrayed in white flowing garments of doubtful cleanness, were sitting in a semi-circle on the floor, holding banners and singing religious chants. Their "mollah," wearing an enormous turban, sat in the centre. Suddenly the tomtoms rolled like thunder and the experiments began. The Fakirs did amazing things. One of them, clad in a sort of white sack with five openings through which passed his head, legs and arms, began to light the sacred fire to the accompaniment of a flute and tambourine, bending over the burning coals into which he threw some essence in order to get dizzy. The barbaric music, struck up faster and a long convulsive shudder shook the Fakir's limbs. Then he took a heated spade and applied it to his arms and face and put his fingers into the brazier, making disorderly jumps, after which he fell on the floor with foam in the corners of his mouth. But it was only a prelude to more horrors. The Fakir who came next terrified me still more by his shouts and wild gestures. He pricked his tongue, lips, cheeks and ears with a long iron spear, and stepped barefooted on the sharp sides of a sword, after which, in a state of wild excitement, he stabbed himself with a poniard, and the blood ran down in abundance. The third Fakir twisted a large serpent round his body and ate a part of it, and then swallowed a scorpion, which the manager had previously shown to the audience. Now came the turn of the last Fakir, who grilled his skin with red hot irons, and made his eyes bulge out of its sockets with the end of a dagger and slowly rolled the eye back into its ordinary position again. Professor Charcot, the celebrated psychologist, who had controlled the experiment, was convinced that it was not a fraud.

Sergy essayed a trip in the "Ballon Captif," which lifted ten persons at a time a hundred metres higher than the Eiffel Tower. From below I breathlessly watched the ascent. Sergy was presented with a medal bearing the inscription: "*Souvenir de mon ascension.*"

Another day we went to see "Buffalo Bill's Wild West," where a troup of "Red Skins" attacked a caravan of travellers, after which they scalped them and showed dramatically all the horrors described by Mayne Reid. Suddenly the Cowboys, with pistols bulging from their belts, came galloping on and drove away the Red Indians.

On July 14th, the day of the Fête Nationale, the usual review of the troops took place at Longchamps. I was ill in bed that day and could not accompany my husband to the review. Military bands played in the streets which were full of noise, and from everywhere shouts of "Vive Boulanger!" were heard. Tables were set in the streets and squares, laid out with dishes for the populace. I saw from my window an Alsacian procession pass by. All the members, dressed in black, were directing their steps towards the Statue of "Strasbourg," in order to adorn it with mourning wreaths. We witnessed on the Place de la Concorde the arrival of the Shah of Persia. Soldiers formed a long line on his way. The Shah drove in a victoria with President Carnot sitting by his side, and was escorted by a squadron of cuirassiers. The General Saussier followed galloping along-side the victoria, and twelve carriages with the suite of the Shah and newspaper correspondents followed. That night, there was a great rush to the Exhibition to see the Shah, who was to make his appearance on the balcony of the "Dome Central." We were carried ahead with the rush, with more than one escape of being crushed to atoms. We raced for chairs, and Sergy got one for me to stand on. A row of red velvet fautueils were placed for the Shah and his suite on the balcony, upon which the Shah appeared arrayed in a beautiful costume all worked with gold and bedecked with diamonds, accompanied by President Carnot with his spouse and a numerous suite. From the exhibition the Shah was driven to the Eiffel Tower. He had gone up only as far as the first floor, and there was no persuading him to ascend higher up. We have been braver than the Shah, as it appears!

M. Prévost-Rousseau and Melle. Camille, having heard of our arrival at Paris, came to see us at the hotel and invited us to come and spend a whole day at Champigny, where they have some property. The very next morning they came up again in their brougham to take us to their Château. It was a two hours' drive, and a very pleasant one, going through Joinville and the Bois de Vincennes. Mme. Prévost came forward to greet us, holding out both hands, and led us to the salon, where we found a group of guests assembled. Our host proposed to all the company to make a tour in the park, which descended in an easy slope to the banks of the Marne. M. Prévost took us for a pull on the river, and showed us afterwards his well kept grounds. The weather had changed for the worse by this time, and M. Prévost thought we ought to be starting home. I lifted up my nose to the clouds from which big drops of rain began to fall. Suddenly a storm burst out, and a shower came down upon us in torrents, accompanied by lightning and peals of thunder, which necessitated a hasty retreat, and we started running back to the Château. Mme. Camille carried me up to her own room to remove my hat and arrange my hair, dishevelled by the wind. After dinner there was to be a little entertainment in the salon, music and recitation, and towards midnight M. Prévost drove us to the railway station in his dog-cart.

Baroness Rothvillers had left Paris when we arrived, nevertheless we went to see her husband, who gave us a warm and kindly welcome. He invited us to dinner on the following day and took us afterwards to the " Cirque d'Eté."

We met at the Exhibition Mme. Diane Bibikoff, a French lady, married to a Russian dignitary, living in Moscow, a very pretty young woman, full of spirits, and Parisienne to her finger tips. One day whilst visiting the Exhibition together, I suggested entering a barrack on the Champs de Mars bearing the inscription, " *On the waves of the sea.*" It appeared to be a carousal with boats rolling over cardboard waves. Mme. Diane stepped into one of these boats, but as I did not like to be sea-sick at shore, I could in no way be persuaded to follow her example, and left poor Mme. Diane to her fate. After the first going round she began to beg for mercy and entreated them to stop the machine, but she had to make the regulation circuits, and stepped out of the boat more dead than alive. The situation was too much for my gravity, and I was seized with a fit of uncontrollable laughter. Mme. Diane will not want to repeat the experience.

CHAPTER LI

TROUVILLE

WE had to leave Paris for the seashore and proceeded to Dieppe, where we took a room in a private house, intending to remain there a fortnight at least, but after our first bath we decided to leave on the morrow to another bathing resort, for the water. wasn't pleasant and the landscape discouragingly rain-blotted. It was to Trouville we gave the preference, and went quietly out of the house with our dressing-bags in rather guilty haste at daybreak, before our landlord was up, to catch the first train to Trouville, feeling like fugitives from justice. We walked on quickly towards the railway station, as there were no cabs about at that early hour. Sergy had to come back again to fetch our boxes and pay our account; he told our bewildered landlord that we were suddenly summoned to Paris on business, but it did not prevent, I am sure, the old man from taking us for a pair of unlawful lovers, who had come stealthily to spend a clandestine night at his house.

I found Trouville a most amusing place: no chance of being dull here! It was the height of the season, and the place was full of people who had come to see the races at Dauville, a pretty Norman coast town on the other side of the river La Touque, possessing a splendid hippodrome, where during one week important races take place. Crowds of people came by special trains from Paris, and omnibuses kept constantly arriving with passengers. Our hotel was crammed to the garrets, and it was difficult to get a seat at any of the tables during our meals. Our landlady, a moustached virago, was almost out of her wits to satisfy all the demands.

Pretty Parisiennes came to Trouville to show off their beautiful toilettes, which they changed three times a day. In the afternoon they sat on the beach under big brown holland umbrellas, chatting and flirting with their cavaliers, whilst their bare-legged babies, armed with tin pails, made sand cakes and paddled in the sea.

We went to Dauville on a raft to see the races, although I do not particularly like that sport, and take the view of the late Shah of Persia, who explained why he would not go to the Derby, during his stay in London, by saying that he had always known that one horse could run faster than another, but that it was a matter of perfect indifference to him which that one horse might be. The hippodrome was filled with a gay and fashionable crowd, who followed the races eagerly. The prize of 10,000 francs was won by the famous " Volcano," whose lucky proprietor was loudly applauded. Rain began to fall and we got wet through because the people behind us wouldn't let us open our umbrellas : my pretty dress was quite spoilt. Whilst we lingered at Dauville the tide had run away, so we had to take an oddly-shaped carriage, with a white awning on it, and drive back to Trouville, being obliged to cross a pontoon bridge, as with low water the little river La Touque becomes almost dry, and the tide retreats so far that fishing-boats were lying upon the banks of sand.

We went one night to the " Eden Concert." Between the acts Sergy left his seat for a few moments to bring me bon-bons, and all at once a handsome woman, in showy dark style, who had been staring at me through her lorgnette in such a nasty way that I became quite uncomfortable, came up and sat by me and gave me her address, entreating me to call upon her the next day. At that very moment my husband returned to his place, very much astonished to see it occupied by that strange person, who gave up her seat very unwillingly, and continued to throw approving glances at me. Funny sort of type that woman !

Another night we went to the theatre to see " Serge Panine," the comedy in vogue. I liked the play, but the spectators did not seem to understand it, and giggled in the most pathetic places. We were very much amused when a dog, who was promenading between the chairs, mounted on the stage and stretched himself comfortably before the prompter's box.

At the end of August we left Trouville and started on our homeward journey.

CHAPTER LII

MOSCOW

MANY renowned artistes visited our old capital this winter, among them Tamagno, the celebrated tenor, whose fame was just then ringing all the world over. After a concert-tour in America he came to Moscow to collect a new harvest of laurels. But I didn't admire particularly his thundering voice, a veritable Jericho trumpet! Ferni-Germano, the ideal "Carmen," for whom Bizet had composed his opera, made a clamorous appearance after Tamagno. She came to see us with a letter of recommendation given to her by one of our friends living in St. Petersburg, but didn't find us at home. I wanted to see her close and went to the hotel where she had put up to pay her a visit. The " diva " didn't gain on close acquaintance; she couldn't stand the ordeal of pitiless sunshine, and sat with her back to the light in discreet semi-obscurity. I saw, nevertheless, that she hadn't had time to rub off the powder which lay an inch thick on her nose. Eleonora Duse, the great Italian tragédienne, had come to Moscow to give a few performances. I saw her in " La Dame aux Camelias," and was immensely pleased with her acting. In all my life I had never seen anything so perfectly beautiful. She seemed to have absolutely converted herself into "Violetta," whom she represented, and put all her soul in her part; most of the women in the audience were in tears. I was also in rapture with Marcella Sembrich, who sang at the Imperial Opera ; her beautiful well-trained voice was something marvellous. I had also the opportunity of seeing the famous ballet-dancer, Virginia Zucchi, in " Esmeralda," and Nikita, a rising young star, recently out of her teens, with whom Europe and America had been enraptured, and who looked like a delicate piece of Dresden china, and was entirely bewitching with her long locks hanging loosely over her shoulders. I enjoyed her singing very much, her voice went straight to the heart of her listeners, and her high notes were as clear as a bird's. Nikita had a brilliant future before her. She was born in America, and sang in public for the first time at the age of six.

There was a gala performance at the Opera-House in

honour of Nasr-ed-Ding, Shah of Persia, who appeared in his box wearing his tall Astrakhan cap and literally ablaze with diamonds. He seemed to have a special appetite for the ladies of the ballet and stared at them fixedly through his opera-glasses, all the time regretting, doubtless, that he could not carry them away to his harem. I was perfectly dazzled by the aspect of the audience in the brilliantly lighted theatre, which presented a most magnificent sight ; the gentlemen in brilliant uniforms and the ladies in beautiful toilets and superb jewels, showed to their greatest advantage.

The Countess Keller, one of the lady patronesses of Moscow, was getting up a charity affair in the hall of the Assembly, an amateur play and "Tableaux." She called upon me to beg me to take part in these Tableaux, and would hear of no refusal. I asked for a day's consideration, for Sergy rather disapproved of the whole thing, but the Countess sent me a note that same evening, imploring me to say "Yes" directly, and Sergy, who was always willing to accede to any wish I expressed, and had not the heart to refuse me anything, gave in.

Our Tableau named "Serenade" in the programme, represented a scene of Venetian life in the sixteenth century. A large gondola was to be moored to the side of a lagoon, with a lady dressed as the wife of a Doge of Venice in it, surrounded by the ladies of her suite, two gondoliers, and a street dancing girl, standing in the middle of the gondola. I was to appear as the dancing girl, in a lovely costume, the exact copy of a well known picture. According to the looking-glass it suited me very well, with my hair hanging down, adorned with a gold net intermingled with pearls. I had been given the choice between a harp, a lyre and a mandoline. The latter I selected for my instrument. We had two rehearsals and everything went smoothly, except that I made several · bitter enemies. The next Tableau was to represent the exit of a troup of masqueraders with their masks off, from a fancy-dress ball. One of my would-be friends took part in that Tableau, she had a tongue as sharp as a sword, and if she could say a bitter thing to wound someone, she never lost the opportunity of doing it. She told me a good many things concerning our Tableau, most of which were more or less disagreeable. Notwithstanding her "darling Vava" here, and "darling Vava" there, she tried to sting me and to spoil my pleasure as thoroughly as possible, in hinting that our gondola was in great danger of being sunk, having such a lot of occupants. As my temper was not of the sweetest that day, I warmed up and paid her back in her own coin by suggesting, that the staircase on which she was to stand during the

Tableau representing the exit from a masked ball, was in far greater danger of giving way, because our Tableau had only ten performers in it whereas a crowd of forty figures appeared in hers. This was a stab which didn't please the young lady; she drew in her claws and bit her lips in vexation that she had been using her weapons in a wrong direction, and that her aim to sting me was not attained. I was mistress of the situation and amply avenged.

Our Tableau was a great success. The curtain fell amid loud applause and went up several times to the sound of an orchestra playing Moschkowsky's "Mandolinata." It was with a sigh of relief that I found myself home. I removed the grease paint off my face and got out of my costume as quickly as I could.

Though we led a quiet life, I had plenty of occupation. I took singing lessons of Mme. Kogan, a delightful teacher, and had some lessons on the cithern, which didn't hold me for long. My participation in the Tableau in which I appeared with a mandoline, suggested to me the idea to study that instrument. Signorina Ciarloni, a soloist on the harp at the Imperial Opera, who played also the mandoline, was invited to give me lessons. Mr. P——, one of the most assiduous frequenters of our "At Homes," a snobbish young man bursting with conceit and thinking a lot of his appearance, proposed to accompany me on the guitar, but our duets came to nothing, for it appeared that my partner could only play Bohemian songs, throwing himself into a sentimental attitude and studying his own reflection, with complacent eyes, in the mirror on the wall beside me, which reflected his proceedings.

Mme. Schwarzenberg, a great friend of ours, who was a splendid pianist and an artist to the finger-tips, asked me to sing at a musical party at her house. I sang there in public for the first time and it amused me very much to be treated as a professional singer. I should be wanting in modesty if I repeated all the compliments I received that night. Somehow or other I felt that I had a call for the stage and had missed my vocation and mistaken my profession of an opera-singer: the vision of treading the stage-boards stood before me night and day.

At Christmas we got up a concert for the benefit of Professor Albrecht, an old violincellist, whose pecuniary, circumstances were not very flourishing just then. My husband's aide-de-camps took the arrangement upon themselves. A raised platform had been put at the end of our hall, and chairs were placed in rows. We invited artists and *dilettanti* to take part in our concert. I had a duet and solo to go through and showed much courage at the rehearsal of the concert. It was poor Sergy who seemed much more excited and nervous, looking forward to that concert with excitement. At last the day of the great event arrived. I hardly knew how to get through it and spent that day like a professional prima-donna, reclining in a long chair and waiting for my triumphs. People began to arrive towards eight o'clock. There were a great many pupils of the Music Academy and the Philharmonic School among the audience. Every seat in the hall was rapidly filled up. We artists gathered behind a screen hidden from view by big plants. The agitation I felt over my *début*, before a select audience of musical critics, may easily be imagined. I had never sung in a concert before and was going to enjoy an entirely novel and exciting experience. Just before the beginning of the performance, whilst I sucked vigorously a pastille to clear my throat, a waiter brought us a bottle of champagne to keep up our courage, to the great alarm of Sergy, who thought that I had been taken by a sudden access of timidity and needed the help of that stimulating drink to hearten me. Before making my appearance on the platform I had an attack of stage-fright, but I soon recovered my self-possession, and after the first note I lost my fear entirely. Taking care not to look at the audience I directed my glances above their heads, trying to persuade myself that all the audience was merely furniture. My first aria was Gounod's " Ave Maria," to the accompaniment of Professor Albrecht on the cello. A storm of applause arose, and I was recalled several times. " Bis, bis," ran round the room and I had to sing again and again. I don't wish to boast, but my triumph was complete. Mr. Schostakowsky, the director of the Philharmonic Society, who was critical to the extreme, approved, nodding his head, and when the first part of the concert was over, he came up to me and complimented me upon my singing. There was a quarter-of-an-hour interval for gossip and refreshment, during which Count Kergaradec, the French Consul, thanked me for the pleasure my singing had given him, telling me that I was equally pleasing to the ear and to the eye. I was very flattered, very excited, very happy, and realised that the stage was my proper sphere. There! I am on the point of failing in modesty, and stop ! When the performance was at an end, and the audience filed out, we invited some friends to supper. I was too excited to go to bed until dawn. Every one agreed that our concert was a wonderful success. Our desire to raise as much money as we could was fulfilled, the collection mounted to over eighty pounds, which we handed over triumphantly to Prosessor Albrecht. We did not expect so large a profit.

Our Governor-General, Prince Dolgorouki, underwent the same fate as Count Brevern de-la-Gardie, my husband's chief;

he was made to understand that it was time for him to give up his post. The uncle of our Emperor, the Grand-Duke Sergius, who was married to Elizaveta Fedorovna, Grand-Duchess of Hessen-Darmstadt, the granddaughter of Queen Victoria and sister of our Empress, was named Governor-General of Moscow in his place. I had to go and meet the Royal pair at the railway station, my name being put in the list with all the ladies, who were to present the image of the Virgin to the Grand Duchess. All the so-called "high-life" of Moscow had assembled at the station. When the train was signalled we went on to the platform covered with red cloth. The Grand-Duke, giving his arm to his spouse, advanced towards the Mayor of the town, who presented them with a silver plate and on it the traditional "Bread and Salt," an ancient Russian custom. On the next day I was presented to the Grand-Duchess, and found myself amidst a lot of ladies standing in a semi-circle in one of the large halls of the palace. The Grand-Duchess was going round, speaking a word of welcome to everyone of us. I was curious to watch the expression of the ladies waiting for the honour of being addressed by Her Imperial Highness; some of them dropped profound courtesies till they almost disappeared.

In May the French Exhibition on the Khodinka Field was inaugurated under the presidence of M. Ditz-Monin, a Senator of the French Republic. There were many interesting things to be seen at the Exhibition. The sections of jewellery and costumes were admirable; beautiful costumes were exhibited by Redfern and Paquin, but the prices were exorbitant: a splendid ball-dress cost neither more nor less than 10,000 francs.

Admiral Gervais visited Kronstadt with the French squadron of ships, and came with all his officers to visit our old city. A banquet was given in their honour at the Exhibition, in the Imperial Pavilion, where everything was done grandly. Caviare was served in a big barrel, and ice-cream was made in the shape of the Eiffel tower with tiny French and Russian flags stuck into the top, which the naval officers pinned in their button-holes as souvenirs. One of the young marine officers exchanged visiting-cards with his neighbour at table, the Vice-Governor of Moscow, who, on returning home, showed it to his wife, and to her great amazement she read on the wrong side of the card the addresses and prices of the most popular courtesans of Moscow, pencilled on it, with the officer's personal valuation of them. I can well imagine how the young mariner felt when he found out his mistake!

The French officers were present at a night retreat on the Khodinka Field, after which a great supper was given in their honour at the Military Club, illuminated *a giorno*. I stood amongst the crowd of lookers-on when the mariners were proceeding to the dining-room. There arose on their passage a mighty shout: "Long live France!" and the French officers shouted: "Long live Russia!" Innumerable toasts were drunk to the prosperity of France and Russia during the repast. My husband pronounced a long discourse in French, after which Admiral Gervais addressed himself to General Malahof, the oldest Russian military commander present, and said that as he hadn't the opportunity to shake hands with all the Russian officers sitting at table, he asked permission to kiss the old General for them all. The champagne had loosened the tongues of the guests, and one of them, having suggested the wish that France and Russia should fight together against Prussia some day, a voice cried: "We'll enter Berlin together!" after which the subject of conversation was diplomatically changed. Next day the French mariners returned to St. Petersburg on their way to Portsmouth, where Queen Victoria was to meet them.

CHAPTER LIII

A TRIP TO EGYPT

THE microbe of globetrotting having entered us, my husband took a month's leave and at the end of September we started on a trip to the East. I was so pleased I could kiss the whole world! We travelled by train to Sebastopol, where an omnibus, drawn by six horses, stood ready for us. There were so many passengers that I hadn't much room for my legs and felt pins and needles in them, and a horrible disjointed feeling, as though my limbs didn't belong to me. The road leading to Yalta was beautiful but very wild, composed of zigzags and terrifying angles ; high cliffs towered on each side of the road. Half way on we drew up at a post house where we had dinner, and arrived at Yalta towards night. We found there my cousin Zoe Zaroudny, who was to travel with us to Constantinople.

The next day we took the "Oleg," a Russian boat going straight to the shores of the Bosphorus. Except ourselves there were only three passengers on board : Mme. Lebedeff, an orientalised European, wearing a scarlet fez, who was returning to Constantinople, and two inhabitants of Alexandria, father and son, whom we took for Greeks, very taciturn-looking both of them. Our crossing was not agreeable, the sea being very rough. I was roused in the night by a terrible squall, which subsided only towards morning.

CHAPTER LIV

CONSTANTINOPLE

TOWARDS midday, when we entered the "Golden Horn," we were plentifully rewarded for our bad passage by the enchanting view of the bay, the harbour of Constantinople being one of the most beautiful in the world. We passed the Citadel and the "Dolman-Baghtcha Palace," where Mourad, the deposed Sultan, is kept prisoner; all around the castle stood sentinels. We glided now along the verdant shores of "Boyouk-Dere," the summer residence of the Ambassadors, and dropped anchor at Constantinople.

The town scrambles up and spreads itself over three sharp-sided hills. It is divided into three quarters: Scutari, on the Asiatic shore, inhabited mostly by Mahometans; Stamboul; and Pera-Galata, on the European side of the "Golden Horn," joined by a long bridge to the Asiatic shore, where all the Embassies, banks and hotels are concentrated.

As soon as we were moored to the shore, a fleet of caïques surrounded us, and a crowd of sallow-faced guides invaded the deck, offering their services. We stepped into a canoe which took us to the Custom-House. After having got our baggage speedily chalked, we called a carriage and drove to the Hôtel de Londres, by narrow and badly paved streets, where appalling beggars and cripples of every description exposed to the eye their sores and insisted upon thrusting their distorted limbs into our faces. It was sickening to look at them!

The streets in Constantinople are awfully dirty, all the refuse is carried out and spilt into the middle of them, and the homeless dogs, who serve here as sweeps, lick them up greedily. Each street has its own band of dogs, who bark and howl throughout the whole night. The carriages and horsemen don't abstain running over them, and the greater part of these poor mongrels are lacking, here a paw, and there a tail. We saw fat Greeks chatting in groups, coffee drinking and smoking before their open shops. The Imams, in white turbans and flowing robes, sat dreaming on the threshold of their dwellings. They are also free to engage in trade, and it is not uncommon to discover that an Imam owns a melon-shop, or proves to be a milkman. Long white veils conceal the form of the Turkish women from head to foot, whenever she leaves her house. I remarked that the old women, to whom age and ugliness permitted their faces to be revealed without offending the Musulman's ideas of propriety, were particularly well wrapped in their *chadras*, leaving only their eyes exposed, but the young and good-looking ones are not averse to show a little more.

The Hôtel de Londres being quite full, we were led into a large saloon, which was hastily converted into a bedroom. It was all windows on one side, and seemed horribly uncomfortable. Looking about me with dissatisfied eyes, my face began to lengthen. I suppose it was very silly, but I felt so tired and out of sorts that I could have cried.

On the day following our arrival we explored the outskirts of Constantinople. The Sultan had the amiability to send his aide-de-camp to go about with us to all the places of interest we should like to visit, and put at our disposal, as often as we pleased to use it, one of his row-boats with ten men. This Turkish officer, a very stylish young man, was the son of Jakir Pacha, ex-Ambassador of Turkey at St. Petersburg, where he has been educated in the Corps-des-Pages. He speaks Russian and French to perfection. He told me that he had a tedious time at Constantinople and was pining for St. Petersburg. In the first place he took us to Dolma-Bachtche Palace, and the Museum of Eski-Sarai, where we saw a throne inlaid with precious stones, dating from the 16th century. We went afterwards to the Cathedral of St. Sofia, transformed now into a Mosque. All the Christian paintings on the walls are scraped out, except a big image of Christ, which the Mussulmans could not manage to rub off. Then we were rowed over to Scutari, on the opposite shore, in a rich yawl with scarlet velvet cushions belonging to the Sultan. Its crew, ten bronzed-skinned men of athletic build, showing bare, muscular brown hands and legs, rowed vigorously bending to the oars. We moored before Belerbey Palace, and entered an immense hall with a marble floor, mirrored walls, and a fountain in the middle, looking out upon the Bosphorus. Before leaving the palace, we visited the sumptuous apartments of the chief of the eunuchs.

The next day we went for a sail in a steam-launch belonging to the Russian Embassy, the swiftest vessel on the Bosphorus. After having moored at Boyouk-Dere we took a long walk in the gardens of the Russian and French Embassies ; the dead autumn leaves covered the paths with a yellow carpet, and were crushed under our feet. On our way back to Constantinople the moon showed above the hills, lighting the Bosphorus.

I repeatedly expressed the desire to be shown the interior of a Mussulman home, jealously kept hidden from the eyes of the curious, in order to see the domestic side of Turkish life. Mme. Lebedeff got the permission for my cousin Zoe and me to visit the harem of one of the Sultan's aide-de-camps, who, like all the modern Turks belonging to the upper classes, had only one wife. After having crossed the Stamboul Bridge, we took a small steamboat which brought us to Scutari. The master of the harem met us on the quay, and, touching his forehead to us, led us to his home, built round a courtyard. We were shown into a large hall, furnished chiefly with sofas draped in different coloured silks along the walls, with lots of cushions and oriental rugs; cigarettes were lavishly strewn on low tables before them. We were cordially welcomed by the Sultaness of the harem, a pretty plump woman saturated with perfume, her cheeks painted red and white, her lips of an unnatural crimson. She wore a fantastic apple-green dress with a broad silver belt which drew attention to the amplitude of her waist, and a small red velvet cap richly embroidered. Our hostess spoke very good French, and seemed very gay, though in the higher ranks of life harem ladies live a dull existence. It is a curious thing that, though they are never seen in public, they take an engrossing interest in their personal appearance, and dress and jewels absorb most of their time and attention. Rouge and other cosmetics are common in harems, and the examination of garments and ornaments is the first and almost the sole form of entertainment when visiting or receiving female friends. Our hostess was surrounded by pretty slave-girls, Circassians for the most part. We were asked to be seated, and soon an enormous old woman, bursting with fat—our hostess's mother-in-law—came in. She wore a dress of crying colours, and a bonnet trimmed with crotcheted flowers. This hippopotamus was treated with great deference. At her appearance everybody rose. She was followed by her daughter with her two little girls, in European dress, and her son, a fine boy of twelve, with fair curly hair, a pretty piece of diminutive manhood dressed like a grown-up, in the last Parisian fashion, his tie fastened with a large emerald pin; a very independent-looking little fellow, who was addressed reverentially as " Bey." Soon after, a slave appeared, a large bundle of keys hanging at her girdle, carrying a large tray covered with a green velvet napkin embroidered in gold, heaped with cakes and preserves flavoured with attar of roses, nauseously sweet, presented with a glass of water to wash them down. A negress followed, handing round coffee, served a la Turca, in tiny little cups like little egg-shells supported in filigree silver, and behind came a mulatto girl holding a silver censer. I felt as if I were at the opera, and the curtain had just gone up on a brilliant act of " Aida."

Presently we were invited into the dining-room, where a dinner of about twelve courses was served, all cooked in olive oil. The dishes were handed to our hostess first, and when she had served herself, the slaves served the guests. We ate our soup with spoons whose bowl was of tortoise-shell, and the handle of ivory tipped with coral. During the repast a band of musician-girls were seated cross-legged on the floor, playing noisily on their weird, strange-looking instruments, and making what they seemed to think was music. One of the slaves began to sing in a falsetto-voice, when suddenly there came a tap at the door and a few words in Turkish, that caused the slave-girls to jump hurriedly to their feet, drawing their veils over their faces. The door was flung open and the master of the house came in, followed by his father-in-law—an ex-Vizier. As a rule no male, except the woman's husband, father-in-law and brother-in-law, ever pass the threshold of the privacy of a harem. At the end of the dinner a slave-girl poured rose-water over our fingers from a copper jug, wiping them with a napkin of damask, after which our hostess threw on a blue cloak and led us into the garden, laid down in terraces, with lemon and orange trees bending under the weight of their fruit. In a large pond gold fish swam, and close by was a large cage filled with canaries. We sat on a hillock, admiring the beautiful birds' eye view of Constantinople and the Bosphorus, whilst the " Bey," the little man-child, picked flowers for Zoe and me. Night was drawing on ; it was time to bid farewell to our amiable hosts and return to the hotel.

My curiosity concerning harem life was not entirely satisfied. I wanted to visit a harem containing several wives. The interpreter of our hotel, a Circassian named Michael, who spoke twelve languages, proposed to show us a harem whose Pasha kept a dozen wives. Sergy did not approve of the expedition, but I had my own way and started off with Zoe and her lady-companion in an open carriage. We drove through narrow, winding streets. While we were slowly mounting a steep slope, we saw two women, wrapped in blue veils, descending almost perpendicular flights of street-steps cut in the rock, making signs to our driver to stop. After a hurried colloquy with Michael, who sat on the box, he had the carriage stopped to take them up, and explained to us that these women were going to serve as interpreters for us in the harem, where he could not be admitted. One of them was a Servian and could jabber a little Russian, and her companion spoke English.

We clambered down a steep bank to which a boat was moored to cross over to the other shore, and dismissed our carriage, having decided to return by steamer. We picked our way through a dingy side-street paved with pointed stones, between which weeds grew, and came up to a house of dubious appearance, with narrow iron-barred windows like those of a prison. At the sound of our bell the door was opened by an eunuch, who took us into a large room with an enormous bedstead, hung with green and gold brocade, standing in the middle. An odour of attar of roses filled the apartment. My curiosity was awfully excited ; I expected to see beautiful "houris," but was greatly disappointed. First of all appeared the Pasha's favourite wife, looking rather pretty, with a flower in her jet-black hair, her fingers stained with henna, and saturated with perfume so strong as to make you sneeze. Behind came the second wife, an insignificant little thing, followed by the third would-be "houri," a wrinkled old guy. For a quarter-of-an hour we stared speechlessly at each other, then losing patience, I asked our interpreter when the other nine wives would make their appearance, and she replied they were all out walking but would soon be back, but I was sure it was all a fib and that they were nothing but a myth. After a while the wife No. 1 began to talk to our interpreters in a low voice, after which they came up and told us that we had to be presented to the master of the house. Here was something that didn't enter our programme, but we had to undergo the ordeal which seems to be the custom here. We were taken into a big room and ushered into the presence of the Pasha, a white-bearded patriarch, wearing an enormous white turban, who was sitting on a low divan upon a pile of cushions, with his legs tucked under him. A little nigger boy, one of his numerous offsprings, was playing at his feet with a wooden horse. The Pasha signalled for us to be seated, and fixed Zoe and me with a long stare over his spectacles, seeming to approve of us. He called one of our interpreters and asked if Zoe and I were sisters, and ordered her to tell us that he wanted to keep us both in his harem. Finding the proceeding of too oriental a fashion, we hurried away under the pretext that my husband was waiting for us outside. The old Satyr appeared very much displeased that we slipped out of his grasp, and when taking leave of us he gripped my hand and squeezed my fingers to make me cry out. Who could have thought of that old man being so inflammable ! We ran down the stairs and rushed out, happy to have got off so cheaply from this mouse-trap. Being too late for the steamer, we took a ferry-boat. It was nearly night when we were back at the hotel, and marched in to dinner, which was half over.

The day of the "Selamlic," the birthday of Mahomed, when the Sultan leaves his palace in great pomp and goes to the neighbouring "Hamidieh Mosque" to public prayers, fell that year on a Friday, the Mahomedan Sabbath. Thanks to Mme. Lebedeff, we had the opportunity to see the ceremonial of the "Selamlic," and the Sultan's State visit to the mosque. She had got cards of admission for us to the terrace of one of the wings of the palace, where places were reserved for the members of the diplomatic corps with their wives and daughters. Mme. Lebedeff came to fetch Zoe and me in her phaeton, in a grand toilet, with a Turkish Order glittering on her breast, which made her look very pompous and very patronising. Great animation reigned in the town ; people crowded in the streets so that our carriage could scarcely move. The windows and house-tops were full of spectators, and the native women seemed to be all out of doors, walking about in groups, wrapped up in long white veils which covered them from head to foot. In a narrow street we had got into the stream of carriages, and nearly ran into a cab. In a moment I was out of the phaeton, just when a platoon of soldiers was advancing on me. Seeing my critical position, a young Turk, who occupied the cab we got into, asked me to get into his carriage, but Mme. Lebedeff drew me back hastily. At length, after many struggles, we arrived at our destination and mounted on the terrace, where Constantinople's high society had gathered in a brilliant throng around us. On the square under our feet were guards of honour and massed troops : twelve battalions, fifteen squadrons and eight military bands, were ranged. We found ourselves just over the bayonets of a regiment of Tunis Zouaves, very good-looking, dark-skinned men. The Muezzin in the minaret began to call to prayers, and there soon appeared a smart coach containing the recluses of the Sultan's harem, preceded by the Grand-master of the eunuchs, and two negro and two white footmen. The numerous sons of the Sultan, armed with spears, came behind cantering on magnificent steeds. An infinite number of Pashas, Beys and Effendies brought up the rear, with a great number of German officers, who had come to Constantinople to teach the military art to the Turkish army ; and then, to the desperate and wild sounds of the Turkish bands, the Sultan appeared, reclining in a victoria with a coachman in Albanian costume. The Padishah was acclaimed with enthusiasm by the populace, and the troops saluted, him putting their hand on the breast and forehead. As soon as the Sultan had entered the Mosque, religious chants were heard. On Friday the service lasts twenty minutes usually, but this time it was prolonged more than an hour through the reading aloud of the Prophet's biography. The Sultan returned to the palace mounted on a fine long-tailed Arab ; the horse's trappings and saddle were covered with precious stones. The Sultan stood at his window whilst the troops defiled before him. After the review paper-bags full of sweets were distributed to the soldiers. I had, as it appeared, conquered the heart of one of the Zouave soldiers, standing just under me, who stared at me with presistence when his officer was away. I looked down upon him and nodded to him to throw me a bonbon and he replied, by gesture, that he was afraid of his officer, who was now watching our little manœuvre. Just then bonbons and cool drinks were being handed on trays to the guests on the terrace, and this time it was my warrior who asked me to throw him a bonbon. An over ripened lady, meagre as a gutter-cat, who stood by me, understood the signal as being addressed to her, and thrusting a coquettish glance at the Zouave, she threw him a chocolate, which he kicked away contemptuously with his boot. As I couldn't help smiling, the affronted lady looked daggers at me, but I didn't mind it a bit and recompensed my bronze-faced admirer by throwing to him a sugar-candy. He stooped down and picked it up, then he raised his hand high, so that I could see that he had the candy in it, and looking up with a smile, he kissed the bonbon and threw it into the pocket of his vest. When the Zouave regiment was leaving the place, and marched away, my soldier took a last look at me and went off, every now and then pausing to look back, and almost broke his neck with efforts to catch a last glimpse of me.

Constantinople did not offer a great deal in the way of distraction ; in the evenings, especially, we were at a loss for amusements. We had quite enough of Turkey and took the " Tzar," a Russian boat bound for Egypt. On our way to the embarkment we entered a Greek church, where a big chandelier bearing the form of a ship, hung from the ceiling, to assure us a safe passage, and get the blessing of St. Nicholas, the patron of the navigators.

Our steamer was a veritable floating hotel, reuniting all the advantages of modern comfort. In the hold were packed 1,800 sheep, a drove of cattle, a large cage full of fowls and three pairs of splendid Russian steppers, who were to be sold at Cairo ; each pair of horses cost 4000 roubles (about four hundred pounds.)

In the night we crossed the Marble Sea, and early the next morning we perceived the Dardanelles, and heard the beat of the drum on the opposite shore. Towards evening we entered the Archipelago, strewn with rocky islands, and passed before Lesbos, with shores scorched by the sun, without a tree or a blade of grass.

CHAPTER LV

ATHENS

WE waited for daybreak to enter the narrow port of Piræus. The Russian military agent, Baron Traubenberg, came to meet us in a launch belonging to a Russian man-of-war, in which we went over to the landing-stage, and then up to Athens by train. The journey was a short one, we got there in twenty minutes. The country is unattractive, deprived of vegetation and looking fearfully burnt up ; the prevalent colour is sandy-yellow.

We had but little time for sight-seeing at Athens, the "Tzar" remaining at anchor only till night. The dusty streets, the want of water and the poverty of the population left a disagreeable impression upon me, and the heat was intense. We were nearly roasted alive by the scorching sun. When passing before the Royal Palace, we were amazed by the simplicity of the railing surrounding it. In the absence of the Royal family the people are allowed to go into the palace, and a lackey offered to escort us over it. The state apartments are worth showing, but the upper suits of rooms are of Spartan simplicity. After having visited the Temple of Theseus, we drove up a long steep hill fringed with spiky cactus plants, leading to the Acropolis, the citadel of ancient Athens, which dominates the whole town.

When we returned to our ship we found new passengers : Lady Denmore, the wife of a high British dignitary, whom she was going to rejoin in India, and a pleasant American pair— Mr. and Mrs. Holland—elderly, childless people, talking with a strong American accent. They were going to Cairo. In the night the sea grew rough, and we were tossed about during two days. On the third day we entered the African waters and perceived a yellow band of sand ; birds, forerunners of land, were flying over our ship, and soon the outlines of the port and the mosques of Alexandria came in view.

CHAPTER LVI

IN PHARAOH LAND

HERE we are on the threshold of the Great Desert! As soon as the "Tzar" dropped anchor, stopping alongside a Russian cruiser, the "Nakhimoff," our vessel was invaded by a crowd of natives who precipitated themselves on our luggage. They were all speaking at once, shouting and gesticulating; the scene reminded me of the attack of savages in "Aida." We looked about us for the right sort of person to accompany us in the capacity of guide to Cairo, and finally hired for the service a dusky Arab named Mahmoud, on whose jersey was embroidered in big white letters: "I speak Russian."

Everybody went on shore, but we decided to pass the night on board and start in the morning to Cairo. We passed a very bad night, the Egyptian sun having turned our cabin into an oven and we could not open the porthole through the close proximity of the cruiser "Nakhimoff," alongside which we were anchored. At six o'clock we took a carriage to drive us to the railway station through the broad streets of Alexandria. The inhabitants we met on our way were for the most part negroes of different shades, and blue-robed, dark-skinned Fellahs. The native women, black-shrouded and veiled, wear a piece of black lustring wrapped round their bodies, making of them formless lumps, and giving them a ghastly aspect; a black veil is suspended on a metal cylinder, which is placed between the eyes with texts out of the Koran inscribed inside.

Before taking the train to Cairo, we had to pass through the preliminaries of the Customs. Thanks to our guide, Mahmoud, we have obtained, by special favour, the permission for our boxes not to be opened. It took three hours to get from Alexandria to Cairo; every few minutes the train halted at a bustling station. At the stoppings the Arabs dusted our cars with long brooms made of ostrich feathers. The journey would have been perfect but for the heat and the dust; eyes, nose, mouth, were choked with it, and by the time we reached Cairo, our hair was quite grey. All through our desert journey I had felt as if I had wandered into a dream of the Old Testament. Egyptian villages, with huts of dry mud of the same colour as the soil, with a maze of dust, of children, of animals and flies, emerged here and there from between the date-palms laden with fruit hanging in big bunches. On the road we saw great brown buffaloes going wearily round and round, turning the irrigating mills. Strings of burdened camels marched slowly along the road. Here is a Bedouin leaning forward upon the neck of his quick stepping horse, outriding a fat Fellah trotting on a small donkey with a woman sitting astride behind him, holding him round the waist. We now passed across the fertile delta of the Nile, through cotton plantations with their white flocks, and fields of ripening grain standing waist-high. In Egypt the land is so fertile that the harvest is got in three times a year. We are speeding along canals on which sailing-boats are gliding ; bands of natives and buffaloes are bathing in them. Here is the Nile, which is very high at this season, all the land between the Biblical river and the sands being hidden beneath the waters. We are approaching the Metropolis of Africa. The windows of every compartment of our train are framed with eager, longing faces, straining for the first glimpse of the Pyramids. There they are, looking quite close in the clear atmosphere. The first view of these colossal piles rather disappointed me : they did not appear on the horizon as big as I thought they would be. We crossed the Nile by a long bridge and arrived at Cairo, halting in a vast domed station. Then we took a carriage and went to the New Hotel, situated in the Esbekieh district, the European quarter of Cairo.

The season had not yet opened, and the hotel was comparatively empty, there being more servants than guests for the moment, but they were expecting a great number of visitors and great preparations were made : carpets were laid down, curtains were put up, and the sights and sounds of these preparations pursued us everywhere.

Everything around seemed so strange to me. There were no chamber-maids in the hotel, and bare-footed Nubians, wearing a flowing white cotton gown from neck straight to heel, served us.

On the day of our arrival we sat up late on the terrace of our hotel, looking out on the Esbekieh Gardens, where the Arab band is playing every night. I was astonished to hear Russian popular airs among their repertoire. Smart British officers, quartered in Cairo, in tight-fitting uniforms, strolled leisurely about the streets. Dignified Arabs, mysterious long-robed figures, appeared to float rather than walk, their white bournouses blowing behind them, native nurses wheeled perambulators, the negresses wrapped up in white veils and the Arab nurses in blue covers. A band of tourists, riding spirited little donkeys, passed along. Egyptian donkeys are fine little animals, holding their heads high like thoroughbreds; they are white for the greater part and shaved in designs. The best donkeys are brought out from Mecca, and valued higher than horses.

Oh, how hot it is in Cairo! It never rains here; sometimes clouds are to be seen on the horizon, but over the town the sky is permanently of azure blue. In the daytime we are bothered by a swarm of flies, and are devoured at night by greedy mosquitoes—a veritable Egyptian plague!

Our apartment is next to the Hollands, our new American friends, who travelled with us on board the "Tzar," from Piræus to Alexandria. Mrs. Holland is a charming lady, but rather despotic; she could twist her husband round her little finger. He was very mild and fond of peace.

Mr. Koyander, the Russian consul, placed himself at our disposal and gave us a great deal of interesting information. It is now the "Ramadan," one of the biggest Mussulman feasts, and the Arab quarter of the town is especially animated. We drove with Mr. Koyander through narrow and dirty streets and arrived at a great open place. I was extremely interested by the panorama of the East which passed before our eyes. We met the most varied types: magnificent Arabs; Syrians in red mantles; Copts—Christians of the Greek faith—wearing black turbans; blue-clad figures of Fellahs in a garb that recalled the ill-omened coat of Joseph; and other specimens of the brown children of the Nile. The Egyptian women have painted chins and a ring stuck through their noses. The eyes of their babies were stuck round with flies, the poor mites being too apathetic to drive them away. This oriental throng, in turbans, stared at us unbenevolently, except a young negress, carrying a naked baby astride on her shoulder, who offered me a piece of sugar-cane, smiling and showing beautiful, glittering white teeth. We passed with some difficulty through the crowd and manœuvred between the tables, laid out with refreshments, set in the middle of the streets, and entered an Arab café to see the dances of the "bayaderes," or Egyptian dancing-girls. At the entry hung a dark curtain, covering the open doorway, which was lifted for us to pass, and we found ourselves in a small hall where three "bayaderes" sat upon a raised platform; they were covered with gauze, with reddened lips and palms, wearing massive golden ear-rings, their hair twisted into innumerable thin ringlets at the end of which hung golden coins, with silver bracelets jingling on their bare ankles and their arms. We waited for their dances in vain, these daughters of the East absolutely refused to exhibit themselves before "Giaours" (Christians), and passed their time in throwing alluring glances at a group of good-looking young "hadjis" (men who had made the pilgrimage to Mecca or Medina), sitting in the first row.

The next day we visited the mosque of "Amrou." Before entering it, we were told to tie on straw slippers upon our shoes. In the shadow of the mosque it was nice and cool. A palm had grown in the second court near a cistern where pilgrims performed their ablutions. The mosque is a large square building containing a whole forest of miraculous columns—"Proof Columns," as they are called—standing very near each other, and giving passage to the "Just" and keeping back the "Perverted." The proof can't be precisely right, for according to it, it is only slim individuals who are ascertained to be the "Just," while those inclined to be fat, always appear to be "Perverse." A "muezzin" was chanting the Koran, in the middle of the mosque, to a throng of pilgrims prostrating themselves in prayer before the tomb of Caliph Amrou, who was buried on the spot where he had been killed during a great slaughter, which took place in the altar during the fight of the Arabs and the Mamelukes.

We mounted on the citadel that same afternoon. Before reaching the old fortress built on the spur of the Mokattam hills, we passed threatening British cannon, which kept watch over the town of Cairo, and passed through the iron-clamped gates to the wide courtyard where stands the mosque of Mohammed-Ali, now converted into barracks. When we returned to the hotel our way was barred by a funeral procession, escorted by a group of dervishes bearing ragged banners and chanting the Koran to the accompaniment of drums, and hired women-mourners, who beat their breasts and scratched their faces wailing lamentably all the time. Behind them the favourite donkey of the deceased was led. Some steps further we were brought to a standstill by a wedding procession. A rich palankeen, bearing the newly married couple appeared, placed on two shafts, to which two splendid dromedaries were harnessed, one behind and one in the front, covered with bright scarlet nets and decorated with tufts of white ostrich feathers and little silver bells. Camels heavily laden with the wedding gifts brought up the rear.

The mighty Pyramids seem to stand quite near to Cairo, and still it takes an hour and a half to drive to them by a long avenue of great trees with meeting branches, stately leafy veterans, whose thick tops, forming a cool vault, prevented the sun from scorching us when we drove on the Ismail Road that leads from Cairo to the Pyramids. We crossed an iron bridge over the Nile, which, though at its fullest now, is not very deep; a drove of buffaloes were crossing it easily. We passed through the mud-built village of Sakhara, a small encampment with a cluster of nomad tents, and saw a circle of Arab-Bedouins, cloaked and white hooded forms, belonging to a nomad tribe, crouching over a fire and cooking their dinner in the plain, under the scanty shade of palm-trees. Their Sheikh, a very tall and dignified Arab, offered us a camel and a donkey to go and see the Sphinx. Sergy mounted the camel and I had to condescend to the donkey. We were followed by a band of Bedouins who offered us their services as guides to the Pyramids. Our escort increased as we went on ; half-naked children ran after us begging baksheesh. Directly after leaving the village we were in the Sahara, with no tree or habitation, only the naked desert with rippling sand-banks. The landscape fatigued the eye by its sand uniformly yellow and its sky uniformly blue. The Pyramids, the greatest of all human monuments, bewildered us by their size when we drove up to them, especially the Pyramid of Cheops, which took a hundred thousand masons twenty-five years to build. The Pyramids are of extreme antiquity, a thousand years before the Christian era. At the time when Abraham undertook his journey to Egypt, the Pyramids had already existed for several centuries back. As soon as a Pharaoh began to reign, in the first place he had his mausoleum built in the form of a Pyramid. Inside, rooms with alabaster walls are shown, and long high galleries containing the huge granite sarcophaguses. We made the tour of the great Pyramid of Cheops. Its blocks consist of a series of steep stone steps. To go up these steps is like walking up a wall. The hard African sun was shining fiercely and it was too hot to undertake the ascent of the Pyramid ; we were contented to contemplate its wonders from the base. A young Bedouin proposed to show us a wonderful feat—his ascent and descent of the Pyramid in nineteen minutes, but we refused to witness that acrobatic performance and rode over the hot yellow sand of the desert to the Sphinx. All around us the great plain extended to the horizon. I was oppressed by the immense solitude. In the desert, in the midst of the sand-ocean, the monstrous Sphinx, the colossus of the past ages, keeps watch on the sands from nearly four thousand years before the birth of Christ, sleeping his eternal and enigmatic sleep. How many centuries have past, and this giant continues contemplating, with a mysterious and condescending smile, the nothingness and instability of the world. Hundreds of years after I am dead the Sphinx would be probably as it is now—silent, grave, crouching there under the scorching sun, its eyes of stone gazing beyond the world of men, and seeming for ever to be smiling ironically on the folly of human vanities and aspirations. I looked at the wonderful beast that lay gazing westward, with mocking, calm and fathomless eyes of everlasting mystery, and was conscious of a sudden sense of smallness. If it hadn't been so hot I should have meditated on the fragility of human greatness. A legend says that Mary, Joseph, and the Holy Child halted here on their long journey, when they fled to the land of Egypt to escape the fury of King Herod, and that the Virgin laid the tired Christ between the paws of the Sphinx to sleep. We had brought a small kodak with us, and Mahmoud immortalised me installed on the back of my peaceable courser, and my husband perched on his high quadruped, both of us surrounded by a multitude of dusky sons of the Sahara. When we got to our carriage we amply recompensed the services of our Bedouin followers, who continued to run after our carriage demanding more tips and shouting "Baksheesh, Sahib, baksheesh!" Mahmoud put out of himself by their effrontery, rose in his seat looking remarkably ferocious, and began to throw stones at them, at which the whole crowd took to their heels. We had to return full speed to Cairo, before the drawbridge was raised for the ships to pass; we tore through the bridge which is a mile long, scattering the foot-passengers who happened to be in our way to right and left.

The next day we went on donkeys to see the "whirling dervishes," an extraordinary and rather terrific sight. We entered a mosque consisting of a square hall, with sheepskins laid down in the middle, on which a score of dervishes, in long white skirts, were ranged in a wide half-circle. Their Sheikh, an old man with a long white beard, stood between them holding the Prophet's banner. The dervishes, their long hair falling to their shoulders, swayed their bodies from side to side, uttering ominous sounds like that of angry lions. I glanced around with an involuntary shiver, and went and sat at the back of the hall, near a group of officers of the Egyptian army, feeling a sense of security in their proximity. Suddenly the Sheikh gave vent to an odd sort of growl which I didn't like at all, it made me think of wolves. The dervishes tried to imitate him and so horribly that I turned cold and measured the distance to the door, wanting frantically to get away. At each howl the dervishes' heads went backward and forward and then from right to left, to the sound of cymbals and blow-pipes, their long hair covering their faces, falling gradually into frantic convulsions, their eyes out of their sockets. One of them entered into such a frenzy that he continued for more than five minutes wagging his head, not being able to stop it by inert force. The long human chain holding each other by the hand, began bending to the ground to the increasing shouts of "Allah, Allah!" At last they fell on the floor inanimate, with foam on their lips. Having gone through all this programme, the dervishes, quietening down, came up to their Sheikh and kissed him.

When we went out of the mosque we had to pass before a sacred goat, a very wicked one, who tried to butt all the passers-by with his horns. We remounted our donkeys and our little cavalcade started off on the long white road. My frisky, little ass trotted swiftly, moving gaily his long ears, and Sergy had great difficulty to keep up to me, being obliged to struggle with his stubborn donkey which was vicious and kicked frantically all the time. We came up to a little desolate village inhabited by Copts, native Christians belonging to the Orthodox faith, and visited in the first place the Coptic church, built on the place where the Virgin Mary, Joseph and the Holy Child are said to have stayed when they fled to Egypt. We stood on the very spot where the Holy Family had rested. The water stood inches deep upon the floor from the overflowing of the Nile. When we went out of the church we saw on the perch a crowd of Coptic beggars who whined in English, "A penny for the love of Christ!"

On our way back we met a carriage preceded by musicians, and thought that it was a wedding, but instead of a newly-married couple we saw a little boy sitting between two natives, and were told that it was the circumcision of the little Egyptian which was being celebrated, by driving him in triumph around the streets of the quarter of the town where his parents lived.

We visited on the same day the enormous Mosque of "Amrou," which will contain about ten thousand people. Upon the floor were stretched hundreds of small bright-red carpets upon which the followers of the Prophet bent, muttering their prayers and went on with the monotonous chanting of "La-illah, illah-llah!" There is an Arabic academy, the "Medressah School" for the education of "softas," (theological students) attached to the mosque. This academy is a grand edifice supported by 180 columns and lighted by a thousand lamps, has accommodation for 11,000 students and 325 professors. When we entered one of the immense halls of the academy, we saw a white-bearded professor, wearing a green turban that means he is a "hadji," and has been to Mecca, sitting on the floor and reading a lecture to a solid mass of white-robed youths, who sat cross-legged before their teacher, bowing and swaying towards him. We were told that before a student becomes an "imam" he must study for fifteen years in order to be admitted formally to the clergy.

Next day Mr Koyander, who was well acquainted with Egyptian antiquities and could decipher indecipherable inscriptions, took us to see the Ghiseh Museum, where in large glass cases lay Egyptian mummies, which had been human beings of flesh and blood three thousand years ago. The bowels of the mummies are put in a box and laid at the feet of their sarcophagus. We saw the mummy of Sette I., the Pharaoh whose daughter had found out baby-Moses on the banks of the Nile, and that of Rameses II., the father of *one hundred and seventy children!* Both mummies are admirably preserved, as well as that of Amanit, the great priestess. She lies upon her back, her mouth open, showing all her teeth ; her long black hair is still attached to the scalp, and the skin to the bones.

We made some excursions out of town. We went one day in the direction of Mataryeh, about five miles from Cairo, to see the Virgin's sycamore-tree, under which the Holy Family took rest. The way leading there gives you the impression of old Bible-times. The vegetation is magnificent, cactuses, bamboos and date-palms everywhere. The grass on the lawns is more than five feet high. We went along shady avenues and crossed lotus, maize, and sugar-cane fields. The Virgin's sycamore is enclosed by a wall which measures about a mile in length. The railing surrounding the tree is locked up. We had it opened and saw a great number of names, to which we added ours, engraved on the mighty trunk of the sycamore, all ragged by lapse of time and intertwined with branches. An ancient legend says that the Holy Family on their flight to Egypt remained two years absent, and lived at the little village of Mataryeh. About fifteen minutes' walk from the spot was the celebrated town of Iliopel, which is mentioned in the Bible. Very few fragments remain of the town, except a high obelisk, which is supposed to be the oldest in Egypt ; it is of granite, and the height is over sixty-five feet. It is there that Moses had been a priest.

We continued our way to the ostrich farm built on the moving sands of the Great Desert. It is kept by a French company, but the men who are occupied with the rearing of the huge birds are all Bedouins. At the entrance there is an inscription in French " *Parc aux auturches* " (Ostrich Park.) It contains about a thousand winged creatures, perched high on their long legs. The males are covered with black curling feathers, only the tail is cream-coloured, and the females are all grey-feathered. The heads of the giant birds reach far above the grating surrounding the farm. The gathering of the feathers, which takes place once a year in May, requires great precautions. The ostrichs gathered into an enclosure are pushed one by one into a kind of box placed on four posts. Closed between the four boards, the bird is unable to fling out his terrible kicks, which could easily smash the operator's legs and arms. Eight men must hold the ostrich during the operation. The section of artificial brooding is very interesting ; it is often practised, as the ostriches, sitting during forty-three days on their eggs, frequently perish. Each ostrich gives yearly about a thousand francs of profit.

Before leaving the farm we bought a dozen beautiful feathers and a pair of enormous ostrich eggs. On our way back to Cairo we saw in the distance in the desert a vast English camp.

On the Isle of Rhoda, the broadest arm of the Nile, there is a Nilometer dating from the time of the Pharaohs. We went to see it, and crossed on the other side of the island in a caïque, in the company of bare-footed Arabs. We moored to the spot where the daughter of the Pharaoh found Moses. The Nile being now in overflow, the Nilometer was submerged in the water to the very top. The native women, with bronze arms, were drawing water from the Nile in stone pitchers, and carried it away, balancing their picturesque burdens, gracefully poised on head and shoulder, recalling the Biblical times.

Every Friday in the "Gisheh," the Hyde Park of Cairo, about sundown, the aristocracy of the city take their drive. We went for a stroll in the park through a wide avenue bordered by thickly planted trees. In the large park-alleys broughams passed containing harem ladies with faces closely veiled with muslin, accompanied by their favourite slaves. A native of high degree came driving in an open carriage, with sandalled, gorgeously-clad syces (carriage runners), with white wing-like sleeves embroidered with gold, running before his carriage and clearing the way for their master. After our drive we had tea at a little inn on the bank of the Nile, where we found a nice sheltered place close to the river. Just in front was moored a *dahabiah*, a large sailing vessel cruising up the Nile as far as the Cataracts. We were immediately surrounded by a crowd of natives; one of them was offering "good bananas," in English, and another one wanted absolutely to clean our shoes.

Our arrival at Cairo had been advertised in the papers. The local authorities were warned and English reporters came to ask Mr. Keyander the reason of our visit to the Metropolis of Africa. They may be perfectly tranquilised, for we certainly have nothing to do with politics, Sergy and I!

It had been our intention to travel in Palestine after our tour in Egypt, but cholera was raging at Mecca, which, much to our disappointment, prevented us from going there.

I was sorry to say good-bye to Mrs. Holland. We parted with mutual regret and promises of letters. Kissing me fondly she said: "I love you awfully, darling; I have never met a more lovely little thing than you!" A few more kisses and we separated to follow our diverse destinies. Mrs. Holland stood on the doorway to see us off and waved her hand in friendly farewell, whilst the omnibus slowly carried us away.

We have learnt through Mr. Koyander that Mr. Abaza, a

very old friend of my family, who had known me at home as a little girl when I was still in short frocks, and whom I had lost sight of for a great many years, had settled in Alexandria. We let him know the day and hour of our arrival, and when we reached Alexandria, as we stepped out of the train, a gentleman came forward with both hands extended, saying, " A hearty welcome to you, Princess Vava ! " My amazement can well be understood, when Mr. Abaza proved to be the silent fellow-passenger who had crossed with us from Sebastopol to Constantinople, whom we had taken for a taciturn Greek. How extraordinary that we should meet like that ! Queer what a little place the world is ! It is so nice to have an old friend turn up in a far country !

We put up at Alexandria at the Hotel Abbat, where our guide Mahmoud served as dragoman. On the following afternoon we went on a visit to Mouchtar Pasha, the ex-commander of the Turkish army during the Russo-Turkish war, who had removed to Egypt, an old general overcharged with years and decorations. Our ancient foe came up with his hand out, welcoming us heartily. We had no need of an interpreter, the Pasha speaking very good French. Our host proposed a little refreshment ; and the next moment a turbaned servant came in with tea and stole out of the room silently, walking backwards.

Next day we went to see Mr. Abaza in Ramle, a little place situated at an hour-and-a-half's journey from Alexandria, where he owned a house of his own. We passed the hippodrome, a broad racing-ground, and a large plain utilised for purposes of recreation by cricketers and lawn-tennis players, arranged by the English colony of Alexandria. We now rolled through an arid and deserted country, swarming with all sorts of vermin, serpents, scorpions, bats, etc. As we approached Ramle the scene changed as if by magic, and we found ourselves in an ocean of verdure. Mr. Abaza came to meet us at the station, and led us to his pretty villa buried among the trees. He regaled us with a Lucullus lunch, with champagne in profusion. The meal was served by Arab servants clad in white, very well groomed and trained. Directly after lunch Sergy had to return to Alexandria to be received in private audience by the Khedive, and I remained at Ramle until night, Mr. Abaza having proposed to see me back safely to Alexandria.

I found my husband enchanted with his visit to the Khedive, who had been charming to him. We sat together with Mr. Abaza on the terrace of our hotel till late, and had a comfortable chat over old times.

CHAPTER LVII

OUR WAY BACK TO RUSSIA

NEXT morning, supplied with tickets from Cook's agency, we sailed for Italy on the " Amphitrite," a splendid steamer belonging to the Austrian Lloyd Company, a veritable floating town filled with every possible requirement. The third bell announcing our departure rung and the boat moved out to sea. Soon Egyptian land disappeared from view. The Adriatic, which is particularly treacherous, promised a stormy passage. There were big black clouds on the horizon and the wind was very strong ; we were in for rough weather ! The whole night our ship tossed about like a cockle-shell, and foaming waves broke against the port-holes of our cabin. I couldn't go to sleep till daybreak. When the liner swung into the familiar waters of the Mediterranean, it was calm as a lake. After the intense heat of Egypt it seemed very cold, but one is never satisfied with the temperature one has !

After six days at sea we arrived at Brindisi, where the formalities of landing are very strict. A pilot-boat came to meet us with a sanitary officer, who had a long conference with our ship's doctor. The pilot, at length, having ascertained himself that everything on board was right, hoisted the sanitary flag and piloted us to the Custom House, after which we took the train to Bari. Two American ladies, mother and daughter, occupied our compartment, and soon conversation began between us. The younger one told us that they came from the new world to the old one to have her trousseau made at Worth's. What a shame to leave her bridegroom for six months for her frivolities. This flighty bride said that in return she bought her sweetheart a collection of neckties in every capital of Europe.

We arrived in the afternoon at Bari, which seems very dull and poor, and took an antediluvian coach drawn by a drowsy nag, sent by the Hôtel Continental to the station. This hotel, the best one in Bari, proved anything but comfortable. A dirty, sleepy waiter showed us into a bare, cold room, and soon after an old witch, who had only one tooth in her mouth and wore enormous copper ear-rings, came to make our beds. After a spare lunch composed of a burnt chicken and a dish of macaroni, we went to visit the famous church where the relics of St. Nicholas repose. The temple swarmed with pilgrims. Two nuns were on their knees before the mausoleum of the Saint, waiting their turn to creep into the narrow nook where the holy remains are laid. We saw them crawling flat on the floor, and the attendant on duty began to drag them out by their legs to give up the place to other pilgrims. Before we left the church the pater put under our noses a big book in which generous travellers, leaving various sums of money as a gift to the church, put their names down. He tried to draw our attention on the signature of a Russian merchant who had bestowed the sum of a hundred roubles, but we did not take the hint, and he had to be satisfied with less than that sum.

When we went back to the hotel, dinner was served in our apartment. We went to bed directly after our meal. The room was like ice. We had to cover ourselves with all the shawls and rugs that we had brought with us, and still we couldn't get warm ; in spite of the cold, voracious mosquitoes ill-treated us the whole night. We got up very early, swallowed hastily a cup of nasty coffee and left for Naples. At the stations our train stopped as long as the guards wanted it. " *Partenza* ! " they cried out, but the train did not move. A lady, who travelled in our compartment, said that there were smugglers on the line, and told us some horrors which fairly made my hair stand on end. While she was going on with stories of smugglers, our train, which was going full speed, stopped suddenly the moment we entered a tunnel ; we were for long minutes in complete darkness and heard voices calling noisily and the sound of smashed glass. Good Heavens ! what could be the matter ? My imagination being awfully excited, I nearly died of fright. It appeared that our guards had forgotten to provide us with candles for the tunnel, and were doing so now, in the dark, breaking to pieces the lantern. I heaved a sigh of relief when we came out of the tunnel into the light again.

On the platform of Naples we were attacked by a swarm of facchini, who took our luggage by force and installed us in a cab, which brought us to the Grand Hôtel on the Chiaia. The traffic in the noisy streets of Naples was bewildering ; we had to proceed cautiously between carriages, heavy cars and laden donkeys. The horses in Naples are not bridled, and therefore very difficult to manage when they happen to be of an independent character. The horse who drew us was of amorous temperament and watched for an opportunity to flirt and bite his rivals all the way, and many a time I was on the point of jumping out of the carriage.

We took an apartment which looked out on to the Piazza Vittorio, where the Municipal band played in the afternoon. The weather was cold and raw, it rained steadily and we were forced to remain indoors.

Naples is not a cheerful place in wet weather and we were ready to turn our back to it and return to Russia, but the weather having cleared up on the third day of our sojourn, we decided to prolong our stay for a fortnight.   We wrapped ourselves up warmly and took the tram to make a tour round the town.   When passing the Emigrant's Office we saw a long line of pale-faced emigrants, with babies and bundles clasped in their arms, who were going to America, sitting on the ground and waiting their turn to subscribe themselves for expatriation.   After our drive, the guide took us through the Royal Palace, where we admired the beautiful Concert Hall, constructed by the Bourbons, with the marble statues of the nine muses standing along the walls.

Profiting by our stay in Naples, I wanted to take a few lessons on the mandoline, and Sergy bought me a costly pearl-inlaid instrument at Vinacio's, the best mandoline-maker.   A lady-teacher, recommended by our hotel-keeper, was engaged to instruct me in the difficulties of the "tremolo" on the strings, but she proved to be a very mediocre teacher and taught me the "tremolo" with her gloves on.   I did not repeat my lesson and Professor D'Ambrosio, a well-known musician and composer, was invited in her place.   I spent hours studying my mandoline, playing scales and exercises.

During the summer and autumn months, the San-Carlo, one of the biggest theatres in the world, is closed, and we went to see "Faust" at a small theatre, where the performance began very early, at six o'clock in the evening. The chairs in the first row cost only two francs.   The conductor of the orchestra seemed little more than a boy and could not be over twenty, and the performance didn't please me : Faust was too fat and Mephistopheles not diabolical enough ; Siebel had a fine mezzo-soprano, but boy's clothes did not suit the outlines of her stout figure, and Margaret had nothing of the woman but the skirt, and struggled against the almost impossible task of the mature woman impersonating a girl of seventeen, and was listening with all the coyness of forty years and six children at home, to the love-making of Faust.   At eight o'clock a new performance of " Don Giovanni " was about to begin, but our eyes closed with sleep and we did not purchase any more tickets.

On the 12th November we took the train to Rome.   I became suddenly aware that one of our fellow passengers, a dandy-looking young Italian, was staring at me over his newspaper.   He wore an eyeglass which made him squint a little and through which he couldn't see, I am sure, but his sight, evidently, was so excellent that he could well afford to sacrifice the vision of one eye, now and then, for the sake of effect.   He faced me with a gaze that made me long to box his ears.   Feeling awfully disturbed I looked anywhere but in his direction, and throwing myself back in my corner, I opened a magazine and pretended to be deeply engrossed in its pages. I slowly turned leaf after leaf; I turned so many that he became impatient and tried, in altering his position by moving up opposite to me, to take a better view of me and catch my eye, but my eye refused to be attracted. Then the persevering man tried to enter into conversation with me in asking permission to smoke. I bent my head in careless assent and pretended to become violently interested in the landscape. "What a splendid scene!" he exclaimed suddenly, but I continued to gaze out of the window and made no reply, laughing inwardly at this little manœuvre and regretting that I had no eyes behind my back to look on the other side and see his discomfiture. When we reached Rome we seized our bags and descended on the platform. We had to cross the railway line, running to catch the Florence train. Whilst my pursuer was calling a facchini to look after his luggage, he lost sight of us in the hurry of changing trains, rather to my regret, I must confess, for like Faust's "Margaret" "*Je voulais bien savoir quel etait ce jeune homme et comment il se nomme,*" I was so sorry that I didn't know who he was and where he came from. We entered an empty car, and Sergy promised the guard a good tip if he would leave us to be sole occupants of the compartment. All at once we saw my " Faust " running about the platform and peeping anxiously into all the cars. He started when he saw me at the window, and prepared to step in, when the guard slammed the carriage door in his face, and I never saw him any more!

When we arrived at Wirballen, the sight of our frontier, the Russian voices, the Russian train, the Russian porters were a joy to me. How nice it is to be home again! We found Moscow in full winter: all the streets were white.

CHAPTER LVIII

PROMOTION OF MY HUSBAND TO THE POST OF GOVERNOR-GENERAL OF THE AMOUR PROVINCES IN EASTERN SIBERIA

THERE was much talk about my husband's appointment to the post of Governor-General of the district of the Amour, including the provinces along the valley of the Amour river and the entire Eastern section of Siberia, instead of Baron Korff, whose health was beginning to fail. About this time my husband was frequently called to St. Petersburg on business. One morning an urgent telegram arrived; the Minister of War summoned my husband without delay to St. Petersburg. Sergy promised to send me a wire containing two words: "Great News," if the question concerned his nomination. I was in a state of great excitment until the telegram arrived. The next evening brought a wire from Sergy, it ran: "Great news!" I had expected it, and yet, it was a shock. But I resigned myself to my lot. I loved Sergy far too well to injure his prospects and I would follow him to the world's end resignedly.

When Sergy returned to Moscow he told me that Baron Korff was not leaving his post at present, but that a temporary function, that of adjunct to the Governor-General of the far east of Siberia, had been proposed to my husband.

It is too serious a resolution to be taken in a hurry, and Sergy went once more to St. Petersburg and took me with him. In the first place we called on Baroness Korff. A hundred questions were burning on my lips, but our visit was rather disappointing. The Baroness described Khabarovsk to us under awfully gloomy aspects, and left us under no illusion about our new abode, which seems as far as the moon to me, describing it as a place where no luxuries of civilisation can be procured, and said that we must be prepared to encounter terrible hardships and great privations. Really, it was not too enthusiastic a description, and did not sound promising at all. I had heard very much the same thing before, but not so emphatically stated. Our fine resolutions flew to the winds, and Sergy decided to refuse his appointment as adjunct to Baron Korff. I could sing victory!

A cloud came soon over our bright sky. An event took

place which completely modified our lives. One morning there come to us a startling and most appalling piece of news, informing us that Baron Korff had departed this life. My husband was summoned by telegram to return instantly to St. Petersburg, where he was told that he was named General-Governor of the Amour province.

My thoughts were in a state of chaos. I was glad to know at least what to expect. That painful uncertainty tortured me ; for days I had been almost without sleep, feeling the sword of Damocles suspended over me.

Sergy wanted me at first to remain in St. Petersburg with my mother, promising to come and fetch me in the middle of the winter ; but the thought that I should be separated from him for so long a time, and that seas should roll between us, was a veritable torture to me. Where he goes, I am bound to go too. I can't let him go alone to that impossible land, I can't and I won't ! My only wish is for Sergy's happiness. I am ready to sacrifice anything for him and to brave a lot of discomforts. I am determined to follow my husband. At least we won't have half the globe between us.

It is very hard, however, to part with our home and to remove to another quarter of the globe. But what is to be, will be. I must submit to the inevitable and look to the future with a firm face.

My husband received the order to start for Siberia within a month. We were making ready to depart and began preparations for our long journey to Khabarovsk, which is a serious undertaking. I had a great deal to think about. Our apartments were turned upside down ; the whole house was topsy-turvy. Packing cases encumbered the floor and professional packers came to pack our trunks. The sight of the empty, denuded rooms depressed me. Our home was broken up ! Our heavy luggage had been consigned to the " Nijni-Novgorod," a merchant vessel belonging to the Volunteer Fleet.

Colonel Serebriakoff, an officer attached to my husband's personal service, and his wife accompanied us on our journey to Khabarovsk, so did Mr. Shaniawski and Mr. Koulomsine, Sergy's private secretaries. Dr. Pokrowski, a surgeon in the Russian army, a dispenser of drugs, was necessary also on our hazardous voyage, and Mme. Beurgier, a former governess of Princess Mimi Troubetzkoy, one of my childhood's greatest friends, made up the party in the capacity of companion. I had sore need of a friend, and it is a great comfort to have dear Mme. Beurgier with me.

The nearer the time approached for our setting out, the more nervous I grew. The hour of our departure was in the papers, and arriving at the railway station we saw a crowd of friends to see us off, with plenty of hand-shakes, kisses and embraces. I was presented with five enormous bouquets, which were distributed in no time by people asking for flowers as souvenirs.

The signal was given for departure and hands and handkerchiefs waved frantically as the train glided out. I felt a lump in my throat on leaving dear old Moscow for good.

On arriving at St. Petersburg, my husband was welcomed on the platform by all the persons composing his staff, except Mr. Shaniawski, who, as an experienced traveller, had been sent out to Paris to arrange for our passage and secure berths for us on the Transatlantic s.s. "La Bourgogne," on which we had to cross the ocean to New York.

My husband received numerous visits of congratulation, and telegrams with testimonies of goodwill reached him from many parts.

We shall now have the Japs and the Chinese for close neighbours. The Ambassadors of both these yellow-faced nations try to get into our good graces. The Ambassador of China came to pay us a call of ceremony, accompanied by his first secretary, Mr. Li, who understands and speaks Russian quite well. This son of the Celestial Empire was our frequent guest and chose to fancy himself in love with me. He accompanied me nearly every night to a concert or a music-hall, under the chaperonship of Mme. Beurgier. He made himself very useful in fetching lemonade and cups of tea, and overloading me with flowers and bon-bons.

The moment had arrived when we could delay our departure no longer. Before leaving, I was bidden to Gatchina, the summer residence of the Empress Dowager, which is an hour by train from St. Petersburg. On arriving at Gatchina I found a carriage from the Imperial stables waiting for me, which took me to the Palace. I was ushered through a long suite of rooms into the one where the Empress sat. Her Majesty came up to me and was most gracious and charming. She said kindly words of welcome and wished me a happy voyage.

CHAPTER LIX

ACROSS THE ATLANTIC

IN the beginning of June we started to Khabarovsk taking the shortest way—*via* America—in order to visit the grand Exhibition that was being held that year at Chicago.

We were met at Paris by Mr. Shaniawski, who had prepared rooms for us at the Hôtel de Calais.

Paris was out of season and looked rather bare. We made a turn in the Bois de Boulogne, which proved a desert. We only met a middle-class wedding-party taking their traditional drive through the park, and nurses in white butterfly-like caps with flowing ribbons, wheeling perambulators and flirting with red-trousered soldiers.

On the following day we took the train to Havre, where we take passage on the "Bourgogne," a Transatlantic liner which is one of the largest, fastest steamers plying between Europe and America. The ship is equipped with baths, electric light and all modern necessaries. We had one of the best cabins situated in the prow, containing two berths, one above the other. I was to have the upper berth and climbed into its narrow proportions by a ladder. In an adjoining cabin I hear the Serebriakoffs stirring, and can chat with them whilst lying in my berth above my husband, through tiny holes cut in the wall for ventilation. The great difficulty that night was to get anything to eat. There was no such thing as a piece of bread to be had in the boat before starting, and we went supperless to bed, having been obliged to wait a long time for the sanitary doctor, as no one is allowed to land in New York without a bill of health.

12th June.—At six o'clock in the morning the steamer gave a long whistle, announcing that the moment for starting had come. I dressed rapidly, and hurried on deck. The ship was all alive and full of the bustle of departure. Good-byes were said in haste, people clung, wept and kissed. The gangway is lifted up, and we begin slowly to move away. I watched the harbour of Havre grow smaller and smaller, until it faded away in the horizon. Swinging in a deck-chair I began to examine our travelling companions in whose company we are going to live for ten days. More than half the first-class passengers on our ship were Americans coming home ; a great many seemed to know each other. I studied the passenger list, and saw that there were two Russians among them : an artillery Colonel, who is sent on business to America, and an old man, aged eighty-one, going to America to take part in a Volapuk Congress. We were taking a great number of emigrants for America. They thronged the foredeck, and crouched on the deck with their heads supported on bundles. Women stood in groups with children in their arms, or clinging to their hands and skirts. Things didn't go well with the emigrants in their old country. They crossed the ocean in search of luck and fortune on the other side of the water, but what was the life to which they were going forth on the steamer, taking them to an unknown fate in an unknown land ?

In the afternoon we passed Trouville and towards evening we perceived the Isle of Wight with its two light-houses pointing on the horizon. The coast soon melted away in the distance. It was our last good-bye to dear old Europe—and *en route* for the New World !

13th June.—I awoke in tears, having dreamt that I was saying good-bye to the nearest and dearest that I had left in Russia. I am miserable and home-sick, which is even more than being sea-sick. I lay flat on my back staring at the ceiling in blank despair. If I had wings I should have flown back to St. Petersburg !

The routine of steamer-life was eating, sleeping, resting in deck-chairs and promenading on the deck. We are fed on board like cattle destined for the slaughter-house. In the morning from nine to ten, breakfast, consisting of broth, tea, coffee or chocolate, and porridge—the first course at every breakfast ; at one o'clock lunch, at six dinner, and at nine tea. A waiter runs through the corridors, ringing a huge bell before each repast. We had a separate table reserved for us. The waiters on board, rigid and dignified, have the manners of a secretary of an embassy ; the waiter who serves at our table looks less Olympian.

The barometer stood high all the time, nevertheless the ocean tosses us pitilessly. Our steamer was rising and falling upon the long Atlantic waves, and now came my first real experience of ocean travelling. I was obliged to leave the table during dinner.

14th June.—Dr Pokrovoski made me go on deck this morning for a little fresh air, and installed me comfortably in my deck chair, tucking me up in my rug. When I came to look at my chair I saw that it had, painted across the top my name in full. The temperature has lowered considerably ; white foam covers the surface of the ocean. There is nothing in sight but a sail or two in the far distance. Suddenly we heard the shriek of a siren and soon perceived a ship coming towards us; it was a transatlantic vessel homeward bound. Lucky beggar!

15th June.—We had unfavourable winds and stood anchored the whole night, beaten by a boisterous sea. My head rolled on the pillow, and I had to hold fast to the edge of my berth not to be thrown out. Of course sleep was out of the question.

The deck to-day offers a lamentable spectacle. Sea-sickness, which had spared the greater part of the passengers, took its revenge now; nearly everybody was ill.

16th June.—The morning is grey and foggy. The siren had been croaking at regular intervals all day. It is Sunday to-day. On the upper-deck the emigrants sang prayers, after which the first-class passengers tossed coins to their offspring. Down poured a shower of small silver and copper, and little boys and girls scrambled to pick it up.

In the afternoon the rolling of the ship increased, the wind blowing steadily across the Atlantic, raised majestic swells. Our steamer pitched and rolled like a walnut. The passengers stumbled and slipped from their chairs and sprawled on all fours without any dignity. I passed the greater part of the day in our cabin, and climbed on deck just before dinner to call Sergy. We executed a *pas-de-deux* in our common effort to meet; my feet suddenly went back, while my body was travelling forward. I got my feet together at last, and clung to the rail not to be swept overboard.

17th June.—We are surrounded again by a thick fog. The syren was blowing all the time. We are in the season of icebergs floating from the Arctic Ocean. About six o'clock in the morning the cabin-steward rapped sharply at the door of our cabin, warning us that there were icebergs in view. I hastened on deck, but the fog was so dense that I couldn't see two steps before me. Besides icebergs there are sandbanks to be avoided in these parts, and the steersman's eye, accustomed to pierce sea-fogs, searched in the darkness; he signalled an iceberg, but I strained my eyes uselessly, when suddenly a gust of wind broke the mist, and we saw a huge mass floating quite close to us.

Towards evening a passing ship signalled to us that there was a great number of icebergs on the way. We were passing now a place called "Devil's Hole," where all the winds meet. The sea was very high and the *Bourgogne* shook and cracked as if it was going to fall to pieces.

18th June.—Again the whole night the syren never ceased blowing. At dawn I was wakened by a formidable noise. I heard footsteps of men running down the deck and the captain's voice roaring out orders to the crew. It appeared that we were in imminent danger, having nearly run into an iceberg three times the size of our ship. If our captain had not been on the bridge at that moment, we should all have perished.

The provisions on board are nearly out, the milk is watered to an atrocious degree, and at breakfast I swallowed, with a grimace, a cup of weak broth instead of tea or coffee. We are fed now on mutton—mutton at luncheon, mutton at dinner. However good the mutton is, one feels towards the end of the week that a change should be welcome.

Every day we put our watches fifty minutes back, the time therefore seems to wile away still longer.

19th June.—Seven pilots have left New York yesterday in fishing-smacks to meet the *Bourgogne.* The pilot who would climb on board first was to receive the sum of 200 dollars. The passengers held wagers, and sweepstakes at five dollars each, had been started among the first-class passengers. One of them gained the sum of 120 dollars on the pilot No. 5, whom we had picked up first. Other pilots appeared after him, but they were told by signals that their services were not required.

20th June.—The sea is very calm to-day, not a breath of air ripples the surface of the ocean. Every morning the passengers look over the map on which our route is marked by small flags. This morning I was awfully happy to see that there was but a short distance left to New York.

After lunch a slight breeze arose, swelling out the sails and making us advance at the rate of twelve knots an hour. To-night the musical talents of the passengers manifested themselves for the first time on board. The *commissaire* played the flute and the second officer sang love ditties. I remained till late on deck, admiring the sea lighted by a magnificent moonshine Suddenly I heard a shrill scream, and one of the lady-passengers ran up to me in her night-gown, shouting for help. It appeared that an enormous rat had been promenading over her during her sleep.

21st June.—To-day the dinner was excellent ; we had awfully good things to eat and champagne *gratis.* The chef had surpassed himself in tarts and all sorts of dainties in honour of our last night on board.

CHAPTER LX

NEW YORK

.

TOWARDS midnight the American coast showed itself to view. In the distance appeared a great multitude of twinkling lights. Our ship fired rockets and burnt Bengal fires. Alike in steerage and first-class saloon, pulses beat fast with joyous anticipation. On the after-deck stood the emigrants full of hope and expectation ; they sang hymns and patriotic songs. I couldn't help thinking of the day when they will wake up to the unpleasant realities of Yankee life. The poor wretches will not find the streets paved with gold.

Bedland Island showed itself afar off with its towering figure of Liberty, the most wonderful statue I ever saw, a majestic giantess holding a torch up to light the world. We saw the statue getting bigger and bigger, and soon New York appeared as bright as day with electricity : one mass of wonderful lights.

A new pilot came on board to take us into port. We advanced cautiously amongst floating lighthouses and dropped anchor in Hudson Bay near the quarantine office, in order to land in the morning.

22nd June.—Sergy woke me at six o'clock and took me up on deck to admire the grand sight of Hudson Bay, with picturesque villas strewn along the banks, and menacing fortresses rising on green hillocks. In the middle of the immense bay, battleships, merchant vessels and yachts are anchored. A big ship, carrying only fishermen, passes by going out into the open sea.

At seven o'clock sanitary and custom officers came on board and stood on guard before the cabins. In this Land of Liberty there were formalities without number to be gone through. Under the fire of cross-examination we had to give our age, name and business, and to explain how long we are going to stay and what was our object in coming; and this is the Land of the Free !

Towards nine o'clock our steamer touched New York quay. We were a long time in getting in and came at last to the broad embankment. Not until eleven were we given permission to land on American ground. A crowd was massed on the dock to welcome the *Bourgogne* and her

passengers. There was a wild waving of hands and handkerchiefs on board. The moment had come to bid the ship
good-bye. Our fellow-passengers hurried to and fro, carrying off their parcels. When all was in order, passengers'
papers looked through and all the formalities over, the
bustle of disembarkment began. Friends are meeting each
other, kisses, hearty greetings are exchanged.

A row of all the letters of the alphabet are printed very
large and black on the wooden wall of the dock. When
stepping from the ship we were taken to the stall bearing
our own letter "D." The "D's" men were busy with our
luggage, also dumped down under the letter "D."

There was much shouting and general tumult. We were
jolted hither and thither by hordes of passengers with their
bundles, baskets, children and pet animals. I felt a little
lost amid all this bustle. Our Russian consul, Mr. Olarowski,
was on the quay to meet us. Thanks to him, a gallant
official of the custom quickly marked crosses on our luggage
without opening it.

Everything was new to us in America. We saw a nurse
holding in her arms a baby in long clothes, about a year old,
adorned with rings and bracelets, who was placidly sucking
his thumb and kicking his feet with delight.

Mr. Shaniawski has been before in America, and his knowledge of American customs was very useful to us. He took
upon himself the task of finding us a lodging. We went to
an hotel called the Clarendon, a sort of boarding-house,
situated in the 18th street, where big and small apartments
are the same price, three dollars and a half for each, including
breakfast, lunch and dinner; there is a bathroom to each
room. The head waiter led us up the handsomely carpeted
stairs to our apartment. The room was pleasant and cool,
with pictures on the walls and a thick carpet.

We were just in time for an early lunch when we arrived
at the hotel. Fruit was served to us before the meal, which
ended with iced-tea. The American custom is having a
vast number of small dishes, each counting separately.

All the men in America are clean-shaven and have the
appearance of actors, and it seemed strange to me that one
of the waiters who served at table-d'hôte, wore a big
moustache. A law had just been promulgated forbidding
the waiters in the restaurants to wear moustaches, but they
all declared that they would obey only if their wages were
increased. Having announced that ultimatum they left
their patrons, and had thus their own way. The servants
in this country are very highly paid, the waiters in our hotel
received eighty dollars a month. They believe in the social
equality of all human beings but do not seem to mind ad-
mitting that there is a class above their's. They just con-

descend to wait upon us, and think they can demonstrate
their equality by being as rude as possible. Dr. Pokrowski
asked à waiter to close the window during dinner, and that
uncivil man answered coolly : "Why don't you do it yourself ? " The day of our arrival happened to be on a Sunday,
and the servants here are very scrupulous about keeping the
Sabbath. Mrs. Serebriakoff called the chambermaid to take
away a broken glass, and the girl, resenting the advent of
visitors on a Sunday, replied impertinently that she did not
work on Sundays. It was also impossible to have our boots
cleaned at the hotel, and we had to go into the street for
that operation.

Our consul came to call upon us with his wife, a smart
young Californian with yellow locks, who looked like a pretty
wax figure in a show-window. She doesn't speak a word
of Russian, though her little daughter, aged six, has had a
Russian nurse since her very birth. The Olarowskis took us
to a music hall on the top of a ten-storied house, lighted
with different coloured lamps, from which you have a bird's-
eye view of the great city. The lift carried us to the roof
of the big house, transformed into a garden. We entered a
vast hall with a glass roof. It was most interesting and quite
without the feeling that you might fall off.

Nearly all the houses in New York are twelve-storeyed,
with terrace roofs which serve sometimes as play-grounds
for school children. In the working quarters the municipality has organised Roof-Gardens, where the poor
people can breathe a purer air than in their hovels. In
Madison Square, one of the richest quarters of New York,
a sculptor has arranged a study on his roof, and in the next
house a sportsman has organised, at the height of ninety
yards above the pavement, a big dog-kennel where he breeds
bull-dogs. In Eighth's Avenue a Protestant church with
a belfry is perched on the roof of an immense building.
The houses here are all divided into flats. In Broadway,
the main street of New York, they are all built in different
styles and architecture, and in the next street, on the
contrary, the houses are all alike.

Next day we went to call on the Hollands, our Cairo
friends, who live at Windsor Hotel. We started down
Fifth Avenue, a street lined with solemn stately buildings with pillared porticoes, all of the self-same pattern. The
height of the houses amazed me, some of them being from
twenty to twenty-five stories high. The streets are mostly
numbered and run in rows. The life in the streets is
tremendous. There was an appalling thunder of trains
rushing every minute above our heads.

Finally we got to the Windsor Hotel which, like all
the big hotels, has its own telegraph and telephone offices,

its milliner, hairdresser, etc.   We were told at the office
that the Hollands had gone the day before to Lake Mohawk.
We sent a wire to tell them that we were here, and started
back to our hotel by the " Elevated," an electric suspended
railway built upon iron struts above the houses, which cuts
through New York in all directions.   It made abrupt turn-
ings, and rushed at a reckless pace over the roofs of the
houses, or raced through tunnels beneath them.   It is great
fun looking through other people's windows, and getting a
peep into comedies and tragedies sometimes.   The train
suddenly stops short with a jerk that sends the passengers
into a conglomerate struggling mass, and throws them into
each other's arms.   The train brought us to the hotel with a
flourish that precipitated me on the knees of my vis-a-vis,
an odious man with a red nose.

The Hollands had wired that they were coming over by
the night train, and early next morning they sent me a
bandbox full of beautiful red roses—so enormous, they
looked like peonies—with a note to ask us when we would
receive them.   The Hollands came to call on us in the
afternoon.   To meet their kind faces again was charming ;
the greetings between us were warm.   I thought dear
Mrs. Holland would never leave off kissing me.

The Hollands offered to drive us in their landau through
Central Park.   The beautiful weather had brought out
all New York, driving, riding, walking.   We returned by
a lovely place called the Riverside Drive, a long road
running along the banks of the Hudson, with charming
houses looking straight out on the river, and bordered by
trees on each side that spread their branches over us and
made the roadway shady.   Between the trees the river
glistened like a silver ribbon.

On the 4th July, the day of the Anniversary of the
Independence of America, we were wakened in the morning
by crackers and rockets.   In the afternoon the Hollands
took us to Coney Island, a fashionable watering-place situated a few miles out of town.   We took the tram to reach
the port, and drove through streets bedecked with flags.
We took places on board the *Taurus*, a pleasure steamer
black with people going out for a boating picnic.   The boat
had a holiday air about it.   The passengers were all workmen with their families, gay, noisy people all of them.   On
the stern a troupe of Neapolitans danced the tarantella.
Leaning on the railing we admired the immense bay of
New York, swarming with ships of different nationalities,
amidst which we saw our *Bourgogne* on the point of leaving
for Europe.   From afar we heard the cannons saluting our
Russian cruiser, the *Admiral Nakhimof*, which was entering
the port just then.   The wind rose suddenly, and it took

more than two hours before we could land at Manhattan Beach. At last we succeeded in dropping anchor. The boat was overcrowded, and all the people on the deck made a rush towards the stern, making the ship incline on one side, and I had to cling fast to Sergy's arm not to be swept overboard.

On landing we took the Elevated, which brought us in a few minutes to Brighton Beach, a seaside resort, the meeting-place for members of fashionable high life. We walked along the seashore and met ladies and gentlemen in bathing suits, and bare-legged children with toy spades, playing merrily with sand and bright sea-washed shells. We found ourselves soon in the midst of a large fair with all sorts of show-tents of various shapes, displaying brilliant banners, and queer little booths where you could get your fortune told. The feast was in full swing. We looked at the many merry-go-rounds, flying wooden horses, donkey races, etc. We mounted, for fun, the flying horses, and had a good gallop. We walked for nearly half-an-hour, exposed to the rays of the pitiless sun. in search of a restaurant ; we had eaten nothing since our breakfast and were horribly hungry. Mr. Holland, who was completely ruled by his imperious spouse, at times had rebellious fits ; he wanted to dine in one place, his wife in another, which made them both cross. He wrangled for about a quarter-of-an-hour ; I was a good deal flushed and so weary that I could scarcely drag myself along. I wasn't able to bear the heat and the fatigue any longer and begged Mr. Holland, who led the party, to take pity on us and pause to draw breath, but he paid no attention whatever to my entreaties and pushed on stubbornly, both hands in his pockets, panting like an engine and mopping his forehead from time to time. There was nothing to do but walk on with a sigh of submission. Mrs. Holland got her way in the end, and announced, in a tone which didn't suffer contradiction, that she would enter the first hotel on our way. We stopped before the porch of the Oriental Hotel, and were told by the porter that there was a table d'hôte at the hotel, at which the lodgers only could partake. We were ready to retreat, famished and awfully disappointed, but Mrs. Holland, flying into a violent temper, forced herself in, declaring authoritatively, " Here we are, and here we remain ! " and made her entrance into the hotel with the step and mien of a woman perfectly determined to have her dinner. Whilst she went to speak to the manager, we came into a large entrance hall, where a long row of negro boys were ranged along the walls, armed with cleaning brushes. They rushed at us and began to dust our clothes. Mrs. Holland must have had a very persuasive way with the head-waiter, for she returned triumphant. We had a very good dinner to which we did ample honour, and were in no way bashful about our appetites. Fortified by our meal, we soon recovered our good spirits, and went by train to Brooklyn. We crossed East River to New York on a ferry full of passengers, horses and carriages. The ferry was sumptuous, the walls of the state cabin entirely of looking-glass.

When we returned to our hotel we found the captain and two ship officers of our cruiser the *Admiral Nakhimoff* who had come to invite us, as well as all our companions, including the Hollands, to come and take a cup of tea on board that night. Being awfully tired, I was not fit for visitors just then, and as our guests settled themselves into a comfortable position in their chairs, making no attempt to go away, I went to my room under the pretext of a bad headache.

Oh! that "Nakhimoff!" I shall never forget the trouble that cruiser gave us. All the way to the port I felt more dead than alive. The streets were transformed into a veritable battle-field, crackers were exploded under our horses' feet, rockets were let off and guns fired in the air for joy. The horses, taking fright, began to fidget and prance. I heaved a sigh of relief when we reached the port. The "Nakhimoff" had sent a boat rowed by fourteen sailors to fetch us. We had already pushed off, when Mrs. Holland suggested that it was dangerous to go on the water to-day, because the captains of the numerous excursion boats must surely be drunk and would sink us in no time. She frightened me out of my wits. I was desperately afraid that our boat would be upset, especially when Mrs. Holland, with a very red face, and an expression of desperate determination, declared that she would jump overboard if we were not rowed back to the shore immediately. "Tell them to go back! I shall go back!" shouted the rebellious lady at the top of her voice. Our husbands tried to persuade us that there was no danger whatever, but they couldn't bring us to reason. They landed us on the beach under the charge of Mr. Shaniawski and were rowed back to the "Nakhimoff." A crowd of spectators, chiefly women, gathered round us and laughed openly at us, bestowing various uncomplimentary remarks on our cowardice. Awfully confused on being the laughing stock of the place, we decided to cross to the "Nakhimoff" at any price, and were so pleased to see the row-boat coming back to fetch us, in case we had changed our minds, with two ship-officers this time. When we stepped into the boat I became aware that the officer at the rudder, who was intrusted to bring us safely on board, wore two pairs of spectacles. He must surely be short-sighted! But come what may! We pushed off and got to the "Nakhimoff" in ten minutes' time, somewhat confused, but awfully pleased to rejoin our husbands. The cruiser had hoisted the Russian flag which made me feel all I don't know how, to look at it hanging there so far from home.

We were taking our tea in the mess-cabin when we heard the sounds of a band striking up our anthem, and shouts of "Hip, hip, hurrah!" We hastened upon the deck, and glancing eagerly in the direction from where the welcome music came we saw an American man-of-war passing before the "Nakhimoff" and saluting us thus gallantly, which roused me to a high pitch of patriotic exaltation. Night coming on, we had to hasten back on shore. The crew of the "Nakhimoff" cheered us as we left her deck and the officers assisted us down the ship's ladder. We reached the coast all right. All is well that ends well!

The next day the papers said that there were about 200 persons killed in the streets of New York and more than 2,000 wounded during the national festivities, and that the rockets had set on fire a great number of houses. We have had a narrow escape, I must say!

New York is full of Russian anarchists. Quite recently a Russian general, Seliverstoff, has been assassinated by one of them. They managed to lay hands on his murderer, whose beard and moustaches are kept by Mr. Olarowski. Oh, the horror!

On the very morning when we read our names in the list of the arrivals at the "Clarendon," Sergy gave audience to a suspicious-looking compatriot of ours, who had come expressly to ask my husband's opinion upon the treaty between Russia and America, concerning the terms on which both countries had to deliver up their respective criminals.

The newspapers were full of us. Our hotel was besieged by reporters waiting in the ante-room for hours to have a word from us. The *Harper's Magazine* asks for our photographs, and a type-writing machine office proposes to issue 250 correspondences concerning my husband. We received a lot of letters from autograph-hunters. Mrs. Vanderbilt, one of the richest women in America, wrote to Sergy requesting his autograph in order that she might add it to her collection of celebrities.

Glancing this morning over an illustrated paper, in the middle of the column I saw our faces, but couldn't believe they were really there, in an American paper. I began to think I wasn't awake yet. I am sure it is the Hollands who have given our photos to the papers, for we are carried about as a show by them. Under our pictures the magazine has printed our biography, with a number of ridiculous stories concerning us. There was a whole sheet with dark hints as to our private lives, every syllable false. My husband, according to the press, was an oppressor of the people, little better than "Nero," and Colonel Serebriakoff, who was not able to hurt a fly, is also said to be noted for his cruelty. How do such revolting things get into papers? It is too ridiculous, but I didn't laugh, I was too angry. The imaginative reporters described me as a Princess with Imperial blood in her veins, endowed with no end of beauty and money, and Mr. Shaniawski as a world-known traveller and explorer. Stupid fellows!

The Hollands are living all the year round at the "Windsor," where they keep a splendid apartment, like a great number of Americans, who live in hotels to avoid the bother of servants and housekeeping. The Hollands had us to dinner at the "Windsor," and Mrs. Holland wanted me to look my best in order to make the conquest of the paper-reporters, who take their meals at the "Windsor." She insisted that I should wear my prettiest dress, but I didn't take any pains to impress the journalists, and put on my walking costume. I wish the Hollands wouldn't put me forward always!

Dinner was at half-past seven. Mr. Holland took me down to the dining-room, a large hall brilliantly illuminated and filled with gentlemen in full dress and bare-shouldered ladies. We made our way to the prettily spread table reserved for us, decorated with bunches of roses. Both Mrs. Holland and Mrs. Olarowski had put on their finest dresses. Of all those present I was the only one to appear in a wrong toilet. My modest frock seemed rather out of place amidst the gorgeous plumes of the other ladies, and Mrs. Holland's eyes swept over me disapprovingly. Nevertheless, I was a great deal stared at and much annoyed, for I felt I was being made a show of, and exhibited as one would exhibit a giant or a dwarf.

We meant to spend a fortnight in New York, but had to leave the city much sooner. When I came down to breakfast one morning, I perceived immediately that something unpleasant had happened. All my companions seemed very preoccupied and gloomy, and ate their breakfasts in silence. After our meal I began turning over the leaves of a daily paper which happened to be on the table close to my hand, and saw an article which made my blood run cold. It ran thus: *Siberia's Governor-General on a visit here—in imminent danger!"* And then I was told that the manager of our hotel had thought fit to warn my husband of the danger to which we were exposed. He had received an anonymous letter that morning, signed *A Victim of Siberia*, in which he was threatened that his hotel would be blown up for having sheltered us. Further on the letter ran thus: *There is now stopping at your hotel a man who is the sworn enemy of thousands of persecuted men and women in far distant Siberia. He has very recently been appointed to the governor-generalship of that accursed spot, but he is a marked man by men of my belief in this country, the Mecca of all, the land of the free. I write this to warn you of a plot to destroy Doukhovskoy, who will now go to rule over the victims of the Tzar in Siberia. But I feel it my duty to warn you to be on your guard against certain members of an organisation of which I am a member.* This letter was sent to the superintendent of the police and he has no doubt made preparations to prevent any attempt at assassination, or at any rate to arrest the assassin, which may not be much comfort to us if there really be a plot. Sergy, however, was not to be frightened easily, but of course I was horribly frightened. What woman would not have been? Another morning paper announced : *General Doukhovskoy will be assassinated with his wife and suite. In any case he wouldn't be allowed to reach Siberia, where he is appointed general-governor to martyrise the people.* And though the *New York Herald* had printed in big black letters a headline six inches tall : *General Doukhovskoy is safe*, we felt ourselves condemned to death.

The first thing to be done was to get away from New York and take the afternoon train to Chicago. I packed in haste and spent a frantic half-hour in thrusting my things in my trunk. The Hollands had invited us to share their box with them at the opera that night, and had announced it in the papers. We telephoned to them that we were obliged to leave New York quite unexpectedly, having been called to Khabarovsk by wire. We also telegraphed to an American lady, who had invited us to visit at her house in Philadelphia, that we were leaving for Boston, in order that they couldn't get on our track.

My husband acceded to my entreaties that for the rest of our journey through America we would not be " The Governor-General and his wife," but a plain party of tourists. After my fright I will enjoy it all, particularly because I could see everything I wanted to see, and that I could not have done if we were pointed out here and there as " The Governor-General and his wife." And thus Sergy changed his name and sent away his luggage ; we will travel across the Continent incognito.

We got hastily into a tram to be driven to the railway station, but we were not destined to go off unobserved. A very unprepossessing-looking individual, with long hair and spectacles, sprang on the steps of the tram and asked Mr. Shaniavski, in very bad English, if General Doukhovskoy was leaving New York for good, Mr. Shaniavski stopping him from entering the car, answered that he knew nothing about General Doukhovskoy. At that very moment the tramway started and we were delivered from the obtrusive spy. At the railway-station Mrs. Serebriakoff and I didn't permit our husbands to leave our sides, and struggled hard to seem unconcerned, mistrusting all the passengers.

CHAPTER LXI

NIAGARA FALLS

THE way is long from New York to San Francisco. We have to pass the Continent from East to West, making about 5000 miles. It took thirty-five days to make that journey before the railway was built. We will touch Niagara on our way to Chicago, and will continue the journey the same day by a later train. To leave America without seeing the Falls of Niagara was impossible.

The train rattled out of New York and crossed the Harlem. We skirted that pretty little river and ran over the prairies. We travel in a splendid "Wagner Express," a rival to "Pullman's Express." All the cars are first-class; it is only the so-named "Colonist trains" which are second-class. Our saloon-car had no compartments in it, there was just one wide corridor with velvet armchairs dotted about. In front of our engine a kind of giant spade is fastened to clear the line from droves of cattle and other encumbrances. A huge bell keeps ringing all the time for the same purpose.

Towards night we removed to the sleeping-car, fitted up with a long double file of two-storeyed bunks, the rows separated by a green calico partition. The railway conductors are shiny black negroes, surnamed "Johnny," all of them. Our Johnny, a most jolly-looking nigger, in white livery, was very talkative, his tongue went like an express train. He plied us with questions and cross-examined us about where we came from, where we were going to. Wasn't he also a spy? At all events we did not reveal our destination. We pretended we were going no further than Niagara. In the night Mme. Beurgier went to drink a glass of water, and when she crawled in, in the dark, she couldn't find out her sleeping-berth, and got into Johnny's couch. When her hands touched the darkie's slippery face, she thought she had touched a frog, and throwing herself back, she bumped her face against the boards, at which her forehead instantly developed a bump of many colours.

The jingle of the breakfast bell and Johnny's piercing voice shouting "First call for breakfast," awakened me in the morning. I had to crouch up and dress on my berth, and succeeded in putting on my frock in a series of contortions.

The Americans are very unceremonious people; peeping through the curtain of my division, I saw unattractive-looking bare legs underneath. All the passengers assembled in the saloon to drink coffee, which was brought in by Johnny and tasted very nasty.

We pass the towns of Rochester and Albion, and are speeding along the wooded banks of Niagara River. The opposite bank is Canada, a territory belonging to England, Johnny began cleaning manipulations over our clothes, proceeding with bold strikes of his brush, as if he were grooming a horse. Then he took off Sergy's hat unceremoniously, gave a vigorously brushing to it, and clapped it upon his head again. After that he made a dash at my hat, but without success, I having jumped back in time.

Here we are at "Niagara Village," an agglomeration of splendid hotels. The next train left at 9·15, and we·had plenty of time to spare. We made our way to "Hôtel National," as we had no porters to carry our things, we had to do it ourselves. We passed before a negro boy perched on a high seat, motionless like a black statue, sticking out both feet adorned with boots shining like twin stars. We were told that the black statue was a boot-boy serving as advertisement to a patent shoe cream.

At the entrance hall of the "National" we found negroes with brushes who made dusting attacks at our clothes.

We are just in time for luncheon. The big hall was filled with tourists who had come to see the Falls, the great wonder of the world. We were served by a staff of waiters, negroes of blackest ebony, the head waiter wore a flower in his buttonhole, and looked awfully smart. During luncheon a pianist played to the accompaniment of an orchestra. After lunch we stretched ourselves comfortably in rocking-chairs on the veranda, looking out into a shady park, and after a good rest, we took a carriage and drove to Goat Island to see the Falls.

Niagara, in the Indian language, means "Thundering Waters," and in fact, from afar the thunder of the Niagara filled the air. We wandered away in the direction of the huge roar. As we advanced the sound became sharper and we had to shout to make ourselves heard above the noise of the cataract. At length we came face to face with the Falls. The sight of the foaming rapids fringed by splendid trees, was awfully grand. Rainbows are reflected in the water. The tumult of the Falls which attained the height of seventy yards, broke in clouds of spray against the rocks. It was well worth travelling all the way to see. Here and there we saw inscriptions: "*Don't venture in dangerous places!*" Leaning over the Falls, I felt very small and strangely attracted by its foaming wonderful sheet of water, just the same as I did whilst standing on Mount Vesuvius, on the very brink of the crater. In a part of the park called " The Cape of the Winds," where the Falls have the form of a horse-shoe, we met a party of audacious tourists, enveloped in yellow mackintoshes, who were slowly groping their way along a narrow bridge thrown across the cataract ; underneath, the Niagara rolled gigantic and majestic in a vast flood. After having rested for a little while on the grass, discoursing about the beauty of the wonderful waterfall, we returned to the hotel just in time for dinner. After the repast, all my companions went out for a sail on the Niagara River ; as for me, I had quite enough of thrilling sensations for that day and pleaded a headache as an excuse for remaining within. They went underneath the Falls in oilskin coats and caps, supplied by the hotel, after which they descended in a lift, and then walked along passages scooped out of the rock, until they were underneath the Falls, which poured over in front of them like a curtain, and then reached a steamboat called " The Maid of the Mist.

When my indefatigable companions returned, we walked across the park to Canada " abroad," as they call it here, and crossed the river by a suspended bridge joining Canada to the United States. We had to pay 25 cents each to cross the Suspension Bridge, which seemed to hang over the water. This bridge had recently collapsed and was now built again.

Whilst our companions explored Canada, I entered with Mrs. Serebriakoff, a white farm-house with green shutters, entirely covered with creeping plants, which announced in large white letters " New Milk," where we regaled ourselves with strawberries and cream.

We were back to the hotel towards sunset and walked to the station laden with our bags and umbrellas, where we arrived just as the train was about to start.

This time our sleeping berths were still more uncomfortable, arranged behind the partition for two persons on one bunk. This is all very well for married couples but is it not particularly cosy for strangers of different sexes to lie down all night side by side. This lot befell Mme. Beurgier ; her berth-mate turned out to be Mr. Koulomzine, who after long parleys succeeded in finding a sleeping berth in the next car.

I slept badly that night and got up very early. We had luncheon in the restaurant-car about a quarter of a mile away from us in the train. Pretty girls waited on us while in continual chorus came from them : " Steaks, chops, ham and eggs, pie or pudding ! " After the repast the waitresses distributed small bouquets to the lady passengers, and dining-car advertisements to the gentlemen.

CHAPTER LXII

CHICAGO

TOWARDS five o'clock Michigan Lake came into view and spread before us as broad as the sea, with tides coming in and going out, and steamships gliding on the blue water. At the last station before Chicago a boy came into the car piled up to his head with advertisements, which he scattered over us ; he was followed by a man with a metal placard on his chest, who thrust into our hands a card setting forth the virtues of Savoie Hotel, and promised to occupy himself with our luggage. Most of the passengers left the train at Hyde Park, the first stoppage at Chicago, but we pushed on to Central Station. Over the city hung a sky laden with smoke ; everywhere black chimneys rose in the air.

Savoie Hotel is situated on the European place, the liveliest quarter of Chicago. We took an apartment in the second storey, for 2 dollars ahead, with board and lodging.

Desirous to keep the strictest incognito, we registered our names in the hotel-book, " Mr. and Mrs. Sergius," for fear of spies. Dr. Pokrovski took the name of "Castorio," which suited his profession admirably.

Our four days' stay at Chicago seemed very short to me. Every morning we went to visit Chicago's World Fair. The exhibition commemorated the fourth century of the discovery of America by Christopher Columbus. The day was Sunday. A holiday crowd pushed and elbowed about the various attractions, middle-class people for the most part, and negro beauties and dandies. We walked through the sections of the Exhibition, where nearly all the exhibited objects are provided with the curt warning : " Hands off ! " The Americans in general, do not shine for their politeness ! Whilst standing before a show-window, a policeman approached us and asked what nation we belonged to. We said we were a company of French tourists who had come to see the World's Fair.

Midway Pleasance is the most animated part of the Exhibition. We entered a theatre where a Japanese play was going on. The actors' faces were covered with terrifying masks, and they were all making atrocious grimaces. After the play a troup of native musicians, sitting on the floor, played "Yankee Doodle" and "God save the Queen" on their national instruments. The spectators in the first row took off their coats and remained in their shirt sleeves without ceremony. Close to the Japanese theatre the Esquimaux performed marvels in the way of throwing lances through rings. They invited the passers-by to enter their enclosure and compete with them in a curious sport, consisting in breaking big sticks into small bits by the means of a long whip. The Esquimaus came from Greenland; they are American subjects but do not speak English, they can say only: "Give money!"

On the quay where stands the monument of Christopher Columbus, the largest elevator in the whole world brought us in the space of one minute, on the roof of the "Liberal Arts," where we visited a beautiful picture gallery containing the works of the most renowned painters of different countries. The Russian pictures occupy the first place, but our manufactory section is very poorly represented. In one of the pavilions of the United States we saw vegetables and fruit piled about in profusion. The fruit of California is three times larger than in any other country; tempting-looking apples and pears, coming from Los Angelos, were enormous in proportion, but quite tasteless.

Foreign artists are greatly appreciated in America, and very highly paid. When walking through the musical section we were agreeably surprised to hear a first-class artiste play one of Chopin's nocturnes in a masterly manner, with a faultless technique and a perfect phrasing.

"Beauties" brought over from all parts of the world black, white and yellow, are exposed in a large hall, in stalls behind a railing, just like wild beasts. One of the prettiest girls, dressed in our Russian national costume, appeared to be a Polish Jewess, who had taken the first prize in a recent "Beauty Competition."

A picture of "Nana," the heroine of Zola's last novel, painted by Soukharowski (a Russian painter), is exhibited in Chicago, and much is made of that canvas.

We went to see a Museum of wax-figures, and saw among other curiosities, a big giant and a negress dwarf with no arms, who played the drum with her toes, and wrote her autograph holding a pen between her toes. Next to her a pretty white-skinned dwarf resembling a pretty wax-doll, attired in a beautiful evening dress, was exhibited, who looked with disdain, mixed with jealousy, at her dusky companion who attracted more attention than her dainty little person. In the adjoining room a gipsy fortune-teller told people's future through examination of the palms of their hands. I wanted my hand read and asked Mr. Shaniavski to accompany me to her booth. From the very beginning the old gipsy woman made formidable mistakes, taking Mr. Shaniavski for my husband. Nevertheless she predicted a lot of charming things to me, and I left her booth with a smiling face. After dinner we went to a Venetian Feast organised on the central basin of Michigan Lake, which was transformed into a Venetian canal. Gondolas floated on the lake, lit up by Chinese lanterns.

Chicago is a dirty, noisy commercial town, and looks a tremendously busy place. The smoke of the factories blacken the sky ; the soot stains the sparrows, making them look quite black. We walked through the broad, straight streets of the Great Grey City, stopping before the s hop, windows. We saw a shop bearing the inscription " Food-and dog's medicine." In a hair-dressing shop a woman was sitting on a high seat with her back to the window with wonderfully splendid hair falling down to the ground. We entered the shop to see if the woman's face corresponded to her beautiful golden hair, but, alas, she appeared to be very unattractive. Her hair served as advertisement for a patent elixir to make the hair grow. How people have sometimes to earn their bread and butter.

The heat is intense. Everybody grumbled at the weather being so hot. The head-porter of our hotel, who is a grand personage, too languid to talk, in order not to be obliged to answer a hundred times a day to the same complaint of the visitors about the heat. Awfully hot, isn't it ? " stuck a placard over the entrance door saying, " Yes, it is very warm to-day ! "

Mme. Beurgier couldn't sleep for the heat, and went one night for a stroll on the outskirts of Michigan Common. She saw heaps of rags here and there on the grass ; she touched one of them with her foot, and oh, what a jump she gave when from the rags strange and somewhat terrifying sounds proceeded, that indicated a drunken sleep. It appeared that the whole place swarmed with houseless vagrants, evidently prepared to camp out-of-doors till morning.

During our four days' stay at Chicago there had been three awful accidents at the Exhibition. First : A collision between two steamboats on the lake. We were crossing the bridge at that moment and saw a man extracted from the water with broken legs. Second : A terrible fire had broken out in the very centre of the Exhibition. An immense building was burnt to the ground. Dr. Pokrovski saw people jumping down from the eighteenth storey and killed on the spot. Third: A captive-balloon had burst, causing the death of all the passengers.

2nd July.—We left Chicago this morning. Our train rolls rapidly towards San Francisco. We have six days of railway. The temperature being very hot, everyone put

himself at his ease ; my travelling-companions also took off
their coats—American fashion. We drink iced-water the
whole day to refresh ourselves. Our "Johnny" lay full
stretched on the sofa in the private saloon ; Mme. Beurgier
tried to make him take a more correct attitude, but to make
remarks to the darkie was as fruitless as to sponge his
nigger face white. He paid no attention whatever to her
reproofs and continued his *dolce far niente*, munching an
apple with beautiful white teeth.

Our train rolls on full speed. We are tossed about as on
the sea. "Johnny" came to make our beds early in the
evening. We had to lie down directly, for when the beds
were made, there was no place to sit down.

3rd July.—The railway line is uninteresting and monotonous and the heat something dreadful. At five o'clock
dinner was served in the restaurant-car, consisting of broth
and roast beef surrounded by slices of oranges.

4th July—We crossed the Mississippi in the night, and are,
rolling through fields of Indian wheat and beetroot. The
heat has still increased and our car is like an overheated
stove ; the dust entering through the windows transformed
us into chimney-sweeps.

We cross now the States of Nebraska and Wyoming.
The villages and towns are all illuminated with electricity.
We read now and then the word "Saloon" gambling house
written on the front of the houses. I have remarked that
at the railway-stations nearly all the doors bear the inscription
"Entrance forbidden." It is curious how many things are
forbidden in this " Free Country !" It is also very odd that
the carriage-roads are not closed before the passage of trains ;
there is only an inscription on wooden poles "Look out for
the cars !"

5th July.—I woke up in the night shivering with cold.
The train was rolling through the states of Utah, across the
Great American Desert. The country is bare and dull, and
very poorly peopled ; not a tree or a blade of grass is to be
seen. The great want in the place is water. A chain of
snow peaks appeared on the horizon. We are crossing the
Cordilleras mountains and find ourselves at eight thousand
feet above the level of the sea. Soon after lunch the
Valley of Salt Lake spread before us. Our train runs amid
green pastures. We pass little hamlets and orchards, which
seem very green and beautiful to me after the long weary
stretches of the desert we had just left. Thatched ranches
(farms) and bungalows peeped from beneath the trees. We
are in the legendary "Far West." Here is a long haired
Red Indian, from Cooper's Books, galloping on the road on a
small lean pony, followed by a cow-boy wearing a broad-
brimmed hat. It only wants "Buffalo-Bill" in person to

complete the picture. Whilst stopping at a station we saw a young Indian "squaw" (woman), sitting cross-legged on the platform, wrapped up in a red blanket, carrying on her back her papoos (baby), lashed up in its hammock. American travellers ought to be accustomed to Red-Indians, nevertheless they surveyed with great interest the young savage female, who showed her nursling to them for the sum of 15 cents. She refused outright to show her "papoos" to a passenger who offered only five cents to her. The local colour begins to disappear in the "Far West," the Red-Indians throw off their plumes and deer-skins for a flannel shirt and a felt hat. They were plentiful enough about here some years ago, but the railroad, with its settlements has swept them back. The railway-line was being built during five years, the Red-Indians destroying it continually. In the olden days, a touch of adventure was lent to the journey by the fear of an attack from hostile Indians. We are told that even now there is danger on the line from Indian bandits. Our train passes with illuminated "Pullmans" in the centre of the plains, and my imagination getting the better of me, I seem to see our train on that lone prairie, surrounded by Red Indians. When I went to sleep, visions of fighting savages woke me up with a suppressed scream, as I fancied I was being scalped, and I find that it is only the shriek of the locomotive, and the war-whoop of the Indians are only the outcries of our pacific "Johnny" announcing that we were approaching Salt Lake City. The capital of the Mormons' State is surrounded by an amphitheatre of hills, over which the Mormons' Hierarchy still dominates. In 1890, Welford Woodruff, the President of the Mormon Church, received, it is said, a revelation from God, commanding that all Mormons should give up their plural wives, and they are satisfied now with one consort.

We are in a long, narrow pass : above us hang abrupt rocks and below flows a serpentine river. Our train makes right angle turns, and it seems as if we were turning all the time on the same spot. Towards night we entered the States of Sierra Nevada ; we are now at only a day's journey from Mexico. The towns, rivers and mountains have Mexican names. A Mexican pedlar selling curios and silver filigree jewellery, entered our car. Sergy bought me a finely worked brooch in the form of a mandoline. We enter a narrow wooden tunnel built to protect the line from stone avalanches, which took a whole hour to go through.

4th July.—At dawn we speeded through the ranches of California, and soon approached the town of Sacramento. Our train dashes now on its way to the Pacific. We felt already the sea breeze, and soon appeared the Gulf of San Francisco and the waters of the Pacific Ocean. Our train was pushed by workmen along an artificial dike to the station of Bonifacio, after which we rolled towards Oakland, where our train after having been divided in three parts, was put on a ferry. When we touched the other shore the train was made up again, and took us straight to San Francisco.

CHAPTER LXIII

SAN FRANCISCO

WE were surrounded at the railway station by a crowd of Negroes, Japs and Chinamen. We drove to the Lyndhurst, a small hotel in Geary Street, where Mr. Shaniavski had secured apartments for us. Nothing was said to the hotel management concerning us, beyond the fact that we were foreign tourists who did not care to go to a large hotel. Our rooms were engaged for a week and paid for in advance.

San Francisco, the Queen of the Pacific, and the glory of the Eastern coast, is a rich and populous city about one hundred years old. After lunch we went out to explore the place. There are but few cabs in the streets, everyone takes the tram or the cable road ; the way in which it climbs the steepest hills is wonderful. We took the cable road to Golden Gate Park, which is very beautiful indeed. Buffaloes graze on the green lawns and strange birds flash among the boughs. I thought that a beetle had settled upon my hat and when I blew it off, it appeared to be a butterfly of fantastical appearance, the size of a bird. In the part of the park called the Children's Garden, all kinds of games and amusements are organised. We saw saddle-horses not bigger than foundland dogs, and baby-coaches drawn by white sheep. We had tea in the Children's Restaurant, where gentlemen are admitted only when accompanied by their families.

On leaving the park we rode out to the Presidio, a military ground with big cannon pointing menacingly on to the Pacific Ocean. We stood with the rest of the crowd to see the President of the United States, who had come down from San Raphaelo, a fashionable sea-bathing place, to review four batteries of artillery, two light-batteries of field pieces and a troop of cavalry. After which the gentlemen of our party went for a stroll through the Chinese part of the town to Cliff House where seals are reared ; these animals come in hundreds to bask in the sun at a few steps only from the cliffs. We ladies preferred to go out shopping. We lingered before the windows of entrancing shops, and listened to an orchestra playing in a music-shop to attract purchasers.

The climate here is perfect, one doesn't suffer at all from the heat, in summer and winter the temperature is nearly always the same. I was very much astonished, however, to see ladies enveloped in furs in July.

We managed to keep up our incognito at the Lyndhurst, and attracted no special attention until after the publication in the *Examiner* of a statement, that "General Doukhovskoy was supposed to have reached San Francisco travelling incognito." After that it was noticed that "The middle-aged gentleman who appeared to be the leader of the party, but whose name was registered in the books of the hotel as 'Mr. Sergius,' didn't go out as frequently as at first." Another San Francisco paper reproduced our portraits, after which Sergy told me to wear my hat when I went down to the dining-room, in order not to be easily recognised by my portrait, copied in different newspapers in which I was reproduced without my hat.

Our first care in the morning was to peruse the earliest editions of the papers to see if we were found out. The reporters were on our track again. A journalist who had been tracking down Mr. Shaniavski all along, step by step, discovered him out at the Lyndhurst, and wanted to have all sorts of information about General Doukhovskoy, and again Mr. Shaniavski told him that he knew nothing about the General.

Sarah, the chambermaid, tried to penetrate our incognito and to learn who and what I was. More than once, while doing up my room, she expressed the desire to see a real Russian General. Looking at my hands she said: "I daresay you have never known what work means, look at your hands, they are much too white!"

It was Mme. Beurgier who had lifted up the veil of our incognito by buying a sewing-machine for me. She had ordered it to be sent to Vladivostock, and the order for the machine gave the information about our party. Happily we were leaving San Francisco on the following day. I was greatly amused by the idea that it was a sewing-machine that had revealed our secret.

CHAPTER LXIV

ACROSS THE PACIFIC

ON the eve of our departure from San Francisco we went to inspect our cabins on the mail-ship, *Peru*, on which we are to cross the Pacific. We are undertaking a long and dangerous voyage. It is not a small affair to settle on board for eighteen days! On our way to the quay we encountered a queer moving house, set on rollers, and being pulled along by a team of horses. The *Peru*, lying on the quay, was getting ready for the sea. The whole of the crew are Chinamen, who are noted to be admirable sailormen. They were taking leave just then of their sweethearts, and offering paper flowers to them as a souvenir.

11th July.—We had to start early in the morning. We hurried over our breakfast and walked rapidly towards the pier and saw the *Peru* getting up steam, impatient to snatch us away. A great crowd was on the quay. Mr. Artsimovitch, the Russian Consul-General at this part, had come to see us off, accompanied by Mr. Haram-Pratt, Vice-Consul, a gallant young man with a large bouquet of the most beautiful pink flowers, called "American Beauties," for me in his hand. I had my flowers put immediately in water, wearing a few of them. The chief of the police was pacing the after-deck followed by two burly private detectives who were appointed to watch over our safety; they lounged around on each side of our party, close enough to see and hear all that was going on, and kept a close eye upon us. This guard was kept until the *Peru* started on her voyage. Tiresome reporters, sent by the papers to get something from us, dogged our steps pencil in hand. My husband had a long chat with a representative of the *New York Herald*. Sergy begged of him not to look upon him as a Governor-General, for he was meanwhile a simple Russian tourist, who had been on a visit to the World's Fair, and is now proceeding on his journey.

" *Vous cherchez un gouverneur-general, il n'y est pas. Vous voulez voir Mr. Doukhovskoy, le voici!* " said my husband to the reporter. Just at that moment I appeared on the deck and Sergy motioned me to approach. "And here," said he, " is the cause of my travelling incognito. It was for her sake that our visit to San Francisco was kept secret."

We were interrupted by a deafening blast from the ship's horn, the first warning for all not passengers to go ashore. There was a tremendous lot of leave-taking, crying, kisses and hand-shaking. Presently the bell clanged violently, and a sailor called out, "All visitors to the shore!"

At last the farewells were over. Groups collected on the wharf and tried to say still more last words and good wishes to their friends crowding against the rail. The *Peru* whistled a prolonged note, the gangway was hauled up, the moorings were cast off, and the steamer glided quietly away from her stopping-place, carrying us to Asiatic shores and an unknown future. Sergy waved his hand cordially to Mr. Artsimovitch and the Vice-Consul. I stood beside him all smiles. A tug-boat towed us with some difficulty among the numerous boats surrounding us, and we sailed through the narrow entrance of San Francisco, known as the Golden Gate. We are hopelessly off from *terra firma* for eighteen days.

The *Peru* is a small vessel little fitted to do battle with such waves as we encountered. The ship is plying ordinarily between America and Panama, and it is quite accidentally that she is bound now to Japan. On her last voyage the *Peru* touched Honolulu.

On board the *Peru* we occupy the cabins 37, 39, 40, known as the cabin state rooms, on the starboard side on the upper deck.

The real names of our party appear upon the ship's list. There was no need of secrecy after we had left America behind us.

Deplorable were the first impressions of our voyage across the ill-named Pacific Ocean. The Pacific had been anything but pacific and peaceful. As soon as we were out of the Gulf of San Francisco the vessel began to roll. At half past eight the gong called us to dinner; after the second dish I returned to my cabin and lay down. I shut my eyes but sleep would not come to me. At dawn, with the aid of Mrs. Berger, the stewardess, I removed to another cabin situated on the lower deck, where the rolling was less felt. I remained in bed the whole day, feeling horribly ill. And we have still seventeen days to live on board!

Mrs. Berger is a really kind-hearted stewardess, and nurses me devotedly. She enters my cabin on tip-toe, bringing a soothing cup of tea with a drop of brandy, when I feel too ill to go down to lunch. But no persuasion of the motherly stewardess could get me out of my cabin, until she called in the ship's doctor, who forced me to go on deck for a little fresh air.

The head-butler, a solemn and majestic-looking mulatto, told me that there were only twenty-five first-class passengers on board. The third-class is full of Japs and Chinamen, who spend their time in playing dominoes. The Celestials are a pest to the ship, their special odour pursues us everywhere. All the boys (in the Far East all the men-servants are called boys, regardless of their age), are Chinamen, who speak a mixture of English, French and German, rather difficult to understand ; they call all the passengers, ladies and gentlemen likewise, Sir. The boys are excellent servants, wonderfully deft and handy. They absolutely watch the passengers, and study their tastes carefully when serving at table ; once let them know your wishes, and everything will be arranged to suit them. What a difference with the rough American servants ! For dinner the boys put on long white sleeves over their blue clothing and stick the ends of their long tresses into their pockets, in order that they should not dangle between their legs. When cleaning the cabins, they roll them round their head. Mme. Beurgier orders the stewards and the boys as if the boat belonged to her. She is a person not lightly to be disobeyed and would have been an excellent Prime Minister. She made friends with all her fellow-travellers and rushed over the entire ship conversing with everyone.

At five o'clock in the morning the sailors begin to clean the boat. The inspection takes place three times daily. At half-past eleven the captain, the ship's doctor and the head-steward walk round the cabins examining minutely if everything is in order ; their commanding eyes swept to-and-fro for the smallest speck of dust discovered in the remotest corner, the delinquent boy is placed for punishment at the wheel on deck for four hours. The boys stand in terrible fear of that rigorous triumvirate. They moved about the cabin flicking off an imperceptible touch of dust here, and straightening a piece of furniture there. Involuntarily I glanced round the carpet for threads, but it was all fearfully tidy, not a speck of dust, not a cobweb anywhere. The duties of inspection over, the boys faces beamed with contentment. With nightfall comes the third inspection ; the triumvirate enters the cabins without ceremony, even when the passengers are in bed.

We do nothing but sleep, eat and drink. At ten o'clock came tiffin (luncheon), consisting of soup, chops, fruit and pancakes ; at four—dinner ; at eight—supper. The days on board are awfully long and tedious. I generally stayed in my cabin between tiffin and dinner, wiling away the weary hours by scribbling my memoirs, and practising on my mandoline. My performances threw our boy Hassan, into ecstasies ; he sat on the floor before my door repeating " Veri nice, veri nice ! " After dinner the music loving passengers assembled in the music-room. Mr. Shaniavski, a very good pianist, is especially appreciated.

There is a whole army of cockroaches in our cabins. Before going to bed, I chase these nasty insects, and wrapping them up in a bit of paper, I throw them into the corridor.

We are now at the extreme end of the world, and have the feeling of standing upside down ; and, in fact, if the globe was being pierced through, we should have found ourselves in that uncomfortable posture conformably to the inhabitants of St. Petersburg. When it is midnight in that city it is midday here.

Severe rules and regulations hang on the wall in my cabin. First rule : The striking of matches forbidden. Second rule : The rush to the life-boats before receiving permission, forbidden. Third rule : Not to take fright when the false alarm of fire was rung. This false alarm takes place once a week for the practice of the crew. Dear me, what a noise they were making! The alarm began by the piercing sound of a whistle, and loud shouts of Fire, Fire! After which the sailors rush on deck to open the fire-pumps, and pour out the water into the ocean, laughing loudly all the time.

Travelling on the same boat with us was a company of Teutonic travellers, with Baron Korff, a German General. One of the youngest members sang German lullabies and love-songs to me, tapping ruefully over the region of his heart and rolling his eyes as if in mute appeal to heaven. His favourite song was *Mit einer Rose in der hand bist Du geboren.* (With a rose in the hand you are born.) The captain of a Mexican sailing vessel, a cadaverous-looking man like Don Quixote, with very black teeth and little hair, fell to my lot as companion at table. An American missionary of grave aspect sat on the other side of me. He was bound to Japan with his wife, a thin and sickly-looking lady, and a whole band of children. The youngest, a baby in arms, was born in America during the missionary's holiday. The children ran wild in the corridor, fighting and quarrelling the whole day, and are as noisy and troublesome as they can be. The boys no sooner heard me go out of my cabin than they were upon me like an avalanche. I could not read or work in the saloon, my attention being constantly disturbed by the children. They were as wild as young colts. One little boy believed himself to be a steam-engine and raced round the saloon driving a tandem of chairs, and his little brother, getting the maximum of sound out of a trumpet, executed a sort of war-dance round me, yelling like a wild Indian. The eldest of the family, a boy of six, was especially ungovernable. The heartless little wretch amused himself in tormenting Mrs. Beurgier's kitten, and I flew to its rescue as soon as I heard the piteous mewing of the poor little animal, which gave me a furious desire to box the little wretch's ears.

On Sunday morning, when I entered the saloon, I saw a notice stuck up on the mirror, announcing that the missionary was going to hold a service in the lower saloon at ten o'clock. At the appointed hour a boy sounded a gong, at which all the passengers assembled in the saloon and joined in the singing of hymns. The servants, baptised Chinamen, stood n a row as near the door as they could get.

July 17th.—Oh, what a night that was! I wonder my hair didn't turn white. We all thought we were going to the bottom. The ship was rolling and pitching violently, every board cracked and quivered, and enormous waves dashed over the deck ; vases in the saloon went down with a fearful crash, and all my things were scattered about my cabin. The captain kept watch on the bridge the whole night. I heard him shouting orders to the crew to take down the sails.

The sentimental German passenger did not coo his romances to me now. He suffered from liver complications and sea-sickness, and lay stretched on a bench on the deck, looking dreadfully green in the face.

July 18th.—The wind abated somewhat towards dawn, nevertheless the rolling continued and I lay in my berth the whole day. My head, finding no support, rolled from right to left on my pillow.

In the afternoon I ventured upon deck. Heavy black clouds hung over us ; a fresh air blew into my face. We are to-day at the extreme point of our voyage, quite near to the Aleutian Islands and Kamtchatka. A lark settled on our mast, and Baron Korff came to congratulate me with this first winged messenger from the distant country which was to be our new home. From San Francisco a pair of big albatrosses followed our ship, resting during night on the masts.

A whole week has past, and we have been on the sea seeing nothing but the sky and the water. The least incident takes the proportions of a whole event in the dreary, tedious life on board. To-day for the first time we perceived in the distance a boat with swelling sails. It was surely a pirate boat going out seal-hunting.

July 19th.—We are half-way over the ocean to-day, and had champagne at dinner for this occasion.

We were near the end of our provisions and starvation stared us in the face. We found at dinner, oysters, ever oysters, which I abhor : oyster soup, oyster vol-au-vent, and so on. I will try and bear all these privations stoically.

July 20th.—The fury of the ocean has increased. Our boat tossed, dipped and shook as a mere plaything. It was a difficult matter to stand upright. Everyone was more or less ill and cross. Dr. Pokrovski was the only one of our company to venture on deck in such weather. A rough movement of the ship threw him rolling out of his chair, and made him turn somersaults. Mme. Beurgier saw our poor Esculapius creep back to his cabin, looking a veritable wreck of humanity, yellow as a marigold, and his necktie all crooked.

July 21st.—To-day we pass the 18th meridian, and have lost a whole day. This is Monday, 21st July, and to-morrow we shall be at Wednesday, 23rd July. We have to put our watches back a whole hour every day.

July 23rd.—I passed again a sleepless night. The ship was rolling a good deal, and the howling of the wind in the rigging was something dreadful. I couldn't remain alone any longer, and stole into Sergy's cabin for company. He persuaded me to go and lie down again, but it was useless to think of sleeping, and I gave up the attempt.

July 24th.—A grey dawn is rising ; white vapours surround us. Our boat, pushed by a favourable wind, makes twelve knots an hour, in spite of the fog. If our captain does not arrive in time at Yokohama, he will have to pay the sum of 500 dollars as penalty.

July 25th.—The colour of the ocean has changed from dark grey to a very bright blue. After dull grey days the sky has suddenly brightened up, and a glittering sun has succeeded the dense haze which enveloped the sea this morning. After ten days of wind, tossing and tempest, all at once an absolute calm. Flying fishes are gamboling all around our ship and two fountains are spouted by whales close by.

July 26th.—To-day is our last Sunday on board. The missionary read prayers in the saloon. He gave out a hymn and all the passengers sang it together. He prayed for the President of the United States, for Queen Victoria and our Emperor, and preached a capital sermon. He said that the passengers, coming from different parts of the world, had gathered here to join together in fervent prayer. In a few days, probably, we shall all have to part for evermore, but in the sight of God we shall always be united.

July 27th.—The weather is quite warm, one feels that we are nearing Japan. Half-naked Japs and Chinamen lay stretched on mats in the hold, fanning themselves lazily, whilst their spouses are occupied in dressing their hair. They grease it with an ointment which makes it stick together, and mould it into a solid mass. This marvellous structure is left without being taken down for a week at a time. These voluntary martyrs sleep with their necks resting on a sort of wooden footstool placed under a thin bolster, which supports the neck, not the head, so that not one hair should be put out of place. They are evidently acquainted with the French proverb which says, *Pour être belle il faut souffrir.*

I was told that an old Chinaman, who had died on board on the third day of our voyage, had been embalmed on the boat. I remember now that the smell of aromas had spread all over the ship that day. Ancestor worship is a striking feature of China. All Chinamen insist on being buried in their native land, and when death overtakes one of them in a foreign country, his remains are always transported to China to be interred there, after the Buddhist rites.

CHAPTER LXV

YOKOHAMA

TOWARDS eight o'clock in the morning we saw a dark outline on the horizon, and made such a fuss over the first lump of sand, as if we were discovering the North Pole. The Island of Goto, precipitous and craggy, was the first sight of Japan; as it fades into greyness behind, there rises far away the high, jagged coast-line of Japan, with mountains in the far distance. Above the eternal snow-line appeared the cone of the sacred mountain Fuji-Yama, with its crown of snow. The peak was visible for a few moments only, retiring again behind the clouds. The Fuji-Yama is an ancient extinct volcano which sprang up in the year 862 before Christ. At the present moment there are four active volcanoes in Japan, which are the cause of frequent earthquakes in this country.

We are surrounded by fishing-smacks, with bronzed fishermen, who wore nothing above the waist-line and not much below it, their whole costume consisting only of a narrow belt. We passed two formidable-looking British cruisers before entering the port of Yokohama, which is rather a difficult undertaking among all this multitude of vessels encumbering the harbour of Yokohama. Sampans, in which stood policemen in snow-white uniform and Japanese quarantine officers scurried towards us. They came to see if we had any ailing passengers on board.

The *Peru* comes to anchor at Yokohama Beach. What joy to touch land after 18 days at sea!

We are met on the quay by the Russian consul, Prince Lobanoff-Rostovski, accompanied by Mr. Vassilieff, attached to the Russian mission at Yokohama, and Mr. Omaio, secretary of the Japanese Embassy at St. Peterburg, who was at home on leave. The Governor of the town has sent five servants to take care of our luggage, and three carriages were put at our disposal. We took our places in a victoria drawn by a pair of ponies, and drove to the Grand Hôtel, through the European quarter of the city with big brick houses and gay cafés and shops. I was very much astonished to see little two-wheeled vehicles called rikshas, drawn by men who trotted between the shafts. They wear a short blue wide-sleeved jacket, close-fitting blue drawers reaching to the ankles, straw sandals and a white mushroom-shaped hat, bearing their name and number ; a blue rag hangs on their shoulder to wipe their perspiration.

We occupied an apartment of two rooms with a balcony at the Grand Hôtel for four Mexican dollars ahead = two American dollars. It is peculiar that the Mexican dollar, though much larger, and containing therefore more silver than the American dollar, is worth only the half. Why is it so ? A mystery of the Exchange Office, I suppose.

The damp heat of Yokohama is very trying. It is well that there are no glasses in the windows ; in the frames and above half of the door are blinds, which let in the soft tropical air and produce an agreeable draught.

We are besieged by tiresomely polite Japanese and Chinese furnishers, tailors, shoe-makers and other purveyors with names almost impossible to pronounce for European tongues. They all bowed a great deal, and thrust their advertisements in our hands. I could not resist the temptation of purchasing a gorgeously embroidered pink satin thing with long, wide sleeves, which can serve as a wonderful tea-dress. I did not recognise myself when I passed before the mirror arrayed in that costume.

We went down to dinner at table-d'hôte and entered a large hall, full of smartly-dressed ladies in low gowns and gentlemen in evening dress. We were served by Japanese boys dressed in kimonos, who spoke very good English. The head-butler is a Chinaman who had his pig-tail cut off. He told us that he could never put his foot in China again, because he would be beheaded for having changed his national head-gear. Human life seems to be regarded rather lightly in the Celestial Empire !

After dinner we went out on the verandah for a breath of fresh air. The verandah, covered with straw mats and furnished with bamboo chairs, was full of loungers, Englishmen mostly, reclining upon their seats with their feet rather higher than their heads, their legs stretched wide apart and resting upon the arms of their rocking-chairs, in order to feel cooler.

28th July.—I woke up in the middle of the night with a suppressed scream and jumped up in my bed. I had been dreaming I was at sea, and the engines of the *Peru* had come to a sudden stand-still. " Why are the engines not working ?" I asked Sergy in an alarmed tone. After he had comforted me and I had pinched myself to be sure I was not dreaming, I fell fast asleep again.

It was an agreeable surprise to wake up and find land all around me. To-day is the birthday of His Majesty the Emperor of Japan. At daybreak I heard the beat of the drum from an English cruiser lying on the Quay, a warship bound to Siam where a mutiny has recently broken out.

Two American cruisers deafened us with artillery discharges. Their admiral, who has put up at our hotel, has sent a military band to play during tiffin. In the afternoon Sergy went to visit a military Japanese school where the officers are taught to inculcate, by suggestion, bravery to their soldiers, and how to vanquish, at the same time, their enemies. I sat by the window awaiting my husband's return, and looked through the chinks of a blind, whence I could see without being seen. Life over here is all new and strange to me. Everything seems elfish—men, trees, houses. Flat-faced aborigines patter along noisily upon wooden clogs, dressed in the garments of old Japan. They seem all alike; when you've seen one, you've seen all. The women are clad in gaily flowered kimonos, girded by a wide sash tied into a gigantic bow, their hair beautifully dressed with mock-flowers and combs and pins, their feet placed on small planes with two little pieces of white wood, in front and behind, just like small stilts. The married women are recognised by their shaved eyebrows and blackened teeth with oxide of iron. They indulge in this fearful custom in the view of alienating all masculine admiration, and remaining faithful to their husbands. But do their husbands remain faithful to their wives, their virtue being so unattractive? That is the question! The Japanese girls grow fast under the Southern sun, and many of them, at the age when little girls in Europe play at dolls, are married materfamilias. I see philosophical-looking babies, with a button of hair at the top of their head, strapped on their mother's back by a scarf, their bald heads falling backwards as though they would drop off. I am unable to recall any single occasion on which I saw a Japanese baby smile. Little children straddle astride on the hip of bigger children, who run after the passers-by with unencumbered hand outstretched. Artisans and tradesmen in blue cotton tunics, with the description of their trades printed in white on their backs, were setting their wares on the pavement, where they thought themselves most sure of attention. Vendors of green cocoa-nuts, slices of melon and sweetmeats, and victual merchants expose for sale in the streets along the walls, on planks, grasshoppers fried in oil and other nasty things. Just in front of our windows is the stand of the rikshas. I see a porter, his face hidden under an immense straw hat, advance towards the riksha-men, stooping under the burden of two cases, at the bottom of which very hot cinders keep the dishes hot. The portions, put into small saucers, are microscopic. The riksha-men, sitting on their heels on the ground, thrust their food into their mouth by the aid of two little sticks.

After lunch we got into rikshas and went for a ride through the streets of Yokohama. The first sensation of having a human being for a horse is not agreeable, but one soon gets accustomed to it. There was a place for one person only in each riksha. Our riksha-men moved briskly in files towards the native quarters of the town, through narrow and dark streets. On each hand was a row of toy-houses mostly unpainted, with the first storeys all open to the street, each standing in a little square of a toy-like garden. We hurried on between two long lines of painted paper lanterns, a festoon of blazing rubies in the intense darkness that surrounds them, suspended before low-thatched shops, constructed chiefly of bamboo, the front wall all doorway with hanging draperies, blue and white, covered with Japanese lettering, before which stood platforms heaped high with tropical fruit. The air was full of that sweet and subtle odour which one has long learned to associate with things imported from Japan. My runner trotted as fast as a horse ; I was rather frightened at first and tried in fantastical language to moderate his ardour. Our riksha-men stopped before a fountain surrounded by dwarf-trees, and after having quenched their thirst, my man-horse began to run with such a frenzy that I began to cry out for help, fearing to be upset. After a quarter of an hour of such mad driving, we arrived at the door of a native theatre lit up with pink and yellow lamps. Our drivers set the shafts of their vehicles on the ground and mopped their faces with a blue towel ; their clothing was drenched with perspiration. We entered a long narrow corridor, and came into a hall lighted by a few oil lamps. The audience consisted of whole families : grand-parents, parents and children of all ages, sitting on the floor on mats. All had their dinners with them, laid on little trays. Each place is separated by a bamboo stick that must be stepped over. A boy rang the bell which was to announce the signal for the beginning of the performance. The musicians began to play upon strange instruments, which made uncanny noises of a sort to make one's flesh creep. We seated ourselves on the floor of our so-called box. The whole representation consisted of a troupe of acrobats who went energetically through their performance and rolled about the stage upon big india-rubber balls.

In a theatre on the opposite side of the street, a parody was played on the ancient Japanese sovereigns. The theatre had no walls ; it was simply supported by columns, and all around was a large crowd struggling to see what took place without paying for the sight. The walls were covered with pictures representing different war scenes between Japs and Chinamen, in which the Chinese were running away and the Japs triumphed all along the line. In Japan the plays have usually fourteen, fifteen acts, and last sometimes two days. The men assume all the female parts.

We ended our nocturnal rambles in rather a fickle manner. We were trotted briskly up to a tea-house, where we were received with many bows by pretty musumés (waiting-girls). After having removed our shoes at the entrance hall, we were conducted up a steep and creaking staircase to the room where the "geishas" dance, and where mats and carpets were the only furniture. We seated ourselves with our feet tucked under us on cushions that the mousumés had set in a half circle on the mats, and waited patiently for the appearance of the geishas—dancing girls—who were occupied elsewhere just then. Presently a musumé slipped in, bearing a tray with all sorts of eatables, and set it before us. There were lobsters and raw-fish, and evil-looking vegetables, and nasty sweetmeats, and green tea in microscopic cups, and unspeakable horror, very strong and salt. The little musumés waited upon us silently and swiftly. The tea that one of them handed me made me feel sick, and after one disgusting mouthful, when I felt myself unobserved, I poured the contents of my cup outside the window on the neighbouring roof. I had cramps, being obliged to sit so long cross-legged, like the rest of the company, expecting the geishas. It was getting late, and having no more patience to wait for them we returned to our hotel.

The next morning Sergy went with the first train to Tokio, the metropolis of Japan, which is three-quarters of an hour's drive by railway from Yokohama, to call upon Mr. Khitrovo, the Russian Ambassador to Japan.

Three days later we left for Tokio, where my husband went to pay his respects to the Emperor of Japan. We called for rikshas and drove off full gallop to the railway station. In the waiting-room we saw a placard stuck up on one side of the wall, bearing the inscription in English "First-Class," and on the opposite wall was written "Second-Class," without any partition at all. All the passengers were Japs, sitting shoeless on their heels on the sofas in monkey-poses.

We took seats in a large car of American pattern, with wooden benches around and a door at each end, and tore through the country with few pauses. The road from Yokohama to Tokio is very picturesque, the shrubs are very green and dense, and the mimosa in full bloom. It is not for nothing that Japan is called "The Garden of Asia." But everything is Lilliputian. We see on our right tiny groves and dwarfed trees. We roll now through maize and rice plantations. Cottages with rush-cane roofs peep out from between the rich vegetation.

CHAPTER LXVI

TOKIO

ON arriving at Tokio we drove in a splendid landau sent to meet us by the Japanese minister of Foreign Affairs, to the Oriental Hotel, where we took an apartment of several rooms. We had barely time to take a little rest, when we received the visit of our Ambassador and the Japanese Naval Minister.

After dinner we sat on the verandah. The city lay in utter darkness before us; the streets were only lighted here and there with paper lanterns carried by the passers-by.

Our Ambassador invited us to his beautiful house close to Tokio, to show us geishas, whose dancing was held to have no equal in Japan. We drove in rikshas through a lovely avenue of cherry trees. When we arrived at the Ambassador's residence we were shown into a large hall hung with many rows of weapons of every description, rifles, revolvers, yataghans, etc., etc. Against the walls stood suits of armour. After having admired the beautiful collection, we entered another hall where four geishas awaited us. They were bare-legged, bare-armed, and with very much painted faces, dressed in bright-coloured kimonos. These little bits of womanhood looked as if they wanted to play at dolls; the eldest of the geishas was barely fifteen. Three musician-girls, arrayed in dark-blue kimonos, were seated cross-legged on the matting. They began to sing melodies resembling the mewing of enamoured cats on the roofs, to the accompaniment of the samissen, a kind of guitar of three strings. The dancing-girls had no more space than an ordinary square rug to dance upon. They were sitting in a circle; one of them rose, and saluting us to the ground, crossed her arms across her chest and began to act a mimic of a blind girl. Her performance could scarcely be called a dance, groping about the matting with her eyes closed. I found her companion's dances rather disappointing also. Their arms twisted and they glided without their body making any movement; a few shuffling steps to-and-fro, a wave of shapely olive bangled arms, all to the nasal twangling of a hideous accompaniment. I began to yawn behind my hand and looked longingly at the clock, and did all I could to keep awake. I should have dropped off to sleep certainly if tea and cakes hadn't come to my rescue. The geishas gathered in a group round us and sat at our feet. They looked at Mrs. Serebriakoff and me as at some object of extraordinary interest. Opening wide their little eyes they examined and tried on bracelets and rings, uttering funny little cries. It was nearly daylight when we returned to Tokio.

The next day my husband, in full military uniform, drove to the Imperial Palace, accompanied by his suite, to be presented to the Emperor of Japan. He returned delighted with his visit to the Taushi-Sama, the Son of Heaven. The word Mikado, by which the Emperor is known in Europe, is never used in Japan. Mikado is an ancient designation which has passed out of date in remote antiquity. The Emperor wore a uniform of European cut, with a Russian order on it, and the Empress was resplendant in a dress that she had ordered from Paris, with the Russian order of St. Catherine worn across her shoulder. The Imperial couple presented my husband with their portraits and their autographs.

On the following day my husband was invited to lunch with the Emperor's uncle, Prince Arissougava. In the afternoon we went to visit the Buddhist Temple of Shiba, to see the tombs of the "shioguns," the ancient Emperors of Japan. Two bonzes (Buddhist priests), enveloped in black gauze, followed by a big dog, served as guides to us. The Temple is surrounded by a magnificent shady park of camphor and other aromatic trees. We inhaled with delight the perfume of myrtle and orange blossoms. We found our way into a courtyard open to the sky, where a fountain played over a marble basin. Beyond is a long, low building, the sides are simple wooden screens. It is the Temple. Men and women kneel and pray before the entrance of the Temple. On each side stand two monster figures, demoniac, with eyes of fury, the guardians of holy things. The custom of offerings is very peculiar in Japan ; pilgrims cast their offerings in a box destined for the purpose, placed before the threshold, consisting of sheets of gilt paper or small coloured incensed tapers. The very poorest throw only a handful of rice into the box. I saw piles of straw sandals thrown at the feet of a huge marble Buddha, seated cross-legged on a bronze pedestal, and was told that it was the modest offering of riksha-men, begging Buddha to grant them strong legs. At the door of the Temple we slipped off our shoes and put on a pair of sandals, for in Japan one may not enter the House of God with shoes on. A white-robed priest with a shaven head appeared and motioned us, with a bow, to enter. The screens slide open and an immense hall is before us, full of unfamiliar sweet smell of Japanese incense, produced by strings of incensed paper which pilgrims burn before their idols. We pass through a great red gateway of the sacred enclosure and enter the mortuary shrines of Setsugu, one of the Shioguns, full of bronze lanterns, which are offerings to the dead from their royal relatives.

About an hour from Tokio stands an Orthodox Cathedral built on a hill. The archbishop, who was by birth Prince Kassatkin Rostovski before he turned monk, has for thirty years already propagated Christianity in this country. He has converted a great number of Japs and has built many schools. In one of these schools Japanese girls are taught the art of painting Russian ikons (holy images). We went to vespers to the cathedral, and all got into rikshas, each with two men, one to pull and the other to push. The road rises steeply to the church porch and our riksha-men had a very fatiguing ascent, perspiration was pouring down their faces. From afar we heard church bells ringing. When we entered the large cathedral, we saw a great number of natives; the men stood grouped on the right side and the women on the left. The priest, a converted Jap, in orthodox clerical attire, officiated in Japanese language. The scholars of the Orthodox school sang in chorus; I could make out only one word, "Amen." When the service was over the archbishop asked us to come and have a cup of tea in his drawing-room.

Next day was Sunday, we went again to the cathedral to hear mass. It was the archbishop who officiated this time and also in Japanese. During the Holy Sacrament he said a few words in Russian to us. The baptised natives were sitting on the floor on their heels. I saw women suckling their babies, and was very much astonished when a little Jap came running to his mother, and springing suddenly on her lap, began to suck her with great appetite. We invited the archbishop to dine with us at the hotel. He was not a bit a bigot, he ate meat and listened with pleasure to the sounds of a waltz played by an orchestra during dinner-time.

Mr. Vassilieff put himself at our disposal during our stay at Tokio. He had been present at the attempt on the life of our Emperor during his voyage to Japan when he was heir to the throne. He was driving in a riksha with the Prince of Greece and a numerous suite in the outskirts of Kioto. Mr. Vassilieff, who was of the party, saw a native policeman rush sword in hand towards the Grand-Duke, at which his riksha-man gave him a kick behind, and the next moment the ruffian was sprawling on the ground. The Prince of Greece fell on him with his stick and struck him full and square on the head. The man died in prison a year after, and the riksha-man who had defended the Grand-Duke has received a medal and a life annuity of a thousand roubles from the Russian Government.

On the day that my husband and his companions had
gone to Nikko, we ladies went out shopping. We stared
into the shop windows, being in search of curios, and bought
right and left with reckless extravagance. The merchants
greeted us with a number of quick, jerky little bows. We
returned laden with parcels, and the result of our struggle in
the curio shops were strewn all over our saloon. Sergy, on
returning from Nikko, had to pay great quantities of bills.
The merchants, having received their money, bowed so low
that it seemed as though they were crawling on all fours.

We were beginning to be tired of Tokio, and on the 5th
August we started to Kobe. The weather was grey and dull,
the crows croaked over us fortelling rain. The road to Kobe
reminded me of the Caucasus by its grand and wild landscape. We entered continually into tunnels. From afar we
heard the splashing of the ocean, and in a short time our
train ran along the shore. Suddenly we were caught in a
terrible storm; the ocean beat violently against the beach.
We were told that the typhon, that terror of seamen, had
just passed over. When a ship is caught in the centre of the
furious whirlwind, she is lost for ever. Our train fought
courageously with the hurricane. The wind rattled the
windows and seemed to threaten to overturn our car. It
won't be agreeable on sea to-morrow!

There was nothing to be got to eat at the stations during
the whole run. At one of the stoppages we bought from an
ambulant vendor an earthen cup and a tea-pot with hot
water, the whole for one cent. At every stoppage we
thought it was Kobe and that we had to get out.

CHAPTER LXVII

KOBE

THE train ran into a station illuminated by electricity; it was Kobe at last! The Russian Consul's interpreter came to meet us at the railway station, but we didn't hear the words through the noise of the gale. The only thing we made out was that we couldn't start for Nagasaki to-morrow on account of the weather. We'll have to wait here until the sea gets calmer. A French ship which had left Kobe in the morning had to return, being unable to continue her voyage.

We drove in rikshas to the Oriental Hotel through dark and empty streets.

Captain Andreieff, the commander of the "Mandchour," a gunboat put at our disposal as far as Vladivostock, came to call upon us; we kept him for luncheon, It was awfully hot during the meal and a boy pulled a "punkah," a gigantic linen fan running the whole length of the dining-room, hanging from the ceiling and moved by a cord.

In the afternoon we again visited the curio shops, where we saw a lot of pretty things, whilst half-naked boys, enveloped only in yellow gauze, were fanning us with wide palm fans, and flourished a feather-duster to keep the mosquitoes off. The master of one of the shops, stout and phlegmatic, sat perched on a high seat, his hands hidden in the long sleeves of his kimono. He rose when we entered, bowing and muttering something we didn't understand. He ordered a pretty Japanese woman to bring us cooling drinks. When Mme. Beurgier asked him, through the interpreter, if the pretty creature was his wife, the fatty replied curtly: "She is my mistress."

After having finished our hunt for curios we returned to the hotel just in time for dinner, and went to bed early, having to start at break of day. About the middle of the night the alarm-bell rang. I quickly got out of bed and ran out on to the gallery where I found myself face to face with a scared English lady in a scanty night attire, who told me that a fire had broken out in the neighbouring house. It was soon extinguished and we returned tranquillised to our beds.

CHAPTER LXVIII

ACROSS THE INLAND SEA

August 6th.—AFTER coffee, we drove to the pier where a steam-launch, with an officer and ten sailors sent by the "Mandchour," carried us off to the ship. We were received by the commander and all the officers in full dress assembled upon the quarter-deck. One hundred and sixty sailors were ranged along the deck, on which stood fourteen cannons. After the commander had presented all his officers to my husband, we were shown to our cabins. A tent made of flags belonging to different nations was set up aft in which we were to have dinner, but the weather changing suddenly, a black cloud appeared on the horizon, and soon a violent storm burst out. The sailors put on their water-proofs and began to execute all kind of manœuvres with the masts and riggings. We left Kobe only at two o'clock of the morning. Just at the starting there had been a rather bad moment. Suddenly there was a shrill whistle followed by a tremendous crash. Mercy on me! What can it be? There was a moment of panic, and everybody rushed on deck. It appeared to be the steersman who did not make out the desperate shouts of the commander of the ship giving him the signal to back, and so he continued to advance, knocking against a Japanese cruiser, on which they had already began to beat the alarm. It was a nice beginning for the voyage! Happily our boat had not been seriously injured, and after the slight damage was repaired, we entered the Inland Sea.

August 7th.—I occupy with Mrs. Serebriakoff the commander's cabin. Early in the morning the officer on service had to come in to consult the chronometer. After breakfast we took a look over the ship. The commander ordered the sailors to show us how they hung their hammocks, for the night. During that operation a big dog, belonging to the crew, who had an aversion to the officers of the ship, cunningly contrived to bite their legs. On the lower deck we saw a group of runaway convicts who were being transported back to Siberia to the Island of Saghalien. They belonged to the Asiatic tribe of "Kurds" (fire worshippers). They were chained together two and two, and guarded by two sentinels. The "Kurds" seemed to be taking their im-

prisonment with amazing apathy.   The presence on the boat
of these evil-looking men, with dark, ferocious faces, will not
give me a calm night.

August 8th.—After tea I mounted on deck and stretched
myself in a rocking-chair.   At midday the officer on duty
came to report to my husband the distance we had run since
yesterday.   We dined on deck under the tent with the
commander and two officers who had been invited to the
commander's table.   It was a custom on board for a certain
number of officers each night to be invited to dinner.   Towards nine o'clock a bell called to evening prayers, after
which we went to bed.

August 9th.—At ten o'clock in the morning on the centre-
deck, before the image of St. Nicholas, the patron of the
mariners, the sailors gathered for prayers, and sang hymns
in chorus.   After lunch a sailor photographed our group
surrounded by all the ship's officers, after which the officers
invited me to take part in a game consisting in throwing
rope-rings on to ciphers drawn in chalk on the deck's floor,
I proved very clumsy, making my first ring fly overboard.

CHAPTER LXIX

NAGASAKI

August 10th.—Towards five o'clock in the morning our vessel glided into the verdure-framed harbour of Nagasaki, a dream of loveliness. High on the three sides rose steep green hills, clothed with forests of palm-trees. On our left the port stretched out, covered with a multitude of junks. Here is the home of Madame Chrysanthemum !

The town of Nagasaki glitters in the sunshine in the distance, buried in verdure. We exchange the habitual salutes with the Japanese men-of-war. One of them had hoisted the Russian flag. I sought refuge on the commander's bridge, where the cannonade was less deafening.

A Japanese officer in full uniform, came in a canoe to welcome and bring us on shore. On the quay the Russian consul, Mr. Kostileff, was expecting us. We climbed up to the Hôtel Belle-Vue by narrow stone steps cut in the rock. The landlady, a respectable Frenchwoman of about forty, came hastening to receive the guests the steamer had brought her.

The hotel is surrounded by galleries on which all the bedrooms open. Our windows look out on the gulf, studded with a multitude of ships. Two British steamers are leaving for America to-night. I do not envy them !

A boy, speaking a few words of Russian, brought in tea with excellent cream and cakes. At Nagasaki the close neighbourhood of Russia is felt, a great number of natives speak our language.

I took refuge in my room from tailors, dress-makers and merchants of every kind, who besieged us the whole day smiling and curtseying at every step and eyeing each other mistrustfully. Here is a thick man entering our apartment with cat-like step, who with much drawing of breath, and bowing as low as his obesity permitted him, introduces himself laconically " Tortoise-shell man," which means that he dealt in wares made of tortoise-shell. When he bowed himself off, another Jap, selling post-cards and pictures, comes in announcing himself " Photograph-man," and so on.

We asked our Consul to dine with us. We were disturbed during the meal by the announcement that two sailors from the "Mandchour" were missed at the evening roll-call. Mr. Kostileff had to get up and make inquiries in the town.

We continue to have no news of the *Nijni-Novgorod* The ship on which my husband's aide-de-camp had embarked with all our household. We asked the consul to cable to Singapore and got the same reply: "No news." We begin to get very anxious.

August 11th.—The rain falls in torrents, and the state of the sky does not promise improvement of the weather for the moment. The tempest-flag is hoisted in the port. Impossible to go out to sea to-morrow!

August 12th.—The sea is much calmer and we sail from Nagasaki to-night. Before embarking we went for a drive in rikshas and met nearly all the officers from the "Mandchour." By night as we approached our ship in a canoe, our rower shouted out the pass-word "An officer," to the question, "Who rows?" of the sailor on duty.

The deck was lighted with different coloured lanterns in our honour. I escaped to my cabin whilst my husband was being greeted by the ship's officers.

CHAPTER LXX

ACROSS THE JAPANESE SEA

August 13th.—We were anchored in the bay the whole night waiting for the break of day, and left Nagasaki at six in the morning. The day is very fine. I lay comfortably stretched in my chair on the deck, covered all over with an awning to ameliorate the ardour of the sun. The crew was exercising on the upper deck. I hear the command of " Fire ! " (powder charges). A second "False alarm " was rung, " Man overboard ! " someone cried, and in the space of three minutes a life-boat was equipped and lowered, manned by two sailors who brought up triumphantly to the officer on duty the huge club, which represented the ship-wrecked man.

August 14th.—The barometer has fallen. The wind is blowing very hard, and the sea is swelling rapidly. I remained shut up in my cabin all day stretched inertia in my narrow berth ; I see the ceiling rise and descend. A very disagreeable feeling indeed !

August 15th.—The sea is something frightful. The wind moans and our ship pitches and groans as if she was going to fall in pieces.

CHAPTER LXXI

SIBERIA

VLADIVOSTOCK

August 17th.—To-day is our last day on board. We pass before the bays of Ulysses, Diomedes, Patrocles, and Ajax. Sergy came to wake me at dawn; the coasts of Siberia were in sight, and the lighthouse on the Island of Askold came to view. After we had seen nothing but waves for so many days, it was exciting to see land again. We advanced slowly in order not to arrive before the appointed hour, nine o'clock to Vladivostock. My husband's standard is hoisted on the *Mandchour* The commander comes to take leave of me and offers me as a souvenir of our voyage, a beautiful bouquet tied with a broad blue ribbon bearing in big gilded letters: Kobe, Nagasaki, Vladivostock,—the three ports we had touched on the *Mandchour*.

My husband went to put on his uniform. When I mounted on the commander's bridge I saw him looking at the coast with his field-glasses. The commander and all his officers were also wearing full uniform.

The town of Vladivostock, built in a semi-circle, is bordered by a chain of mountains. We are entering the port. Salvoes of artillery are fired from the men-of-war; military bands played on these cruisers until we were out of hearing distance. The Japanese men-of-war saluted us, while a band played our anthem. We stopped the engines to drift by them slowly. We pass now between the Russian and Japanese fleets, ranged at the entrance of the port. The citadel furnished with 190 guns, saluted us with 21 cannon-shots; the *Mandchour* responded with deafening discharges. On all the cruisers the men stood in rows along the yards. We cross the "Bosphorus," and drop anchor in the "Golden Horn," recalling Constantinople's "Golden Horn." Admiral Engelm, the chief of the port arrived on board in a steam-launch, accompanied by a numerous suite. We saw another canoe approaching, carrying Admiral Tirtoff the chief of the Russian fleet cruising at Vladivostock, with a Japanese Admiral. As soon as the welcomes were over, we got into a steam-launch with the General-Governor's flag hoisted on it, which took us to the shore.

My husband was received on the pier, carpeted with a red cloth, by all the military and civil authorities of the town We were bowing to right and left as we proceeded between a living hedge of officers and smart ladies. The soldiers of the garrison saluted Sergy with loud hurrahs. The Mayor of the town came up and presented my husband, according to the Russian custom, with "Bread and Salt" on a beautiful silver dish, and pronounced a long welcoming discourse. Chinese and Corean deputations also presented "Bread and Salt." I received a whole lot of bouquets tied with ribbons bearing welcoming inscriptions.

After my husband had thanked the authorities for their warm welcome, a "troika" (a carriage with three horses) was brought up. The horses were rather troublesome and I was quite foolishly terrified to drive in the carriage; having a nervous dread of horses, after the accident on the day of our marriage, when our horses took fright and bolted, and nearly did away with us. I entreated Sergy to proceed on foot to General Unterberger's house (the governor of the town). We were escorted through the streets in triumph. Vladivostock had put itself into festival array; flags hung from the house-tops, in the town and from the masts in the harbour. The troops formed a wall from the pier to the governor's house. We advanced to the sound of marches between two rows of soldiers, amidst peals of loud hurrahs. I was somewhat dazzled by all these manifestations. We marched now between rows of scholars belonging to different schools of Khabarovsk. The pupils of the young ladies' gymnasium curtseyed to me as we passed. One of the smallest girls came up to me and presented me with an enormous bouquet, tied with a pink ribbon, whilst the head-mistress delivered a little speech to me. I stood there at a loss what to say and blushed perfectly scarlet, which was very silly of me. I could not maintain my dignity at all, and felt for the moment tongue-tied.

On our way we entered the cathedral full of people. The Bishop in a few hearty words bade us welcome to Vladivostock. Many curious glances were turned on us and it was a veritable torture to me to be stared at like that.

At last we arrived at the Governor's house. Mrs. Unterberger welcomed me with a bouquet in her hand, and took me to my apartment. Six rooms had been allotted to the rest of our company at the house of Mr. Langeletti, a rich merchant from Hamburg.

I hadn't time to rest and was called down to the dining-room to be present at a Te Deum of thanksgiving for the happy termination of our voyage across the treacherous Japanese sea. There were many people in the room and no end of presentations and exchanging of greetings, after which my husband went to pay his official call on the admirals, who received him with cannon-shots when he stepped on board. At night the town was beautifully illuminated in our honour.

I awoke in the middle of the night with a heavy heart; feeling myself expatriated and shut up in a golden cage: I cried bitterly. What would I have not given to be back at St. Petersburg again!

The next day a grand dinner was given by General Unterberger. About sixty guests sat at a long table richly decorated with flowers and silver; a band of the Siberian navy played during the repast. The dinner was very gay; numerous toasts were drunk. General Unterberger raising his glass drank to my health and the whole company rose to touch my glass. The Japanese Admiral addressed in flowery native language a long speech to me, translated rather badly by his interpreter. I was crimson with the effort to control my laughter and bit my lips to blood. I did not venture to look at Mrs. Serebriakoff who was also assailed with a fit of giggling, and kept my eyes on my plate.

I got an invitation to a ball given on the cruiser *Admiral Nakhimoff*, but found a plausible pretext not to accept it, preferring to slumber in my bed, lulled to sleep and wafted into the land of dreams by the soft music of a military band played on the cruiser, which floated faintly from afar through the night air; there came to me through the window the faint strains of a waltz which personified to me just then the sense of my favourite waltz "Loin du Bal."

The next day I visited the young ladies' gymnasium of which I am Honorary President. I was welcomed at the entrance by Mrs. Unterberger and the Vice-Governor of Vladivostock. The directress of the gymnasium presented to me all the members of her administration. After which the pupils presented me with a beautiful embroidered serviette of their own work.

August 22nd.—To-day Sergy started for Nikolskoe, a large military settlement above 150 miles away from Vladivostock to review the troops and be present, at the same time, at the inauguration of the railway-line which is to join Vladivostock and Khabarovsk. Nikolskoe is inhabited by Russian colonists, who live well, each family possessing above 100 acres of land. The troops quartering in the surroundings of Nikolskoe consist of three batteries of artillery, a brigade of riflemen, five batteries containing a thousand men each, and a brigade of cavalry. I was also expected at Nikolskoe and the officers of the garrison begged Sergy to transmit to me a beautiful bouquet.

All day long streams of visitors came; I felt a stranger among them, and so lonely without Sergy! One soon grows old here. One of the visitors, a colonel with a very wrinkled face, was only forty years of age but would have passed for seventy easily. I do hope we won't make a long stay here, not only because of home-sickness but also from coquetry.

We had to pay some calls, driving in a beautiful "troika," belonging to General Unterberger. We made a great sensation in the streets. Our cortège was triumphal ; the Prefect of the Police drove before us and a numerous escort of Cossacks galloped behind our carriage. We were cheered by the crowd on our way ; hats and caps flew in the air. My neck was nearly dislocated, having to bow right and left all the time.

The town of Vladivostock is scattered about on hillocks ; up one street we went and down another. Half the shops of the town are Chinese ; they are in constant competition with the Russian shops, taking away all their customers. A Russian tailor came to ask my husband to remove into another place his Chinese neighour, who was a dangerous rival to him on account of his low prices. Certainly Sergy did not accede to his request.

The climate of Vladivostock is extremely damp ; the perpetual fogs act perniciously upon the nerves ; the percentage of suicide is high and cases of madness are very frequent here. I am very happy that my desire to help the afflicted poor is beginning to be fulfilled. At my request the mayor of the town has collected five thousand roubles in the space of a few days to build an asylum for lunatics. One bed has already been established bearing my name.

The service of the post leaves very much to be desired. We have received a letter from Russia dated six months ago ; the missive had arrived first at Khabarovsk, but as at that time there was no communication between these two towns, on account of the bad state of the roads, this letter had returned to Russia to be sent back again to Vladivostock via Japan.

The admirals and the commander of the *Nakhimoff* came to ask me to fix a day for the ball that they wanted to give at the marine club in my honour. In order to make it more attractive to me the marine officers have decided to open it by a concert. I was received like a queen at the ball. Admiral Engelm gave me his arm, leading me across the brilliantly illuminated ball-room. I was loaded with two enormous bouquets, rather heavy to carry. When I entered the crowded hall all eyes were turned on me, and I struggled with an overwhelming inclination towards instant flight. As soon as we got to our places in the first row, the concert began. It lasted about two hours, after which I mounted on an estrade, and glued to my chair, decided to remain as looker-on at the ball, when I saw Admiral Engelm coming up to me as a spokesman from the marine officers, to ask if I might accord them a dance, but I declined the invitation, with thanks, and passed my time in looking at the dancers, eating bonbons. It was near day-light when we returned home.

Bad news has been received regaridng the ship *Nijni-Novgorod*. A telegram came from Mascat from the captain of the ship saying that they had encountered a terrible storm which had driven them out of their course. They had been forced to take refuge in an Arabian port, and thus the ship can't be due at Vladivostock before October, when the roads are blocked for weeks, and all communication stopped between Vladivostock and Khabarovsk.

Mrs. Unterberger is awfully nice to me, and full of kind attentions. She proposes drives and boat-parties, but it was only Mme. Beurgier who profited by them. She went one day to lay a wreath of flowers on the tomb of a young officer of the French navy, who had been murdered recently in the outskirts of Vladivostock by a convict, who profited by his uniform to run away.

Sergy went in a steam-launch along the Gulf to visit the villages inhabited by Russian colonists. I had made myself quite ill by this time with the thought that we could not expect our household and things before Christmas. I felt awfully discouraged thinking of all the privations we should have to endure. The path of a General Governor's wife is not always strewn with roses. How many thorns there are for a few flowers! I can never reconcile myself with the life in this wretched land. I suffered miseries of home-sickness, and had the desire of a caged bird to fly. I dream only of going back to St. Petersburg, but it is foolish of me, I may as well ask for the moon. I, who from my very infancy had only to stretch my hand to gather all the joys of life, was I going to doubt my lucky star now?

A doctor who had the reputation of making a good diagnosis had to be summoned to me. After having tapped me here and there, he said I was a bundle of nerves and prescribed a gayer mode of life for me, nothing more.

The day after Sergy's departure there was a tremendous storm at sea, destroying innumerable fishing-boats. I passed an anxious night listening to the roar of the wind outside, threatening to overturn the house. The windows rattled in their frames, and doors were burst open. Mme. Beurgier came in the morning with terrible stories of damage done by the storm. Boats were torn from their moorings and blown on to the land, and a great number of Chinese junks were tossed on the shore. A score of soldiers, who were crossing the bay on a raft to bring hay from the opposite shore, were obliged to drop anchor not far from the coast, in order to await for the tempest to abate. They were caught by the storm and their raft was torn away and shattered to pieces against the rocks. At dawn, eight soldiers only succeeded in landing, after having swum on the wrecks for many miles ; all the rest had perished. And my husband was out at sea at that moment! I was beside myself with anxiety.

I didn't expect Sergy before three days, and taking up a piece of needle-work, sat in a restless mood talking with Mrs. Unterberger, when suddenly I heard the report of a gun, followed by a second report. It was my husband who was returning to Vladivostock sooner than we expected.

On the 30th August, our Emperor's namesday, my husband reviewed the troops on the Square, surrounded by a crowd of officers of all ranks. The soldiers passed before our windows with an even step. After the review Sergy gave a lunch to all the military and civil authorities of the town. In the evening we went to a garden-party given in the Admiralty Grounds, with all sorts of games, and so on.

CHAPTER LXXII

OUR JOURNEY TO KHABAROVSK

September 2nd.—We leave Vladivostock with its mists and fogs to-day. I, for my part, shall be heartily glad when we can be comfortably by ourselves at Khabarovsk.

A great number of officers accompanied us as far as the boat on the Soungatcha river. We had a brilliant leave-taking. I received so many bouquets that I almost disappeared amongst the flowers. The railway-station was decked out with flags. A great crowd had assembled on the platform which was covered with red cloth ; a special train, with a dinner-car attached to it, was awaiting us. Two sentinels were placed before our saloon-carriage. Whistles are given to signal our departure. The train steamed out of the station amid the ringing cheers of the crowd. Standing at the window we answer the salutes and hand-wavings. Our train crept along at the pace of a snail, making only twenty miles an hour. Our way leads along the sea-shore for some time, and then we enter a wide plain, disturbing the tiger with the locomotive.

At the first stoppage we are received in pomp. A triumphal arch has been raised, bearing our initials. A deputation of inhabitants came up to my husband and presented him with " Bread and Salt," and the workmen of the railway-line handed me a bouquet almost too big to carry.

We move very cautiously and slowly, because yesterday the train which had been run on trial, went off the rails in this place. We see a number of mansas, Chinese workmen, repairing the line.

At five o'clock we arrived at the point at which the railway ended and stopped at Nikolskoe, a large military station. We were four hours late. Dr. Pokrovski and Mr. Koulomsine take from here the boat on the lake Khanka. They will await our arrival at a place called the " Third Post." We chose to go by way of the carriage road, which will prolong our journey for at least a day or two.

My husband was received on the platform by General Kopanski, the commander of the troops, who drove us to his abode, situated about eight miles distant from the railway station. A group of peasants were awaiting my husband on the square before the church to offer up their petitions, very queer ones some of them. An old woman went on her knees holding her request on the top of her head, in which she asked Sergy to indicate to her the shortest way to Jerusalem! Our drive through the village caused a great sensation. The inhabitants stood on their thresholds and stared at us. I saw some peer at us from the windows, through opera-glasses. Before General Kopanski's house a guard of honour presented arms to my husband, and a platoon of Cossacks defiled before him.

We are here for three days. Our host, though an old bachelor, knew how to make us as comfortable as possible.

September 3rd.—General Kopanski gave a grand dinner to-day in our honour. During the repast a military band played selections from "Faust." The music led me to a far-away place; I had closed my eyes and saw St. Petersburg in vision. I kept back my tears with difficulty.

September 4th.—I did not leave my room until dinner-time, reading a heap of newspapers which had been forwarded from Khabarovsk; but the news was two months old. One is obliged to live behind date in this far-away country.

After dinner we went to the camp to assist at the evening retreat. The big camp, situated about five miles from Nikolshoe, was decorated with flags and lanterns of different colours. The soldiers received us with shouts and cheers. When prayers were ended, the drums beat the salute and a salvo of twenty-six cannons was fired, after which the spouse of the chief of the brigade offered us tea in a big tent.

September 5th.—To-day we are undertaking the most difficult part of our journey, and shall have to endure the misery of atrocious roads. At six o'clock in the morning our tarantass, a rattling post-chaise, was at the door. An escort of two hundred Cossacks on horseback is trotting close behind our carriage and on both sides of it, until our first stoppage where we have to change horses. A third hundred of Cossacks was sent on before, to be divided into parties of six men to escort us all the way.

Our cortège consists of seven carriages. Whilst we traverse the camp the soldiers forming a line on each side of us cheer us loudly; military bands play marches as we drive along. We plodded on steadily the whole morning and were shaken a good deal on the badly-made roads. The two first stations were kept by the post department, but at the third stopping-place a team of three horses, belonging to different Russian colonists, harnessed together with utter disregard to size, breed, and disposition, were awaiting us. The harness was rusty and mended with strings. The driver was with great difficulty inspired to action, and totally incapable of transmitting such inspiration to his animals, by coaxing

A*

words or whip. At last the poor hacks moved on, one pulling to the right, the other to the left. The road was completely deserted; we didn't meet a living creature on our way. I was told that these spots were frequented by tigers, and when I asked a Cossack of our escort if we had no risk of meeting one, the man answered coolly that it might happen very easily. Not much comfort from that Cossack.

The roads were very bad, very hilly and rough. We climbed with difficulty the steep ascents, and descended with still greater difficulty. Our driver, a peasant boy of about sixteen, drove artrociously, cutting corners and racing down steep hills. At a descent, which he took at a tremendous pace, a part of the harness gave way and the horses became uncontrollable. I was on the act of jumping out of the carriage when the Cossack, who sat on the box, succeeded in holding in the horses.

At each stage the colonists welcomed us with " Bread and Salt." My husband received a great number of petitions from the emigrants, for the greater part complaints from the new settlers against the colonists, who demanded one hundred roubles for the right of settling down with them, and oppressed them in every way.

Towards evening we reached a large village, and passed under a triumphal arch bearing the inscription " Welcome ! " We had an hour's stop at the village-inn, where we pulled up for dinner. We did honour to the frugal repast, consisting of cabbage-soup and roasted chicken, served by pretty village girls arrayed in their Sunday best.

After a drive of less than an hour, we came to a village where we stopped to rest for the night at the house of the Commissary of Rural Police.

September 6th.—We went in the morning to hear mass in the village chapel. The peasant girls were in their national dress, their long tresses interlaced with gay-coloured ribbons. After church, we continued our journey. We have yet many miles before us. At the next station we found a relay of four powerful horses belonging to the Prison Department. The Inspector of the Prisons, Mr. Komorski, was at the station to meet us. Our escort was increased by two Cossack officers. The horses fretted at standing, and I found them a bit over fresh; they started at a brisk pace. Our driver is a convict transported for life to Siberia, who had just terminated his ten years of penal servitude, and will be made a colonist in a short time. On the way we stopped at the house of a young engineer who is taking part in the construction of the railway-line beyond the Lake Baikal, after the Caspian Sea and the Sea of Aral, the largest lake in Asia. As soon as the horses were sufficiently rested, we proceeded on a road which had been growing from bad to worse. It is constructed on marshy ground and is full of ruts and holes in which we jolted and tossed about. The shocking roads aren't like roads at all, more like ploughed fields, inches deep in mud, and so rough that our vehicle seemed to be propelled by a succession of earthquakes wallowing in mud half-way deep. Our horses had hard work, sinking almost to their shoulders at every step. Our Heir to the throne on his tour to the Orient, when passing this way, had to be drawn by oxen.

At last we reached the convict settlement where Mr. Kopanski resides, superintending the work on the railway-line of the convicts sentenced to hard labour. At the present moment he has under his command three thousand convicts, and one thousand soldiers to guard them.

Mr. Komorski's house stands on a small eminence surrounded by barracks inhabited by convicts, dressed in long grey coats; the greater part are in chains. A long line of prisoners had half of their heads shaved, they were runaway convicts, who were brought back again to these parts. They cheered my husband gaily. A monk stood on the threshold of the chapel, where a Te Deum was sung by the convicts.

Mr. Komorski showed us a great deal of hospitality. He has contrived to give our apartment quite an air of cosiness. On my dressing-table I saw a bottle of scent bearing the name of "Bouquet d'Amour" quite a fitting denomination, for we are now in the provinces of the "Amour."

All the servants in the house are convicts, who fulfil their duty perfectly well, nevertheless these surroundings made me feel so nervous and miserable, that I did not want to be present at dinner and went to bed immediately after our arrival, under the pretext of a bad headache. Oh! how horrid it was to hear the sounds of a gay waltz played by an orchestra of convicts during the repast! I buried my head in my pillow and had a good cry. I hated our host ferociously at that moment.

September 7th.—Early in the morning Sergy visited the prisons, and at eight o'clock we proceeded on our journey. The road had recently been laid out specially to transport provisions from the boat to Mr. Komorski's abode. After a drive of two hours we arrived at a spot where a copious lunch awaited us in a pavilion set up near the railway-line. We suddenly came upon a gang of chained convicts breaking stones on the road, who worked under the eager eyes of guards with ever-ready revolvers. Whistles were heard giving the signal to these wretched men to take off their caps at our approach. I was told that work was assigned to them for twelve hours of labour. Their food is good, the daily rations consisting of a plate of soup with 250 grams of meat and a kilogram of bread. In a group of convicts we saw the son of a General we had known at St. Petersburg. That unfortunate young man had belonged to one of the brilliant Guard regiments, and had been sent to the galleys and put to hard labour for life, for having shot one of his comrades, (*Cherchez la femme!*) His pale, haggard face was so painful to behold.

The last miles leading to the boat were as bad as bad could be. We were tumbled about like nuts in a bag. We reached towards four p.m. the Third Post on the banks of the "Soungatcha," with aching bones and stiffened limbs There were our fellow-travellers on the quay awaiting us, and whom should I see among them but Mr. Li, the *attaché* of the Chinese Embassy at St. Petersburg, my summer cavalier of Music Halls. I must say I was surprised! And I thought I should never see him again. The world's small! Mr. Li passed through Vladivostock on his way to China, on a holiday. When we met our companions on Lake Khanka, he decided to come all this long way to see us. He will return to Lake Khanka to-morrow morning. The director of the Navigation Company on the Amour-river was also on the quay to meet us. He presented my husband " Bread and Salt " on a beautiful silver dish, and I received an enormous bouquet.

We are going to travel now by water as far as Khabarovsk. A handsome steam-yacht named " Ingoda " was lying alongside the quay, ordered for our use—a vessel gaily tricked out with flags, with my husband's standard floating on the overdeck. The yacht was apparently quite new, all white and gold, with steam-heating and electricity. We were to travel luxuriously on that dainty thing. I have a charming cabin with real windows and bed, not a hard shelf, but quite a wide, springy bed, and blue silk tapestries on the walls ; the covering of the furniture and the curtains are of the same stuff. I have a toilet-table adorned with white muslin curtains tied with blue ribbon. The cookery on board is excellent; the head-cook is a Chinaman. The captain provided soft-moving Chinese waiters and a Russian maid for me.

We shall weigh anchor only to-morrow morning, because it is dangerous to sail on the "Soungatcha" by night, the river being very narrow and winding. After supper the sailors lighted up the boat with Bengal fires, and barrels of burning tar were placed along the banks of the river. I sat up half the night on deck, stretched in a basket-chair chatting with Mr. Li about St. Petersburg, and awakening so many far-off memories.

Sept. 8th.—We started at 8 o'clock in the morning. Our boat glided down the swift river advancing very slowly. Our way wound in cork-screw curves, and the raftsman had to do some clever piloting to make the turns. On the left side of the "Soungatcha" was China. Here and there appeared to sight Chinese thatched huts. Natives, with long tresses, floated in junks on the river. On our side there is no vestige of habitation; all around the silence was profound; we seemed to have the world to ourselves. Now we steam on along lovely green banks fringed with tall trees bending their branches low over the water and reflected in it as in a mirror. Wild ducks swept over us, and long-legged herons came quite near to the edge of the water.

By the time the moon rose we had come to the first halt, a Cossack settlement situated in the hollow of a valley, where we cast anchor for the night. Smoke rose over the thatched roofs of the village; church-bells were ringing for vespers. Two "atamans" (Cossack delegates) are standing on the quay, holding their huge staffs of command. A deputation of Cossacks presented "Bread and Salt" on a glass dish to my husband, and I received as a gift a wild kid. We saw two men advancing, carrying between them, across their shoulders, a long pole upon which hung an enormous sturgeon. There was scarcely room enough on board for the gigantic fish.

We took a stroll through the village, where we visited the home of a rich Cossack inhabitant. My husband signed himself as godfather to his little son, who lay shrieking in his cot. The wee Cossack was still unbaptised, as there was no priest in the neighbourhood.

Sept. 9th.—The captain waited for the sun to rise to weigh anchor. Towards ten o'clock we enter the river "Oussouri," which is considerably broader than the "Soungatcha." An eagle is ascending high up in the skies. The air is so transparent that mountains which are scores of miles away are distinctly visible. The freshness of the vegetation is surprising. The furze attains the height of three yards. We slide along rich verdant valleys strewn with sweet-smelling flowers. The fresh breeze brings us a penetrating perfume of new-mown hay.

The next stopping-place was Krasnoyarsk, a big Cossack settlement. The inhabitants presented us wine in bottles entwined with branches of grapes. I remained on deck till midnight, admiring the large river on which the full moon reflected its opal glimmer.

Sept. 10th.—The wind that had risen in the night brought rain. We intended pushing on to Khabarovsk for the night, but the fog being very dense, we dropped anchor before Kasakewitchi, a large village scattered on a hillock.

Sept. 11th.—We are passing the most shallow part of the "Oussouri." The water is so shallow that we advance with great difficulty. We dropped anchor five miles off Khabarovsk. Two barges with sails were sent to meet us with an officer and thirty rowers, in case we could not advance further on our boat, and it came out that it was the barges that had to be helped, for during the night a squall arose, followed by a shower, which nearly submerged the barges. The officer and soldiers had to be taken on board.

Sept. 12th.—We are at our journey's end. Our next station will be Khabarovsk. We advance very slowly in order not to arrive at Khabarovsk before the appointed hour—nine o'clock in the morning.

CHAPTER LXXIII

KHABAROVSK

WE approach Khabarovsk, which, like ancient Rome, is built on seven slopes divided by deep ravines. Each slope has its own principal street, cut by transversal lanes which descend to the ravines. Khabarovsk stands at the joining of two grand rivers, the " Amour " and the " Oussouri." In about ten minutes a large building came to view. It was the so-called "Castle," our future residence, an imposing red-brick house with the General-Governor's flag waving from the roof.

We were received at Khabarovsk with much display of military pomp, and cheered by the entire population, which was on the pier to see us land. The quay was spread out with red cloth and decorated with flags. All Khabarovsk appeared to turn out: men, women, and children. There was a salute of one hundred and one cannon-shots from the batteries to welcome us. My husband was received on the quay by the authorities and the Municipality of the town. After a speech of welcome, they presented him with " Bread and Salt" on a silver salver. The Mayor of the town, an exiled Pole, addressed a few flattering words to me, saying that great things were expected from me. I was very much embarrassed, and stood there with burning cheeks.

I entreated Sergy, just the same as at Vladivostock, to walk on to the "Castle." We made quite an imposing procession. The town was dressed all over with flags and the balconies ornamented with draperies. The streets were lined with people all the way down to the "Castle." The windows of the houses were full of faces gazing at us. A double row of soldiers were placed on each side of the road. All along the way we were loudly greeted by the people, and showers of flowers fell at my feet when we passed through the streets. On our way we entered the cathedral. The church was crowded. The bishop, in full sacerdotal costume, waited to receive us and to officiate a solemn mass. Baron Korff, my husband's predecessor, is buried inside the cathedral. Sergy laid upon his tomb a large silver wreath which he had brought up from Moscow. The schools of Khabarovsk stood in a line from the cathedral right up to our house. The school girls strewed roses in my path. Then we went into the "Castle." The first arrival in my new home was not encouraging, thanks to the awkwardness of one of my husband's secretaries, who gave me a very unpleasant piece of information, breaking to me the news that the boat *Nijni-Novgorod* with all our household, had been wrecked on the coast of Aden. I could scarcely keep from bursting into tears. I departed to the privacy of my room and fell into a chair without taking off my hat. I sat and wondered how I would take to this life. Here I was in a foreign land, a fearful distance from home! I felt utterly desolate in this great strange house and looked a picture of forlorn misery. I could control myself no longer, and burying my face in my hands, I wept and sobbed unrestrainedly. But I must put a good face upon things before Sergy. I must and I will!

In the evening there was a display of fireworks which we admired from our verandah. In front of the entrance blazed an immense shield with "Welcome" in transparencies, and the initials "B. S." (Barbara, Sergius) on it. A military band was playing in the pavilion of the assembly just opposite us. The idea came to me to go for a stroll incognito as far as the monument of Count Mouravieff-Amourski, the conqueror of the Provinces of the Amour. The statue stands in front of the river on a huge pedestal dominating the whole plain of the "Amour." My incognito was soon discovered, and people made way to us as we walked past the row of curious eyes, on the boulevard all flaming with garlands of fire. I hate nothing so much as exhibiting myself. It was very creepy to be stared at like that!

On the next day Sergy sent a telegram to Vladivostock to the agent of the Volunteer Fleet with inquiries about the fate of the *Nijni-Novgorod* and received on the same night a reassuring answer that the boat was safe and sound, and had just left Colombo.

Our house is so large that we can easily be lost in it. One of the immense halls is decorated with life-size portraits of our Emperor and the Heir to the throne, under which, on a silver plate, was engraved that His Imperial Highness had stopped in the house during his recent visit to the Orient. From my windows I could look at the "Amour," flowing along deep and broad. I enjoyed seeing the ships crowded with tourists go past.

The first days at Khabarovsk were hard to me. I thought nothing could make me like the country; nothing except duty would make one come here! My new home put me in mind of a gilt cage. For everybody I was the wife of the Governor-General, and treated, therefore with a deference which I abhor. A new life began for me. I had duties to perform: official dinners, official receptions—a duty which was not particularly enjoyable to me. I had to follow my husband everywhere with outward pleasure and inward rebellion—a martyr to politeness.

In my quality of President of the Committee of Benevolent Ladies, I had to send invitations to all the members asking them to attend a meeting in our house. It was for the first time in my life that I had assisted at a committee, and being new to my work, I began to get awfully shy, and stupidly got very red. The flush on my cheek was scarlet when I was called upon to make a little speech. I felt so shy that I seemed entirely to have lost the use of my tongue, and forgot all the words I had learnt by heart. It is terrible that feeling when people are expecting you to do something and you are sure to disappoint them. The committee lasted three hours at least. Colonel Alexandroff, the secretary of the Benevolent Society, began by reading aloud the account of the previous month. It is concerts, theatricals, and lotteries which form the essential income of the Society. The lady-patronesses were long in dividing the poor of the town by districts between themselves ; differences of opinion arising, and the sitting lasted three hours at least. At the second one I was over my first fit of shyness, and even gave a short discourse when opening the meeting. I was chosen President of the " musical and dramatic circles " that day.

My husband works very hard from morning till night ; he rarely had a moment he could call his own, and hadn't a second for me, except at meal-times, and then there was always somebody present.

With what impatience we are awaiting the *Nijni-Novgorod* with all our household. In the meantime we are served by convicts who, at the end of their penal servitude in the Isle of Sakhalin, had been transferred to Khabarovsk, their place of exile. The head-gardener, who was sent to the galleys for having drowned his sweetheart, lives here as man and wife with our laundress, who has poisoned her husband (a pretty couple indeed !) The principal barber of the town, when shaving my husband one day, tried to raise his pity, calling himself a poor orphan bereaved of father and mother, and it turned out that it was the poor orphan who had sent both parents *ad patres*. The locksmith who had been called to mend my trunk, appeared to have been with Sergy at the military school. The man was deported to Siberia for having strangled his wife.

My husband happening to visit a prison, saw a man who had stolen a sturgeon. The law-suit had been going on for three years, and it is only now that he was sentenced to three months' imprisonment. During this long lapse of time his wife had died, leaving him as legacy four little children who were wearing away in the close atmosphere of the gloomy prison cell, which they shared with their father, having no other shelter. In one of the sittings of the "Benevolent Society" we found means to give the poor brats a more comfortable home.

My husband has promulgated a new regulation. The soldiers who were sent here to serve terms of three years, have the right—after having ended their terms, to remain at Khabarovsk for another three years engaged in diverse works—to be sent, after the lapse of this time, to Russia, on account of the Government. By these means the convicts and Chinese servants can easily be supplanted.

Ths richest shop at Khabarovsk, situated in a street called "Straight," which isn't straight at all, belongs to a rich Chinese merchant named Tifountai, where you can buy everything necessary and desirable, beginning with clothes down to furniture, and all sort of provisions which are of a fabulous price here, milk products especially : a pint of cream costs two roubles (four shillings.) We had to buy three cows and grow vegetables ourselves in hot-houses, and have thus vegetables all the year round.

Settlers who went out to seek fortune in the Far East, were beginning to arrive at Khabarovsk. Thirty families of emigrants, coming from the south of Russia, are quartered in barracks a few miles from the town. My husband wants to stock with inhabitants the outskirts of Khabarovsk, flattering himself with the hope that they will supply the town with provisions. In spring portions of ground will be distributed to them. In Russia the peasants receive one acre of land and in this country they will get forty acres of good land.

There is a good dress-maker in Khabarovsk, the widow of an officer, who after the death of her husband was left absolutely destitute, and to support herself took in sewing, making dresses for Khabarovsk belles.

I lead a regular life : music and books fill up my time. In the evening I played duets with Mr. Shaniavski, who is an accomplished musician. A young officer of the garrison, playing the violin, comes frequently to make up a trio. Our performance lasted sometimes till after midnight, and Sergy assured me that my partners, thoroughly tired out, were visibly growing thinner and thinner, and became real spectres at the end of the performance. Mr. Shaniavski offered to teach me Italian and Spanish ; he is a fine linguist, speaking fluently several languages. I need music and work to drive away my blue devils, and have decided to keep friends with Mr. Shaniavski without paying attention to evil tongues. People are so interested in what I do, that a hundred-eyed Argus would not be enough to look after me. Wicked things will be said of me, I am sure, but the calumnies of the world do not trouble me a bit. What are they really worth ?

News from Russia arrives only three times a week. As soon as the mail-post is perceived from the belfry, one flag is hoisted to signal the mail from Vladivostock (*via* America), two flags the post coming from Blagovestchensk (*via* Siberia) and three flags the courier from Nikolskoe (the small local mail). It took long for letters to come ; by the time you get an answer to the questions you made, you may forget what you were asking about. In October I got mother's letter written in July. Only far echoes come of what is going on in the world outside. I hadn't got the patience to read the belated accounts that arrive by post weeks after the events. Here is an example of how long it takes for news from the civilised world to reach Khabarovsk. Captain Olsoufieff, Baron Korffs *aide-de-camp*, had been sent by the Baron on business to a remote part of Siberia, and has learnt only now, on returning to Khabarovsk, that Baron Korff is dead, and that my husband was his successor ! In October the rivers began to freeze, and the mails were delayed for some weeks. We got our correspondence by land across the snow-covered mountains by means of pack-horses, and in what a state can well be imagined. Our letters were all torn and wet, and it was difficult to decipher the contents.

Sergy received one day a curious letter from Hackenberg, a small town in Prussia, from an individual named Wilhelm Dukhow, who informed Sergy that his grandfather had entered the Russian military service in 1812, during the retreat of Napoleon, and had disappeared without vestige. Having learnt by the papers that the family name of the newly appointed General-Governor of the Amour provinces was Doukhovskoy, he begged my husband to inform him if he was not a descendant of his ancestor.

The agents of the Volunteer Fleet gave us constant news of the *Nijni-Novgorod*. The last news were rather alarming. The boat had left Hong-Kong on the 28th September and hadn't arrived at Nagaski at the end of October. Days rolled on and nothing further was heard of the missing ship. At last we had a satisfactory telegram from Vladivostock, announcing that our household and trunks had arrived in safety. The unloading of the boat was done at once, and our servants took the train to Nikolskoe. A boat named the *Khanka* was waiting for them on the " Oussouri " river. Our servants must hurry as fast as possible in order to arrive at Khabarovsk before the " Amour " was frozen. In the beginning of November our trunks had not yet reached Krasnoyarsk, and the " Amour " was beginning to get covered with ice ; in a short time all communication with this Cossack settlement, which is three hundred miles away from Khabarovsk, will be interrupted. Sergy wired to the captain of the *Khanka* offering the sum of one hundred roubles to his crew, if they managed to arrive at "Novo-Michailovsk" before the river was altogether frozen, but the captain did not manage it however, and we got news that the *Khanka* with its thirty-five passengers, was caught by the ice within a few miles of a small village called Kroutoberejnaia, where the boat will be obliged to winter. Some of the passengers, a travelling dramatic company going to act at Khabarovsk among them, managed to make their way to that village. The passengers could find only one cottage to shelter them all. My parrot, who travelled with our household, helped to keep everybody in good temper, repeating his favourite cry "stuff and nonsense!" And thus, thanks to "Polly" good-humour was re-established, but not for very long, for no supplies could be got in the surroundings of Kroutoberejnaia, and the provisions on the boat coming to an end, the passengers had the prospect of starvation, as well as the danger of being attacked by "hounhouses" (Chinese bandits.) My husband sent a dozen Cossacks to protect them. It was with great difficulty that these men got to the village where the passengers of the *Khanka* were sequestered, the roads being almost impracticable. However my husband succeeded in sending a hundred carts to bring over our luggage. The first transport had arrived at last, but instead of our pelisses, for which we waited with such impatience, the trunks contained only our summer things, and in what a lamentable state! The band-boxes containing my hats were completely turned into pancakes. On the 29th November the last transport arrived with 120 big cases. All day long the unpacking was going on, the work of convicts, while joiners and upholsterers were busy mending our furniture. Many valuable things were completely ruined.

Every year in October, during the full moon, the Chinese aborigines of Khabarovsk feasted that planet. They thrust into the "Amour," from the top of a mountain, lanterns of all the colours of the rainbow. Bands of Chinamen walked about the streets perched on high stilts, shouting and gamboling, to the great joy of the populace.

Every Sunday I go to church, where I try to hide myself behind one of the pillars, having the uncomfortable sensation of being stared at. The deacon of the cathedral is a legendary personage. He was born in America from a Russian colonist and a negress. In his early youth he embarked as ship-boy on board an American vessel which was wrecked on the shores of Vladivostock. One day, as the boy sat on the beach-seat overlooking the sea, forming plans for his future, dressed in rags and famished, he attracted the attention of a rich Austrian merchant, who took him to his house and employed him as aid to his cook. But the castaway, hearing the silent call of the sea, ran away to America, where he became a sailor and ultimately an officer. His second escape from shipwreck was still more romantic, The current sent him with two comrades on a block of ice on which they passed eight days. Being famished, they began by eating their boots, and then decided that one of them should be sacrificed to be devoured by his companion, they drew lots and that terrible fate fell upon the poor castaway who offered up a prayer for preservation, and vowed that if this miracle was vouchsafed, he would become a priest. He had given himself up for lost and was about to blow out his brains, when they perceived, quite close, a black mass. It was an enormous seal which they killed on the spot, and which served as a sumptuous feeding-ground until they were rescued by a passing ship. The future deacon, in gratitude, carried out his promise.

One Sunday morning, before Mass, a group of strange wild people, belonging to the " Golde " tribe, dressed in seal-skins presented my husband with a stag's head. These " Goldes " are a curious tribe—pagans to the bottom of their hearts. They are baptised twice sometimes, because it is the custom to give them a shirt and a small sum of money when they pass through the ritual of Christianity. The priests, therefore, have to make minute inquiries to be quite sure that the new candidate had not been baptised before. The " Goldes " have prominent cheek-bones, a broad nose, and very coarse and straight hair. Their faces long remain hairless, a scanty beard grows only in their old age. They are dirty people like all nomads, and smell awfully bad ; the atmosphere in our apartments was filled with the perfume of their persons. These malodorous men examined everything with great curiosity ; the parquet-floors, especially, attracted their attention. We offered tea to the " Goldes," who carried away the remains of the bread and sugar ; it is lucky they didn't take away the tea-things. I saw from my window two pairs of dogs, harnessed to sledges, being driven at full gallop across the ice to the other side of the Amour. It will be a difficult task for my husband to tame these savages, who camp in winter in the woods, and live on what they hunt, killing the animal with their arrows. As the " Goldes " have no ready-money in their commerce they pay with sable-furs instead of coins.

On the following day the " Goldes " were celebrating their " Feast of the Bear." They bring up all the year round a young bear and devour it on that day. After lunch a " Golde " brought his two wives to be presented to me. They offered me a model of their national costume, richly embroidered.

Mme. Beurgier has invented a new pastime. Having become a strong adept of spiritualism, she occupies herself with table-turning, and is always discovering some new occult genius, who promises to show her some wonderful manifestations from spirit land. At night she frightens out of her wits poor Mrs. Serebriakoff, whose apartment was next to hers, by conversing with the spirits of the defuncts, who guide her in every smallest action of her life. She had been very sulky and cross for some time past, and said that the spirits advised her to leave Khabarovsk as fast as possible. I did not try to detain her, most certainly. Her luggage was already sent to the railway station, when she came up to bid me good-bye, and when I asked her if she would write to me from time to time, she replied " No," curtly. And that was her last word to me. Nevertheless I rushed after her, racing downstairs and kissed her warmly, which softened the poor old lady. She began to weep and went to announce to Sergy that it was beyond her power to leave me. She left us for good, however, a week afterwards.

We have now been three months at Khabarovsk. I can't get accustomed to this life. If I could but follow the example of Mme. Beurgier and fly away from here ! All my brightness has gone and my nerves are put out of order. I don't know what is the matter with me at all ; for no reason on earth I suddenly burst into tears and cry for hours. Sergy tried to rouse me from the apathy into which I was falling deeper and deeper every day. I shook myself at last, and am getting back my spirits and my colour. I certainly was not going to let myself grow into a moping misanthrope.

The winter is splendid at Kharbarovsk; the sky always clear of clouds and no wind whatever, and for that reason one does not feel the cold so much, though the thermometer shows over twenty degrees of frost every day. The snow falls only once, in the beginning of winter, and keeps white until spring. But the weather has no effect whatever upon me, and very often when the sky is of azure blue, black thoughts overwhelm me ; and vice versa. The air in the apartments is excessively dry. I am often awakened at night by the creaking of the furniture. We have to suspend wet blankets in our bedroom as it is impossible to sleep otherwise.

We have learned by a newspaper-telegram from St. Petersburg that an earthquake, preceded by a formidable underground noise, had shaken Khabarovsk. It is very strange that nobody had felt it here. It comes out that it is from a writing in a local paper, describing an earthquake at the distance of 800 miles from Khabarovsk, but the correspondent of St. Petersburg had omitted the 800 miles, and it is thus that the false report spread out.

Every Sunday we give a grand dinner with a military

band playing during the meal. Our head-gardener is a veritable artist in the arrangement of the dinner-table. There were always pretty bunches of flowers before each plate. At the sound of a drum the gentlemen offered their arms to their respective ladies and marched to the dining-room. One Sunday my cavalier was a Chinese General, who had just arrived from Pekin. He watched the way his neighbours were eating but made, nevertheless, fearful blunders, and did everything wrong with his knife and fork. The French proverb that "Nul n'est prophete dans son pays," has no hold over that important personage of the Celestial Empire, who is reckoned as an oracle in Pekin. He has learnt thoroughly the mystic sciences from Indian fakirs. When drinking my health he congratulated me, through his interpreter, at the forthcoming birth of a son. He said he could read it in my eyes. Foolish man! The mandarin gave me his visiting-card printed on a piece of red paper on which was stated, in Chinese hieroglyphics, that he was the bravest man in the army, and his wife, the most important lady in the land. He was not very modest, the maggot.

Another day we had to dinner Mr. De Windt, an English writer, who came for a few days to Khabarovsk, after having visited the Island of Saghalien. In remembrance of our short acquaintance, he sent me his last work from London, a very interesting novel.

A great Charity Bazaar was planned for Christmas. The biggest prizes were to be a horse, a cow, a baby-bear, twelve suckling pigs and a couple of rabbits. We made a great deal of money at the bazaar. I was doing splendidly, and in about an hour or two there were no more tickets in my wheel.

On the third day of the Christmas week, the Goldes organised dogs' races on the ice. Five pairs of dogs dragged the sledges. The fancy took me to experience that mode of polar locomotion. I established myself sideways on the shaft with my legs projecting over the sledge, and was afraid all the time of the dogs who ran behind me biting at my heels ; they really looked as if they contemplated making their lunch off my legs.

I have been starved of music for long, and was enchanted when Kostia Doumtcheff, a boy violinist, gave a concert at Khabarovsk. He is only thirteen years old and has already toured the world as a "Wunderkind." His execution is quite extraordinary for so young a performer.

With the Chinese every month begins with the new moon. This year the 14th January was their New Year's day. The Chinese quarter of the town was brilliantly illuminated, and a procession of monsters made of paste-board, marched through the streets. An enormous dragon made of paper, a nightmare beast, was carried by Chinamen hidden from view, giving the complete illusion that it was creeping along. The monster is so long that a score of men is required to carry it. Behind the dragon came Chinamen oddly arrayed, carrying garlands of coloured paper-flowers and chains of fantastical form hanging on long poles, bearing huge banners with different religious devices. All this was accompanied by a loud flourish of trumpets, and the gongs made all the time an infernal noise.

Towards the middle of April, when the weather became milder, a military band played three times a week in the square. I listened to it lying back on a rocking-chair on the veranda, feeling quite safe from observation.

We have a veritable menagerie in our garden. General Kopanski sent me a pair of beautiful white swans from Nikolskoe; Tifountai presented me with a deer; and a Golde brought me two sables, very wicked little animals, who watched for every opportunity to snap at the legs of the passers-by through the bars of the cage.

At the end of the month of May, Mrs. Kohan, my singing mistress, arrived from Moscow with her two little daughters. Her husband has recently been appointed military doctor at Khabarovsk.

In June Sergy went to inspect the troops beyond the Baikal mountains. He will be away about two or three weeks. I dreaded to let him go so far away, and decided to rejoin him on his way back at Sretensk, a town situated at 2,500 miles from Khabarovsk.

10th July.—Except Mrs. Serebriakoff, who accompanied me on my voyage to Stretensk, there were only two passengers on our steamer; one of the directors of the Navigation Companies on the Amour, and a German pastor from Vladivostock. We started at noon. A brilliant welcome was given me at our first stopping place, a rich Cossack settlement; but I didn't leave my cabin, for I hate to share my husband's honours when I am travelling with him, and hate it still more when I am alone. Directly the darkness came, we dropped anchor before another settlement, awaiting the rising of the sun.

July 11th.—We started at dawn. The banks are very picturesque. We are passing the green mountains of Hingan, which are clearly outlined on the blue sky. Beyond these mountains one comes upon rich gold mines.

July 12th.—Towards night we dropped anchor on the coast of a Chinese village on the left bank of the river.

13th July.—Early in the morning we passed Argon, a dirty Chinese town with big pools of water here and there; one would need stilts to walk across the unpaved streets full of children, pigs and evil smells. Towards noon, we arrived at Blagovestchensk, a large and populous town.

Declining the honours the authorities of Blagovestchensk wished to bestow on me, I telegraphed to General Arsenieff, the governor of the town, that I could receive no one on board, having decided to play the invalid, and was disagreeably surprised to see that a great crowd awaited me on the quay. Mrs. Arsenieff forced my cabin door open and and transmitted to me three big bouquets tied with broad ribbons, sent by her husband, the chief of the Cossack regiment quartered at Blagovestchensk, and the Prefect of the Police.

July 15th.—The weather is lovely. We glide rapidly on the calm water. The banks are deprived of life. I have the impression of travelling in the land of the "Sleeping Beauty," not a sound around us.

July 16th.—We stopped at midday before a Cossack settlement. The steps leading to the quay were covered with red cloth and strewn with flowers ; a triumphal arch was erected, bearing at the top my monogram. Under the arch stood two "atamans." A group of young girls, dressed in their best, came to offer me flowers.

July 17th.—This morning we met a steam-launch carrying on board the Archbishop of Blagovestchensk, going to inspect his diocese. Towards night, we saw a raft, twice as large as our boat, transporting emigrants. A wooden fire was burning in the middle of the raft, around which horses and peasant-carts were piled. We came to grief at night, running on the bank in the dark, and had to drop anchor on the Chinese shore before a small town, having broken the screw. Navigation is difficult in these parts because of the strong current.

July 18th.—At dawn my maid came to wake me. She told me that a Chinese General, the Governor of the town before which we were anchored, was standing on the quay, sword in hand, waiting to be presented to me. But our interview didn't take place. We sent a rocket by way of compliment to the warrior of the Celestial Empire, and glided past him. After dinner, we came alongside a large Cossack village where we were to halt. A number of girls with their school-mistress and a platoon of Cossacks were standing on the quay. The chief of the platoon sent up a loud cheer for me, and his men threw up their caps in the air and shouted themselves hoarse.

July 19th.—We are passing the whole day before the stations named "The Seven Capital Sins." Towards night we stopped before the "Fourth Sin." These stations have been fitly named : their aspect takes away every desire to sin. I never saw such God-forsaken places !

July 20th.—We glide through districts completely submerged by the recent overflowing of the rivers. Whole villages disappeared under the waters. There was great

B*

distress and great poverty everywhere; my heart ached for the poor inhabitants. Steadily the waters ascended and the raging torrent tore off the trees, breaking them away. It was a scene of desolation like the deluge. The houses, the cattle, the fields, all were destroyed. Now a window, now a door tore past; chimneys, slates, tiles, whirled about like so much paper.

July 21st.—We passed this morning before a Cossack settlement without stopping. On the quay a platoon of Cossacks was ranged. The men started running after our boat along the bank, shouting hurrahs to me as to a queen. Indifferent to all their honours, I only counted the hours which separated me from my husband.

Towards mid-day we approached Sretensk. Sergy was waiting for me on the quay, surrounded by a large suite and a group of ladies, who came up to greet me. I immediately went over to Sergy's boat on which I received many visitors. During dinner we suddenly heard loud shouts of alarm. It was a big raft full of emigrants which had broken loose from the shore and was drifted straight on to us. It had been rather a bad moment. In less time than it takes to write, I had jumped out on the quay, and just in time, for a collision took place; the raft struck against our boat and was carried away further by the torrent. A steam-launch was sent after it, which brought it back safe and sound to the port. In the evening there were fireworks on the quay.

July 22nd.—A Te Deum has been performed this morning on the square before the church, after which my husband reviewed the troops. Before leaving Blagovestchensk, Sergy gave a grand lunch to all the military chiefs on board.

We started back to Khabarovsk in the afternoon. A large company of ladies and officers accompanied us in a steam-launch to the first stoppage. We landed and walked through the village and visited a Cossack one hundred years old.

July 23rd.—We are going swiftly down the "Amour." Towards evening we landed at Mokho, a large Chinese town, where we were invited to dinner by a Chinese General, the chief of the district. We saw him advancing towards our boat with measured steps, accompanied by his suite. He greeted us with great dignity, and when the usual ceremonies were terminated, after much bowing and scraping, according to Chinese fashion, the Mandarin conducted us to his abode, a small cottage with a dilapidated-looking roof. Before the cottage my husband was received by a Chinese guard of honour, who after having presented arms, threw themselves face downwards on the ground. At the sound of an enormous drum they stood up, shouting piercingly, and raising up their halberds in the air, whilst all around rifles were being fired. Chinese soldiers were standing in groups, carrying signs of their rank on their back and chest, written on disks of white stuff. We entered a square room and took our place at long table set with Asiatic dishes, amongst which a sucking-pig occupied the first place. I sat on the right of our host, who was very attentive to my wants; he piled my plate high by means of small ivory sticks. The table was spread with all sorts of curious looking foods. This wonderful dinner did not come in courses, but the whole of it was placed on the table at once—a Gargantuan meal: soft-shell crabs, sausages of mouse-meat, little fried animals looking like spiders and other horrid things stood in a long procession. Every dish was unfamiliar; I didn't know at all what I was eating. Having at last discovered a dish to my taste, I helped myself with a fresh portion of it, and oh, horror! it appeared to be dog's meat. The Chinese General clinked his empty goblet with my glass full to the brim, which signified that I had to drink the whole contents of it. Our host never cuts his nails as it seems, for they were of phenomenal length, veritable claws. I was told afterwards that the length of the nails of a Chinaman are a sign of aristocracy: it means he never works. Through the half-opened door we saw a crowd of Chinese soldiers straining their necks to peep over each other's heads and satisfy their curiosity. At parting, our host bade us a courteous farewell, and presented me with several pieces of silk.

24th July.—We travelled to-day from sunrise to sunset without stopping.

25th July.—We arrived at Blagovestchensk in the afternoon, and will leave to-morrow at dawn. The Governor and his family came to dine on board.

26th July.—It was about three o'clock in the afternoon when we arrived at Khabarovsk. A great crowd was on the quay to greet us. I was glad to find old friends and bowed and smiled from right to left, shaking hands with people as we passed. I received a whole harvest of flowers.

The railway between Khabarovsk and Vladivostock is opened. Vladivostock can be reached now in four days.

In September Sergy had to go up to Vladivostock, where he had some business to attend to. He sent me news regularly. On the 11th September, the anniversary of our sojourn at Khabarovsk, Sergy thanked me by wire for having shared his exile during a whole year.

The inauguration of the gymnasium for young ladies took place on the 30th August. The head-mistress and the architect who constructed the gymnasium, met us at the door at our arrival, followed by one of the youngest pupils, a pretty little girl, who recited an ode composed in favour of my husband, with a little complimentary address to me, after which the bishop performed a Te Deum before the image of

St. Barbara, my Patroness, which was painted from my portrait.

There is a museum at Khabarovsk in which, amongst other local curiosities, I saw horrid busts of different murderers who had died at Khabarovsk during their penal servitude. The most repulsive bust is that of a convict who had killed and devoured his comrade. I could not have believed it possible to put such a thoroughly ferocious creature into wax.

A steamer has just come in, towing a large barge with about one hundred women sentenced to penal servitude, who are to be taken to the Island of Saghalien, where women are in a minority, in order to cohabit with the male convicts.

We were dreadfully struck and grieved to hear of my brother's death, and soon after came a telegram from St. Petersburg announcing that our Emperor had departed this life. His Majesty fell dangerously ill during his stay in the Crimea, and died in October. The oath of loyalty to Nicholas II., who succeeded to the throne, was given in the cathedral by all the military and civil functionaries serving in Khabarovsk. The town is in mourning; there is not a yard of crape left in the shops. In November the betrothal of Nicolas II. with Princess Alice of Hessen, the granddaughter of Queen Victoria, took place.

The "hounhouses" (Chinese bandits) cause a great panic amongst the officials serving on the railway line. Quite recently the brigands attacked a railway station, and murdered the station-master and his family. It was found out that the bandits were Chinese soldiers, by a standard that they had dropped at the station.

On Christmas Eve the village children came up from the nearest villages to sing their carols under our windows. On Christmas night a giant Christmas-tree was set up in our hall for the school children. It was sparkling from top to foot with decorations of fringed and coloured paper and glittering glass-balls; the dark green boughs were hung with gilded apples, pears, walnuts, etc. On the table round the Christmas-tree lay the gifts to the children, who walked into the hall by twos and twos. I handed out the presents to the girls, and Sergy to the boys. Every girl received a present adapted to her wants and her wishes. On Christmas Eve the head-mistress of the gymnasium had disguised her porter into Santa Claus, the children's friend, who looked a real Father Christmas with a large white beard. The girls had to write a letter to the good saint, and to explain in it what they wanted Santa Claus to send them for their Christmas present. The pupils of the small classes asked for dolls, except one little girl, a premature coquette, who had chosen a looking-glass for her Christmas gift.

On Easter night a group of emigrants, who were returning

home after midnight service, whilst crossing the cemetery, heard a voice screaming pitifully for help. The cry was repeated at short intervals. They stared at one another perplexedly. "What's that?" they called out loudly. "It's I!" said someone close at hand. It was a vagabond who had fallen into a newly-dug grave, together with a goat which he had just stolen. The emigrants knotted their sashes and slipped down the improvised cord, ordering the man to recite the Lord's prayer to be convinced that it was not the evil spirit who was playing tricks with them. The vagabond had the unhappy thought to tie his goat first to the rope, and when the emigrants perceived a long beard and a pair of horns, they took to their heels and ran away, leaving the vagabond to his sad fate, persuaded that they had seen the devil. It was only at daybreak that the vagabond was hoisted up, in a very pitiful state.

At last we are going to have some good music. A travelling opera-troup, making a tour in Siberia, has just arrived at Khabarovsk to give a series of performances. The lady who substituted the orchestra and accompanied the artists on the piano, came to invite us to assist at their first performance, given in the Social Club. She told us how she despaired because she was unable to find black tights for Siebel, which had been torn on the way. No such thing was to be procured in Khabarovsk. We went to hear "Faust." Sitting in a corner of our box I listened to Gounod's divine music, and the thought of my pleasant life at Moscow came upon me with a sharp pang. I was on the point of bursting into tears. The performers were all second-rate artists. Faust had no great voice, Margaret looked rather clumsy, Mephistopheles was always in danger of degenerating into a buffoon, and Siebel, in darned tights, had a fine mezzo-soprano, but was too fat. (There is nearly always something too much or too little with everybody.)

The baritone of the opera-troup was at the same time a piano-tuner, and came to tune our "Erard." It was only once a year that a professional tuner came from Blagovestchensk to repair pianos for 25 roubles per instrument. We have an amateur tuner at Khabarovsk, a colonel, who repairs the pianos for three roubles only, for the benefit of the Benevolent Society, but it is true that in his tuning there is more benevolence than skill.

I was not in very good health for the present time and had fits of depression and apathy at the thought of all the dear ones left in Russia. Sergy, who was terribly worried about me, decided that I needed daily exercise, and made me walk up and down our large hall, counting all the time I went round, to make one mile. But I didn't become rosier for all that, because it is not exercise I wanted, but cheering up.

Rumours of strained relations between China and Japan spread about. A colonel of the general staff, sent by my husband to Tokio, gave us alarming news. Complications burst out between the two countries and soon war broke out. At the first combat of the outposts the Japs put to defeat the sons of the Celestial Empire. It was a headlong flight; twenty thousand Chinese soldiers went over to the enemy, abandoning their rifles. The Japs have sunk several Chinese cruisers, and have invaded Manchuria, where everything is put to fire and sword. There was an armistice of three weeks between China and Japan, during which Likhoundjan, the viceroy of China, was sent to Japan as Ambassador for negotiations of peace. He was wounded by a pistol-shot by a Jap. Fearing to be poisoned by the enemies of his country, he refused to be treated by Japanese doctors, and a German physician had to be sent to him from Berlin. For some time uncertain news arrived from the seat of war. At last we were informed that peace had been signed, when a second despatch was received, telling us that the Emperor of Japan had refused to ratify peace. Russia, together with France and Germany, insisted that the Japanese troops quit Manchuria, but the Japs insist on remaining and become more and more arrogant.

They say that Russia is going to occupy Manchuria, but they say such a lot of things! Sergy has received a cipher telegram from St. Petersburg, from the chief-commissary, asking him what is the quantity of provender necessary for the Siberian army, in case of war. Sergy is very much disturbed; the feeling of his responsibility weighs upon him. If our troops are sent out to Manchuria we shall remain quite helpless and unprotected here!

Japan having taken a menacing attitude towards Russia, my husband has received the order to prepare his troops to be ready for battle. The mobilisation must be completed in the month of April. At the thought that war was about to be proclaimed, my courage failed me. When I called to mind all ths hardships I had to endure during the Russo-Turkish war, I could do away with myself.

A subsidy has been given to the officers in order they might supply themselves with saddle-horses. We have organised a committee of Sisters of Mercy. The three Governors subordinated to my husband are now at Khabarovsk. Every night they deliberate in our house on different preparations for war, together with a great number of generals and officers.

As soon as the misunderstanding with Japan began, a great number of functionaries sent out their families to Russia, by land; one couldn't travel by sea for the moment, because Japanese men-of-war swarmed in the neighbourhood of Vladivostock. Sergy wanted to follow their example, and me away, but I would not part with him now, and announced positively that I should not move from here.

The Chinese inhabitants of Kharbarovsk, fearing the invasion of the Japs, sell their houses, their furniture, their shops. The Bishop performed a Te Deum on the square before the cathedral to the troops quartered at Khabarovsk. When the service was over, my husband said a few words to the soldiers concerning the war that was going to break out. Our brave warriors shouted in chorus " We are ready to fight to the last drop of our blood !"

Our fleet started for Tchifou, to cut all communications with the Japanese army, in case the Japs would not consent to our proposals for giving up Manchuria to China. We are waiting for the decisive answer to Japan concerning the ratification of peace. God grant that it may be satisfactory!

Hurrah! On the 20th of April the Minister of War sent a telegram to my husband announcing that Japan had consented to our terms. I could jump for joy!

Though peace was signed, the Embassies and Consulates continue to be guarded by the troops in Japan.

At last we are completely tranquillized. My husband has received orders to clear away all the mines from the Japanese Sea.

A false report has been spread at St. Petersburg, that Sergy had ordered all the Japs to leave the Provinces of the Amour. He hastened to inform the Minister of War that, on the contrary, six hundred Japanese workmen had just arrived to construct the Manchur railway-line.

Hot weather has set in. Swarms of mosquitos and midges fill the air.

When sitting after dinner on our terrace, we hear the drums beating for the evening retreat. At nine o'clock punctual, three rockets are fired; a military band begins to play and march, and the musicians walk all round the Public Gardens; on returning to the music-kiosque they sing the Lord's Prayer and our anthem. One night a retreat on the water was organised. The musicians were placed in a large barge towed by a steamer. The Amour, lighted by the full moon, and the barge decorated with different-coloured lanterns, gliding smoothly on the water, producing a fairy-like scene.

Two Frenchmen, who were passing through Khabarovsk on their way from Japan, were invited to dinner by Sergy: Mr. Lallo, a correspondent of the " Illustration," and the Vicomte de Labry, the military agent of Tokio, who was resplendent in his uniform of the " Chasseurs d'Afrique."

An Italian yacht, the " Christopher Columbus," bearing the Prince of the Abruzzes, the nephew of King Humbert, has arrived at Vladivostock, but the Prince didn't proceed further on to Kharbarovsk.

A body of a thousand soldiers, was sent back to Russia, *via* India and Odessa, on a ship belonging to the Volunteer Fleet. It is for the first time that they have been sent by water; they had to travel before through the whole continent of Oriental Siberia. At the moment when the boat was to start, one of the soldiers was arrested. His crime had just been discovered: he had poisoned his wife, wanting to return solo to his native land. He was already shouting hurrah in chorus with his comrades, when he was seized and conducted to prison.

There came an urgent telegram calling my husband to St. Petersburg on business. It was too good to be true! I felt like an escaped prisoner, and counted the hours when we should start to Russia.

On my last reception-day, Colonel Alexandroff, the secretary of the Benevolent Society, addressed a panegyric to me, and presented an album with the photographic group of all the members of the Benevolent Society with their signatures.

CHAPTER LXXIV

OUR VOYAGE AROUND THE WORLD

August 24th.—The day for leaving Khabarovsk came at last. We started this afternoon for the Land of Desire, to St. Petersburg, darling place. Colonel Serebriakoff, his wife and Mr. Shaniavski, accompanied us on our long voyage.

There was a great crowd on the quay to see us off and wish us a pleasant journey. We embarked on the ship *Neptune* to Iman, from where we take the train to Vladivostok. We hasten to say our good-byes. The flying-bridge is taken off, the last whistle is blown, and we are off to Europe.

It was growing dark when we weighed anchor at Kasake-vitchi, a Cossack settlement, where a Te Deum was sung in the village chapel for our safe journey. Log-fires burnt along the shore, and the Cossacks cheered us enthusiastically.

August 26th.—It was about seven in the morning when we arrived at Iman and made our way to the special train which was waiting for us. It was composed of three saloon-cars. We advance slowly, with great precautions, going twenty miles an hour only, because the ballast is not firmly set yet. Just about a year ago we drove in these parts in an ante-diluvian carriage, by impossible roads covered with untrodden forests, and now we proceed by train, with all the comfort of modern communication. It took formerly a whole week to reach Vladivostock, and now the journey is made in three days! Scores of "manzas," Chinese workmen, are complet-ing the railway-line. Their heads are enveloped in a rag, to protect them from the bites of the mosquitoes, which abound here. We do not stop at the stations because of the cholera raging in these parts.

August 27th.—We arrived at Nikolskoe two hours late, and put up again at the house of General Kopanski. We'll stay a few days here, for Sergy wants to assist at the manœuvres.

August 28th.—I accompanied my husband to the camp this morning. The soldiers cheered loudly as we passed. After the manœuvres my husband invited to dinner all the com-manders of the troops.

August 30th.—The weather is heavy and stormy; it has been raining for the last twenty-four hours. I remained all day indoors.

August 31st.—We left Nikolskoe this morning. A platoon of Cossacks escorted us to the railway station, where a great crowd had gathered to see us off. Sergy stood at the window of his car answering the loud cheers of the population.

We passed in the afternoon a sandy slope called "Gliding Hill," which approaches progressively the railway line, and soon perceived the sea in the distance. Towards midday we arrived at Vladivostock where the reception was enthusiastic.

The house of the Military Club is put at our disposal. Our windows look on the "Golden Horn." Russian and foreign cruisers are anchored in the vast bay. Every day a new steamer arrives. Here is a trading vessel carrying the Dutch flag, advancing towards the pier. I see numerous fishing-smacks plying towards the open sea.

Official visits have been exchanged between my husband and the admirals. Sergy went over to the cruisers in a steam-launch carrying his standard. He called first on Admiral Tirtoff, the chief of the Russian fleet, on his man-of-war *Pamiat Azova*, on which our Emperor made his voyage around the world when he was heir to the throne. According to naval etiquette, every time my husband left a vessel cannons were fired.

September 1st.—This morning we were awakened by a loud cannonade; it was the cruisers who were saluting each other as they usually do every morning. To-day we are giving a dinner to a hundred guests. All the admirals and commanders of the troops are invited with their families.

September 5th.—This afternoon twenty-five naval officers came to be presented to me; they were sent by their commanders, who wanted to entertain me on their cruisers.

September 6th.—There came an invitation to dinner to-day from Admiral Tirtoff, which I wanted to decline because Sergy was unwell, but I had to go all the same. I started off at seven o'clock in a steam-launch, accompanied by Colonel and Mrs. Serebriakoff, Mr. Shaniavski, and one of Sergy's aide-de-camps. Before boarding the cruiser we had to undergo an examination. On seeing our approach the officer on duty shouted out: "Who are you?" and the lieutenant who commanded our launch gave him the pass-word: "Officer." The cruiser was illuminated in our honour by lamps of different colours. The officers helped me along the foot-bridge, and Admiral Tirtoff advanced to meet us. He offered me his arm and took me to the brilliantly illuminated dining-room flooded with electric light and full of guests. The Admiral put me at his right hand. I was made much of; the officers were charming to me. Everyone seemed in the best of spirits and everything was unceremonious and cosy. I enjoyed myself tremendously. Here I was in the midst of life once more; formalities were quickly forgotten, and my modesty was not a bit shocked by the complimentary speeches of our amiable hosts. I also was in one of my most reckless and vivacious moods, and threw all my reserves to the winds. It was delightful to be treated without any manner of deference by our hosts, and I had rather be admired than esteemed. I am not made of wood altogether! Directly after dinner the pet of the crew was presented to me : a baby-bear. The animal was very clever, he performed many tricks, and amused us with his antics ; he drank champagne at a gulp, straight from the bottle, and got drunk. I was suddenly aware that it was getting late, but it was in vain that Mrs. Serebriakoff tried to hurry me home ; our hosts would not let me go, and I, on my part, had no wish to leave the ship, just when the fun was at its height. It was not often I got a chance of amusing myself like that ! It was past midnight when we said good-bye to the gallant mariners The second officer escorted us back to the shore. An enormous electric search-light showed us our way. During our short crossing the officer found time to tell me that I did not look at all like a hermit, and was not made for dull existence ; he pitied me that my social position hindered me from profiting of the joys of life, and advised me to shake myself up a bit. Wicked Mephistopheles !

September 7th.—Sergy went to the camp to inspect the troops, together with the representatives of the civil, military and naval forces. Before they left the camp, reciprocal hurrahs cheered our Emperor, the army and the navy.

September 10th.—Our stay at Vladivostock was a long round of gaiety and pleasure. I lived in a whirl of excitement. To-day we were invited to dine on the flagship "Nicholas II." As we approached the cruiser we heard the sounds of a band striking up a march. The officer gave us a warm reception and the Admiral offered me a big bouquet tied with a lovely piece of Japanese silk, embroidered with fantastical arabesques. I saw in the dining-room amongst other guests a young opera singer, Señorita Estrella Bellinfanti, a pupil of Tosti, who had arrived from Japan for a few days. The young diva is going on to America on a tournée, escorted by a lady-companion. After a long illness that she has gone through, the poor señorita begins to lose her sight. She told me that in the space of another year she would be quite blind, which will oblige her to abandon the artistic career, which she adores. Seeing her so gay and bright, nobody could dream of the tragedy awaiting the poor girl. After dinner we had an improvised concert. One of the officers sat down at the piano to accompany Señorita Estrella, who sang in a sweet mezzo-soprano voice lovely Spanish songs, after which the officers sang in chorus Russian songs, in very good time and rhythm, to the accompaniment of guitars.

I was asked to play on the mandolin; the officers were so insistant that it was not easy to refuse, and finally I yielded to their entreaties, but I couldn't be induced to sing. The officers, thinking that it was my husband's presence which kept me back, proposed to detain him on deck during my performance, but it was all in vain, I would not sing. We returned on shore very late and went to bed with the evening star.

September 11th.—We have visited the young ladies' gymnasium this afternoon. The pupils presented me with a richly embroidered table-cloth of their own work.

September 12th.—Sergy has gone to Possiette, to the extreme point of Oriental Siberia on the frontier of Corea, to review the troops. The Admirals accompanied him on their cruisers.

September 14th.—My husband has returned to-day from his voyage. How long the time has seemed to me in his absence!

A steamer has just arrived, bringing a battalion of sappers. The boat had nearly perished on its way, having been caught by a tempest near Singapore. When the boat moored to the quay a band struck up a march to the sappers, with a flourish of trumpets, whilst the soldiers stood in ranks on the deck and shouted hurrah.

September 15th.—To-day the naval officers arranged a concert for me at the Naval Club. The entertainment was quite a success. Señorita Estrella took part in it; sitting on the floor, she sang Spanish songs charmingly, to her own accompaniment on the guitar. She was much applauded and sang song after song. The audience crowded around the platform and threw flowers to her. The marine officers sang in chorus Russian folk songs, and shared Señorita Estrella's success, sending the audience wild. One of the officers played a solo on the balalaika. He is a virtuoso of that Russian national instrument; it was marvellous how he could draw such rich sounds from that primitive three-corded thing.

CHAPTER LXXV

ON OUR WAY TO JAPAN

September 17th.—I am quite worn out with all this dissipation, and very pleased to leave Vladivostock and see regions unknown to me.

This morning we took our passage on the *Khabarovsk*, a steamer of the volunteer fleet specially built for the voyages of the Governor-General of the Amour provinces. We go straight to Shanghai. Notwithstanding the early hour a great crowd assembled on the quay, and a row of officers and ladies stood on deck to wish us a happy passage. I gave many shake-hands and smiled to right and left. The Bishop performed a Te Deum on board, after which it was time to weigh anchor. Three loud whistles pierced the air, and our steamer left her moorings amidst artillery salutes and loud cheers. After the last exchange of salutes with a Japanese man-of-war, on which the sailors, ranged in rows, rendered military honours to my husband, who was standing on the captain's bridge, we left the bay on our way to the Japanese Sea. The troops lined the shore for several miles. We began to put on steam, and Vladivostock soon disappeared from view.

The *Khabarovsk* was built in England. It is lighted all over with electricity. We are the only passengers on board, except two American travellers to whom Sergy gave permission to take passage with us. They had to go in all haste to Japan, and the regular boat was only to sail next week.

September 18th.—The day is gloomy, with a low, leaden sky. The rain is falling in torrents since morning. The sea begins to foam and our boat tosses, tosses! I lie in my cabin inert, suffering greatly from sea-sickness, and powerless to lift a finger. It was such a fearful night! We were nearly caught in a cyclone. The tempest raged awfully; the body of the vessel cracked in an alarming manner, and all the objects in my cabin danced a mad jig. In the middle of the night I heard shouts of voices bellowing out commands overhead. What could be the matter? I sprang out of my berth and opening the door called Sergy who occupied the cabin just opposite mine. But it was not easy to make oneself heard; I made myself hoarse in vain, Sergy could not hear me. I wanted to rush to the staircase and began to dress quickly, but I was so agitated I could not get my arms into my sleeves. In that critical moment the captain, clad in a dripping yellow oilskin coat, knocked at my door; he came to comfort me, assuring me that there was nothing to be afraid of. Foreseeing a strong gale he had given the order to go out into open sea fearing to split on a rock. He said that in a few hours we might run out of bad weather. Somewhat tranquillised I lay down, to start off my sleep again, being nearly thrown out of my berth. The awful wind bent our boat on to her side, the screw was quite out of the water. We were obliged to drop anchor and to be pitilessly tossed by furious billows until morning. I thought that daylight would never come.

September 19th.—Little by little morning appeared through the portholes. The wind continued to blow a hurricane. Towards seven o'clock we moved forward. The coasts of Japan were outlined in the distance. It is the deserted island of Dalegetta, surrounded by mountains 4,800 feet high.

Towards midday the wind abated, we were off the cyclone circle. The weather has become beautiful. Large white birds hover over us. After dinner I sat on deck in the moonlight, breathing with delight the fresh night air.

September 20th.—The ocean is quite calm. We are going along the coasts of Corea. Our first stoppage was Fusan, a rocky Corean spot, which will play, one day, a big part in the history of the far Orient. That port being in close proximity with Japan, is of great strategic importance for the Japs, who have occupied it during the war with China. We have been perceived from the shore, rousing the suspicion of the Japs, who looked with no kindly eyes upon our intrusion. We saw a vessel coming towards us with two Japan officials, who asked who we were and whence we came. Our captain told them that we had to stop at this port to repair damage caused by the storm to the rudder. After the captain had given them the desired information, we were allowed to move on.

September 21st.—The crossing from Fusan to Nagasaki is not a very long one. At seven o'clock in the evening we moored to the quay of that lovely Japanese town.

CHAPTER LXXVI

NAGASAKI

If Ireland is called " Erin," (Green Island), this name would suit Japan still better. After the bare coasts of Siberia and Corea, the eye rests with delight on the beautiful verdure of the Japanese Islands.

The Bay of Nagasaki is very animated for the moment. After the end of the war all the fleet of the Pacific Ocean has assembled here : English, French, Russian and American cruisers, and monster ironclads, filled the harbour with their menace.

We went on to land in a steam-launch put at our disposal by Mr. Guinzburg, a German merchant who has grown awfully rich by being the official supplier of the Russian fleet. Our Consul, Mr. Kostileff, was on the pier to meet us, and walked with us to the Grand Hotel, where we decided to take a few hours of rest. Out flew our hostess all smiles and a hearty welcome, highly pleased to see us return to her hotel.

A printed placard, hanging up outside the bureau, announced that a big English steamer, the *Empress of China* belonging to the Canadian Line, starts to-morrow for Vancouver *via* Shanghai. The idea came to us to continue our voyage on that boat for a change, but we were told that there was no place on board.

After tiffin, we took five rikshas and went to call upon the Consul's wife, but didn't find her at home. After having made a round of the curio shops, we drove through broad streets full of drinking dens, with Russian and English signboards. On the threshold stood girls with very much painted faces, clad in European dress, who—as a bait—surveyed the sailors of different nations, who swung along arm in arm and came here to take a bite at their fishing-line, after their long and virtuous crossing. These girls are for the most part Russian Jewesses, to be found in nearly all the ports of the far East. After dinner we returned on board the *Khabarovsk*.

September 23rd.—I was wakened very early by the sound of military bands playing the Russian and English anthems, and the Marseillaise, on different cruisers. In the afternoon we left for Shanghai.

CHAPTER LXXVII

FROM NAGASAKI TO SHANGHAI

September 24th.—We cross the treacherous Japanese Sea, on which the monsoons, disagreeable north-east winds, are raging in this season. We went on deck for a breath of fresh air and had a chat with the captain. He told us of the danger we were running during our stay at Nagasaki, because of the hatred of the Japs towards Russians. Every time we left the hotel we were followed by two detectives to protect us. The captain, as it appears, always carried a loaded pistol in his pocket when he accompanied us in the streets.

We saw a black spot advancing rapidly towards us ; we are going to have a storm. Soon wind began to blow furiously, and the ship staggered and pitched. The captain promised better weather for to-morrow ; yes, but it is to-day that we have to go through !

September 25th.—Yellow spots appear on the water, it means that we are going to enter the great Yang-tse-kiang, the sacred Blue River ; a false nomenclature, as the river is not blue but yellow ; just the same as the Blue Danube, which nobody has ever seen of azure colour. We anchored at the mouth of the Woosung, nine miles off Shanghai and have to wait till morning, the water being very low.

September 27th.—I was up and dressed at dawn and mounted half asleep on deck. The rising tide was beginning to put all the anchored vessels afloat. The entrance into the harbour of Shanghai being rather dangerous, we put out signs calling the pilot, and soon perceived his fragile skiff, which the waves seemed to swallow up at every moment. Our sailors had to pull the pilot up by means of a rope, after which we went up the Woosung river, of dirty dark brown colour. The banks are low and scattered all over with habitations. The pilot brought us into the port, filled with cruisers of all nationalities.

CHAPTER LXXVIII

SHANGHAI

AFTER having said a hearty farewell to our captain and his officers, we mounted a canoe steered with one oar, and went ashore. Mr. Redding, our Consul, was on the quay to meet us. He proposed for us to put up at his house, but the invitation was declined with thanks. We preferred to stop at the Hôtel des Colonies, situated in the French Concession, to which we drove in Mr. Redding's carriage. The French Concession is a real French corner with its own law court, municipality, pólice, etc.

The city rather disappointed me with its modern appearance, and wide crowded streets bearing French names, lined with houses of European architecture and brilliant shops. Shanghai is the city of great international commerce in the extreme Orient. The French, English and Americans possess concessions which they rent from the Chinese Government. Each concession has its own Consul.

All the first storey of our hotel is put to our disposal, each apartment has its own bathroom. I had to lock myself in to avoid the native merchants, who enter without knocking at the door, all smiles and making funny little bows.

In the afternoon we started in a litter, carried on the shoulders of four porters, to inspect the curiosities of the native town. It was a new mode of locomotion to us. The streets for the most part are two or three yards broad, and full of local colour. I looked out at everything with wondering eyes, it's all so strange ! The houses of the rich are built of stone, and those of the poor, with lumps of earth mixed with chopped straw. Nearly every house has a small courtyard surrounded by a high wall, a low door is cut in this wall giving access to the street. We see a fat Chinese merchant dressed in a blue silk robe, sitting in front of one of these doors, fanning himself in a melancholy manner. At the next door a barber is shaving his client in the open air. We are carried now through a street full of shops ; their fronts disappear completely behind gilded planks hung up vertically, bearing hieroglyphic signs. The shopkeeper sits on the floor of his shop, surrounded by his various goods. He never rises to customers, for everything is within reach of his hand.

c*

Women never meddle with trade, which is solely in the hands of the men. "Ladies first," we say in the west; in the east it is "ladies last"; their sphere is the back-room. The whole duty of a woman is to worship and wait upon her husband, who is lord and master in its most exacting sense.

The streets are full of life and movement. Chinese women, enveloped in long blue shirts, plod on their deformed feet. Fat, grotesque-looking Chinese maggots sprawl in splendid victorias. Curious one-wheeled vehicles are pushed by a vigorous coolie, bearing one passenger only, sitting at one end of a plank put on the top of the enormous wheel, making balance to his goods and chattels placed on the other end of the plank. As "time is not money" in the Orient, the fare of a run which lasts sometimes half-a-day, with many halts, is only one farthing! We met a "towkee," or mandarin, arrayed in a marvellous costume embroidered with silk and gold, who was conveyed in a rich palanquin, surrounded by many attendants who beat the drum all the way. Further on our carriers stopped to make way for a funeral procession, preceded by Chinamen sounding the horn and beating the drum. The deceased is carried in a large box ornamented with a metal dragon. Behind came the hired women mourners, with their plaintive wail. The whole procession is arrayed in white, the mourning colour in China. On our way back we passed along the Bund, in the English section, a pleasant little park to which no Chinaman, be he a coolie or a mandarin, was admitted, and traversed the broad, grassy Maidan, the European rendezvous, where Englishmen and Americans, in spotless flannels, played cricket or football. On the pier we saw a flag signalling a tempest coming on. How annoying! We shall have to wait here until the typhoon passes away. In different places placards announced the arrival of Antoine Kontski, the celebrated pianist, Beethoven's last disciple.

September 28th.—My husband was invited by the French authorities to visit Zi-ka-wai, a small colony established by the Jesuits, two miles from Shanghai. The reverend fathers on leaving France take an oath never to return to their native land. On arriving in this far-away country, they put on the Chinese costume, and, cross in hand—their only weapon—they go about fearlessly, preaching Christianity in the very centre of fanaticism and hatred of the white race. Sergy saw a group of monks sitting under the palms, watching their long-tressed pupils who played tennis.

September 29th.—To-day our Consul gave a dinner-party at which Kontski was present. The old maestro is 82 years old, but does not appear more than 60. He has much humour in him, and kept the attention of the whole table with his amusing anecdotes.

September 30th.—We took passage to-day on the *Melbourne* one of the finest steamers of the Messageries Maritimes. We slipped down the Woosung on board the *Chenan* a small steamboat which transported the passengers from Shanghai to the big ocean vessels, which could not enter the mouth of the Woosung.

When we stepped on board the *Melbourne* the captain met us in full naval uniform with big epaulettes and a three-cornered hat. The commander of a Russian cruiser moored in the harbour, and the chief admiral of the French fleet came also to pay their respects to my husband.

We started in the afternoon on our way to the equatorial regions. Whilst we passed before the *Khabarovsk*, the sailors waved their caps and cheered us loudly.

There are about fifty first-class passengers on the *Melbourne*. Kontski and his wife have also taken passage on that boat. The celebrated Polish pianist proved a most cheery and entertaining companion. Though the aged maestro has passed his eightieth birthday, his spring-like vigour and abounding vitality are surprising ; he defies the march of time. Kontski speaks five languages with equal facility. His wit is sparkling. During five o'clock tea he told us a number of rather risky anecdotes which kept his neighbours in fits of laughter. When I handed the old maestro his cup of tea, asking him if he had sugar enough, he said, "Everything proceeding from the hands of Your Excellence can't be otherwise than excellent!" Gallant old man!

Between the hours of five and seven the passengers take their siesta on deck, sitting down in canvas chairs and fading slowly into a deep slumber, conscious of the rhythmic throbbing of the engine and of the beat of warm air on their cheek.

At eight o'clock the gong sounded for dinner. The captain would have me placed next him ; at my left hand sat the Director of the French Post, a Corsican bearing the high-sounding name of Casanova. That compatriot of Bonaparte leads, as it seems to me, the depraved life that his famous namesake did before him. He said gallant things to me, and related scandalous stories about his amorous exploits.

After dinner we expected that Kontski would play the piano, but he said he would do it, for my sole benefit, at Hong-Kong.

October 1st.—I had little sleep last night, for the ship was rolling a good deal. I climbed on deck at sunrise. Sergy tucked me up in my chair and I soon fell into a deep slumber. When I woke the rolling had ceased and the sea was quite calm. I was so comfortable I didn't want to get out of my rug, and took my breakfast on deck.

October 2nd.—This morning, whilst we took our coffee,

a weird procession of gentlemen, in extremely impromptu costume, with towels over their arms, passed by on their way to the bath-cabin. After luncheon the captain led us over the inner mysteries of the ship. We went down the deck ladder into the engine-room, where he, who would taste purgatory, had but to find employment there. The stokers are all niggers, who support better that stifling atmosphere than their white brethren.

After dinner we sat on deck, seeking in vain for a breath of fresh air. It was fire that we inhaled. We are now in the straits of Formosa and have reached the tropics.

After tea we had music in the salon. I sat down at the piano and played four hands with Mr. Shaniavski. Our fellow passengers, crowding round, applauded, and begged us to play on. Kontski turned over the leaves and approved of our performance. In recompense he improvised, on the spot, a song which he dedicated to me, and entitled " Mes Adieux."

CHAPTER LXXIX

HONG-KONG

October 3rd.—At dawn the island of Hong-Kong appeared to view. We slipped into the horse-shoe harbour of Victoria Town, the most beautiful and picturesque place I have ever seen. The shores of the splendid bay are crowned with long rows of tropical villas. Victoria Town is a handsome, well-built city. One can see we are in a British colony ; English flags float everywhere. We got into a small boat to go ashore, and walked to the Hotel Hong-Kong, having to pass over a long bridge. The Hotel Hong-Kong is a large seven-storied building, surrounded on all sides by a gallery with about a dozen shops. I shut myself up in my room with all the blinds closed ; the semi-darkness gave me a sense of coolness, but when I opened the window such a stifling breath of air flew into the room that I had to shut it hurriedly. After the hour of siesta had passed, we went up the steep funicular railway to Victoria Peak, a perpendicular mountain 1,850 feet high. The funicular creeps straight up the side of the hill ; while one car creeps up the mountain, the other crawls down. In about three minutes time we found ourselves on the Esplanade, where we had palanquins to take us to the cool summit where a big hotel is built. Many travellers come here to look down from the height of the Peak upon the great harbour of Hong-Kong. A flag floated at the top of the Peak, announcing the mailboat from Japan. The big steamer seemed from there but a black spot. Picnic parties often come to the Peak, and the hotel is always full, thanks to the temperature, which is several degrees lower than in town. We had dinner at the hotel where the food is considered very good for the English palates, but far too spiced for ours. It was long before I recovered from my first mouthful of chicken plentifully seasoned wirh coarse red-pepper.

We took a bright green palanquin with three men at the foot of the hill, and went at a swinging pace through the outskirts of Victoria-Town. I had all the blinds pulled up whilst we were carried through the " Happy-alley " to the cathedral. There was a long file of pretty, dark-haired señoritas marching soberly to church, holding their prayer-books devoutly in their hands, attended by black-gowned, sharp-eyed duennas. The congregation consists of diverse nationalities, and the priest is obliged to preach in four languages—in English, Portuguese, Malay and Malabar. Macaites (aborigines of Macas) abound in Hong-Kong: they are a mixture of Portuguese and Chinese. Though wearing the European costume, these half-castes remain inwardly Chinese. It is a race of degenerates, whereas cross-breeding between English and French creoles with the Chinese, form a splendid race.

The dinner at table-d'hôte was announced for seven o'clock. We entered the large dining-room full of grand gentlemen and smart ladies in evening dress. Dinner was served at small separate tables; it consisted of oyster soup, followed by a dish of frogs, strongly spiced *cari*, served with hot rice, and tropical fruit for dessert, unknown in Europe: the jack-fruit, of the size and appearance of a water-melon, and a sort of great orange four times its natural size, named grape-fruit; you have it on your plate cut in two halves with ice on each, and you scoop the inside out of a lot of tiny pockets with a tea-spoon. I was glad of the coolness of the big hall; a punkah-boy on the verandah pulled drowsily at the cords that moved the great fan. The usual language spoken here between Europeans and natives is called " pigeon-English "—a mixture of English, French, and German. It was difficult to make ourselves understood by the boys. We had to explain ourselves mostly by signs.

Directly after dinner we went out in palanquins. The fare is only one dollar for the whole day. We were carried swiftly up broad streets bordered by palm trees and bamboos covered with mould because of the damp, tepid air. Queen's Road, the principal street, is a large avenue bordered with beautiful English shops, and reminds one of London, only instead of commonplace constables, it is Punjabs—Hindoos—in big red turbans who keep order in the streets. On our way to the Botanic Gardens we saw English soldiers exercising in a large square. We admired—in the beautiful Gardens, amongst the innumerable wonders of tropical vegetation—a large basin with lotuses in full bloom. We returned to the hotel through the native quarter of the town, lined with straw huts between hedges of banana and cocoa-nut trees.

After dinner we stayed out on the veranda till nearly midnight, with Kontski and his wife, who are also stopping at Hotel Hong-Kong. An intoxicating perfume of flowers came from the garden below; only the tinkle of a fountain and the ceaseless chanting of myriads of insects tempered the stillness of the beautiful tropical night. The old mæstro is a most interesting and brilliant talker, with an unending store of anecdote and reminiscence; you could listen to him for hours. He recalled the days of his youth, and told us that at the age of four he played the piano. When he was twelve years old it was decided that he was to enter the musical profession. His father brought him to Vienna to be introduced so Beethoven, who was already half-deaf at that time. He listened to his performance with ear-trumpets to his ears, and accepted Kontski as a pupil. One day, during the lesson, a card bearing the name of Beethoven's brother, with whom he was not on the best of terms, was brought to him. *Beethoven, Rittergut-Besitzer* (possessor of a feudal estate) was printed on it. The great composer greeted it with a growl. He took his note-book from his pocket, tore out a leaf and hastily scribbled on it: *Beethoven, Gehirn-Besitzer* (possessor of brains), and, handing it to his servant, he said: " There, give him that and tell him that I am occupied and cannot receive him." After having studied four years with Beethoven, Kontski returned to Warsaw, where his father taught French in a college in which he ended his education, together with Chopin. The friendship between them lasted unclouded until Chopin's death broke it.

We talked a lot of music with Kontski, who had known many celebrated artists, and had been on the best of terms with Rachel. During his stay in Paris in 1836, Kontski had been invited to a dinner-party given by Rothschild, at which many celebrities were present, famous people in the world of music: Chopin, Rossini, Liszt, Thalberg, and a host of others. After dinner the great musicians were asked to play. Thalberg complied readily, but Chopin refused point blank, saying that he had grown too heavy after the copious repast. Liszt followed his example and would not play. Then Rothschild, addressing himself to Rossini, who owed the nick-name of "Papa Rossini," thanks to his fat and round figure, asked him to persuade Liszt to play something to them. But there was little sympathy between these two geniuses, and Rossini exclaimed perfidiously: " Liszt, mon ami, play us one of your admirable compositions which you give out ordinarily as an improvisation." Liszt, furious to be turned into ridicule, sat down ragingly at the piano, bending his face over the keys, and began to play one of his most brilliant rhapsodies, with high technique and rare poetic insight. His performance enchanted everyone in the room, except Rossini, who had not succeeded in ridiculing Liszt.

October 4th.—This morning we accompanied Kontski to a music-shop, where he went to choose a piano for his forth-coming concert. There was only a cracked old "Pleyel" for the choice. The old maestro kept his promise and played most enchantingly some selections of "Faust" of his own transposition. I cannot understand how he could manage to get such lovely notes out of such a decrepit old instrument; by his magic touch he persuaded it to give forth delicious music. I could have listened all day long.

On our way back to the hotel, we entered a farm bearing a placard with the alluring inscription: "New Milk." The hostess, a fat negress with an orange kerchief tied round her head, ran up to us, smiling and shewing two rows of very white teeth in a very black face. She offered tea with excellent cream and bread and butter.

We dined in haste at the hotel and walked to the quay, where we took the steam-launch belonging to the hotel to be transported to the *Melbourne*. I felt at home when I stepped over her familiar side. Some of the old faces were among the crew, and the head steward was the same.

At four o'clock in the afternoon we were on our way to Saigon. The steward told me that amongst the passengers on board we had Theo, the well-known French actress, accompanied by her maid, a pretty mulatto-girl, dressed in a yellow and red striped cotton frock, with a silk kerchief on her head. The dark charms of this dusky maiden conquered the hearts of a great number of the crew. European fashions reach these remote parts. Sergy's neighbour at table, a Japanese young lady, very tall for her Liliputian race, had discarded the kimono and wears the white woman's tailor-made dress. Many of the men in Japan get their clothes from London, as their wives do from Paris. What a pity! Soon there will be no special customs or dress left. We shall all be exactly alike.

October 5th.—The atmosphere in my cabin being unbearable, I settled down on deck, seeking refuge under an awning, with books and work, and stretched myself comfortably in my own bamboo-chair that I had bought at Hong-Kong. By my side a Portuguese girl read aloud Psalms to a group of nuns wearing white caps floating in the air, whilst her friend, a Chinese girl, did needlework. The Good Sisters had recruited both girls into their Order. They sat telling their rosaries, their lips reverently framing words of prayer; I could hear the click of their beads. The opposite side of the deck was occupied by a Chinese school, a class of about thirty little boys, their long tresses entwined with pink ribbon. The teacher stood at one end of the rank and sang a single line of his lessons, and all the children sang it after him. Then came the second line, and they repeated it.

October 6th.—The coasts of Annam are outlined on the horizon. Dark grey clouds, precursors of rain, sweep rapidly, driven by the wind which had risen suddenly, and one of these tempests of the equinox came to fall upon us. The squall lasted only a few minutes, but we couldn't go on the deck, which was drenched by the deluge.

October 7th.—I couldn't sleep the whole night for the heat. The temperature continues to rise ; as soon as the sun gets up it is already scorching. The tropics are making themselves strongly felt. We are only 600 miles from the equator.

Towards midnight the steward knocked at my door, begging me to close the port-holes in order to give room to the rope-ladder for the pilot. We are at the mouth of the river Saigon. The tide was already too low for us to enter the harbour, and we anchored outside.

October 8th.—We are moving on at last, making great windings on the river which is very narrow in these parts. All the passengers were on deck. The banks are flat, planted with high palms. Insolent black-faced monkeys gambol on the tree-tops and chat vivaciously as they scamper from branch to branch, making grimaces at us. Birds of all the colour of the rainbow are perched on the branches. One of the passengers assured me that he had perceived a crocodile, but strain my eyes as I might, I could not see the monster.

CHAPTER LXXX

SAIGON

THE smell of earth reached us already, as well as the perfume of amber and tropical flowers. We are in Cochin-China, in fairy-like decorations. I thought myself in dreamland and had to pinch myself to be sure I was awake.

The town of Saigon, buried in banyan and palm trees, is a city of splendid wonders. The French colours floated everywhere. Small omnibuses harnessed with a Malay pony were waiting under the banyan trees on the quay. An aide-de-camp of the Governor-General of Cochin-China invited us, in the name of his chief, to put up at his house, but we preferred to drive independently to the Grand Hôtel, and mounted an omnibus drawn by a Liliputian pony, with a native coachman on the box, dressed in white linen with a red turban. We drove through streets that tried to be French, and boulevards surrounded by mimosas and laurel trees. All Saigon sleeps between the hours of two and five. The houses of commerce are closed and every business stops. Most of the window-shades were down, and there was no sign of life in the streets ; we only saw a man sleeping in an angle of a wall, flies above his head. It seemed a very long drive to the Grand Hôtel. The coachman. to whom we had explained ourselves in a language of signs, didn't understand where we wanted to go, and instead of driving us to the Grand Hôtel he brought us to the Botanic Gardens, through long alleys of red sand. Once we were at the door of the gardens, we decided to visit them, though it wasn't at all an afternoon pastime in such awful heat. In this tropical land, one of the hottest on the globe, there are often cases of sunstroke amongst the Europeans. As to the natives, they are accustomed to receive the caresses of the hot rays of the sun, which is at its zenith in these parts.

On our way back to the hotel we saw the statue of Gambetta on the square. The fancy of the sculptor has attired the great man in a fur-lined coat, which looks rather queer in this country, where everyone would prefer to be completely deprived of clothes.

A spacious gallery with hermetically closed shutters stretches the whole length of our hotel. Directly after tiffin, we went up to our apartment and indulged in a pleasant siesta. I was awfully thirsty, taking up a decanter to pour out a glass of water, what was my horror to find a drowned scorpion at the bottom of it. It was enough to disgust you of the Tropics for ever! I rang the bell and my summons were quickly answered by a barefooted Annamite boy, with nothing but a bit of stuff wrapped round his loins. I pointed out to him, with an indignant gesture, the contents of the decanter, trying by an expressive gesture to let him see all my disgust, but the boy didn't appear shocked, he only grinned, showing his shining teeth from ear to ear. When going to bed I looked in and underneath the bed for relatives of the drowned scropion and have discovered an enormous tarantula on my mosquito-net. The whole night swarms of noisy lizards crawled round the walls and on the ceiling, making a very disagreeable concert. I was expecting them to come down upon my head all the time. The lizards are generally quite inoffensive, except a dangerous species called " to-que," according to the sound they produce. Before putting on our boots in the morning we looked inside, lest a scorpion may be lying in ambush.

My husband was invited to dinner by the General-Governor, Mr. Prévost, together with the Resident of Kambodge. The Palace is closed nearly all the year round, because Mr. Prévost inhabits Hanoi-in-Tonkin. He is passing now through Saigon on his way to Europe, on a holiday. I dined comfortably with Mrs. Serebriakoff at a private table by an open window. After the repast, we settled ourselves at a little table on the boulevard, reminding one of the Paris boulevards, with well-dressed white men sitting at small tables, smoking, drinking syrups and eating ices; only instead of white-aproned Parisian waiters, it is Chinese boys, resembling women with their long white robes and tresses hanging down their backs, who serve the customers. We sat contemplating the movements of the crowd on the boulevard, full of Europeanised negro swells, Hindoos with a cast-mark on their forehead, and officers of the French army. Two French regiments and two Annamite battalions are quartered at Saigon. The Annamite soldiers are bare-footed and wear straw hats of conical form. There is no cavalry in Cochin-China, because horses, except Annamite ponies, cannot stand the climate.

Mr. Prévost had invited my husband and his suite to share his box at the opera, which was " Faust." We saw their carriage stop before the theatre just in front of the boulevard. We could hear the sound of our Anthem and the Marseillaise, played by a military band in the garden belonging to the theatre, and the clapping of hands and bravoes. Between the acts the little tables on the boulevard were taken by storm by the audience, and rapidly abandoned at the moment when an Annamite boy began to run up and down the boulevard ringing the bell, which was to be the signal for the beginning of the following act.

A guard of honour was placed this morning at the entrance-door of our hotel, in honour of my husband. The French soldiers were replaced in the afternoon by Annamite warriors, who grasped their guns and saluted Sergy as he passed them and presented arms. After tiffin Mr. Rousseau called upon us with his son. They are going to sail with us as far as Singapore. Before dinner Sergy went to visit the barracks with General Corona, the chief of the troops. The soldiers, locked up for punishment, were set free to commemorate my husband's inspection of the barracks.

At nightfall we went on board the *Melbourne*, and saw on the upper deck a great number of French officers who had come to wish Mr. Rousseau a happy voyage.

October 12th.— The heat is something dreadful, and I had to converse with Mr. Rousseau. After tiffin I shut myself up, having decided to keep to my cabin for the remainder of the voyage, until we reached Singapore.

Towards evening we approached the great Hindoo-Chinese city. We are now in the neighbourhood of the equator, at the distance of half a degree only. We have the pilot on board, because this port is dangerous, many vessels having perished here. We entered the bay with some difficulty, and passed before the wreck of a ship. We dropped anchor amongst a number of steamers of different nationalities. The harbour is beautiful and traversed in all directions by canoes mounted by natives, whose want of dress amused me: it was a mere fig-leaf of coloured rag.

CHAPTER LXXXI

SINGAPORE

OUR captain had sent a boat ashore to warn the authorities of our arrival. We were afraid we should be in quarantine owing to the plague raging at the time in India. We had to undergo a sanitary inspection and waited a long time for the doctor. At last, a boat flying a yellow flag, bearing the inscription: "Health Officer," came off to us It contained the port-doctor. It is dreadful if we have to perform a quarantine! It's all right. The native passangers only passed the ordeal of medical examination. They showed their tongues and their eyelids to the doctor, and after he had examined the state of their health, we were permitted to land. We were instantly surrounded by a whole fleet of junks full of howling natives, who attacked our boat offering their different wares insistingly in funny English: "You bye laidee, veree nice, you bye!" Naked bronze-coloured boys, screaming out "A la mer!" dived into the water after the coins dropped overboard by passengers, and came to the surface smiling, holding the coins between their teeth. They won't trouble themselves to search for coppers, and discover them in the deep with their lynx eyes.

We were in a dense crowd of Hindoos, Negroes and half-castes, when we stepped on shore. Enterprising natives attacked us, each of them seeming determined to carry some portion of us away with them. They were not ruffians demanding our money or our lives, as they seemed doing, but were simply peaceable porters and guides, hoping to earn an honest penny. An elegant victoria drawn by a pair of fine horses, with a native coachman—wearing a red fez—on the box, was placed at our disposal by a rich rajah, but I preferred to drive to the Hotel d'Europe in a carriage belonging to our Consul.—Mr. Kleimenoff,—drawn by a pacific pony. The Consul's "Kawass," a negro of the blackest black, wearing on his shoulder a belt with the Russian arms—the double eagle—embroidered on it, was sitting on the box. We are again on British territory. The names of the streets and all the signboards are written in English. Every nationality seemed to be represented in the streets: all shades of black, brown and yellow—Chinese,

Malays, Hindoos and Europeans from all countries. The Hindoos are slender and handsome men, with firm polished bodies like bronze statuetts. The negroes are also splendid specimens of manhood, robust and square-built; they wear round their necks, arms and legs silver bands ornamented with coral beads. Both sexes walk about in the streets in the primitive simplicity of nature, naked and unashamed. The women with silver rings in their nostrils and clinking bangles round their arms and ankles, wear nothing above the waist and not much below. They grow old very early, and at the age of twenty look forty at least. Little black children, resembling each other as two drops of ink, are playing in the tropical sunlight in the dust. Good-looking English soliders promenade, stick in hand, and English officials drive importantly in victorias.

The Hôtel d'Europe is composed of several separate pavilions, with high ceilinged bare rooms, with white-washed walls and mat-covered floors. The hotel is draughty and perfectly adapted to the tropics. The doors do not touch the floor and the ceilings and the walls between each room are also open at the top, leaving an interval for the air to circulate freely; every sound, therefore, is heard in the next apartment.

October 13th.—After tiffin, we went to the Botanic Gardens, the most wonderful in the world, a vision of loveliness. I had not eyes enough to admire it properly. On our way back we passed the race-courses and saw a line of smart carriages standing on the road. The race days in Singapore resemble Sunday in London, nothing can be got in the city, all the shops and banks are closed.

October 14th.—Our Consul gave us to-day a first rate dinner. His house is very stylish: all his servants are christened Chinamen, who have come from Pekin, where they form a large colony. Their ancestors were Cossacks taken prisoners by the Chinese in the seventeetnh century.

October 15th.—To-day, we start for Java, in the Dutch East Indies, on the *Godavéri* a steamboat of the Méssageries Maritimes. The ship makes the trip in thirty-six hours. What a chance to see the most beautiful country in the world! The voyage will not be a pleasant one however, because we are sure to be roasted alive, our cabin being on the sunny side. The captain, fat and jovial, is a weather-beaten experienced old seaman, who has had long practice in these far away waters; it is twenty-five years already that he has plied between Singapore and Java, fighting with the waves. The gallant old mariner has hoisted the Russian flag in our honour. The passengers for the greater part are Dutchmen, and half-castes (a cross-breed between Dutch colonists and Japanese.)

October 16th.—To-day we are upon the equator and enter the south hemisphere. We cross the great meridian—the 180th degree of longitude, and are close to the centre of the globe. We drop out a day of our lives; yesterday it was October 15th (Sunday), to-day it is October 17th (Tuesday). We did not celebrate the passage of the line, and had no foolish ceremonies, no fantastics, no ducking at sea, which consisted in sprinkling with salt-water the neophyte who crossed the equator for the first time. All that sort of thing has gone out. One of the passengers exclaimed for fun that he saw the equator and a naive lady-passenger took up her opera-glasses and began to stare round about, which made everybody laugh. We remained long on deck, enjoying the beautiful tropical night. The sky was sown with stars. Good-by the "Old Bear," and welcome the "Southern Cross." It is not particularly large nor strikingly bright, but it does, after a fashion, suggest a cross not carefully shaped, consisting of four large stars and a little one. We saw also the black patch of the sky which the sailors call the "soot-bag." We had music on deck, where the piano was carried out. I played duets together with Mr. Shaniavski, and the commissaire scraped on the mandoline. I have remarked that it is always the commissaires who constitute the musical element on French steamers.

CHAPTER LXXXII

JAVA—BATAVIA

October 16th.—We see an island on our right. It is Java, the Garden of the East, one of the most splendid spots in the world, to which nature has been prodigal with beauties and wonders. In the distance we perceive the port of Batavia, the capital of Netherland India, with Dutch flags flying. It was a strange land to come to. I seemed to be in a dream all the time, and felt as if transported into another planet. It was like being in a theatre where all the scenery was real and the curtain never came down.

Our Consul—Mr. Bakounine—was on the quay. It was nice meeting someone from the part of the world I was born in. The warm and damp climate of Java had not suited our Consul ; he looked very thin and white. Mr. Bakounine was extremely kind and gave all his time to us.

On the quay exemplary order reigned. The natives are treated by the Dutch as pariahs, and ruled with a hand of iron. They are not allowed to speak Dutch, and as we were not acquainted with the native language, we had the universal language, that of the signs, left to us. The Dutch also evince great contempt for the Chinese, and treat them as if they were dirt. Coolies are not permitted to ride in tramways with white-faced Europeans ; only high-caste Parsees may ride with sahibs in second-class compartments

Batavia is the reunion of three separate towns : Weltewredeu, the new town, buried in luxuriant vegetation, with low-built white houses, surrounded by verandas, groves of palm and cocoa-nut, gives one the impression of a series of villas built in a large park ; the Pettah, (old town) is an agglomeration of bamboo-huts forming narrow streets, inhabited by the natives, and separated from the European quarter by a cricket-ground ; the so-called Chinese Town is inhabited only by Chinamen.

We took the train, which brought us in twenty minutes to Batavia. Whilst we crossed a beautiful cocoa and palm-wood, Mr. Bakounine said that he would have exchanged willingly one single birch-tree of far-away Russia for all the palms in the world. How I understand him ! I also would have gladly exchanged all this luxurious tropical vegetation and blue sky for the grey skies of dear old Petersburg.

When we arrived at Batavia, we were driven in a cab, with a native coachman on the box, to the Hôtel de Java. I had got hold of some Japanese words and kept repeating to him : " Plan, plan," which means "go slowly." The inhabitants were probably taking their "siesta," during the sweltering heat of mid-day : troops, natives, animals, were all asleep. Batavia seemed deserted, all the houses had dropped their blinds. We only saw lizards in the streets, warming themselves in the sun.

The Hôtel de Java is a square, one storied building with an open courtyard in the middle and a veranda supported by pillars on the whole length of the front. The rooms are barely furnished, the floors covered with mats ; there are wire nettings in the doors and windows to keep away the midges, who weren't even honourable enough to wait until sunset before attacking you. There are no bells in the hotel and I grew hoarse calling the Malay "boy" for some information I wanted. With many gesticulations he began to gabble in an unknown tongue to me, and I was obliged to write down my requests on a bit of paper which the "boy" carried to the office. One may well imagine how promptly my demands were satisfied.

The veranda was full of creole ladies seeking relief from the sunshine outside and whiling away the dreary mid-day hours reclining in hammocks and cane-lounges, clad in loose transparent night-jackets, stockingless, with their hair in curling-pins, their discarded shoes lying on the floor. The climate makes them indolent. They enjoyed their "siesta" smoking cigarettes and drinking iced lemonade.

We had tiffin in the dining-room. The Dutch cooking does not please me. Tiffin always begins with the traditional "reistafel," a dish of chipped meat and rice, without any seasoning to it. The meat is lean and unsavoury, and the dairy products are very bad. The cattle in Java are very small, looking more like goats than cows. The natives are not exacting in this country, cocoa-nuts serve them both as food and drink ; they eat the pulp and drink the milk.

Towards evening, the town became animated ; the streets were full of bustle. Europeans go out in the streets bareheaded, and seem to have forgotten their hats.

We drove in a tram through the three towns. Batavia is a city of many canals ; it reminded me of Rotterdam. We saw lots of natives bathing in the Grand Canal. When passing the Portuguese Gate, we were shown a big cannon which is the object of a queer sort of pilgrimage for barren Malay women, who bring offering to the cannon in order not to remain childless in their wedded life.

October 17th.—I passed a wretched night, tossing and turning in my bed, half smothered with mosquito-curtains,

D*

which effectually keep off any little breath of air there is. In that awful heat sleep was out of the question. As soon as I lay down I felt myself devoured by quantities of famished recatures who greedily awaited their prey, and with which I I fought a desperate battle, persevering in the chase with a fine sporting spirit until morning.

Batavia does not enchant me. The heat is tremendous. We have determined to-day to go and seek freshness on the wooded slopes of Buitenzorg, the summer resort of the Dutch Resident, situated a few hours out of Batavia. The railway-line from Batavia to Buitenzorg is one of the most picturesque in the world. Marvellous landscapes spread out before our admiring eyes. What vegetation! There are thick mighty palms, bananas and dense tropical jungle. The road is very steep and we ascended slowly along wide precipices, stopping only twice at neat little railway-stations. The higher we mounted the fresher the air became. We rolled now between sugar-cane, vanilla and cotton plantations, with trees covered with white flakes, and passed picturesque villas with tall cocoanut palms casting cool shadows on the low flat roofs. The tropical sun made the train like a furnace. After three hours' drive we saw a settlement of low dwellings, at the foot of blue hills, half hidden in an eucalyptus forest and gigantic mimosas. It was Buitenzorg!

When we left the train, an aide-de-camp of the Resident came up to my husband and offered his carriage to drive us to the Hôtel du Chemin de Fer. The hotel is kept by a Frenchman. We entered a courtyard surrounded by several low buildings. Our apartment disappointed me by the doubtful cleanliness of its beds denuded of coverlets and sheets. Lizards were running about the ceiling and the walls. A barefooted "boy" arrayed in a white loose jacket, armed with a feather-brush and a duster, came to tidy our bedroom. He first swept the petroleum lamp (there are no candles to be had in this corner of the globe) and then began to dust our beds with the same brush. It won't be an easy task to civilise him!

Our windows looked out into the garden. Green coffee-trees covered with white flowers and ripe fruit, peeped into our room, and a sweet musky aromatic odour pervaded the air.

The year, in all tropical countries, is divided into two seasons, summer and winter. Summer begins towards October to end in May, which is winter-time here. The wet season has set in, the season of ceaseless, abundant rain and suffocating heat. In these abominable regions, when summer ends and the intense heat of January has passed, tepid rain begins to fall every day from four to six o'clock with astonishing persistency. The air is clear and yet full of moisture; everything grows musty. If a pair of boots have not been cleaned for two days, they get covered with green mould. Leaves and branches grow now and then on the telegraph posts, transforming them into trees, which obliges the railway companies, sometimes, to use iron instead of wooden posts. Watches and all metal objects when exposed to the air become covered with rust.

October 18th.—Foreigners come rarely to Java and, except our company, there are only two Dutch families in our hotel, who arrived a few days ago from Borneo.

Snakes, centipedes and all sorts of filthy vermin abound here. One must look out for poisonous serpents hidden in the grass; they often creep into the houses. Quite recently an enormous boa, measuring over three yards, penetrated into the Resident's courtyard, and after having regaled himself with a fowl, that he snapped up on his way, the formidable reptile crept into the Palace and coiled himself into a comfortable position under the Resident's writing-table. One of the Dutch ladies stopping at the hotel went down into the drawing-room this afternoon to play the piano and perceived a huge cobra-capella, a serpent of the most dangerous species, taking his nap under the instrument.

I heard a dog barking under my window. It appeared to be a little subterranean animal called "Earth dog," who barks loudly each time anyone passes before his hole.

Before dinner Sergy went to pay a visit to the Resident, who had sent his carriage for him, drawn by a team of four horses, with a Javanese coachman on the box and two barefooted footmen in splendid livery, wearing helmets.

The Resident is absolute sovereign in these parts; his surroundings transport one at the end of the nineteenth century to the epoch of feudalism. During the reception barefooted servants presented trays charged with wine and champagne, in humble attitudes, bending the knee before their master, and retreated backwards bowing very low.

The Resident invited Sergy for a drive in his carriage. They crossed large fields alloted to the culture of tobacco, cacao, pepper, indigo and coffee. A long street of small huts, with roofs that may be opened, all of the same shape and size, spreads in the coffee plantations, serving for the drying of the grains. As soon as the sun appears, the roofs are opened and the coffee grains are spread on the floor to be dried. From thence Sergy was driven to the Piradenia Gardens, containing a rich collection of queer tropical plants, trees of the rarest species, and beautiful flower-beds. To see the gardens took hours. Sergy was dazzled by the beauty of all he saw. On his way back to the hotel, a storm broke out; it was one of those formidable equatorial rains of such violence, that it seemed as if the sky was emptying itself upon the earth.

As soon as dinner was over, we went for a walk round Buitenzorg. After the shower there was a delicious perfume of plants and damp earth. We strolled through broad streets lined with huts built of bamboo and thatched with cocoa-nut leaves, hidden in the dense foliage.

October 19th.—To-day the Resident gave a grand dinner to my husband, a Lucullus-like feast. Sergy was entertained in great state by his host, who did things royally. The marble steps of the wide staircase were decorated with bare-footed lackeys in showy livery and powdered wigs, standing all the way up at equal distances. The brilliantly lighted reception-rooms of the Palace were full of elegantly dressed gentlemen and ladies in low dresses, showing all their jewellery and shoulders. The table was beautifully laid ; before each stool stood a native servant. Champagne flowed abundantly, but Sergy was too hot to enjoy the meal, for there are no punkahs in Java, because the Dutch find that these huge fans tend to induce bald heads.

I find it a bit dull here. There is positively nothing to do in the evening but to sit on the veranda and admire the beautiful tropical night, which falls suddenly without twilight. Everything is queer in these equatorial regions. The moon is right over our heads, the sickle pointing upwards, and the shade caused by the planet spreads right under our feet.

October 22nd.—We took the train back to Batavia this morning, and put up this time at the Hôtel Niderlander, a cool white building with deep pillared verandas, carpeted with cocoa-nut mattings and strewn with tables and easy cane chairs. We sat on the veranda after dinner, listening to the band playing in Waterloo-Square, just opposite. Strolling merchants bothered us, offering their wares ; we sent them off by saying "piggie," meaning in Javanese "get off with you," at which they beat a hasty retreat.

October 24th.—We are leaving Java to-day without regret. The hideous climate is depressing, the hot, steamy atmosphere awfully enervating. The head-manager came to knock at our door at four o'clock in the morning to inform us that it was time to go to the railway station. Mr. Bakounine and the agent of the Méssageries Maritimes rode down with us to the port, a veritable inferno, full of mosquitoes and pestered by malarial fever, in which deadly miasmas seem to evaporate from the unwholesome soil.

The *Godavéri* set sail at ten o'clock in the morning. Adieu, Java !

We are about twenty passengers on board. There is a young half-caste among them, the proprietor of a rich tea-estate, sent back for his health to Europe.

CHAPTER LXXXIII

SINGAPORE

October 25th.—At dawn we approached Singapore. We put up at the Hôtel d'Europe. After tiffin, we visited the cisterns which supply the inhabitants with potable water. There are no wells in Singapore, the natives must be satisfied with the water produced by the rains, which is gathered and kept in large ponds. On our way we met natives driving in chariots drawn by small bisons, who have not the lazy drag of their western brethren, but trot briskly as horses. The aborigines, clad with a band of stuff round their thighs, held burning torches in their hands, and beat the tom-tom with all their might to chase away the spirits of darkness, because evil spirits, according to their belief, shun daylight.

October 26th.—We spent the whole afternoon on the veranda bargaining with natives who carried trays of precious stones. One has to be very careful with these vendors, who frequently sell worthless stones for precious ones. Sergy bought me a beautiful moonstone necklace.

Before dinner, Sergy called upon the Governor-General of Singapore, who had governed the Fiji Islands for a long time.

October 27th.—At 8 o'clock in the evening we took our passage on the *Océanien*, a steamer bound to Marseilles. If the temperature permitted, I would jump for joy at the thought that it was our boat to Europe.

It was night when we left the port. Amongst the passengers we have on board the wife of the Japanese Ambassador in London, who was going to join her husband. She was accompanied by her sister and a lady companion, with whom she practised English and took lessons in geography on deck. Both Japanese ladies are dressed in the latest Parisian fashion, and it is only their small turned-up eyes and high-boned cheeks, which betray their nationality.

October 28th.—The children of a native couple bound to the Isles de la Réunion, romp in the corridor making a terrible row. They are awfully ill-bred and boil over with perversity, and pass their time in fighting and playing tricks and putting their tongues out to their " ayah " (nurse), an old negress wearing a yellow kerchief on her head, the ends of which passed through her large straw hat. She endeavoured to teach the naughty brats better manners, but it was all in vain; they continued to behave shockingly. I was sorely tempted to give them a sound shaking when they shrieked when taken to bed at night.

October 29th, 30th, 31st.—All these days there was no land in view, nothing but the endless blue of the sky and the endless waters of the Indian Ocean.

November 1st.—The sea is quite smooth and still our ship rocks very unpleasantly. We are approaching the verdant island of Ceylon, the most marvellous meridional point of India. The air is so pure that we perceive the Peak of Adam, at thirty miles off from Ceylon, the legendary site of Adam's burial ground.

CHAPTER LXXXIV

COLOMBO ·

TOWARDS night we arrived at Colombo and moored two miles off the low coast, bordered with cocoa-nut trees crowned with green palms. A long greystone breakwater with a round-topped tower at the end ran out into the sea, and over it in the distance Colombo with its red-tiled houses lay half hidden in deep green vegetation. Canoes brought on board Singhalese merchants with stuffs and other products of the land. We see everywhere British flags flying. We are on English ground under the tropic sun of Ceylon. From afar we perceive Adam's Peak, the region where Paradise was. On the summit of the Peak there is the impress of a gigantic foot, the first footstep of Adam out of Paradise, according to the Christian legends, of Siva for the Brahmins, of Buddha for the Buddhists.

The *Océanien* is going to stop here twenty-four hours to discharge coal. I saw Singhalese porters, with sacks on their heads, mounting on deck and plunging down into the hold to come out again bent in two under their loads. We walked to the Great Oriental Hotel, which stands on the quay, quite near to the port, a large building surrounded on all sides by the broad veranda. There are colonnades underneath the hotel with shops.

The heat and damp of Ceylon are just as terrible as in Java. I passed a wretched night. I went to bed but not to sleep—oh, dear, no! for I just began to doze when swarms of mosquitoes recalled me to reality very soon.

November 2nd.—I was glad to return to the *Océanien* early in the morning. I stood on deck until we unmoored, watching a band of bronzed natives, in a state of almost Adamic nudity, beautifully shaped men unconscious of immodesty, their wardrobe reduced to a rag replacing the traditional fig-leaf swinging to and fro in a canoe and singing "Tarra-Boumbia" at the top of their voices, with a great supply of gesticulations and grimaces, slapping themselves energetically on the hips at the same time.

The *Oceanien* has weighed anchor. The Isle of Ceylon decreases more and more in the distance. The ocean is as smooth as a lake, and as blue as the sky over us.

November 3rd.—Between Ceylon and Aden the voyage is long and tedious. The *Océanien* makes the trip in seven days. I had a very bad headache and went on deck for a breath of fresh air. The ship's doctor, a physician without patients just now, as all the passengers are in perfect health, appropriated the empty chair next my own and stared at me fixedly as if he wanted to know me by heart, and then made notes in his copy-book. He was writing a novel, in which I was to take the principal part, as it appeared, because I had a very strong resemblance to his first love. This doctor has kept his heart of seventeen through thrice seventeen summers. Wherever I went, there he was, and a little manœuvring was always necessary to prevent him from sitting near me and paying me compliments, whilst his bulging eyes stared at me as if he had the intention to devour me. He was ridiculous with his gallantry, having scarcely any hair on his head. He was stout, jolly-looking and effusive, and seemed to have stepped out of a comic opera.

Nearly everyone on board has a flirtation going on. At nightfall in nice flirting corners, on the part of the deck far away and out of the sphere of electricity, couples sat hand in hand deeply immersed in their eager whispers, out of the lights of the ship's lanterns.

November 4th.—When I mounted on deck this morning, my fat Esculapius came up to me, and crushed my fingers in his grasp; I gave a little squeak, for he had forgotten my rings. He had a drooping appearance, and looked profoundly miserable and martyrlike because yesterday I avoided him and looked the other way when he drew near. Nevertheless he took a chair in a way that told me distinctly of his intention not to desert me, and as I felt at the moment that I would have given anything to be deserted, I pretended to be absorbed in a thrilling novel. A long drawn sigh which escaped him failed to produce the intended effect. He said now in low, mournful accents, that I made fun of him, and doubted whether I had any heart at all.

November 5th.—We pass near the African coast, and the peninsula of Socotra. These parts were formerly the terror of the navigators; many ships have gone to pieces in this treacherous place, where strong hurricanes prevail. The Portuguese sailormen have named that cape Guardafui, which means " Be on your guard." But the great boats of our days laugh at the danger, though a terrible rolling and tossing is always felt in these parts.

Sea-sickness is a very good remedy for cooling down love. My fat doctor has become indifferent and mute. He lay stretched in his deck-chair, looking dreadfully green in the face.

CHAPTER LXXXV

ADEN

November 7th.—At the first break of day we reached the sun-baked city of Aden, a British possession on the southern coast of Arabia, lying on the Red Sea trade route between Europe and the East. The multiplicity of rocks, and the absence of trees, are the two most striking features of the landscape. Not a blade of grass is to be seen anywhere, and all around there is desolation. Aden looked rather a dreary spot : just a little cluster of white buildings lying at the feet of slate-coloured rocks. The burning sand, the sun, and the flies render the town quite unbearable. Opposite the port of Aden is Sirah, where the Arabs pretend that Cain, after the murder of Abel, came to take refuge. The town has but little local colouring. It was founded specially as a maritime station ; it gives shelter to traders and about a dozen hotel-managers. The town looked baking hot. The want of water is cruelly felt. Stone reservoirs have been constructed to catch rain-water, as there is no other natural supply whatever. The only difficulty is that it practically never rains, so the reservoirs stand empty. It is nearly three years since it rained in these parts. The water is distilled now from the sea, and an immense manufactory to fabricate artificial ice has been built, changing completely the condition of local life. The inhabitants have now plenty of water, and can refresh themselves with iced drinks *ad libitum*. They are even undertaking to arrange a square with verdure and trees out of a sand plot. Every morning hundreds of camels bring the necessary provisions for the daily use of the inhabitants, from the oases of the interior.

The water not being deep enough for landing, we had to moor some miles from the coast, at "Steamer point." The passengers are obliged to take a small Arab boat to get on shore. Sergy and his companions went to visit Aden, but the town was so little interesting that I preferred to remain on board with Mrs. Serebriakoff. We watched from the deck a band of negro boys with only a belt round their waist, with the words "Diving Boy," written in English. The harbour is infected with sharks, the monsters of the deep, and tragedies have happened more than once. Quite recently a shark made swift work of the life of a "diving boy," who was crushed up by the jaws of the monster in the presence of many passengers. Nevertheless his comrades were not afraid of sharks, they dived very deep under our boat and came out on the other side, holding between their teeth the coins that the passengers threw into the water, and scrambled again on board their boats. The local negroes belong to the "Somali" tribe; they are very ugly, with perfectly flat noses, immense teeth and woolly, crisp hair dyed a rich brick-red. It was too hot to remain long on deck, and I went to lie down in my cabin until the return of my husband. The order was given to close the port holes because of the loading of coal. I was scarcely to be recognised, being quickly transformed into a negress, my garments covered with oily soot.

Directly after dinner we weighed anchor and left Aden.

November 8th.—We are on the waters of the Red Sea, which is rightly considered one of the hottest parts of the globe. We suffer terribly from the heat; the ventilators give but a faint illusion of fresh air.

Towards evening the breeze seemed to rise, the surface of the sea began to ripple, and soon a veritable squall arose. During our dinner a big wave dashed into the dining-room through the portholes. After dinner, when we mounted on deck to look at the boisterous sea, a spray of water splashed right into my face. I gazed deeply impressed at the elements in fury. How small is man in the presence of such a struggle! It was difficult to keep one's equilibrium on the rocking deck, and I tumbled out of my chair rolling with it to the other end of the deck. One of the passengers laid hold of me by my dress and hauled me out of danger, just in time, for without his aid I should have slipped overboard.

November 9th.—We go full speed between the two parts of the world. On our left—the grand African Desert, and on our right—the Desert of Asia. We have over us the scorching sun, and below—the almost boiling water, and are suffering the tortures of hell. The captain promises that in the course of three days we shall feel the first touches of the north breeze.

It is etiquette on all the boats of the Méssageries Maritimes that before eight o'clock one may wander on the decks in the *négligé* of early morning in the tropics, but on the stroke of eight bells, one must disappear very promptly to array oneself for breakfast. This morning amongst the passengers scattered here and there on the deck, in various stages of undress, I saw my fat admirer curiously arrayed, muffled into a sort of poplin of very light material, which gave him a most comical appearance and set off rather too well every curve of his anatomy.

November 10th.—The temperature is supportable. In the

afternoon a breeze arose which revived us somewhat.   After dinner, there was music, and I was asked to sing, but objected, saying that my music was packed up.   The captain told me that as soon as we get to Suez, he would write to Port Said for my favourite parts of "Margaret" and "Rosina."

November 11th.—We are coasting along Egypt and glide quite near the Sinai Mountains, on the top of which Moses wrote the Ten Commandments.   Already the liner had left the rocky perils of the treacherous Red Sea, studded with hidden shelves, which are not marked on the charts.

CHAPTER LXXXVI

SUEZ

THE heroic statue of Ferdinand de Lesseps, who has given to the world the Suez Canal, standing for ever at the gateway he opened to the East, was plainly visible before we caught the first glimpse of land. We dropped anchor at a small distance from Suez, having to wait for the canal to be free. Our binoculars showed us a row of white houses with trees and a railway-line. That was the town of Suez. I stood on deck watching the animation on the canal. Hundreds of small boats hovered near, filled with eager vendors of curios and ostrich feathers. A great homeward-bound troop-ship filled with French soldiers, who were returning from the expedition to Madagascar, had just arrived. The climate didn't agree with the soldiers, they were all in a wretched condition, knocked up with malarial fever. Here is a sanitary "sampan," carrying a flag with the inscription, *Santé*, coming alongside our rope-ladder. The pilot allowed us at last to enter the Suez Canal, which is considerably narrower than the Thames. It's queer to know that but for the narrow passage in which the vessel moves, you are on dry land. Our way is marked out with floating red barrels. The moving sands of the Sahara border the banks of the canal ; the sky above the yellow sand looked extremely blue. From time to time tall palms with bushy tops appear. All around is an immense stillness. There is a caravan of camels marching slowly with rhythmical gait, on the sands of the desert, conveyed by Arabs in billowy white bournouses. On the opposite shore a flock of large white birds with long red legs stand contemplative each on a single leg. A crowd of half-naked little Arabs are running along the edge of the bank. They follow us laughing and begging as gaily as if begging were a game, catching the pennies thrown by the passengers.

We have very little breeze and sunshine in profusion until the stifling afternoon had passed. It is evening now ; the sun has set and the freshness of the desert night is delightful. Our ship is steaming at half speed through the placid canal. An immense electric light shows us our way. A big vessel comes to meet us. Our sailors having taken the ship for a Russian cruiser, began to shout, " *Vive la Russie!* " but it appeared to be a Spanish mail-boat.

CHAPTER LXXXVII

PORT-SAID

November 12th.—We reached the end of the Suez Canal about eight o'clock in the morning, and caught the first glimpse of land, a narrow stretch of reddish desert land beyond Port-Said, a town standing on the threshold of Europe, at the Mediterranean entrance of the Suez Canal. This is almost home ! As soon as we had disembarked we were assailed by a throng of natives who offered to serve as guides to us. We gave ourselves up to the care of a gigantic negro, Mustapha by name, clad in a red jersey with the words, *Mustapha molodetz*, which means in Russian " clever fellow," worked in yellow worsted on it.

We had just time enough to run over the town in a tram-car drawn by a pair of sad-looking mules. There are only two or three streets properly paved, everywhere else you sink up to the ankle in the sand. The streets lined with little shops are a mass of moving colour in which swarm a variety of Arabs, Egyptians, Negros, East-Indians and a few Europeans, generally in white. We passed small taverns from which floated stray snatches of music either awfully barbaric or quite modern. Our guide brought us to the " Eldorado," a large establishment with a roulette, a sort of bar. We were ushered into a courtyard pompously named " garden," with two or three ricketty trees growing in it, and then entered a large hall with an estrade on which played a small orchestra composed of a dozen European girls with painted faces. Thanks to the overheated temperature, the black paint of their eyes was running down their cheeks. We tried our luck at the " roulette," and took part in games where you are sure to be cheated. I lost two francs and Mr. Shaniawski, who was in a run of good luck, gained a louis d'or, which afterwards appeared to be a false coin.

The sharp sound of the syren from the *Oceanien* warned us that it was time to return to the boat. Towards two o'clock in the afternoon our ship finished loading coal, and we left Port-Said on our way to Marseilles.

CHAPTER LXXXVIII

ON THE MEDITERRANEAN

November 11th.—The crossing from Suez to Marseilles does not take more than three or four days. The weather grew perceptibly colder. We entered the Mediterranean in the afternoon and found it very disagreeable in this season. Great billows are rising on the water and the steamer begins to rock.

November 12th.—The night has been abominable, the sirocco was blowing very hard all day.

November 13th.—The snow-covered summit of Mount Etna appears on the horizon. We have been assailed by a terrible tempest when passing the coasts of Calabra. All the passengers are prostrated with sea-sickness.

November 14th.—A grey sky, grey rocks, and a grey sea! The wind has gone down and everybody is on deck. On a placid sea we sped westward, sighting the mountain ranges of Corsica and Sardinia.

CHAPTER LXXXIX

MARSEILLES

November 15th.—In the middle of the night the stopping of the screw woke me. The white cliffs of France had come to sight at last. I heaved a sign of relief when the *Océanien* dropped anchor at Marseilles, and only thought of a comfortable bed and a good fire. It was a day of "mistral," and whilst we drove to the Hôtel de Noailles, I had to protect myself with my umbrella against the terrible gusts of wind which played havoc with my hat and hair.

November 16th.—I have enjoyed my first night on *terrafirma*, snug and warm in my soft, immovable bed, and forgot all the miseries we have passed through during our long voyage. The sky is slate-coloured, a cold wind blows in the street ; nevertheless I decided to go to Monte-Carlo with the Serebriakoffs and Mr. Shaniawski. Sergy had to remain at Marseilles in order to confer with some French officials about the traffic carried on between Marseilles and Oriental Siberia. I sent traffic to the deuce.

CHAPTER XC

MONTE-CARLO

WE put up for the night at the Hôtel de Paris, where the prices are exorbitant. We had dinner at a small hotel which boasted of a table d' hôte at 2 francs 25 centimes per head. Sixty boarders sat down at table, inveterate roulette-players all of them. The game was the sole conversation during the meal. After dinner we went to the Casino to see the fireworks and listen to the splendid orchestra playing in the concert-hall. I tried my luck at the gambling-tables and lost about ten francs, but Sergy gained heaps of money. The run of bad luck had completely emptied the purse of an old lady sitting on my right—she looked so wretched, the poor old thing!

CHAPTER XCI

NICE

November 17th.—We started with the first train for Nice, where we stopped at the Hôtel Julien, hidden among lemon trees. Directly after lunch I went out for a walk. Whilst I stood gazing into a jewellery-shop, an old gentleman came up, and touching my arm, began to whisper compliments into my ear. I cast an indignant glance at the old satyr and hastened back to the hotel, walking very fast, and it was by an effort that my pursuer kept me in sight, for my legs were long and his were not.

Before dinner we sat on the boulevard at a small table. We ordered coffee, and listened to exciting Hungarian *czardas* that Tziganes were playing at a neighbouring restaurant on our left. On our right a troup of Neapolitan singers sang national songs in chorus.

The whole night I shivered with cold in my bed under two quilts scented with lavender. Notwithstanding the chilly atmosphere, persecuting mosquitoes strove to cover us with their stings.

November 18th.—We came back to Marseilles to-day. I was half out of the window of our car, watching for Sergy who was waiting for us on the platform, his face beaming with pleasure. We had some dinner at the station and took the train for Paris.

E*

CHAPTER XCII

PARIS

November 19th.—We arrived at Paris in the afternoon and stopped as usual at the Hôtel de Calais. It was very cold in our apartment and we had a fire all day.

After dinner we went to the opera to see "Tannhauser." I felt tired and asked Sergy what was the time every minute. After the second act, he took me out on to the boulevard to eat ices.

November 21st.—We had to get up very early in the morning to catch the express. It was six o'clock when we drove to the Gare du Nord. There were few people about. We only saw the milk-carts on their morning rounds, and the street-sweepers at work.

Our long journey is nearing its end. In another two days we shall be back in Russia.

WE went round all the world and returned more satisfied than ever with our capital. I feel like an escaped prisoner.

A few days after our arrival, my husband presented to the Emperor a deputation composed of representatives of different tribes inhabiting Oriental Siberia, who offered to His Majesty, according to custom, a silver dish with "Bread and Salt" and beautiful sable-skins. The corridors in the Grand Hôtel, where we had taken an apartment, were crowded with people wanting to get a glimpse of the deputies. One of them, Tifountai, one of the richest Chinese merchants of Khabarovsk, who had prominent oriental ideas about women when passing through Paris, led a dissipated life in the Great Babylon, that went on for a week, and did not arrive in time for the presentation. The representatives of different countries began to arrive at St. Petersburg on their way to Moscow, where the Coronation of Nicolas II. was to take place. One of the first arrivals was the Ambassador of the Chinese Emperor, the famous Li Hung Chang who had been treacherously wounded in Japan. Notwithstanding his eighty-two years, he looks very alert and vigilant. My husband had an interview with the old diplomatist, after which he presented his suite to him. According to Chinese etiquette the mandarin addressed to everyone two stereotype questions translated by his dragoman into French : "What is your name," and "How old are you?" Henritzi, the youngest of Sergy's *aide-de-camps*, who was of German origin and spoke his national tongue better than French, when answering to the last questions, said that he was twenty-four years old, German-fashion : "*Quatre-vingt,*" *vier und zwanzig,* which means eighty-four in French. The dragoman casting an astonished glance at the young octogénarian, translated his answer to the letter. The old mandarin never winced, and rising from his seat, bowed low to the "*Ninon de l'Encles*" of the unfair sex. (I beg your pardon, gentlemen !) In China old age is greatly venerated. If you wish to make a Chinaman perfectly happy, all you need to say is "How old you look!" When the reception was over, Li Hung Chang remitted to my husband the Chinese order of the "Double Dragon," bearing the imprinted inscription " Before this the liorg will grow pale and the tiger mute."

Little by little, St. Petersburg was getting empty. The railway-line to Moscow, notwithstanding its twenty-four trains a day, could hardly supply all the passengers proceeding to the old capital ; they had to book their places a a month beforehand.

A great many crowned heads had gathered in Moscow. Amongst the European guests there were several exotic personages who had come from Siam, Japan and other distant countries.

In the beginning of May Sergy went to Moscow to be present at the Coronation, which was to take place on the 15th May. That day at ten o'clock in the morning all the church-bells in St. Petersburg began ringing, and at noon volleys of artillery announced the beginning of the ceremony in the Kremlin, and at the end of the ceremony the Coronation was made known by a salute and one-hundred-and-one cannon shots.

I learned from the papers that during the festivals there occurred a terrible accident at Moscow, which claimed some thousand victims, and darkened the Coronation of Nicolas II. On the 19th May, a colossal festival was organised for the populace on the Khodinka-Field. Long tables with all sorts of refreshment were laid on the brink of an enormous ditch. Towards two o'clock in the afternoon about 6000 persons hurried to the spot where free dinners were distributed. Tumultuous crowds continued to arrive unceasingly. The first arrivals couldn't resist the great pressure of the on-comers, and fell headlong into the ditch. The catastrophe took place in twenty times less than it takes to describe it.

The moment of our departure for Khabarovsk approached. It was decided at first that Sergy would go alone. He promised to come back to St. Petersburg in six months' time. I dreaded the moment of his departure, and the moment was not far off. No! I could not bear to part with Sergy. I always yielded to impulse under any circumstances. I told him that nothing should induce me to stay away, and that I would follow him a second time to the end of the world. But Sergy absolutely refused to hear of it. His opposition made me only the more distinctly determined to have my own way. I simply didn't know what "No" meant, and Sergy consented after a good deal of coaxing to take me with him.

The Serebriakoffs could not accompany us. The Colonel was promoted to the grade of general, and had received a new appointment at Moscow. I was awfully sorry to part with Mrs. Serebriakoff with whom I had gone through many hardships during our first tour around the world.

We have engaged a young lady to hold the position of companion, Maria Michaelovna Titoff by name. She is a very gay and lively girl, who will help to make my life at Khabarovsk a little more cheery. Mr. Shaniavski, Mr. Scherbina and Henritzi accompany us on our journey.

CHAPTER XCIV

OUR WAY BACK TO KHABAROVSK VIA ODESSA

WE left St. Petersburg on the 17th June, and are on our way for a second tour around the world. This time we sail from Odessa on the *Orel* a boat belonging to the Volunteer Fleet, which will take us straight to Vladivostock.

June 19th.—Towards noon we arrived at Odessa where I was happy to find my mother, who had come from Moscow to see us off. We put up together at the Hôtel de Londres.

June 20th.—This morning Sergy reviewed the recruits who are to sail with us on the *Orel.*

June 21st.—At three o'clock in the afternoon we went on board the *Orel* our new dwelling for many days. I took the best place I could find at the side of the ship to see the last of Russia and mother, with whom I parted shedding abundant tears. After the last embraces we separated, our boat gave the third whistle, and slowly we moved away from the dense crowd that covered the wharf. I sent my good-byes to mother, waving wildly my handkerchief to her. I saw the shore separating us, and knew that we couldn't meet for a very long time.

We are in the open sea, the wind is favourable, the sails are up, and our boat advances rapidly.

The *Orel* had on board 1300 recruits and 280 first-class passengers, Russian officers for the most part, going out to serve in Siberia, accompanied by their families. We occupy one of the largest state-cabins, with mirrors, carpets, electric light, and electric ventilators, which make, it is true, more noise than ventilation.

We sit down to meals four times a day. At nine o'clock breakfast, at one—tiffin, at four—tea, at seven—dinner. The food is good, but a trifle heavy for the tropics. To-day after dinner, the officer upon duty came up to Sergy to show him the log-book in which all the incidents of the day are noted. At nine o'clock precisely the sailors sang the evening prayers, after which all the passengers went to bed.

June 22nd.—We are on the Black Sea, between sky and water, with no land in view. The weather is beautiful, but the ship rolls dreadfully all the same. I try to brave sea-sickness, and do needlework, whilst Maria Michaelovna reads aloud to me.

June 23rd.—At ten o'clock in the morning we enter the Bosporus and anchor in the Golden Horn. Sergy with all his companions and almost all the passengers had landed in order to stroll about Constantinople. I was tired of sight-seeing and lessons of history, and was the only one of our party who remained on board. At eight o'clock in the evening the *Orel* weighed anchor. To-day is Saturday, and our ship's priest performed vespers on the lower deck.

June 24th.—To-day we passed the Dardanelles and entered the Archipelago, and found ourselves near the point where ancient Troy stood.

June 25th.—It is getting hotter and hotter. My hair is out of curl, but never mind ; this awful heat takes away all attempt at coquetry. A tent has been spread on deck, under which we take our repasts, protected from the rays of the scorching sun. We have given to this tent the poetical name of " Villa Borghese." During our dinner the recruits danced a wild jig on the deck, to the accompaniment of five violins, a tambourine and a blow-pipe. One of the men began to whistle artistically, imitating the nightingale, whilst another recruit gambolled and turned somersaults, representing a trained monkey. It is pleasant to see the good relations between the recruits and the chief of their battalion, surnamed by his men " Captain Tempest," on account of his fiery temper. He raged and stormed a great deal, but was adored by the recruits, notwithstanding his rough tongue.

CHAPTER XCV

PORT SAID

June 26th.—At dawn the African coast, scorched by the sun, came into view. We enter the port and stop opposite the Russian Consulate. Our boat will enter the Suez Canal only at night, and we shall have time to make a short trip to Cairo. When we arrived at the railway station we saw the tail end of the Cairo express passing before our noses. As the next train left only at six o'clock, we had to put off Egypt, and were glad to find shelter in a cool little bar surrounded by a tiny garden, where we sat in the shade and sipped iced drinks, after which we returned on board. Our boat was loading coal, and all the portholes had to be closed in order not to get black. I ventured on deck and was instantly transformed into a negress.

At ten o'clock in the evening we entered the Suez Canal. On our right, spread as far as the eye could see, Lake Monzaleh. The railway runs along the shore, separated from the canal by a narrow embankment. We only make five knots an hour, nevertheless we get before a French warship, from which they shouted to us, "*Vive la Russie!*" Our captain gave order to hoist the French flag, whilst our recruits shouted loud hurrahs. Here comes another steamer with the flag of Britain above it ; her funnels are covered with salt. The ship has surely been a good deal tossed about in the Indian Ocean. It does not promise us a smooth passage.

June 27th.—We are on Lake Timsah. The railway runs along the shore as far as Ismailia, to continue its way to Cairo. Flocks of odd white birds swim on the surface of the lake and chase the fish. On the coast, a little Arab, completely nude, raced us for a short distance, begging *baksheesh*. The recruits, having nothing better, throw him crusts of black bread. On the opposite bank we see pilgrims going to Mecca, and a caravan of camels off to Suez across the desert, resting under the shade of a gigantic fig-tree. Egyptian policemen, on camel-back, keep watch on the banks of the canal here and there. This morning, whilst we took our breakfast, Sergy was informed that a vessel, bearing the Italian flag, was approaching us. The ship is returning from Masowah, bringing back to Europe hollow-cheeked and worn-out looking soldiers, mere shadows of human beings, covered with parchment skin.

CHAPTER XCVI

SUEZ

AT eleven o'clock we entered the port of Suez. On the African coast rises the chain of the Dakhi Mountains; opposite, on the Arabian coast, we see the high peak of Mount Sinai, and an oasis of palm trees surnamed the "Fountain of Moses." The ship was going to stay here for two or three hours only; it was not worth while going on shore.

Towards five o'clock we have got over the 64 kilomètres of the maritime canal, and are in the stifling heat of the Red Sea.

During night the wind arose. I was wakened by the horrid rolling of the ship. Piercing whistles were blown and the sailors climbed hurriedly up the masts in pitch darkness, trying to catch the end of the sails which the storm was tearing into pieces.

June 28th.—We are in the tropics. The air is like fire and the temperature of the water is very high. The stewardess advised me to lie down on the floor under the open port-hole over which she spread a sheet. I had a nice little nap, thanks to this improvised punkah.

June 29th.—There is not the slightest breeze; we live in a furnace. The sky, always blue, gives me the nostalgia of the cloud. This afternoon we crossed the Strait of Bab-el-Mandeb.

June 30th.—I could not sleep the whole night. I tried to lie down on the floor under the improvised punkah, but it didn't help a bit. I was quite worn out and had a good cry. Maria Michaelovna and my maid Feoktista came to keep me company. The moon was beginning to pale when Sergy took me on the deck, where matresses had been laid down for us on the floor. Whilst we passed along the lower deck we had to step over the recruits who lay on the deck one beside the other.

July 1st.—This morning we came into the narrow channels of the fortified Perim Islands, a bare rock with a few houses on it, without any traces of vegetation. And to think that it was political conditions which forced unfortunate British officers to pass a part of their lives in such an infernal hole!

CHAPTER XCVII

ADEN

July 2nd.—Early in the morning we came in view of Aden. Our boat sets off at six o'clock in the evening, and we had plenty of time to visit the town. We landed at Steamer Point and found ourselves in a territory over which the British flag flies. We took a carriage with a negro coachman, and drove to see the cisterns, following a beautifully kept road. At a steep turning we met a long caravan of camels. To jump out of the carriage was the affair of a minute for me. I continued the ascent trudging under a broiling sun, spoiling my complexion, foot-sore and ill-tempered. A most unpleasant walk it was; the trees were too thin to give any shade, the ground was parched and cracked and scorching hot, one could easily bake an egg in it.

When we were back at Aden, we had lunch at the Hotel d' Europe. After our meal I went out to rest on the verandah, whilst Sergy visited the English Hospital, to which one of our recruits, who had fallen ill during the voyage, had been removed.

Towards five o'clock we were back on board, and left Aden at six. Before starting, one of our ship-officers standing on the deck got sunstroke.

The monsoon rages at this season in these parts. When we came into the open sea the long swell began to lift and toss the steamer like a cork. The passengers became immediately sea-sick and sought their berths. One of the cows on board broke her leg during the horrid rocking and had to be killed. I rolled my deck-chair into the corridor under a ventilator broken through the ceiling, which allowed me to overhear all the conversation which took place on the upper deck; the rolling was less here. Maria Michaelovna brought me some tea and a lot of nice things with it. Over my head, through the pipe of the ventilator, I heard the recruits conversing. Two men began to pick a quarrel, and nearly came to blows. Both of them were put under arrest. Whilst they were being led away, one of the quarrellers complained to the officer on duty that his antagonist, in an access of fury, had pricked him with a pin, and the other one defended himself, advancing that he had been pricked the, first with a crust of bread !

The rolling of the ship drove my chair in all directions about the corridor. I was obliged to return to my cabin.

In the night the wind increased, and the anchor ran out with a rattle and a roar of cable. It was stifling in my cabin; I imprudently opened the porthole and an avalanche of water rushed in, threatening to drown me.

July 3rd.—The sea is the colour of ink, and I am ill, ill! . . . Towards noon great black clouds came upon us rapidly and very soon the whole sky was covered, it was almost as dark as night; a heavy storm was coming on. The recruits are put down in the hold. The long menacing waves were advancing upon our ship like big mountains. Sounds of broken crockery are heard; two beautiful Chinese vases, standing on the side-board in the saloon, were thrown out on the floor and went to pieces.

Though we have six cows on board they cannot be milked for the rolling of the ship, and I had to drink my coffee without cream; it tasted like medicine to me.

July 4th.—A terrible night had followed. The ship rolled over fifty degrees from the perpendicular on each side. The situation was becoming more and more perilous. The shouts of the watch-officer mingled with the whistle of the quarter-master, and the shrieks of the siren were something awful. Hearing a commotion above, shouting and rushing footsteps, I thought we were going to sink. I dressed in a hurry and rushed to the staircase, where I met Sergy, who persuaded me to return to my cabin and lie down, but I felt it was quite useless to try to sleep.

July 5th.—I passed again the whole of the night in the corridor; Maria Michaelovna followed my example and came up with her pillow and coverlet, and slipped into the narrow space between me and my maid. Towards noon the direction of the wind changed, we are out of the cyclone centre.

July 6th, 7th.—The temperature all these days is something awful. We are dying of thirst and all our provision of ice on board has melted.

A bird which followed our boat all the way from Aden, rested this night on the main mast and was captured by the sailors who want to tame it.

CHAPTER XCVIII

COLOMBO

July 8th.—We enter the harbour of Colombo and moor pretty far away from the coast, to the great disappointment of the recruits. Scores of sampans with Singhalese rowers came to bring us ashore. We stopped again at the Grand Hôtel. I had tea in a nice shady corner of the verandah, which runs round the two sides of the hotel. The first half of it is lined with tables and easy-chairs and the other is nothing but a succession of shops, where Hindoo merchants are installed. We could see from here all that was going on in the street, and observe all passers to and fro. The feminine-looking Singhalese walk bareheaded, their long hair saturated in cocoa-oil, gathered in a knot chignon-fashion, and fastened by a huge tortoishell circle-comb. The Singhalese women wear only a short skirt and a short waist bodice between which several inches of brown skin are visible.

After luncheon we set off in six rikshas to explore the city of Colombo. Our men-horses trotted off at full speed, regardless of my protestations. The principal streets are planted with great overhanging trees and bordered with beautiful several-storied houses. Opposite the shipping office, in the heart of the European section, lay Gordon Gardens, a park full of flowers and grateful shade, the rendezvous of the elite of the city, white and brown. We went down the smooth red road that lies almost level with the sea, with emerald, velvety grass and cool shady bungalows. In the distance towered the Queen's House, Governor Black's residence, set well back from the broad highway in a grove of palms, a spacious, imposing edifice, where large entertainments are given. The governor, for the moment, was away on tour to some distant district of the island. We met on our way covered waggons drawn by two little hump-necked, strangely tattooed bullocks, and elegant dog-carts driven by English women. Dark came on suddenly and our rikshamen stopped to light their paper-lanterns, and hurried us back to the hotel. The second dinner-bell sounded as we entered the dining-room, as big as a cathedral and ventilated by twelve punkahs.

July 9th.—Our boat does not leave for another ten days ;

we will profit by it and go on a trip to Kandy, the ancient city of the sovereigns of Ceylon, situated in the hills some 2,000 feet above the level of the sea, which can boast of a climate in many respects superior to that of Colombo.

A Singhalese boy brought in my coffee very early in the morning, and tried to explain to me that the train for Kandy left at 8 o'clock. It took some time for both of us to make ourselves understood, for I addressed the boy in English and he replied in Malay language; however, with a good deal of pantomime, we got along somehow.

It is a three hours' ride from Colombo to Kandy. Ceylon wears rightly the title of the "Switzerland of the Tropics;" only fairy islands can surpass the scenery. I could but gaze and gaze, and felt what poor things words had suddenly become. A riot of luxuriant tropical vegetation spread out on every hand, and aromas of strong smelling flowers scented the air. A series of moving pictures glided past us. We are rolling through fields of lotuses, sugar-cane plantations and vast plots of ground planted with coffee-trees, with shining leaves like porcelain, cut small to facilitate the gathering of the fruit. Cocoa and date-palms and bread-fruit are at your service, all you have to do is to pick the fruit—and luncheon is ready. The train is speeding along thick bamboo-clumps, through which peered the red-tiled roofs of bungalows and negro villages with palm-thatched huts shaded by immense banana-trees. We are in the harvest season. In the fields men and women were at work, occupied in gathering in the coffee. Natives sitting in ox-waggons drive slowly along the road. Here is an enormous elephant covered over with a rich carpet, carrying four natives on his back. The huge animal's offspring, a baby-elephant as big as a bull, is running clumsily alongside. The railway stations are hidden amid cocoa-palms. On the platforms water-carriers and fruit-sellers briskly plied their trades. At one of the stoppages a Hindoo in white skirts came up to offer us bananas and cocoa-nuts full of milk, and red juicy fruit which I found very tasty; but I was awfully disgusted when I learned that it was the fruit of the castor-oil plant. Our train was moving away when a negro boy thrust into my lap, through the window, a small serpent of tender green colour, which I took at first for a blade of grass. Though these reptiles are quite inoffensive, I didn't like the present. The ascent began. We climbed on steadily into the cooler regions. The steamy atmosphere was left behind, we were welcomed now by draughts of delicious air. We are crossing a thick-set wood, and are in the mysterious primitive jungle which the foot of man has seldom penetrated, and where elephants and tigers wander about. The train continues to wind its way upwards to the mountains, plunging through numerous tunnels. Coming out of them we see the road which we had just crossed just beneath us now. The place is rightly named "Sensational Rock"—it is a succession of precipices and torrents. We are rolling along ledges cut in the rock, twisting and turning above sheer abysses.

When we arrived at Kandy, we ran on the platform in pursuit of our luggage, which a swarm of vociferous natives had confiscated and carried off. Having overtaken them, we climbed into an omnibus which brought us to Queen's Hotel; situated on the shore of a miniature lake.

After lunch we went to see the Pyradenia Gardens, about six miles from Kandy, situated on the right bank of the river Manhavilla-Ganga. These gardens are renowned for their splendid flowers. There are trees as high as ship-masts and strange plants with large blossoms monstrous of shape and gorgeous in colour. Most things are highly coloured as in Java: birds, butterflies and luxuriant vegetation. I am not sent easily into fits of ecstasy, nevertheless I admired everything until my vocabulary of exclamations was exhausted and my head whirled.

We were back for dinner at the table d'hôte. We had just finished our meal under the cooling caresses of the punkah and were going up to our room to take a siesta, when a boy announced to us that Hindoo snake-charmers were going to give a performance on the veranda. We were amazed by their startling experiments. They played the flute to their reptiles, who crawled out of a basket and rolled round their bodies, and they juggled with them as with balls. After that the jugglers performed the astonishing feat of producing spontaneous vegetation. They made a tree grow from seed to foliage before our eyes ; they dug a fruit-stone into a little heap of sand, making cabalistic signs with their wand, and the stone grew visible and soon became a shrub covered with branches and leaves !

July 10th.—Directly after breakfast Sergy went into the mountains to see the sacred elephants. He was shown a pair of huge savage animals recently caught in these parts.

When my husband returned, we went to visit the famous Hindoo temple where the Tooth of Buddha is preserved, braving the scorching tropical sun, whose rays fell just over our heads, so that I didn't see my shadow, but only the circle of my umbrella. Tradition says, there was found in Burma one of the teeth of Gautama (Buddha). An embassy from the King of Burma bore the relic to Ceylon, and over it was erected the celebrated Temple of the Tooth. Kandy is a holy city ; Buddhists not merely of Ceylon, but of India and the equatorial islands, make pilgrimages to the ancient shrine, which is an object of veneration for the four hundred million of Buddhists inhabiting Asia. The Kings of

Siam and Burma contribute to the keeping up of the temple,
in sending rich gifts to the priests every year.

The streets were alive with crowds on their way to the
temple, a structure of grey stone with a red roof, set in a
lotus grove on the shores of a lake. A large avenue leads to
the courtyard of the temple, the ground all strewn with white
sweet-smelling jasmine flowers, which deadened the sound
of our steps. Within the gates, under the vaulted archways,
crowds of people gathered around a dozen of Singhalese,
devoted to the sale of candles, the white sacred flowers to
be laid in the lap of the statue of Buddha. Flaming torches
burnt at the entrance of the temple. The whole spectacle
was fantastical, just like a decoration of Lakmě. Under the
portico of the temple, a band of native musicians beat loudly
the tom-tom and buck-skinned calabashes. On the top of
the broad steps leading into the interior of the temple, we
removed our shoes and were taken over the temple by
apathetic saffron-robed bonzes (Buddhist priests) with shaven
heads, and arms and feet bare. They led us by way of
many tile-paved corridors lit by lamps suspended from
roofs of arabesque cedar-wood, and strongly incensed candles,
The temple is of marvellous richness; the altar and the
doors are of carved ivory, large frescoes cover the walls
representing hell with flames, devils and so on, In every
nook and corner we saw the effigies of Buddha. There was
an important service in the temple just now. A group of
bonzes, after having washed their heads and their feet,
advanced towards the sacred relic, suspended in a tabernacle
over a symbolic lotus flower with golden petals studded with
precious stones. The chief priest fell on his knees, muttering
a prayer, and then drew from the tabernacle a gold casket,
from it he took a second then a third, a fourth, and a fifth.
With the opening of every box the priests repeated their
genuflexions. There appeared at last the innermost,
and soon the receptacle, set with diamonds and rubies. Then
the priests carefully opened and discovered to view an
enormous tooth yellow with age, which assuredly never grew
in any human mouth. During the whole time the tom-toms
and other barbarian instruments made a horrible noise. Two
simple rules govern the production of native music—First:
make as much noise as possible all the time; and, second,
to heighten the effect, make more. There was a heavy
perfume of flowers and incense—very enervating—inside the
temple, which made us hurry away. Buddhist priestesses,
with shaved heads like the priests, dressed in long yellow
robes, accompanied us to the door, throwing at us sacred
flowers, jasmine and lotuses. Crowds of Brahmin beggars,
demanding money, were gathered in the porch.

After dinner we took the train back, and were shown into

a compartment occupied by a honeymooning Anglo-Indian couple of planters, whose wedding day was only twenty days old. They didn't seem pleased to be disturbed, especially the young bride, who vented her ill-humour upon her husband, and was decidedly inclined to be disagreeable to him. The evil temper of his consort forced the young planter to take refuge in the corridor.

On arriving at Colombo we went straight on board the *Orel* and weighed anchor in the night.

July 11th.—As soon as we entered the gulf of Bengal, the rocking of the ship became so unpleasant, that I shut myself up in my cabin for the whole day.

July 12th.—The sea continues to be very rough. Towards night, when we approached the lighthouse at the entrance of the Bay of Malacca, the rolling of the boat ceased suddenly.

July 15th.—We approach Sumatra. The bay is strewn with treacherous coral-shelves. This morning, whilst I was dressing, the alarm bell sounded. I heard voices shouting "Help, help, man overboard!" It was a manœuvre of false alarm, which nearly came to end by a veritable catastrophe. Whilst dropping a life-boat one of the sailors fell himself into the sea, but help, fortunately, came in time.

CHAPTER XCIX

SINGAPORE

July 16th.—We arrived at Singapore this morning and put up at the Hôtel d'Europe. Before dinner we went for a drive out of town, passing through a Malay village perched on piles in cocoa plantations. The hillocks are strewn with villas, like the outskirts of London. On our way back we crossed the Square, the centre of European commerce, with large bazaars and markets.

Singapore, according to its population, is a veritable Tower of Babel. We are amidst natives of every variety of shade, from sepia to chocolate: Majestic Arabs, arrayed in long flowing robes, Hindoos in white tunics and bright red turbans, Malays, Chinamen, Persians, etc. The Malay women are very black, with the fewest clothes that it was possible to wear and nose-rings and beads hanging everywhere. They carry on their backs black babies with woolly hair and white eyes like nice Newfoundland puppies. Ambulant cooks walk amongst the crowd ; they carry two round chests, containing a small stove, on which they fry nasty-smelling roasts ; in another box, on wooden trays, are placed bowls containing minced meats of all kinds ; a whole lot of little horrors, which the natives snap up with the aid of long chopsticks, sitting on their heels on the ground and turning their backs to the passers-by. Black policemen, dressed European fashion, with a white stick in their hand, keep order in the streets.

F*

CHAPTER C

FROM SINGAPORE TO NAGASAKI

July 18th.—To-day we returned to our ship. A Portuguese cruiser, which had just arrived at Singapore, has sent out one of her officers to salute my husband on board. I sat on deck and looked about me. A troop of jugglers, who begged leave to give a performance, swallowed swords, transformed sand into rice, and showed us how a tree may spring up from seed they had just sown. They produced a paper from their pockets, filled with earth, which they strew out into a pot, and when it was full, they set a seed in it and covered it over with a handkerchief. We saw a movement beneath that handkerchief, it fluttered, and was lifted higher and higher. Finally the magicians whisked it off, and there was a shrub, leaf and stem—all complete. This was really marvellous! A little Hindoo girl, aged five, performed the *Danse du ventre*, after which she settled herself on the knees of our Portuguese guest, and pulled very unceremoniously at his moustache, demanding "baksheesh." Around us glided, backwards and forwards, small boats filled with half-naked natives, who dived into the water for coins, and came on the surface smiling, with cheeks puffed up like a well-filled purse.

July 19th, 20th.—Great was the desire of all the passengers to visit the celebrated cigar-manufactory of Manilla, but our captain opposed our landing on the Phillipine Islands, because cholera had broken out in the town, and thus, Manilla was black-balled.

July 21st.—We are in the sphere of a cyclone, and battle with the swell of the ocean. We mount, descend, and roll from right to left. Enormous billows throw clouds of foam as high as a mountain on the deck, and two liquid walls meet to swallow us up. A terrible gust of wind tore the great sail, shredding it to pieces, and its tatters floated like old banners on the top of the mast. I passed the night on the floor in the corridor, and woke up after three hours of poor sleep, feeling something tickling my nose. It was the tail of a rat the size of a kitten, which was promenading over my face.

July 22nd.—Daybreak came at last to put an end to my torments. The tempest began to abate. To-day is the

namesday of our Empress Dowager, and the boat has
assumed a holiday aspect. At dinner Sergy regaled us with
champagne, and offered up libations to the recruits and the
crew. He raised his glass to the health of Her Majesty ;
the sailors shouted loud hurrahs and got up a dance on
the deck.

July 23rd.—Early in the morning we perceived in the
distance the coasts of Formosa. We have to go to-day
through dangerous parts filled with coral banks, and sadly
famed for numerous shipwrecks.

July 24th, 25th.—The weather is very fine, the sea—a
polished mirror. A favourable wind sends us forward, all
the sails are up, and the *Orel* is running at the rate of fifteen
miles an hour.

CHAPTER CI

NAGASAKI

July 26th.—This morning at ten o'clock we arrived at Nagasaki, and anchored alongside the *Voronege*, a Russian boat, bringing back to Russia a thousand soldiers. These men, who had just finished their military service in Siberia, and our recruits, who had not begun it, exchanged frenzied hurrahs.

We stepped on shore and walked to the Hôtel Belle-Vue. After lunch we took rikshas and wandered about the town. Our riksha-men stopped of their own accord before a tea-house, muttering laconically, "Something to see!" But there was only a big picture on the wall to be seen, representing a sea-battle between the Japs and the Chinese, where all the Chinese boats went down to the bottom.

July 27th.—This morning my husband went with a party of recruits to be present at a funeral service in the Christian cemetery of Nagasaki, where a great number of our sailors are buried.

July 28th.—We left Nagasaki in the afternoon, and were soon out of sight of the Japanese Islands.

July 29th.—I was wakened in the middle of the night by the piercing shrieking of the siren. We had entered a dense fog and were advancing slowly, the horns blowing all the time.

July 30th.—Since dawn our sailors were preparing to land at Possiet. A steam-launch came up to us with the chief of the brigade quartered there. At noon we dropped anchor in the middle of the bay.

Possiet is marked as a town on the map, but it looks more like a large village. We saw from afar a triumphal arch erected on the quay. The crowd on the pier cheered us loudly. Nine big barges approached our steamer and the disembarking of our soldiers began. Sergy went on shore to visit the camp, situated twenty-eight miles from Possiet. As to me, I installed myself with my book on deck, awaiting his return. A fresh breeze succeeded to the stifling atmosphere. How nice it was!

Sergy returned on board towards night, accompanied by a whole flotilla of boats carrying a number of officers with their families and a military band. The quay was decorated with different coloured lanterns. We had an impromptu dance on board, and weighed anchor after midnight.

CHAPTER CII

VLADIVOSTOCK

July 31st.—Towards midday the harbour of Vladivostock came to view. We have reached the end of our long voyage. I am so happy to get away from the *Orel* where we have been cooped up for forty-one days.

Before landing, a Te Deum of thanksgiving, for having reached Vladivostock in safety, was sung on the deck. On the red-carpeted pier a roar of cheering went up as we passed. The faces all seemed familiar. I hastened to distribute greetings and nods among a number of the crowd. The daughter of the agent of the Volunteer Fleet presented me with an enormous bouquet, tied with a broad pink ribbon, bearing the inscription, " Welcome ! "

We walked to the military club, where apartments were prepared for us. To-morrow we leave for Khabarovsk. At night the town and the ships in the harbour were beautifully illuminated.

August 1st.—We left Vladivostock by an express train on a moonless night. Two rows of Chinese coolies, each holding a Japanese lantern over his head, lined our way from the military club to the railway station. Many officers and engineers accompanied us as far as Iman, where we shall take the boat to Khabarovsk.

August 2nd.—The rain is falling all the time, transforming the roads into liquid mud. We met with an accident this morning. The last car of our train ran off the track, and we had to stop in the middle of a field, and it was two hours before we could continue our journey. Everybody had to descend. Chinese coolies, who were working on the railway line, brought a long narrow plank on which we crossed to the other side of the road, balancing like dancers on the cord. Two engineers supported me, picking their way among the rain-pools. At last all was repaired, and our train set forward *piano-pianissimo* ; it could beat the world's record for its slowness, it simply crawled, and we arrived at Iman only at night-fall, and took the boat to Khabarovsk.

August 3rd.—At six o'clock in the evening we moored at Khabarovsk. Our arrival was announced as usual by cannon-shots. I saw a crowd of friendly faces on the quay, and shook hands all around. Khabarovsk looked very bright. Troops lined all the way to our house.

CHAPTER CIII

KHABAROVSK

OUR life went on much as usual. I have just come back, and the longing for St. Petersburg overcame me already. The weather is horrid. The rain beats against the window-panes. Pressing my face against the glass, I looked at the Amour, black and tempestuous, and my nerves began to give way. Oh, I do want to go back to Russia so badly!

There has been a great inundation at Nikolaievsk, caused by the diluvian rains which had filled the Amour to over-flowing. The streets were transformed into torrents, and many houses are completely ruined by the flood. The corn in the fields, the wood for fuel—all has been carried away by the water.

Tigers have appeared in the neighbourhood of Khabarovsk. They come at night, travelling long distances from inland to drink; their roar is heard some miles around. Quite recently a man-eating tiger had devoured a soldier who was washing his linen on the banks of the Amour. Only his head and a few bones were found. A hunt has been organised, and several tigers were shot near Khabarovsk.

Tifountai, the rich Chinese merchant, introduced his new wife to me. He had brought her recently from Shanghai. She advanced slowly towards me on her deformed little feet, supported by her husband, gorgeously dressed in brocade silks and covered with jewels. She had a quantity of paint put on her face, which bore an expression of idleness and ennui.

The brother of the late Queen of Corea, who had been murdered by her subjects, passed through Khabarovsk on his way to St. Petersburg, where he went to ask the Emperor to take under his protection and ensure the safety of the King of Corea, who was hiding at the Russian mission at Seoul, the capital of Corea. We gave a grand dinner to this im-portant personage.

I began to learn the English concertina. Sergy has ordered one from London for me. I took a great liking to this melodious instrument, on which all the musical literature written for the violin can be produced. I now play the mandolin only in my spare moments.

In April Sergy went on a tour through Siberia ; he visited Kamtchatka and the island of Saghalien, to which the Russian government transports convicts. He will be away a month at least, and I shall miss him terribly. A month is such a long time to wait. In his absence I remained in complete seclusion, refusing myself to callers.

On the 6th May, the Emperor's namesday, Sergy landed at Petropavlovsk, the capital of Kamtchatka, with only 400 inhabitants in it. There was still snow on the ground in this polar region, and the breaking of ice had not yet commenced. Visitors are quite unknown in this desolate place, and Sergy's arrival created the greatest excitement, nothing like it had been known for years. There, in far off Kamtchatka, the inhabitants don't hear much of what happens in the world. All the town was upside down. That same day the population of Petropavlovsk celebrated the second centenary of the occupation of the territory of Kamtchatka by the Russians. After stepping on shore, Sergy and his suite were driven to the cathedral to hear mass, in sleighs drawn by a team of dogs, who barked and made a terrible noise during the service. Before the arrival of my husband the inhabitants of that dreary, God-forsaken place were as if cut off from everything, and had no communication whatever with the outer world for several months. Whilst the authorities of the town were presented to my husband, they asked in the first place what day it was—they had confounded the dates—and then inquired if the Empress had not given birth to an heir to the throne. When Sergy told the magistrates that it was high time to join Petropavlovsk by telegraphic cable with the other parts of the world, they replied that they had done perfectly well without any telegraph, and would continue to do without it. Some time before, an officer had been sent by my husband to teach the inhabitants of Petropavlovsk target-shooting. In the first place they asked their teacher if he could hit the eye of a sable at three hundred paces with his gun, and the officer replied that he couldn't. "Then we have nothing to learn from you," exclaimed his unsubmissive pupils, " for we never miss our aim even with our old-fashioned guns ! "

From Kamtchatka Sergy went to the Commander Islands, where a number of seals were caught in his presence. It is the only spot in the world where seals gather in masses in summer ; in winter they emigrate to the South Pole.

On his way back Sergy was overtaken by a terrible storm in the Sea of Okhotsk. His steamer arrived at Vladivostock covered with ice.

In August my husband made a second long voyage beyond the Baikal Lake. Since his departure I have not known an hour of peace. I followed him in my thoughts through the washed-away roads by a recent flood. The streams had become rivers, bridges had been carried far away by the rush of the waters; the horses harnessed to Sergy's carriage had to ford the river with water up to their knees. For a fortnight I had no news of my husband; the telegraph didn't work and the postal communications were interrupted. One afternoon that I was especially out of sorts, I had a telegram from Antoine Kontski, asking if he might come with his wife and spend a few days with us on their return journey to Europe. Though I didn't feel able in the present to enjoy anybody's society, I proposed to them, nevertheless, to stop at our house. I never left my bedroom during their stay pleading indisposition. Mrs. Kontski came up to keep me company; as to her husband I only saw him on the day of his departure, when he came to bid me good-bye. Before leaving he played for me his famous *Reveil du Lion* I had all the doors opened, and I could hear the piano plainly. It was refreshing to hear good music after having been deprived of it so long. Kontski gave three concerts during his stay at Khabarovsk, with immense success. When his evenings were unnoccupied the old mæstro was deeply engrossed in a game of chess with his wife, or played patience

The chief of the Japanese army, Viscount Kawakami, who belonged to the small number of Japs well disposed to Russia, came to Khabarovsk during Sergy's absence and dropped a card for me.

Oh, joy! At last my husband announced his arrival by wire. He was to arrive on board the *Ataman*, on the 23rd August, towards six o'clock in the evening. I sat on the window-sill watching for the longed-for ship, and looked at the clock every three minutes, but it did not make it go any faster, nor would sitting at the window make Sergy arrive the sooner. The dinner hour came, and still there was no sign of my husband. I began to be seriously anxious; perhaps something might have happened to him! Eleven, twelve o'clock struck, but Sergy did not come. I wandered about the room unable to rest, and went from one window to the other, imitating a wild beast in his cage. At last, after seven mortal hours of watch, I saw a bright spot advancing on the "Amour." It was the *Ataman* bringing back my husband! A slight damage to the boat was the cause of her long delay. And thus, Sergy has gone all over the vast territory of the Amour, from the Commandor Islands to the Lake Baikal, having travelled about eight thousand miles.

A great event occurred, the completion of the new railway-line between Khabarovsk and Vladivostock. My husband went by an express-train, about eight miles beyond Khabarovsk, to the station "Doukhovskaia," named thus in our honour. Another train arrived at the same time, bringing among other authorities Count **Permodan**, the French military agent at Pekin. Several hundred workmen were hurrying to join both lines. The last bolt was driven in by my husband and both trains advanced simultaneously, joining each other in the dead of night, to the dim lights of some lanterns taken from the engines. Thus, the first train which united the Pacific Ocean to the Amour, arrived at Khabarovsk on the 1st September, 1897. Over the portal of the railway-station an inscription bears: " 9,877 verstes from St. Petersburg." How far away we are from the world !

CHAPTER CIV

BACK TO RUSSIA

IT'S such great news that Sergy was bringing to me! He has received a leave of eight months. We are going to spend the winter at St. Petersburg and make a trip abroad in the summer. I felt nearly crazy with joy! I am so happy to cast off the trammels of a Governor General's wife and live for some time as a simple mortal. I should have liked to say good-bye to Khabarovsk for ever!

December 19th.—We took this morning a special train to Vladivostock and are on our way for a third voyage round the world. About three hundred persons were assembled at the station to wish us a happy and safe journey. The train slowly moved away, followed by loud cheers. Leaning out of the window I sent my smiles to everyone.

There is a terrible frost outside, but our carriage is well heated and we do not feel the cold at all. There is a silver plate on the door of my saloon, engraved with large letters with the announcement that the Oussouri railway was founded by His Imperial Highness the Heir to the Throne on the 19th May, 1891, and underneath was the following inscription : " His Excellence General Doukhovskoy, Governor-General of the Amour Provinces, has opened, on the 27th August, 1897, the railway-line between Khabarovsk and Vladivostock."

At the station a deputation of Cossacks offered " Bread and Salt " to my husband on a napkin on which was embroidered : " God save thee on the seas."

CHAPTER CV

VLADIVOSTOCK

December 20th.—We arrived at Vladivostock in the morning, and were met on the platform by all the military and civil authorities of the town. We embark to-morrow on the *Khabarovsk* which the Volunteer Fleet puts at our disposal as far as Shanghai.

December 21st.—At seven o'clock in the morning the command of the captain resounded, and the engines began to throb, but the boat, held by the ice, did not move, and hope had been abandoned of starting to-day. It will be a polar cruise that we shall have to undertake, as it appears.

December 22nd.—We were obliged to have recourse to an ice-breaker, which came to our rescue. We are moving at last. The boat had to saw her way through the ice, which came breaking against her sides. We are in the open sea which is greeting us with a terrible gust of wind. We are going to have a fine dance on the water.

December 23rd.—The squall has confined nearly all the passengers to their cabins. Although accustomed to many sails across the ocean, I was beginning to feel a slight dizziness and had to lie down. The ship's doctor, trying to recover me from an attack of sea-sickness which had prostrated me, made me swallow a tablet of antipyrine.

December 24th.—The rolling continues, the wind roars, great waves splash overdeck. I am dreadfully ill and keep my bed. Okaia, the Japanese stewardess, crouches upon the floor at the foot of my bed, watching me with the eyes of a faithful dog.

December 25th.—To-day is Christmas day. Two French tradesmen, Kahn by name, to whom Sergy gave permission to sail with us as far as Shanghai, have sent me a large box filled with fruit. The barometer begins to rise and shows one degree above zero.

December 26th.—The weather is very mild, and there are already twelve degrees of warmth. After having suffered from the cold, we are going to experience now the torture of tropical heat. The one is worth the other.

NAGASAKI

IT is very calm to-day. We are going full speed, making about 16 knots an hour. At eight o'clock in the morning we perceived a vague shadow without outlines—it is land! We soon enter the port of Nagasaki and pass before an American cruiser in gala attire on the occasion of Christmas. Pine branches, holly and mistletoe hung in festoons about the masts. We stopped alongside a Russian man-of-war, which welcomed us by the sound of a march. A steam-launch belonging to the Russian marine squadron, stationed for the moment at Nagasaki under the command of Admiral Doubassoff, was sent to bring us on shore.

We put up again at the Hôtel Belle-Vue, and again the hostess stood on the steps with a smiling welcome. On the entrance door a board bore the inscription in English: "A happy Christmas and New Year!"

Scarcely had I time to take off my hat when a boy brought me a harvest of beautiful roses forming quite a large tray. It is the Kahns who have sent me this odoriferous Christmas offering.

In the afternoon, whilst we were sunning ourselves on the terrace, Admiral Doubassoff called upon us with his wife, whom he is sending back to Russia to-morrow. The order of the day perscribed that all Russian subjects should leave the country in forty-eight hours. Clouds are gathering on the political horizon. There are rumours of war between Russia and Japan, and things are working up for an excursion to Manchuria.

December 27th.—It is awfully cold in our apartment. I had to get up in the night and make up the fire which had gone out.

We returned on board after dinner, and shall weigh anchor early to-morrow morning. The Kahns have to hurry to Shanghai and are taking a Japanese steamer to-night. Before leaving they have sent a beautiful bouquet in a "cloisonné" vase to me, with a card bearing their name, and underneath stood "*Pour remplacer avantageusement.*"

An English liner, which had entered the harbour at night, warned us that a north-east wind was blowing hard out at sea. We have to wait again until to-morrow.

December 29th.—After ten this morning we weighed anchor. Whilst passing before our cruisers, the officers stood in rows on the deck, and the sailors ranged along the sail-yards shouted loud hurras, Admiral Doubassoff was standing on the bridge, making the military salute.

The weather is grey and the sea is swelling. We were scarcely out of harbour when our boat began to be roughly tossed about.

December 30th.—The hurricane is pitiless, the anchor rolls out with a rattle and roar of cable ; our steamer leans first on one side then on the other, and piercing whistles are heard on the upper deck all the time. The captain shouts order to tack. We change direction and turn back, and thus all the nightmare night was lost in vain. The portholes were closed and I was almost faint with the want of air. Staggering under the rolling of the sea, I crept into the saloon and stretched myself on the sofa. We enter the mouth of the Voosung, but the pilot refuses to lead us further because of the fog. We have to cast anchor until to-morrow.

January 1st.—The siren was shrieking the whole night. I was in a terrible fright all the time lest a boat should run against us in the dark.

CHAPTER CVII

SHANGHAI

WE weighed anchor early in the morning, and soon entered the harbour of Shanghai. A little steamer, belonging to the Russian-Chinese Bank, came to take us on land, and moored opposite the French Consulate. We found the Russian Consul waiting for us in his carriage, in which we drove to the Hôtel des Colonies, where we arrived just in time for tiffin. During the meal a large bouquet of heliotrope, surrounded by white lillies, was sent to me by the director of the Russian-Chinese Bank. In the afternoon the Governor of the town, accompanied by other Chinese authorities, came to congratulate my husband on the occasion of New Year's Day.

January 2nd.—We took our passage on the *Salasie* one of the swiftest boats of the Messageries Maritimes, bound for Hong-Kong. We leave Shanghai in splendid weather; the sea is beautiful, the sky of an azure blue.

We have about two hundred passengers on board. Every one chooses his company according to one's taste. I have remarked that people on board ship impart their affairs to utter strangers after a fashion that would seem impossible on land. Soon we all became known to one another.

At six o'clock the gong called us to dinner. I was placed just opposite the captain, an experienced mariner who had sailed for the last twenty-eight years in these parts. After dinner there was music in the saloon. The *commissaire*, who had a magnificent baritone voice, with looks of anticipated success, cleared his voice and began to sing love ditties. His assistant was induced to exhibit his skill on the mandoline, after which the Attorney-General of Tonkin, a creole, born at the Assumption Islands, sang opera airs, all the soprano, tenor and baritone parts, in his *basso profundo* voice.

January 3rd.—The *Salasie* is like a splendid hotel on treacherous waters. After lunch we went over the steamer and admired it greatly. The crew is composed of 180 sailors—Chinamen all of them. At six o'clock in the morning they begin to clean the boat, polishing brass things so beautifully that they can easily be used as mirrors.

CHAPTER CVIII

HONG-KONG

January 6th.—In the afternoon we entered the calm harbour of Hong-Kong, and moored at New Harbour, where the boats come in to take coal. When we stepped on shore, chocolate-coloured natives, speaking all at once, fought for our luggage and snatched our bags out of our hands. We hailed a carriage which brought us to Windsor Hotel, where we took a suite of several rooms.

After dinner we were carried in palanquins about Victoria Town. Our porters panted like short-breathed horses whilst ascending the steep streets, which wasn't pleasant at all.

January 7th.—It is Christmas in Russia to-day. Hard luck to spend Christmas in these far away parts, when one wants to have one's dear people about one! It makes me feel horribly home-sick. It is a dull day, chill and cloudy; long gusts of wind come down the street. We have a fire burning in the grate; fine tropics indeed! The Chinese inhabitants walk about muffled up in big coats lined with sheep-skins. In the extreme Orient it is the yellow race who predominates. I have had quite enough of the Chinese, who resemble each other as two ears of corn.

January 9th.—We will make a flying visit to Canton to-day, going up the Si-Kiang, or Pearl River, in a large English steamer bearing the Chinese name of *Fat-Chan* The Si-Kiang is so broad that one can't see across from bank to bank. The crossing takes only eight hours, and is comfortably made in large floating palaces, plying between Hong-Kong and the towns of the inner country. Except ourselves there are only two first-class passengers. I caught sight in the saloon of stacks of rifles, swords and revolvers, with printed instructions to the passengers to use them if necessary, the river-steamers having been known to be attacked by pirates, who rove in junks about the river and assail pssing ships. Last year a band of pirates boarded the *Fat-Chan* as passengers. As soon as Hong-Kong was out of view, the brigands, after having bound with cords the captain and his crew, cut the throats of all the passengers and threw their bodies overboard. Soldiers now accompany every steamer, and the third-class passengers are locked up for the night in the hold behind an iron rail, at the entrance to which stand sentinels. We have three hundred Chinamen as third-class passengers, and it did not make me feel safe at all. The captain took us down into the hold after tiffin to show us the human ant's nest. We saw the Chinese passengers heaped up pell-mell, men, women and children. The men were smoking opium or playing dice, and looked quite peaceful.

CHAPTER CIX

CANTON

FROM afar appeared the numerous pagodas of Canton, with their domes adorned with little gold bells. Our boat nosed her way into the crowded river, traversed by a perpetual scurry of launches, and we were at once surrounded by a flotilla of numerous sampans ornamented with golden devices. We were deafened by the screams and the dreadful noise. Canton is a veritable town of amphibians. There is not room enough on land for the two million inhabitants, who spend all their lives on the water in floating huts. There are families who have never stepped on shore. Their floating houses have platforms on each end, on which their babes pass a part of their lives until the age of three, tied with a long cord to a post. Canoes propelled by strong Chinese women, clad in broad trousers, come alongside our ship; some of them carry a baby tied on their backs. The women pile up the luggage and transport passengers on shore, together with long cases of opium, which compose the principal cargo of the *Fat-Chan*.

On landing we crossed the French Bridge leading to the Isle of Shamin, and entered the cantonment and the European sections. The Isle of Shamin is a community which consists of a gathering of buildings and gardens forming a kind of European village. Concessions of ground-plots are granted by the Chinese government to England, France, America and Germany. On these diverse pieces of ground the Consulates of the different countries are established; over each Consulate the national flag is hoisted. The Chinese bear no good-will towards Europeans, whom they have surnamed " Devils of the Western countries." One of these days they threw stones at a party of travellers who were crossing the bridge. Chinese sentinels are placed on both ends of the bridge to keep order, but these warriors of the Celestial Empire inspire but little confidence and I felt safe only when we stepped into Shamin. It is only the Chinese inhabitants of Shamin who are allowed to cross the French and English bridges leading to the small island; for the natives living in Canton it is *terra prohibita*.

We put up at the Victoria Hotel. Our room is large and desolate-looking; it has but little furniture: two uncomfortable little iron bedsteads, shrouded with mosquito-nets, a table and three chairs. The floor is stone; on the whitewashed walls hangs the portrait of Queen Victoria sitting

G*

side by side with our Empress-Dowager, holding on her knee her first-born, Nicolas II. From our window I perceive a corner of the quay of Canton, from where resounded an appalling noise of tom-toms and cymbals.

The French Consul came to pay his respects to my husband in the afternoon, accompanied by Mr. Emelianoff, a young compatriot of ours who teaches Russian in one of the schools in Canton. We kept them for dinner. The cooking is abominable. Among other unappetising dishes we had an underdone beefsteak surrounded with slices of oranges. But the milk products are good ; a Dutch settler has brought out of Australia a score of beautiful cows, and has established an excellent dairy-farm at Shamin.

The town of Canton is surrounded by a thick wall. Every street in the city has a gate which is locked at eight every night, the heavy iron doors are bolted and no one is allowed to enter or go out of Canton. All the junks and sampans stand in a line along the bank and are strictly forbidden to come alongside Shamin at night. At nine o'clock in the evening the guards on the bridges beat the retreat, making a terrible noise with drums, maddening tom-toms and pipes several yards long. Thousands of crackers are let off. To crown all the retreat ends by loud gun-shots.

We went to bed in the dark, our sole light consisted of a piece of candle stuck on a tea-saucer. We passed a troublesome, sleepless night, trembling with cold. The dampness mounted from the river by an aperture broken through the ceiling for ventilation. The deafening sound of gongs seemed to rend the air at equal intervals, making noise enough to wake the " Sleeping Beauty." Every quarter of an hour the sound of tom-toms resounded, and immediately after, the sentinels sent up their watch-cry accompanied by the beating of drums and the ringing of bells. The Chinese make all this noise through superstition to chase away the evil spirit !

January 10th.—In spite of our fireless, chilly room, we did not escape the bites of vicious mosquitos and were half devoured by swarms of wretched insects.

At six o'clock in the morning a boy naked down to the waist, his long plait rolled round his head, brought us our coffee. It is Sunday to-day. Being too late for Mass, both in the Cathedral and the Protestant church, we went for a walk round Shamin, which took us altogether half an hour. Before the " English Settlement," joining the " French Concession," there spreads a large tennis-ground.

After tiffin six palanquins were at the door to carry us through the town of Canton. Our guide advised us to dress quietly so as not to attract too much attention. Our palanquin-carriers, thin, emaciated creatures, started at a small trot. As soon as we had crossed the French Bridge and entered Canton, I began to feel seriously uneasy. We were carried through the labyrinth of narrow, muddy evil-smelling streets crowded with humanity; pigs and rooks are their only cleaners. Our carriers advanced with difficulty through the crowd, elbowing the people. There is no foot-way, and at the corners our porters shouted "ho-ho, hi-ha!" to make the people avoid the path, scattering them to right and left. The streets are full of shops, banners, Chinese lanterns, bizarre sign-boards hang down to the ground. On the portico of the houses we saw hideous faced idols, guardians of the thresholds, to whom the Chinese burn red candles with painted flowers and little incense Joss-sticks" (Joss is a god) to propitiate the demons. A Chinese "Punch and Judy" were acting on a little stage in a street. We saw legions of lepers at each corner, and were accosted by sordid beings exposing terrible sores. I had a creepy sensation as we passed groups of evil-looking natives eyeing us with evident malevolent curiosity, which threatened to become hostile. Angry murmurs rose behind us. We heard strong epithets used on our behalf; they shouted after us "Fan-Quai," which meant "Dogs of the West," and made menacing gestures. It was old women and children who were the most aggressive; a little boy pulled a tongue a yard long to me. I felt suddenly a hand grasping my arm, and a brutal-looking young Chinaman gave me such a stare that I felt quite uncomfortable. I endeavoured to look uncon-cerned, but did not know what to do all the same, whether to smile or to maintain a stern countenance. I heaved a sigh of relief when our carriers stopped before the "Pagoda of the five hundred geniuses," which contains life-sized statues made of gilded wood, one more grotesque than the other, placed on granite pedestals, an idol with six eyes and ears down to the neck, poured down from four pairs of hands his blessings; another with three faces held a sort of mandoline in his hands. A statue with European features and clothes, wearing a Rembrandt hat, personified "Marco Polo" the renowned Venetian explorer of the sixteenth century, the first European who penetrated into China. I wonder how that personage had come to attain the rank of a god. We were carried afterwards to the Roman Catholic cathedral, where Christian natives, in Chinese dress, knelt near the altar listen-ing to the litanies sung in Chinese language by a priest wearing the Chinese costume. We went slowly round the cathedral and admired the beautiful stained glass-windows, in which figures of saints stood, and paintings representing diverse subjects from the Bible adapted to Chinese life. The figure of Christ blessing a Chinese woman with children clinging to her skirts, especially attracted our attention.

I was delighted when we were brought back to Shamin.

CHAPTER CX

MACAO

January 11th.—This morning we took our passage to Macao on an English steamer named *The White Cloud*. I turned my back to Canton with great pleasure. I think China is a frightful country and wish I had never set foot in it.

After eight hours of crossing, the Portuguese peninsula came to view. We saw about a hundred cannons on the high forts, protecting Macao from the side of the sea. Two hundred years have gone by since the shores of Macao, the oldest European Colony in the Orient, were first visited by Europeans; in 1720 the Portuguese landed and took possession of it in the name of their Sovereign. The front of the town bears the inscription in Portuguese: *Cita de nome de Dios, nas ha outra mas leal.* (City in the name of God, there does not exist a more loyal one.)

On the quay men besieged us with their cards and prospectuses, each of them trying to lead us into the hotel that they were charged to represent. We took a Chinese interpreter called Fun, who spoke a few words of English, and promised to show us all the sights of Macao. He took us to the Hotel Hing-Kee, standing on the marine esplanade called " Praia-Grande," where a military band plays every evening. The hotel is built Portuguese fashion, with a gallery running around the four sides of the " patio " leading into the various rooms. The gallery is divided in several parts by wooden partitions communicating by doors which we opened, appropriating thus the whole gallery. Outside the air is mild, but it is very cold indoors ; we were obliged to have a fire. In front of our hotel a boat, belonging to the Portuguese Customs, is moored ; the opposite shore belongs to China.

January 13th.—We went about all day in palanquins, seeing the sights of Macao. Nearly all the streets bear clerical names: " Rua Padre Antonio," " Callada de bon Jesus," " Traversa de San Agosto." Macao is a very pretty town. The houses are generally not more than one storey high, most of them painted blue, pink, or yellow, with green shutters, and terraces instead of roofs, all having overhanging balconies reaching out to one another in friendly wise across the narrow streets, which swarm with Chinamen, who, contrary to their fellow-countrymen in Canton, look very peaceful. One of the particular features of the streets of Macao is the abundance of Portuguese priests, wearing long black beards, and women enveloped from head to foot in black mantillas. The natives of Macao are not attractive-looking. They are a race of half-castes—Portuguese father and Chinese mother, resembling orang-outangs, with their prominent jaws.

Fun suggested that we should visit a silk manufactory, where about six-hundred Chinese women were employed. Their Superintendent, a fat Portuguese dame, with a cigarette between her lips, forbad our gentlemen to pass before the rows of workwomen. After showing us through a dozen rooms, Fun brought us into a large hall where numbers of Chinese coolies, in Adam-like dress except the rag-vine-leaf, were occupied in boiling silk cocoons.

We were carried from the manufactory to the frontier of Macao and China. Our porters clambered up the stony ladder-staircases bearing the name of streets, which are all two yards broad, veritable corridors paved with sharp stones, with grass growing between them. We passed through the Chinese quarters of the town, where all the fronts of the houses have recesses containing grotesque-looking idols with twisted legs, the gods of prosperity, before which incenses are burnt.

Here we are on the frontier called "Porta Portuguese" Chinese soldiers guard the boundary. After having set foot on Chinese ground, we were carried back to Macao by a winding staircase-like path, and passed before the grotto of Luis Camoens, the celebrated Portuguese poet of the sixteenth century, exiled in the year 1556 for his daring liberal ideas. The great poet, who had been shipwrecked in these inhospitable seas, gained the shore of this newly-founded Portuguese colony, and took refuge in a grotto situated in a chaotic assemblage of rocks, in the hollow of a dale, where a monument has been erected to his memory. The site is desolate and wild, looking upon the Chinese Empire and the ocean, where there is no land before the icy polar regions. Camoens lamented here his life of exile, and glorified his country in verse. By the side of the monument, on a large stone, a book is sculptured in the rock, bearing the names of all the works of the great poet.

Before returning to the hotel, we went to a Chinese photographer to have our group taken in palanquins. Our carriers were quite amusingly afraid of the aparatus, it being against the teaching of their religion to have their pictures taken, especially together with white-faced men. They paused, undecided what to do, to fly or to remain, and the next moment they suddenly disappeared ; look where we would, we could in no manner discover them, and had our group taken sitting in palanquins placed on the ground.

Macao is a sort of Monte-Carlo of the East, where the principal industry is play. All the numerous gambling saloons are kept by Chinamen. After dinner Fun took us to one of these play-houses, where a risky game named "fonton" goes on. We sat over the gambling tables on the top of a gallery where the game is carried on also. Our gambling neighbours put their stakes into a basket which was dropped down into the hall by the means of a long cord. We saw a venerable white-bearded Chinese croupier take a handful of counters which he placed on the middle of the table and began to count them with a long rod. I also tried my fortune and lost a dollar. Things are done here very unceremoniously ; our croupier feeling hot, undressed and remained almost without clothes !

I wanted very much to see opium-smokers, and Fun led us by a queer old back-street to a bamboo barrack where a score of half-naked Chinamen lay on the floor in different stages of intoxication produced by the effect of opium, with ghastly smiles, their faces expressing the ecstatic delight of extraordinary bliss ; the "haschish" carrying them away into paradisaical dreams. Beside each smoker a small cocoa-oil lamp was burning, to light their long pipes saturated with opium. After two or three puffs, the smokers fell into ecstacies, and swoon away showing the white of the eyes and looking altogether horrible. The smoke in the room blinded me and my head swam from the nasty smell of the opium.

January 14th.—To-day we visited the seminary of San Paula, built by the Jesuits. When we entered the cathedral, a young Irish monk, in the brown habit of the Franciscan order, girded with a thick cord, came towards us, breviary in hand, clinking his sandals on the flag-stones. He took my husband and his companions to show them over the seminary ; he said that ladies are not admitted within the walls of the seminary, and I had to remain in the cathedral with Maria Michaelovna. We went over the church and read all the inscriptions, after which we became a little bored and were pleased when our gentlemen came back, accompanied this time by the prior of the seminary, a grey-bearded Portuguese padre, round-faced and benevolent, who happened to be less Puritan than his young colleague, and invited me to come and drink a glass of Malaga in the refectory, but I refused point-blank this time.

We were back at the hotel just in time for the table d'hôte. After dinner we went to the pier, where we admired the phosphorescence of the sea, produced by the myriads of animalcules with which the ocean is infested at certain periods. The evening was fine and the air very mild. When we passed before the Governor's abode, a sort of pavilion surrounded by a small garden named "Villa Flora," we seated ourselves on a broad stone parapet and listened to the band playing in the "patio" of the villa. How jolly it was to throw etiquette to the winds, and feel like simple mortals!

January 15th.—This afternoon my husband called upon the Governor, who returned his visit an hour later; as to me, I exchanged visiting-cards with his wife.

January 16th.—This morning we left for Hong-Kong on the boat *Scha*. Our steamer tugged a barge loaded with cases of opium, for the sum of forty thousand Mexican dollars. The cargo will be transhipped afterwards on to another boat bound for the Sandwich Islands and San Francisco. Our steamer is escorted by a detachment of Portuguese soldiers. After three hours' sail we arrived at Hong-Kong.

January 17th.—The weather is very bad, the rain is falling in torrents. This morning a boy brought me, instead of tea, a tepid undrinkable potion as black as ink. When I told him to add some water to my tea, he found nothing better but to mix it with water that he had taken from the top of our bath, and then, wanting to convince himself that my tea was not too hot, he put his dirty finger into my cup.

It is Sunday to-day. After breakfast we were carried in palanquins to St. John's Cathedral, where English ladies sang prayers in chorus.

Maria Michaelovna made us laugh at tiffin; each time when the boy handed her the menu to point out the extras, she repeated mechanically in Russian "*Vot eto*," which means, "Give me that," and the boy, confounding the sound of *vot eto* with potatoe, served her with each course a perpetual supply of potatoes, even with ice cream.

At four o'clock in the afternoon we attended the evening service at the cathedral. This time the chorus consisted of Chinamen. A young Mexican padre mounted a pulpit and began preaching a long sermon in Portuguese language. As we did not understand what he said, we returned to the hotel, where we found visiting-cards left for us by General Wilson Black, the Commander of the English troops at Hong-Kong, who had called upon us with his wife and daughter.

The *Salasie* has arrived this morning, and to-morrow we sail on that ship for Saigon.

January 18th.—We went on board directly after lunch. All the passengers were still on land, except a buxom Russian nurse, who was rocking in her arms a squalling baby. There are nine families of Russian marine officers on board. My husband was invited to dinner, with his suite, at General Wilson Black's, but I refused the invitation and locked myself up in my cabin until Sergy's return. In the saloon next to my cabin I heard the officers, who had returned on board by this time, flirting with Melle. Jeanne Mougin, a pretty French girl, full of animation and merriment, with a face all laughter and dimples, with whom I made acquaintance on deck in the evening. Sergy described to me in detail the dinner party at the Wilson Black's. Everything was done in grand style ; the table, set out with silver-plate and crystal, was beautifully decorated with flowers. After dinner Miss Lilie, the General's daughter, sang English songs, accompanying herself on the guitar.

January 19th.—We weighed anchor at noon. The sea is very rough, and I remained in bed all day, preparing myself for a bad crossing.

January 20th.—It begins to get hot. The double doors of the dining-room are taken off, and the piano is brought out on the deck. The passengers have put on their white clothes for dinner. We are approaching the equator zone, and pass the Strait of Tonkin by moonlight.

January 21st.—The heat is intense. Towards midday we enter the Saigon River.

CHAPTER CXII

SAIGON

At four o'clock we are at Saigon. We put up at the Hôtel Continental, the top flat of which is occupied by the "Cercle Colonial." We dined at table d'hôte. The dining-room was thronged with officers of the Colonial Infantry, dressed all in white, who quartered in the garrison. They were very gay and talked all at once. After dinner we went to the opera. The performance was *La Fille du Régiment*, and the singers very good. The theatre looked very elegant, the men all in white, the ladies in low gowns. Between the acts we went to eat ices on the boulevard. Hindoos, draped in white, with the blue tattoo mark on their forehead, promenaded before us. Towards midnight we were back on board.

January 22nd.—We left the harbour of Saigon at seven in the morning, when the tide was in. We passed before huge English and German cargo-ships anchored in a line along the banks of the river. It is terribly hot, we are all at roasting point.

January 23rd.—Full calm. Intolerable heat.

CHAPTER CXIII

SINGAPORE

January 24th.—It was night when the *Salasie* came in sight of Singapore. We are going to stop here about a fortnight, waiting for the *Laos*, a French boat, bound to Colombo and Marseilles. We put up again at the Hôtel d' Europe.

January 25th.—An English officer and his family occupy the apartment next door to ours. The children are shamefully spoilt by their mother, who never reproves them. They can't keep quiet one minute and get into everybody's way, getting hideous sounds out of two combs, and beating the drum into our ears. When they were attacked by a fit of bad humour, nobody could approach them in safety. They lay down on the floor and kicked and howled. Their manners at table d'hôte were of the worst, for they made as much noise as they could with their spoons and knives. I found this morning the youngest of the family, the best-loved child, an extremely troublesome little Saxon, beating his *ayah* (nurse) with the leg of his rocking-horse, which had come off. That insupportable brat has been instantly dispatched to bed by his father. The room opposite to us is occupied by a Dutch opera-singer, who is going on a tour to Siam. I heard her practising her exercises the whole morning.

January 26th.—Our Consul, Mr. Kleimenoff, is awfully nice to me. To-day he sent to me a bottle of milk, a rarity in these parts.

January 28th.—It is dreadfully hot. The tropical rain, which falls from time to time, does not refresh the air. Sergy intneded to make an excursion to Bankok, but the signals of tempest are hoisted in the port, and I am wickedly pleased, for Sergy will remain at home.

January 29th.—The young Sultan of Johore paid an unexpected call to us in the afternoon, a fabulous creature, all covered with diamonds. This Hindoo prince is enormously rich, the greatest part of Malacca belonging to him.

Opposite our windows spreads a spacious lawn and pleasure grounds, where Englishmen, who carry their habits with them in all parts of the world, give themselves up to every kind of outdoor sport : golf, cricket, tennis, etc. The players look very nice in their white flannels and blue caps.

In Singapore it is the Chinese who possess the largest fortunes ; the whole commerce of the place is in their hands. Every evening the Chinese merchants, after having ended their business in the city, drive round the Esplanade in smart carriages, drawn by big Australian horses, with a white groom on the back seat.

February 5th.—It is my birthday to-day. Our Consul gave me for my birthday gift a large basket with enormous cocoa-nuts filled with milk. This native beverage is very cool and refreshing.

The Hindoo colony of Singapore invited us to be present at a great annual festivity in honour of Siva, the god of good and evil. The whole town rushed to the famous heathen temple from which the procession was to proceed. We saw an enormous chariot of carved silver advancing, drawn by two sacred white bulls covered with rich clothes, shining with gold embroideries and spangles, their legs and horns decorated with bracelets. We were told that the chariot cost eighty thousand dollars. It held the statue of the Hindoo Trinity—Brahma, Vishnu and Siva—crowned with flowers. A great throng of natives, their faces and hands daubed with ashes, in the simplest of costumes—a mere white linen band, five fingers wide, passing round the hips, escorted the chariot, holding lighted torches. We left our shoes in charge of a turbaned man, and proceeded to the temple to which many thousands of people came from all parts to pay their vows. Thousands of pilgrims crowded through the gates, all straining towards the enclosure of the temple. About sixty men, dressed in white, beat tom-toms and howled in a piercing voice. We were deafened by the hideous music. We entered a magnificent hall, full of enormous columns, lit by Arabian lamps with glass panes framed in carved copper. On the floor stood a big copper incense-burner, loading the atmosphere with perfume. The interior of the temple is a veritable bazaar. A fantastic crowd surrounded us ; they beat the drums, they sang, they danced. A group of bonzes (priests), naked to the waist, girded with a thick cord, came up to pour strong perfume on our hands, and offered us armfuls of fragrant jasmine, which spread a violent odour all over the temple. I was somewhat scared by all this noise, and giddy with the scent of crushed flowers heaped on the floor.

February 6th.—To-day my husband went with his suite to visit the Rajah of Johore in his dominions on the coast of Malacca. It took them two hours to reach his States. They crossed the strait that divides Singapore from Johore in a steam-boat, and made the rest of the journey in rikshas.

The Rajah wasn't at home ; my husband, nevertheless, was shown over the Palace, which had nothing remarkable about it. Numbers of articles, without any artistic value, were heaped up in the apartments. Sergy lunched at the Johore Club, from which he sent me a letter with a Johore post stamp for my collection.

February 7th.—I was awakened this morning by a voice, proceeding from the corridor, wildly vociferating, " My money ! I want my money ! " It was an American traveller who had been robbed at the hotel of the sum of eleven thousand dollars. He had gone down for breakfast, and when he returned some minutes later, he found the drawer forced and his money gone. The police was summoned, and his apartment turned upside down. The porfolio was found out under the mattress, and one of the boys, serving at the hotel, confessed to the robbery, and was marched off to gaol. I saw a constable dragging the culprit by his long tail, whilst the whole household regaled him with blows and kicks.

FROM SINGAPORE TO SUEZ

February 9th.—To-day we take our passage on the *Laos*. A Prussian officer, with an unpronounceable name, who was stopping with us at the hotel, came on board to see us off. He had just returned from a tour in Sumatra, where cannibalism still exists, and narrated to us, with Teutonical phlegm, his experiences among man-eaters. In that barbarian country the tribes engaged in war eat their prisoners. Those who slaughter them are also risking their life, for if one single drop of blood falls upon the executioner, he is devoured in his turn. This officer brought back from Sumatra the head and the hands of a man who had been eaten in his presence. Ugh—the horror!

The *Laos* is a veritable floating palace. There are about one hundred first-class passengers on board. I found some old acquaintances from the *Salasie*, Melle. Jeanne Mougin amongst them, merry and pleasant as ever. She threw herself stormingly upon my neck; I was very pleased, in my turn, to have such a gay companion during our crossing. The steamer included among its passengers a nuncio of the Pope, a Pole, Zalessky by name, a high personage of the Church, who will soon be appointed to the rank of Cardinal. He inhabits Kandy and is now making the round of his diocese. *Monseigneur*, as he is called on board, wears a broad violet waistband over his black cassock. He is awfully nice, without a particle of bigotry. He told me, as we paced up and down the long deck, that he had been very fond of society in the days of his youth, and that it had been extremely hard for him to take final vows and to part with his moustache.

February 12th.—After dinner everyone who had pretensions to music played or sang in the salon. The wife of a French officer, who was returning to Toulon after having ended his military service in Cochin-China, favoured the company with arias and cavatinas. The lady is very smart and elegant, but her warbling does not suit her plumage, her musical gifts not being of an extraordinary order. At first she was somewhat nervous and, in her agitation, dropped all her notes. Another would-be prima donna, an old hen that imagined that she could crow, and whose singing would make the dogs howl, with many simpers began to squeak love songs as high as she could reach, with a voice particularly discordant with tune. She accompanied herself on the piano, and thumped the poor instrument enough to destroy the keys. Her performance put my teeth on edge, and I cast her no tender glances; but my neighbour, a meagre exalted German lady, went into raptures, showing the whites of her eyes and repeating, " *Famos, colossal!* " A pretentious and bad pianist took her place, and massacred, with the greatest assurance, one of Chopin's most beautiful compositions. After the pianist a young girl sat down at the piano, whose musical gift didn't go further than " *La prière d'une vierge.*" After two hours of such anti-musical performance, the salon emptied little by little, and her solo was executed, so to speak, to empty seats.

February 13th.—We arrived at Colombo this morning, and immediately took passage on the *Armand Behic* an ocean liner sailing to Suez from Australia. We have abandoned the *Laos* to avoid the quarantine at Bombay, where the ship was to stop. Nearly all her passengers passed over on the *Armand Behic* There were many Australians and Japs on board and some French officers who are returning from Tonkin, very pale and suffering, whilst the Australians are all blooming with health. There were different sets, of course, among a throng of four hundred passengers. There was the " gay set," who got up plays and dances on board, the " cultured set," the " musical set," etc., etc.

A concert with tombola is being got up on board for the benefit of the families of the sailors who have perished at sea. A subscription has been started amongst the first-class passengers. I consented to take part in the concert and to play a solo on the concertina. Active preparations are made. The piano of the salon has been screwed down to the floor, the piano of the second-class was carried out on the deck, which is transformed into a veritable concert-hall.

February 14th.—In the afternoon we all went to draw the lottery. A jolly French colonel took upon himself to be auctioneer at the tombola. He presided with extraordinary gravity, hammer in hand, and kept the whole company alive by puffing his wares unblushingly. The programmes of our concert, painted by one of the Australian lady-passengers, were sold by auction, 12 francs each; the bids rose finally to 40 francs. Our concert yielded about 1,500 francs. The evening wound up with a ball. Between the dances tea and all sorts of refreshments were being carried round by sailors. I had no notion of the hour and found it was three o' clock when I got to bed.

February 15th.—The Chinese element has disappeared on

board, but in return, the number of Hindoos, Malays and Arabs have increased. They are all on the fore and aft of the ship, piled up on heaps of luggage.

Our boat has brought a parcel bearing my address at St. Petersburg, postmarked Sydney. The message over the seas was a book written by O'Ryan, an Australian doctor who had served in the Turkish army during the Russian-Turkish war, whom I had met many years ago at Erzeroum. The book is entitled, " Under the Red Crescent." It is mentioned in it that the author had fallen in love with me at first sight, and could not forget me till now. It was a strange coincidence that the book travelled in the same mail-bag, going to the same country, and it was very queer this unexpected discovery of an Australian adorer of long vanished times.

February 16th.—Our list of acquaintances has increased on board. There is among the passengers a Creole family bound to Marseilles, Crémazy by name. Mr. Crémazy has occupied for a long time the post of President of the Court of Justice at Saigon. His pretty daughters, Melles. Paule and Blanche, were born in the Colonies and represent the real Creole type. They are very pleasant girls, and in a few days we had become fast friends.

Another French girl, Melle. Louise Martel, is an invalid ; she lay back in her deck-chair all day amidst a pile of pillows, carefully wrapped in a thick shawl, though exposed to the rays of a tropical sun. She is dying of consumption and looks very ill and sad, her face drawn and sharpened by suffering. The poor young creature is cold and indifferent to every one. She took a fancy to me nevertheless, and to-day, when I came up to bid her good-morning, her face lit up with a poor, sickly, little smile.

As a contrast to the young invalid, we have a jolly opera-singer on board, who flirts and appropriates all the passengers of the unfair sex. She especially set her cap at Mr. Schaniavski, and bored him with requests to accompany her vicious little songs.

There is a particularly nice young man on board, an Australian, according to the information of the head steward. He didn't stare at me during the meals, he was too well-bred, but when I looked the other way, he looked at me. He sketched caricatures wickedly well, and I asked him to make a drawing of me, but it wasn't a caricature at all, too flattering I should say. To-day the young man made a rush for a seat near me at table. I had noticed that he had put on a becoming tie adorned with a pin with a beautiful opal set in it, which I had imprudently admired, and which had cost a considerable sum of money. After dinner he came up to me and laid in my lap a little vellum box, in it was the famous opal pin, which he tried to make me accept as a souvenir, but of course I refused his offering, telling him that in Russia the opal is considered an unlucky stone. He was awfully vexed and sulked the whole evening, following me with eyes of gloomy disappointment. The Australian endeavoured to throw himself in my way everywhere ; he passed beside the windows of my cabin when he couldn't catch me elsewhere. I was not quite indifferent to the adventure, for he was very attractive that young Australian. But it appears that I was playing with fire. He placed himself close to me on deck this evening and taking my hand, which he retained in his grasp, his eyes speaking a number of things to me, he began to talk of love, murmuring a torrent of passionate words. He told me of the sleepless nights he spent in thinking of me, and said I had cast a kind of spell upon him, and that since the hour he had seen me, he had thought only of how he might see me again. His attentions became so pressing that I found it time to put a stop to them. " I think, if you don't mind," I said to him heartlessly whilst he was talking of his flame to me, " that I'd rather speak of the weather." He didn't look pleased, the poor boy, I must say.

February 20th.—We are crossing to-day the Strait of Bab-el-Mandeb, (the Gate of Tears.) The mariners try to pass this dangerous place by daylight.

There has been a deal of cricket-playing this afternoon on board. It seems a queer game for a ship, but the promenade-deck has nettings to keep the balls from flying overboard.

For dinner the Australians dressed as if for a ball, the ladies in low dresses, the gentlemen in smokings. The *cuisine* is very good on board ; all the provisions are brought from Australia. The Australian passengers monopolised the salon after dinner, sitting there as if the whole place belonged to them. Someone played the piano and they all sang Australian songs in chorus.

February 21st.—The air is cool and fresh, and the Japanese passengers begin to freeze. In Australia it is summer in November, December, January and February, and thus our Australian passengers, going out to Europe for twelve months will enjoy summer the whole year round.

February 22nd.—The monotony of our crossing had begun to weary every one. The passengers saw far too much of each other, and the good-understanding between them was cooling down. They began to pick quarrels with each other and lived in strife for the remainder of the voyage.

CHAPTER CXV

SUEZ

WE were obliged to take leave of our pleasant steamer friends at Suez. I was very sorry to part with the Crémazy, who hoped we might meet again and promised to write to me from time to time. When it came to saying good-bye to my Australian admirer, he hurt my hand squeezing it and pressing my fingers made me cry, whilst he expressed his despair at parting from me.

We lowered a boat that carried us on shore. When we entered it, my Australian waved his farewell tome and shouted from the deck, " I am so sorry to lose you!"

We had the intention on arriving at Suez to make an excursion along the banks of the Nile, and then to catch the *Laos* at Port Said. When we set foot on African soil, the train for Cairo had already started, and we were obliged to wait patiently until the next day. We set out *piano pianissimo* through the intense heat to seek rooms at the Hôtel Continental. Suez is in the full Carnival ; masked groups walk about the streets. A man dressed like a cook, holding an immense sauce-pan, in which he was stirring with a big spoon a sort of gruel, sprinkled with this nasty mixture all the passers-by, shouting, " *Vive la France!* " Knowing that he was at our heels, we hastened to the hotel.

CHAPTER CXVI

CAIRO

February 24th.—We started for Cairo with the first train, and followed for a long time the Suez Canal. We are rolling now by the side of the Nile. The passengers, their faces at the windows, are looking out for the Pyramids. We came in sight of one Pyramid, and ten minutes afterwards, we enter Cairo station.

The winter season at Cairo was in full swing; the city was full of tourists and it was difficult to find a shelter. We made a tour of the hotels, but not a single room was to be had: " full up," came the curt reply. We went to Shepherd's Hotel, and the next hotel, and the next to that, and received the same answer everywhere. At last we found shelter at the Hôtel Bristol, but for two days only, as all the apartments were already let to a number of American tourists who were to arrive with the next boat from Alexandria.

February 25th.—The chances were that we should remain at Cairo for some days to come. We had just been informed that we must wait a whole week to catch the *Laos* at Port-Said. Directly after breakfast we set to work to find lodgings, which was not an easy thing to do. At last we got apartments, consisting of a bedroom and a sitting-room, in the second floor of a private house, where we were made as comfortable as circumstances would allow. We'll pay five shillings a day for our board and lodging. Our travelling companions have found rooms in the same house.

February 26th.—I am laid up with a bad cold and look hideous with my nose twice its size and my eyes half theirs. I wonder if my Australian admirer would keep faithful to me if he saw me just now? Sergy wanted absolutely to send for the doctor, but I said that it was quite unnecessary and had my own way.

Sergy, with all our travelling companions, went to the Pyramids this afternoon, and I felt very lonely all by myself at home. I listened to the chant of the "muezzin" calling for prayers from many a minaret, and at the same time from the Esbekieh Gardens came the music of the native military band playing Arabian airs.

February 28th.—When the morning came I was burning

with fever and could not raise my head from the pillow, but the *Laos* had arrived at Port-Said, and we must leave Cairo to-day absolutely. It will not suit my cold to be sure! Before leaving I swallowed a large dose of quinine.

The railway-line leading to Port-Said is very narrow and looks more like a tramway-line. The road ran close along the Suez Canal. A steamer crawled by close at hand as our train wheezed on from Ismailia to the coast; we soon left the ship behind us. Our way lay now through sugar-cane and cotton-fields. I felt very unwell all the time and lay stretched on my narrow bench, feeling very miserable. Notwithstanding the large dose of quinine my temperature was up, and I was shivering with fever. I hope I shall not fall seriously ill!

PORT-SAID

WE were at Port-Said at six o'clock in the evening. As soon as we arrived at the hotel I got to bed at once.

February 29th.—I kept my bed the whole day. It is Carnival-time and the streets are full of laughing crowds dressed in fantastic costumes, who showered confetti on each other. I could see from my bed all that was going on in Lesseps Square. Sergy went out for a walk and returned accompanied by an Italian youth with a performing monkey arrayed in a red jacket and fez, perched upon his shoulder. The ugly little animal, whilst turning somersaults, was watching slyly the opportunity to jump upon my bed.

March 1st.—We had to go on board the *Laos* in the middle of the night. I did not at all like to be turned out of my warm bed, and felt so miserably weak that I could hardly stand on my feet.

We rocked on the waves in a small rowing-boat for more than an hour, awaiting permission to step on board the *Laos* at the appointed hour. A little fleet of barges loaded with coal, surrounded us; their close neighbourhood made us look like chimney-sweeps. When we mounted the *Laos* we were as black as negroes.

March 2nd.—The gradual lowering of the temperature is very sensible. Since yesterday the punkahs in the salon had ceased to work and the light dresses and straw hats on board have been replaced by warm coats and woollens of all kinds. The wind is getting fresher and the sea begins to ripple. It is the "mistral" coming on; we are rolling terribly on the Mediterranean. It is not at all jolly, especially with the perspective of quarantine at Marseilles.

During the stay of the *Laos* at Bombay many new passengers boarded the ship, amongst them a rich Indian nabob with a face like a wicked monkey, who is going to London to be presented to the Queen. He is dressed in European garb, which doesn't suit him at all and makes him look more like an ape than a human being. But the Hindoo was thoroughly unconscious of his own deficiencies. He sat next to Mr. Shaniavski at dinner and found fault with all the passengers during the repast; especially with those belonging to the yellow race, and said that the Chinese and the Japs were all monkey-faced creatures. And he himself—whom does he look like, I should like to know?

March 5th.—Thank God we are close to Marseilles. At seven o'clock in the morning the washing of the deck was already over and the boat had put on her best toilet. At ten the French coasts were in sight. Shall we be able to come into the harbour or shall we be confined to quarantine? That is the question which preoccupies us all.

Hurrah! the sanitary state of our boat is declared satisfactory and we are permitted to land.

We decided to rest one day at Marseilles at the Hôtel de Noailles. I could think of nothing else but bed and the bliss of laying my ailing body down to rest between clean sheets that smelt of lavender.

March 7th.—We are on our way to Paris. I am so happy to see the miles added to miles, and the distance separating me from darling St. Petersburg decreasing visibly. The whole country is covered with a deep mantle of snow. I wanted snow so badly in the tropics, and must be satisfied now!

CHAPTER CXVIII

ST. PETERSBURG

WE are back from our exile; home in Russia! At last our wanderings have come to an end. We have crossed the globe almost in all directions by land and sea, but I know of no place as dear as St. Petersburg.

·We are staying at the Grand Hôtel, and have had such a good time since we came here, and no end of a better one in prospect. I feel myself free of all constraint and étiquette; all my words and acts are not taken up and discussed as at Khabarovsk. We were full of lovely plans for spending the summer abroad, but man proposes and circumstances master him. We have just been at St. Petersburg for a week, when an event occurred which upset all our plans. My husband was offered, quite unexpectedly, the brillant post of Governor-General of Turkestan, a territory in Central Asia, between Siberia and Afghanistan. He accepted the post. I was awfully taken by the rapidity of the events—it gave me quite a shock! All my little castles in the air have been shattered at one blow, and my day-dreams have come to nothing. It was such a sorrow for me to leave St. Petersburg, and a great sacrifice to give up going abroad. I am so tired of being a bird of passage, hunting about from place to place, until I could scream for rest, leading a life of constant travel in overheated trains and on rolling seas. And we are obliged now to undertake another long journey! A new existence is in store for us at the other extremity of our spacious native country. A new home, a new life! What will it be like? But the die is cast; there is nothing to do but submit. I must be reasonable and look the matter fairly in the face and endeavour to take a philosophic view of what can't be helped.

It is said in a Persian sacred book, the " Zend-Avesta," written two hundred years before Christ, that Turkestan is one of the most ancient cradles of humanity. Tashkend, our new home, is a city a thousand years old. It was captured in 1865 by General Tsherniaeff. That country is as big as France and England put together, and has a population of eight millions.

The Emir of Bokhara, Said-Abdul-ul-Akhad-Khan, announced to my husband by wire his forthcoming arrival at St. Petersburg. He came to call on us, accompanied by his ministers, speechless with awe and veneration in his presence. The Sovereign of Bokhara was very magnificently clad in a superb khalat of brocade, a long robe cut straight, girded with a silver sash, wearing on his head a turban studded with precious stones, his breast adorned with decorations. When the official compliments were exchanged, it was my turn to entertain the Emir with the aid of an interpreter. Somewhat at a loss to open the conversation, I was trying to think of something to say that was suitable for the situation, and nearly began to make unnecessary announcements about the weather. In taking leave the Emir bestowed on my husband the Bokharian Order studded with big diamonds, and that same day there came a package for me from the Emir, a golden case containing a beautiful necklace of massive gold of the finest Oriental work, inlaid with precious stones.

It is impossible to postpone our journey to Tashkend any longer, my husband being called to his new post of duty because of the disturbances taking place in Andidjan, the capital of Fergan, a district of Turkestan. During the night from the 17th to 18th May, a revolt burst out. A band of Mussulmans, about 1,000 men, under the command of their ishan Mahomet-Ali-Halif, attacked the camp of our garrison from the side of the village Don Kishlak, adjoining the camp. The natives crept stealthily to the first barrack in which our soldiers were sleeping peacefully, and began to cut their throats. Starting up out of their sleep, the men of the neighbouring barracks drove their assailants back with the points of their bayonets. All the camp was soon astir and the Mussulmans retreated, carrying away their wounded. The "imam," a pilgrim from Mecca, was one of the first to be killed, whilst he was reading the Koran to the rioters, who, in attacking our garrison, had planned the extermination of the whole Russian population, and putting everything to fire and sword, after having taken possession of our camp. The agitation in the country is settled down and active measures are taken against the rebels. The "ishan" is sentenced to death, together with the principal mutineers, whilst 500 natives will be exported to penal servitude to the Isle of Saghalien. I do pity these poor fanatics! Legends are told about this ishan; the story goes that some time before the last rebellion, a message from the Sultan had delivered to him a venerable relic, the hair and beard of the prophet, with the permission to commence a sacred war against the infidels. The population of Fergan, recently submitted to Russia, had attempted several times to raise a general rebellion against the Russians, nourishing towards them an implacable hatred. My husband will have to take strong measures to avoid a new outburst.

CHAPTER CXIX

OUR JOURNEY TO TASHKEND

May 26.—We started for Tashkend to-day. I will return to St. Petersburg in September to confer about the publishing of my " Memories,"·which I issue for the benefit of the gymnasium of young ladies at Tashkend.

It is a long and tedious journey from St. Petersburg to Tashkend ; we have to cover 4,600 miles to reach our new far-away abode.

A crowd of people had come to see us off and stood before the car which was put at our disposal as far as Petrovsk, one of the largest ports of the Caucasus. The next car was reserved for my husband's suite.

The hour for departure approached. The train is moving and carrying us away on our long journey. I left St. Petersburg in a flood of tears.

May 30th.—We arrived at Petrovsk at eight o'clock in the morning, and took passage on the *Alexis* a boat bound to Krasnovodsk, the chief port of the Transcaspian provinces. We weighed anchor at 10 o'clock. Our voyage began under favourable auspices ; the weather is very mild, not the slightest breeze ruffles the smooth surface of the water, but unfortunately, in even the most splendid weather, the rolling is felt in the Caspian Sea.

May 31st.—Nine o'clock in the morning. In the distance the coasts of the Caucasus rise with snow-clad mountains. We soon reach Baku, the town of petroleum. A noisy crowd of Persians, Tartars and Armenians throng on the quay ; the hubbub of voices was almost deafening. My husband profited by the stoppage of our ship to visit the town. He was shown the famous Black Town, where the naphtha is exported. According to the most recent theory, the substance of naphtha is the produce of the petrification of animals and marine plants. It is not easy to make a fountain of naphtha spout out, sometimes it is only after two years of boring, the layer of ground penetrated being sometimes twenty metres thick.

June 1st.—The weather has taken a turn for the worse. The sky is overclouded, the wind is rising and the ship rolls horribly. We have shut ourselves in our cabins.

June 2nd.—The sun was not yet up when the coasts of Asia appeared on the horizon in long white lines. Towards seven o'clock in the morning we entered Krasnovodsk. Flags flutter on the quay, and a triumphal arch is erected with our initials and "Welcome" written in large letters. All the administrative officials of the town have come to present themselves to my husband, who is greeted with the greatest enthusiasm. We come on land and walk between two lines of lookers-on. Prince Toumanoff, the chief of the Transcaspian provinces, came up to me with a large bouquet, whilst a military band was playing a march.

A special train was waiting on the quay. All the cars are painted white. I have my private car provided with every possible comfort and luxury. At one end is the sitting-room containing sofas, armchairs, a large writing-table, shelves, etc. The furniture is covered with red silk brocade to match the window curtains. At the other end a suite consisting of a bedroom with a bed with splendid springs, a bath and dining-room.

Whilst Sergy was visiting the town, my car was taken to the railway station, a large white building of oriental design and ornamentation. Elegantly dressed ladies and officers in full uniform were waiting my husband on the platform. I leant far back, to conceal myself from view, in nervous horror of being stared at. To amuse me a musical band executed the best pieces of their repertoire, in turns with another band composed of wandering minstrels. An old white-bearded man began to sing in a broken voice a bizarre melody to the accompaniment of a zourna, a national instrument. My heart went out to the poor old troubadour with infinite pity.

As soon as my husband arrived, the train steamed away amidst loud cheers.

From Krasnovodsk to Tashkend, we have to make 1,800 kilometres by rail. Prince Toumanoff and a group of engineers accompany us as far as Samarkand. We have invited the whole company to lunch with us.

It was awfully stifling in my car and I was too hot to talk, I was too exhausted to eat, but devoured with thirst. As soon as lunch was over, I hastened to get into my dressing-gown and stretched myself on the sofa.

Our road lay for a long time along the Caspian. The moist, warm air that blew through the carriage windows brought a salt taste from the sea. The stretch of country through which we are now passing is flat and uninteresting. Along the roadway the dust rose in clouds which poured in through the curtains ; to crown all we are devoured by flies. I am furious with the nasty insects, with the heat, with the dust, with everything !

At all the stations the military and civil dignitaries meet

my husband ; enthusiastic receptions are made : speeches, music, etc., etc.   Crowds of natives welcome us with Eastern greetings of hands to lips and forehead.

June 3rd.—I didn't close my eyes during the whole night ; I turned and turned in my bed, but sleep would not come.

The barometer continues to rise, it shows already 32 degrees over zero.   Such a tedious journey, and we had a long, long way to go still !   I lay motionless on my sofa— hot as a grill, and began to heave sighs hard enough to split a rock, but it did not trouble my travelling companions at all, quite on the contrary : if I had ceased to moan, they would have come to see what was the matter with me, because they had grown accustomed to my groans and complaints.

We enter now the arid steppes of Central Asia.   We are in the open desert, desolate and immense.   As far as the eye could see on each side, the plain spreads before us, nothing but unlimited sand all round, and great monstrous yellow waves come closing in from all sides, threatening to engulf us. Such a wild, solitary landscape !   Anything more dreary is impossible to imagine ; there was neither water, tree, nor vegetation of any kind, nothing but glaring sun.   It seemed as if we had been transported into a forlorn land.   We were the only living things in a dead world ; no sign of man or beast , not even a wandering bird was to be seen.   The monotonous click of the engine was the only sound that broke the silence.   The stations appear at great intervals in the midst of the desert.   Life mustn't be sweet here !

As we drew near Kizil-Arvat the landscape changed in character ; verdure begins to appear.   We are crossing an oasis.   In the distance we see a caravan of camels advancing slowly.   At sundown we approach Geok-Tepe, and our train stops before the tombs of our soldiers killed during the assault of the town, whilst a requiem was chanted for the repose of their souls.   Much blood has been spilt here !   We passed before the ruins of the fortress made famous by the heroic defence of the natives during a whole month.   The walls of the fortress stretch for several kilometres.

Towards evening we arrived at Askhabad.   In spite of the want of water, the vegetation is luxuriant in these parts.   My uncle, General Roehrberg, was the founder of the town.   After the conquest of Akhal-Teke by General Skobeleff in 1881, the Grand Duke Michael, commander in chief of the army of the Caucasus, proposed to my uncle who was at that time General of Division, to occupy the post of chief of the Transcaspian provinces.   He was ordered to Askhabad which was but a small village inhabited by wandering tribes.   My uncle established peace and tranquillised the country which he began to rule as the Khan (Asiatic despot).   In the first place he had to organise the distribution of ground-plots among the natives, the army and the Russian inhabitants, and plan out the town. A few years ago my uncle visited Askhabad and found it in a flourishing state. It has at present 47,000 inhabitants exclusive of the nomad population, (a tribe bearing the name of Tekintzi,) and has two gymnasiums for boys and girls, three municipal schools, and other public establishments.

June 4th.—The night was so fresh that I had to take out my warm blanket. Early in the morning we arrived at Merv. Repetition of yesterday's greetings with the offering of " Bread and Salt " on a silver dish besides. A few minutes from Merv is Mourgab, a beautiful estate belonging to the Emperor, extending to the very frontier of Persia. At the station of Amou-Daria a wagon was put at the rear of the train, an observation car ; all the back was in glass to view the country. We had to cross the Amou-Daria, one of the greatest rivers of the world, on a temporary slender wooden bridge, which swung and quivered under us. An iron bridge about three kilometres long, is in construction, a masterpiece of engineering skill, which will cost a large sum to build. I was awfully uneasy whilst we traversed the bridge, and turned to my husband with a frightened face, but Sergy who had strong nerves, was looking provokingly calm, and laughed at my fears, and nothing was so aggravating as calmness for me at that moment. At the other side of the river we came into a land of beauty and fertility, and rolled through maize and tobacco plantations. I looked around with admiring eyes. Here again was life ! The bushes were full of warbling birds.

The sun had set when we arrived at Kermine in the domains of the Emir of Bokhara. The railway station is situated at ten kilometres from the capital of Bokhara bearing the same name. I was told that the customs in that barbarian country reminded one of prehistoric times. The prison at Kermine consists of three deep pits in which swarm pell-mell women, men, and children. On approaching the station we saw fires lighted in tar-barrels, showing two battalions of Bokhara soldiers ranged along the railway-line. In the semi-darkness we could have easily taken these men dressed in Russian-cut uniforms, for Russian soldiers, especially whilst they shouted in chorus loud hurras when my husband appeared at the door of his car.

The Emir, who was in Moscow at the time, was represented by three high dignitaries. A large tent had been erected just opposite the station, in which was prepared an abundant *dastarkhan* (native dainties of all kinds.) The long table covered with a white table-cloth reminded one of European customs, but the throng of natives in long khalats and turbans, the bizarre sounds of the native music and all this Oriental

mise-en-scène, testified that we were very far from Europe, in
the centre of Mohametanism, on a visit to an Asiatic sovereign.
I was peeping through the blinds of the window and watched
the crowd on the platform.   I saw the glare of the torches,
carried by the natives, on the faces and the moving forms.
The whole Russian colony was assembled on the platform.
A deputation of Bokharans came up to present " Bread and
Salt " to my husband.   Before leaving Kermine Sergy sent a
telegram to the Emir to thank him for the friendly reception
which had been made to him by his representatives.

June 5th.—The train crosses fresh green valleys ; the soil
is rich and easy to irrigate.   The burning sun gives two
harvests a year.   It is chiefly cotton-shrubs which are
cultivated here.   Turcomen, wearing enormous fur caps,
are working in the fields.   We see a group of wandering
Kirghees sitting on the ground before their tents.   The men
of this tribe breed cattle and horses, and fabricate a fermented
drink made of mare's milk, called *koumiss.*

We approach Samarkand station ; the city of Samarkand
is some miles distant.   It represents a bushy forest in the
middle of which low-roofed houses, towers and minarets are
scattered.   It was annexed to Russia in 1868, after the taking
of Bokhara.   Samarkand has been one of the most famous
cities of the Mussulman world, and had only the town of
Pekin as rival in Asia ; its princes were equal to the
Emperors of China.   The glory of Samarkand is departed ;
alone and desolate stand the ruins, the remnants of ancient
splendour.   Samarkand has seen fine old doings.   My
thoughts wandered back to the time when it had echoed to
the tramp of the Greek legions, as they thundered forth on
their way to India, under the command of Alexander the
Great, King of Macedonia, who had rested here during his
triumphal march.   It is here that the sun of the power of
Timur or Tamerlane, the greatest King of the country, who
reigned in the fourteenth century, rose and set.   Ruins and
sandy plains replace now Tamerlane's beautiful palaces and
magnificent gardens.   On what does human greatness hang !
These ruins of ancient splendour surpass the ruins of Rome
and Greece by their magnificence, and can be compared only
with the ruins of Egypt.   Unfortunately, these vestiges of
vanished civilisation are destroyed, little by little, by frequent
earthquakes, and still more by the inhabitants who continue
to pull them unmercifully to pieces for their new buildings.
In one of the streets of Samarkand a house was pointed out
to my husband whose whole front had been taken from the
ruins of one of the most beautiful minarets of the town.

On the platform of the railway station, adorned with flags
and wreaths of flowers, the Governor of Samarkand presented
to Sergy a deputation of Sartes, one of the richest tribes of

Turkestan. Behind the station all the soldiers of the garrison of Samarkand, ranged in lines, cheered my husband by loud hurrahs, which produced a great effect upon the natives.

I was not in a condition to respond to civilities just now, looking very hot, dusty and unbrushed, and presented altogether a very disreputable appearance. I would not be seen in such a state, and as it was too late to pay tribute to vanity, I feigned a bad headache in order not to take part at the dinner which had been prepared for us in the state rooms of the stations, transformed into beautifully arrayed saloons.

The railway-line from Samarkand to Tashkend is not yet inaugurated officially, and the whole way is guarded by patrols to prevent the damage frequently caused to the line by hostile natives.

June 6th.—We have crossed this night the so-named Starving Plain. This waste land is well worthy of its denomination. There was nothing but plain, endless plain, always the same dull colour. The soil is arid, and the want of water seemed more pronounced as we went on. The Grand Duke Nicolas Constantinovitch, uncle to our Emperor, who inhabited Turkestan for more than seventeen years, spent the greatest part of his life in this desert, occupying himself with irrigation works in the plain, a part of which he has furrowed with canals. The Grand Duke has spent more than a million roubles already for the digging of these canals, which are to transform the barren soil of the Starving Plain into fertile fields some day. It is a splendid plan, but how is one to get the quantity of water necessary for this purpose?

CHAPTER CXX

TASHKEND

AT ten o'clock in the morning the train stopped at Tashkend station, where we met a royal reception. A great crowd was on the platform and all around the station. The courtyard was full of carriages and natives curious to see us. I think all the inhabitants were gathered there to stare. We mounted into our carriage, drawn by a pair of splendid long-tailed horses which my husband had bought from the widow of the late Governor-General. A hundred Cossacks, and a great number of natives on horseback, escorted us from the station to our house, called a palace. The horses flew along the streets full of people ; enthusiastic cheers resounded as we passed. We nodded to right and left. Great preparations were made to greet us ; the streets were all dressed with flags, the windows and balconies hung with carpets and wreaths of flowers. The photographers made the best of their opportunities and prepared their kodaks for action. We drove fast and soon reached the cathedral, where a Te Deum was sung in our honour. The Bishop in a few hearty words bade us welcome to Tashkend, and pointed out to Sergy that it was the third Asiatic country already which had been confided to him—Erzeroum, Khabarovsk and Tashkend.

From the cathedral we walked to the palace ; a very large crowd, which was waiting outside the church, followed us.

The excitement of the day had utterly exhausted me. I had gone to rest, and slept the sleep of the weary and the just, when the Grand Duke called upon my husband and asked him to give me a beautiful bouquet of roses, freshly cut by the Grand Duke from the garden of his palace, bound with a sand-coloured ribbon, the emblem of the Starving Plain, which was also welcoming me.

On the next day after our arrival, Sergy, surrounded by a brilliant escort of generals and officers, gave audience, as representative of His Imperial Majesty Nicolas II., to the members of Municipal Council, wearing voluminous turbans, who presented to him different deputations. First came a deputation of native notables who delivered to my husband the sum of four thousand roubles, all in gold, offered by the natives for the benefit of the bereaved families of the soldiers killed during the mutiny in Andidjan. They asked Sergy to transmit many expressions of loyalty to the Tzar, as well as their profound indignation on account of the murder of our soldiers. Sergy promised to carry out their wishes, but when the deputies began to comb their beards with their fingers, expressing their satisfaction by sounds reminding one of the howls of wild beasts, my husband, who knew that they were not to be trusted for all their promises and soft speeches, told them, by the aid of an interpreter, that he would take great care that they should keep their word to the very letter. He said besides that the Tzar had more than one hundred and fifty million subjects, and such numbers of soldiers that, in case of a new rebellion, a whole battalion could easily be quartered in every village of Turkestan. The deputies' faces showed disappointment, and fell several degrees. Whence came the representatives of a deputation from the Hindoo colony established at Tashkend, fire-worshippers and traders most of them, bizarre-looking individuals dressed in a sort of long frock-coat, with black velvet caps on their heads? After the presentation was over, Sergy visited the Mussulman quarters of the town and gave his portrait to some of the most notable natives. One of the "imams," who could express himself in Russian pretty well, said to my husband that up to the present the inhabitants of Tashkend celebrated yearly two great feasts— the *Ramadan* and the *Bairam*—but henceforth, after Sergy's appearance amongst them, they would celebrate a third one— his visit to them. For flattering words the Oriental people have not their equal.

Our house is furnished with every luxury one can imagine. There is a fine suite of state rooms with beautiful tapestry and pictures. A sitting-room is coloured mosaic, the ball-room of immense size, with full-length portraits of our Imperial Family hung on the walls, is capable of accommodating about three hundred persons. In the library long tables are covered with illustrated magazines and papers. The centre of the house is topped with a dome of glass; under it is a large winter garden full of beautiful palms and flourishing plants. In the middle of it a fountain bubbled up in a basin of white marble. The house is surrounded by extensive grounds with long shady alleys; it is cool under them even in the most intense heat. Kiosques, grottos and rustic bridges are scattered here and there. A waterfall, three metres high, rushes into a reservoir just opposite my bed-room windows. The gardens are overloaded with fruit, peaches, grapes, apricots, melons, ripening on every side. In Turkestan, fruit of all kind abounds; peaches and apricots are here a common food for pigs. White and black swans swim in the broad arik (canal) winding like a river in the park. A troop of deer walk about freely on the meadows; they come up and examine us fearlessly. About a dozen foxes live at the end of the park, in a large den formerly occupied by a family of bears. In a big cage walk peacocks who wake me every morning by their piercing shrieks.

Our park is a veritable labyrinth; it is surrounded by a wall twenty feet high. Sergy lost himself when he went out riding in the park for the first time.

Our numerous household is cosmopolitan; it consists of Sartes, Tartars, Poles, Cossacks and Germans. At twelve o'clock punctually, when the cannon is fired from the citadel, the head-butler, a very solemn personage, comes to announce that luncheon is on the table. He wears a Bokharian decoration and looks very important with his star. A smart waiter arrayed in a magnific "khalat" attends behind my husband's chair. The aide-de-camps and functionaries on duty are invited to lunch and dinner every day.

The balcony of my bedroom looks out into the park. I used to lounge there for hours in a rocking-chair after dinner. The steps of the sentinel, walking to-and-fro with his gun on his shoulder, were sharply audible. I did not move, I was so cosy here, listening to the monotonous splash of the fountain and the gentle rustling of the wind amongst the branches of the trees. The light breeze brought me the perfume of flowers; from the garden came the scent of heliotropes from a bed beneath the balcony. My thoughts flew away—far, very far, to darling St. Petersburg.

For two days the rain never ceased pouring; there are mud-pools of water everywhere. When the sun had sufficiently dried the streets, we went for a drive through the town, escorted by a platoon of Cossacks. We drove through wide, tree-shaded streets. The flat-topped houses, generally not more than a storey high, are covered with verdure. It is dangerous to build high edifices in the country because of the frequent earthquakes. We were in the hottest part of the day and saw but few people in the streets. From noon to four o'clock the inhabitants of Tashkend take their siesta. When the heat decreases, the native quarters begin to fill with life and local colour. We drove along arcaded streets like narrow corridors towards the bazaar, passing by numerous "tschai-khans" (tea-houses), and were saluted on our passage by profound salaams; the natives pass their hands over their faces and beards, a gesture which signifies that their sentiments towards us are as clear as a well-washed face. Steady-handed barbers are shaving customers on the threshold of their shops. Vociferating sellers sit on low tables behind piles of fruit and vegetables. Imperturbable and passive Sartes, sitting cross-legged on rugs, smoke their kalyans and appear to be plunged in profound meditation. Here is a group of "douvanas" (Mecca pilgrims) wearing sharp-pointed caps; they are listening to a "maddah" (street story-teller). The Sarte women leave their houses hidden beneath their "farandja," a dark mantle which covers them from head to foot, and makes them look like guys. They follow more strictly than any other daughters of the Orient the principles of the Mussulman religion, and cover their faces with black horse-hair nets. I have seen veiled Turkish women at Constantinople, but in such a transparent manner, that they differed but little from our European ladies wearing slight veils over their hats. At Cairo the veils are thicker, but for that, the Egyptian women leave their eyes uncovered. The Mussulman women in India go out in the streets unveiled, just the same as our Kirghis women. The natives are very fond of music; in every tent of the nomad tribes, in every "khaoul" (house) one can see a two-stringed instrument called "doutarra," a sort of guitar. The Sarte makes even of his "arba," a massive cart, an instrument of barbaric music, putting a stick into the wheels, so that the stick catching the spokes, reproduces the sound of the drum, which resounds through the streets of Tashkend, to the accompaniment of the monotonous singing of the proprietor of the "arba," a wailing, winding chant which, as it had no end, may well have had no beginning. The Sarte sings always in a high-pitched voice, for to sing in a basso voice is considered unbecoming. The "arba" is put upon two enormous wooden wheels and driven by one horse, on whose back sits astride the carter, his legs stretched on the shafts. The Sartes never grease their "arbas," and the noise produced by these screeching wheels compose a terrible discord, accompanied by the piercing cry of the camels, and the howling of vagrant dogs.

The Sartes are perfectly indifferent to the change of temperature; neither heat nor cold affects them in any way. They have no stoves in their houses; a hole in the floor is the family cooking-place, and an opening is broken through the roof for the emission of smoke.

The streets are watered several times a day, which lays the dust, but contributes also to increase pernicious fevers. The climate is very unwholesome in Turkestan; immediately after sunset it becomes so damp that it is dangerous to remain out of doors. In June the heat is intolerable.

I held a reception once a week; between two and five about a hundred persons would pass through our saloons. The day I held my first reception, the large drawing-room was crowded with guests. I had to take up the subject of politics and be amiable to everyone. I was so tired with having had to talk all the time that my tongue, having refused to obey me, I said good-bye instead of good-afternoon to a belated visitor. The Grand-Duke was amongst our guests and gained my sympathy at once. He is not a bit haughty and altogether charming, and I felt perfectly at ease with him. He is such a nice-looking man, towering nearly a head over everyone. When taking leave the Duke asked me to come and drink a cup of chocolate the next day. He was awfully amiable to me, and took me all over his palace—a veritable museum. Amongst other curiosities he showed me a watch made by Briguet, which goes without being wound up. It is put into the pocket, and after you have taken a few steps, the watch is already set going for twenty-four hours. There exists only two examples of such watches; Briguet valued them at ten thousand francs each. Alexander II. possessed the first one. Being free from all household management, I feel myself on a visit here. The first days of my arrival, I did not know how to while away the time, wishing for even the mildest adventure, something that would put a little spice into the insipidity of our lives. I would like a row now and then just to enliven things a little. For distraction I tried to pick a quarrel with Sergy, making tragedies of pure nonsense, but it takes two to make a quarrel, and Sergy is a man of peace and is a desperately calm person, and finds it necessary for the sake of domestic quiet to put up with all my tempers; nothing could put him out of patience.

Every day I grew more and more home-sick. I often was in tears, not taking interest in anything. The awful climate was injurious to my health. I have no appetite, no sleep. The pink has gone out of my cheeks. Someone had cast an evil eye upon me to be sure. I've got so thin and pale that I am afraid to look at myself in the glass. Sergy, who reads my face, which is a mirror of all passive emotions, like a familiar book, grew alarmed and called in a doctor, but no doctor's prescriptions were any good for my complaint. Mephistopheles whispered into my ear that instead of making me swallow horrid mixtures, the best remedy for me would be to fly back to Petersburg, but I have decided not to let myself be tempted by the enemy of mankind. At the end of a month I began to feel myself at home.

I work hard at my book and give much time to my English concertina. This melodious instrument leads to the transmission of the most difficult violin literature. I am passionately fond of music; having inherited that passion from my father who had the true artistic temperament and was a gifted musician and a splendid pianist.

The life that I had to lead was entirely out of my line. I hate state receptions, state manners; grandeurs weigh heavily upon me, and etiquette to the laws of which I must submit. I have got a court like a little queen, everyone is charming to me, but I, ungrateful being, should have liked warm friendship far better than respectful homage. I had hundreds of acquaintances, and not a single intimate friend, and I was badly in need of one. I hated my reception days when callers flocked in on us, and I had to talk to people, only for the sake of talking, pretending to be pleased when all the time I want to say "Oh, do go away!" One of the disadvantages of being the wife of a Governor-General was the necessity of suffering bores gladly. As soon as the clock struck six, and the last guest had departed, I hastened to step down from my pedestal and put on with delight my dressing-gown and stretch myself in an easy chair. How I long to get away from all these ties of public life, to stay at St. Petersburg and live the life of a simple mortal, independent, and apart from the so-called world, and be free of all pomp. But there is no use my thinking about it. It's silly to want the moon.

I am selected for President of the Benevolent Society of the city of Tashkend. The meetings of the committee are held in our house. I presided at a long table covered with green cloth. At the first assembly I felt timid and embarrassed for many eyes were on me, and for the moment I almost forgot how to get on with the formal little speech I had learned so carefully. I was grateful when Sergy, who sat opposite to me, came to my relief and did all the talking for me. All at once my courage returned to me, and I took an animated part in the project to found an asylum for old men and women. It was decided to organise for that purpose a great charity feast with theatricals, bazaar, tombola, and what not! I issued about 700 invitations, with an indirect allusion to the subject of offerings which I claimed for the forthcoming lottery.

The opening of the new asylum was celebrated with great pomp. The Directress of the establishment hurried forward to meet us and led us straight to the chapel where a Te Deum was sung, after which we were shown through the asylum, containing 600 old people of both sexes. It gave also shelter to an officer's daughter who was not quite right in her mind. Her bridegroom had been mixed up in some political affair and sent to the galleys and she had gone mad from the shock. The poor insane woman is barely thirty years old, but looks fifty at least, arrayed in a costume which our grandmothers wore in their youth. She leads a very secluded life, and never speaks to anyone. We saw her walking in the garden her eyes fixed on the ground, pretending not to see us.

On that same day we visited an asylum for the lunatics. The whole staff of doctors came up to meet us. We walked first to the womens' section. The patients were wandering in the park in groups. One of them came up to my husband to entreat him to release her, asserting that she was in perfect health, but would certainly go raving mad if she was forced to spend one more night in such company. That woman had come a few days ago to ask Sergy to permit her to embrace the Mussulman religion. She told him also that in hatred of one of the high dignitaries of the city, she had written to him, that she cursed him and all his family. It appeared she bought a revolver with the intention of shooting him. She was seized in time, luckily, and brought into this lunatic asylum to test her sanity. Another insane creature, grinning idiotically, approached me and stared at me from head to foot. She became very fierce all at once, and began to abuse me, calling me all sorts of bad names, and accused me of having stolen her best frock. When we approached the section of the raving lunatics, roars and shouts reached our ears. Though trembling with fear I would not be led away and kept tight hold of Sergy's arm, clinging fast to him. Behind an iron-barred window we saw a horrible moustached creature, standing with her arms folded across her chest, glaring ferociously at us with an expression so malignant, that Satan would have been jealous of her. She believes herself to be a man and becomes terribly agitated when she sees a woman. She beckoned to me suddenly making dreadful gestures and demoniac grimaces. Sergy hurried me away. We made but a short visit to the men's section. We saw a man mad with love for the Empress. The poor maniac writes long letters every day to his lady-love, but receiving no answer, he guesses that everybody plays him false and that his letters are not sent. He was lying on his bed when we approached him and turned suddenly his face to the wall and his back to us. I heaved a sigh of relief when we left these sad quarters.

In July great festivals were arranged to clelebrate the twenty-third anniversary of the taking of Tashkend. There was a parade of troops on the square before the palace, after which my husband proceeded to the tomb of our soldiers killed during the siege of the town and laid a wreath on their grave.

We gave a grand dinner that same day for about one hundred guests. An amusing incident occurred during this meal. Among the guests there were some important natives who had come from the end of the country. One of these men, who had never tasted European cooking, took a pot of mustard for a separate dish, and swallowed a whole spoonful of it. He naturally gasped, choked, whilst tears ran in rivulets down his cheeks. His neighbour at table, who had not noticed the proceeding with the mustard, asked him the cause of his grief. The native, heaving a deep sigh, answered that he had just called to mind his deceased father, and that to-day was the anniversary of his death; he had been drowned in the Amou-Daria, whilst sailing on the river in a small boat. Meanwhile his left hand neighbour, a compatriot of his, had followed his example, having also regaled himself with mustard, and with the same consequences, of course. The son of the drowned man was wickedly rejoiced at his blunder, and asked in his most velvety tone, "Why does my brother cry?" "Because I regret that thou did'st not disappear beyond the mysterious regions of the Amou-Daria together with thy father!" was the cunning reply. Everybody laughed when the interpreter translated this dialogue between the two natives.

Our life had many dark moments. There had been a great excitement these last few days; bad news had arrived, a new rebellion was apprehended. We stood on a volcano that might explode at any moment; the only thing to ask ourselves was when will it begin to pour out its flames. Anonymous letters, splashed with blood, announced to my husband that on the night of the 30th July, a holy war would break out. What troublesome times we are living through!

One side of our park is joined to the native quarters of the town, and a little shiver ran down my back each time the clear voice of the muezzin chanted from the minaret of the neighbouring mosque, calling the faithful to prayer: "*Allah il Allah.*" (There is no God but God.)

Though things had looked serious for some time, they seemed to have quieted down again. Thanks to energetic means, the agitation in the country was soon calmed down.

When Autumn arrived, I started for St. Petersburg. It was arranged that my husband was to rejoin me in a few weeks' time, and that we should return together to Tashkend in the Spring. I hated to part from Sergy; I shall want him horribly, but I must see to the publishing of the first part of my book and end the last part; absolute quiet is essential for rapid work. Our separation would not be a very prolonged one, and Sergy was to write every day.

August 9th.—My husband had to go on business to Bokhara and Andidjan, the place of the recently appeased mutiny. I will profit by it by making a part of the journey with him.

We started to-day at ten o'clock in the morning. The station was quite full. All the military and civil authorities of the town, and all the members of the committee of the Benevolence Society, came to wish me a happy journey and safe return. I had to shake hands with such a lot of people that my glove burst in several places, and I received such a lot of bouquets that they were hard to hold; the supply of beautiful flowers in my car made it look like a flower-shop.

August 11th.—This morning I had to part with Sergy and

we went each our several ways. My car was coupled to the express, and when the time for parting with my husband came, I cried so awfully that I had to borrow Sergy's pocket-handkerchief It was a very painful moment and I found it hard to tear myself away; it seemed as if we could never finish saying good-bye. The guide gave the signal and the train moved off. Soon Sergy's face was out of sight and I was left to my thoughts and to my loneliness. The know-ledge that the train was bearing me further and further from Sergy, and that every moment was increasing the distance between us, made me wild. I threw myself back in the corner of the carriage and had a good cry.

I am well taken care of. Sergy had given me into the charge of one of his aide-de-camps who was going to Kras-novodsk, and asked him to take me to the steamer.

August 12th.—The same scenery is repeated with fatiguing uniformity; the desolate sun-baked desert spread out, and the yellow steppes joined with the horizon. The journey seems to last ages.

August 13th.—The heat is not so intense to-day. The sky is grey and big drops of rain begin to fall. At 8 o'clock in the morning we arrived at Krasnovodsk, where I was received by the agent of the steamboat company, an old admiral retired from the service. The *Tropic*, a boat built in England, was reserved for my crossing. I have the best cabin; a placard placed over the door bears the following iscription in English: "To accommodate four seamen," but one could easily place a dozen of men in it. It proves to what an extent the English consider the comfort of their sailors.

I went to my lonely bed in rather a depressed frame of mind. Sleep would not come. I was seized with an ungovernable longing to see Sergy, to hear his voice, and my mind was filled with only one thought I must go back! It was too late to turn back now. The captain came at the door to wish me good-night, but it was rather a mockery, under the circumstances, for I never closed my eyes, thanks to my blue devils and the horrid rolling of the boat.

August 14th.—We had very rough weather in the night and were dancing all the time on formidable waves; our boat was creaking in every joint. I heard the sailors running on the upper-deck and the watch-officer shouting orders in a voice of thunder. What did all this uproar mean? In a terrible fright I jumped out of bed and dressing speedily hurried on deck. It was our boat changing its course and going out into the open sea instead of following the shore to avoid the breakers. The captain came to tell me that I had nothing to be afraid of and could go to sleep in security. He promised for to-morrow a sea as calm as a lake.

The captain is awfully nice to me, and performs an endless series of little attentions, looking to my comfort. He has, as it appears, the intention to fatten me up like the cattle destined for the slaughter-house, but sea-sickness takes away all my appetite.

August 15th.—The distant coasts of the Caucasus appear like a grey outline. Towards ten o'clock in the morning the *Tropic* landed us at Petrovsk five hours behind time. The captain insisted upon my passage being free, which cost me a great deal more in tips for the crew. He accompanied me with his officers to the railway-station.

CHAPTER CXXI

ST. PETERSBURG

August 18th.—It was pouring with rain this morning when we arrived at St. Petersburg. My mother was at the stati n to meet me, and took me to the new house my husband had bought in one of the most fashionable quarters of the city.

I had a letter four pages long from Sergy, full of interesting detail about his interview with the Emir at Kerminch, and of his journey to Andidjan, where the recent mutiny had taken place. A crowd of prostrated figures, their faces against the ground, were awaiting his arrival. After a Te Deum sung on the square before the cathedral, my husband distributed to the wounded soldiers a whole lot of crosses of the order of St. George, whilst cannons were fired. From Andidjan Sergy travelled on to Asch, a town situated near the frontier of the Pamir, in a mountainous region named The Roof of the World. An old Kirghise woman, called The Queen of the Alai, aged 87, came up to my husband supported by her two sons, white-bearded old men. This Asiatic Princess reminded one of the antique " Mother of the Gracchi." A few days after his return to Tashkend Sergy received the visit of the heir to the throne of Khiva.

I saw no visitors and went nowhere, working hard at my book till late in the night, keeping awake with black coffee. At the end of the week I found solitude intolerable and began to feel awfully dull. Every day was the same, the hours seemed years. It was so hard to be alone here! I had seldom experienced much of my own society and was sick of my own company. Sergy being absent, the world seemed one great blank. I never had him out of my thoughts for one minute. Sometimes I had the impulse to take the first train and fly back to Tashkend.

October had passed and Sergy did not come. I bombarded him with desperate letters full of exclamation points, always putting the stereotyped question when he would arrive.

I read in the papers that the plague had broken out near Samarkand, carrying away every day a great many victims, and that the Prince of Oldenbourg was going there with a medical expedition. I was getting awfully anxious about Sergy and felt tempted to throw up everything and rush back to him. I had the most awful dreams and imagined all sorts of calamities and spoiled my eyes with tears, having only one thought, to rejoin my husband. I could endure my suspense no longer and telegraphed to Sergy, imploring him to let me come to Tashkend. I waited with feverish impatience for his permission to start instantly, but my husband, who never refused me in trifles, did not give in when it concerned serious matters. He would not of hear this; he firmly opposed my arrival, and wired to me to be reasonable and have patience; but patience, alas, was contrary to my temperament. My hundred and one wishes were always fulfilled until now, and when it has come to the hundred and second wish—stop? Oh on! Sergy's opposition made me only the more obstinately determined to have my own way. I despatched him a long letter, an ultimatum in fact. I wrote that if he did not arrive at St. Petersburg in the course of a fortnight, I should start to Tashkend without awaiting his permission. I worried Sergy till I finally got him to consent to my going over to rejoin him. My maid brought me a telegram from my husband with my tea one morning. I opened it, and read one word. "Come!" I wanted to leave at once in spite of mother and some friends who tried to make me understand the danger I was running in going to meet the plague; but I am a fatalist and fear nothing. All their persuasions fell on stony ground. If they think that they will stop me, they are very much mistaken; no consideration of wisdom will ever induce me not to do what I want to do. I would not hear reason and was in a hurry to go back to Tashkend. With me to think has always been to act. The sooner I start the better.

October 17th.—I am off to Tashkend to-day, with Maria Michaelovna and my maid Mina. All the cars of our train are occupied by the members of the medical expedition sent to Tashkend to fight against the plague. It consists of forty doctors and ten sisters of mercy. The rain is coming down in torrents, but when I felt happy I was not in the least aware that the sun was not shining, and I am so happy now to rejoin Sergy! Our train is an express and rushes past nearly all the stations. We hadn't time for dinner and snatched a sandwich at a railway buffet, that had probably been waiting more than a week for travellers to arrive.

October 21st.—We are at Petrovsk at ten o'clock in the morning. I saw the *Tzarevitch*, a great ship ready for sea, with steam up, making ready to cast off and be gone; the gang way was just about to be withdrawn when we got on board.

I am again on the hateful element. The sea is covered with foam, the wind blows impetuously, rising in enormous billows. We have to struggle both with the hurricane and the swift current which does not permit us to approach the coasts of Derbent where we had to put in. I suffer a great deal from sea-sickness, although I have made three voyages round the world. All the passengers look green and miserable.

October 22nd.—At eleven o'clock we arrived at Baku, where a very disagreeable surprise awaited us. We have to leave the boat and go over to the *Prince Bariatinsky*, a poor little thing, little more than a yacht. The *Tzarevitch* is retained for the Prince of Oldenbourg.

We made ourselves as comfortable as we could in our stuffy little cabin. Towards evening we entered a dense fog, and could not see four paces ahead. The captain does not leave the poop, and every five minutes the fog-horn throws piercing shrieks into the black night.

October 23rd.—At daybreak the fog cleared away. The sea is quite smooth. We are going full speed, making fifteen knots an hour.

At ten o'clock we entered the port of Krasnovodsk. My car was attached to the express of the Prince of Oldenbourg, who arrived in the afternoon on the *Tzarevitch*. Before starting the Prince sent his aide-de-camp to ask if I could receive him. I replied that I felt very tired for the moment but hoped that I should be able to see His Highness during our long railway journey.

October 25th.—I found a telegram from Sergy waiting for me at Karmineh, telling me by what train he would meet me at the station of Kata-Kourgan. I am happy, happy, happy!

We had a long time to wait at Kermineh because the Emir had come to see the Prince of Oldenbourg, and our train was not due to start for two mortal hours. I must just have patience and wait, but as patience is an unknown word in my vocabulary, I grumbled awfully at the delay. This time I travelled incognito and was left in peace ; my blinds were scrupulously drawn down. Trying to shorten the hours that separated me from my husband, I went to bed directly after dinner. Oh, I wish it was to-morrow !

October 26th.—It was only in the middle of the night that we arrived at Kata-Kourgan, where Sergy's waggon was joined to our train. I can't find words to express my joy !

It was about eleven o'clock when we stopped at the station of Samarkand. Everywhere was the smell of pungent disinfectant. We are going to remain two days here. Sergy put up at the house of General Fedoroff, Governor of Samarkand. The town is ten miles from the station, but I prefer to remain in my car, standing alone in a side-track of the line. The road leading to the station was illuminated at night with different coloured lanterns hanging from the trees.

October 27th.—The chief of the station, who took care of

my sleep, and was afraid that I should be aroused by the shrieks of the manœuvring engines, gave order to the engine-drivers to moderate their transports when blowing their whistles.

The Medical Expedition has arrived this morning. Four lady-physicians, accompanied by twelve sisters of mercy, called upon me in the afternoon. They told me that a part of the expedition had been sent to Anzob, a pestilence-stricken village, and got there with great difficulty. There was no carriage-road and they had to make their way by precipitous paths in the mountains.

My husband proposed to the Medical Expedition to organise an ocular ambulatory inspection during their stay at Samarkand which was especially necessary in this country, where eye-diseases predominate, thanks to the rare and superficial connection of the natives with water. Their famous religious ablutions consist in the submersion of their hands in a vase filled with water of doubtful cleanliness, in which they wash away their sins ; and after that they dash the water over their faces, and it happens sometimes that a whole crowd of natives have already performed their ablutions in that basin of water ! One can easily imagine the hygiene of this ceremony.

October 28th.—This morning a group of Asiatic princes were presented to my husband in his railway-car ; amongst them there was the pretender to the throne of Afghanistan Isaac-Khan—leading his little son by the hand. Before that Prince several pretenders to the throne of Afghanistan had chosen Samarkand for their residence, amongst them the famous Abdurakham, who, after having been raised to the throne, had shown his gratitude to the friendliness of the Russians, by playing false, Under pain of death, the entrance of Russian subjects into his territory was forbidden. Isaac-Khan is poor as a rat ; he is living on a petty allowance of the Russian government, and though he has very little hope of succeeding to the throne of Afghanistan, he brings up his son as if the throne would belong to him one day or other. When the boy is asked who he is, he answers with an air of great importance : " I am Grand Sirdar " (General-in Chief), but for the moment his army consists only of half a dozen ragged servants. I took an instinctive dislike to his father, and saw " Borgia " written all over him. In fact I believe the prince a man capable of anything, and though honied words come readily to his lips, his eyes flash an evil look, and hardly ever meet those of the person with whom he talks. There was something in his appearance which distinctly alarmed me. He would have made a perfect villain in a melodrama, with a beard growing almost reaching his eyes. It was not a face that one would care to meet when alone in the dark. Amongst the exotic princes I saw the suzerain of a small principality, who after having become a Russian subject, received as recompense the grade of major. He wears a "khalat" with Russian epaulettes, girded with a green sash, a sign that he is a descendant of the Prophet. When the presentations ended, my husband distributed medals and "khalats" to the native notables who came up to him preparing their most engaging smiles. After having received their gift, they retired backwards murmuring profuse thanks and touching their forehead, mouth and heart, contriving to stimulate on their faces sentiments of profound gratitude, though nourishing a profound hatred towards the Russians. From these treacherous people one can expect anything; it is an eternal armed-peace with them.

October 30th.—At ten o'clock precisely we arrived at Tashkend-station. My unexpected arrival was welcomed with joy and cordiality. I distributed my nods and smiles on each hand; the back of my neck was sore with bowing.

Energetic measures are being taken to check the progress of the epidemic. The plague is daily decreasing, and the Emperor charged the Prince of Oldenbourg to thank my husband for the energetic measures he had taken to battle with it.

The first leaves begin to fall and the park looks very dismal. The weather is horrible, the sky leaden-grey. I hear the monotonous wail of the wind and the rain beating against the window-panes.

This time my stay at Tashkend was but a very short one. At the end of a fortnight I was on my way back to St. Petersburg.

November 12th.—When I arrived at Samarkand, a telegram from the Emir was brought to me. The Asiatic Sovereign asked to be warned in advance, so that I could be received with fitting ceremony at Kermineh where he wanted to meet me, but I refused and begged him by wire not to trouble himself, because we passed Kermineh by night.

November 14th.—The Amu-Daria is very low at this season. The big river in several places forms wide sandbanks, and this time I was not a bit afraid to cross the bridge.

November 16th.—We arrived this morning at Krasnovodsk, where I took my passage on the *Korniloff.* The weather is bright and clear; the sea is shining in the sun, promising us a favourable crossing.

November 17th.—The wind has changed during the night, bringing bad weather. After dinner the captain came to ask how I was and told me that the lights of Petrovsk had been sighted, and that another half-hour will find us on shore. We had four hours to wait before the train started.

November 21st.—I arrived safe and sound at St. Petersburg, having had quite enough of railway and sea.

Our capital was very animated this season : soirées, dinners, concerts, the whirl went on, but I shut myself within four walls and scarcely saw anyone, I can't enjoy anything when Sergy is not there. I am reckoned as being eccentric in leading the life of a nun in her cell—a very spacious one, it is true—but I have a sublime indifference to public opinion, having my own way of looking at things, and am not, as a rule, meddling with other people's business ; why do they meddle with mine? I am free of my own actions, and can do as I like, I suppose! Goethe says: " The happiest of mortals is he who finds his happiness in his own home." I can, therefore, be placed among the happy ones.

It is music which is my passion. In my spare moments I had some lessons on the guitar, but I soon put an end to them, the cords of the instrument hurting my fingers. Then I bought a cithern, the cords of which hurt me still more, and resolved to give myself up, as before, to the concertina.

At last I decided to come out of my shell and went sometimes to theatres and concerts. Volodia Rougitzki, a gifted boy-pianist of thirteen, enchanted me by his performance of the works of Chopin, Liszt and Rubinstein. I wonder if this " Wunderkind " will ever become a " Wundermann ! "

Antonine Kontski came to St. Petersburg to give a concert. He had a tremendous success ; the audience was enthusiastic and the applause was deafening. I enjoyed his concert a great deal and applauded so much that I split my gloves. For the last encore the audience demanded " Lé Reveil du Lion," one of Kontski's masterpieces. Then the old maestro returned and bowed to the wildly excited people and said : " My Lion is weary, he is going to bed, but next week I'll bring out my wild animal, if you still desire to hear his roaring."

My husband is promoted to the rank of General-in-Chief. He was Brigadier-General when I married him, and it is now the third and last rank that I enjoy with him.

In the middle of December Sergy sent me a telegram to say that he had taken a six months' leave. We decided to spend Christmas in Mertchik, the beautiful estate belonging to my husband's elder brother, situated in the government of Kharkoff. I started for Mertchik to meet Sergy in the highest of spirits. A week later, we were both back to St. Petersburg.

When Spring came on, I began to learn to ride the bicycle. After some inevitable tumbles, I soon surmounted the difficulties of this sport.

May 17th.—The day of our departure for Tashkend has come. This time we decided to steam down the Volga from Nijni-Novgorod to Astrakhan. When we arrived at Nijni-Novgorod we went straight to the boat. Numerous porters with heavy loads on their backs invaded the deck; they are able to bear extraordinary burdens. We saw a man carrying a piano, coming up a narrow plank on to our steamer, just as easily as a world-famed athlete would have performed it.

Our boat has weighed anchor. The weather is beautiful. After dinner we lay stretched on our rocking-chairs on deck, inhaling with delight the fresh evening breeze; sea-gulls followed us. An obliging sailor, a good-looking sun-tanned young fellow, brought me big lumps of black bread to feed them. We ply between two low and flat banks, only reeds round about and fishing men's huts here and there. I must say, though it is not very patriotic of me, that the Volga is not to be compared to the romantic Rhine, which, in its turn, is not to be compared to the lovely shores of the Amour, one of the most beautiful rivers in the world. During our numerous voyages we had seen the Mississippi, the Yan-tze-Kiang, the river of Saint Lawrence and many other big rivers, and I find that the Amour surpasses them all by the beauty of its banks.

May 18th.—This morning we arrived at Kazan. Large barges come up to unload our cargo of coal. We remained here till six o'clock and Sergy went to see the Governor of the city, having to discuss different questions concerning the Mussulmans, who compose the ninth part of the population of Russia. The principal centre of their domicile is the Caucasus, Crimea, Turkestan and the Government of Kazan. At first sight it seems that the Mussulmans of Turkestan and those of Kazan differ widely in conditions and characteristics. They have different histories, and last but not least, quite different modes of life, but in reality it is not so, the dream of the splendour and glory of their Prophet unites them all. That refers not only to the Mussulmans inhabiting Russia, but just as much to the millions of believers peopling India, Turkey and other Mussulman countries. The task of administering equal justice to Moslems and Christians is a difficult one. The Mussulmans are all clever diplomatists from their youth. Talleyrand said that the tongue was given to the man to hide his thoughts, and the Mussulmans, who have understood it long before him, profit largely by this principle. I was present at an interesting interview which took place between my·husband and some Buriate syndics during our travel through the Transbaikalia provinces; they were Buddhists all of them. The interview took place soon after the nomad Buriates were placed on a level with the Russian population, perhaps not quite to the satisfaction of the Buriates. When Sergy asked them if they were satisfied with the change of their social position, the syndics replied frankly that they were but tolerably pleased. With these people one could come to an understanding somehow, but it is quite different with the Mussulmans. This is a discourse that my husband held with a group of Moslem syndics who were presented to him in one of his voyages in the provinces of Turkestan, all standing with sweeping salaams from floor to forehead, their turbaned heads bent low. Sergy's words were translated into their native tongue by an interpreter : " Do you remember the everlasting wars you had in the time when you were under the dominion of your khans, when nobody knew that, leading a peaceful and easy-going life to-day, your blood would not be shed to-morrow? Do you not feel happier now, when the labourer can gather in his harvest quietly, and the merchant sell his wares in safety?" And all the syndics, smoothing their long white beards, replied in chorus : " *Hosch, Taksir!*" (It is true, master) " Do you remember that not long ago spears were driven into you and that you were condemned to death without any judgment? Are you punished now without any plausible cause? " *Hosch, Taksir!*" asserted the syndics bowing very low. " Did your administrators ever build schools, hospitals, nicely-paved roadways? Did they give you an impartial court of justice, and incorruptible functionaries?" At these last words a swift change swept over their faces with a malicious smile they exchanged a look, and their countenances again remained expressionless, as if carved in wood, and the same stereotype answer was heard : " *Hosch, Taksir!*" And only accidentally, you could learn from the junior natives, that their elders remembered with veneration the time when they were not sure of the following day and when they were pierced through with spears. They weren't in want of any innovation either, provided that their " Crescent " should be glorified everywhere. In such conditions, when the population does not come to meet the enterprises of the administration, all the measures concerning the Mussulmans, scattered about Russia, must be taken by the administrators. It is precisely on this subject that my husband had conferred with the Governor of Kazan, whilst I pined alone in my stuffy cabin.

As soon as Sergy returned on board, we continued our way. The smell of naphtha pursues us. The surface of the water is covered with large spots of naphtha all the colours of the rainbow. It is pretty to look at, but this substance is injurious to the fish ; the best species of which have disappeared from the Volga.

The night is splendid, the sky is all studded with stars, and I have no wish to go to bed.

May 20th.—The weather has changed, and the Volga is stirred into little rippling waves by the passing of the wind.

We are at Samarkand in the afternoon. A large company

of young ladies, pupils of the Institute of Orenbourg and scholars of the corps of cadets, came on board our steamer; they are bound for Turkestan to spend their summer holidays. An elderly grandmother of one of the cadets had charge of the young people. The officers and functionaries serving in Taskhend have the right to send their children to be educated in Orenbourg on the government's account.

From Samara to Saratov the Volga is more like a lake than a river. We pass under an immense iron bridge, the building of which cost seven million roubles. I remained all the time on deck, admiring the beautiful banks along which rise forest-clothed hills.

Towards four o'clock in the afternoon we arrived at Saratov. A company of Cossacks took passage on our boat. The men came from Orenbourg and are going to serve their time in Turkestan for three years. After dinner the Cossacks sang in chorus and danced wild jigs on the deck, whilst, on the other hand, a man with a green turban, which indicated that he was a Mecca pilgrim, went through the necessary forms of prayer on the rug at his feet, with his face to the East, first standing, then kneeling, then prostrating himself.

May 21st.—The banks of the Volga are low and sandy in these parts; the sky has become grey, the water has taken a dull colour, and the rain is beginning to fall heavily.

In the afternoon we arrived at Astrakhan and were immediately surrounded by a noisy crowd of Kalmucks, Tartars and Persians. We had a jolly dinner on deck. My husband's aide-de-camps and attachés were so amusing and merry. They ordered champagne and drank my health. Mr. Baumgarten, one of the attachés, the soul of the company, when raising his glass to me, made a most charming speech; he said that my presence embellished their journey and that they regretted awfully that our arrival at Tashkend would put an end to the pleasure of having a good deal of my company, for we only met at meals.

Dinner over, we had music in the saloon. After my solo on the concertina, Mr. Baumgarten, who had been inspired by my performance, and was by nature somewhat of a poet, improvised a piece of poetry of the most tender nature, with the following dedication: "To Mrs. Barbara Doukhovskoy, in remembrance of a never-to-be-forgotten night on the Volga." It is spoken there of love, moon and the rest. The poetry ended with the words, "Oh, enchanting night on the Volga, can I ever forget thee?" How sweetly poetical! Who could have believed fat Mr. Baumgarten to be so gifted!

May 22nd.—The Volga is so broad that the shores disappear; only a narrow yellow line of bank is to be seen. At dawn we changed our steamer for a larger one—the *Equator*. We had to part from the Volga here; our boat stole out towards the open sea.

The neigbourhood of Astrakhan plays a great part in the life of the Transcaspian provinces; all sorts of wares and products are imported there in great quantity. This time our steamer is loaded with barrels of beer.

The wind raises great waves, which sweep our deck. We shall have a good tossing about on the treacherous Caspian Sea, no doubt.

May 23rd.—I have slept very badly the whole night, because of the intense heat and the horrid rolling of the ship; every hour I heard the change of watch ringing. At last I saw the morning twilight entering by the port-hole. A brown-coloured lamb, brought by our sailors from Persia, squeezed himself through the half-open door of my cabin; he was on friendly terms with my little pug-nosed Chinese dog, Mokho, and both animals began to chase each other, making an awful noise.

May 24th.—Horrible night! A heavy gale blowing all the time. The sailors couldn't hear the words of command; we rolled unmercifully.

We arrived in the morning at Krasnovodsk and walked to the train which was waiting for us near the pier. During the short walk I had to fight against the wind, which did its utmost to carry off my hat, and blew my umbrella into a sail.

Before starting we were shown the railway-carriage which had just been presented to the Emir by our Emperor; it impressed me by its splendour. This carriage, painted blue and ornamented with golden stars, will be very useful to the Emir when the Orenbourg railway-line is terminated, for he goes for a cure to the Caucasus every year.

May 25th.—What a heat! The roof of my car is covered with a thick layer of earth to protect it from the rays of the burning sun, but it is of no use, we are roasted alive all the same.

This morning we nearly ran over a camel. The encounter with these quadrupeds is very disagreeable, for it is only by repeated loud whistles that our engine-driver can make them leave the rails; they kept running before the train all the time.

May 26th.—It is Sunday to-day. When we approached the station of Merv, church-bells began to toll. It was a church-car which was waiting to be hooked on to our train, and thus we had Mass whilst crossing the vast desert.

May 27th.—At seven o'clock in the morning we are at Kermineh, where the Emir had come to welcome us. Opposite the platform was erected a large tent in which a copious lunch was prepared ; but I did not leave my car, feigning a bad headache. A band of native musicians came to divert me with their weird music, which made me grind my teeth. A beautiful bouquet was brought to me from the Emir, together with a rich casket containing a pair of ear-rings with diamonds as large as hazel nuts.

The Emir invited my husband and his suite to dine at his summer residence, eight miles from the station. In their absence the soldiers of the Bokharian watch-guard were lying stretched out full length in the shade, under the trees, indulging in a *dolce far niente*.

My husband returned late in the night and we continued on our way. To Sergy the palace of the Emir proved a disappointment. It is an ugly building of no particular kind of architecture ; the apartments are decorated with pictures, statues and ornaments of every sort, stuck up anyhow and everywhere. The Emir regaled my husband with a Lucullus repast, with champagne in profusion, but the Emir drank only lemonade, fermented drinks being forbidden by the Koran.

May 28th.—At last we are nearing Tashkend. Towards noon our train stopped at the railway-station, full of people. After having gone through the proceedings of hasty greetings with all present, we went to our carriage. On our passage native musicians blew with all their might into pipes of enormous length, raising them to the skies. They performed such beastly sounds that I feared our horses would take fright and bolt.

A few days after our arrival, three foreign tourists paid an unexpected visit to Tashkend : Sven-Hedin, the renowned Swedish Pamir and Thibet explorer, who had written a book about these countries ; MacSwinee, an English colonel going out to India to command a Bengal regiment ; and Mr. Herbert Powell, an English traveller going to try the shortest way leading from London to India, the future railway-line. For the present the English make this journey, *via* Brindisi and the Suez Canal, in three weeks' time, but as soon as the Russian and British railroad join, the trip will take but eight days. Only five hundred miles are wanting for the line to be completed, but political com-binations are hindering the work. Mr. Powell had passed one month in Moscow to study the Russian language, so difficult for strangers. Nevertheless, many English officers serving in India speak our language, and it is a great pity that the same cannot be said of the Russian officers who serve in Turkestan. Notwithstanding their long sojourn in that country, they do not speak the native language. It is quite recently that a school was organised where the Hindu-stani language is taught. We had also a visit from a French

Academician, Mr. St. Yves, a member of the French Academy, who was going to Thibet to explore the lake Koukou-Nor, and of an English engineer, Mr. Wilson, who had come to Tashkend to study the system of local irrigation. The greater part of the soil of Turkestan, as that of India, would have presented long ere this a veritable earthly paradise if it were not for the want of water. The Government and the inhabitants are doing everything in their power to overcome this difficulty. They profit by the proximity of every river, and if there is no river, they dig artesian wells.

The English, in general, are very much interested in everything concerning Turkestan. I read an article about my husband which came out in the *Daily Chronicle*. I quote the following from the London newspaper :—" Every English officer, who understands the problem of Oriental politics, must know of what great importance is the centralisation of Russian powers in Asia. For the moment sixty thousand men are united under the command of General Doukhovskoy, one of the most able officers of the Russian army." We gave a great dinner to the foreign travellers. After the end of the repast, we went into the park, illuminated with coloured lanterns to let them see the dances of the " batchas " (native boys arrayed in woman's dress). The women in the Orient are not allowed to participate at public performances, and their parts are always taken by men. The courts of the suzerains of Central Asia and India boast of their troops of " batchas," effeminate boys with long plaited hair, arrayed in sumptuous silk robes. In Tashkend the " batchas " are quite different. It was grown-up youths who were brought up to us, wearing white calico shirts and heavy boots which had not seen any polish for a long time. A band of native musicians, sitting on their heels on a carpet spread upon the grass, began to beat the cords of a kind of cithern, and the would-be " batchas " started turning around, whilst the musicians accelerated their time. The performance could scarcely be called a dance ; it was rather a swift walk within a circle. Suddenly wild shrieks were heard, and the " batchas " began turning round like a spinning-top, whilst the musicians accelerated their time, and the " batchas " made rather clumsy jumps.

Our menagerie is enlarged. A native inhabitant of Tashkend presented me with a wild horse caught in the mountains, striped like a zebra, with long donkey ears. The animal was placed in the same enclosure with the reindeers, and a she-donkey was given to him as a spouse, which helped to tame the wild horse. Donkeys are very cheap in Turkestan. One can get a splendid specimen for the sum of twelve roubles, and a working ass for five roubles.

A few miles from Tashkend there is a Leper Settlement.

When my husband visited it, he saw only ten lepers. He made inquiries, and was told that all the rest were begging in the streets of Tashkend. Sergy ordered them to be packed off immediately to their own dwelling. A collection, for the benefit of these poor wretches, is now in the press. I take part in it, and publish our crossing of the Pacific Ocean from San Francisco to Yokohama.

CHAPTER CXXII

A SHORT PEEP AT ST. PETERSBURG AND BACK TO TASHKEND

August 10th.—To-day I started for St. Petersburg, where I am going to spend two months. There were many people to see me off. The Grand Duke was at the station. He handed me a big bouquet and a beautiful rose-coloured satin box of bonbons. I received so many bouquets that my husband's aide-de-camps had not arms enough to hold them. One of the lady members of our collective book for the benefit of the lepers, presented me with an enormous bouquet, bound with a white ribbon with a swallow perched on a telegraphic wire painted on it, and underneath "*Revenez*" was imprinted in golden letters, with the signature of all the writers concerned in the book. Before the train started the Grand Duke told me he was very pleased that I entered my car holding his bouquet, without any rivals to it.

August 12th.—I saw a mirage to-day : a lake with some trees around appeared on the horizon. In the desert in fine weather, mirages are often to be seen, but they always appear in the form of water.

August 13th.—I arrived this morning at Krasnovodsk where I had to wait for the steamboat until to-morrow. My car was rolled on to the pier and two sentinels were placed at its door. There is stillness all around, I only heard the wash of the waves on the shore, some steps distant. It made me feel drowsy, and I soon fell asleep, lulled by the whispering ripple of the sea.

August 14th.—I woke at dawn. The morning dew spread around in a white mist. Somewhere in the distance a cock crowed and another answered the challenge. At seven o'clock I took passage on the steamer *Tzarevitch*. The weather is splendid, the sea like a mirror. A slight breeze enters my cabin, flapping the muslin curtains. After dinner I went upon deck. On the sky bright stars were shining, and the fresh breeze swept my face.

August 15th.—The weather has changed for the worse ; heavy black clouds hang over the billowy sea. The wind is getting stronger ; we are awfully tossed about. I have really no chance on the sea ; as soon as I step on board, Neptune never fails to be very disagreeable.

We arrived at Petrovsk far behind time. My car was attached to our train as far as St. Petersburg.

I only spent three weeks on the banks of the Neva. I was miserable without Sergy, and my solitude becoming unbearable, I returned with my mother to Tashkend.

We have borne the voyage capitally and had a good crossing this time. The weather was fine, the sun shone brightly on a very calm sea ; we had no rolling at all. We accomplished also our journey by rail without any accident.

My sudden and unexpected appearance at Tashkend created quite a commotion in the town. My mother was very much impressed by all our surroundings. To amuse her we arranged, every night, card-parties. There appeared to be a great number of whist-players in Tashkend ; partners were never wanting. Mother's partners presented her with a green cloth with all their autographs embroidered on it. They tried to entice me into their play, but I was no card-player, and at my first essay, my face openly expressed : " I am bored to death." I thrust furtive glances at the clock all the time, watching for the hands to show the hour of my deliverance. I did not repeat my experiment.

Tashkend is thrown into wild agitation by the arrival of General Toutolmine, the aide of the Grand Duke Nikolai Nikolaevitch. This General had been in the same military school with my husband ; he was accompanied by several smart officers in the guards, Prince Jaime de Bourbon, the son of Don Carlos, among them. The Prince is a legitimist claimant of the Spanish throne, serving in the Russian army in the regiment of the Hussars. He is a dashing, showy, cavalry officer, of the type that finds favour with women ; like Cæsar he came, saw, and conquered. The Prince is accustomed to win all hearts and does not believe it possible for any creature of the fair sex to do so much as look at him without falling in love with him. I found him very entertaining, but did not lose my heart. He sat beside me at dinner and was very bright and witty. He told me that a gipsy had foretold him three things : a great gain, a wound and a crown. The first of the predictions came true, he has won at a lottery the sum of 2000 roubles ; will the the other two prophecies come true ? " Qui vivra verra ! " After dinner I mounted my bicycle, accompanied by Prince Jaime and his comrades. We made a long run, I rode fast, going at a pace almost equal to that of an express train ; my cavaliers were completely exhausted, trying to keep up with me.

The Emir has sent a delegation to my husband with numerous rich presents. The delegates wore beautiful khalats and white turbans made of very thin stuff, twisted round their shaved heads. These turbans cost scores of pounds ;

it was India which supplied them, but now they are fabricated in Moscow much cheaper. After the deputies had been presented to Sergy, they were ushered into my sitting-room. The most talkative of the party was Astanakul-Divan-Begui, the first minister of the Emir; his companions sat down on the edge of their chairs, smoothing their knees with their hands, scarcely lifting their eyes from the carpet, and would only say "yes" and "no." After a copious "dastarkhan," (lunch) served in the winter-garden, the deputies presented us with numerous gifts sent by their Sovereign, which lay piled about the long terrace. Six Bokharian attendants stood like ancient slaves before this amassed wealth : superb carpets, muskets, pistols, daggers set with precious stones, gilt caskets with splendid jewellery, a dream from the "Thousand and One Arabian Nights."

We gave a grand dinner for two hundred persons in honour of the delegates. An invisible band placed in the park played during the repast. Champagne flowed in abundance and numerous toasts were drunk, accompanied by a flourish of trumpets. I sat between two laconic deputies, who answered with low sounding monosyllables to all the questions I put to them with seraphic patience. I felt glad when dinner was over.

That same night I took part in a concert got up by the Benevolence Society in our house. The ball was brilliantly lighted ; every seat was taken. The Bokharian deputies were present at the concert and I wore in their honour the heavy golden necklace presented to me by the Emir. It is fortunate that I had to play instead of singing, because for the great weight of the necklace I could not have drawn one single note out of my throat. I was seized with an access of shyness, before mounting the platform, and had to swallow soothing drops to quiet my nerves ; nevertheless I thought I should die of fright when I appeared before the audience and was conscious of an inclination to run away, but giving a swift glance to the public confronting me, I soon recovered my self-possession entirely, and performed my solo on the concertina with great success, gathering frenzied bravos, and I had to play no fewer than five encores. All the same I had too good sense not to understand that my success was due especially to the position I held, much more than to my talent ; it was only green paper laurels that I got, and I should have liked to win real ones and play in other surroundings, with veritable artists and amongst a less partial audience. The concert brought a large profit, more than one hundred pounds. All the ladies who took part in it received a bouquet bound with white ribbons bearing the Red Cross.

On the next day the delegates were present at a children's feast arranged on the square opposite our house. The entertainment was given especially to attract the little natives; we wanted to tame these little savages and show them that the Russians were not so terrible as they are made to believe. The whole population, except a small part of civilised natives bring up their children inculcating in them the fear of the Russians. The entertainment began about three o'clock and went on till quite late in the evening. There were about two thousand children. It amused me to watch their enjoyment and see the expression of mistrust, stamped on their small faces, change suddenly into one of keen delight when sweets and toys were being distributed to them. It is to be hoped that the little Sartes returned to their homes carrying sentiments of friendship to the Russians in their small hearts.

The opening of the Agricultural Exhibition took place whilst the deputies were at Tashkend. All the productions of Turkestan were gathered there: fruit, flowers, seeds, preserved vegetables, bon-bons, domestic animals, etc. A great number of venomous insects, which abound in the Famished Steppe, were also exhibited; scorpoins, phalanxes, and spiders of every kind. A mollusk, which is to be found in all the bathing establishments of Tashkend, is particularly disgusting; that little monster is scarcely perceptible in the water, being half transparent, like jelly. Ugh, the horror!

Summer passed quickly. Autumn came on. The dead leaves fell silently and covered the alleys of our park with a yellow carpet. In November, snow fell in abundance and the trees bent under the heavy flakes. The trains are obliged to stop for several days, the line being encumbered with snow,

On Christmas night a group of maskers, wrapped up in red dominoes, with little round bells hanging all around, appeared unexpectedly, followed by a band of music. After having performed a kind of ballet, they took off their dominoes and we saw before us a fantastical crowd of people in fancy dress. There were clowns daubed with chalk among them, and pirates, monks, pierrots, Columbines, etc. One of the aide-de-camps proved a tremendous success; he represented a gigantic doll dressed all in red, and walking on stilts right up to the ceiling. In one of the corners of the big hall suddenly a small booth appeared, in which an old wizard began selling curious advertisements. He offered, for instance, ten thousand roubles for a faithful woman. (And for the fidelity of a man it is ten millions that he ought to offer, shouldn't he?) The people who approached this booth were caught by the hook of this old man, who sprinkled them all over with scent out of an invisible sprinkler. Everybody seemed to enjoy themselves thoroughly. The floor was strewn with confetti. I did not at all like to have bits of paper poured down my back. The ball-room presented a very gay appearance with its merry couples swinging to-and-fro to the music of one of Tashkend's best bands. I had not danced for years, not since I was married, and enjoyed it greatly, I must confess. We did not stop dancing till late. When the last people went away it was broad daylight.

The winter this year was a particularly severe one. The thermometer has gone down very low. Our apartments though supposed to be thoroughly heated, are very chilly. The wind whistles down the chimney its monotonous song, and I am so dull, so dull! Oh, how I long to leave Tashkend for good and all!

My wish was realised sooner than I expected. In the middle of January my husband was called away to St. Petersburg on business. It semmed too good to be true! St. Petersburg was to me the summit of earthly bliss. I longed for the life, the beauty, the movement of the Great City.

January 6th.—We started to-day for St. Petersburg. Our train advances very slowly because of the snow which covers the line. We have recourse to means used in America : a sort of brush is fastened to our engine to clear the way and sweep away the snow.

January 9th.—The weather is horrible. A snowstorm arose. The wind whistles and howls in the plain ; flakes of snow adhere to the glass and it is impossible to see anything outside.

January 10th.—The cold keeps increasing. It is difficult to believe that it was a hot inferno I had to endure in these places not very long ago.

January 11th.—The cold keeps increasing ; though well wrapped up with furs, I sat shivering in the train. The pale rays of the sun appear from time to time, piercing the sky clouds, and the road covered with a heavy carpet of snow shines like diamonds.

Early in the morning we arrived at Kizil-Arvat, having to stop here for twenty-four hours : the train could not move for the heaps of snow on the line and soldiers were sent out to clear the way for us. The principal offices of the railroad are stationed here. There is a working-men's club with a bar, but without alcoholic drinks, a library and a large hall where concerts and theatricals are held. It would have been desirable to increase the number of such clubs, for it is not only by tedious, boring preaching that the workmen are kept away from drunkenness, and if you made them happy and comfortable they would not want to go off in the evening to public ale-houses.

January 12th.—We continued our journey at daybreak. When I awoke I found the snow had completely disappeared. Towards noon we arrived at Krasnovodsk and took our passage on the *Tropic.*

We are once more convinced that the geographers are often

mistaken. The Caspian Sea, which never freezes according to them, appears to be frozen for forty miles out. It is not an agreeable prospect to have to cut through the ice, but we have a compensation—we shall not be tossed about.

January 13th.—At dawn we weighed anchor. It gives one the shivers to hear the ice grating against the thin body of our ship. As the Caspian never freezes the ships are not equipped for polar-crossing, and the *Tropic* does not resemble in the least the ice breaker, which was of such use to us during our crossing from Vladivostock to Nagasaki in the winter.

January 14th.—During the whole night we found ourselves in the position of Nansen. It is only towards morning that the sea was free from the ice. The barometer mounts visibly ; the proximity of the Caucasus is perceptible.

Towards night we arrived at Baku,where we have a special train placed at our disposal. The railway between Baku and Petrovsk is not open officially, and we had to advance at a snail's pace. I thought we should never get to Petrovsk if we crawled like that.

January 15th.—We have passed the night in the open field because the trains do not run yet in the dark. Early in the morning we began to advance at the rate of four miles an hour ; in risky places the guards walked on in front to examine the line.

January 16th.—We arrived at Petrovsk in the afternoon. We are in Europe here, and although we have got a three days' railway journey before us, St. Petersburg seems quite near.

PARIS WORLD'S FAIR

My husband's health had failed a good deal of late, and the doctors have ordered him an absolute change and rest. Sergy was overworked and a good holiday will set him right. He wants to take a long leave and go abroad for some time. Kissingen was recommended by the doctors, but we meant to have a jolly good time and went first to Paris to visit the World's Fair. Mr. Shaniavski was nominated as representative of the Turkestan section and was sent before us to Paris. He met us at the Gare du Nord, accompanied by four Bokharians and a Turkoman, sent to the Exhibition to look after the rich objects exposed by the Emir, and to serve also as a vivid decoration in the Asiatic section, where the place of honour was assigned to Turkestan. These decorative personages, when passing through St. Petersburg, attracted much curiosity by their magnificent costumes, it is not astonishing therefore that they produced a great sensation in Paris. When our train came to stop at the platform, we saw a crowd of eager spectators waiting to see the arrival of the exotic personages whom the Orientals had come to meet, expecting to see no less a person than a Rajah. People stood on chairs to get a peep at us, and great was their disappointment, when simple mortals clad in European dress, stepped out of the train.

We took a carriage and went to Passy, a western suburb of Paris, where a villa, overgrown with lilacs, bearing the name of Villa des Lilas, was secured for us by Mr. Shaniavski, in the quietest part of Paris, in the neighbourhood of the Exhibition.

Mr. Shaniavski had put up with his Bokharians in a house in the Passage des Eaux, described by Zola in his novel *Une page d'Amour*. The small Asiatic colony consists of a Bokharian colonel, a captain, a merchant who speaks a few words of French and serves as interpreter, and four servants. The Bokharians, arrayed in rich "khalats," walk about the streets quite indifferent to the stare of wondering Parisians. When they go out shopping, they are taken for princes, and are made to pay princely prices. One day, when visiting the Grands Magasins du Louvre, they were received at the entrance door by the directeur, surrounded by his assistants, who proposed to the princes to show them through the house, expecting to fleece the Bokharians, who asked the prices of everything they saw without any views as to purchasing them. After having visited in detail the section of jewellery, tapestry and other fancy goods, they made the insignificant purchase of half a dozen crockery plates, after which the splendid directeur, and his satellites, disappeared as by magic, forsaking the stingy Bokharians.

Though the Exhibition has been opened a whole month, the section of Central Asia is not quite ready yet ; it is only the section of Turkestan which came to an end, thanks to the energy of our delegate. Next to it are the sections of the Caucasus and Siberia. A crowd of Russian workmen, wearing red shirts, put the finishing stroke to them.

The best place at the Exhibition is assigned to Central Asia, called " Russie des Indes," quite near the Trocadero. This section, which is a duplicate in miniature of the Kremlin, in Moscow, is surrounded by a high crenelated wall with a row of turrets ornamented with the Russian Double Eagle. When you enter it, the Russian architecture gives place to an Arabian style. An immense panorama represents a large square in Samarkand, with a lively crowd of natives ; only when seen quite close, one perceives that it is but a picture, not a reality. Our section is striking by its vivid and bright colouring. A fountain plays in the middle of an immense hall, decorated with beautiful Asiatic carpets and armour, and filled with all kinds of products of our possessions in Central Asia. The best appreciators of a remarkable collection of plants and seeds, appeared to be a legion of mice ; these gnawing little animals arranged for themselves, in broad daylight, Lucullus-like repasts, without being disturbed in the least by the crowd of visitors. The grains disappeared visibly, and poison was put in every attractive place, but the cunning mice, preferring the tasty grains, carried their victory on to the battle-field.

Next to our Asiatic section stands the pavilion of Polar Russia. The morose Siberian nature is such a contrast with our bright Turkestan. The panels on the walls represent a seal-chase ; all sorts of stuffed polar animals fill the big halls, as well as an ethnographic collection of manikins, which represents in a very life-like manner, different types of the inhabitants of Siberia. The model of a sledge, harnessed with a team of dogs, reminded me vividly of our drive on the frozen Amour during carnival-week at Khabarovsk. On long tables, in the middle of the hall, lay all sorts of furs : beautiful sables, blue fox, beaver, etc. It is curious that according to official information, only 7—8 beavers are killed yearly in Kamtchatka. How can we explain then that hundreds of real beaver skins are sold in Russia. (It is the fur-traders only who can unriddle the thing).

The Caucasus section is just opposite. In a large separate building a panorama represents the new Siberian railway-line. The Sleeping-car Company has exposed the model of a Transcaspian train, composed of an engine and three cars belonging to the International Company, in which one experiences the illusion of a journey through Siberia. The guard whistles, the train seems to move, but in reality it is only the panorama on the walls which is put into motion by a special mechanism. The travellers perceive through the windows the whole way leading from Moscow right to the terminus station—Pekin. When you pass through all the cars, to the other end of the hall, you are in the Chinese section, where the front gate represents a part of the walls of the city of Pekin.

The next day after our arrival at Paris, the section of Central Asia was inaugurated. To get there we had to elbow our way through a throng. A Te Deum was sung by the singers of the Russian Church, whilst all the Kremlin bells were ringing a full peal at which my Russian heart bounded with joy. That day we spent six hours at the Exhibition, and did not sit down for one minute. I was awfully hungry, having eaten only one *croissant* since morning, and Sergy carried me off to the Trocadero to have dinner in one of the best restaurants. The hall was full of guests. Two very disreputable-looking creatures sat at the table next our own; they were painted with cheap cosmetics, and the heat took off their paint, which came out in the wrong places, and very soon the powder on their faces was becoming paste, and the red on their cheeks and the black of their eyebrows began to run down in streaks, metamorphosing them into tattooed papouses, which didn't hinder them in the least from casting coquettish glances around. They tried to make eyes at my cavaliers, but it was all in vain; their charms left them quite unmoved. We were too tired to walk home and got into a cab whose driver, with folded arms and bowed head, was nodding on his seat, his nose buried in an open newspaper. Both coachman and horse were dozing the whole way, and it is only a miracle that we got to our villa without running into other carriages.

Next day President Loubet visited our section, where he was presented with a map of France worked " in relievo," in a frame of jasper; the seas were made of marble, the rivers of silver and the towns of precious stones, got from the Ural mountains. The huge emerald representing the city of Marseilles cost eight thousand roubles. President Loubet is a very different sort of person from what I had expected the ruler of France to be; he is an insignificant-looking little old man, saluting cordially from right to left. A Russian lady, who heard us speaking our mother-tongue, mingled into our conversation. Before leaving our section she favoured me with a condescending nod and a limp hand-shake, but when she heard our interpreter addressing me by my rank, she rushed back and squeezed my fingers effusively. Nasty woman!

We visited that day the Algerian village in the Trocadero Gardens. Superb natives, arrayed in rich costumes, sat on the threshold of their open booths, shrieking out the virtues of their wares. Close to the village stands the Dahomey pavilion, with its straw-thatched roof. Black natives stood on watch, perched on the top of a high tower. In the Singhalese village I patted the small brown babies, calling to mind my sojourn in Colombo. We entered a barrack close by, from which resounded the frantic strains of weird native music. Inside, women clad in Oriental costumes, gleaming with golden coins on their waists and wrists, performed the *Danse du Ventre* to the accompaniment of clapping hands. One of the beautiful "odalisques" stepped down from the estrade and passed round with a plate into which people dropped money. One glance was enough to show that this would-be Daughter of the Desert was a typical "Parisienne" from the "quartier des Batignolles."

The pavilions of the different States are picturesquely scattered along the banks of the Seine. All these magnificent buildings, made of plaster, will be in three months' time reduced to the level of the "Champ de Mars." One can't believe that these enormous palaces are only temporary visitors, like the people, and will be destroyed in a few months, after the closing of the Exhibition. It is only the "Palais des Beaux Arts," built of brick and mortar, which will not be thrown down. A most beautiful and interesting collection of old masters is exhibited in this building. We became so fascinated with some of these wonders, that we could hardly get away from the place. It amused me to see how insufficiently cloaked statues upset the decorum of a pair of prim old maids in, large turned-down hats surrounded by green gauze veils, unlovely and unloved creatures, belong-ing to that sort of Puritans who do not admit kisses because no one ever kissed them. This part of the Exhibition is situated near the principal entry on the side of the Place de la Concorde, with the famous "Parisienne" made of stone and perched very high on the top of a triumphal arch. It is queer to see the reproduction of a fashionable lady dressed up-to-date, posted in such a dangerous and un-comfortable place; we are accustomed to see symbolic figures in that risky position, defying in posture to the laws of equilibrium.

There was a great crowd walking about the Exhibition, a constant going to-and-fro of people who had come from all quarters of the globe. The human whirlpool made me quite giddy. Several bands play in different parts of the grounds near the "Pont Alexandre III.," which illustrates in stone and bronze the famous Russian Czar. We listened to the music of an American orchestra led by Sousa, the king of marches, in like manner as Strauss and Waldteufel had been the kings of the waltz in times of yore.

Our walks through the Exhibition lightened visibly our pockets. The prices of all the objects exposed for sale are exorbitant, money melted like snow and we came home utterly penniless.

There are different means of locomotion through the great extent of the Exhibition, beginning by the Tonquinoise " puss-puss," to the last technical invention—the "trottoir roulant," moving sidewalks, three rows of which run along without stopping. The first row moves very slowly, and it is easy to jump on it ; the second row moves faster, and the third one races with the swiftness of an express train. Great agility is needed to pass from one trottoir to the other, and it happens sometimes that the backs of clumsy pedestrians rest on one trottoir, whilst his legs are being dragged on the neighbouring one.

In the Rue de Paris, near the Eiffel Tower, different attractions are to be found : bearded women, mermaids, and other marvels of past, present, and future life. In a miorama we crossed from Marseilles to Constantinople without leaving Paris. Another panorama gives the illusion of a sea-voyage round the world. In the Palais des Optiques we went down under the sea, and were introduced to horrid monsters. We came upon a gigantic telescope showing the moon at the distance of sixty kilometres. A huge wheel 177 metres high, with thirty-two waggons, wheels round intrepid passengers. The Palais de la Femme contains amazing toilettes of past and ultra modern times. I fell in love with a costume of the last note of modernity, which Sergy wanted to purchase, but I was reasonable enough to refuse the present, for the price was unheard of. The Panorama du Mont Blanc shows a group of excursionists climbing up the Alps, which reminded me of our ascent on the Mont Blanc.

To come into the Vieux Paris representing the Paris of past centuries, we had to cross a draw-bridge and enter through a tower-gate guarded by sentinels of the middle ages, holding long lances, into the Rue des Remparts, a corner of a street in the fourteenth century, with dwellings filled with mediæval attributes. On the front of the houses, instead of numbers, the pictures of different birds are reproduced. In the narrow, tortuous streets we found ourselves surrounded by people dressed according to the fashion of ancient times ; knights in armour and ladies of the middle-ages walked to-

and-fro. My imagination travelled, transporting me to the days of long ago, and I felt as if the clock had been put back several centuries. When we passed the Tour du Châtelet, the fourteenth century had vanished by magic into the time of the Tudors, making a jump through the space of over two hundred years. Chants resounded from the church of St. Julien, which belonged formerly to the "Minstrels Brotherhood." On the Square we saw the gibbet watched over by mousquetaires armed with muskets and wearing three-cornered hats. In the Rue des Vieilles Écoles, the house inhabited by Moliére is exactly reproduced. Ladies in paniers and powdered perukes promenaded, escorted by their cavaliers dressed as marquesses. Different processions circulated. Here is a band of clerks directing their steps towards the Court of Justice, with inkstands adjusted to their girdles, carrying in their hands burning torches. In the Criminal Hall, instead of law suits, Mysteries are represented.

Not far from the Vieux Paris is the Andalousie du temps des Maures. The entry represents the exact copy of the Alcazar in Seville; on the Plaza de Toros, instead of horrid bull-fights, pretty Andalusian gitanas (Spanish gypsies) with a rose placed above the left ear in their jet-black hair, dance seguedillas and habaneras. It was fire which ran in their veins. I was very much astonished to see our Turkoman promenading amongst the audience. We were told that the impressario had invited him to come every night gratis to his establishment, as a living decoration. I cannot conceive what can be in common between an inhabitant from Central Asia and Spanish life.

Opposite Andalousia an Alpine village has spread itself ungeographically, with its cattle, shepherds, watchmaker-shops and wooden toy-makers. Amidst natural glaciers and water-falls, an animated crowd dressed in the costumes of all the Swiss cantons, walk about. We saw the house where Bonaparte passed the night on his march with his army of 30,000 men across the St. Gothard pass, with all the furniture just as it was then. There was the arm-chair by the hearth in which the great man sat, gazing into the glowing coals. What pictures did he see in the flames? Did his thoughts wander back to Josephine, or to new laurels and glory?

The Exhibition opened at ten. We went there as soon as the gates were thrown open and left it only when we found ourselves almost too tired to stand. We met there many friends from Russia, Mr. Radde amongst them, director of the Museum in Tiflis, an eminent biologist versed in all the antiquities and questions of the past. He is awfully abstruse-minded, and always looking as if he just descended from the clouds. One day, when Mr Radde called upon us at the Villa des Lilas, he made the acquaintance of our landlord,

L*

who had nothing of the Adonis about him, with his round moon face, and a tiny baby nose disappearing between his fat cheeks. In a fit of absent-mindedness he began to pity the cherub-faced gentleman for having such a terrible inflammation, and on both sides of the face all the more. Our landlord thanked him for his compassion, but said that happily, he never suffered from toothache, and was not afflicted therefore, with inflammation of any kind. I had to make a desperate effort to be serious when witnessing this comic scene.

We knew our Paris well, and had a jolly good time at night, enjoying theatres and café-chantants. I did feel gay going to naughty places in the quartier Montmartre without caring whether it was proper or not. At the Chat Noir the programme was very varied, exhibiting celebrities dressed in a costume remarkable for its lack of stuff, and famed for the height to which they could raise one leg and knock their own noses with it while standing upon the other. We visited the Cabaret du Ciel and the Cabaret de l'Enfer, two rather disreputable establishments with quaint representations of bliss in heaven and tortures in hell. In the first cabaret the customers are received by a bevy of white-winged, long-haired masculine beings, and in the second one, an establishment where the lights blaze red, the attendants, attired as devils, greet the visitors making demoniac grimaces. The Cabaret Alexandre Bruyant is very amusing ; the proprietor of this establishment well merits his surname of Bruyant—(noisy.) He meets his guests shouting in a voice of thunder, and making mocking jeers. When an old lady with orange-coloured hair and a very powdered face came in, he exclaimed, " *Oh, la belle brune, n'a-t-elle pas un teint eclatant ?* (Oh, the dark beauty, hasn't she got a dazzling complexion?) A general laugh arose. Then he came up to me and patting my shoulder roared, " *Pauvre petite créature, comme elle a l'air maladif !* " (Poor little thing, how ailing and sickly she looks !") The newcomers, feeling rather scared at being addressed in such a rough manner, and displeased at being made to appear ridiculous, wanted to get away, but when they saw that this queer reception was one of the peculiarities of the house, they settled themselves comfortably at separate little tables, and laughed in their turn good-humouredly at the reception of new arrivals.

The distribution of prizes at the Exhibition took place a few days before we left Paris. My husband received for our Turkestan section the Great Cross of the Légion d'Honneur. The Russian Commissaire, when packing up different objects, found it difficult to bring back to Tashkend a huge " arba " (a two-wheeled cart) and it was decided to leave it here and present it to some collector of curiosities. But no one wanted such a gift, and the commissaires had recourse to another means of getting rid of this encumbering " arba," they asked a carter, promising him a good tip, to harness his horse to the cart and take it along as far as the highway leading to Versailles, and then leave it there to its own fate.

EVERY day in Paris was too short for me, and I left the Great Babylon with immense regret. Sergy went to Kissingen to begin his cure, and I returned to St. Petersburg to publish my book.

About a week after my arrival I was on my way to Kissingen. Sergy wrote to me entreating me to come, as he couldn't do without me, and had been very miserable since we parted. He said that he would give up his cure and start for St. Petersburg if I would not rejoin him. I telegraphed back that I was starting off immediately.

Spoilt by the comforts of my travels in Turkestan, I felt very uncomfortable in a train full of passengers. We were crowded together like herrings in a barrel. I squeezed myself into my place in the corner of the carriage, pressing close my elbows. My fellow-passengers were going straight to Berlin and I couldn't stretch my legs the whole night to get the cramp out of them. We looked at one another with no great love in our eyes. I was placed by the side of a well preserved lady of about fifty years of age, trying to pass off for thirty, who had still the remains of what she had been in her young days and did not like to part with them. I caught her practising her fascinations in the mirror. She was accompanied by her daughter, a grown-up girl of about eighteen, clad in a short frock, with her hair down her back in a plait. When I heard them say " I reckon," I knew they were Americans. My neighbour opened her basket and offered a part of her supper to me. She was most communicative respecting her own concerns, and chatted away like a magpie. She told me that they were going to do Paris, and spoke all the time of her conquests, stating to me that she had got all the men at her feet. I scarcely listened to her prattle, but she chatted on, accustomed to do without answers. Opposite me, sat a full contrast to that chatter-box, a placid materfamilias endowed with three babies aged respectively five, four and two, who kept singing praises to the many charms and wondrous perfection of her offsprings. The children were petted and fondled by their mother, who crammed them all the way with bon-bons and cake in profusion. Her little girl hugging in her arms an immense doll, began quarreling with her brother, an ugly and anything but well-behaved brat, with nose and mouth blackened with chocolate; they kicked and screamed until they were both black in the face. I only just stopped short of throwing my book at their heads. The baby, the pet of the family, was cutting a tooth and kept roaring the whole night.

We arrived early in the morning at the frontier of Prussia. At the Customs my trunks were unmercifully turned topsy-turvy, the horrid officials stirring them up as I used to do with my nursery pudding when all the plums had sunk to the bottom.

When we approached Kissingen, I thrust my head out of the railway-carriage, with my body half out of the window, to catch the first sight of my husband's face. As we drew up at the station I perceived him on the platform, beaming with delight. I jumped out of the train joyfully, and the next moment I was in Sergy's arms.

Kissingen is surrounded by mountains and buried in verdure. It is the favourite meeting-place for aristocratic Europe. There is a great rush of ailing humanity towards these healing waters.

I found Sergy comfortably established in a villa belonging to Doctor Sautier, by whom he was treated. The next day I accompanied my husband when he made his visit to the doctor. The drawing-room was crowded with patients who had arrived from all parts of the world. They perused magazines, and plunged their heads into large books of photographs, awaiting their turn to appear before the esculapius.

Early in the morning, as soon as I heard the postilion sounding his horn, I hastened to jump out of bed, and accompanied Sergy to the Kurhaus, where he took his waters. A beautiful string-orchestra entertained the Kurhaus guests from six to eight. The sick, undergoing a cure, walk in the broad alley, carrying their glasses with them. They stroll from one spring to another, sipping the water on the way. We saw invalids in wheeled chairs, basking in the sun with a shawl over their legs, discussing and comparing their various diseases.

The outskirts of Kissingen are beautiful. We made long walks every afternoon; exercise gave me a ravenous appetite, and I was far from being satisfied with our meagre dinner when we returned home, being put on low diet like my husband, for company's sake We were kept with a discipline that was worse than that of a convent, and were all put to bed at nine o'clock, in accordance with the doctor's order. I didn't like at all to be under hospital rules, and began to revolt against this tedious discipline. At the end of three days I longed for change of air and surroundings, and wanted much to run away. I am sick to death of seeing the same faces every day and of hearing the same sort of talk of people drinking disgusting waters and occupied only with the engrossing pastime of taking care of one's health. We have also become imaginary sufferers, and very often came upon Maria Michaelovna looking at her tongue in the glass.

The weather is bad again, it is raining all the time. The sick are promenading sulky and morose under their umbrellas, emptying their glasses in a melancholy way.

Sergy has accomplished his cure at Kissingen; the treatment had proved successful and his health was now gradually returning. I felt reassured for the moment. But Sergy, instead of seeking a spot for an after-treatment, hastened back to Tashkend, where he at once resumed his work, which had become more complicated than ever, thanks to the Boxer's rising in China. The foreign diplomatists living in Pekin, are besieged by a hostile crowd of natives. The Boxers have attacked the newly-built Manchuria railway. When my husband was Governor-General of the Amour Provinces, and there was no sign whatever of a misunderstanding between China and European countries, he formed the project of building a railway-line along the Amour banks, being against the construction of the Manchuria railway on a foreign land, but he was uot listened to, and we see now the deplorable consequences.

CHAPTER CXXV

BACK TO TASHKEND FOR THE LAST TIME

MEANWHILE I had a very tedious time at St. Petersburg, where I was to remain until autumn. It is odd that Sergy had not written to me for quite ten days. I was tortured by the fear that something had happened to him. I got at last a letter in which he told me that his health had changed again for the worse, and that he pined for me to such an extent as to lose his appetite and sleep, and that his lips had forgotten to smile. I must come back and cheer him a bit. Such a longing for Sergy came over me that I decided to leave for Tashkend on the following day.

I was in a fever to reach the end of my journey, and it seemed to me that the train was creeping at a snail's pace. At one of the stations I received a telegram from Mr. Shaniavski, informing me that my husband was unwell and that the doctors had ordered him to remain in bed. I was awfully upset by that telegram, and my spirits sank lower and lower. I was haunted in the night by a nightmare of frightful reality; I stood before the cathedral in Tashkend, surrounded by a crowd of soldiers; suddenly an officer came out of the church and announced in a loud voice, "General Doukhovskoy has just passed away." Oh! the horror of it! I woke in tears with a start, full of agony.

The more the time drew near for my arrival at Tashkend, the more nervous I became. My impatience increased from minute to minute. One can well imagine my amazement when, stopping at the station nearest to Tashkend, I saw my husband on the platform. He had left his bed to come and meet me. Sergy met me open-armed, whilst my heart beat so violently that I feared he would hear it. He had altered a good deal, and I was awfully shocked by the drawn look of his features. There was a large lump in my throat and I could not speak for the risk of tears, but I made a strong effort, and, trying to conceal my anxiety, I forced a poor smile, and did my utmost to look composed and cheerful.

As soon as we arrived at Tashkend, Sergy went to bed again, but was all right on the following morning. The sight of my face was the best medicine he could have.

The clouds thickened on the political horizon, and questions concerning China began to occupy the public mind. The European powers, feeling alarmed, marched conjointly on Pekin; there were thirty thousand troops assembled there. They say that Russia is going to take an active part, and we have to apprehend a catastrophe any moment on the frontier of Turkestan. Our Russian consul, who did not feel safe at Kuldja—a Chinese town near our frontier—asked my husband to send a platoon of Cossacks to protect him.

My husband's governorship was not a bed of roses. It is a difficult career, requiring much patience, perseverance and delicate handling. Sergy did not know fatigue, working from early morning till late at night, and even when he went to bed, he tried to remember the things he had done and the things he had to do, instead of falling off to sleep. He was a man who had never seemed to flinch from duty, either for himself or others, and he required the same from his subordinates, but didn't find the necessary support in them he ought to have had in such troublesome times. He looks awfully careworn and worn-out. The doctors spoke again of rest and change, and Sergy applied for leave. He thought of resigning altogether, to my greatest joy.

CHAPTER CXXVI

DEFINITE DEPARTURE FOR ST. PETERSBURG

I COUNTED the last hours of my stay at Tashkend. At last the happy day of our departure arrived. Swarms of people came to see us start and wish a happy journey and a safe and speedy return to them. The leave-taking was very warm. How happy I should have been to say good-bye to Tashkend for ever! " *Au revoir*," said my lips, and " *adieu* " whispered to me the presentiment that we shall never meet again.

The train began to move amidst loud cheers. I stood at the window of my car, with my arms full of flowers, exchanging smiles and nods.

We are back at St. Petersburg. I am so happy to push etiquette aside and live the life of a simple mortal. But the sword of Damocles was hanging over my head all the time. My husband's illness had taken a sudden turn for the worse ; he became thinner and paler every day, and the doctors ordered him a complete rest. This put an end to Sergy's hesitations, and he begged the Emperor to permit him to resign his post in Turkestan.

On New Year's Day my husband was named member of the State Council. Oh, how blessed it was to have done with Tashkend and all! Our wandering life was over now, the thing I had longed for year after year. I lulled myself with such sweet dreams for the future. But my joy was a short one. I soon saw sinister black clouds darkening my bright sky. Sergy was sinking fast, and was confined to his bed. I hated to see him in pain, and would have given all my blood to save him, but the Almighty predetermined it otherwise. On March 1, my beloved husband passed away. The awful circumstances of my dream, during my railway-journey to Tashkend, were realised, and the world suddenly took a cold and dismal aspect ; everything around and within me grew dark and chill. Ever since I was born, good fortune had marked me her own ; there were many fairies at my cradle. Life had been too smooth for me, and so it took vengeance now for all my felicity of bygone years !

The Emperor was present at a Requiem-Mass sung in our house. His Majesty said kind words of condolence to me, but I scarcely heard them.   Happiness, peace, all that was scattered to the ground like a house built on sand, nothing remained of it !

There are griefs that are too deep to speak of, and too secret for pen and ink.   I end my remembrances by these sad words :—

" Sic transit gloria mundi."

THE END

John Long, Ltd., Publishers, London. 1917

INDEX